THE COLLECTED NOVELS OF THOMAS HARDY

VOLUME II

THE COLLECTED NOVELS OF THOMAS HARDY

VOLUME II

TESS OF THE D'URBERVILLES

JUDE THE OBSCURE

THE MODERN LIBRARY
NEW YORK

1994 Modern Library Edition

Printed on recycled, acid-free paper.

Library of Congress Cataloging-in-Publication Data is available

ISBN 0-679-60078-7

Manufactured in the United States of America

2 4 6 8 9 7 5 3 1

THOMAS HARDY

THOMAS HARDY was born on June 2, 1840, in a thatched-roof cottage in upper Bockhampton, Dorset, England, a prophetic birthplace that lay in the center of 'Wessex,' the fictional region of southwest England which would serve as the backdrop for his novels. The eldest son of a prosperous builder and stonemason, Hardy was educated at the village school and apprenticed at the age of sixteen to a local architect and church restorer John Hicks. In 1862 he went to London to pursue his architectural career; he also began writing at this time. Hardy returned to Dorset in 1867 to become assistant to John Hicks and wrote his first novel, *The Poor Man and the Lady*, of which only fragments remain. Although George Meredith, who was reader for Chapman & Hall publishers, advised against its publication, he encouraged Hardy to keep writing, preferably a story with a more complicated plot. Over the next several years he produced three more novels: *Desperate Remedies* (1871) and *Under the Greenwood Tree* (1872) were published anonymously, but *A Pair of Blue Eyes* (1873) bore the author's name.

In November 1872, Leslie Stephen, the distinguished critic and editor, wrote to Hardy inviting him to contribute a novel for serialization in the *Cornhill Magazine*, a prestigious monthly that had published the work of such established writers as Anthony Trollope. Hardy accepted and in his letter to Stephen added that 'the chief characters would probably be a young woman-farmer, a shepherd, and a sergeant of cavalry.' He wrote *Far from the Madding Crowd* both in and out of doors at Bockhamptom as if possessed. 'Occasionally without a scrap of paper at the very moment when [I] felt volumes . . . [I] would use large dead leaves, white chips left by the woodcutters, or pieces of stone or slate that came to hand,' Hardy later recalled. Published anonymously in 1874, *Far from the Madding Crowd* sold out in just over two months and marked the turning point in Hardy's literary career. As Virginia Woolf later noted: 'The subject was right; the method was right; the poet and the countryman, the sensual man, the sombre reflective man, the man of learning, all enlisted to produce a book which, however fashions may chop and change, must hold its place among the great English novels.'

The success of *Far from the Madding Crowd* in 1874 encouraged Hardy to abandon architecture and devote himself entirely to the craft of fiction. His next novel, *The Hand of Ethelberta* (1876), also appeared in the *Cornhill Magazine* but did not repeat the success of its predecessor. In 1874 Hardy married Emma Lavinia Gifford, and the couple soon settled in an idyllic cottage overlooking the Dorset Stour, at Sturminster Newton, where Hardy wrote *The Return of the Native* (1878). In 1878 he moved to London. Although he became a well-known figure in literary circles and was considered a catch for hostesses, Hardy wrote three disappointing 'minor' novels during his years there: *The Trumpet-Major* (1880), *A Laodicean* (1881), and *Two on a Tower* (1882).

This fallow period in his career seemed to lift in 1885 with his return to Dorset to live at Max Gate. Over the next three years he published *The Mayor of Casterbridge* (1886), which many regard as his greatest tragic novel, *The Woodlanders* (1887), and his first collection of short stories, *Wessex Tales* (1888). In 1891 *Tess of the d'Urbervilles* appeared, and in 1895 Hardy's final novel, *Jude the Obscure*, came out. The book sent shock waves of indignation rolling across Victorian England. It was denounced as pornography and subjected the author to an avalanche of abuse. Hardy's disgust at the public's reaction led him to announce in 1896 that he would never again write fiction.

During the remaining years of his life, Hardy devoted himself to poetry, publishing his first book of verse, *Wessex Poems*, in 1898. A second collection, *Poems of the Past and Present*, appeared in 1901. Over the next five years Hardy wrote *The Dynasts*, an epic drama about the Napoleonic War. In 1912 he made a final revision of his novels for the authoritative Wessex Editions. Hardy's wife died suddenly the same year. In February 1914 he married his longtime secretary, Florence Emily Dugdale. Over the next decade Hardy continued to write poetry and to work on his autobiography, *The Early Life of Thomas Hardy*, which was supposedly authored by his second wife and published posthumously. Thomas Hardy died in

Dorset on January 11, 1928. His heart was buried in the Wessex countryside in the parish churchyard at Stinsford; his ashes were placed next to those of Charles Dickens in the Poets' Corner of Westminster Abbey.

Contents

Tess of the d'Urbervilles

A Pure Woman

'. . . Poor wounded name! My bosom as a bed
Shall lodge thee.'

—William Shakespeare

Contents

Explanatory Note to the First Edition

The main portion of the following story appeared—with slight modifications—in the *Graphic* newspaper; other chapters, more especially addressed to adult readers, in the *Fortnightly Review* and the *National Observer*, as episodic sketches. My thanks are tendered to the editors and proprietors of those periodicals for enabling me now to piece the trunk and limbs of the novel together, and print it complete, as originally written two years ago.

I will just add that the story is sent out in all sincerity of purpose, as an attempt to give artistic form to a true sequence of things; and in respect of the book's opinions and sentiments, I would ask any too genteel reader, who cannot endure to have said what everybody nowadays thinks and feels, to remember a well-worn sentence of St Jerome's: If an offence come out of the truth, better it is that the offence come than that the truth be concealed.

November 1891 T.H.

Author's Preface to the Fifth and Later Editions

This novel being one wherein the great campaign of the heroine begins after an event in her experience which has usually been treated as fatal to her part of protagonist, or at least as the virtual ending of her enterprises and hopes, it was quite contrary to avowed conventions that the public should welcome the book, and agree with me in holding that there was something more to be said in fiction than had been said about the shaded side of a well-known catastrophe. But the responsive spirit in which *Tess of the d'Urbervilles* has been received by the readers of England and America, would seem to prove that the plan of laying down a story on the lines of tacit opinion, instead of making it to square with the merely vocal formulae of society, is not altogether a wrong one, even when exemplified in so unequal and partial an achievement as the present. For this responsiveness I cannot refrain from expressing my thanks; and my regret is that, in a world where one so often hungers in vain for friendship, where even not to be wilfully misunderstood is felt as a kindness, I shall never meet in person these appreciative readers, male and female, and shake them by the hand.

I include among them the reviewers—by far the majority—who have so generously welcomed the tale. Their words show that they, like the others, have only too largely repaired my defects of narration by their own imaginative intuition.

Nevertheless, though the novel was intended to be neither didactic nor aggressive, but in the scenic parts to be representative simply, and in the contemplative to be oftener charged with impressions than with convictions, there have been objectors both to the matter and to the rendering.

The more austere of these maintain a conscientious difference of opinion concerning, among other things, subjects fit for art, and reveal an inability to associate the idea of the sub-title adjective with any but the artificial and derivative meaning which has resulted to it from the ordinances of civilization. They ignore the meaning of the word in Nature, together with all aesthetic claims upon it, not to mention the spiritual interpretation afforded by the finest side of their own Christianity. Others dissent on grounds which are intrinsically no more than an assertion that the novel embodies the view of life prevalent at the end of the nineteenth century, and not those of an earlier and simpler generation—an assertion which I can only hope may be well founded. Let me repeat that a novel is an impression, not an argument; and there the matter must rest; as one is reminded by a passage which occurs in the letters of Schiller to Goethe on judges of this class: 'They are those who seek only their own ideas in a representation, and prize that which should be as higher than what is. The cause of the dispute, therefore, lies in the very first principles, and it would be utterly impossible to come to an understanding with them.' And again: 'As soon as I observe that any one, when judging of poetical representations, considers anything more important than the inner Necessity and Truth, I have done with him.'

In the introductory words to the first edition I suggested the possible advent of the genteel person who would not be able to endure something or other in these pages. That person duly appeared among the aforesaid objectors. In one case he felt upset that it was not possible for him to read the book through three times, owing to my not having made that critical effort which 'alone can prove the salvation of such an one'. In another, he objected to such vulgar articles as the Devil's pitchfork, a lodging-house carving knife, and a shame-bought parasol, appearing in a respectable story. In another place he was a gentleman who turned Christian for half-an-hour the better to express his grief that a disrespectful phrase about the Immortals should have been used; though the same innate gentility compelled him to excuse the author in words of pity that one cannot be too thankful for: 'He does but give us of his best.' I can assure this critic that to exclaim illogically against the gods, singular or plural, is not such an original sin of mine as he seems to imagine. True, it may have some local originality; though if Shakespeare were an authority on history, which perhaps he is not, I could show that the sin was introduced into Wessex as early as Heptarchy itself. Says Glo'ster in *Lear*, otherwise Ina, king of that country:

> As flies to wanton boys are we to the gods;
> They kill us for their sport.

The remaining two or three manipulators of *Tess* were of the predetermined sort whom most writers and readers would gladly forget; professed literary boxers, who put on their convictions for the occasion; modern 'Hammers of Heretics'; sworn Discouragers, ever on the watch to prevent the tentative half-success from becoming the whole success later on; who pervert plain meanings, and grow personal under the name of practising the great historical method. However, they may have causes to advance, privileges to guard, traditions to keep going; some of which a mere tale-teller, who writes down how the things of the world strike him, without any ulterior intentions whatever, has overlooked, and may by pure inadvertence have run foul of when in the least aggressive mood. Perhaps some passing perception, the outcome of a dream hour, would, if generally acted on, cause such an assailant considerable inconvenience with respect to position, interests, family, servant, ox, ass, neighbour, or neighbour's wife. He therefore valiantly hides his personality behind a publisher's shutters, and cries 'Shame!' So densely is the world thronged that any shifting of positions, even the best warranted advance, galls somebody's kibe. Such shiftings often begin in sentiment, and such sentiment sometimes begins in a novel.

July 1892

The foregoing remarks were written during the early career of this story, when a spirited public and private criticism of its points was still fresh to the feelings. The pages are allowed to stand for what they are worth, as something once said; but probably they would not have been written now. Even in the short time which has elapsed since the book was first published, some of the critics who provoked the reply have 'gone down into silence', as if to remind one of the infinite unimportance of both their say and mine.

January 1895

The present edition of this novel contains a few pages that have never appeared in any previous edition. When the detached episodes were collected as stated in the preface of 1891, these pages were overlooked, though they were in the original manuscript. They occur in Chapter X.

Respecting the sub-title, to which allusion was made above, I may add that it was appended at the last moment, after reading the final proofs, as being the estimate left in a candid mind of the heroine's character—an estimate that nobody would be likely to dispute. It was disputed more than anything else in the book. *Melius fuerat non scribere*. But there it stands.

The novel was first published complete, in three volumes, in November 1891.

March 1912 T.H.

PHASE THE FIRST

THE MAIDEN

I

On an evening in the latter part of May a middle-aged man was walking homeward from Shaston to the village of Marlott, in the adjoining Vale of Blakemore or Blackmoor. The pair of legs that carried him were rickety, and there was a bias in his gait which inclined him somewhat to the left of a straight line. He occasionally gave a smart nod, as if in confirmation of some opinion, though he was not thinking of anything in particular. An empty egg-basket was slung upon his arm, the nap of his hat was ruffled, a patch being quite worn away at its brim where his thumb came in taking it off. Presently he was met by an elderly parson astride on a gray mare, who, as he rode, hummed a wandering tune.

'Good night t'ee,' said the man with the basket.

'Good night, Sir John,' said the parson.

The pedestrian, after another pace or two, halted, and turned round.

'Now, sir, begging your pardon; we met last market-day on this road about this time, and I zaid "Good night", and you made reply "*Good night, Sir John*", as now.'

'I did,' said the parson.

'And once before that—near a month ago.'

'I may have.'

'Then what might your meaning be in calling me "Sir John" these different times, when I be plain Jack Durbeyfield, the haggler?'

The parson rode a step or two nearer.

'It was only my whim,' he said; and, after a moment's hesitation: 'It was on account of a discovery I made some little time ago, whilst I was hunting up pedigrees for the new county history. I am Parson Tringham, the antiquary, of Stagfoot Lane. Don't you really know, Durbeyfield, that you are the lineal representative of the ancient and knightly family of the d'Urbervilles, who derive their descent from Sir Pagan d'Urberville, that renowned knight who came from Normandy with William the Conqueror, as appears by Battle Abbey Roll?'

'Never heard it before, sir!'

'Well it's true. Throw up your chin a moment, so that I may catch the profile of your face better. Yes, that's the d'Urberville nose and chin—a little debased. Your ancestor was one of the twelve knights who assisted the Lord of Estremavilla in Normandy in his conquest of Glamorganshire. Branches of your family held manors over all this part of England; their names appear in the Pipe Rolls in the time of King Stephen. In the reign of King John one of them was rich enough to give a manor to the Knights Hospitallers; and in Edward the Second's time your forefather Brian was summoned to Westminster to attend the great Council there. You declined a little in Oliver Cromwell's time, but to no serious extent, and in Charles the Second's reign you were made Knights of the Royal Oak for your loyalty. Aye, there have been generations of Sir Johns among you, and if knighthood were hereditary, like a baronetcy, as it practically was in old times, when men were knighted from father to son, you would be Sir John now.'

'Ye don't say so!'

'In short,' concluded the parson, decisively smacking his leg with his switch, 'there's hardly such another family in England.'

'Daze my eyes, and isn't there?' said Durbeyfield. 'And here have I been knocking about, year after year, from pillar to post, as if I was no more than the commonest feller in the parish . . . And how long hev this news about me been knowed, Pa'son Tringham?'

The clergyman explained that, as far as he was aware, it had quite died out of knowledge, and could hardly be said to be known at all. His own investigations had begun on a day in the preceding spring when, having been engaged in tracing the vicissitudes of the d'Urberville family, he had observed Durbeyfield's name on his waggon, and had thereupon been led to make inquiries about his father and grandfather till he had no doubt on the subject.

'At first I resolved not to disturb you with such a useless piece of information,' said he. 'However, our impulses are too strong for our judgment sometimes. I thought you might perhaps know something of it all the while.'

'Well, I have heard once or twice, 'tis true, that my family had seen better days afore they came to Blackmoor. But I took no notice o't, thinking it to mean that we had once kept two horses where we now keep only one. I've got a wold silver spoon, and a wold graven seal at home, too; but, Lord, what's a spoon and seal? . . . And to think that I and these noble d'Urbervilles were one flesh all the time. 'Twas said that my gr't-grandfer had secrets, and didn't care to talk of where he came from . . . And where do we raise our smoke, now, parson, if I may make so bold; I mean, where do we d'Urbervilles live?'

'You don't live anywhere. You are extinct—as a county family.'

'That's bad.'

'Yes—what the mendacious family chronicles call extinct in the male line—that is, gone down—gone under.'

'Then where do we lie?'

'At Kingsbere-sub-Greenhill: rows and rows of you in your vaults, with your effigies under Purbeck-marble canopies.'

'And where be our family mansions and estates?'

'You haven't any.'

'Oh? No lands neither?'

'None; though you once had 'em in abundance, as I said, for your family consisted of numerous branches. In this county there was a seat of yours at Kingsbere, and another at Sherton, and another at Millpond, and another at Lullstead, and another at Wellbridge.'

'And shall we ever come into our own again?'

'Ah—that I can't tell!'

'And what had I better do about it, sir?' asked Durbeyfield, after a pause.

'Oh—nothing, nothing; except chasten yourself with the thought of "how are the mighty fallen". It is a fact of some interest to the local historian and genealogist, nothing more. There are several families among the cottagers of this county of almost equal lustre. Good night.'

'But you'll turn back and have a quart of beer wi' me on the strength o't, Pa'son Tringham? There's a very pretty brew in tap at The Pure Drop—though, to be sure, not so good as at Rolliver's.'

'No, thank you—not this evening, Durbeyfield. You've had enough already.' Concluding thus the parson rode on his way, with doubts as to his discretion in retailing this curious bit of lore.

When he was gone Durbeyfield walked a few steps in a profound reverie, and then sat down upon the grassy bank by the roadside, depositing his basket before him. In a few minutes a youth appeared in the distance, walking in the same direction as that which had been pursued by Durbeyfield. The latter, on seeing him, held up his hand, and the lad quickened his pace and came near.

'Boy, take up that basket! I want 'ee to go on an errand for me.'

The lath-like stripling frowned. 'Who be you, then, John Durbeyfield, to order me about and call me "boy"? You know my name as well as I know yours!'

'Do you, do you? That's the secret—that's the secret! Now obey my orders, and take the message I'm going to charge 'ee wi' . . . Well, Fred, I don't mind telling you that the secret is that I'm one of a noble race—it has been just found out by me this present afternoon, P.M.' And as he made the announcement, Durbeyfield, declining from his sitting position, luxuriously stretched himself out upon the bank among the daisies.

The lad stood before Durbeyfield, and contemplated his length from crown to toe.

'Sir John d'Urberville—that's who I am,' continued the prostrate man. 'That is if knights were baronets—which they be. 'Tis recorded in history all about me. Dost know of such a place, lad, as Kingsbere-sub-Greenhill?'

'Ees. I've been there to Greenhill Fair.'

'Well, under the church of that city there lie—'

''Tisn't a city, the place I mean; leastwise 'twaddn' when I was there—'twas a little one-eyed, blinking sort o' place.'

'Never you mind the place, boy, that's not the question before us. Under the church of that there parish lie my ancestors—hundreds of 'em—in coats of mail and jewels, in gr't lead coffins weighing tons and tons. There's not a man in the county o' South-

Wessex that's got grander and nobler skillentons in his family than I.'

'Oh?'

'Now take up that basket, and goo on to Marlott, and when you've come to The Pure Drop Inn, tell 'em to send a horse and carriage to me immed'ately, to carry me hwome. And in the bottom o' the carriage they be to put a noggin o' rum in a small bottle, and chalk it up to my account. And when you've done that goo on to my house with the basket, and tell my wife to put away that washing, because she needn't finish it, and wait till I come hwome, as I've news to tell her.'

As the lad stood in a dubious attitude, Durbeyfield put his hand in his pocket, and produced a shilling, one of the chronically few that he possessed.

'Here's for your labour, lad.'

This made a difference in the young man's estimate of the position.

'Yes, Sir John. Thank 'ee. Anything else I can do for 'ee, Sir John?'

'Tell 'em at hwome that I should like for supper,—well, lamb's fry if they can get it; and if they can't, black-pot; and if they can't get that, well, chitterlings will do.'

'Yes, Sir John.'

The boy took up the basket, and as he set out the notes of a brass band were heard from the direction of the village.

'What's that?' said Durbeyfield. 'Not on account o' I?'

''Tis the women's club-walking, Sir John. Why, your da'ter is one o' the members.'

'To be sure—I'd quite forgot it in my thoughts of greater things! Well, vamp on to Marlott, will ye, and order that carriage, and maybe I'll drive round and inspect the club.'

The lad departed, and Durbeyfield lay waiting on the grass and daisies in the evening sun. Not a soul passed that way for a long while, and the faint notes of the band were the only human sounds audible within the rim of blue hills.

II

THE village of Marlott lay amid the north-eastern undulations of the beautiful Vale of Blakemore or Blackmoor aforesaid, an engirdled and secluded region, for the most part untrodden as yet by tourist or landscape-painter, though within a four hours' journey from London.

It is a vale whose acquaintance is best made by viewing it from the summits of the hills that surround it—except perhaps during the droughts of summer. An unguided ramble into its recesses in bad weather is apt to engender dissatisfaction with its narrow, tortuous, and miry ways.

This fertile and sheltered tract of country, in which the fields are never brown and the springs never dry, is bounded on the south by the bold chalk ridge that embraces the prominences of Hambledon Hill, Bulbarrow, Nettlecombe-Tout, Dogbury, High Stoy, and Bubb Down. The traveller from the coast, who, after plodding northward for a score of miles over calcareous downs and corn-lands, suddenly reaches the verge of one of these escarpments, is surprised and delighted to behold, extended like a map beneath him, a country differing absolutely from that which he has passed through. Behind him the hills are open, the sun blazes down upon fields so large as to give an unenclosed character to the landscape, the lanes are white, the hedges low and plashed, the atmosphere colourless. Here, in the valley, the world seems to be constructed upon a smaller and more delicate scale; the fields are mere paddocks, so reduced that from this height their hedgerows appear a network of dark green threads overspreading the paler green of the grass. The atmosphere beneath is languorous, and is so tinged with azure that what artists call the middle distance partakes also of that hue, while the horizon beyond is of the deepest ultramarine. Arable lands are few and limited; with but slight exceptions the prospect is a broad rich mass of grass and trees, mantling minor hills and dales within the major. Such is the Vale of Blackmoor.

The district is of historic, no less than of topographical interest. The Vale was known in former times as the Forest of White Hart, from a curious legend of King Henry III's reign, in which the killing by a certain Thomas de la Lynd of a beautiful white hart which the king had run down and spared, was made the occasion of a heavy fine. In those days, and till comparatively recent times, the country was densely wooded. Even now, traces of its earlier condition are to be found in the old oak copses and irregular belts of timber that yet survive upon its slopes, and the hollow-trunked trees that shade so many of its pastures.

The forests have departed, but some old customs of their shades remain. Many, however, linger only in a metamorphosed or disguised form. The May-Day dance, for instance, was to be discerned on the afternoon under notice, in the guise of the club revel, or 'club-walking', as it was there called.

It was an interesting event to the younger inhabitants of Marlott, though its real interest was not observed by the participators in the ceremony. Its singularity lay less in the retention of a custom of walking in procession and dancing on each anniversary than in the members being solely women. In men's clubs such celebrations were, though expiring, less uncommon; but either the natural shyness of the softer sex, or a sarcastic attitude on the part of male relatives, had denuded such women's clubs as remained (if any other did) of this their glory and consummation. The club of Marlott alone lived to uphold the local Cerealia. It had walked for hundreds of years, if not as benefit-club, as votive sisterhood of some sort; and it walked still.

The banded ones were all dressed in white gowns—a gay survival from Old Style days, when cheerfulness and May-time were synonyms—days before the habit of taking long views had reduced emotions to a monotonous average. Their first exhibition of themselves was in a processional march of two and two round the parish. Ideal and real clashed slightly as the sun lit up their figures against the green hedges and creeper-laced house-fronts; for, though the whole troop wore white garments, no two whites were alike among them. Some approached pure blanching; some had a bluish pallor; some worn by the older characters (which had possibly lain by folded for many a year) inclined to a cadaverous tint, and to a Georgian style.

In addition to the distinction of a white frock, every woman and girl carried in her right hand a peeled willow wand, and in her left a bunch of white flowers. The peeling of the former, and the selection of the latter, had been an operation of personal care.

There were a few middle-aged and even elderly women in the train, their silver-wiry hair and wrinkled faces, scourged by time and trouble, having almost a grotesque, certainly a pathetic, appearance in such a jaunty situation. In a true view, perhaps, there was more to be gathered and told of each anxious and experienced one, to whom the years were drawing nigh when she should say, 'I have no pleasure in them', than of her juvenile comrades. But let the elder be passed over here for those under whose bodices the life throbbed quick and warm.

The young girls formed, indeed, the majority of the band, and their heads of luxuriant hair reflected in the sunshine every tone of gold, and black, and brown. Some had beautiful eyes, others a beautiful nose, others a beautiful mouth and figure: few, if any, had all. A difficulty of arranging their lips in this crude exposure to public scrutiny, an inability to balance their heads, and to dissociate self-consciousness from their features, was apparent in them, and showed that they were genuine country girls, unaccustomed to many eyes.

And as each and all of them were warmed without by the sun, so each had a private little sun for her soul to bask in; some dream, some affection, some hobby, at least some remote and distant hope which, though perhaps starving to nothing, still lived on, as hopes will. Thus they were all cheerful, and many of them merry.

They came round by The Pure Drop Inn, and were turning out of the high road to pass through a wicket-gate into the meadows, when one of the women said

'The Lord-a-Lord! Why, Tess Durbeyfield, if there isn't thy father riding hwome in a carriage!'

A young member of the band turned her head at the exclamation.

She was a fine and handsome girl—not handsomer than some others, possibly—but her mobile peony mouth and large innocent eyes added eloquence to colour and shape. She wore a red ribbon in her hair, and was the only one of the white company who could boast of such a pronounced adornment. As she looked round Durbeyfield was seen moving along the road in a chaise belonging to The Pure Drop, driven by a frizzle-headed brawny damsel with her gown-sleeves rolled above her elbows. This was the cheerful servant of that establishment, who, in her part of factotum, turned groom and ostler at times. Durbeyfield, leaning back, and with his eyes closed luxuriously, was waving his hand above his head, and singing in a slow recitative—

'I've-got-a-gr't-family-vault-at-Kingsbere—and knighted-fore-fathers-in-lead-coffins-there!'

The clubbists tittered, except the girl called Tess—in whom a slow heat seemed to rise at the sense that her father was making himself foolish in their eyes.

'He's tired, that's all,' she said hastily, 'and he has got a lift home, because our own horse has to rest to-day.'

'Bless thy simplicity, Tess,' said her companions. 'He's got his market-nitch. Haw-haw!'

'Look here; I don't walk another inch with you, if you say any jokes about him!' Tess cried, and the colour upon her cheeks spread over her face and neck. In a moment her eyes grew moist, and her glance drooped to the ground. Perceiving that they had really pained her they said no more, and order again prevailed. Tess's pride would not allow her to turn her head again, to learn what her father's meaning was, if he had any; and thus she moved on with the whole body to the enclosure where there was to be dancing on the green. By the time the spot was reached she had recovered her equanimity, and tapped her neighbour with her wand and talked as usual.

Tess Durbeyfield at this time of her life was a mere vessel of emotion untinctured by experience. The dialect was on her tongue to some extent, despite the village school: the characteristic intonation of that dialect for this district being the voicing approximately rendered by the syllable UR, probably as rich an utterance as any to be found in human speech. The pouted-up deep red mouth to which this syllable was native had hardly as yet settled into its definite shape, and her lower lip had a way of thrusting the middle of her top one upward, when they closed together after a word.

Phases of her childhood lurked in her aspect still. As she walked along to-day, for all her bouncing handsome womanliness, you could sometimes see her twelfth year in her cheeks, or her ninth sparkling from her eyes; and even her fifth would flit over the curves of her mouth now and then.

Yet few knew, and still fewer considered this. A small minority, mainly strangers, would look long at her in casually passing by, and grow momentarily fascinated by her freshness, and wonder if they would ever see her again: but to almost everybody she was a fine and picturesque country girl, and no more.

Nothing was seen or heard further of Durbeyfield in his triumphal chariot under the conduct of the ostleress, and the club having entered the allotted space, dancing began. As there were no men in the company the girls danced at first with each other, but when the hour for the close of labour drew on, the masculine inhabitants of the village, together with other idlers and pedestrians, gathered round the spot, and appeared inclined to negotiate for a partner.

Among these on-lookers were three young men of a superior class, carrying small knapsacks strapped to their shoulders, and stout sticks in their hands. Their general likeness to each other, and their consecutive ages, would almost have suggested that they might be, what in fact they were, brothers. The eldest wore the white tie, high waistcoat, and thin-brimmed hat of the regulation curate; the second was the normal undergraduate; the appearance of the third and youngest would hardly have been sufficient to characterize him; there was an uncribbed, uncabined aspect in his eyes and attire, implying that he had hardly as yet found the entrance to his professional groove. That he was a desultory tentative student of something and everything might only have been predicted of him.

These three brethren told casual acquaintance that they were spending their Whitsun holidays in a walking tour through the Vale of Blackmoor, their course being south-westerly from the town of Shaston on the north-east.

They leant over the gate by the highway, and inquired as to the meaning of the dance and the white-frocked maids. The two elder of the brothers were plainly not intending to linger more than a moment, but the spectacle of a bevy of girls dancing without male partners seemed to amuse the third, and make him in no hurry to move on. He unstrapped his knapsack, put it, with his stick, on the hedge-bank, and opened the gate.

'What are you going to do, Angel?' asked the eldest.

'I am inclined to go and have a fling with them. Why not all of us—just for a minute or two—it will not detain us long?'

'No—no; nonsense!' said the first. 'Dancing in public with a troop of country hoydens—suppose we should be seen! Come along, or it will be dark before we get to Stourcastle, and there's no place we can sleep at nearer than that; besides, we must get through another chapter of *A Counterblast to Agnosticism* before we turn in, now I have taken the trouble to bring the book.'

'All right—I'll overtake you and Cuthbert in five minutes; don't stop; I give my word that I will, Felix.'

The two elder reluctantly left him and walked on, taking their brother's knapsack to relieve him in following, and the youngest entered the field.

'This is a thousand pities,' he said gallantly, to two or three of the girls nearest him, as soon as there was a pause in the dance. 'Where are your partners, my dears?'

'They've not left off work yet,' answered one of the boldest. 'They'll be here by and by. Till then, will you be one, sir?'

'Certainly. But what's one among so many!'

'Better than none. 'Tis melancholy work facing and footing it to one of your own sort, and no clipsing and colling at all. Now, pick and choose.'

''Ssh—don't be so for'ard!' said a shyer girl.

The young man, thus invited, glanced them over, and attempted some discrimination; but, as the group were all so new to him, he could not very well exercise it. He took almost the first that came to hand, which was not the speaker, as she had expected; nor did it happen to be Tess Durbeyfield. Pedigree, ancestral skeletons, monumental record, the d'Urberville lineaments, did not help Tess in her life's battle as yet, even to the extent of attracting to her a dancing-partner over the heads of the commonest peasantry. So much for Norman blood unaided by Victorian lucre.

The name of the eclipsing girl, whatever it was, has not been handed down; but she was envied by all as the first who enjoyed the luxury of a masculine partner that evening. Yet such was the force of example that the village young men, who had not hastened to enter the gate while no intruder was in the way, now dropped in quickly, and soon the couples became leavened with rustic youth to a marked extent, till at length the plainest woman in the club was no longer compelled to foot it on the masculine side of the figure.

The church clock struck, when suddenly the student said that he must leave—he had been forgetting himself—he had to join his companions. As he fell out of the dance his eyes lighted on Tess Durbeyfield, whose own large orbs wore, to tell the truth, the faintest aspect of reproach that he had not chosen her. He, too, was sorry then that, owing to her backwardness, he had not observed her; and with that in his mind he left the pasture.

On account of his long delay he started in a flying-run down the lane westward, and had soon passed the hollow and mounted the next rise. He had not yet overtaken his brothers, but he paused to get breath, and looked back. He could see the white figures of the girls in the green enclosure whirling about as they had whirled when he was among them. They seemed to have quite forgotten him already.

All of them, except, perhaps, one. This white shape stood apart by the hedge alone. From her position he knew it to be the pretty maiden with whom he had not danced. Trifling as the matter was, he yet instinctively felt that she was hurt by his oversight. He wished that he had asked her; he wished that he had inquired her name. She was so modest, so expressive, she had looked so soft in her thin white gown that he felt he had acted stupidly.

However, it could not be helped, and turning, and bending himself to a rapid walk, he dismissed the subject from his mind.

III

As for Tess Durbeyfield, she did not easily dislodge the incident from her consideration. She had no spirit to dance again for a long time, though she might have had plenty of partners; but, ah! they did not speak so nicely as the strange young man had done. It was not till the rays of the sun had absorbed the young stranger's retreating figure on the hill that she shook off her temporary sadness and answered her would-be partner in the affirmative.

She remained with her comrades till dusk, and participated with a certain zest in the dancing; though, being heart-whole as yet, she enjoyed treading a measure purely for its own sake; little divining when she saw 'the soft torments, the bitter sweets, the pleasing pains, and the agreeable distresses' of those girls who had been wooed and won, what she herself was capable of in that kind. The struggles and wrangles of the lads for her hand in a jig were an amusement to her—no more; and when they became fierce she rebuked them.

She might have stayed even later, but the incident of her father's odd appearance and manner returned upon the girl's mind to make her anxious, and wondering what had become of him she dropped away from the dancers and bent her steps towards the end of the village at which the parental cottage lay.

While yet many score yards off, other rhythmic sounds than those she had quitted became audible to her; sounds that she knew well—so well. They were a regular series of thumpings from the interior of the house, occasioned by the violent rocking of a cradle upon a stone floor, to which movement a feminine voice kept time by singing, in a vigorous gallopade, the favourite ditty of 'The Spotted Cow'—

I saw her lie do′-own in yon′-der green gro′-ove;
Come, love!′ and I'll tell′ you where!′

The cradle-rocking and the song would cease simultaneously for a moment, and an exclamation at highest vocal pitch would take the place of the melody.

'God bless thy diment eyes! And thy waxen cheeks! And thy cherry mouth! And thy Cubit's thighs! And every bit o' thy blessed body!'

After this invocation the rocking and the singing would recommence, and the 'Spotted Cow' proceed as before. So matters stood when Tess opened the door, and paused upon the mat within it surveying the scene.

The interior, in spite of the melody, struck upon the girl's senses with an unspeakable dreariness. From the holiday gaieties of the field—the white gowns, the nosegays, the willow-wands, the whirling movements on the green, the flash of gentle sentiment towards the stranger—to the yellow melancholy of this one-candled spectacle, what a step! Besides the jar of contrast there came to her a chill self-reproach that she had not returned sooner, to help her mother in these domesticities, instead of indulging herself out-of-doors.

There stood her mother amid the group of children, as Tess had left her, hanging over the Monday washing-tub, which had now, as always, lingered on to the end of the week. Out of that tub had come the day before—Tess felt it with a dreadful sting of remorse—the very white frock upon her back which she had so carelessly greened about the skirt on the damping grass—which had been wrung up and ironed by her mother's own hands.

As usual, Mrs Durbeyfield was balanced on one foot beside the tub, the other being engaged in the aforesaid business of rocking her youngest child. The cradle-rockers had done hard duty for so many years, under the weight of so many children, on that flagstone floor, that they were worn nearly flat, in consequence of which a huge jerk accompanied each swing of the cot, flinging the baby from side to side like a weaver's shuttle, as Mrs Durbeyfield, excited by her song, trod the rocker with all the spring that was left in her after a long day's seething in the suds.

Nick-knock, nick-knock, went the cradle; the candle-flame stretched itself tall, and began jigging up and down; the water dribbled from the matron's elbows, and the song galloped on to the end of the verse, Mrs Durbeyfield regarding her daughter the while. Even now, when burdened with a young family, Joan Durbeyfield was a passionate lover of tune. No ditty floated into Blackmoor Vale from the outer world but Tess's mother caught up its notation in a week.

There still faintly beamed from the woman's features something of the freshness, and even the prettiness, of her youth; rendering it probable that the personal charms which Tess could boast of were in main part her mother's gift, and therefore unknightly, unhistorical.

'I'll rock the cradle for 'ee, mother,' said the daughter gently. 'Or I'll take off my best frock and help you wring up? I thought you had finished long ago.'

Her mother bore Tess no ill-will for leaving the house-work to her singlehanded efforts for so long; indeed, Joan seldom upbraided her thereon at any time, feeling but slightly the lack of Tess's assistance whilst her instinctive plan for relieving herself of her labours lay in postponing them. To-night, however, she was even in a blither mood than usual. There was a dreaminess, a preoccupation, an exaltation, in the maternal look which the girl could not understand.

'Well, I'm glad you've come,' her mother said, as soon as the last note had passed out of her. 'I want to go and fetch your father; but what's more'n that, I want to tell 'ee what have happened. Y'll be fess enough, my poppet, when th'st know!' (Mrs Durbeyfield habitually spoke the dialect; her daughter who had passed the Sixth Standard in the National School under a London-trained mistress, spoke two languages; the dialect at home, more or less; ordinary English abroad and to persons of quality.)

'Since I've been away?' Tess asked.

'Ay!'

'Had it anything to do with father's making such a mommet of himself in thik carriage this afternoon? Why did 'er! I felt inclined to sink into the ground with shame!'

'That wer all a part of the larry! We've been found to be the greatest gentlefolk in the whole county—reaching all back long before Oliver Grumble's time—to the days of the Pagan Turks—

with monuments, and vaults, and crests, and 'scutcheons, and the Lord knows what all. In Saint Charles's days we was made Knights o' the Royal Oak, our real name being d'Urberville! . . . Don't that make your bosom plim? 'Twas on this account that your father rode home in the vlee; not because he'd been drinking, as people supposed.'

'I'm glad of that. Will it do us any good, mother?'

'O yes! 'Tis thoughted that great things may come o't. No doubt a mampus of volk of our own rank will be down here in their carriage as soon as 'tis known. Your father learnt it on his way hwome from Shaston and he has been telling me the whole pedigree of the matter.'

'Where is father now?' asked Tess suddenly.

Her mother gave irrelevant information by way of answer: 'He called to see the doctor to-day in Shaston. It is not consumption at all, it seems. It is fat round his heart, 'a says. There, it is like this.' Joan Durbeyfield, as she spoke, curved a sodden thumb and forefinger to the shape of the letter C, and used the other forefinger as a pointer. ' "At the present moment," he says to your father, "your heart is enclosed all round there, and all round there; this space is still open," 'a says. "As soon as it do meet, so," '—Mrs Durbeyfield closed her fingers into a circle complete—' "off you will go like a shadder, Mr Durbeyfield," 'a says. "You mid last ten years; you mid go off in ten months, or ten days." '

Tess looked alarmed. Her father possibly to go behind the eternal cloud so soon, notwithstanding this sudden greatness!

'But where *is* father?' she asked again.

Her mother put on a deprecating look. 'Now don't you be bursting out angry! The poor man—he felt so rafted after his uplifting by the pa'son's news—that he went up to Rolliver's half an hour ago. He do want to get up his strength for his journey to-morrow with that load of beehives, which must be delivered, family or no. He'll have to start shortly after twelve to-night, as the distance is so long.'

'Get up his strength!' said Tess impetuously, the tears welling in her eyes. 'O my God! Go to a public-house to get up his strength! And you as well agreed as he, mother!'

Her rebuke and her mood seemed to fill the whole room, and to impart a cowed look to the furniture, and candle, and children playing about, and to her mother's face.

'No,' said the latter touchily, 'I be not agreed. I have been waiting for 'ee to bide and keep house while I go to fetch him.'

'I'll go.'

'O no, Tess. You see, it would be no use.'

Tess did not expostulate. She knew what her mother's objection meant. Mrs Durbeyfield's jacket and bonnet were already hanging slily upon a chair by her side, in readiness for this contemplated jaunt, the reason for which the matron deplored more than its necessity.

'And take the *Compleat Fortune-Teller* to the outhouse,' Joan continued, rapidly wiping her hands, and donning the garments.

The *Compleat Fortune-Teller* was an old thick volume, which lay on a table at her elbow, so worn by pocketing that the margins had reached the edge of the type. Tess took it up, and her mother started.

This going to hunt up her shiftless husband at the inn was one of Mrs Durbeyfield's still extant enjoyments in the muck and muddle of rearing children. To discover him at Rolliver's, to sit there for an hour or two by his side and dismiss all thought and care of the children during the interval, made her happy. A sort of halo, an occidental glow, came over life then. Troubles and other realities took on themselves a metaphysical impalpability, sinking to mere mental phenomena for serene contemplation, and no longer stood as pressing concretions which chafed body and soul. The youngsters, not immediately within sight, seemed rather bright and desirable appurtenances than otherwise; the incidents of daily life were not without humorousness and jollity in their aspect there. She felt a little as she had used to feel when she sat by her now wedded husband in the same spot during his wooing, shutting her eyes to his defects of character, and regarding him only in his ideal presentation as lover.

Tess, being left alone with the younger children, went first to the outhouse with the fortune-telling book, and stuffed it into the thatch. A curious fetichistic fear of this grimy volume on the part of her mother prevented her ever allowing it to stay in the house all night, and hither it was brought back whenever it had been consulted. Between the mother, with her fast-perishing lumber of superstitions, folk-lore, dialect, and orally transmitted ballads, and the daughter, with her trained National teachings and Standard knowledge under an infinitely Revised Code, there was a gap of two hundred years as ordinarily understood. When they were together the Jacobean and the Victorian ages were juxtaposed.

Returning along the garden path Tess mused on what the mother could have wished to ascertain from the book on this particular day. She guessed the recent ancestral discovery to bear upon it, but did not divine that it solely concerned herself. Dismissing this, however, she busied herself with sprinkling the linen dried during the daytime, in company with her nine-year-old brother Abraham, and her sister Eliza-Louisa of twelve and a half, called ''Liza-Lu', the youngest ones being put to bed. There was an interval of four years and more between Tess and the next of the family, the two who had filled the gap having died in their infancy, and this lent her a deputy-maternal attitude when she was alone with her juniors. Next in juvenility to Abraham came two more girls, Hope and Modesty; then a boy of three, and then the baby, who had just completed his first year.

All these young souls were passengers in the Durbeyfield ship—entirely dependent on the judgment of the two Durbeyfield adults for their pleasures, their necessities, their health, even their existence. If the heads of the Durbeyfield household chose to sail into difficulty, disaster, starvation, disease, degradation, death, thither were these half-dozen little captives under hatches compelled to sail with them—six helpless creatures, who had never been asked if they wished for life on any terms, much less if they wished for it on such hard conditions as were involved in being of the shiftless house of Durbeyfield. Some people would like to know whence the poet whose philosophy is in these days deemed as profound and trustworthy as his song is breezy and pure, gets his authority for speaking of 'Nature's holy plan'.

It grew later, and neither father nor mother reappeared. Tess looked out of the door, and took a mental journey through Marlott.

The village was shutting its eyes. Candles and lamps were being put out everywhere: she could inwardly behold the extinguisher and the extended hand.

Her mother's fetching simply meant one more to fetch. Tess began to perceive that a man in indifferent health, who proposed to start on a journey before one in the morning, ought not to be at an inn at this late hour celebrating his ancient blood.

'Abraham,' she said to her little brother, 'do you put on your hat—you bain't afraid?—and go up to Rolliver's, and see what has gone wi' father and mother.'

The boy jumped promptly from his seat, and opened the door, and the night swallowed him up. Half an hour passed yet again; neither man, woman, nor child returned. Abraham, like his parents, seemed to have been limed and caught by the ensnaring inn.

'I must go myself,' she said.

'Liza-Lu then went to bed, and Tess, locking them all in, started on her way up the dark and crooked lane or street not made for hasty progress; a street laid out before inches of land had value, and when one-handed clocks sufficiently subdivided the day.

IV

Rolliver's inn, the single alehouse at this end of the long and broken village, could only boast of an off-licence; hence, as nobody could legally drink on the premises, the amount of overt accommodation for consumers was strictly limited to a little board about six inches wide and two yards long, fixed to the garden palings by pieces of wire, so as to form a ledge. On this board thirsty strangers deposited their cups as they stood in the road and drank, and threw the dregs on the dusty ground to the pattern of Polynesia, and wished they could have a restful seat inside.

Thus the strangers. But there were also local customers who felt the same wish; and where there's a will there's a way.

In a large bedroom upstairs, the window of which was thickly curtained with a great woollen shawl lately discarded by the landlady Mrs Rolliver, were gathered on this evening nearly a dozen persons, all seeking beatitude; all old inhabitants of the nearer end of Marlott, and frequenters of this retreat. Not only did the distance to The Pure Drop, the fully-licensed tavern at the further part of the dispersed village, render its accommodation practically unavailable for dwellers at this end; but the far more serious question, the quality of the liquor, confirmed the prevalent opinion that it was better to drink with Rolliver in a corner of the housetop than with the other landlord in a wide house.

A gaunt four-post bedstead which stood in the room afforded sitting-space for several persons gathered round three of its sides; a couple more men had elevated themselves on a chest of drawers; another rested on the oak-carved 'cwoffer'; two on the washstand; another on the stool; and thus all were, somehow, seated at their ease. The stage of mental comfort to which they had arrived at this hour was one wherein their souls expanded beyond their skins, and spread their personalities warmly through the room. In this process the chamber and its furniture grew more and more dignified and luxurious; the shawl hanging at the window took upon itself the richness of tapestry; the brass handles of the chest of drawers were as golden knockers; and the carved bed-posts seemed to have some kinship with the magnificent pillars of Solomon's temple.

Mrs Durbeyfield, having quickly walked hitherward after parting from Tess, opened the front door, crossed the downstairs room, which was in deep gloom, and then unfastened the stair-door like one whose fingers knew the tricks of the latches well. Her ascent of the crooked staircase was a slower process, and her face, as it rose into the light above the last stair, encountered the gaze of all the party assembled in the bedroom.

'—Being a few private friends I've asked in to keep up club-walking at my own expense,' the landlady exclaimed at the sound of footsteps, as glibly as a child repeating the Catechism, while she peered over the stairs. 'Oh, 'tis you, Mrs Durbeyfield—Lard—how you frightened me!—I thought it might be some gaffer sent by Gover'ment.'

Mrs Durbeyfield was welcomed with glances and nods by the remainder of the conclave, and turned to where her husband sat. He was humming absently to himself, in a low tone: 'I be as good as some folks here and there! I've got a great family vault at Kingsbere-sub-Greenhill, and finer skillentons than any man in Wessex!'

'I've something to tell 'ee that's come into my head about that—a grand projick!' whispered his cheerful wife. 'Here, John, don't 'ee see me?' She nudged him, while he, looking through her as through a window-pane, went on with his recitative.

'Hush! Don't 'ee sing so loud, my good man,' said the landlady; 'in case any member of the Gover'ment should be passing, and take away my licends.'

'He's told 'ee what's happened to us, I suppose?' asked Mrs Durbeyfield.

'Yes—in a way. D'ye think there's any money hanging by it?'

'Ah, that's the secret,' said Joan Durbeyfield sagely. 'However, 'tis well to be kin to a coach, even if you don't ride in 'en.' She dropped her public voice, and continued in a low tone to her husband: 'I've been thinking since you brought the news that there's a great rich lady out by Trantridge, on the edge o' The Chase, of the name of d'Urberville.'

'Hey—what's that?' said Sir John.

She repeated the information. 'That lady must be our relation,' she said. 'And my projick is to send Tess to claim kin.'

'There *is* a lady of the name, now you mention it,' said Durbeyfield. 'Pa'son Tringham didn't think of that. But she's nothing beside we—a junior branch of us, no doubt, hailing along since King Norman's day.'

While this question was being discussed neither of the pair noticed, in their preoccupation, that little Abraham had crept into the room, and was awaiting an opportunity of asking them to return.

'She is rich, and she'd be sure to take notice o' the maid,' continued Mrs Durbeyfield; 'and 'twill be a very good thing. I don't see why two branches o' one family should not be on visiting terms.'

'Yes; and we'll all claim kin!' said Abraham brightly from under the bedstead. 'And we'll all go and see her when Tess has gone to live with her; and we'll ride in her coach and wear black clothes!'

'How do you come here, child? What nonsense be ye talking! Go away, and play on the stairs till father and mother be ready! . . . Well, Tess ought to go to this other member of our family. She'd be sure to win the lady—Tess would; and likely enough 'twould lead to some noble gentleman marrying her. In short, I know it.'

'How?'

'I tried her fate in the *Fortune-Teller*, and it brought out that very thing! . . . You should ha' seen how pretty she looked to-day; her skin is as sumple as a duchess's.'

'What says the maid herself to going?'

'I've not asked her. She don't know there is any such lady-relation yet. But it would certainly put her in the way of a grand marriage, and she won't say nay to going.'

'Tess is queer.'

'But she's tractable at bottom. Leave her to me.'

Though this conversation had been private, sufficient of its import reached the understandings of those around to suggest to them that the Durbeyfields had weightier concerns to talk of now than common folks had, and that Tess, their pretty eldest daughter, had fine prospects in store.

'Tess is a fine figure o' fun, as I said to myself to-day when I zeed her vamping round parish with the rest,' observed one of the elderly boozers in an undertone. 'But Joan Durbeyfield must mind that she don't get green malt in floor.' It was a local phrase which had a peculiar meaning, and there was no reply.

The conversation became inclusive, and presently other footsteps were heard crossing the room below.

'—Being a few private friends asked in to-night to keep up club-walking at my own expense.' The landlady had rapidly re-used the formula she kept on hand for intruders before she recognized that the newcomer was Tess.

Even to her mother's gaze the girl's young features looked sadly out of place amid the alcoholic vapours which floated here as no unsuitable medium for wrinkled middle-age; and hardly was a reproachful flash from Tess's dark eyes needed to make her father and mother rise from their seats, hastily finish their ale, and descend the stairs behind her, Mrs Rolliver's caution following their footsteps.

'No noise, please, if ye'll be so good, my dears; or I mid lose my licends, and be summons'd, and I don't know what all! 'Night t'ye!'

They went home together, Tess holding one arm of her father, and Mrs Durbeyfield the other. He had, in truth, drunk very little—not a fourth of the quantity which a systematic tippler could carry to church on a Sunday afternoon without a hitch in his eastings or genuflections; but the weakness of Sir John's constitution made mountains of his pretty sins in this kind. On reaching the fresh air he was sufficiently unsteady to incline the row of three at one moment as if they were marching to London, and at another as if they were marching to Bath—which produced a comical effect, frequent enough in families on nocturnal homegoings; and, like most comical effects, not quite so comic after all. The two women valiantly disguised these forced excursions and counter-marches as well as they could from Durbeyfield their cause, and from Abraham, and from themselves; and so they approached by degrees their own door, the head of the family bursting suddenly into his former refrain as he drew near, as if to fortify his soul at sight of the smallness of his present residence—

'I've got a fam-ily vault at Kingsbere!'

'Hush—don't be so silly, Jacky,' said his wife. 'Yours is not the only family that was of 'count in wold days. Look at the Anktells, and Horseys, and the Tringhams themselves—gone to seed a'most as much as you—though you was bigger folks than they, that's true. Thank God, I was never of no family, and have nothing to be ashamed of in that way!'

'Don't you be so sure o' that. From your nater 'tis my belief you've disgraced yourselves more than any o' us, and was kings and queens outright at one time.'

Tess turned the subject by saying what was far more prominent in her own mind at the moment than thoughts of her ancestry—

'I am afraid father won't be able to take the journey with the beehives tomorrow so early.'

'I? I shall be all right in an hour or two,' said Durbeyfield.

It was eleven o'clock before the family were all in bed, and two o'clock next morning was the latest hour for starting with the beehives if they were to be delivered to the retailers in Casterbridge before the Saturday market began, the way thither lying by bad roads over a distance of between twenty and thirty miles, and the horse and waggon being of the slowest. At half-past one Mrs Durbeyfield came into the large bedroom where Tess and all her little brothers and sisters slept.

'The poor man can't go,' she said to her eldest daughter, whose great eyes had opened the moment her mother's hand touched the door.

Tess sat up in bed, lost in a vague interspace between a dream and this information.

'But somebody must go,' she replied. 'It is late for the hives already. Swarming will soon be over for the year; and if we put off taking 'em till next week's market the call for 'em will be past, and they'll be thrown on our hands.'

Mrs Durbeyfield looked unequal to the emergency. 'Some young feller, perhaps, would go? One of them who were so much after dancing with 'ee yesterday,' she presently suggested.

'O no—I wouldn't have it for the world!' declared Tess proudly. 'And letting everybody know the reason—such a thing to be ashamed of! I think *I* could go if Abraham could go with me to kip me company.'

Her mother at length agreed to this arrangement. Little Abraham was aroused from his deep sleep in a corner of the same apartment, and made to put on his clothes while still mentally in the other world. Meanwhile Tess had hastily dressed herself; and the twain, lighting a lantern, went out to the stable. The rickety little waggon was already laden, and the girl led out the horse Prince, only a degree less rickety than the vehicle.

The poor creature looked wonderingly round at the night, at the lantern, at their two figures, as if he could not believe that at that hour, when every living thing was intended to be in shelter and at rest, he was called upon to go out and labour. They put a stock of candle-ends into the lantern, hung the latter to the off-side of the load, and directed the horse onward, walking at his shoulder at first during the uphill parts of the way, in order not to overload an animal of so little vigour. To cheer themselves as well as they could, they made an artificial morning with the lantern, some bread and butter, and their own conversation, the real morning being far from come. Abraham, as he more fully awoke (for he had moved in a sort of trance so far), began to talk of the strange shapes assumed by the various dark objects against the sky; of this tree that looked like a raging tiger springing from a lair; of that which resembled a giant's head.

When they had passed the little town of Stourcastle, dumbly somnolent under its thick brown thatch, they reached higher ground. Still higher, on their left, the elevation called Bulbarrow or Bealbarrow, well-nigh the highest in South Wessex, swelled into the sky; engirdled by its earthen trenches. From hereabout the long road was fairly level for some distance onward. They mounted in front of the waggon, and Abraham grew reflective.

'Tess!' he said in a preparatory tone, after a silence.

'Yes, Abraham.'

'Bain't you glad that we've become gentlefolk?'

'Not particular glad.'

'But you be glad that you 'm going to marry a gentleman?'

'What?' said Tess, lifting her face.

'That our great relation will help 'ee to marry a gentleman.'

'I? Our great relation? We have no such relation. What has put that into your head?'

'I heard 'em talking about it up at Rolliver's when I went to find father. There's a rich lady of our family out at Trantridge, and mother said that if you claimed kin with the lady, she'd put 'ee in the way of marrying a gentleman.'

His sister became abruptly still, and lapsed into a pondering silence. Abraham talked on, rather for the pleasure of utterance than for audition, so that his sister's abstraction was of no account. He leant back against the hives, and with upturned face made observations on the stars, whose cold pulses were beating amid the black hollows above, in serene dissociation from these two wisps of human life. He asked how far away those twinklers were, and whether God was on the other side of them. But ever and anon his childish prattle recurred to what impressed his imagination even more deeply than the wonders of creation. If Tess were made rich by marrying a gentleman, would she have money enough to buy a spy-glass so large that it would draw the stars as near to her as Nettlecombe-Tout?

The renewed subject, which seemed to have impregnated the whole family, filled Tess with impatience.

'Never mind that now!' she exclaimed.

'Did you say the stars were worlds, Tess?'

'Yes.'

'All like ours?'

'I don't know; but I think so. They sometimes seem to be like the apples on our stubbard-tree. Most of them splendid and sound—a few blighted.'

'Which do we live on—a splendid one or a blighted one?'

'A blighted one.'

‘’Tis very unlucky that we didn’t pitch on a sound one, when there were so many more of ’em!’

‘Yes.’

‘Is it like that *really*, Tess?’ said Abraham, turning to her much impressed, on reconsideration of this rare information. ‘How would it have been if we had pitched on a sound one?’

‘Well, father wouldn’t have coughed and creeped about as he does, and wouldn’t have got too tipsy to go this journey; and mother wouldn’t have been always washing, and never getting finished.’

‘And you would have been a rich lady ready-made, and not have had to be made rich by marrying a gentleman?’

‘O Aby, don’t—don’t talk of that any more!’

Left to his reflections Abraham soon grew drowsy. Tess was not skilful in the management of a horse, but she thought that she could take upon herself the entire conduct of the load for the present, and allow Abraham to go to sleep if he wished to do so. She made him a sort of nest in front of the hives, in such a manner that he could not fall, and taking the reins into her own hands, jogged on as before.

Prince required but slight attention, lacking energy for superfluous movements of any sort. With no longer a companion to distract her, Tess fell more deeply into reverie than ever, her back leaning against the hives. The mute procession past her shoulders of trees and hedges became attached to fantastic scenes outside reality, and the occasional heave of the wind became the sigh of some immense sad soul, conterminous with the universe in space, and with history in time.

Then, examining the mesh of events in her own life, she seemed to see the vanity of her father’s pride; the gentlemanly suitor awaiting herself in her mother’s fancy; to see him as a grimacing personage, laughing at her poverty, and her shrouded knightly ancestry. Everything grew more and more extravagant, and she no longer knew how time passed. A sudden jerk shook her in her seat, and Tess awoke from the sleep into which she, too, had fallen.

They were a long way further on than when she had lost consciousness, and the waggon had stopped. A hollow groan, unlike anything she had ever heard in her life, came from the front, followed by a shout of 'Hoi there!'

The lantern hanging at her waggon had gone out, but another was shining in her face—much brighter than her own had been. Something terrible had happened. The harness was entangled with an object which blocked the way.

In consternation Tess jumped down, and discovered the dreadful truth. The groan had proceeded from her father's poor horse Prince. The morning mail-cart, with its two noiseless wheels, speeding along these lanes like an arrow, as it always did, had driven into her slow and unlighted equipage. The pointed shaft of the cart had entered the breast of the unhappy Prince like a sword, and from the wound his life's blood was spouting in a stream, and falling with a hiss into the road.

In her despair Tess sprang forward and put her hand upon the hole, with the only result that she became splashed from face to skirt with the crimson drops. Then she stood helplessly looking on. Prince also stood firm and motionless as long as he could; till he suddenly sank down in a heap.

By this time the mail-cart man had joined her, and began dragging and unharnessing the hot form of Prince. But he was already dead, and, seeing that nothing more could be done immediately, the mail-cart man returned to his own animal, which was uninjured.

'You was on the wrong side,' he said. 'I am bound to go on with the mail-bags, so that the best thing for you to do is to bide here with your load. I'll send somebody to help you as soon as I can. It is getting daylight, and you have nothing to fear.'

He mounted and sped on his way; while Tess stood and waited. The atmosphere turned pale, the birds shook themselves in the hedges, arose, and twittered; the lane showed all its white features, and Tess showed hers, still whiter. The huge pool of blood in front of her was already assuming the iridescence of coagulation; and when the sun rose a hundred prismatic hues were reflected from it. Prince lay alongside still and stark; his eyes half open, the hole in his chest looking scarcely large enough to have let out all that had animated him.

''Tis all my doing—all mine!' the girl cried, gazing at the spectacle. 'No excuse for me—none. What will mother and father live on now? Aby, Aby!' She shook the child, who had slept soundly through the whole disaster. 'We can't go on with our load—Prince is killed!'

When Abraham realized all, the furrows of fifty years were extemporized on his young face.

'Why, I danced and laughed only yesterday!' she went on to herself. 'To think that I was such a fool!'

''Tis because we be on a blighted star, and not a sound one, isn't it, Tess?' murmured Abraham through his tears.

In silence they waited through an interval which seemed endless. At length a sound, and an approaching object, proved to them that the driver of the mail-cart had been as good as his word. A farmer's man from near Stourcastle came up, leading a strong cob. He was harnessed to the waggon of beehives in the place of Prince, and the load taken on towards Casterbridge.

The evening of the same day saw the empty waggon reach again the spot of the accident. Prince had lain there in the ditch since the morning; but the place of the blood-pool was still visible in the middle of the road, though scratched and scraped over by passing vehicles. All that was left of Prince was now hoisted into the waggon he had formerly hauled, and with his hoofs in the air, and his shoes shining in the setting sunlight he retraced the eight or nine miles to Marlott.

Tess had gone back earlier. How to break the news was more than she could think. It was a relief to her tongue to find from the faces of her parents that they already knew of their loss, though this did not lessen the self-reproach which she continued to heap upon herself for her negligence.

But the very shiftlessness of the household rendered the misfortune a less terrifying one to them than it would have been to a striving family, though in the present case it meant ruin, and in the other it would only have meant inconvenience. In the Durbeyfield countenances there was nothing of the red wrath that would have burnt upon the girl from parents more ambitious for her welfare. Nobody blamed Tess as she blamed herself.

When it was discovered that the knacker and tanner would

give only a very few shillings for Prince's carcase because of his decrepitude, Durbeyfield rose to the occasion.

'No,' said he stoically, 'I won't sell his old body. When we d'Urbervilles was knights in the land, we didn't sell our chargers for cat's meat. Let 'em keep their shillings! He've served me well in his lifetime, and I won't part from him now.'

He worked harder the next day in digging a grave for Prince in the garden than he had worked for months to grow a crop for his family. When the hole was ready, Durbeyfield and his wife tied a rope round the horse and dragged him up the path towards it, the children following in funeral train. Abraham and 'Liza-Lu sobbed, Hope and Modesty discharged their griefs in loud blares which echoed from the walls; and when Prince was tumbled in they gathered round the grave. The bread-winner had been taken away from them; what would they do?

'Is he gone to heaven?' asked Abraham, between the sobs.

Then Durbeyfield began to shovel in the earth, and the children cried anew. All except Tess. Her face was dry and pale, as though she regarded herself in the light of a murderess.

V

THE haggling business, which had mainly depended on the horse, became disorganized forthwith. Distress, if not penury, loomed in the distance. Durbeyfield was what was locally called a slack-twisted fellow; he had good strength to work at times; but the times could not be relied on to coincide with the hours of requirement; and, having been unaccustomed to the regular toil of the day-labourer, he was not particularly persistent when they did so coincide.

Tess, meanwhile, as the one who had dragged her parents into this quagmire, was silently wondering what she could do to help them out of it; and then her mother broached her scheme.

'We must take the ups wi' the downs, Tess,' said she; 'and never could your high blood have been found out at a more called-for moment. You must try your friends. Do ye know that there is a very rich Mrs d'Urberville living on the outskirts o' The Chase, who must be our relation? You must go to her and claim kin, and ask for some help in our trouble.'

'I shouldn't care to do that,' says Tess. 'If there is such a lady, 'twould be enough for us if she were friendly—not to expect her to give us help.'

'You could win her round to do anything, my dear. Besides, perhaps there's more in it than you know of. I've heard what I've heard, good-now.'

The oppressive sense of the harm she had done led Tess to be more deferential than she might otherwise have been to the maternal wish; but she could not understand why her mother should find such satisfaction in contemplating an enterprise of, to her, such doubtful profit. Her mother might have made inquiries, and have discovered that this Mrs d'Urberville was a lady of unequalled virtues and charity. But Tess's pride made the part of poor relation one of particular distaste to her.

'I'd rather try to get work,' she murmured.

'Durbeyfield, you can settle it,' said his wife, turning to where he sat in the background. 'If you say she ought to go, she will go.'

'I don't like my children going and making themselves beholden to strange kin,' murmured he. 'I'm the head of the noblest branch o' the family, and I ought to live up to it.'

His reasons for staying away were worse to Tess than her own objection to going. 'Well, as I killed the horse, mother,' she said mournfully, 'I suppose I ought to do something. I don't mind going and seeing her, but you must leave it to me about asking for help. And don't go thinking about her making a match for me—it is silly.'

'Very well said, Tess!' observed her father sententiously.

'Who said I had such a thought?' asked Joan.

'I fancy it is in your mind, mother. But I'll go.'

Rising early next day she walked to the hill-town called Shaston, and there took advantage of a van which twice in the week ran from Shaston eastward to Chaseborough, passing near Trantridge, the parish in which the vague and mysterious Mrs d'Urberville had her residence.

Tess Durbeyfield's route on this memorable morning lay amid the north-eastern undulations of the Vale in which she had been born, and in which her life had unfolded. The Vale of Blackmoor was to her the world, and its inhabitants the races thereof. From the gates and stiles of Marlott she had looked down its length in the wondering days of infancy, and what had been mystery to her then was not much less than mystery to her now. She had seen daily from her chamber-window towers, villages, faint white mansions; above all the town of Shaston standing majestically on its height; its windows shining like lamps in the evening sun. She had hardly ever visited the place, only a small tract even of the Vale and its environs being known to her by close inspection. Much less had she been far outside the valley. Every contour of the surrounding hills was as personal to her as that of her relatives' faces; but for what lay beyond her judgment was dependent on the teaching of the village school, where she had held a leading place at the time of her leaving, a year or two before this date.

In those early days she had been much loved by others of her own sex and age, and had used to be seen about the village as one of three—all nearly of the same year—walking home from school side by side; Tess the middle one—in a pink print pinafore, of a finely reticulated pattern, worn over a stuff frock that had lost its original colour for a nondescript tertiary—marching on upon long stalky legs, in tight stockings which had little ladder-like holes at the knees, torn by kneeling in the roads and banks in search of vegetable and mineral treasures; her then earth-coloured hair hanging like pot-hooks; the arms of the two outside girls resting round the waist of Tess; her arms on the shoulders of the two supporters.

As Tess grew older, and began to see how matters stood, she felt quite a Malthusian towards her mother for thoughtlessly giving her so many little sisters and brothers, when it was such a trouble to nurse and provide for them. Her mother's intelligence was that of a happy child: Joan Durbeyfield was simply an additional one, and that not the eldest, to her own long family of waiters on Providence.

However, Tess became humanely beneficent towards the small ones, and to help them as much as possible she used, as soon as she left school, to lend a hand at haymaking or harvesting on neighbouring farms; or, by preference, at milking or butter-making processes, which she had learnt when her father had owned cows; and being deft-fingered it was a kind of work in which she excelled.

Every day seemed to throw upon her young shoulders more of the family burdens, and that Tess should be the representative of the Durbeyfields at the d'Urberville mansion came as a thing of course. In this instance it must be admitted that the Durbeyfields were putting their fairest side outward.

She alighted from the van at Trantridge Cross, and ascended on foot a hill in the direction of the district known as The Chase, on the borders of which, as she had been informed, Mrs d'Urberville's seat, The Slopes, would be found. It was not a manorial home in the ordinary sense, with fields, and pastures, and a grumbling farmer, out of whom the owner had to squeeze an income for himself and his family by hook or by crook. It was more, far more; a country-house built for enjoyment pure and simple, with not an acre of troublesome land attached to it beyond what was required for residential purposes, and for a little fancy farm kept in hand by the owner, and tended by a bailiff.

The crimson brick lodge came first in sight, up to its eaves in dense evergreens. Tess thought this was the mansion itself till, passing through the side wicket with some trepidation, and onward to a point at which the drive took a turn, the house proper stood in full view. It was of recent erection—indeed almost new—and of the same rich red colour that formed such a contrast with the evergreens of the lodge. Far behind the corner of the house—which rose like a geranium bloom against the subdued colours around—stretched the soft azure landscape of The Chase—a truly venerable tract of forest land, one of the few remaining woodlands in England of undoubted primaeval date, wherein Druidical mistletoe was still found on aged oaks, and where enormous yew-trees, not planted by the hand of man, grew as they had grown when they were pollarded for bows. All this sylvan antiquity, however, though visible from The Slopes, was outside the immediate boundaries of the estate.

Everything on this snug property was bright, thriving, and well kept; acres of glass-houses stretched down the inclines to the copses at their feet. Everything looked like money—like the last coin issued from the Mint. The stables, partly screened by Austrian pines and evergreen oaks, and fitted with every late appliance, were as dignified as Chapels-of-Ease. On the extensive lawn stood an ornamental tent, its door being towards her.

Simple Tess Durbeyfield stood at gaze, in a half-alarmed attitude, on the edge of the gravel sweep. Her feet had brought her onward to this point before she had quite realized where she was; and now all was contrary to her expectation.

'I thought we were an old family; but this is all new!' she said, in her artlessness. She wished that she had not fallen in so readily with her mother's plans for 'claiming kin', and had endeavoured to gain assistance nearer home.

The d'Urbervilles—or Stoke-d'Urbervilles, as they at first called themselves—who owned all this, were a somewhat unusual family to find in such an old-fashioned part of the country. Parson

Tringham had spoken truly when he said that our shambling John Durbeyfield was the only really lineal representative of the old d'Urberville family existing in the county, or near it; he might have added, what he knew very well, that the Stoke-d'Urbervilles were no more d'Urbervilles of the true tree than he was himself. Yet it must be admitted that this family formed a very good stock whereon to regraft a name which sadly wanted such renovation.

When old Mr Simon Stoke, latterly deceased, had made his fortune as an honest merchant (some said money-lender) in the North, he decided to settle as a county man in the South of England, out of hail of his business district; and in doing this he felt the necessity of recommencing with a name that would not too readily identify him with the smart tradesman of the past, and that would be less commonplace than the original bald stark words. Conning for an hour in the British Museum the pages of works devoted to extinct, half-extinct, obscured, and ruined families appertaining to the quarter of England in which he proposed to settle, he considered that *d'Urberville* looked and sounded as well as any of them: and d'Urberville accordingly was annexed to his own name for himself and his heirs eternally. Yet he was not an extravagant-minded man in this, and in constructing his family tree on the new basis was duly reasonable in framing his intermarriages and aristocratic links, never inserting a single title above a rank of strict moderation.

Of this work of imagination poor Tess and her parents were naturally in ignorance—much to their discomfiture; indeed, the very possibility of such annexations was unknown to them; who supposed that, though to be well-favoured might be the gift of fortune, a family name came by nature.

Tess still stood hesitating like a bather about to make his plunge, hardly knowing whether to retreat or to persevere, when a figure came forth from the dark triangular door of the tent. It was that of a tall young man, smoking.

He had an almost swarthy complexion, with full lips, badly moulded, though red and smooth, above which was a well-groomed black moustache with curled points, though his age could not be more than three- or four-and-twenty. Despite the touches of bar-

barism in his contours, there was a singular force in the gentleman's face, and in his bold rolling eye.

'Well, my Beauty, what can I do for you?' said he, coming forward. And perceiving that she stood quite confounded: 'Never mind me. I am Mr d'Urberville. Have you come to see me or my mother?'

This embodiment of a d'Urberville and a namesake differed even more from what Tess had expected than the house and grounds had differed. She had dreamed of an aged and dignified face, the sublimation of all the d'Urberville lineaments, furrowed with incarnate memories representing in hieroglyphic the centuries of her family's and England's history. But she screwed herself up to the work in hand, since she could not get out of it, and answered—

'I came to see your mother, sir.'

'I am afraid you cannot see her—she is an invalid,' replied the present representative of the spurious house; for this was Mr Alec, the only son of the lately deceased gentleman. 'Cannot I answer your purpose? What is the business you wish to see her about?'

'It isn't business—it is—I can hardly say what!'

'Pleasure?'

'Oh no. Why, sir, if I tell you, it will seem—'

Tess's sense of a certain ludicrousness in her errand was now so strong that, notwithstanding her awe of him, and her general discomfort at being here, her rosy lips curved towards a smile, much to the attraction of the swarthy Alexander.

'It is so very foolish,' she stammered; 'I fear I can't tell you!'

'Never mind; I like foolish things. Try again, my dear,' said he kindly.

'Mother asked me to come,' Tess continued; 'and, indeed, I was in the mind to do so myself likewise. But I did not think it would be like this. I came, sir, to tell you that we are of the same family as you.'

'Ho! Poor relations?'

'Yes.'

'Stokes?'

'No; d'Urbervilles.'

'Ay, ay; I mean d'Urbervilles.'

'Our names are worn away to Durbeyfield; but we have several proofs that we are d'Urbervilles. Antiquarians hold we are,—and—and we have an old seal, marked with a ramping lion on a shield, and a castle over him. And we have a very old silver spoon, round in the bowl like a little ladle, and marked with the same castle. But it is so worn that mother uses it to stir the pea-soup.'

'A castle argent is certainly my crest,' said he blandly. 'And my arms a lion rampant.'

'And so mother said we ought to make ourselves beknown to you—as we've lost our horse by a bad accident, and are the oldest branch o' the family.'

'Very kind of your mother, I'm sure. And I, for one, don't regret her step.' Alec looked at Tess as he spoke, in a way that made her blush a little. 'And so, my pretty girl, you've come on a friendly visit to us, as relations?'

'I suppose I have,' faltered Tess, looking uncomfortable again.

'Well—there's no harm in it. Where do you live? What are you?'

She gave him brief particulars; and responding to further inquiries told him that she was intending to go back by the same carrier who had brought her.

'It is a long while before he returns past Trantridge Cross. Supposing we walk round the grounds to pass the time, my pretty Coz?'

Tess wished to abridge her visit as much as possible; but the young man was pressing, and she consented to accompany him. He conducted her about the lawns, and flower-beds, and conservatories; and thence to the fruit-garden and green-houses, where he asked her if she liked strawberries.

'Yes,' said Tess, 'when they come.'

'They are already here.' D'Urberville began gathering specimens of the fruit for her, handing them back to her as he stooped; and, presently, selecting a specially fine product of the 'British Queen' variety, he stood up and held it by the stem to her mouth.

'No—no!' she said quickly, putting her fingers between his hand and her lips. 'I would rather take it in my own hand.'

'Nonsense!' he insisted; and in a slight distress she parted her lips and took it in.

They had spent some time wandering desultorily thus. Tess eating in a half-pleased, half-reluctant state whatever d'Urberville offered her. When she could consume no more of the strawberries he filled her little basket with them; and then the two passed round to the rose trees, whence he gathered blossoms and gave her to put in her bosom. She obeyed like one in a dream, and when she could affix no more he himself tucked a bud or two into her hat, and heaped her basket with others in the prodigality of his bounty. At last, looking at his watch, he said, 'Now, by the time you have had something to eat, it will be time for you to leave, if you want to catch the carrier to Shaston. Come here, and I'll see what grub I can find.'

Stoke-d'Urberville took her back to the lawn and into the tent, where he left her, soon reappearing with a basket of light luncheon, which he put before her himself. It was evidently the gentleman's wish not to be disturbed in this pleasant *tête-à-tête* by the servantry.

'Do you mind my smoking?' he asked.

'Oh, not at all, sir.'

He watched her pretty and unconscious munching through the skeins of smoke that pervaded the tent, and Tess Durbeyfield did not divine, as she innocently looked down at the roses in her bosom, that there behind the blue narcotic haze was potentially the 'tragic mischief' of her drama—one who stood fair to be the blood-red ray in the spectrum of her young life. She had an attribute which amounted to a disadvantage just now; and it was this that caused Alec d'Urberville's eyes to rivet themselves upon her. It was a luxuriance of aspect, a fulness of growth, which made her appear more of a woman than she really was. She had inherited the feature from her mother without the quality it denoted. It had troubled her mind occasionally, till her companions had said that it was a fault which time would cure.

She soon had finished her lunch. 'Now I am going home, sir,' she said, rising.

'And what do they call you?' he asked, as he accompanied her along the drive till they were out of sight of the house.

'Tess Durbeyfield, down at Marlott.'

'And you say your people have lost their horse?'

'I—killed him!' she answered, her eyes filling with tears as she gave particulars of Prince's death. 'And I don't know what to do for father on account of it!'

'I must think if I cannot do something. My mother must find a berth for you. But, Tess, no nonsense about "d'Urberville";—"Durbeyfield" only, you know—quite another name.'

'I wish for no better, sir,' said she with something of dignity.

For a moment—only for a moment—when they were in the turning of the drive, between the tall rhododendrons and conifers, before the lodge became visible, he inclined his face towards her as if—but no: he thought better of it, and let her go.

Thus the thing began. Had she perceived this meeting's import she might have asked why she was doomed to be seen and coveted that day by the wrong man, and not by some other man, the right and desired one in all respects—as nearly as humanity can supply the right and desired; yet to him who amongst her acquaintance might have approximated to this kind, she was but a transient impression, half forgotten.

In the ill-judged execution of the well-judged plan of things the call seldom produces the comer, the man to love rarely coincides with the hour of loving. Nature does not often say 'See!' to her poor creature at a time when seeing can lead to happy doing; or reply 'Here!' to a body's cry of 'Where?' till the hide-and-seek has become an irksome, outworn game. We may wonder whether at the acme and summit of the human progress these anachronisms will be corrected by a finer intuition, a closer interaction of the social machinery than that which now jolts us round and along; but such completeness is not to be prophesied, or even conceived as possible. Enough that in the present case, as in millions, it was not the two halves of a perfect whole that confronted each other at the perfect moment; a missing counterpart wandered independently about the earth waiting in crass obtuseness till the late time came. Out of which maladroit delay sprang anxieties, disappointments, shocks, catastrophes, and passing-strange destinies.

When d'Urberville got back to the tent he sat down astride on a chair reflecting, with a pleased gleam in his face. Then he broke into a loud laugh.

'Well, I'm damned! What a funny thing! Ha-ha-ha! And what a crumby girl!'

VI

Tess went down the hill to Trantridge Cross, and inattentively waited to take her seat in the van returning from Chaseborough to Shaston. She did not know what the other occupants said to her as she entered, though she answered them; and when they had started anew she rode along with an inward and not an outward eye.

One among her fellow-travellers addressed her more pointedly than any had spoken before: 'Why, you be quite a posy! And such roses in early June!'

Then she became aware of the spectacle she presented to their surprised vision: roses at her breast; roses in her hat; roses and strawberries in her basket to the brim. She blushed, and said confusedly that the flowers had been given to her. When the passengers were not looking she stealthily removed the more prominent blooms from her hat and placed them in the basket, where she covered them with her handkerchief. Then she fell to reflecting again, and in looking downwards a thorn of the rose remaining in her breast accidentally pricked her chin. Like all the cottagers in Blackmoor Vale, Tess was steeped in fancies and prefigurative superstitions; she thought this an ill omen—the first she had noticed that day.

The van travelled only so far as Shaston, and there were several miles of pedestrian descent from that mountain-town into the vale to Marlott. Her mother had advised her to stay here for the night, at the house of a cottage-woman they knew, if she should feel too tired to come on; and this Tess did, not descending to her home till the following afternoon.

When she entered the house she perceived in a moment from her mother's triumphant manner that something had occurred in the interim.

'Oh yes; I know all about it! I told 'ee it would be all right, and now 'tis proved!'

'Since I've been away? What has?' said Tess rather wearily.

Her mother surveyed the girl up and down with arch approval, and went on banteringly: 'So you've brought 'em round!'

'How do you know, mother?'

'I've had a letter.'

Tess then remembered that there would have been time for this.

'They say—Mrs d'Urberville says—that she wants you to look after a little fowl-farm which is her hobby. But this is only her artful way of getting 'ee there without raising your hopes. She's going to own 'ee as kin—that's the meaning o't.'

'But I didn't see her.'

'You zid somebody, I suppose?'

'I saw her son.'

'And did he own 'ee?'

'Well—he called me Coz.'

'An' I knew it! Jacky—he called her Coz!' cried Joan to her husband. 'Well, he spoke to his mother, of course, and she do want 'ee there.'

'But I don't know that I am apt at tending fowls,' said the dubious Tess.

'Then I don't know who is apt. You've be'n born in the business, and brought up in it. They that be born in a business always know more about it than any 'prentice. Besides, that's only just a show of something for you to do, that you midn't feel beholden.'

'I don't altogether think I ought to go,' said Tess thoughtfully. 'Who wrote the letter? Will you let me look at it?'

'Mrs d'Urberville wrote it. Here it is.'

The letter was in the third person, and briefly informed Mrs Durbeyfield that her daughter's services would be useful to that lady in the management of her poultry-farm, that a comfortable room would be provided for her if she could come, and that the wages would be on a liberal scale if they liked her.

'Oh—that's all!' said Tess.

'You couldn't expect her to throw her arms round 'ee, an' to kiss and to coll 'ee all at once.'

Tess looked out of the window.

'I would rather stay here with father and you,' she said.

'But why?'

'I'd rather not tell you why, mother; indeed, I don't quite know why.'

A week afterwards she came in one evening from an unavailing search for some light occupation in the immediate neighbourhood. Her idea had been to get together sufficient money during the summer to purchase another horse. Hardly had she crossed the threshold before one of the children danced across the room, saying, 'The gentleman's been here!'

Her mother hastened to explain, smiles breaking from every inch of her person. Mrs d'Urberville's son had called on horseback, having been riding by chance in the direction of Marlott. He had wished to know, finally, in the name of his mother, if Tess could really come to manage the old lady's fowl-farm or not; the lad who had hitherto superintended the birds having proved untrustworthy. 'Mr d'Urberville says you must be a good girl if you are at all as you appear; he knows you must be worth your weight in gold. He is very much interested in 'ee—truth to tell.'

Tess seemed for the moment really pleased to hear that she had won such high opinion from a stranger when, in her own esteem, she had sunk so low.

'It is very good of him to think that,' she murmured; 'and if I was quite sure how it would be living there, I would go any-when.'

'He is a mighty handsome man!'

'I don't think so,' said Tess coldly.

'Well, there's your chance, whether or no; and I'm sure he wears a beautiful diamond ring!'

'Yes,' said little Abraham, brightly, from the window-bench; 'and I seed it! and it did twinkle when he put his hand up to his mistarshers. Mother, why did our grand relation keep on putting his hand up to his mistarshers?'

'Hark at that child!' cried Mrs Durbeyfield, with parenthetic admiration.

'Perhaps to show his diamond ring,' murmured Sir John, dreamily, from his chair.

'I'll think it over,' said Tess, leaving the room.

'Well, she's made a conquest o' the younger branch of us, straight off,' continued the matron to her husband, 'and she's a fool if she don't follow it up.'

'I don't quite like my children going away from home,' said the haggler. 'As the head of the family, the rest ought to come to me.'

'But do let her go, Jacky,' coaxed his poor witless wife. 'He's struck wi' her—you can see that. He called her Coz! He'll marry her, most likely, and make a lady of her; and then she'll be what her forefathers was.'

John Durbeyfield had more conceit than energy or health, and this supposition was pleasant to him.

'Well, perhaps, that's what young Mr d'Urberville means,' he admitted; 'and sure enough he mid have serious thoughts about improving his blood by linking on to the old line. Tess, the little rogue! And have she really paid 'em a visit to such an end as this?'

Meanwhile Tess was walking thoughtfully among the gooseberry-bushes in the garden, and over Prince's grave. When she came in her mother pursued her advantage.

'Well, what be you going to do?' she asked.

'I wish I had seen Mrs d'Urberville,' said Tess.

'I think you mid as well settle it. Then you'll see her soon enough.'

Her father coughed in his chair.

'I don't know what to say!' answered the girl restlessly. 'It is for you to decide. I killed the old horse, and I suppose I ought to do something to get ye a new one. But—but—I don't quite like Mr d'Urberville being there!'

The children, who had made use of this idea of Tess being taken up by their wealthy kinsfolk (which they imagined the other family to be) as a species of dolorifuge after the death of the horse, began to cry at Tess's reluctance, and teased and reproached her for hesitating.

'Tess won't go—o—o and be made a la—a—dy of!—no, she says she wo—o—on't!' they wailed, with square mouths. 'And we shan't have a nice new horse, and lots o' golden money to buy fairlings! And Tess won't look pretty in her best cloze no mo—o—ore!'

Her mother chimed in to the same tune: a certain way she had of making her labours in the house seem heavier than they were by prolonging them indefinitely, also weighed in the argument. Her father alone preserved an attitude of neutrality.

'I will go,' said Tess at last.

Her mother could not repress her consciousness of the nuptial Vision conjured up by the girl's consent.

'That's right! For such a pretty maid as 'tis, this is a fine chance!'

Tess smiled crossly.

'I hope it is a chance for earning money. It is no other kind of chance. You had better say nothing of that silly sort about parish.'

Mrs Durbeyfield did not promise. She was not quite sure that she did not feel proud enough, after the visitor's remarks, to say a good deal.

Thus it was arranged; and the young girl wrote, agreeing to be ready to set out on any day on which she might be required. She was duly informed that Mrs d'Urberville was glad of her decision, and that a spring-cart should be sent to meet her and her luggage at the top of the Vale on the day after the morrow, when she must hold herself prepared to start. Mrs d'Urberville's handwriting seemed rather masculine.

'A cart?' murmured Joan Durbeyfield doubtingly. 'It might have been a carriage for her own kin!'

Having at last taken her course Tess was less restless and abstracted, going about her business with some self-assurance in the thought of acquiring another horse for her father by an occupation which would not be onerous. She had hoped to be a teacher at the school, but the fates seemed to decide otherwise. Being mentally older than her mother she did not regard Mrs Durbeyfield's matrimonial hopes for her in a serious aspect for a moment. The light-minded woman had been discovering good matches for her daughter almost from the year of her birth.

VII

On the morning appointed for her departure Tess was awake before dawn—at the marginal minute of the dark when the grove is still mute, save for one prophetic bird who sings with a clear-voiced conviction that he at least knows the correct time of day, the rest preserving silence as if equally convinced that he is mistaken. She remained upstairs packing till breakfast-time, and then came down in her ordinary week-day clothes, her Sunday apparel being carefully folded in her box.

Her mother expostulated. 'You will never set out to see your folks without dressing up more the dand than that?'

'But I am going to work!' said Tess.

'Well, yes,' said Mrs Durbeyfield; and in a private tone, 'at first there mid be a little pretence o't . . . But I think it will be wiser of 'ee to put your best side outward,' she added.

'Very well; I suppose you know best,' replied Tess with calm abandonment.

And to please her parent the girl put herself quite in Joan's hands, saying serenely—'Do what you like with me, mother.'

Mrs Durbeyfield was only too delighted at this tractability. First she fetched a great basin, and washed Tess's hair with such thoroughness that when dried and brushed it looked twice as much as at other times. She tied it with a broader pink ribbon than usual. Then she put upon her the white frock that Tess had worn at the club-walking, the airy fulness of which, supplementing her enlarged *coiffure*, imparted to her developing figure an amplitude which belied her age, and might cause her to be estimated as a woman when she was not much more than a child.

'I declare there's a hole in my stocking-heel!' said Tess.

'Never mind holes in your stockings—they don't speak! When I was a maid, so long as I had a pretty bonnet the devil might ha' found me in heels.'

Her mother's pride in the girl's appearance led her to step back, like a painter from his easel, and survey her work as a whole.

'You must zee yourself!' she cried. 'It is much better than you was t'other day.'

As the looking-glass was only large enough to reflect a very small portion of Tess's person at one time, Mrs Durbeyfield hung a black cloak outside the casement, and so made a large reflector of the panes, as it is the wont of bedecking cottagers to do. After this she went downstairs to her husband, who was sitting in the lower room.

'I'll tell 'ee what 'tis, Durbeyfield,' said she exultingly; 'he'll never have the heart not to love her. But whatever you do, don't zay too much to Tess of his fancy for her, and this chance she has got. She is such an odd maid that it mid zet her against him, or against going there, even now. If all goes well, I shall certainly be for making some return to that pa'son at Stagfoot Lane for telling us—dear, good man!'

However, as the moment for the girl's setting out drew nigh, when the first excitement of the dressing had passed off, a slight misgiving found place in Joan Durbeyfield's mind. It prompted the matron to say that she would walk a little way—as far as to the point where the acclivity from the valley began its first steep ascent to the outer world. At the top Tess was going to be met with the spring-cart sent by the Stoke-d'Urbervilles, and her box had already been wheeled ahead towards this summit by a lad with trucks, to be in readiness.

Seeing their mother put on her bonnet the younger children clamoured to go with her.

'I do want to walk a little-ways wi' Sissy, now she's going to marry our gentleman-cousin, and wear fine cloze!'

'No,' said Tess, flushing and turning quickly, 'I'll hear no more o' that! Mother, how could you ever put such stuff into their heads?'

'Going to work, my dears, for our rich relation, and help get enough money for a new horse,' said Mrs Durbeyfield pacifically.

'Good-bye, father,' said Tess, with a lumpy throat.

'Good-bye, my maid,' said Sir John, raising his head from his breast as he suspended his nap, induced by a slight excess this morning in honour of the occasion. 'Well, I hope my young friend will like such a comely sample of his own blood. And tell'n, Tess, that being sunk, quite, from our former grandeur, I'll sell him the title—yes, sell it—and at no onreasonable figure.'

'Not for less than a thousand pound!' cried Lady Durbeyfield.

'Tell'n—I'll take a thousand pound. Well, I'll take less, when I come to think o't. He'll adorn it better than a poor lammicken feller like myself can. Tell'n he shall hae it for a hundred. But I won't stand upon trifles—tell'n he shall hae it for fifty—for twenty pound! Yes, twenty pound—that's the lowest. Dammy, family honour is family honour, and I won't take a penny less!'

Tess's eyes were too full and her voice too choked to utter the sentiments that were in her. She turned quickly, and went out.

So the girls and their mother all walked together, a child on each side of Tess, holding her hand, and looking at her meditatively from time to time, as at one who was about to do great things; her mother just behind with the smallest; the group forming a picture of honest beauty flanked by innocence, and backed by simple-souled vanity. They followed the way till they reached the beginning of the ascent, on the crest of which the vehicle from Trantridge was to receive her, this limit having been fixed to save the horse the labour of the last slope. Far away behind the first hills the cliff-like dwellings of Shaston broke the line of the ridge. Nobody was visible in the elevated road which skirted the ascent save the lad whom they had sent on before them, sitting on the handle of the barrow that contained all Tess's worldly possessions.

'Bide here a bit, and the cart will soon come, no doubt,' said Mrs Durbeyfield. 'Yes, I see it yonder!'

It had come—appearing suddenly from behind the forehead of the nearest upland, and stopping beside the boy with the barrow. Her mother and the children thereupon decided to go no farther, and bidding them a hasty good-bye Tess bent her steps up the hill.

They saw her white shape draw near to the spring-cart, on which her box was already placed. But before she had quite reached it another vehicle shot out from a clump of trees on the summit, came round the bend of the road there, passed the luggage-cart, and halted beside Tess, who looked up as if in great surprise.

Her mother perceived, for the first time, that the second vehicle was not a humble conveyance like the first, but a spick-and-span gig or dog-cart, highly varnished and equipped. The driver was a young man of three- or four-and-twenty, with a cigar between his teeth; wearing a dandy cap, drab jacket, breeches of the same hue, white neckcloth, stick-up collar, and brown driving-gloves—in short, he was the handsome, horsey young buck who had visited Joan a week or two before to get her answer about Tess.

Mrs Durbeyfield clapped her hands like a child. Then she looked down, then stared again. Could she be deceived as to the meaning of this?

'Is dat the gentleman-kinsman who'll make Sissy a lady?' asked the youngest child.

Meanwhile the muslined form of Tess could be seen standing still, undecided, beside this turn-out, whose owner was talking to her. Her seeming indecision was, in fact, more than indecision: it was misgiving. She would have preferred the humble cart. The young man dismounted, and appeared to urge her to ascend. She turned her face down the hill to her relatives, and regarded the little group. Something seemed to quicken her to a determination: possibly the thought that she had killed Prince. She suddenly stepped up; he mounted beside her, and immediately whipped on the horse. In a moment they had passed the slow cart with the box, and disappeared behind the shoulder of the hill.

Directly Tess was out of sight, and the interest of the matter as a drama was at an end, the little ones' eyes filled with tears. The youngest child said, 'I wish poor, poor Tess wasn't gone away to be a lady!' and, lowering the corners of his lips, burst out crying. The new point of view was infectious, and the next child did likewise, and then the next, till the whole three of them wailed loud.

There were tears also in Joan Durbeyfield's eyes as she turned to go home. But by the time she had got back to the village she was passively trusting to the favour of accident. However, in bed that night she sighed, and her husband asked her what was the matter.

'Oh, I don't know exactly,' she said. 'I was thinking that perhaps it would ha' been better if Tess had not gone.'

'Oughtn't ye to have thought of that before?'

'Well, 'tis a chance for the maid—Still, if 'twere the doing again, I wouldn't let her go till I had found out whether the gentleman is really a good-hearted young man and choice over her as his kinswoman.'

'Yes, you ought, perhaps, to ha' done that,' snored Sir John.

Joan Durbeyfield always managed to find consolation somewhere: 'Well, as one of the genuine stock, she ought to make her way with 'en, if she plays her trump card aright. And if he don't marry her afore he will after. For that he's all afire wi' love for her any eye can see.'

'What's her trump card? Her d'Urberville blood, you mean?'

'No, stupid; her face—as 'twas mine.'

VIII

Having mounted beside her, Alec d'Urberville drove rapidly along the crest of the first hill, chatting compliments to Tess as they went, the cart with her box being left far behind. Rising still, an immense landscape stretched around them on every side; behind, the green valley of her birth, before, a gray country of which she knew nothing except from her first brief visit to Trantridge. Thus they reached the verge of an incline down which the road stretched in a long straight descent of nearly a mile.

Ever since the accident with her father's horse Tess Durbeyfield, courageous as she naturally was, had been exceedingly timid on wheels; the least irregularity of motion startled her. She began to get uneasy at a certain recklessness in her conductor's driving.

'You will go down slow, sir, I suppose?' she said with attempted unconcern.

D'Urberville looked round upon her, nipped his cigar with the tips of his large white centre-teeth, and allowed his lips to smile slowly of themselves.

'Why, Tess,' he answered, after another whiff or two, 'it isn't a brave bouncing girl like you who asks that? Why, I always go down at full gallop. There's nothing like it for raising your spirits.'

'But perhaps you need not now?'

'Ah,' he said, shaking his head, 'there are two to be reckoned with. It is not me alone. Tib has to be considered, and she has a very queer temper.'

'Who?'

'Why, this mare. I fancy she looked round at me in a very grim way just then. Didn't you notice it?'

'Don't try to frighten me, sir,' said Tess stiffly.

'Well, I don't. If any living man can manage this horse I can:—

I won't say any living man can do it—but if such has the power, I am he.'

'Why do you have such a horse?'

'Ah, well may you ask it! It was my fate, I suppose. Tib has killed one chap; and just after I bought her she nearly killed me. And then, take my word for it, I nearly killed her. But she's touchy still, very touchy; and one's life is hardly safe behind her sometimes.'

They were just beginning to descend; and it was evident that the horse, whether of her own will or of his (the latter being the more likely), knew so well the reckless performance expected of her that she hardly required a hint from behind.

Down, down, they sped, the wheels humming like a top, the dog-cart rocking right and left, its axis acquiring a slightly oblique set in relation to the line of progress; the figure of the horse rising and falling in undulations before them. Sometimes a wheel was off the ground, it seemed, for many yards; sometimes a stone was sent spinning over the hedge, and flinty sparks from the horse's hoofs outshone the daylight. The aspect of the straight road enlarged with their advance, the two banks dividing like a splitting stick; one rushing past at each shoulder.

The wind blew through Tess's white muslin to her very skin, and her washed hair flew out behind. She was determined to show no open fear, but she clutched d'Urberville's rein-arm.

'Don't touch my arm! We shall be thrown out if you do! Hold on round my waist!'

She grasped his waist, and so they reached the bottom.

'Safe, thank God, in spite of your fooling!' said she, her face on fire.

'Tess—fie! that's temper!' said d'Urberville.

''Tis truth.'

'Well, you need not let go your hold of me so thanklessly the moment you feel yourself out of danger.'

She had not considered what she had been doing; whether he were man or woman, stick or stone, in her involuntary hold on him. Recovering her reserve she sat without replying, and thus they reached the summit of another declivity.

'Now then, again!' said d'Urberville.

'No, no!' said Tess. 'Show more sense, do, please.'

'But when people find themselves on one of the highest points in the county, they must get down again,' he retorted.

He loosened rein, and away they went a second time. D'Urberville turned his face to her as they rocked, and said, in playful raillery: 'Now then, put your arms round my waist again, as you did before, my Beauty.'

'Never!' said Tess independently, holding on as well as she could without touching him.

'Let me put one little kiss on those holmberry lips, Tess, or even on that warmed cheek, and I'll stop—on my honour, I will!'

Tess, surprised beyond measure, slid farther back still on her seat, at which he urged the horse anew, and rocked her the more.

'Will nothing else do?' she cried at length, in desperation, her large eyes staring at him like those of a wild animal. This dressing her up so prettily by her mother had apparently been to lamentable purpose.

'Nothing, dear Tess,' he replied.

'Oh, I don't know—very well; I don't mind!' she panted miserably.

He drew rein, and as they slowed he was on the point of imprinting the desired salute, when, as if hardly yet aware of her own modesty, she dodged aside. His arms being occupied with the reins there was left him no power to prevent her manoeuvre.

'Now, damn it—I'll break both our necks!' swore her capriciously passionate companion. 'So you can go from your word like that, you young witch, can you?'

'Very well,' said Tess, 'I'll not move since you be so determined! But I—thought you would be kind to me, and protect me, as my kinsman!'

'Kinsman be hanged! Now!'

'But I don't want anybody to kiss me, sir!' she implored, a big tear beginning to roll down her face, and the corners of her mouth trembling in her attempts not to cry. 'And I wouldn't ha' come if I had known!'

He was inexorable, and she sat still, and d'Urberville gave her the kiss of mastery. No sooner had he done so than she flushed with shame, took out her handkerchief, and wiped the spot on her cheek that had been touched by his lips. His ardour was nettled at the sight, for the act on her part had been unconsciously done.

'You are mighty sensitive for a cottage girl!' said the young man.

Tess made no reply to this remark, of which, indeed, she did not quite comprehend the drift, unheeding the snub she had administered by her instinctive rub upon her cheek. She had, in fact, undone the kiss, as far as such a thing was physically possible. With a dim sense that he was vexed she looked steadily ahead as they trotted on near Melbury Down and Wingreen, till she saw, to her consternation, that there was yet another descent to be undergone.

'You shall be made sorry for that!' he resumed, his injured tone still remaining, as he flourished the whip anew. 'Unless, that is, you agree willingly to let me do it again, and no handkerchief.'

She sighed. 'Very well, sir!' she said. 'Oh—let me get my hat!'

At the moment of speaking her hat had blown off into the road, their present speed on the upland being by no means slow. D'Urberville pulled up, and said he would get it for her, but Tess was down on the other side.

She turned back and picked up the article.

'You look prettier with it off, upon my soul, if that's possible,' he said, contemplating her over the back of the vehicle. 'Now then, up again! What's the matter?'

The hat was in place and tied, but Tess had not stepped forward.

'No, sir,' she said, revealing the red and ivory of her mouth as her eye lit in defiant triumph; 'not again, if I know it!'

'What—you won't get up beside me?'

'No; I shall walk.'

''Tis five or six miles yet to Trantridge.'

'I don't care if 'tis dozens. Besides, the cart is behind.'

'You artful hussy! Now, tell me—didn't you make that hat blow off on purpose? I'll swear you did!'

Her strategic silence confirmed his suspicion.

Then d'Urberville cursed and swore at her, and called her everything he could think of for the trick. Turning the horse suddenly he tried to drive back upon her, and so hem her in between the gig and the hedge. But he could not do this short of injuring her.

'You ought to be ashamed of yourself for using such wicked words!' cried Tess with spirit, from the top of the hedge into which she had scrambled. 'I don't like 'ee at all! I hate and detest you! I'll go back to mother, I will!'

D'Urberville's bad temper cleared up at sight of hers; and he laughed heartily.

'Well, I like you all the better,' he said. 'Come, let there be peace. I'll never do it any more against your will. My life upon it now!'

Still Tess could not be induced to remount. She did not, however, object to his keeping his gig alongside her; and in this manner, at a slow pace, they advanced towards the village of Trantridge. From time to time d'Urberville exhibited a sort of fierce distress at the sight of the tramping he had driven her to undertake by his misdemeanour. She might in truth have safely trusted him now; but he had forfeited her confidence for the time, and she kept on the ground, progressing thoughtfully, as if wondering whether it would be wiser to return home. Her resolve, however, had been taken, and it seemed vacillating even to childishness to abandon it now, unless for graver reasons. How could she face her parents, get back on her box, and disconcert the whole scheme for the rehabilitation of her family on such sentimental grounds?

A few minutes later the chimneys of The Slopes appeared in view, and in a snug nook to the right the poultry-farm and cottage of Tess's destination.

IX

The community of fowls to which Tess had been appointed as supervisor, purveyor, nurse, surgeon, and friend, made its headquarters in an old thatched cottage standing in an enclosure that had once been a garden, but was now a trampled and sanded square. The house was overrun with ivy, its chimney being enlarged by the boughs of the parasite to the aspect of a ruined tower. The lower rooms were entirely given over to the birds, who walked about them with a proprietary air, as though the place had been built by themselves, and not by certain dusty copyholders who now lay east and west in the churchyard. The descendants of these bygone owners felt it almost as a slight to their family when the house which had so much of their affection, had cost so much of their forefathers' money, and had been in their possession for several generations before the d'Urbervilles came and built here, was indifferently turned into a fowlhouse by Mrs Stoke-d'Urberville as soon as the property fell into hand according to law. ''Twas good enough for Christians in grandfather's time,' they said.

The rooms wherein dozens of infants had wailed at their nursing now resounded with the tapping of nascent chicks. Distracted hens in coops occupied spots where formerly stood chairs supporting sedate agriculturists. The chimney-corner and once blazing hearth was now filled with inverted beehives, in which the hens laid their eggs; while out of doors the plots that each succeeding householder had carefully shaped with his spade were torn by the cocks in wildest fashion.

The garden in which the cottage stood was surrounded by a wall, and could only be entered through a door.

When Tess had occupied herself about an hour the next morning in altering and improving the arrangements, according to her skilled ideas as the daughter of a professed poulterer, the door in the wall opened and a servant in white cap and apron entered. She had come from the manor-house.

'Mrs d'Urberville wants the fowls as usual,' she said; but perceiving that Tess did not quite understand, she explained, 'Mis'ess is a old lady, and blind.'

'Blind!' said Tess.

Almost before her misgiving at the news could find some time to shape itself she took, under her companion's direction, two of the most beautiful of the Hamburghs in her arms, and followed the maid-servant, who had likewise taken two, to the adjacent mansion, which, though ornate and imposing, showed traces everywhere on this side that some occupant of its chambers could bend to the love of dumb creatures—feathers floating within view of the front, and hencoops standing on the grass.

In a sitting-room on the ground-floor, ensconced in an armchair with her back to the light, was the owner and mistress of the estate, a white-haired woman of not more than sixty, or even less, wearing a large cap. She had the mobile face frequent in those whose sight has decayed by stages, has been laboriously striven after, and reluctantly let go, rather than the stagnant mien apparent in persons long sightless or born blind. Tess walked up to this lady with her feathered charges—one sitting on each arm.

'Ah, you are the young woman come to look after my birds?' said Mrs d'Urberville, recognizing a new footstep. 'I hope you will be kind to them. My bailiff tells me you are quite the proper person. Well, where are they? Ah, this is Strut! But he is hardly so lively to-day, is he? He is alarmed at being handled by a stranger, I suppose. And Phena too—yes, they are a little frightened—aren't you, dears? But they will soon get used to you.'

While the old lady had been speaking Tess and the other maid, in obedience to her gestures, had placed the fowls severally in her lap, and she had felt them over from head to tail, examining their beaks, their combs, the manes of the cocks, their wings, and their claws. Her touch enabled her to recognize them in a moment, and to discover if a single feather were crippled or draggled. She handled their crops, and knew what they had eaten, and if too little or too much; her face enacting a vivid pantomime of the criticisms passing in her mind.

The birds that the two girls had brought in were duly returned to the yard, and the process was repeated till all the pet cocks and hens had been submitted to the old woman—Hamburghs, Bantams, Cochins, Brahmas, Dorkings, and such other sorts as were in fashion just then—her perception of each visitor being seldom at fault as she received the bird upon her knees.

It reminded Tess of a Confirmation, in which Mrs d'Urberville was the bishop, the fowls the young people presented, and herself and the maid-servant the parson and curate of the parish bringing them up. At the end of the ceremony Mrs d'Urberville abruptly asked Tess, wrinkling and twitching her face into undulations, 'Can you whistle?'

'Whistle, Ma'am?'

'Yes, whistle tunes.'

Tess could whistle like most other country girls though the accomplishment was one which she did not care to profess in genteel company. However, she blandly admitted that such was the fact.

'Then you will have to practise it every day. I had a lad who did it very well, but he has left. I want you to whistle to my bullfinches; as I cannot see them I like to hear them, and we teach 'em airs that way. Tell her where the cages are, Elizabeth. You must begin to-morrow, or they will go back in their piping. They have been neglected these several days.'

'Mr d'Urberville whistled to 'em this morning, ma'am,' said Elizabeth.

'He! Pooh!'

The old lady's face creased into furrows of repugnance, and she made no further reply.

Thus the reception of Tess by her fancied kinswoman terminated, and the birds were taken back to their quarters. The girl's surprise at Mrs d'Urberville's manner was not great; for since seeing the size of the house she had expected no more. But she was far from being aware that the old lady had never heard a word of the so-called kinship. She gathered that no great affection flowed between the blind woman and her son. But in that, too, she was mistaken. Mrs d'Urberville was not the first mother compelled to love her offspring resentfully, and to be bitterly fond.

In spite of the unpleasant initiation of the day before, Tess inclined to the freedom and novelty of her new position in the morning when the sun shone, now that she was once installed there; and she was curious to test her powers in the unexpected direction asked of her, so as to ascertain her chance of retaining her post. As soon as she was alone within the walled garden she sat herself down on a coop, and seriously screwed up her mouth for the long-neglected practice. She found her former ability to have degenerated to the production of a hollow rush of wind through the lips, and no clear note at all.

She remained fruitlessly blowing and blowing, wondering how she could have so grown out of the art which had come by nature, till she became aware of a movement among the ivy-boughs which cloaked the garden-wall no less than the cottage. Looking that way she beheld a form springing from the coping to the plot. It was Alec d'Urberville, whom she had not set eyes on since he had conducted her the day before to the door of the gardener's cottage where she had lodgings.

'Upon my honour!' cried he, 'there was never before such a beautiful thing in Nature or Art as you look, "Cousin" Tess ["Cousin" had a faint ring of mockery]. I have been watching you from over the wall—sitting like *Im*-patience on a monument, and pouting up that pretty red mouth to whistling shape, and whooing and whooing, and privately swearing, and never being able to produce a note. Why, you are quite cross because you can't do it.'

'I may be cross, but I didn't swear.'

'Ah! I understand why you are trying—those bullies! My mother wants you to carry on their musical education. How selfish of her! As if attending to these curst cocks and hens here were not enough work for any girl. I would flatly refuse, if I were you.'

'But she wants me particularly to do it, and to be ready by to-morrow morning.'

'Does she? Well then—I'll give you a lesson or two.'

'Oh no, you won't!' said Tess, withdrawing towards the door.

'Nonsense; I don't want to touch you. See—I'll stand on this side of the wire-netting, and you can keep on the other; so you may feel quite safe. Now, look here; you screw up your lips too harshly. There 'tis—so.'

He suited the action to the word, and whistled a line of 'Take, O take those lips away.' But the allusion was lost upon Tess.

'Now try,' said d'Urberville.

She attempted to look reserved; her face put on a sculptural severity. But he persisted in his demand, and at last, to get rid of him, she did put up her lips as directed for producing a clear note; laughing distressfully, however, and then blushing with vexation that she had laughed.

He encouraged her with 'Try again!'

Tess was quite serious, painfully serious by this time; and she tried—ultimately and unexpectedly emitting a real round sound. The momentary pleasure of success got the better of her; her eyes enlarged, and she involuntarily smiled in his face.

'That's it! Now I have started you—you'll go on beautifully. There—I said I would not come near you; and, in spite of such temptation as never before fell to mortal man, I'll keep my word . . . Tess, do you think my mother a queer old soul?'

'I don't know much of her yet, sir.'

'You'll find her so; she must be, to make you learn to whistle to her bullfinches. I am rather out of her books just now, but you will be quite in favour if you treat her live-stock well. Good morning. If you meet with any difficulties and want help here, don't go to the bailiff, come to me.'

It was in the economy of this *régime* that Tess Durbeyfield had undertaken to fill a place. Her first day's experiences were fairly typical of those which followed through many succeeding days. A familiarity with Alec d'Urberville's presence—which that young man carefully cultivated in her by playful dialogue, and by jestingly calling her his cousin when they were alone—removed much of her original shyness of him, without, however, implanting any feeling which could engender shyness of a new and tenderer kind. But she was more pliable under his hands than a mere companionship would have made her, owing to her unavoidable dependence upon his mother, and, through that lady's comparative helplessness, upon him.

She soon found that whistling to the bullfinches in Mrs d'Urberville's room was no such onerous business when she had regained the art, for she had caught from her musical mother numerous airs that suited those songsters admirably. A far more satisfactory time than when she practised in the garden was this whistling by the cages each morning. Unrestrained by the young man's presence she threw up her mouth, put her lips near the bars, and piped away in easeful grace to the attentive listeners.

Mrs d'Urberville slept in a large four-post bedstead hung with heavy damask curtains, and the bullfinches occupied the same apartment, where they flitted about freely at certain hours, and made little white spots on the furniture and upholstery. Once while Tess was at the window where the cages were ranged, giving her lesson as usual, she thought she heard a rustling behind the bed. The old lady was not present, and turning round the girl had an impression that the toes of a pair of boots were visible below the fringe of the curtains. Thereupon her whistling became so disjointed that the listener, if such there were, must have discovered her suspicion of his presence. She searched the curtains every morning after that, but never found anybody within them. Alec d'Urberville had evidently thought better of his freak to terrify her by an ambush of that kind.

X

Every village has its idiosyncrasy, its constitution, often its own code of morality. The levity of some of the younger women in and about Trantridge was marked, and was perhaps symptomatic of the choice spirit who ruled The Slopes in that vicinity. The place had also a more abiding defect; it drank hard. The staple conversation on the farms around was on the uselessness of saving money; and smockfrocked arithmeticians, leaning on their ploughs or hoes, would enter into calculations of great nicety to prove that parish relief was a fuller provision for a man in his old age than any which could result from savings out of their wages during a whole lifetime.

The chief pleasure of these philosophers lay in going every Saturday night, when work was done, to Chaseborough, a decayed market-town two or three miles distant; and, returning in the small hours of the next morning, to spend Sunday in sleeping off the dyspeptic effects of the curious compounds sold to them as beer by the monopolizers of the once independent inns.

For a long time Tess did not join in the weekly pilgrimages. But under pressure from matrons not much older than herself—for a field-man's wages being as high at twenty-one as at forty, marriage was early here—Tess at length consented to go. Her first experience of the journey afforded her more enjoyment that she had expected, the hilariousness of the others being quite contagious after her monotonous attention to the poultry-farm all the week. She went again and again. Being graceful and interesting, standing moreover on the momentary threshold of womanhood, her appearance drew down upon her some sly regards from loungers in the streets of Chaseborough; hence, though sometimes her journey to the town was made independently, she always searched for her fellows at nightfall, to have the protection of their companionship homeward.

This had gone on for a month or two when there came a

Saturday in September, on which a fair and a market coincided; and the pilgrims from Trantridge sought double delights at the inns on that account. Tess's occupations made her late in setting out, so that her comrades reached the town long before her. It was a fine September evening, just before sunset, when yellow lights struggle with blue shades in hair-like lines, and the atmosphere itself forms a prospect without aid from more solid objects, except the innumerable winged insects that dance in it. Through this low-lit mistiness Tess walked leisurely along.

She did not discover the coincidence of the market with the fair till she had reached the place, by which time it was close upon dusk. Her limited marketing was soon completed; and then as usual she began to look about for some of the Trantridge cottagers.

At first she could not find them, and she was informed that most of them had gone to what they called a private little jig at the house of a hay-trusser and peat-dealer who had transactions with their farm. He lived in an out-of-the-way nook of the townlet, and in trying to find her course thither her eyes fell upon Mr d'Urberville standing at a street corner.

'What—my Beauty? You here so late?' he said.

She told him that she was simply waiting for company homeward.

'I'll see you again,' said he over her shoulder as she went on down the back lane.

Approaching the hay-trussers she could hear the fiddled notes of a reel proceeding from some building in the rear; but no sound of dancing was audible—an exceptional state of things for these parts, where as a rule the stamping drowned the music. The front door being open she could see straight through the house into the garden at the back as far as the shades of night would allow; and nobody appearing to her knock she traversed the dwelling and went up the path to the outhouse whence the sound had attracted her.

It was a windowless erection used for storage, and from the open door there floated into the obscurity a mist of yellow radiance, which at first Tess thought to be illuminated smoke. But on drawing nearer she perceived that it was a cloud of dust, lit by candles within the outhouse, whose beams upon the haze carried forward the outline of the doorway into the wide night of the garden.

When she came close and looked in she beheld indistinct forms racing up and down to the figure of the dance, the silence of their footfalls arising from their being overshoe in 'scroff'—that is to say, the powdery residuum from the storage of peat and other products, the stirring of which by their turbulent feet created the nebulosity that involved the scene. Through this floating, fusty *débris* of peat and hay, mixed with the perspirations and warmth of the dancers, and forming together a sort of vegeto-human pollen, the muted fiddles feebly pushed their notes, in marked contrast to the spirit with which the measure was trodden out. They coughed as they danced, and laughed as they coughed. Of the rushing couples there could barely be discerned more than the high lights—the indistinctness shaping them to satyrs clasping nymphs—a multiplicity of Pans whirling a multiplicity of Syrinxes; Lotis attempting to elude Priapus, and always failing.

At intervals a couple would approach the doorway for air, and the haze no longer veiling their features, the demigods resolved themselves into the homely personalities of her own next-door neighbours. Could Trantridge in two or three short hours have metamorphosed itself thus madly!

Some Sileni of the throng sat on benches and hay-trusses by the wall; and one of them recognized her.

'The maids don't think it respectable to dance at "The Flower-de-Luce",' he explained. 'They don't like to let everybody see which be their fancy-men. Besides, the house sometimes shuts up just when their jints begin to get greased. So we come here and send out for liquor.'

'But when be any of you going home?' asked Tess with some anxiety.

'Now—a'most directly. This is all but the last jig.'

She waited. The reel drew to a close, and some of the party were in the mind for starting. But others would not, and another dance was formed. This surely would end it, thought Tess. But it merged in yet another. She became restless and uneasy; yet, having waited so long, it was necessary to wait longer; on account of the fair the roads were dotted with roving characters of possibly ill intent; and, though not fearful of measurable dangers, she feared the unknown. Had she been near Marlott she would have had less dread.

'Don't ye be nervous, my dear good soul,' expostulated, between his coughs, a young man with a wet face, and his straw hat so far back upon his head that the brim encircled it like the nimbus of a saint. 'What's yer hurry? To-morrow is Sunday, thank God, and we can sleep it off in church-time. Now, have a turn with me?'

She did not abhor dancing, but she was not going to dance here. The movement grew more passionate: the fiddlers behind the luminous pillar of cloud now and then varied the air by playing on the wrong side of the bridge or with the back of the bow. But it did not matter; the panting shapes spun onwards.

They did not vary their partners if their inclination were to stick to previous ones. Changing partners simply meant that a satisfactory choice had not as yet been arrived at by one or other of the pair, and by this time every couple had been suitably matched. It was then that the ecstasy and the dream began, in which emotion was the matter of the universe, and matter but an adventitious intrusion likely to hinder you from spinning where you wanted to spin.

Suddenly there was a dull thump on the ground: a couple had fallen, and lay in a mixed heap. The next couple, unable to check its progress, came toppling over the obstacle. An inner cloud of dust rose around the prostrate figures amid the general one of the room, in which a twitching entanglement of arms and legs was discernible.

'You shall catch it for this, my gentleman, when you get home!' burst in female accents from the human heap—those of the unhappy partner of the man whose clumsiness had caused the mishap; she happened also to be his recently married wife, in which assortment there was nothing unusual at Trantridge as long as any affection remained between wedded couples; and, indeed, it was not uncustomary in their later lives, to avoid making odd lots of the single people between whom there might be a warm understanding.

A loud laugh from behind Tess's back, in the shade of the garden, united with the titter within the room. She looked round, and saw the red coal of a cigar: Alec d'Urberville was standing there alone. He beckoned to her, and she reluctantly retreated towards him.

'Well, my Beauty, what are you doing here?'

She was so tired after her long day and her walk that she confided her trouble to him—that she had been waiting ever since he saw her to have their company home, because the road at night was strange to her. 'But it seems they will never leave off, and I really think I will wait no longer.'

'Certainly do not. I have only a saddle-horse here to-day; but come to "The Flower-de-Luce", and I'll hire a trap, and drive you home with me.'

Tess, though flattered, had never quite got over her original mistrust of him, and, despite their tardiness, she preferred to walk home with the work-folk. So she answered that she was much obliged to him, but would not trouble him. 'I have said that I will wait for 'em, and they will expect me to now.'

'Very well, Miss Independence. Please yourself . . . Then I shall not hurry . . . My good Lord, what a kick-up they are having there!'

He had not put himself forward into the light, but some of them had perceived him, and his presence led to a slight pause and a consideration of how the time was flying. As soon as he had re-lit a cigar and walked away the Trantridge people began to collect themselves from amid those who had come in from other farms, and prepared to leave in a body. Their bundles and baskets were gathered up, and half an hour later, when the clock-chime sounded a quarter past eleven, they were straggling along the lane which led up the hill towards their homes.

It was a three-mile walk, along a dry white road, made whiter to-night by the light of the moon.

Tess soon perceived as she walked in the flock, sometimes with this one, sometimes with that, that the fresh night air was producing staggerings and serpentine courses among the men who had partaken too freely; some of the more careless women also were wandering in their gait—to wit, a dark virago, Car Darch, dubbed Queen of Spades, till lately a favourite of d'Urberville's; Nancy, her sister, nick-named the Queen of Diamonds; and the young married woman who had already tumbled down. Yet however terrestrial and lumpy their appearance just now to the mean unglamoured eye, to themselves the case was different. They followed the road with a sensation that they were soaring along in a supporting medium, possessed of original and profound thoughts, themselves and surrounding nature forming an organism of which all the parts harmoniously and joyously interpenetrated each other. They were as sublime as the moon and stars above them, and the moon and stars were as ardent as they.

Tess, however, had undergone such painful experiences of this kind in her father's house, that the discovery of their condition spoilt the pleasure she was beginning to feel in the moonlight journey. Yet she stuck in the party, for reasons above given.

In the open highway they had progressed in scattered order; but now their route was through a field-gate, and the foremost finding a difficulty in opening it they closed up together.

This leading pedestrian was Car the Queen of Spades, who carried a wicker-basket containing her mother's groceries, her own draperies, and other purchases for the week. The basket being large and heavy, Car had placed it for convenience of porterage on the top of her head, where it rode on in jeopardized balance as she walked with arms akimbo.

'Well—whatever is that a-creeping down thy back, Car Darch?' said one of the group suddenly.

All looked at Car. Her gown was a light cotton print, and from the back of her head a kind of rope could be seen descending to some distance below her waist, like a Chinaman's queue.

''Tis her hair falling down,' said another.

No; it was not her hair: it was a black stream of something oozing from her basket, and it glistened like a slimy snake in the cold still rays of the moon.

''Tis treacle,' said an observant matron.

Treacle it was. Car's poor old grandmother had a weakness for the sweet stuff. Honey she had in plenty out of her own hives, but treacle was what her soul desired, and Car had been about to give her a treat of surprise. Hastily lowering the basket the dark girl found that the vessel containing the syrup had been smashed within.

By this time there had arisen a shout of laughter at the extraordinary appearance of Car's back, which irritated the dark queen into getting rid of the disfigurement by the first sudden means available, and independently of the help of the scoffers. She rushed excitedly into the field they were about to cross, and flinging herself flat on her back upon the grass, began to wipe her gown as well as she could by spinning horizontally on the herbage and dragging herself over it up upon her elbows.

The laughter rang louder; they clung to the gate, to the posts, rested on their staves, in the weakness engendered by their convulsions at the spectacle of Car. Our heroine, who had hitherto held her peace, at this wild moment could not help joining in with the rest.

It was a misfortune—in more ways than one. No sooner did the dark queen hear the soberer richer note of Tess among those of the other work-people than a long smouldering sense of rivalry inflamed her to madness. She sprang to her feet and closely faced the object of her dislike.

'How darest th' laugh at me, hussy!' she cried.

'I couldn't really help it when t'others did,' apologized Tess, still tittering.

'Ah, th'st think th' beest everybody, dostn't, because th' beest first favourite with He just now! But stop a bit, my lady, stop a bit! I'm as good as two of such! Look here—here's at 'ee!'

To Tess's horror the dark queen began stripping off the bodice of her gown—which for the added reason of its ridiculed condition she was only too glad to be free of—till she had bared her plump neck, shoulders, and arms to the moonshine, under which they looked as luminous and beautiful as some Praxitelean creation, in their possession of the faultless rotundities of a lusty country girl. She closed her fists and squared up at Tess.

'Indeed, then, I shall not fight!' said the latter majestically; 'and if I had known you was of that sort, I wouldn't have so let myself down as to come with such a whorage as this is!'

The rather too inclusive speech brought down a torrent of vituperation from other quarters upon fair Tess's unlucky head, particularly from the Queen of Diamonds, who having stood in the relations to d'Urberville that Car had also been suspected of, united with the latter against the common enemy. Several other women also chimed in, with an animus which none of them would have been so fatuous as to show but for the rollicking evening they had passed. Thereupon, finding Tess unfairly browbeaten, the husbands and lovers tried to make peace by defending her; but the result of that attempt was directly to increase the war.

Tess was indignant and ashamed. She no longer minded the loneliness of the way and the lateness of the hour; her one object was to get away from the whole crew as soon as possible. She knew well enough that the better among them would repent of their passion next day. They were all now inside the field, and she was edging back to rush off alone when a horseman emerged almost silently from the corner of the hedge that screened the road, and Alec d'Urberville looked round upon them.

'What the devil is all this row about, work-folk?' he asked.

The explanation was not readily forthcoming; and, in truth, he did not require any. Having heard their voices while yet some way off he had ridden creepingly forward, and learnt enough to satisfy himself.

Tess was standing apart from the rest, near the gate. He bent over towards her. 'Jump up behind me,' he whispered, 'and we'll get shot of the screaming cats in a jiffy!'

She felt almost ready to faint, so vivid was her sense of the crisis. At almost any other moment of her life she would have refused such proffered aid and company, as she had refused them several times before; and now the loneliness would not of itself have forced her to do otherwise. But coming as the invitation did at the particular juncture when fear and indignation at these adversaries could be transformed by a spring of the foot into a triumph over them, she abandoned herself to her impulse, climbed the gate, put her toe upon his instep, and scrambled into the saddle behind him. The pair were speeding away into the distant gray by the time that the contentious revellers became aware of what had happened.

The Queen of Spades forgot the stain on her bodice, and stood beside the Queen of Diamonds and the new-married, staggering young woman—all with a gaze of fixity in the direction in which the horse's tramp was diminishing into silence on the road.

'What be ye looking at?' asked a man who had not observed the incident.

'Ho-ho-ho!' laughed dark Car.

'Hee-hee-hee!' laughed the tippling bride, as she steadied herself on the arm of her fond husband.

'Heu-heu-heu!' laughed dark Car's mother, stroking her moustache as she explained laconically: 'Out of the frying-pan into the fire!'

Then these children of the open air, whom even excess of alcohol could scarce injure permanently, betook themselves to the field-path; and as they went there moved onward with them, around the shadow of each one's head, a circle of opalized light, formed by the moon's rays upon the glistening sheet of dew. Each pedestrian could see no halo but his or her own, which never deserted the head-shadow, whatever its vulgar unsteadiness might be; but adhered to it, and persistently beautified it; till the erratic motions seemed an inherent part of the irradiation, and the fumes of their breathing a component of the night's mist; and the spirit of the scene, and of the moonlight, and of Nature, seemed harmoniously to mingle with the spirit of wine.

XI

THE twain cantered along for some time without speech, Tess as she clung to him still panting in her triumph, yet in other respects dubious. She had perceived that the horse was not the spirited one he sometimes rode, and felt no alarm on that score, though her seat was precarious enough despite her tight hold of him. She begged him to slow the animal to a walk, which Alec accordingly did.

'Neatly done, was it not, dear Tess?' he said by and by.

'Yes!' said she. 'I am sure I ought to be much obliged to you.'

'And are you?'

She did not reply.

'Tess, why do you always dislike my kissing you?'

'I suppose—because I don't love you.'

'You are quite sure?'

'I am angry with you sometimes!'

'Ah, I half feared as much.' Nevertheless, Alec did not object to that confession. He knew that anything was better than frigidity. 'Why haven't you told me when I have made you angry?'

'You know very well why. Because I cannot help myself here.'

'I haven't offended you often by love-making?'

'You have sometimes.'

'How many times?'

'You know as well as I—too many times.'

'Every time I have tried?'

She was silent, and the horse ambled along for a considerable distance, till a faint luminous fog, which had hung in the hollows all the evening, became general and enveloped them. It seemed to hold the moonlight in suspension, rendering it more pervasive than in clear air. Whether on this account, or from absent-mindedness, or from sleepiness, she did not perceive that they had long ago passed the point at which the lane to Trantridge branched from the highway, and that her conductor had not taken the Trantridge track.

She was inexpressibly weary. She had risen at five o'clock every morning of that week, had been on foot the whole of each day, and on this evening had in addition walked the three miles to Chaseborough, waited three hours for her neighbours without eating or drinking, her impatience to start them preventing either; she had then walked a mile of the way home, and had undergone the excitement of the quarrel, till, with the slow progress of their steed, it was now nearly one o'clock. Only once, however, was she overcome by actual drowsiness. In that moment of oblivion her head sank gently against him.

D'Urberville stopped the horse, withdrew his feet from the stirrups, turned sideways on the saddle, and enclosed her waist with his arm to support her.

This immediately put her on the defensive, and with one of those sudden impulses of reprisal to which she was liable she gave him a little push from her. In his ticklish position he nearly lost his balance and only just avoided rolling over into the road, the horse, though a powerful one, being fortunately the quietest he rode.

'That is devilish unkind!' he said. 'I mean no harm—only to keep you from falling.'

She pondered suspiciously; till, thinking that this might after all be true, she relented, and said quite humbly, 'I beg your pardon, sir.'

'I won't pardon you unless you show some confidence in me. Good God!' he burst out, 'what am I, to be repulsed so by a mere chit like you? For near three mortal months have you trifled with my feelings, eluded me, and snubbed me; and I won't stand it!'

'I'll leave you to-morrow, sir.'

'No, you will not leave me to-morrow! Will you, I ask once more, show your belief in me by letting me clasp you with my arm? Come, between us two and nobody else, now. We know each other well; and you know that I love you, and think you the prettiest girl in the world, which you are. Mayn't I treat you as a lover?'

She drew a quick pettish breath of objection, writhing uneasily on her seat, looked far ahead, and murmured, 'I don't know—I wish—how can I say yes or no when—'

He settled the matter by clasping his arm round her as he desired, and Tess expressed no further negative. Thus they sidled slowly onward till it struck her they had been advancing for an unconscionable time—far longer than was usually occupied by the short journey from Chaseborough, even at this walking pace, and that they were no longer on hard road, but in a mere trackway.

'Why, where be we?' she exclaimed.

'Passing by a wood.'

'A wood—what wood? Surely we are quite out of the road?'

'A bit of The Chase—the oldest wood in England. It is a lovely night, and why should we not prolong our ride a little?'

'How could you be so treacherous!' said Tess, between archness and real dismay, and getting rid of his arm by pulling open his fingers one by one, though at the risk of slipping off herself. 'Just when I've been putting such trust in you, and obliging you to please you, because I thought I had wronged you by that push! Please set me down, and let me walk home.'

'You cannot walk home, darling, even if the air were clear. We are miles away from Trantridge, if I must tell you, and in this growing fog you might wander for hours among these trees.'

'Never mind that,' she coaxed. 'Put me down, I beg you. I don't mind where it is; only let me get down, sir, please!'

'Very well, then, I will—on one condition. Having brought you here to this out-of-the-way place, I feel myself responsible for your safe-conduct home, whatever you may yourself feel about it. As to your getting to Trantridge without assistance, it is quite impossible; for, to tell the truth, dear, owing to this fog, which so disguises everything, I don't quite know where we are myself. Now, if you will promise to wait beside the horse while I walk through the bushes till I come to some road or house, and ascertain exactly our whereabouts, I'll deposit you here willingly. When I come back I'll give you full directions, and if you insist upon walking you may; or you may ride—at your pleasure.'

She accepted these terms, and slid off on the near side, though not till he had stolen a cursory kiss. He sprang down on the other side.

'I suppose I must hold the horse?' said she.

'Oh no; it's not necessary,' replied Alec, patting the panting creature. 'He's had enough of it for to-night.'

He turned the horse's head into the bushes, hitched him on to a bough, and made a sort of couch or nest for her in the deep mass of dead leaves.

'Now, you sit there,' he said. 'The leaves have not got damp as yet. Just give an eye to the horse—it will be quite sufficient.'

He took a few steps away from her, but, returning, said, 'Bye the bye, Tess, your father has a new cob to-day. Somebody gave it to him.'

'Somebody? You!'

D'Urberville nodded.

'O how very good of you that is!' she exclaimed, with a painful sense of the awkwardness of having to thank him just then.

'And the children have some toys.'

'I didn't know—you ever sent them anything!' she murmured, much moved. 'I almost wish you had not—yet, I almost wish it!'

'Why, dear?'

'It—hampers me so.'

'Tessy—don't you love me ever so little now?'

'I'm grateful,' she reluctantly admitted. 'But I fear I do not—' The sudden vision of his passion for herself as a factor in this result so distressed her that, beginning with one slow tear, and then following with another, she wept outright.

'Don't cry, dear, dear one! Now sit down here, and wait till I come.' She passively sat down amid the leaves he had heaped, and shivered slightly. 'Are you cold?' he asked.

'Not very—a little.'

He touched her with his fingers, which sank into her as into down. 'You have only that puffy muslin dress on—how's that?'

'It's my best summer one. 'Twas very warm when I started, and I didn't know I was going to ride, and that it would be night.'

'Nights grow chilly in September. Let me see.' He pulled off a light overcoat that he had worn, and put it round her tenderly.

'That's it—now you'll feel warmer,' he continued. 'Now, my pretty, rest there; I shall soon be back again.'

Having buttoned the overcoat round her shoulders he plunged into the webs of vapour which by this time formed veils between the trees. She could hear the rustling of the branches as he ascended the adjoining slope, till his movements were no louder than the hopping of a bird, and finally died away. With the setting of the moon the pale light lessened, and Tess became invisible as she felt into reverie upon the leaves where he had left her.

In the meantime Alec d'Urberville had pushed on up the slope to clear his genuine doubt as to the quarter of The Chase they were in. He had, in fact, ridden quite at random for over an hour, taking any turning that came to hand in order to prolong companionship with her, and giving far more attention to Tess's moonlit person than to any wayside object. A little rest for the jaded animal being desirable, he did not hasten his search for landmarks. A clamber over the hill into the adjoining vale brought him to the fence of a highway whose contours he recognized, which settled the question of their whereabouts. D'Urberville thereupon turned back; but by this time the moon had quite gone down, and partly on account of the fog The Chase was wrapped in thick darkness, although morning was not far off. He was obliged to advance with outstretched hands to avoid contact with the boughs, and discovered that to hit the exact spot from which he had started was at first entirely beyond him. Roaming up and down, round and round, he at length heard a slight movement of the horse close at hand; and the sleeve of his overcoat unexpectedly caught his foot.

'Tess!' said d'Urberville.

There was no answer. The obscurity was now so great that he could see absolutely nothing but a pale nebulousness at his feet, which represented the white muslin figure he had left upon the dead leaves. Everything else was blackness alike. D'Urberville stooped; and heard a gentle regular breathing. He knelt and bent lower, till her breath warmed his face, and in a moment his cheek was in contact with hers. She was sleeping soundly, and upon her eyelashes there lingered tears.

Darkness and silence ruled everywhere around. Above them rose the primeval yews and oaks of The Chase, in which were poised gentle roosting birds in their last nap; and about them stole the hopping rabbits and hares. But, might some say, where was Tess's guardian angel? where was the providence of her simple faith? Perhaps, like that other god of whom the ironical Tishbite spoke, he was talking, or he was pursuing, or he was in a journey, or he was sleeping and not to be awaked.

Why it was that upon this beautiful feminine tissue, sensitive as gossamer, and practically blank as snow as yet, there should have been traced such a coarse pattern as it was doomed to receive; why so often the coarse appropriates the finer thus, the wrong man the woman, the wrong woman the man, many thousand years of analytical philosophy have failed to explain to our sense of order. One may, indeed, admit the possibility of a retribution lurking in the present catastrophe. Doubtless some of Tess d'Urberville's mailed ancestors rollicking home from a fray had dealt the same measure even more ruthlessly towards peasant girls of their time. But though to visit the sins of the fathers upon the children may be a morality good enough for divinities, it is scorned by average human nature; and it therefore does not mend the matter.

As Tess's own people down in those retreats are never tired of saying among each other in their fatalistic way: 'It was to be.' There lay the pity of it. An immeasurable social chasm was to divide our heroine's personality thereafter from that previous self of hers who stepped from her mother's door to try her fortune at Trantridge poultry-farm.

END OF PHASE THE FIRST

PHASE THE SECOND

MAIDEN NO MORE

XII

The basket was heavy and the bundle was large, but she lugged them along like a person who did not find her especial burden in material things. Occasionally she stopped to rest in a mechanical way by some gate or post; and then, giving the baggage another hitch upon her full round arm, went steadily on again.

It was a Sunday morning in late October, about four months after Tess Durbeyfield's arrival at Trantridge, and some few weeks subsequent to the night ride in The Chase. The time was not long past daybreak, and the yellow luminosity upon the horizon behind her back lighted the ridge towards which her face was set—the barrier of the vale wherein she had of late been a stranger—which she would have to climb over to reach her birthplace. The ascent was gradual on this side, and the soil and scenery differed much from those within Blakemore Vale. Even the character and accent of the two peoples had shades of difference, despite the amalgamating effects of a roundabout railway; so that, though less than twenty miles from the place of her sojourn at Trantridge, her native village had seemed a far-away spot. The field-folk shut in there traded northward and westward, travelled, courted, and married northward and westward, thought northward and westward; those on this side mainly directed their energies and attention to the east and south.

The incline was the same down which d'Urberville had driven with her so wildly on that day in June. Tess went up the remainder of its length without stopping, and on reaching the edge of the escarpment gazed over the familiar green world beyond, now half-veiled in mist. It was always beautiful from here; it was terribly beautiful to Tess to-day, for since her eyes last fell upon it she had learnt that the serpent hisses where the sweet birds sing, and her views of life had been totally changed for her by the lesson. Verily another girl than the simple one she had been at home was she who, bowed by thought, stood still here, and turned to look behind her. She could not bear to look forward into the Vale.

Ascending by the long white road that Tess herself had just laboured up, she saw a two-wheeled vehicle, beside which walked a man, who held up his hand to attract her attention.

She obeyed the signal to wait for him with unspeculative repose, and in a few minutes man and horse stopped beside her.

'Why did you slip away by stealth like this?' said d'Urberville, with upbraiding breathlessness; 'on a Sunday morning, too, when people were all in bed! I only discovered it by accident, and I have been driving like the deuce to overtake you. Just look at the mare. Why go off like this? You know that no-body wished to hinder your going. And how unnecessary it has been for you to toil along on foot, and encumber yourself with this heavy load! I have followed like a madman, simply to drive you the rest of the distance, if you won't come back.'

'I shan't come back,' said she.

'I thought you wouldn't—I said so! Well, then, put up your baskets, and let me help you on.'

She listlessly placed her basket and bundle within the dog-cart, and stepped up, and they sat side by side. She had no fear of him now, and in the cause of her confidence her sorrow lay.

D'Urberville mechanically lit a cigar, and the journey was continued with broken unemotional conversation on the commonplace objects by the wayside. He had quite forgotten his struggle to kiss her when, in the early summer, they had driven in the opposite direction along the same road. But she had not, and she sat now, like a puppet, replying to his remarks in monosyllables. After some miles they came in view of the clump of trees beyond which the village of Marlott stood. It was only then that her still face showed the least emotion, a tear or two beginning to trickle down.

'What are you crying for?' he coldly asked.

'I was thinking that I was born over there,' murmured Tess.

'Well—we must all be born somewhere.'

'I wish I had never been born—there or anywhere else!'

'Pooh! Well, if you didn't wish to come to Trantridge why did you come?'

She did not reply.

'You didn't come for love of me, that I'll swear.'

''Tis quite true. If I had gone for love o' you, if I had ever sincerely loved you, if I loved you still, I should not so loathe and hate myself for my weakness as I do now! . . . My eyes were dazed by you for a little, and that was all.'

He shrugged his shoulders. She resumed—

'I didn't understand your meaning till it was too late.'

'That's what every woman says.'

'How can you dare to use such words!' she cried, turning impetuously upon him, her eyes flashing as the latent spirit (of which he was to see more some day) awoke in her. 'My God! I could knock you out of the gig! Did it never strike your mind that what every woman says some women may feel?'

'Very well,' he said, laughing; 'I am sorry to wound you. I did wrong—I admit it.' He dropped into some little bitterness as he continued: 'Only you needn't be so everlastingly flinging it in my face. I am ready to pay to the uttermost farthing. You know you need not work in the fields or the dairies again. You know you may clothe yourself with the best, instead of in the bald plain way you have lately affected, as if you couldn't get a ribbon more than you earn.'

Her lip lifted slightly, though there was little scorn, as a rule, in her large and impulsive nature.

'I have said I will not take anything more from you, and I will not—I cannot! I *should* be your creature to go on doing that, and I won't!'

'One would think you were a princess from your manner, in addition to a true and original d'Urberville—ha! ha! Well, Tess, dear, I can say no more. I suppose I am a bad fellow—a damn bad fellow. I was born bad, and I have lived bad, and I shall die bad in all probability. But, upon my lost soul, I won't be bad towards you again, Tess. And if certain circumstances should arise—you understand—in which you are in the least need, the least difficulty, send me one line, and you shall have by return whatever you require. I may not be at Trantridge—I am going to London for a time—I can't stand the old woman. But all letters will be forwarded.'

She said that she did not wish him to drive her further, and they stopped just under the clump of trees. D'Urberville alighted, and lifted her down bodily in his arms, afterwards placing her articles on the ground beside her. She bowed to him slightly, her eye just lingering in his; and then she turned to take the parcels for departure.

Alec d'Urberville removed his cigar, bent towards her, and said—

'You are not going to turn away like that, dear? Come!'

'If you wish,' she answered indifferently. 'See how you've mastered me!'

She thereupon turned round and lifted her face to his, and remained like a marble term while he imprinted a kiss upon her cheek—half perfunctorily, half as if zest had not yet quite died out. Her eyes vaguely rested upon the remotest trees in the lane while the kiss was given, as though she were nearly unconscious of what he did.

'Now the other side, for old acquaintance' sake.'

She turned her head in the same passive way, as one might turn at the request of a sketcher or hairdresser, and he kissed the other side, his lips touching cheeks that were damp and smoothly chill as the skin of the mushrooms in the fields around.

'You don't give me your mouth and kiss me back. You never willingly do that—you'll never love me, I fear.'

'I have said so, often. It is true. I have never really and truly loved you, and I think I never can.' She added mournfully, 'Perhaps, of all things, a lie on this thing would do the most good to me now; but I have honour enough left, little as 'tis, not to tell that lie. If I did love you I may have the best o' causes for letting you know it. But I don't.'

He emitted a laboured breath, as if the scene were getting rather oppressive to his heart, or to his conscience, or to his gentility.

'Well, you are absurdly melancholy, Tess. I have no reason for flattering you now, and I can say plainly that you need not be so sad. You can hold your own for beauty against any woman of these parts, gentle or simple; I say it to you as a practical man and well-wisher. If you are wise you will show it to the world more than you do before it fades . . . And yet, Tess, will you come back to me? Upon my soul I don't like to let you go like this!'

'Never, never! I made up my mind as soon as I saw—what I ought to have seen sooner; and I won't come.'

'Then good morning, my four months' cousin—good-bye!'

He leapt up lightly, arranged the reins, and was gone between the tall redberried hedges.

Tess did not look after him, but slowly wound along the crooked lane. It was still early, and though the sun's lower limb was just free of the hill, his rays, ungenial and peering, addressed the eye rather than the touch as yet. There was not a human soul near. Sad October and her sadder self seemed the only two existences haunting that lane.

As she walked however, some footsteps approached behind her, the footsteps of a man; and owing to the briskness of his advance he was close at her heels and had said 'Good morning' before she had been long aware of his propinquity. He appeared to be an artisan of some sort, and carried a tin pot of red paint in his hand. He asked in a business-like manner if he should take her basket, which she permitted him to do, walking beside him.

'It is early to be astir this Sabbath morn!' he said cheerfully.

'Yes,' said Tess.

'When most people are at rest from their week's work.'

She also assented to this.

'Though I do more real work to-day than all the week besides.'

'Do you?'

'All the week I work for the glory of man, and on Sunday for the glory of God. That's more real than the other—hey? I have a little to do here at this stile.' The man turned as he spoke to an opening at the roadside leading into a pasture. 'If you'll wait a moment,' he added, 'I shall not be long.'

As he had her basket she could not well do otherwise; and she waited, observing him. He set down her basket and the tin pot, and stirring the paint with the brush that was in it began painting large square letters on the middle board of the three composing the stile, placing a comma after each word, as if to give pause while that word was driven well home to the reader's heart—

THY, DAMNATION, SLUMBERETH, NOT.

2 PET. ii. 3.

Against the peaceful landscape, the pale, decaying tints of the copses, the blue air of the horizon, and the lichened stileboards, these staring vermilion words shone forth. They seemed to shout themselves out and make the atmosphere ring. Some people might have cried 'Alas, poor Theology!' at the hideous defacement—the last grotesque phase of a creed which had served mankind well in its time. But the words entered Tess with accusatory horror. It was as if this man had known her recent history; yet he was a total stranger.

Having finished his text he picked up her basket, and she mechanically resumed her walk beside him.

'Do you believe what you paint?' she asked in low tones.

'Believe that tex? Do I believe in my own existence!'

'But,' said she tremulously, 'suppose your sin was not of your own seeking?'

He shook his head.

'I cannot split hairs on that burning query,' he said. 'I have walked hundreds of miles this past summer, painting these texes on every wall, gate, and stile in the length and breadth of this district. I leave their application to the hearts of the people who read 'em.'

'I think they are horrible,' said Tess. 'Crushing! killing!'

'That's what they are meant to be!' he replied in a trade voice. 'But you should read my hottest ones—them I kips for slums and seaports. They'd make ye wriggle! Not but what this is a very good tex for rural districts . . . Ah—there's a nice bit of blank wall up by that barn standing to waste. I must put one there—one that it will be good for dangerous young females like yerself to heed. Will ye wait, missy?'

'No,' said she; and taking her basket Tess trudged on. A little way forward she turned her head. The old gray wall began to advertise a similar fiery lettering to the first, with a strange and unwonted mien, as if distressed at duties it had never before been called upon to perform. It was with a sudden flush that she read and realized what was to be the inscription he was now half-way through –

THOU, SHALT, NOT, COMMIT—

Her cheerful friend saw her looking, stopped his brush, and shouted –

'If you want to ask for edification on these things of moment, there's a very earnest good man going to preach a charity-sermon to-day in the parish you are going to—Mr Clare of Emminster. I'm not of his persuasion now, but he's a good man, and he'll expound as well as any parson I know. 'Twas he began the work in me.'

But Tess did not answer; she throbbingly resumed her walk, her eyes fixed on the ground. 'Pooh—I don't believe God said such things!' she murmured contemptuously when her flush had died away.

A plume of smoke soared up suddenly from her father's chimney, the sight of which made her heart ache. The aspect of the interior, when she reached it, made her heart ache more. Her mother, who had just come down stairs, turned to greet her from the fireplace, where she was kindling barked-oak twigs under the breakfast kettle. The young children were still above, as was also her father, it being Sunday morning, when he felt justified in lying an additional half-hour.

'Well!—my dear Tess!' exclaimed her surprised mother, jumping up and kissing the girl. 'How be ye? I didn't see you till you was in upon me! Have you come home to be married?'

'No, I have not come for that, mother.'

'Then for a holiday?'

'Yes—for a holiday; for a long holiday,' said Tess.

'What, isn't your cousin going to do the handsome thing?'

'He's not my cousin, and he's not going to marry me.'

Her mother eyed her narrowly.

'Come, you have not told me all,' she said.

Then Tess went up to her mother, put her face upon Joan's neck, and told.

'And yet th'st not got him to marry 'ee!' reiterated her mother. 'Any woman would have done it but you, after that!'

'Perhaps any woman would except me.'

'It would have been something like a story to come back with, if you had!' continued Mrs Durbeyfield, ready to burst into tears of vexation. 'After all the talk about you and him which has reached us here, who would have expected it to end like this! Why didn't ye think of doing some good for your family instead o' thinking only of yourself? See how I've got to teave and slave, and your poor weak father with his heart clogged like a dripping-pan. I did hope for something to come out o' this! To see what a pretty pair you and he made that day when you drove away together four months ago! See what he has given us—all, as we thought, because we were his kin. But if he's not, it must have been done because of his love for 'ee. And yet you've not got him to marry!'

Get Alec d'Urberville in the mind to marry her! He marry *her*! On matrimony he had never once said a word. And what if he had? How a convulsive snatching at social salvation might have impelled her to answer him she could not say. But her poor foolish mother little knew her present feeling towards this man. Perhaps it was unusual in the circumstances, unlucky, unaccountable; but there it was; and this, as she had said, was what made her detest herself. She had never wholly cared for him, she did not at all care for him now. She had dreaded him, winced before him, succumbed to adroit advantages he took of her helplessness; then, temporarily blinded by his ardent manners, had been stirred to confused surrender awhile: had suddenly despised and disliked him, and had run away. That was all. Hate him she did not quite; but he was dust and ashes to her, and even for her name's sake she scarcely wished to marry him.

'You ought to have been more careful if you didn't mean to get him to make you his wife!'

'O mother, my mother!' cried the agonized girl, turning passionately upon her parent as if her poor heart would break. 'How could I be expected to know? I was a child when I left this house four months ago. Why didn't you tell me there was danger in men-folk? Why didn't you warn me? Ladies know what to fend hands against, because they read novels that tell them of these tricks; but I never had the chance o' learning in that way, and you did not help me!'

Her mother was subdued.

'I thought if I spoke of his fond feelings and what they might lead to, you would be hontish wi' him and lose your chance,' she murmured, wiping her eyes with her apron. 'Well, we must make the best of it, I suppose. 'Tis nater, after all, and what do please God!'

XIII

The event of Tess Durbeyfield's return from the manor of her bogus kinsfolk was rumoured abroad, if rumour be not too large a word for a space of a square mile. In the afternoon several young girls of Marlott, former schoolfellows and acquaintances of Tess, called to see her, arriving dressed in their best starched and ironed, as became visitors to a person who had made a transcendent conquest (as they supposed), and sat round the room looking at her with great curiosity. For the fact that it was this said thirty-first cousin, Mr d'Urberville, who had fallen in love with her, a gentleman not altogether local, whose reputation as a reckless gallant and heart-breaker was beginning to spread beyond the immediate boundaries of Trantridge, lent Tess's supposed position, by its fearsomeness, a far higher fascination than it would have exercised if unhazardous.

Their interest was so deep that the younger ones whispered when her back was turned—

'How pretty she is; and how that best frock do set her off! I believe it cost an immense deal, and that it was a gift from him.'

Tess, who was reaching up to get the tea-things from the corner-cupboard, did not hear these commentaries. If she had heard them, she might soon have set her friends right on the matter. But her mother heard, and Joan's simple vanity, having been denied the hope of a dashing marriage, fed itself as well as it could upon the sensation of a dashing flirtation. Upon the whole she felt gratified, even though such a limited and evanescent triumph should involve her daughter's reputation; it might end in marriage yet, and in the warmth of her responsiveness to their admiration she invited her visitors to stay to tea.

Their chatter, their laughter, their good-humoured innuendoes, above all, their flashes and flickerings of envy, revived Tess's spirits also; and, as the evening wore on, she caught the infection of their excitement, and grew almost gay. The marble hardness left her face, she moved with something of her old bounding step, and flushed in all her young beauty.

At moments, in spite of thought, she would reply to their inquiries with a manner of superiority, as if recognizing that her experiences in the field of courtship had, indeed, been slightly enviable. But so far was she from being, in the words of Robert South, 'in love with her own ruin,' that the illusion was transient as lightning; cold reason came back to mock her spasmodic weakness; the ghastliness of her momentary pride would convict her, and recall her to reserved listlessness again.

And the despondency of the next morning's dawn, when it was no longer Sunday, but Monday; and no best clothes; and the laughing visitors were gone, and she awoke alone in her old bed, the innocent younger children breathing softly around her. In place of the excitement of her return, and the interest it had inspired, she saw before her a long and stony highway which she had to tread, without aid, and with little sympathy. Her depression was then terrible, and she could have hidden herself in a tomb.

In the course of a few weeks Tess revived sufficiently to show herself so far as was necessary to get to church one Sunday morning. She liked to hear the chanting—such as it was—and the old Psalms, and to join in the Morning Hymn. That innate love of melody, which she had inherited from her ballad-singing mother, gave the simplest music a power over her which could well-nigh drag her heart out of her bosom at times.

To be as much out of observation as possible for reasons of her own, and to escape the gallantries of the young men, she set out before the chiming began, and took a back seat under the gallery, close to the lumber, where only old men and women came, and where the bier stood on end among the churchyard tools.

Parishioners dropped in by twos and threes, deposited themselves in rows before her, rested three-quarters of a minute on their foreheads as if they were praying, though they were not; then sat up, and looked around. When the chants came on one of her favourites happened to be chosen among the rest—the old double chant 'Langdon'—but she did not know what it was called, though she would much have liked to know. She thought, without exactly wording the thought, how strange and godlike was a composer's power, who from the grave could lead through sequences of emotion, which he alone had felt at first, a girl like her who had never heard of his name, and never would have a clue to his personality.

The people who had turned their heads turned them again as the service proceeded; and at last observing her they whispered to each other. She knew what their whispers were about, grew sick at heart, and felt that she could come to church no more.

The bedroom which she shared with some of the children formed her retreat more continually than ever. Here, under her few square yards of thatch, she watched winds, and snows, and rains, gorgeous sunsets, and successive moons at their full. So close kept she that at length almost everybody thought she had gone away.

The only exercise that Tess took at this time was after dark; and it was then, when out in the woods, that she seemed least solitary. She knew how to hit to a hair's-breadth that moment of evening when the light and the darkness are so evenly balanced that the constraint of day and the suspense of night neutralize each other, leaving absolute mental liberty. It is then that the plight of being alive becomes attenuated to its least possible dimensions. She had no fear of the shadows; her sole idea seemed to be to shun mankind—or rather that cold accretion called the world, which, so terrible in the mass, is so unformidable, even pitiable, in its units.

On these lonely hills and dales her quiescent glide was of a piece with the element she moved in. Her flexuous and stealthy figure became an integral part of the scene. At times her whimsical fancy would intensify natural processes around her till they seemed a part of her own story. Rather they became a part of it; for the world is only a psychological phenomenon, and what they seemed they were. The midnight airs and gusts, moaning amongst the tightly-wrapped buds and bark of the winter twigs, were formulae of bitter reproach. A wet day was the expression of irremediable grief at her weakness in the mind of some vague ethical being whom she could not class definitely as the God of her childhood, and could not comprehend as any other.

But this encompassment of her own characterization, based on shreds of convention, peopled by phantoms and voices anti-pathetic to her, was a sorry and mistaken creation of Tess's fancy—a cloud of moral hobgoblins by which she was terrified without reason. It was they that were out of harmony with the actual world, not she. Walking among the sleeping birds in the hedges, watching the skipping rabbits on a moonlit warren, or standing under a pheasant-laden bough, she looked upon herself as a figure of Guilt intruding into the haunts of Innocence. But all the while she was making a distinction where there was no difference. Feeling herself in antagonism she was quite in accord. She had been made to break an accepted social law, but no law known to the environment in which she fancied herself such an anomaly.

XIV

It was a hazy sunrise in August. The denser nocturnal vapours, attacked by the warm beams, were dividing and shrinking into isolated fleeces within hollows and coverts, where they waited till they should be dried away to nothing.

The sun, on account of the mist, had a curious sentient, personal look, demanding the masculine pronoun for its adequate expression. His present aspect, coupled with the lack of all human forms in the scene, explained the old-time heliolatries in a moment. One could feel that a saner religion had never prevailed under the sky. The luminary was a golden-haired, beaming, mild-eyed, God-like creature, gazing down in the vigour and intentness of youth upon an earth that was brimming with interest for him.

His light, a little later, broke through chinks of cottage shutters, throwing stripes like red-hot pokers upon cupboards, chests of drawers, and other furniture within; and awakening harvesters who were not already astir.

But of all ruddy things that morning the brightest were two broad arms of painted wood, which rose from the margin of a yellow cornfield hard by Marlott village. They, with two others below, formed the revolving Maltese cross of the reaping-machine, which had been brought to the field on the previous evening to be ready for operations this day. The paint with which they were smeared, intensified in hue by the sunlight, imparted to them a look of having been dipped in liquid fire.

The field had already been 'opened'; that is to say, a lane a few feet wide had been hand-cut through the wheat along the whole circumference of the field, for the first passage of the horses and machine.

Two groups, one of men and lads, the other of women, had come down the lane just at the hour when the shadows of the eastern hedge-top struck the west hedge midway, so that the heads of the groups were enjoying sunrise while their feet were still in the dawn. They disappeared from the lane between the two stone posts which flanked the nearest field-gate.

Presently there arose from within a ticking like the love-making of the grasshopper. The machine had begun, and a moving concatenation of three horses and the aforesaid long rickety machine was visible over the gate, a driver sitting upon one of the hauling horses, and an attendant on the seat of the implement. Along one side of the field the whole wain went, the arms of the mechanical reaper revolving slowly, till it passed down the hill quite out of sight. In a minute it came up on the other side of the field at the same equable pace; the glistening brass star in the forehead of the fore horse first catching the eye as it rose into view over the stubble, then the bright arms, and then the whole machine.

The narrow lane of stubble encompassing the field grew wider with each circuit, and the standing corn was reduced to smaller area as the morning wore on. Rabbits, hares, snakes, rats, mice, retreated inwards as into a fastness, unaware of the ephemeral nature of their refuge, and of the doom that awaited them later in the day when, their covert shrinking to a more and more horrible narrowness, they were huddled together, friends and foes, till the last few yards of upright wheat fell also under the teeth of the unerring reaper, and they were every one put to death by the sticks and stones of the harvesters.

The reaping-machine left the fallen corn behind it in little heaps, each heap being of the quantity for a sheaf; and upon these the active binders in the rear laid their hands—mainly women, but some of them men in print shirts, and trousers supported round their waists by leather straps, rendering useless the two buttons behind, which twinkled and bristled with sunbeams at every movement of each wearer, as if they were a pair of eyes in the small of his back.

But those of the other sex were the most interesting of this company of binders, by reason of the charm which is acquired by woman when she becomes part and parcel of outdoor nature, and is not merely an object set down therein as at ordinary times. A field-man is a personality afield; a field-woman is a portion of the field; she has somehow lost her own margin, imbibed the essence of her surrounding, and assimilated herself with it.

The women—or rather girls, for they were mostly young—wore drawn cotton bonnets with great flapping curtains to keep off the sun, and gloves to prevent their hands being wounded by the stubble. There was one wearing a pale pink jacket, another in a cream-coloured tight-sleeved gown, another in a petticoat as red as the arms of the reaping-machine; and others, older, in the brown-rough 'wropper' or over-all—the old-established and most appropriate dress of the field-woman, which the young ones were abandoning. This morning the eye returns involuntarily to the girl in the pink cotton jacket, she being the most flexuous and finely-drawn figure of them all. But her bonnet is pulled so far over her brow that none of her face is disclosed while she binds, though her complexion may be guessed from a stray twine or two of dark brown hair which extends below the curtain of her bonnet. Perhaps one reason why she seduces casual attention is that she never courts it, though the other women often gaze around them.

Her binding proceeds with clock-like monotony. From the sheaf last finished she draws a handful of ears, patting their tips with her left palm to bring them even. Then stooping low she moves forward, gathering the corn with both hands against her knees, and pushing her left gloved hand under the bundle to meet the right on the other side, holding the corn in an embrace like that of a lover. She brings the ends of the bond together, and kneels on the sheaf while she ties it, beating back her skirts now and then when lifted by the breeze. A bit of her naked arm is visible between the buff leather of the gauntlet and the sleeve of her gown; and as the day wears on its feminine smoothness becomes scarified by the stubble, and bleeds.

At intervals she stands up to rest, and to retie her disarranged apron, or to pull her bonnet straight. Then one can see the oval face of a handsome young woman with deep dark eyes and long heavy clinging tresses, which seem to clasp in a beseeching way anything they fall against. The cheeks are paler, the teeth more regular, the red lips thinner than is usual in a country-bred girl.

It is Tess Durbeyfield, otherwise d'Urberville, somewhat changed—the same, but not the same; at the present stage of her existence living as a stranger and an alien here, though it was no strange land that she was in. After a long seclusion she had come to a resolve to undertake outdoor work in her native village, the busiest season of the year in the agricultural world having arrived, and nothing that she could do within the house being so remunerative for the time as harvesting in the fields.

The movements of the other women were more or less similar to Tess's, the whole bevy of them drawing together like dancers in a quadrille at the completion of a sheaf by each, every one placing her sheaf on end against those of the rest, till a shock, or 'stitch' as it was here called, of ten or a dozen was formed.

They went to breakfast, and came again, and the work proceeded as before. As the hour of eleven drew near a person watching her might have noticed that every now and then Tess's glance flitted wistfully to the brow of the hill, though she did not pause in her sheafing. On the verge of the hour the heads of a group of children, of ages ranging from six to fourteen, rose above the stubbly convexity of the hill.

The face of Tess flushed slightly, but still she did not pause.

The eldest of the comers, a girl who wore a triangular shawl, its corner draggling on the stubble, carried in her arms what at first sight seemed to be a doll, but proved to be an infant in long clothes. Another brought some lunch. The harvesters ceased working, took their provisions, and sat down against one of the shocks. Here they fell to, the men plying a stone jar freely, and passing round a cup.

Tess Durbeyfield had been one of the last to suspend her labours. She sat down at the end of the shock, her face turned somewhat away from her companions. When she had deposited herself a man in a rabbit-skin cap and with a red handkerchief tucked into his belt, held the cup of ale over the top of the shock for her to drink. But she did not accept his offer. As soon as her lunch was spread she called up the big girl her sister, and took the baby off her, who, glad to be relieved of the burden, went away to the next shock and joined the other children playing there. Tess, with a curiously stealthy yet courageous movement, and with a still rising colour, unfastened her frock and began suckling the child.

The men who sat nearest considerately turned their faces towards

The men who sat nearest considerately turned their faces towards the other end of the field, some of them beginning to smoke; one, with absent-minded fondness, regretfully stroking the jar that would no longer yield a stream. All the women but Tess fell into animated talk, and adjusted the disarranged knots of their hair.

When the infant had taken its fill the young mother sat it upright in her lap, and looking into the far distance dandled it with a gloomy indifference that was almost dislike; then all of a sudden she fell to violently kissing it some dozens of times, as if she could never leave off, the child crying at the vehemence of an onset which strangely combined passionateness with contempt.

'She's fond of that there child, though she mid pretend to hate en, and say she wishes the baby and her too were in the churchyard,' observed the woman in the red petticoat.

'She'll soon leave off saying that,' replied the one in buff. 'Lord, 'tis wonderful what a body can get used to o' that sort in time!'

'A little more than persuading had to do wi' the coming o't, I reckon. There were they that heard a sobbing one night last year in The Chase; and it mid ha' gone hard wi' a certain party if folks had come along.'

'Well, a little more, or a little less, 'twas a thousand pities that it should have happened to she, of all others. But 'tis always the comeliest! The plain ones be as safe as churches—hey, Jenny?' The speaker turned to one of the group who certainly was not ill-defined as plain.

It was a thousand pities, indeed; it was impossible for even an enemy to feel otherwise on looking at Tess as she sat there, with her flower-like mouth and large tender eyes, neither black nor blue nor gray nor violet; rather all those shades together, and a hundred others, which could be seen if one looked into their irises—shade behind shade—tint beyond tint—around pupils that had no bottom; an almost standard woman, but for the slight incautiousness of character inherited from her race.

A resolution which had surprised herself had brought her into the fields this week for the first time during many months. After wearing and wasting her palpitating heart with every engine of regret that lonely inexperience could devise, commonsense had illumined her. She felt that she would do well to be useful again—to taste anew sweet independence at any price. The past was past; whatever it had been it was no more at hand. Whatever its consequences, time would close over them; they would all in a few years be as if they had never been, and she herself grassed down and forgotten. Meanwhile the trees were just as green as before; the birds sang and the sun shone as clearly now as ever. The familiar surroundings had not darkened because of her grief, nor sickened because of her pain.

She might have seen that what had bowed her head so profoundly—the thought of the world's concern at her situation—was founded on an illusion. She was not an existence, an experience, a passion, a structure of sensations, to anybody but herself. To all humankind besides Tess was only a passing thought. Even to friends she was no more than a frequently passing thought. If she made herself miserable the livelong night and day it was only this much to them—'Ah, she makes herself unhappy.' If she tried to be cheerful, to dismiss all care, to take pleasure in the daylight, the flowers, the baby, she could only be this idea to them—'Ah, she bears it very well.' Moreover, alone in a desert island would she have been wretched at what had happened to her? Not greatly. If she could have been but just created, to discover herself as a spouseless mother, with no experience of life except as the parent of a nameless child, would the position have caused her to despair? No, she would have taken it calmly, and found pleasures therein. Most of the misery had been generated by her conventional aspect, and not by her innate sensations.

Whatever Tess's reasoning, some spirit had induced her to dress herself up neatly as she had formerly done, and come out into the fields, harvest-hands being greatly in demand just then. This was why she had borne herself with dignity, and had looked people calmly in the face at times, even when holding the baby in her arms.

The harvest-men rose from the shock of corn, and stretched their limbs, and extinguished their pipes. The horses, which had been unharnessed and fed, were again attached to the scarlet machine. Tess, having quickly eaten her own meal, beckoned to her eldest sister to come and take away the baby, fastened her dress, put on the buff gloves again, and stooped anew to draw a bond from the last completed sheaf for the tying of the next.

In the afternoon and evening the proceedings of the morning were continued, Tess staying on till dusk with the body of harvesters. Then they all rode home in one of the largest waggons, in the company of a broad tarnished moon that had risen from the ground to the eastwards, its face resembling the outworn gold-leaf halo of some worm-eaten Tuscan saint. Tess's female companions sang songs, and showed themselves very sympathetic and glad at her reappearance out of doors, though they could not refrain from mischievously throwing in a few verses of the ballad about the maid who went to the merry green wood and came back a changed state. There are counterpoises and compensations in life; and the event which had made of her a social warning had also for the moment made her the most interesting personage in the village to many. Their friendliness won her still farther away from herself, their lively spirits were contagious, and she became almost gay.

But now that her moral sorrows were passing away a fresh one arose on the natural side of her which knew no social law. When she reached home it was to learn to her grief that the baby had been suddenly taken ill since the afternoon. Some such collapse had been probable, so tender and puny was its frame; but the event came as a shock nevertheless.

The baby's offence against society in coming into the world was forgotten by the girl-mother; her soul's desire was to continue that offence by preserving the life of the child. However, it soon grew clear that the hour of emancipation for that little prisoner of the flesh was to arrive earlier than her worst misgivings had conjectured. And when she had discovered this she was plunged into a misery which transcended that of the child's simple loss. Her baby had not been baptized.

Tess had drifted into a frame of mind which accepted passively the consideration that if she should have to burn for what she had done, burn she must, and there was an end of it. Like all village girls she was well grounded in the Holy Scriptures, and had dutifully studied the histories of Aholah and Aholibah, and knew the inferences to be drawn therefrom. But when the same question arose with regard to the baby, it had a very different colour. Her darling was about to die, and no salvation.

It was nearly bedtime, but she rushed downstairs and asked if she might send for the parson. The moment happened to be one at which her father's sense of the antique nobility of his family was highest, and his sensitiveness to the smudge which Tess had set upon that nobility most pronounced, for he had just returned from his weekly booze at Rolliver's Inn. No parson should come inside his door, he declared, prying into his affairs, just then, when, by her shame, it had become more necessary than ever to hide them. He locked the door and put the key in his pocket.

The household went to bed, and, distressed beyond measure, Tess retired also. She was continually waking as she lay, and in the middle of the night found that the baby was still worse. It was obviously dying—quietly and painlessly, but none the less surely.

In her misery she rocked herself upon the bed. The clock struck the solemn hour of one, that hour when fancy stalks outside reason, and malignant possibilities stand rock-firm as facts. She thought of the child consigned to the nethermost corner of hell, as its double doom for lack of baptism and lack of legitimacy; saw the arch-fiend tossing it with his three-pronged fork, like the one they used for heating the oven on baking days; to which picture she added many other quaint and curious details of torment sometimes taught the young in this Christian country. The lurid presentment so powerfully affected her imagination in the silence of the sleeping house that her nightgown became damp with perspiration, and the bedstead shook with each throb of her heart.

The infant's breathing grew more difficult, and the mother's mental tension increased. It was useless to devour the little thing with kisses; she could stay in bed no longer, and walked feverishly about the room.

'O merciful God, have pity; have pity upon my poor baby!' she cried. 'Heap as much anger as you want to upon me, and welcome; but pity the child!'

She leant against the chest of drawers, and murmured incoherent supplications for a long while, till she suddenly started up.

'Ah! perhaps baby can be saved! Perhaps it will be just the same!'

She spoke so brightly that it seemed as though her face might have shone in the gloom surrounding her.

She lit a candle, and went to a second and a third bed under the wall, where she awoke her young sisters and brothers, all of whom occupied the same room. Pulling out the washingstand so that she could get behind it, she poured some water from a jug, and made them kneel around, putting their hands together with fingers exactly vertical. While the children, scarcely awake, awe-stricken at her manner, their eyes growing larger and larger, remained in this position, she took the baby from her bed—a child's child—so immature as scarce to seem a sufficient personality to endow its producer with the maternal title. Tess then stood erect with the infant on her arm beside the basin, the next sister held the Prayer-Book open before her, as the clerk at church held it before the parson; and thus the girl set about baptizing her child.

Her figure looked singularly tall and imposing as she stood in her long white nightgown, a thick cable of twisted dark hair hanging straight down her back to her waist. The kindly dimness of the weak candle abstracted from her form and features the little blemishes which sunlight might have revealed—the stubble scratches upon her wrists, and the weariness of her eyes—her high enthusiasm having a transfiguring effect upon the face which had been her undoing, showing it as a thing of immaculate beauty, with a touch of dignity which was almost regal. The little ones kneeling round, their sleepy eyes blinking and red, awaited her preparations full of a suspended wonder which their physical heaviness at that hour would not allow to become active.

The most impressed of them said:

'Be you really going to christen him, Tess?'

The girl-mother replied in a grave affirmative.

'What's his name going to be?'

She had not thought of that, but a name suggested by a phrase in the book of Genesis came into her head as she proceeded with the baptismal service, and now she pronounced it:

'Sorrow, I baptize thee in the name of the Father, and of the Son, and of the Holy Ghost.'

She sprinkled the water, and there was silence.

'Say "Amen", children.'

The tiny voices piped in obedient response 'Amen!'

Tess went on:

'We receive this child'—and so forth—'and do sign him with the sign of the Cross.'

Here she dipped her hand into the basin, and fervently drew an immense cross upon the baby with her forefinger, continuing with the customary sentences as to his manfully fighting against sin, the world, and the devil, and being a faithful soldier and servant unto his life's end. She duly went on with the Lord's Prayer, the children lisping it after her in a thin gnat-like wail, till, at the conclusion, raising their voices to clerk's pitch, they again piped into the silence, 'Amen!'

Then their sister, with much augmented confidence in the efficacy of this sacrament, poured forth from the bottom of her heart the thanksgiving that follows, uttering it boldly and triumphantly in the stopt-diapason note which her voice acquired when her heart was in her speech, and which will never be forgotten by those who knew her. The ecstasy of faith almost apotheosized her; it set upon her face a glowing irradiation, and brought a red spot into the middle of each cheek; while the miniature candle-flame inverted in her eye-pupils shone like a diamond. The children gazed up at her with more and more reverence, and no longer had a will for questioning. She did not look like Sissy to them now, but as a being large, towering, and awful—a divine personage with whom they had nothing in common.

Poor Sorrow's campaign against sin, the world, and the devil was doomed to be of limited brilliancy—luckily perhaps for himself, considering his beginnings. In the blue of the morning that fragile soldier and servant breathed his last, and when the other children awoke they cried bitterly, and begged Sissy to have another pretty baby.

The calmness which had possessed Tess since the christening remained with her in the infant's loss. In the daylight, indeed, she felt her terrors about his soul to have been somewhat exaggerated; whether well founded or not she had no uneasiness now, reasoning that if Providence would not ratify such an act of approximation she, for one, did not value the kind of heaven lost by the irregularity—either for herself or for her child.

So passed away Sorrow the Undesired—that intrusive creature, that bastard gift of shameless Nature who respects not the social law; a waif to whom eternal Time had been a matter of days merely, who knew not that such things as years and centuries ever were; to whom the cottage interior was the universe, the week's weather climate, new-born babyhood human existence, and the instinct to suck human knowledge.

Tess, who mused on the christening a good deal, wondered if it were doctrinally sufficient to secure a Christian burial for the child. Nobody could tell this but the parson of the parish, and he was a new-comer, and did not know her. She went to his house after dusk, and stood by the gate, but could not summon courage to go in. The enterprise would have been abandoned if she had not by accident met him coming homeward as she turned away. In the gloom she did not mind speaking freely.

'I should like to ask you something, sir.'

He expressed his willingness to listen, and she told the story of the baby's illness and the extemporized ordinance.

'And now, sir,' she added earnestly, 'can you tell me this—will it be just the same for him as if you had baptized him?'

Having the natural feelings of a tradesman at finding that a job he should have been called in for had been unskilfully botched by his customers among themselves, he was disposed to say no. Yet the dignity of the girl, the strange tenderness in her voice, combined to affect his nobler impulses—or rather those that he had left in him after ten years of endeavour to graft technical belief on actual scepticism. The man and the ecclesiastic fought within him, and the victory fell to the man.

'My dear girl,' he said, 'it will be just the same.'

'Then will you give him a Christian burial?' she asked quickly.

The vicar felt himself cornered. Hearing of the baby's illness, he had conscientiously gone to the house after nightfall to perform the rite, and, unaware that the refusal to admit him had come from

Tess's father and not from Tess, he could not allow the plea of necessity for its irregular administration.

'Ah—that's another matter,' he said.

'Another matter—why?' asked Tess, rather warmly.

'Well—I would willingly do so if only we two were concerned. But I must not—for certain reasons.'

'Just for once, sir!'

'Really I must not.'

'O sir!' She seized his hand as she spoke.

He withdrew it, shaking his head.

'Then I don't like you!' she burst out, 'and I'll never come to your church no more!'

'Don't talk so rashly.'

'Perhaps it will be just the same to him if you don't? . . . Will it be just the same? Don't for God's sake speak as saint to sinner, but as you yourself to me myself—poor me!'

How the Vicar reconciled his answer with the strict notions he supposed himself to hold on these subjects it is beyond a layman's power to tell, though not to excuse. Somewhat moved, he said in this case also—

'It will be just the same.'

So the baby was carried in a small deal box, under an ancient woman's shawl, to the churchyard that night, and buried by lantern-light, at the cost of a shilling and a pint of beer to the sexton, in that shabby corner of God's allotment where He lets the nettles grow, and where all unbaptized infants, notorious drunkards, suicides, and others of the conjecturally damned are laid. In spite of the untoward surroundings, however, Tess bravely made a little cross of two laths and a piece of string, and having bound it with flowers, she stuck it up at the head of the grave one evening when she could enter the churchyard without being seen, putting at the foot also a bunch of the same flowers in a little jar of water to keep them alive. What matter was it that on the outside of the jar the eye of mere observation noted the words 'Keelwell's Marmalade'? The eye of maternal affection did not see them in its vision of higher things.

XV

'By experience,' says Roger Ascham, 'we find out a short way by a long wandering.' Not seldom that long wandering unfits us for further travel, and of what use is our experience to us then? Tess Durbeyfield's experience was of this incapacitating kind. At last she had learned what to do; but who would now accept her doing?

If before going to the d'Urbervilles' she had vigorously moved under the guidance of sundry gnomic texts and phrases known to her and to the world in general, no doubt she would never have been imposed on. But it had not been in Tess's power—nor is it in anybody's power—to feel the whole truth of golden opinions while it is possible to profit by them. She—and how many more—might have ironically said to God with Saint Augustine: 'Thou hast counselled a better course than Thou hast permitted.'

She remained in her father's house during the winter months, plucking fowls, or cramming turkeys and geese, or making clothes for her sisters and brothers out of some finery which d'Urberville had given her, and she had put by with contempt. Apply to him she would not. But she would often clasp her hands behind her head and muse when she was supposed to be working hard.

She philosophically noted dates as they came past in the revolution of the year; the disastrous night of her undoing at Trantridge with its dark background of The Chase; also the dates of the baby's birth and death; also her own birthday; and every other day individualized by incidents in which she had taken some share. She suddenly thought one afternoon, when looking in the glass at her fairness, that there was yet another date, of greater importance to her than those; that of her own death, when all these charms would have disappeared; a day which lay sly and unseen and among all the other days of the year, giving no sign or sound when she annually passed over it; but not the less surely there. When was it?

Why did she not feel the chill of each yearly encounter with such a cold relation? She had Jeremy Taylor's thought that some time in the future those who had known her would say? 'It is the —th, the day that poor Tess Durbeyfield died'; and there would be nothing singular to their minds in the statement. Of that day, doomed to be her terminus in time through all the ages, she did not know the place in month, week, season, or year.

Almost at a leap Tess thus changed from simple girl to complex woman. Symbols of reflectiveness passed into her face, and a note of tragedy at times into her voice. Her eyes grew larger and more eloquent. She became what would have been called a fine creature; her aspect was fair and arresting; her soul that of a woman whom the turbulent experiences of the last year or two had quite failed to demoralize. But for the world's opinion those experiences would have been simply a liberal education.

She had held so aloof of late that her trouble, never generally known, was nearly forgotten in Marlott. But it became evident to her that she could never be really comfortable again in a place which had seen the collapse of her family's attempt to 'claim kin'—and, through her, even closer union—with the rich d'Urbervilles. At least she could not be comfortable there till long years should have obliterated her keen consciousness of it. Yet even now Tess felt the pulse of hopeful life still warm within her; she might be happy in some nook which had no memories. To escape the past and all that appertained thereto was to annihilate it, and to do that she would have to get away.

Was once lost always lost really true of chastity? she would ask herself. She might prove it false if she could veil bygones. The recuperative power which pervaded organic nature was surely not denied to maidenhood alone.

She waited a long time without finding opportunity for a new departure. A particularly fine spring came round, and the stir of germination was almost audible in the buds; it moved her, as it moved the wild animals, and made her passionate to go. At last, one day in early May, a letter reached her from a former friend of her mother's, to whom she had addressed inquiries long before—a person whom she had never seen—that a skilful milkmaid was required at a dairy-house many miles to the southward, and that the dairyman would be glad to have her for the summer months.

It was not quite so far off as could have been wished; but it was probably far enough, her radius of movement and repute having been so small. To persons of limited spheres, miles are as geographical degrees, parishes as counties, counties as provinces and kingdoms.

On one point she was resolved: there should be no more d'Urberville air-castles in the dreams and deeds of her new life. She would be the dairymaid Tess, and nothing more. Her mother knew Tess's feeling on this point so well, though no words had passed between them on the subject, that she never alluded to the knightly ancestry now.

Yet such is human inconsistency that one of the interests of the new place to her was the accidental virtue of its lying near her forefathers' country (for they were not Blakemore men, though her mother was Blakemore to the bone). The dairy called Talbothays, for which she was bound, stood not remotely from some of the former estates of the d'Urbervilles, near the great family vaults of her granddames and their powerful husbands. She would be able to look at them, and think not only that d'Urberville, like Babylon, had fallen, but that the individual innocence of a humble descendant could lapse as silently. All the while she wondered if any strange good thing might come to her being in her ancestral land; and some spirit within her rose automatically as the sap in the twigs. It was unexpended youth, surging up anew after its temporary check, and bringing with it hope, and the invincible instinct towards self-delight.

END OF PHASE THE SECOND

PHASE THE THIRD

THE RALLY

XVI

On a thyme-scented, bird-hatching morning in May, between two and three years after the return from Trantridge—silent reconstructive years for Tess Durbeyfield—she left her home for the second time.

Having packed up her luggage so that it could be sent to her later, she started in a hired trap for the little town of Stourcastle, through which it was necessary to pass on her journey, now in a direction almost opposite to that of her first adventuring. On the curve of the nearest hill she looked back regretfully at Marlott and her father's house, although she had been so anxious to get away.

Her kindred dwelling there would probably continue their daily lives as heretofore, with no great diminution of pleasure in their consciousness, although she would be far off, and they deprived of her smile. In a few days the children would engage in their games as merrily as ever without the sense of any gap left by her departure. This leaving of the younger children she had decided to be for the best; were she to remain they would probably gain less good by her precepts than harm by her example.

She went through Stourcastle without pausing, and onward to a junction of highways, where she could await a carrier's van that ran to the south-west; for the railways which engirdled this interior tract of country had never yet struck across it. While waiting, however, there came along a farmer in his spring-cart, driving approximately in the direction that she wished to pursue. Though he was a stranger to her she accepted his offer of a seat beside him, ignoring that its motive was a mere tribute to her countenance. He was going to Weatherbury, and by accompanying him thither she could walk the remainder of the distance instead of travelling in the van by way of Casterbridge.

Tess did not stop at Weatherbury, after this long drive, further than to make a slight nondescript meal at noon at a cottage to which the farmer recommended her. Thence she started on foot, basket in hand, to reach the wide upland of heath dividing this district from the low-lying meads of a further valley in which the dairy stood that was the aim and end of her day's pilgrimage.

Tess had never before visited this part of the country, and yet she felt akin to the landscape. Not so very far to the left of her she could discern a dark patch in the scenery, which inquiry confirmed her in supposing to be trees marking the environs of Kingsbere—in the church of which parish the bones of her ancestors—her useless ancestors—lay entombed.

She had no admiration for them now; she almost hated them for the dance they had led her; not a thing of all that had been theirs did she retain but the old seal and spoon. 'Pooh—I have as much of mother as father in me!' she said. 'All my prettiness comes from her, and she was only a dairymaid.'

The journey over the intervening uplands and lowlands of Egdon, when she reached them, was a more troublesome walk than she had anticipated, the distance being actually but a few miles. It was two hours, owing to sundry wrong turnings, ere she found herself on a summit commanding the long-sought-for vale, the Valley of the Great Dairies, the valley in which milk and butter grew to rankness, and were produced more profusely, if less delicately, than at her home—the verdant plain so well watered by the river Var or Froom.

It was intrinsically different from the Vale of Little Dairies, Blackmoor Vale, which, save during her disastrous sojourn at Trantridge, she had exclusively known till now. The world was drawn to a larger pattern here. The enclosures numbered fifty acres instead of ten, the farmsteads were more extended, the groups of cattle formed tribes hereabout; there only families. These myriads of cows stretching under her eyes from the far east to the far west outnumbered any she had ever seen at one glance before. The green lea was speckled as thickly with them as a canvas by Van Alsloot or Sallaert with burghers. The ripe hue of the red and dun kine absorbed the evening sunlight, which the white-coated animals returned to the eye in rays almost dazzling, even at the distant elevation on which she stood.

The bird's-eye perspective before her was not so luxuriantly beautiful, perhaps, as that other one which she knew so well; yet it was more cheering. It lacked the intensely blue atmosphere of the rival vale, and its heavy soils and scents; the new air was clear, bracing, ethereal. The river itself, which nourished the grass and cows of these renowned dairies, flowed not like the streams in Blackmoor. Those were slow, silent, often turbid; flowing over beds of mud into which the incautious wader might sink and vanish unawares. The Froom waters were clear as the pure River of Life shown to the Evangelist, rapid as the shadow of a cloud, with pebbly shallows that prattled to the sky all day long. There the water-flower was the lily; the crowfoot here.

Either the change in the quality of the air from heavy to light, or the sense of being amid new scenes where there were no invidious eyes upon her, sent up her spirits wonderfully. Her hopes mingled with the sunshine in an ideal photosphere which surrounded her as she bounded along against the soft south wind. She heard a pleasant voice in every breeze, and in every bird's note seemed to lurk a joy.

Her face had latterly changed with changing states of mind, continually fluctuating between beauty and ordinariness, according as the thoughts were gay or grave. One day she was pink and flawless; another pale and tragical. When she was pink she was feeling less than when pale; her more perfect beauty accorded with her less elevated mood; her more intense mood with her less perfect beauty. It was her best face physically that was now set against the south wind.

The irresistible, universal, automatic tendency to find sweet pleasure somewhere, which pervades all life, from the meanest to the highest, had at length mastered Tess. Being even now only a young woman of twenty, one who mentally and sentimentally had not finished growing, it was impossible that any event should have left upon her an impression that was not in time capable of transmutation.

And thus her spirits, and her thankfulness, and her hopes, rose higher and higher. She tried several ballads, but found them inadequate; till, recollecting the psalter that her eyes had so often wandered over of a Sunday morning before she had eaten of the tree of knowledge, she chanted: 'O ye Sun and Moon . . . O ye Stars . . . ye Green Things upon the Earth . . . ye Fowls of the Air . . . Beasts and Cattle . . . Children of Men . . . bless ye the Lord, praise Him and magnify Him for ever!'

She suddenly stopped and murmured: 'But perhaps I don't quite know the Lord as yet.'

And probably the half-unconscious rhapsody was a Fetichistic utterance in a Monotheistic setting; women whose chief companions are the forms and forces of outdoor Nature retain in their souls far more of the Pagan fantasy of their remote forefathers than of the systematized religion taught their race at later date. However, Tess found at least approximate expression for her feelings in the old *Benedicite* that she had lisped from infancy; and it was enough. Such high contentment with such a slight initial performance as that of having started towards a means of independent living was a part of the Durbeyfield temperament. Tess really wished to walk uprightly, while her father did nothing of the kind; but she resembled him in being content with immediate and small achievements, and in having no mind for laborious effort towards such petty social advancement as could alone be effected by a family so heavily handicapped as the once powerful d'Urbervilles were now.

There was, it might be said, the energy of her mother's unexpended family, as well as the natural energy of Tess's years, rekindled after the experience which had so overwhelmed her for the time. Let the truth be told—women do as a rule live through such humiliations, and regain their spirits, and again look about them with an interested eye. While there's life there's hope is a conviction not so entirely unknown to the 'betrayed' as some amiable theorists would have us believe.

Tess Durbeyfield, then, in good heart, and full of zest for life, descended the Egdon slopes lower and lower towards the dairy of her pilgrimage.

The marked difference, in the final particular, between the rival vales now showed itself. The secret of Blackmoor was best discovered from the heights around; to read aright the valley before her it was necessary to descend into its midst. When Tess had accomplished this feat she found herself to be standing on a carpeted level, which stretched to the east and west as far as the eye could reach.

The river had stolen from the higher tracts and brought in particles to the vale all this horizontal land; and now, exhausted, aged, and attenuated, lay serpentining along through the midst of its former spoils.

Not quite sure of her direction Tess stood still upon the hemmed expanse of verdant flatness, like a fly on a billiard-table of indefinite length, and of no more consequence to the surroundings than that fly. The sole effect of her presence upon the placid valley so far had been to excite the mind of a solitary heron, which, after descending to the ground not far from her path, stood with neck erect, looking at her.

Suddenly there arose from all parts of the lowland a prolonged and repeated call—

'Waow! waow! waow!'

From the furthest east to the furthest west the cries spread as if by contagion, accompanied in some cases by the barking of a dog. It was not the expression of the valley's consciousness that beautiful Tess had arrived, but the ordinary announcement of milking-time—half-past four o'clock, when the dairymen set about getting in the cows.

The red and white herd nearest at hand, which had been phlegmatically waiting for the call, now trooped towards the steading in the background, their great bags of milk swinging under them as they walked. Tess followed slowly in their rear, and entered the barton by the open gate through which they had entered before her. Long thatched sheds stretched round the enclosure, their slopes encrusted with vivid green moss, and their eaves supported by wooden posts rubbed to a glossy smoothness by the flanks of infinite cows and calves of bygone years, now passed to an oblivion almost inconceivable in its profundity. Between the posts were ranged the milchers, each exhibiting herself at the present moment to a whimsical eye in the rear as a circle on two stalks, down the centre of which a switch moved pendulum-wise; while the sun, lowering itself behind this patient row, threw their shadows accurately inwards upon the wall. Thus it threw shadows of these obscure and homely figures every evening with as much care over each contour as if it had been the profile of a Court beauty on a palace wall; copied them as diligently as it had copied Olympian shapes on marble *façades* long ago, or the outline of Alexander, Caesar, and the Pharaohs.

They were the less restful cows that were stalled. Those that would stand still of their own will were milked in the middle of the yard, where many of such better behaved ones stood waiting now—all prime milchers, such as were seldom seen out of this valley, and not always within it; nourished by the succulent feed which the water-meads supplied at this prime season of the year. Those of them that were spotted with white reflected the sunshine in dazzling brilliancy, and the polished brass knobs on their horns glittered with something of military display. Their large-veined udders hung ponderous as sandbags, the teats sticking out like the legs of a gipsy's crock; and as each animal lingered for her turn to arrive the milk oozed forth and fell in drops to the ground.

XVII

THE dairymaids and men had flocked down from their cottages and out of the dairy-house with the arrival of the cows from the meads; the maids walking in pattens, not on account of the weather, but to keep their shoes above the mulch of the barton. Each girl sat down on her three-legged stool, her face sideways, her right cheek resting against the cow; and looked musingly along the animal's flank at Tess as she approached. The male milkers, with hat-brims turned down, resting flat on their foreheads and gazing on the ground, did not observe her.

One of these was a sturdy middle-aged man—whose long white 'pinner' was somewhat finer and cleaner than the wraps of the others, and whose jacket underneath had a presentable marketing aspect—the master-dairyman, of whom she was in quest, his double character as a working milker and buttermaker here during six days, and on the seventh as a man in shining broad-cloth in his family pew at church, being so marked as to have inspired a rhyme—

Dairyman Dick
All the week:
On Sundays Mister Richard Crick.

Seeing Tess standing at gaze he went across to her.

The majority of dairymen have a cross manner at milking-time, but it happened that Mr Crick was glad to get a new hand—for the days were busy ones now—and he received her warmly; inquiring for her mother and the rest of the family—(though this as a matter of form merely, for in reality he had not been aware of Mrs Durbeyfield's existence till apprised of the fact by a brief business-letter about Tess).

'Oh—ay, as a lad I knowed your part o' the country very well,' he said terminatively. 'Though I've never been there since. And a aged woman of ninety that used to live nigh here, but is dead and gone long ago, told me that a family of some such name as yours in Blackmoor Vale came originally from these parts, and that 'twere a old ancient race that had all but perished off the earth—though the new generations didn't know it. But, Lord, I took no notice of the old woman's ramblings, not I.'

'Oh no—it is nothing,' said Tess.

Then the talk was of business only.

'You can milk 'em clean, my maidy? I don't want my cows going azew at this time o' year.'

She reassured him on that point, and he surveyed her up and down. She had been staying indoors a good deal, and her complexion had grown delicate.

'Quite sure you can stand it? 'Tis comfortable enough here for rough folk; but we don't live in a cowcumber frame.'

She declared that she could stand it, and her zest and willingness seemed to win him over.

'Well, I suppose you'll want a dish o' tay, or victuals of some sort, hey? Not yet? Well, do as ye like about it. But faith, if 'twas I, I should be as dry as a kex wi' travelling so far.'

'I'll begin milking now, to get my hand in,' said Tess.

She drank a little milk as temporary refreshment—to the surprise—indeed, slight contempt—of Dairyman Crick, to whose mind it had apparently never occurred that milk was good as a beverage.

'Oh, if ye can swaller that, be it so,' he said indifferently, while one held up the pail that she sipped from. ''Tis what I hain't touched for years—not I. Rot the stuff; it would lie in my innerds like lead. You can try your hand upon she,' he pursued, nodding to the nearest cow. 'Not but what she do milk rather hard. We've hard ones and we've easy ones, like other folks. However, you'll find out that soon enough.'

When Tess had changed her bonnet for a hood, and was really on her stool under the cow, and the milk was squirting from her fists into the pail, she appeared to feel that she really had laid a new foundation for her future. The conviction bred serenity, her pulse slowed, and she was able to look about her.

The milkers formed quite a little batallion of men and maids, the men operating on the hard-teated animals, the maids on the kindlier natures. It was a large dairy. There were nearly a hundred milchers under Crick's management, all told; and of the herd the master-dairyman milked six or eight with his own hands, unless away from home. These were the cows that milked hardest of all; for his journey-milkmen being more or less casually hired, he would not entrust this half-dozen to their treatment, lest, from indifference, they should not milk them fully; nor to the maids, lest they should fail in the same way for lack of finger-grip; with the result that in course of time the cows would 'go azew'—that is, dry up. It was not the loss for the moment that made slack milking so serious, but that with the decline of demand there came decline, and ultimately cessation, of supply.

After Tess had settled down to her cow there was for a time no talk in the barton, and not a sound interfered with the purr of the milk-jets into the numerous pails, except a momentary exclamation to one or other of the beasts requesting her to turn round or stand still. The only movements were those of the milkers' hands up and down, and the swing of the cows' tails. Thus they all worked on, encompassed by the vast flat mead which extended to either slope of the valley—a level landscape compounded of old landscapes long forgotten, and, no doubt, differing in character very greatly from the landscape they composed now.

'To my thinking,' said the dairyman, rising suddenly from a cow he had just finished off, snatching up his three-legged stool in one hand and the pail in the other, and moving on to the next hard-yielder in his vicinity; 'to my thinking, the cows don't gie down their milk to-day as usual. Upon my life, if Winker do begin keeping back like this, she'll not be worth going under by midsummer.'

''Tis because there's a new hand come among us,' said Jonathan Kail. 'I've noticed such things afore.'

'To be sure. It may be so. I didn't think o't.'

'I've been told that it goes up into their horns at such times,' said a dairymaid.

'Well, as to going up into their horns,' replied Dairyman Crick dubiously, as though even witchcraft might be limited by anatomical possibilities, 'I couldn't say; I certainly could not. But as nott cows will keep it back as well as the horned ones, I don't quite agree to it. Do ye know that riddle about the nott cows, Jonathan? Why do nott cows give less milk in a year than horned?'

'I don't!' interposed the milkmaid. 'Why do they?'

'Because there bain't so many of 'em,' said the dairyman. 'Howsomever, these gam'sters do certainly keep back their milk to-day. Folks, we must lift up a stave or two—that's the only cure for't.'

Songs were often resorted to in dairies hereabout as an enticement to the cows when they showed signs of withholding their usual yield; and the band of milkers at this request burst into melody—in purely business-like tones, it is true, and with no great spontaneity; the result, according to their own belief, being a decided improvement during the song's continuance. When they had gone through fourteen or fifteen verses of a cheerful ballad about a murderer who was afraid to go to bed in the dark because he saw certain brimstone flames around him, one of the male milkers said—

'I wish singing on the stoop didn't use up so much of a man's wind! You should get your harp, sir; not but what a fiddle is best.'

Tess, who had given ear to this, thought the words were addressed to the dairyman, but she was wrong. A reply, in the shape of 'Why?' came as it were out of the belly of a dun cow in the stalls; it had been spoken by a milker behind the animal, whom she had not hitherto perceived.

'Oh yes; there's nothing like a fiddle,' said the dairyman. 'Though I do think that bulls are more moved by a tune than cows—at least that's my experience. Once there was a old aged man over at Mellstock—William Dewy by name—one of the family that used to do a good deal of business as tranters over there, Jonathan, do ye mind?—I knowed the man by sight as well as I know my own brother, in a manner of speaking. Well, this man was a coming home-along from a wedding where he had been playing his fiddle, one fine moonlight night, and for shortness' sake he took a cut across Forty-acres, a field lying that way, where a bull was out to grass. The bull seed William, and took after him, horns aground, begad; and though William runned his best, and hadn't *much* drink in him (considering 'twas a wedding, and the folks well off), he found he'd never reach the fence and get over in time to save himself. Well, as a last thought, he pulled out his fiddle as he runned, and struck up a jig, turning to the bull, and backing towards the corner. The bull softened down, and stood still, looking hard at William Dewy, who fiddled on and on; till a sort of a smile stole over the bull's face. But no sooner did William stop his playing and turn to get over hedge than the bull would stop his smiling and lower his horns towards the seat of William's breeches. Well, William had to turn about and play on, willy-nilly; and 'twas only three o'clock in the world, and 'a knowed that nobody would come that way for hours, and he so leery and tired that 'a didn't know what to do. When he had scraped till about four o'clock he felt that he verily would have to give over soon, and he said to himself, "There's only this last tune between me and eternal welfare! Heaven save me, or I'm a done man." Well, then he called to mind how he'd seen the cattle kneel o' Christmas Eves in the dead o' night. It was not Christmas Eve then, but it came into his head to play a trick upon the bull. So he broke into the 'Tivity Hymn, just as at Christmas carol-singing; when, lo and behold, down went the bull on his bended knees, in his ignorance, just as if 'twere the true 'Tivity night and hour. As soon as his horned friend were down, William turned, clinked off like a long-dog, and jumped safe over hedge, before the praying bull had got on his feet again to take after him. William used to say that he'd seen a man look a fool a good many times, but never such a fool as that bull looked when he found his pious feelings had been played upon, and 'twas not Christmas Eve . . . Yes, William Dewy, that was the man's name; and I can tell you to a foot where's he a-lying in Mellstock Churchyard at this very moment—just between the second yew-tree and the north aisle.'

'It's a curious story; it carries us back to mediaeval times, when faith was a living thing!'

The remark, singular for a dairy-yard, was murmured by the

voice behind the dun cow; but as nobody understood the reference no notice was taken, except that the narrator seemed to think it might imply scepticism as to his tale.

'Well, 'tis quite true, sir, whether or no. I knowed the man well.'

'Oh yes; I have no doubt of it,' said the person behind the dun cow.

Tess's attention was thus attracted to the dairyman's interlocutor, of whom she could see but the merest patch, owing to his burying his head so persistently in the flank of the milcher. She could not understand why he should be addressed as 'sir' even by the dairyman himself. But no explanation was discernible; he remained under the cow long enough to have milked three, uttering a private ejaculation now and then, as if he could not get on.

'Take it gentle, sir; take it gentle,' said the dairyman. ''Tis knack, not strength that does it.'

'So I find,' said the other, standing up at last and stretching his arms. 'I think I have finished her, however, though she made my fingers ache.'

Tess could then see him at full length. He wore the ordinary white pinner and leather leggings of a dairy-farmer when milking, and his boots were clogged with the mulch of the yard; but this was all his local livery. Beneath it was something educated, reserved, subtle, sad, differing.

But the details of his aspect were temporarily thrust aside by the discovery that he was one whom she had seen before. Such vicissitudes had Tess passed through since that time that for a moment she could not remember where she had met him; and then it flashed upon her that he was the pedestrian who had joined in the club-dance at Marlott—the passing stranger who had come she knew not whence, had danced with others but not with her, had slightingly left her, and gone on his way with his friends.

The flood of memories brought back by this revival of an incident anterior to her troubles produced a momentary dismay lest, recognizing her also, he should by some means discover her story. But it passed away when she found no sign of remembrance in him. She saw by degrees that since their first and only encounter his mobile face had grown more thoughtful, and had acquired a young man's shapely moustache and beard—the latter of the palest straw colour where it began upon his cheeks, and deepening to a warm brown farther from its root. Under his linen milking-pinner he wore a dark velveteen jacket, cord breeches and gaiters, and a starched white shirt. Without the milking-gear nobody could have guessed what he was. He might with equal probability have been an eccentric landowner or a gentlemanly ploughman. That he was but a novice at dairywork she had realized in a moment, from the time he had spent upon the milking of one cow.

Meanwhile many of the milkmaids had said to one another of the new-comer, 'How pretty she is!' with something of real generosity and admiration, though with a half hope that the auditors would qualify the assertion—which, strictly speaking, they might have done, prettiness being an inexact definition of what struck the eye in Tess. When the milking was finished for the evening they straggled indoors, where Mrs Crick, the dairyman's wife—who was too respectable to go out milking herself, and wore a hot stuff gown in warm weather because the dairymaids wore prints—was giving an eye to the leads and things.

Only two or three of the maids, Tess learnt, slept in the dairy-house besides herself; most of the helpers going to their homes. She saw nothing at supper-time of the superior milker who had commented on the story, and asked no questions about him, the remainder of the evening being occupied in arranging her place in the bed-chamber. It was a large room over the milk-house, some thirty feet long; the sleeping-cots of the other three indoor milk-maids being in the same apartment. They were blooming young women, and, except one, rather older than herself. By bedtime Tess was thoroughly tired, and fell asleep immediately.

But one of the girls who occupied an adjoining bed was more wakeful than Tess, and would insist upon relating to the latter various particulars of the homestead into which she had just entered. The girl's whispered words mingled with the shades, and, to Tess's drowsy mind, they seemed to be generated by the darkness in which they floated.

'Mr Angel Clare—he that is learning milking, and that plays the harp—never says much to us. He is a pa'son's son, and is too much taken up wi' his own thoughts to notice girls. He is the dairyman's pupil—learning farming in all its branches. He has learnt sheep-farming at another place, and he's now mastering dairy-work . . . Yes, he is quite the gentleman-born. His father is the Reverent Mr Clare at Emminster—a good many miles from here.'

'Oh—I have heard of him,' said her companion, now awake. 'A very earnest clergyman, is he not?'

'Yes—that he is—the earnestest man in all Wessex, they say—the last of the old Low Church sort, they tell me—for all about here be what they call High. All his sons, except our Mr Clare, be made pa'sons too.'

Tess had not at this hour the curiosity to ask why the present Mr Clare was not made a parson like his brethren, and gradually fell asleep again, the words of her informant coming to her along with the smell of the cheeses in the adjoining cheese-loft, and the measured dripping of the whey from the wrings downstairs.

XVIII

ANGEL Clare rises out of the past not altogether as a distinct figure, but as an appreciative voice, a long regard of fixed, abstracted eyes, and a mobility of mouth somewhat too small and delicately lined for a man's, though with an unexpectedly firm close of the lower lip now and then; enough to do away with any inference of indecision. Nevertheless, something nebulous, preoccupied, vague, in his bearing and regard, marked him as one who probably had no very definite aim or concern about his material future. Yet as a lad people had said of him that he was one who might do anything if he tried.

He was the youngest son of his father, a poor parson at the other end of the county, and had arrived at Talbothays Dairy as a six months' pupil, after going the round of some other farms, his object being to acquire a practical skill in the various processes of farming, with a view either to the Colonies, or the tenure of a home-farm, as circumstances might decide.

His entry into the ranks of the agriculturists and breeders was a step in the young man's career which had been anticipated neither by himself nor by others.

Mr Clare the elder, whose first wife had died and left him a daughter, married a second late in life. This lady had somewhat unexpectedly brought him three sons, so that between Angel, the youngest, and his father the vicar there seemed to be almost a missing generation. Of these boys the aforesaid Angel, the child of his old age, was the only son who had not taken a University degree, though he was the single one of them whose early promise might have done full justice to an academical training.

Some two or three years before Angel's appearance at the Marlott dance, on a day when he had left school and was pursuing his studies at home, a parcel came to the vicarage from the local bookseller's, directed to the Reverend James Clare. The vicar having opened it and found it to contain a book, read a few pages; whereupon he jumped up from his seat and went straight to the shop with the book under his arm.

'Why has this been sent to my house?' he asked peremptorily, holding up the volume.

'It was ordered, sir.'

'Not by me, or any one belonging to me, I am happy to say.'

The shopkeeper looked into his order-book.

'Oh, it has been misdirected, sir,' he said. 'It was ordered by Mr Angel Clare, and should have been sent to him.'

Mr Clare winced as if he had been struck. He went home pale and dejected, and called Angel into his study.

'Look into this book, my boy,' he said. 'What do you know about it?'

'I ordered it,' said Angel simply.

'What for?'

'To read.'

'How can you think of reading it?'

'How can I? Why—it is a system of philosophy. There is no more moral, or even religious, work published.'

'Yes—moral enough; I don't deny that. But religious!—and for *you*, who intend to be a minister of the Gospel!'

'Since you have alluded to the matter, father,' said the son, with anxious thought upon his face, 'I should like to say, once for all, that I should prefer not to take Orders. I fear I could not conscientiously do so. I love the Church as one loves a parent. I shall always have the warmest affection for her. There is no institution for whose history I have a deeper admiration; but I cannot honestly be ordained her minister, as my brothers are, while she refuses to liberate her mind from an untenable redemptive theolatry.'

It had never occurred to the straightforward and simple-minded Vicar that one of his own flesh and blood could come to this! He was stultified, shocked, paralyzed. And if Angel were not going to enter the Church, what was the use of sending him to Cambridge? The University as a step to anything but ordination seemed, to this man of fixed ideas, a preface without a volume. He was a man not merely religious, but devout; a firm believer—not as the phrase is now elusively construed by theological thimble-riggers in the Church and out of it, but in the old and ardent sense of the Evangelical school: one who could

> Indeed opine
> That the Eternal and Divine
> Did, eighteen centuries ago
> In very truth . . .

Angel's father tried argument, persuasion, entreaty.

'No, father; I cannot underwrite Article Four (leave alone the rest), taking it "in the literal and grammatical sense" as required by the Declaration; and, therefore, I can't be a parson in the present state of affairs,' said Angel. 'My whole instinct in matters of religion is towards reconstruction: to quote your favourite Epistle to the Hebrews, "the removing of those things that are shaken, as of things that are made, that those things which cannot be shaken may remain".'

His father grieved so deeply that it made Angel quite ill to see him.

'What is the good of your mother and me economizing and stinting ourselves to give you a University education, if it is not to be used for the honour and glory of God?' his father repeated.

'Why, that it may be used for the honour and glory of man, father.'

Perhaps if Angel had persevered he might have gone to Cambridge like his brothers. But the Vicar's view of that seat of learning as a stepping-stone to Orders alone was quite a family tradition; and so rooted was the idea in his mind that perseverance began to appear to the sensitive son akin to an intent to misappropriate a trust, and wrong the pious heads of the household, who had been and were, as his father had hinted, compelled to exercise much thrift to carry out this uniform plan of education for the three young men.

'I will do without Cambridge,' said Angel at last. 'I feel that I have no right to go there in the circumstances.'

The effects of this decisive debate were not long in showing themselves. He spent years and years in desultory studies, undertakings, and meditations; he began to evince considerable indifference to social forms and observances. The material distinctions of rank and wealth he increasingly despised. Even the 'good old family' (to use a favourite phrase of a late local worthy) had no aroma for him unless there were good new resolutions in its representatives. As a balance to these austerities, when he went to live in London to see what the world was like, and with a view to practising a profession or business there, he was carried off his head, and nearly entrapped by a woman much older than himself, though luckily he escaped not greatly the worse for the experience.

Early association with country solitudes had bred in him an unconquerable, and almost unreasonable, aversion to modern town life, and shut him out from such success as he might have aspired to by following a mundane calling in the impracticability of the spiritual one. But something had to be done; he had wasted many valuable years; and having an acquaintance who was starting on a thriving life as a Colonial farmer, it occurred to Angel that this might be a lead in the right direction. Farming, either in the Colonies, America, or at home—farming at any rate, after becoming well qualified for the business by a careful apprenticeship—that was a vocation which would probably afford an independence without the sacrifice of what he valued even more than a competency—intellectual liberty.

So we find Angel Clare at six-and-twenty here at Talbothays as a student of kine, and, as there were no houses near at hand in which he could get a comfortable lodging, a boarder at the dairyman's.

His room was an immense attic which ran the whole length of the dairy-house. It could only be reached by a ladder from the cheese-loft, and had been closed up for a long time till he arrived and selected it as his retreat. Here Clare had plenty of space, and could often be heard by the dairy-folk pacing up and down when the household had gone to rest. A portion was divided off at one end by a curtain, behind which was his bed, the outer part being furnished as a homely sitting-room.

At first he lived up above entirely, reading a good deal, and strumming upon an old harp which he had bought at a sale, saying when in a bitter humour that he might have to get his living by it in the streets some day. But he soon preferred to read human nature by taking his meals downstairs in the general dining-kitchen, with the dairyman and his wife, and the maids and men, who all together formed a lively assembly; for though but few milking hands slept in the house, several joined the family at meals. The longer Clare resided here the less objection had he to his company, and the more did he like to share quarters with them in common.

Much to his surprise he took, indeed, a real delight in their companionship. The conventional farm-folk of his imagination—personified by the pitiable dummy known as Hodge—were obliterated after a few days' residence. At close quarters no Hodge was to be seen. At first, it is true, when Clare's intelligence was fresh from a contrasting society, these friends with whom he now hobnobbed seemed a little strange. Sitting down as a level member of the dairyman's household seemed at the outset an undignified proceeding. The ideas, the modes, the surroundings, appeared retrogressive and unmeaning. But with living on there, day after day, the acute sojourner became conscious of a new aspect in the spectacle. Without any objective change whatever, variety had taken the place of monotonousness. His host and his host's household, his men and his maids, as they became intimately known to Clare, began to differentiate themselves as in a chemical process. The thought of Pascal's was brought home to him: 'A mesure qu'on a plus d'esprit, on trouve qu'il y a plus d'hommes originaux. Les gens du commun ne trouvent pas de différence entre les hommes.' The typical and unvarying Hodge ceased to exist. He had been disintegrated into a number of varied fellow-creatures—beings of many minds, beings infinite in difference; some happy, many serene, a few depressed, one here and there bright even to genius, some stupid, others wanton, others austere; some mutely Miltonic, some potentially Cromwellian; into men who had private views of each other, as he had of his friends; who could applaud or condemn each other, amuse or sadden themselves by the contemplation of each other's foibles or vices; men every one of whom walked in his own individual way the road to dusty death.

Unexpectedly he began to like the outdoor life for its own sake, and for what it brought, apart from its bearing on his own proposed career. Considering his position he became wonderfully free from the chronic melancholy which is taking hold of the civilized races with the decline of belief in a beneficent Power. For the first time of late years he could read as his musings inclined him, without any eye to cramming for a profession, since the few farming handbooks which he deemed it desirable to master occupied him but little time.

He grew away from old associations, and saw something new in life and humanity. Secondarily, he made close acquaintance with phenomena which he had before known but darkly—the seasons in their moods, morning and evening, night and noon, winds in their different tempers, trees, waters and mists, shades and silences, and the voices of inanimate things.

The early mornings were still sufficiently cool to render a fire acceptable in the large room wherein they breakfasted; and, by Mrs Crick's orders, who held that he was too genteel to mess at their table, it was Angel Clare's custom to sit in the yawning chimney-corner during the meal, his cup-and-saucer and plate being placed on a hinged flap at his elbow. The light from the long, wide, mullioned window opposite shone in upon his nook, and, assisted by a secondary light of cold blue quality which shone down the chimney, enabled him to read there easily whenever disposed to do so. Between Clare and the window was the table at which his companions sat, their munching profiles rising sharp against the panes; while to the side was the milk-house door, through which were visible the rectangular leads in rows, full to the brim with the morning's milk. At the further end the great churn could be seen revolving, and its slip-slopping heard—the moving power being discernible through the window in the form of a spiritless horse walking in a circle and driven by a boy.

For several days after Tess's arrival Clare, sitting abstractedly reading from some book, periodical, or piece of music just come by post, hardly noticed that she was present at table. She talked so little, and the other maids talked so much, that the babble did not strike him as possessing a new note, and he was ever in the habit of neglecting the particulars of an outward scene for the general impression. One day, however, when he had been conning one of his music-scores, and by force of imagination was hearing the tune in his head, he lapsed into listlessness, and the music-sheet rolled to the hearth. He looked at the fire of logs, with its one flame pirouetting on the top in a dying dance after the breakfast-cooking and boiling, and it seemed to jig to his inward tune; also at the two chimney crooks dangling down from the cotterel or cross-bar, plumed with soot which quivered to the same melody; also at the half-empty kettle whining an accompaniment. The conversation at the table mixed in with his phantasmal orchestra till he thought: 'What a fluty voice one of those milkmaids has! I suppose it is the new one.'

Clare looked round upon her, seated with the others.

She was not looking towards him. Indeed, owing to his long silence, his presence in the room was almost forgotten.

'I don't know about ghosts,' she was saying; 'but I do know that our souls can be made to go outside our bodies when we are alive.'

The dairyman turned to her with his mouth full, his eyes charged with serious inquiry, and his great knife and fork (breakfasts were breakfasts here) planted erect on the table, like the beginning of a gallows.

'What—really now? And is it so, maidy?' he said.

'A very easy way to feel 'em go,' continued Tess, 'is to lie on the grass at night and look straight up at some big bright star; and, by fixing your mind upon it, you will soon find that you are hundreds and hundreds o' miles away from your body, which you don't seem to want at all.'

The dairyman removed his hard gaze from Tess, and fixed it on his wife.

'Now that's a rum thing, Christianner—hey? To think o' the miles I've vamped o' starlight nights these last thirty year, courting, or trading, or for doctor, or for nurse, and yet never had the least notion o' that till now, or feeled my soul rise so much as an inch above my shirt-collar.'

The general attention being drawn to her, including that of the dairyman's pupil, Tess flushed and remarking evasively that it was only a fancy, resumed her breakfast.

Clare continued to observe her. She soon finished her eating, and having a consciousness that Clare was regarding her, began to trace imaginary patterns on the tablecloth with her forefinger with the constraint of a domestic animal that perceives itself to be watched.

'What a fresh and virginal daughter of Nature that milkmaid is!' he said to himself.

And then he seemed to discern in her something that was familiar, something which carried him back into a joyous and unforeseeing past, before the necessity of taking thought had made the heavens gray. He concluded that he had beheld her before; where he could not tell. A casual encounter during some country ramble it certainly had been, and he was not greatly curious about it. But the circumstance was sufficient to lead him to select Tess in preference to the other pretty milkmaids when he wished to contemplate contiguous womankind.

XIX

In general the cows were milked as they presented themselves, without fancy or choice. But certain cows will show a fondness for a particular pair of hands, sometimes carrying this predilection so far as to refuse to stand at all except to their favourite, the pail of a stranger being unceremoniously kicked over.

It was Dairyman Crick's rule to insist on breaking down these partialities and aversions by constant interchange, since otherwise, in the event of a milkman or maid going away from the dairy, he was placed in a difficulty. The maids' private aims, however, were the reverse of the dairyman's rule, the daily selection by each damsel of the eight or ten cows to which she had grown accustomed rendering the operation on their willing udders surprisingly easy and effortless.

Tess, like her compeers, soon discovered which of the cows had a preference for her style of manipulation, and her fingers having become delicate from the long domiciliary imprisonments to which she had subjected herself at intervals during the last two or three years, she would have been glad to meet the milchers' views in this respect. Out of the whole ninety-five there were eight in particular—Dumpling, Fancy, Lofty, Mist, Old Pretty, Young Pretty, Tidy, and Loud—who, though the teats of one or two were as hard as carrots, gave down to her with a readiness that made her work on them a mere touch of the fingers. Knowing, however, the dairyman's wish, she endeavoured conscientiously to take the animals just as they came, excepting the very hard yielders which she could not yet manage.

But she soon found a curious correspondence between the ostensibly chance position of the cows and her wishes in this matter, till she felt that their order could not be the result of accident. The dairyman's pupil had lent a hand in getting the cows together of late, and at the fifth or sixth time she turned her eyes, as she rested against the cow, full of sly inquiry upon him.

'Mr Clare, you have ranged the cows!' she said, blushing; and in making the accusation symptoms of a smile gently lifted her upper lip in spite of her, so as to show the tips of her teeth, the lower lip remaining severely still.

'Well, it makes no difference,' said he. 'You will always be here to milk them.'

'Do you think so? I *hope* I shall! But I don't *know*.'

She was angry with herself afterwards, thinking that he, unaware of her grave reasons for liking this seclusion, might have mistaken her meaning. She had spoken so earnestly to him, as if his presence were somehow a factor in her wish. Her misgiving was such that at dusk, when the milking was over, she walked in the garden alone, to continue her regrets that she had disclosed to him her discovery of his considerateness.

It was a typical summer evening in June, the atmosphere being in such delicate equilibrium and so transmissive that inanimate objects seemed endowed with two or three senses, if not five. There was no distinction between the near and the far, and an auditor felt close to everything within the horizon. The soundlessness impressed her as a positive entity rather than as the mere negation of noise. It was broken by the strumming of strings.

Tess had heard those notes in the attic above her head. Dim, flattened, constrained by their confinement, they had never appealed to her as now, when they wandered in the still air with a stark quality like that of nudity. To speak absolutely, both instrument and execution were poor; but the relative is all, and as she listened Tess, like a fascinated bird, could not leave the spot. Far from leaving she drew up towards the performer, keeping behind the hedge that he might not guess her presence.

The outskirt of the garden in which Tess found herself had been left uncultivated for some years, and was now damp and rank with juicy grass which sent up mists of pollen at a touch; and with tall blooming weeds emitting offensive smells—weeds whose red and yellow and purple hues formed a polychrome as dazzling as that of cultivated flowers. She went stealthily as a cat through this profusion of growth, gathering cuckoo-spittle on her skirts, cracking snails that were underfoot, staining her hands with thistle-milk and slug-slime, and rubbing off upon her naked arms sticky blights which, though snow-white on the apple-tree trunks, made madder stains on her skin; thus she drew quite near to Clare, still unobserved of him.

Tess was conscious of neither time nor space. The exaltation which she had described as being producible at will by gazing at a star, came now without any determination of hers; she undulated upon the thin notes of the second-hand harp, and their harmonies passed like breezes through her, bringing tears into her eyes. The floating pollen seemed to be his notes made visible, and the dampness of the garden the weeping of the garden's sensibility. Though near nightfall, the rank-smelling weed-flowers glowed as if they would not close for intentness, and the waves of colour mixed with the waves of sound.

The light which still shone was derived mainly from a large hole in the western bank of cloud; it was like a piece of day left behind by accident, dusk having closed in elsewhere. He concluded his plaintive melody, a very simple performance, demanding no great skill; and she waited, thinking another might be begun. But, tired of playing, he had desultorily come round the fence, and was rambling up behind her. Tess, her cheeks on fire, moved away furtively, as if hardly moving at all.

Angel, however, saw her light summer gown, and he spoke; his low tones reaching her, though he was some distance off.

'What makes you draw off in that way, Tess?' said he. 'Are you afraid?'

'Oh no, sir . . . not of outdoor things; especially just now when the apple-blooth is falling, and everything so green.'

'But you have your indoor fears—eh?'

'Well—yes, sir.'

'What of?'

'I couldn't quite say.'

'The milk turning sour?'

'No.'

'Life in general?'

'Yes, sir.'

'Ah—so have I, very often. This hobble of being alive is rather serious, don't you think so?'

'It is—now you put it that way.'

'All the same, I shouldn't have expected a young girl like you to see it so just yet. How is it you do?'

She maintained a hesitating silence.

'Come, Tess, tell me in confidence.'

She thought that he meant what were the aspects of things to her, and replied shyly—

'The trees have inquisitive eyes, haven't they?—that is, seem as if they had. And the river says,—"Why do ye trouble me with your looks?" And you seem to see numbers of tomorrows just all in a line, the first of them the biggest and clearest, the others getting smaller and smaller as they stand farther away; but they all seem very fierce and cruel and as if they said, "I'm coming! Beware of me! Beware of me!" . . . But *you*, sir, can raise up dreams with your music, and drive all such horrid fancies away!'

He was surprised to find this young woman—who though but a milkmaid had just that touch of rarity about her which might make her the envied of her housemates—shaping such sad imaginings. She was expressing in her own native phrases—assisted a little by her Sixth Standard training—feelings which might almost have been called those of the age—the ache of modernism. The perception arrested him less when he reflected that what are called advanced ideas are really in great part but the latest fashion in definition—a more accurate expression, by words in *logy* and *ism*, of sensations which men and women have vaguely grasped for centuries.

Still, it was strange that they should have come to her while yet so young; more than strange; it was impressive, interesting, pathetic. Not guessing the cause, there was nothing to remind him that experience is as to intensity, and not as to duration. Tess's passing corporeal blight had been her mental harvest.

Tess, on her part, could not understand why a man of clerical family and good education, and above physical want, should look upon it as a mishap to be alive. For the unhappy pilgrim herself there was very good reason. But how could this admirable and poetic man ever have descended into the Valley of Humiliation, have felt with the man of Uz—as she herself had felt two or three years ago—'My soul chooseth strangling and death rather than my life. I loathe it; I would not live alway.'

It was true that he was at present out of his class. But she knew that was only because, like Peter the Great in a shipwright's yard, he was studying what he wanted to know. He did not milk cows because he was obliged to milk cows, but because he was learning how to be a rich and prosperous dairyman, landowner, agriculturist, and breeder of cattle. He would become an American or Australian Abraham, commanding like a monarch his flocks and his herds, his spotted and his ring-straked, his men-servants and his maids. At times, nevertheless, it did seem unaccountable to her that a decidedly bookish, musical, thinking young man should have chosen deliberately to be a farmer, and not a clergyman, like his father and brothers.

Thus, neither having the clue to the other's secret, they were respectively puzzled at what each revealed, and awaited new knowledge of each other's character and moods without attempting to pry into each other's history.

Every day, every hour, brought to him one more little stroke of her nature, and to her one more of his. Tess was trying to lead a repressed life, but she little divined the strength of her own vitality.

At first Tess seemed to regard Angel Clare as an intelligence rather than as a man. As such she compared him with herself; and at every discovery of the abundance of his illuminations, of the distance between her own modest mental standpoint and the unmeasurable, Andean altitude of his, she became quite dejected, disheartened from all further effort on her own part whatever.

He observed her dejection one day, when he had casually mentioned something to her about pastoral life in ancient Greece. She was gathering the buds called 'lords and ladies' from the bank while he spoke.

'Why do you look so woebegone all of a sudden?' he asked.

'Oh 'tis only—about my own self,' she said, with a frail laugh of sadness, fitfully beginning to peel 'a lady' meanwhile. 'Just a sense of what might have been with me! My life looks as if it had been wasted for want of chances! When I see what you know, what you have read, and seen, and thought, I feel what a nothing I am! I'm like the poor Queen of Sheba who lived in the Bible. There is no more spirit in me.'

'Bless my soul, don't go troubling about that! Why,' he said with some enthusiasm, 'I should be only too glad, my dear Tess, to help you do anything in the way of history, or any line of reading you would like to take up –'

'It is a lady again,' interrupted she, holding out the bud she had peeled.

'What?'

'I meant that there are always more ladies than lords when you come to peel them.'

'Never mind about the lords and ladies. Would you like to take up any course of study—history, for example?'

'Sometimes I feel I don't want to know anything more about it than I know already.'

'Why not?'

'Because what's the use of learning that I am one of a long row only—finding out that there is set down in some old book somebody just like me, and to know that I shall only act her part; making me sad, that's all. The best is not to remember that your nature and past doings have been just like thousands' and thousands', and that your coming life and doings 'll be like thousands' and thousands'.'

'What, really, then, you don't want to learn anything?'

'I shouldn't mind learning why—why the sun do shine on the just and the unjust alike,' she answered, with a slight quaver in her voice. 'But that's what books will not tell me.'

'Tess, fie for such bitterness!' Of course he spoke with a conventional sense of duty only, for that sort of wondering had not been unknown to himself in bygone days. And as he looked at the unpractised mouth and lips, he thought that such a daughter of the soil could only have caught up the sentiment by rote. She went on peeling the lords and ladies till Clare, regarding for a moment the wave-like curl of her lashes as they drooped with her bent gaze on her soft cheek, lingeringly went away. When he was gone she stood awhile, thoughtfully peeling the last bud; and then, awakening from her reverie, flung it and all the crowd of floral nobility impatiently on the ground, in an ebullition of displeasure with herself for her *niaiseries*, and with a quickening warmth in her heart of hearts.

How stupid he must think her! In an access of hunger for his good opinion she bethought herself of what she had latterly endeavoured to forget, so unpleasant had been its issues—the identity of her family with that of the knightly d'Urbervilles. Barren attribute as it was, disastrous as its discovery had been in many ways to her, perhaps Mr Clare, as a gentleman and a student of history, would respect her sufficiently to forget her childish conduct with the lords and ladies if he knew that those Purbeck-marble and alabaster people in Kingsbere Church really represented her own lineal forefathers; that she was no spurious d'Urberville, compounded of money and ambition like those at Trantridge, but true d'Urberville to the bone.

But, before venturing to make the revelation, dubious Tess indirectly sounded the dairyman as to its possible effect upon Mr Clare, by asking the former if Mr Clare had any great respect for old county families when they had lost all their money and land.

'Mr Clare,' said the dairyman emphatically, 'is one of the most rebellest rozums you ever knowed—not a bit like the rest of his family; and if there's one thing that he do hate more than another 'tis the notion of what's called a' old family. He says that it stands to reason that old families have done their spurt of work in past days, and can't have anything left in 'em now. There's the Billetts and the Drenkhards and the Greys and the St Quintins and the Hardys and the Goulds, who used to own the lands for miles down this valley; you could buy 'em all up now for an old song a'most. Why, our little Retty Priddle here, you know, is one of the Paridelles—the old family that used to own lots o' the lands out by King's-Hintock now owned by the Earl o' Wessex, afore even he or his was heard of. Well, Mr Clare found this out, and spoke quite scornful to the poor girl for days. "Ah!" he says to her, "you'll never make a good dairymaid! All your skill was used up ages ago in Palestine, and you must lie fallow for a thousand years to git strength for more deeds!" A boy came here t'other day asking for a job, and said his name was Matt, and when we asked him his surname he said he'd never heard that 'a had any surname, and when we asked why, he said he supposed his folks hadn't been 'stablished long enough. "Ah! you're the very boy I want!" says Mr Clare, jumping up and shaking hands wi'en; "I've great hopes of you"; and gave him half-a-crown. O no! he can't stomach old families!'

After hearing this caricature of Clare's opinions poor Tess was glad that she had not said a word in a weak moment about her family—even though it was so unusually old as almost to have gone round the circle and become a new one. Besides, another dairy-girl was as good as she, it seemed, in that respect. She held her tongue about the d'Urberville vault, and the Knight of the Conqueror whose name she bore. The insight afforded into Clare's character suggested to her that it was largely owing to her supposed untraditional newness that she had won interest in his eyes.

XX

The season developed and matured. Another year's instalment of flowers, leaves, nightingales, thrushes, finches, and such ephemeral creatures, took up their positions where only a year ago others had stood in their place when these were nothing more than germs and inorganic particles. Rays from the sunrise drew forth the buds and stretched them into long stalks, lifted up sap in noiseless streams, opened petals, and sucked out scents in invisible jets and breathings.

Dairyman Crick's household of maids and men lived on comfortably, placidly, even merrily. Their position was perhaps the happiest of all positions in the social scale, being above the line at which neediness ends, and below the line at which the *convenances* begin to cramp natural feeling, and the stress of threadbare modishness makes too little of enough.

Thus passed the leafy time when arborescence seems to be the one thing aimed at out of doors. Tess and Clare unconsciously studied each other, ever balanced on the edge of a passion, yet apparently keeping out of it. All the while they were converging, under an irresistible law, as surely as two streams in one vale.

Tess had never in her recent life been so happy as she was now, possibly never would be so happy again. She was, for one thing, physically and mentally suited among these new surroundings. The sapling which had rooted down to a poisonous stratum on the spot of its sowing had been transplanted to a deeper soil. Moreover she, and Clare also, stood as yet on the debatable land between predilection and love; where no profundities have been reached; no reflections have set in, awkwardly inquiring, 'Whither does this new current tend to carry me? What does it mean to my future? How does it stand towards my past?'

Tess was the merest stray phenomenon to Angel Clare as yet—

a rosy warming apparition which had only just acquired the attribute of persistence in his consciousness. So he allowed his mind to be occupied with her, deeming his preoccupation to be no more than a philosopher's regard of an exceedingly novel, fresh, and interesting specimen of womankind.

They met continually; they could not help it. They met daily in that strange and solemn interval, the twilight of the morning, in the violet or pink dawn; for it was necessary to rise early, so very early, here. Milking was done betimes; and before the milking came the skimming, which began at a little past three. It usually fell to the lot of some one or other of them to wake the rest, the first being aroused by an alarm-clock; and, as Tess was the latest arrival, and they soon discovered that she could be depended upon not to sleep through the alarm as the others did, this task was thrust most frequently upon her. No sooner had the hour of three struck and whizzed, than she left her room and ran to the dairyman's door; then up the ladder to Angel's, calling him in a loud whisper; then woke her fellow-milkmaids. By the time that Tess was dressed Clare was downstairs and out in the humid air. The remaining maids and the dairyman usually gave themselves another turn on the pillow, and did not appear till a quarter of an hour later.

The gray half-tones of daybreak are not the gray half-tones of the day's close, though the degree of their shade may be the same. In the twilight of the morning light seems active, darkness passive; in the twilight of evening it is the darkness which is active and crescent, and the light which is the drowsy reverse.

Being so often—possibly not always by chance—the first two persons to get up at the dairy-house, they seemed to themselves the first persons up of all the world. In these early days of her residence here Tess did not skim, but went out of doors at once after rising, where he was generally awaiting her. The spectral, half-compounded, aqueous light which pervaded the open mead, impressed them with a feeling of isolation, as if they were Adam and Eve. At this dim inceptive stage of the day Tess seemed to Clare to exhibit a dignified largeness both of disposition and physique, an almost regnant power, possibly because he knew that at that preternatural time hardly any woman so well endowed in person as she was likely to be walking in the open air within the boundaries of his horizon; very few in all England. Fair women are usually asleep at midsummer dawns. She was close at hand, and the rest were nowhere.

The mixed, singular, luminous gloom in which they walked along together to the spot where the cows lay, often made him think of the Resurrection hour. He little thought that the Magdalen might be at his side. Whilst all the landscape was in neutral shade his companion's face, which was the focus of his eyes, rising above the mist stratum, seemed to have a sort of phosphorescence upon it. She looked ghostly, as if she were merely a soul at large. In reality her face, without appearing to do so, had caught the cold gleam of day from the north-east; his own face, though he did not think of it, wore the same aspect to her.

It was then, as has been said, that she impressed him most deeply. She was no longer the milkmaid, but a visionary essence of woman—a whole sex condensed into one typical form. He called her Artemis, Demeter, and other fanciful names half teasingly, which she did not like because she did not understand them.

'Call me Tess,' she would say askance; and he did.

Then it would grow lighter, and her features would become simply feminine; they had changed from those of a divinity who could confer bliss to those of a being who craved it.

At these non-human hours they could get quite close to the waterfowl. Herons came, with a great bold noise as of opening doors and shutters, out of the boughs of a plantation which they frequented at the side of the mead; or, if already on the spot, hardily maintained their standing in the water as the pair walked by, watching them by moving their heads round in a slow, horizontal, passionless wheel, like the turn of puppets by clockwork.

They could then see the faint summer fogs in layers, woolly, level, and apparently no thicker than counterpanes, spread about the meadows in detached remnants of small extent. On the gray moisture of the grass were marks where the cows had lain through the night—dark-green islands of dry herbage the size of their carcases, in the general sea of dew. From each island proceeded a serpentine trail, by which the cow had rambled away to feed after getting up, at the end of which trail they found her; the snoring puff from her nostrils, when she recognized them, making an intenser little fog of her own amid the prevailing one. Then they drove the animals back to the barton, or sat down to milk them on the spot, as the case might require.

Or perhaps the summer fog was more general, and the meadows lay like a white sea, out of which the scattered trees rose like dangerous rocks. Birds would soar through it into the upper radiance, and hang on the wing sunning themselves, or alight on the wet rails subdividing the mead, which now shone like glass rods. Minute diamonds of moisture from the mist hung, too, upon Tess's eyelashes, and drops upon her hair, like seed pearls. When the day grew quite strong and commonplace these dried off her; moreover, Tess then lost her strange and ethereal beauty; her teeth, lips, and eyes scintillated in the sunbeams, and she was again the dazzlingly fair dairymaid only, who had to hold her own against the other women of the world.

About this time they would hear Dairyman Crick's voice, lecturing the non-resident milkers for arriving late, and speaking sharply to old Deborah Fyander for not washing her hands.

'For Heaven's sake, pop thy hands under the pump, Deb! Upon my soul, if the London folk only knowed of thee and thy slovenly ways, they'd swaller their milk and butter more mincing than they do a'ready; and that's saying a good deal.'

The milking progressed, till towards the end Tess and Clare, in common with the rest, could hear the heavy breakfast table dragged out from the wall in the kitchen by Mrs Crick, this being the invariable preliminary to each meal; the same horrible scrape accompanying its return journey when the table had been cleared.

XXI

There was a great stir in the milk-house just after breakfast. The churn revolved as usual, but the butter would not come. Whenever this happened the dairy was paralyzed. Squish, squash, echoed the milk in the great cylinder, but never arose the sound they waited for.

Dairyman Crick and his wife, the milkmaids Tess, Marian, Retty Priddle, Izz Huett, and the married ones from the cottages; also Mr Clare, Jonathan Kail, old Deborah, and the rest, stood gazing hopelessly at the churn; and the boy who kept the horse going outside put on moon-like eyes to show his sense of the situation. Even the melancholy horse himself seemed to look in at the window in inquiring despair at each walk round.

‘'Tis years since I went to Conjuror Trendle's son in Egdon—years!' said the dairyman bitterly. ‘And he was nothing to what his father had been. I have said fifty times, if I have said once, that I don't believe in en. And I *don't* believe in en. But I shall have to go to 'n if he's alive. O yes, I shall have to go to 'n, if this sort of thing continnys!'

Even Mr Clare began to feel tragical at the dairyman's desperation.

‘Conjuror Fall, t'other side of Casterbridge, that they used to call “Wide-O”, was a very good man when I was a boy,' said Jonathan Kail. ‘But he's rotten as touchwood by now.'

‘My grandfather used to go to Conjuror Mynterne, out at Owlscombe, and a clever man a' were, so I've heard grandf'er say,' continued Mr Crick. ‘But there's no such genuine folk about nowadays!'

Mrs Crick's mind kept nearer to the matter in hand.

‘Perhaps somebody in the house is in love,' she said tentatively. ‘I've heard tell in my younger days that that will cause it. Why,

Crick—that maid we had years ago, do ye mind, and how the butter didn't come then—'

'Ah yes, yes!—but that isn't the rights o't. It had nothing to do with the lovemaking. I can mind all about it—'twas the damage to the churn.'

He turned to Clare.

'Jack Dollop, a 'hore's-bird of a fellow we had here as milker at one time, sir, courted a young woman over at Mellstock, and deceived her as he had deceived many afore. But he had another sort o' woman to reckon wi' this time, and it was not the girl herself. One Holy Thursday, of all days in the almanack, we was here as we mid be now, only there was no churning in hand, when we zid the girl's mother coming up to the door, wi' a great brass-mounted umbrella in her hand that would ha' felled an ox, and saying "Do Jack Dollop work here?—because I want him! I have a big bone to pick with he, I can assure 'n!" And some way behind her mother walked Jack's young woman, crying bitterly into her handkercher. "O Lard, here's a time!" said Jack, looking out o' winder at 'em. "She'll murder me! Where shall I get—where shall I—? Don't tell her where I be!" And with that he scrambled into the churn through the trap-door, and shut himself inside, just as the young woman's mother busted into the milk-house. "The villain—where is he?" says she, "I'll claw his face for'n, let me only catch him!" Well, she hunted about everywhere, ballyragging Jack by side and by seam, Jack lying a'most stifled inside the churn, and the poor maid—or young woman rather—standing at the door crying her eyes out. I shall never forget it, never! 'Twould have melted a marble stone! But she couldn't find him nowhere at all.'

The dairyman paused, and one or two words of comment came from the listeners.

Dairyman Crick's stories often seemed to be ended when they were not really so, and strangers were betrayed into premature interjections of finality; though old friends knew better. The narrator went on –

'Well, how the old woman should have had the wit to guess it I could never tell, but she found out that he was inside that there churn. Without saying a word she took hold of the winch (it was turned by handpower then), and round she swung him, and Jack began to flop about inside. "O Lard! stop the churn! let me out!" says he, popping out his head, "I shall be churned into a pummy!" (he was a cowardly chap in his heart, as such men mostly be). "Not till ye make amends for ravaging her virgin innocence!" says the old woman. "Stop the churn, you old witch!" screams he. "You call me old witch, do ye, you deceiver!" says she, "when ye ought to ha' been calling me mother-law these last five months!" And on went the churn, and Jack's bones rattled round again. Well, none of us ventured to interfere; and at last 'a promised to make it right wi' her. "Yes—I'll be as good as my word!" he said. And so it ended that day.'

While the listeners were smiling their comments there was a quick movement behind their backs, and they looked round. Tess, pale-faced, had gone to the door.

'How warm 'tis to-day!' she said, almost inaudibly.

It was warm, and none of them connected her withdrawal with the reminiscences of the dairyman. He went forward, and opened the door for her, saying with tender raillery—

'Why, maidy' (he frequently, with unconscious irony, gave her this pet name), 'the prettiest milker I've got in my dairy; you mustn't get so fagged as this at the first breath of summer weather, or we shall be finely put to for want of 'ee by dogdays, shan't we, Mr Clare?'

'I was faint—and—I think I am better out o' doors,' she said mechanically; and disappeared outside.

Fortunately for her the milk in the revolving churn at that moment changed its squashing for a decided flick-flack.

''Tis coming!' cried Mrs Crick, and the attention of all was called off from Tess.

That fair sufferer soon recovered herself externally; but she remained much depressed all the afternoon. When the evening milking was done she did not care to be with the rest of them, and went out of doors wandering along she knew not whither. She was wretched—O so wretched—at the perception that to her companions the dairyman's story had been rather a humorous narration than otherwise; none of them but herself seemed to see the sorrow of it; to a certainty, not one knew how cruelly it touched the tender place in her experience. The evening sun was now ugly to her, like a great inflamed wound in the sky. Only a solitary cracked-voiced reed-sparrow greeted her from the bushes by the river, in a sad, machine-made tone, resembling that of a past friend whose friendship she had outworn.

In these long June days the milkmaids, and, indeed, most of the household, went to bed at sunset or sooner, the morning work before milking being so early and heavy at a time of full pails. Tess usually accompanied her fellows upstairs. To-night, however, she was the first to go to their common chamber; and she had dozed when the other girls came in. She saw them undressing in the orange light of the vanished sun, which flushed their forms with its colour; she dozed again, but she was reawakened by their voices, and quietly turned her eyes towards them.

Neither of her three chamber-companions had got into bed. They were standing in a group, in their nightgowns, barefooted, at the window, the last red rays of the west still warming their faces and necks, and the walls around them. All were watching somebody in the garden with deep interest, their three faces close together: a jovial and round one, a pale one with dark hair, and a fair one whose tresses were auburn.

'Don't push! You can see as well as I,' said Retty, the auburn-haired and youngest girl, without removing her eyes from the window.

''Tis no use for you to be in love with him any more than me, Retty Priddle,' said jolly-faced Marian, the eldest, slily. 'His thoughts be of other cheeks than thine!'

Retty Priddle still looked, and the others looked again.

'There he is again!' cried Izz Huett, the pale girl with dark damp hair and keenly cut lips.

'You needn't say anything, Izz,' answered Retty. 'For I zid you kissing his shade.'

'*What* did you see her doing?' asked Marian.

'Why—he was standing over the whey-tub to let off the whey, and the shade of his face came upon the wall behind, close to Izz, who was standing there filling a vat. She put her mouth against the wall and kissed the shade of his mouth; I zid her, though he didn't.'

'O Izz Huett!' said Marian.

A rosy spot came into the middle of Izz Huett's cheek.

'Well, there was no harm in it,' she declared, with attempted coolness. 'And if I be in love wi'en, so is Retty, too; and so be you, Marian, come to that.'

Marian's full face could not blush past its chronic pinkness.

'I!' she said. 'What a tale! Ah, there he is again! Dear eyes—dear face—dear Mr Clare!'

'There—you've owned it!'

'So have you—so have we all,' said Marian, with the dry frankness of complete indifference to opinion. 'It is silly to pretend otherwise amongst ourselves, though we need not own it to other folks. I would just marry 'n tomorrow!'

'So would I—and more,' murmured Izz Huett.

'And I too,' whispered the more timid Retty.

The listener grew warm.

'We can't all marry him,' said Izz.

'We shan't, either of us; which is worse still,' said the eldest. 'There he is again!'

They all three blew him a silent kiss.

'Why?' asked Retty quickly.

'Because he likes Tess Durbeyfield best,' said Marian, lowering her voice. 'I have watched him every day, and have found it out.'

There was a reflective silence.

'But she don't care anything for 'n?' at length breathed Retty.

'Well—I sometimes think that too.'

'But how silly all this is!' said Izz Huett impatiently. 'Of course he won't marry any one of us, or Tess either—a gentleman's son, who's going to be a great landowner and farmer abroad! More likely to ask us to come wi'en as farm-hands at so much a year!'

One sighed, and another sighed, and Marian's plump figure sighed biggest of all. Somebody in bed hard by sighed too. Tears came into the eyes of Retty Priddle, the pretty red-haired youngest—the last bud of the Paridelles, so important in the county annals. They watched silently a little longer, their three faces still close together as before, and the triple hues of their hair mingling. But the unconscious Mr Clare had gone indoors, and they saw him no more; and, the shades beginning to deepen, they crept into their beds. In a few minutes they heard him ascend the ladder to his own room. Marian was soon snoring, but Izz did not drop into forgetfulness for a long time. Retty Priddle cried herself to sleep.

The deeper-passioned Tess was very far from sleeping even then. This conversation was another of the bitter pills she had been obliged to swallow that day. Scarce the least feeling of jealousy arose in her breast. For that matter she knew herself to have the preference. Being more finely formed, better educated, and, though the youngest except Retty, more woman than either, she perceived that only the slightest ordinary care was necessary for holding her own in Angel Clare's heart against these her candid friends. But the grave question was, ought she to do this? There was, to be sure, hardly a ghost of a chance for either of them, in a serious sense; but there was, or had been, a chance of one or the other inspiring him with a passing fancy for her, and enjoying the pleasure of his attentions while he stayed here. Such unequal attachments had led to marriage; and she had heard from Mrs Crick that Mr Clare had one day asked, in a laughing way, what would be the use of his marrying a fine lady, and all the while ten thousand acres of Colonial pasture to feed, and cattle to rear, and corn to reap. A farm-woman would be the only sensible kind of wife for him. But whether Mr Clare had spoken seriously or not, why should she, who could never conscientiously allow any man to marry her now, and who had religiously determined that she never would be tempted to do so, draw off Mr Clare's attention from other women, for the brief happiness of sunning herself in his eyes while he remained at Talbothays?

XXII

THEY came downstairs yawning next morning; but skimming and milking were proceeded with as usual, and they went indoors to breakfast. Dairyman Crick was discovered stamping about the house. He had received a letter, in which a customer had complained that the butter had a twang.

'And begad, so 't have!' said the dairyman, who held in his left hand a wooden slice on which a lump of butter was stuck. 'Yes—taste for yourself!'

Several of them gathered round him; and Mr Clare tasted, Tess tasted, also the other indoor milkmaids, one or two of the milking-men, and last of all Mrs Crick, who came out from the waiting breakfast-table. There certainly was a twang.

The dairyman, who had thrown himself into abstraction to better realize the taste, and so divine the particular species of noxious weed to which it appertained, suddenly exclaimed—

''Tis garlic! and I thought there wasn't a blade left in that mead!'

Then all the old hands remembered that a certain dry mead, into which a few of the cows had been admitted of late, had, in years gone by, spoilt the butter in the same way. The dairyman had not recognized the taste at that time, and thought the butter bewitched.

'We must overhaul that mead,' he resumed; 'this mustn't continny!'

All having armed themselves with old pointed knives they went out together. As the inimical plant could only be present in very microscopic dimensions to have escaped ordinary observation, to find it seemed rather a hopeless attempt in the stretch of rich grass before them. However, they formed themselves into line, all assisting, owing to the importance of the search; the dairyman at the upper end with Mr Clare, who had volunteered to help; then Tess, Marian, Izz Huett, and Retty; then Bill Lewell, Jonathan, and the married dairywomen—Beck Knibbs, with her woolly black hair and rolling eyes; and flaxen Frances, consumptive from the winter damps of the watermeads—who lived in their respective cottages.

With eyes fixed upon the ground they crept slowly across a strip of the field, returning a little further down in such a manner that, when they should have finished, not a single inch of pasture but would have fallen under the eye of some one of them. It was a most tedious business, not more than half a dozen shoots of garlic being discoverable in the whole field; yet such was the herb's pungency that probably one bite of it by one cow had been sufficient to season the whole dairy's produce for the day.

Differing one from another in natures and mood so greatly as they did, they yet formed, bending, a curiously uniform row—automatic, noiseless; and an alien observer passing down the neighbouring lane might well have been excused for massing them as 'Hodge'. As they crept along, stooping low to discern the plant, a soft yellow gleam was reflected from the buttercups into their shaded faces, giving them an elfish, moonlit aspect, though the sun was pouring upon their backs in all the strength of noon.

Angel Clare, who communistically stuck to his rule of taking part with the rest in everything, glanced up now and then. It was not, of course, by accident that he walked next to Tess.

'Well, how are you?' he murmured.

'Very well, thank you, sir,' she replied demurely.

As they had been discussing a score of personal matters only half-an-hour before, the introductory style seemed a little superfluous. But they got no further in speech just then. They crept and crept, the hem of her petticoat just touching his gaiter, and his elbow sometimes brushing hers. At last the dairyman, who came next, could stand it no longer.

'Upon my soul and body, this here stooping do fairly make my back open and shut!' he exclaimed, straightening himself slowly with an excruciated look till quite upright. 'And you, maidy Tess, you wasn't well a day or two ago—this will make your head ache finely! Don't do any more, if you feel fainty; leave the rest to finish it.'

Dairyman Crick withdrew, and Tess dropped behind. Mr Clare

also stepped out of line, and began privateering about for the weed. When she found him near her, her very tension at what she had heard the night before made her the first to speak.

'Don't they look pretty?' she said.

'Who?'

'Izzy Huett and Retty.'

Tess had moodily decided that either of these maidens would make a good farmer's wife, and that she ought to recommend them, and obscure her own wretched charms.

'Pretty? Well, yes—they are pretty girls—fresh looking. I have often thought so.'

'Though, poor dears, prettiness won't last long!'

'O no, unfortunately.'

'They are excellent dairywomen.'

'Yes: though not better than you.'

'They skim better than I.'

'Do they?'

Clare remained observing them—not without their observing him.

'She is colouring up,' continued Tess heroically.

'Who?'

'Retty Priddle.'

'Oh! Why is that?'

'Because you are looking at her.'

Self-sacrificing as her mood might be Tess could not well go further and cry, 'Marry one of them, if you really do want a dairy-woman and not a lady; and don't think of marrying me!' She followed Dairyman Crick, and had the mournful satisfaction of seeing that Clare remained behind.

From this day she forced herself to take pains to avoid him—never allowing herself, as formerly, to remain long in his company, even if their juxtaposition were purely accidental. She gave the other three every chance.

Tess was woman enough to realize from their avowals to herself that Angel Clare had the honour of all the dairymaids in his keeping, and her perception of his care to avoid compromising the happiness of either in the least degree bred a tender respect in Tess for what she deemed, rightly or wrongly, the self-controlling sense of duty shown by him, a quality which she had never expected to find in one of the opposite sex, and in the absence of which more than one of the simple hearts who were his housemates might have gone weeping on her pilgrimage.

XXIII

THE hot weather of July had crept upon them unawares, and the atmosphere of the flat vale hung heavy as an opiate over the dairy-folk, the cows, and the trees. Hot steaming rains fell frequently, making the grass where the cows fed yet more rank, and hindering the late hay-making in the other meads.

It was Sunday morning; the milking was done; the outdoor milkers had gone home. Tess and the other three were dressing themselves rapidly, the whole bevy having agreed to go together to Mellstock Church, which lay some three or four miles distant from the dairy-house. She had now been two months at Talbothays, and this was her first excursion.

All the preceding afternoon and night heavy thunderstorms had hissed down upon the meads, and washed some of the hay into the river; but this morning the sun shone out all the more brilliantly for the deluge, and the air was balmy and clear.

The crooked lane leading from their own parish to Mellstock ran along the lowest levels in a portion of its length, and when the girls reached the most depressed spot they found that the result of the rain had been to flood the lane over-shoe to a distance of some fifty yards. This would have been no serious hindrance on a week-day; they would have clicked through it in their high pattens and boots quite unconcerned; but on this day of vanity, this Sun's-day, when flesh went forth to coquet with flesh while hypocritically affecting business with spiritual things; on this occasion for wearing their white stockings and thin shoes, and their pink, white, and lilac gowns, on which every mud spot would be visible, the pool was an awkward impediment. They could hear the churchbell calling—as yet nearly a mile off.

'Who would have expected such a rise in the river in summer-time!' said Marian, from the top of the roadside-bank on which they had climbed, and were maintaining a precarious footing in the hope of creeping along its slope till they were past the pool.

'We can't get there anyhow, without walking right through it, or else going round the Turnpike way; and that would make us so very late!' said Retty, pausing hopelessly.

'And I do colour up so hot, walking into church late, and all the people staring round,' said Marian, 'that I hardly cool down again till we get into the That-it-may-please-Thees.'

While they stood clinging to the bank they heard a splashing round the bend of the road, and presently appeared Angel Clare, advancing along the lane towards them through the water.

Four hearts gave a big throb simultaneously.

His aspect was probably as un-Sabbatarian a one as a dogmatic parson's son often presented; his attire being his dairy clothes, long wading boots, a cabbage-leaf inside his hat to keep his head cool, with a thistlespud to finish him off.

'He's not going to church,' said Marian.

'No—I wish he was!' murmured Tess.

Angel, in fact, rightly or wrongly (to adopt the safe phrase of evasive controversialists), preferred sermons in stones to sermons in churches and chapels on fine summer days. This morning, moreover, he had gone out to see if the damage to the hay by the flood was considerable or not. On his walk he observed the girls from a long distance, though they had been so occupied with their difficulties of passage as not to notice him. He knew that the water had risen at that spot, and that it would quite check their progress. So he had hastened on, with a dim idea of how he could help them—one of them in particular.

The rosy-cheeked, bright-eyed, quartet looked so charming in their light summer attire, clinging to the roadside bank like pigeons on a roof-slope, that he stopped a moment to regard them before coming close. Their gauzy skirts had brushed up from the grass innumerable flies and butterflies which, unable to escape, remained caged in the transparent tissue as in an aviary. Angel's eye at last fell upon Tess, the hindmost of the four; she, being full of suppressed laughter at their dilemma, could not help meeting his glance radiantly.

He came beneath them in the water, which did not rise over his long boots; and stood looking at the entrapped flies and butterflies.

'Are you trying to get to church?' he said to Marian, who was in front, including the next two in his remark, but avoiding Tess.

'Yes, sir; and 'tis getting late; and my colour do come up so—'

'I'll carry you through the pool—every Jill of you.'

The whole four flushed as if one heart beat through them.

'I think you can't, sir,' said Marian.

'It is the only way for you to get past. Stand still. Nonsense—you are not too heavy! I'd carry you all four together. Now, Marian, attend,' he continued, 'and put your arms round my shoulders, so. Now! Hold on. That's well done.'

Marian had lowered herself upon his arm and shoulder as directed, and Angel strode off with her, his slim figure, as viewed from behind, looking like the mere stem to the great nosegay suggested by hers. They disappeared round the curve of the road, and only his sousing footsteps and the top ribbon of Marian's bonnet told where they were. In a few minutes he reappeared. Izz Huett was the next in order upon the bank.

'Here he comes,' she murmured, and they could hear that her lips were dry with emotion. 'And I have to put my arms round his neck and look into his face as Marian did.'

'There's nothing in that,' said Tess quickly.

'There's a time for everything,' continued Izz, unheeding. 'A time to embrace, and a time to refrain from embracing; the first is now going to be mine.'

'Fie—it is Scripture, Izz!'

'Yes,' said Izz, 'I've always a' ear at church for pretty verses.'

Angel Clare, to whom three-quarters of this performance was a commonplace act of kindness, now approached Izz. She quietly and dreamily lowered herself into his arms, and Angel methodically marched off with her. When he was heard returning for the third time Retty's throbbing heart could be almost seen to shake her. He went up to the red-haired girl, and while he was seizing her he glanced at Tess. His lips could not have pronounced more plainly, 'It will soon be you and I.' Her comprehension appeared in her face; she could not help it. There was an understanding between them.

Poor little Retty, though by far the lightest weight, was the most troublesome of Clare's burdens. Marian had been like a sack of meal, a dead weight of plumpness under which he had literally staggered. Izz had ridden sensibly and calmly. Retty was a bunch of hysterics.

However, he got through with the disquieted creature, deposited her, and returned. Tess could see over the hedge the distant three in a group, standing as he had placed them on the next rising ground. It was now her turn. She was embarrassed to discover that excitement at the proximity of Mr Clare's breath and eyes, which she had contemned in her companions, was intensified in herself; and as if fearful of betraying her secret she paltered with him at the last moment.

'I may be able to clim' along the bank perhaps—I can clim' better than they. You must be so tired, Mr Clare!'

'No, no, Tess,' said he quickly. And almost before she was aware she was seated in his arms and resting against his shoulder.

'Three Leahs to get one Rachel,' he whispered.

'They are better women than I,' she replied, magnanimously sticking to her resolve.

'Not to me,' said Angel.

He saw her grow warm at this; and they went some steps in silence.

'I hope I am not too heavy?' she said timidly.

'O no. You should lift Marian! Such a lump. You are like an undulating billow warmed by the sun. And all this fluff of muslin about you is the froth.'

'It is very pretty—if I seem like that to you.'

'Do you know that I have undergone three-quarters of this labour entirely for the sake of the fourth quarter?'

'No.'

'I did not expect such an event to-day.'

'Nor I . . . The water came up so sudden.'

That the rise in the water was what she understood him to refer to, the state of her breathing belied. Clare stood still and inclined his face towards hers.

'O Tessy!' he exclaimed.

The girl's cheeks burned to the breeze, and she could not look into his eyes for her emotion. It reminded Angel that he was somewhat unfairly taking advantage of an accidental position; and he went no further with it. No definite words of love had crossed their lips as yet, and suspension at this point was desirable now. However, he walked slowly, to make the remainder of the distance as long as possible; but at last they came to the bend, and the rest of their progress was in full view of the other three. The dry land was reached, and he set her down.

Her friends were looking with round thoughtful eyes at her and him, and she could see that they had been talking of her. He hastily bade them farewell, and splashed back along the stretch of submerged road.

The four moved on together as before, till Marian broke the silence by saying—

'No—in all truth; we have no chance against her!' She looked joylessly at Tess.

'What do you mean?' asked the latter.

'He likes 'ee best—the very best! We could see it as he brought 'ee. He would have kissed 'ee, if you had encouraged him to do it, ever so little.'

'No, no,' said she.

The gaiety with which they had set out had somehow vanished; and yet there was no enmity or malice between them. They were generous young souls; they had been reared in the lonely country nooks where fatalism is a strong sentiment, and they did not blame her. Such supplanting was to be.

Tess's heart ached. There was no concealing from herself the fact that she loved Angel Clare, perhaps all the more passionately from knowing that the others had also lost their hearts to him. There is contagion in this sentiment, especially among women. And yet that same hungry heart of hers compassionated her friends.

Tess's honest nature had fought against this, but too feebly, and the natural result had followed.

'I will never stand in your way, nor in the way of either of you!' she declared to Retty that night in the bedroom (her tears running down). 'I can't help this, my dear! I don't think marrying is in his mind at all; but if he were even to ask me I should refuse him, as I should refuse any man.'

'Oh! would you? Why?' said wondering Retty.

'It cannot be! But I will be plain. Putting myself quite on one side, I don't think he will choose either of you.'

'I have never expected it—thought of it!' moaned Retty. 'But O! I wish I was dead!'

The poor child, torn by a feeling which she hardly understood, turned to the other two girls who came upstairs just then.

'We be friends with her again,' she said to them. 'She thinks no more of his choosing her than we do.'

So the reserve went off, and they were confiding and warm.

'I don't seem to care what I do now,' said Marian, whose mood was tuned to its lowest bass. 'I was going to marry a dairyman at Stickleford, who's asked me twice; but—my soul—I would put an end to myself rather'n be his wife now! Why don't ye speak, Izz?'

'To confess, then,' murmured Izz, 'I made sure to-day that he was going to kiss me as he held me; and I lay still against his breast, hoping the hoping, and never moved at all. But he did not. I don't like biding here at Talbothays any longer! I shall go hwome.'

The air of the sleeping-chamber seemed to palpitate with the hopeless passion of the girls. They writhed feverishly under the oppressiveness of an emotion thrust on them by cruel Nature's law—an emotion which they had neither expected nor desired. The incident of the day had fanned the flame that was burning the inside of their hearts out, and the torture was almost more than they could endure. The differences which distinguished them as individuals were abstracted by this passion, and each was but portion of one organism called sex. There was much frankness and so little jealousy because there was no hope. Each one was a girl of fair common sense, and she did not delude herself with any vain conceits, or deny her love, or give herself airs, in the idea of outshining the others. The full recognition of the futility of their infatuation, from a social point of view; its purposeless beginning; its self-bounded outlook; its lack of everything to justify its existence in the eye of civilization (while lacking nothing in the eye of Nature); the one fact that it did exist, ecstasizing them to a killing joy; all this imparted to them a resignation, a dignity, which a practical and sordid expectation of winning him as a husband would have destroyed.

They tossed and turned on their little beds, and the cheese-wring dripped monotonously downstairs.

'B' you awake, Tess?' whispered one, half-an-hour later.

It was Izz Huett's voice.

Tess replied in the affirmative, whereupon also Retty and Marian suddenly flung the bedclothes off them, and sighed—

'So be we!'

'I wonder what she is like—the lady they say his family have looked out for.'

'I wonder,' said Izz.

'Some lady looked out for him?' gasped Tess, starting. 'I have never heard o' that!'

'O yes—'tis whispered; a young lady of his own rank, chosen by his family; a Doctor of Divinity's daughter near his father's parish of Emminster; he don't care for her, they say. But he is sure to marry her.'

They had heard so very little of this; yet it was enough to build up wretched dolorous dreams upon, there in the shade of the night. They pictured all the details of his being won round to consent, of the wedding preparations, of the bride's happiness, of her dress and veil, of her blissful home with him, when oblivion would have fallen upon themselves as far as he and their love were concerned. Thus they talked, and ached, and wept till sleep charmed their sorrow away.

After this disclosure Tess nourished no further foolish thought that there lurked any grave and deliberate import in Clare's attentions to her. It was a passing summer love of her face, for love's own temporary sake—nothing more. And the thorny crown of this sad conception was that she whom he really did prefer in a cursory way to the rest, she who knew herself to be more impassioned in nature, cleverer, more beautiful than they, was in the eyes of propriety far less worthy of him than the homelier ones whom he ignored.

XXIV

AMID the oozing fatness and warm ferments of the Var Vale, at a season when the rush of juices could almost be heard below the hiss of fertilization, it was impossible that the most fanciful love should not grow passionate. The ready bosoms existing there were impregnated by their surroundings.

July passed over their heads, and the Thermidorean weather which came in its wake seemed an effort on the part of Nature to match the state of hearts at Talbothays Dairy. The air of the place, so fresh in the spring and early summer, was stagnant and enervating now. Its heavy scents weighed upon them, and at mid-day the landscape seemed lying in a swoon. Ethiopic scorchings browned the upper slopes of the pastures, but there was still bright green herbage here where the watercourses purled. And as Clare was oppressed by the outward heats, so was he burdened inwardly by waxing fervour of passion for the soft and silent Tess.

The rains having passed the uplands were dry. The wheels of the dairyman's spring cart, as he sped home from market, licked up the pulverized surface of the highway, and were followed by white ribands of dust, as if they had set a thin powder-train on fire. The cows jumped wildly over the five-barred barton-gate, maddened by the gad-fly; Dairyman Crick kept his shirt-sleeves permanently rolled up from Monday to Saturday: open windows had no effect in ventilation without open doors, and in the dairy-garden the blackbirds and thrushes crept about under the current-bushes, rather in the manner of quadrupeds than of winged creatures. The flies in the kitchen were lazy, teasing, and familiar, crawling about in unwonted places, on the floor, into drawers, and over the backs of the milkmaids' hands. Conversations were concerning sunstroke; while butter-making, and still more butter-keeping, was a despair.

They milked entirely in the meads for coolness and convenience, without driving in the cows. During the day the animals obsequiously followed the shadow of the smallest tree as it moved round the stem with the diurnal roll; and when the milkers came they could hardly stand still for the flies.

On one of these afternoons four or five unmilked cows chanced to stand apart from the general herd, behind the corner of a hedge, among them being Dumpling and Old Pretty, who loved Tess's hands above those of any other maid. When she rose from her stool under a finished cow Angel Clare, who had been observing her for some time, asked her if she would take the aforesaid creatures next. She silently assented, and with her stool at arm's length, and the pail against her knee, went round to where they stood. Soon the sound of Old Pretty's milk fizzing into the pail came through the hedge, and then Angel felt inclined to go round the corner also, to finish off a hard-yielding milcher who had strayed there, he being now as capable of this as the dairyman himself.

All the men, and some of the women, when milking, dug their foreheads into the cows and gazed into the pail. But a few—mainly the younger ones—rested their heads sideways. This was Tess Durbeyfield's habit, her temple pressing the milcher's flank, her eyes fixed on the far end of the meadow with the quiet of one lost in meditation. She was milking Old Pretty thus, and the sun chancing to be on the milking-side it shone flat upon her pink-gowned form and her white curtain-bonnet, and upon her profile, rendering it keen as a cameo cut from the dun background of the cow.

She did not know that Clare had followed her round, and that he sat under his cow watching her. The stillness of her head and features was remarkable: she might have been in a trance, her eyes open, yet unseeing. Nothing in the picture moved but Old Pretty's tail and Tess's pink hands, the latter so gently as to be a rhythmic pulsation only, as if they were obeying a reflex stimulus, like a beating heart.

How very lovable her face was to him. Yet there was nothing ethereal about it; all was real vitality, real warmth, real incarnation. And it was in her mouth that this culminated. Eyes almost as deep and speaking he had seen before, and cheeks perhaps as fair; brows as arched, a chin and throat almost as shapely; her mouth he had seen nothing to equal on the face of the earth. To a young man with the least fire in him that little upward lift in the middle of her red top lip was distracting, infatuating, maddening. He had never before seen a woman's lips and teeth which forced upon his mind with such persistent iteration the old Elizabethan simile of roses filled with snow. Perfect, he, as a lover, might have called them off-hand. But no—they were not perfect. And it was the touch of the imperfect upon the would-be perfect that gave the sweetness, because it was that which gave the humanity.

Clare had studied the curves of those lips so many times that he could reproduce them mentally with ease: and now, as they again confronted him, clothed with colour and life, they sent an *aura* over his flesh, a breeze through his nerves, which wellnigh produced a qualm; and actually produced, by some mysterious physiological process, a prosaic sneeze.

She then became conscious that he was observing her; but she would not show it by any change in position, though the curious dream-like fixity disappeared, and a close eye might easily have discerned that the rosiness of her face deepened, and then faded till only a tinge of it was left.

The influence that had passed into Clare like an excitation from the sky did not die down. Resolutions, reticences, prudences, fears, fell back like a defeated battalion. He jumped up from his seat, and, leaving his pail to be kicked over if the milcher had such a mind, went quickly towards the desire of his eyes, and, kneeling down beside her, clasped her in his arms.

Tess was taken completely by surprise, and she yielded to his embrace with unreflecting inevitableness. Having seen that it was really her lover who had advanced, and no one else, lips parted, and she sank upon him in her momentary joy, with something very like an ecstatic cry.

He had been on the point of kissing that too tempting mouth, but he checked himself, for tender conscience' sake.

'Forgive me, Tess dear!' he whispered. 'I ought to have asked. I—did not know what I was doing. I do not mean it as a liberty. I am devoted to you, Tessy, dearest, in all sincerity!'

Old Pretty by this time had looked round, puzzled; and seeing two people crouching under her where, by immemorial custom, there should have been only one, lifted her hind leg crossly.

'She is angry—she doesn't know what we mean—she'll kick over the milk!' cried Tess, gently striving to free herself, her eyes concerned with the quadruped's actions, her heart more deeply concerned with herself and Clare.

She slipped up from her seat, and they stood together, his arm still encircling her. Tess's eyes, fixed on distance, began to fill.

'Why do you cry, my darling?' he said.

'O—I don't know!' she murmured.

As she saw and felt more clearly the position she was in she became agitated and tried to withdraw.

'Well, I have betrayed my feeling, Tess, at last,' said he, with a curious sigh of desperation, signifying unconsciously that his heart had outrun his judgment. 'That I—love you dearly and truly I need not say. But I—it shall go no further now—it distresses you—I am as surprised as you are. You will not think I have presumed upon your defencelessness—been too quick and unreflecting, will you?'

'N'—I can't tell.'

He had allowed her to free herself; and in a minute or two the milking of each was resumed. Nobody had beheld the gravitation of the two into one; and when the dairyman came round by that screened nook a few minutes later there was not a sign to reveal that the markedly sundered pair were more to each other than mere acquaintance. Yet in the interval since Crick's last view of them something had occurred which changed the pivot of the universe for their two natures, something which, had he known its quality, the dairyman would have despised, as a practical man; yet which was based upon a more stubborn and resistless tendency than a whole heap of so-called practicalities. A veil had been whisked aside; the tract of each one's outlook was to have a new horizon thenceforward—for a short time or for a long.

END OF PHASE THE THIRD

PHASE THE FOURTH

THE CONSEQUENCE

XXV

Clare, restless, went out into the dusk when evening drew on, she who had won him having retired to her chamber.

The night was as sultry as the day. There was no coolness after dark unless on the grass. Roads, garden-paths, the house-fronts, the barton-walls were warm as hearths, and reflected the noontide temperature into the noctambulist's face.

He sat on the east gate of the dairy-yard, and knew not what to think of himself. Feeling had indeed smothered judgment that day.

Since the sudden embrace, three hours before, the twain had kept apart. She seemed stilled, almost alarmed, at what had occurred, while the novelty, unpremeditation, mastery of circumstance disquieted him—palpitating, contemplative being that he was. He could hardly realize their true relations to each other as yet, and what their mutual bearing should be before third parties thenceforward.

Angel had come as pupil to this dairy in the idea that his temporary existence here was to be the merest episode in his life, soon passed through and early forgotten; he had come as to a place from which as from a screened alcove he could calmly view the absorbing world without, and, apostrophizing it with Walt Whitman—

> Crowds of men and women attired in the usual costumes,
> How curious you are to me!—

resolve upon a plan for plunging into that world anew. But, behold, the absorbing scene had been imported hither. What had been the engrossing world had dissolved into an uninteresting outer dumb-show; while here, in this apparently dim and unimpassioned place, novelty had volcanically started up, as it had never, for him, started up elsewhere.

Every window of the house being open Clare could hear across the yard each trivial sound of the retiring household. That dairy-house, so humble, so insignificant, so purely to him a place of constrained sojourn that he had never hitherto deemed it of sufficient importance to be reconnoitred as an object of any quality whatever in the landscape; what was it now? The aged and lichened brick gables breathed forth 'Stay!' The windows smiled, the door coaxed and beckoned, the creeper blushed confederacy. A personality within it was so far-reaching in her influence as to spread into and make the bricks, mortar, and whole overhanging sky throb with a burning sensibility. Whose was this mighty personality? A milkmaid's.

It was amazing, indeed, to find how great a matter the life of the obscure dairy had become to him. And though new love was to be held partly responsible for this it was not solely so. Many besides Angel have learnt that the magnitude of lives is not as to their external displacements, but as to their subjective experiences. The impressionable peasant leads a larger, fuller, more dramatic life than the pachydermatous king. Looking at it thus he found that life was to be seen of the same magnitude here as elsewhere.

Despite his heterodoxy, faults, and weaknesses, Clare was a man with a conscience. Tess was no insignificant creature to toy with and dismiss; but a woman living her precious life—a life which, to herself who endured or enjoyed it, possessed as great a dimension as the life of the mightiest to himself. Upon her sensations the whole world depended to Tess; through her existence all her fellow-creatures existed, to her. The universe itself only came into being for Tess on the particular day in the particular year in which she was born.

This consciousness upon which he had intruded was the single opportunity of existence ever vouchsafed to Tess by an unsympathetic First Cause—her all; her every and only chance. How then should he look upon her as of less consequence than himself; as a pretty trifle to caress and grow weary of; and not deal in the greatest seriousness with the affection which he knew that he had awakened in her—so fervid and so impressionable as she was under her reserve; in order that it might not agonize and wreck her?

To encounter her daily in the accustomed manner would be to develop what had begun. Living in such close relations, to meet meant to fall into endearment; flesh and blood could not resist it; and, having arrived at no conclusion as to the issue of such a tendency, he decided to hold aloof for the present from occupations in which they would be mutually engaged. As yet the harm done was small.

But it was not easy to carry out the resolution never to approach her. He was driven towards her by every heave of his pulse.

He thought he would go and see his friends. It might be possible to sound them upon this. In less than five months his term here would have ended, and after a few additional months spent upon other farms he would be fully equipped in agricultural knowledge, and in a position to start on his own account. Would not a farmer want a wife, and should a farmer's wife be a drawing-room wax-figure, or a woman who understood farming? Notwithstanding the pleasing answer returned to him by the silence he resolved to go his journey.

One morning when they sat down to breakfast at Talbothays Dairy some maid observed that she had not seen anything of Mr Clare that day.

'O no,' said Dairyman Crick. 'Mr Clare has gone hwome to Emminster to spend a few days wi' his kinsfolk.'

For four impassioned ones around the table the sunshine of the morning went out at a stroke, and the birds muffled their song. But neither girl by word or gesture revealed her blankness.

'He's getting on towards the end of his time wi' me,' added the dairyman, with a phlegm which unconsciously was brutal; 'and so I suppose he is beginning to see about his plans elsewhere.'

'How much longer is he to bide here?' asked Izz Huett, the only one of the gloom-stricken bevy who could trust her voice with the question.

The others waited for the dairyman's answer as if their lives hung upon it; Retty, with parted lips, gazing on the table-cloth, Marian with heat added to her redness, Tess throbbing and looking out at the meads.

'Well, I can't mind the exact day without looking at my memorandum-book,' replied Crick, with the same intolerable unconcern. 'And even that may be altered a bit. He'll bide to get a little practice in the calving out at the straw-yard, for certain. He'll hang on till the end of the year I should say.'

Four months or so of torturing ecstacy in his society—of 'pleasure girdled about with pain'. After that the blackness of unutterable night.

At this moment of the morning Angel Clare was riding along a narrow lane ten miles distant from the breakfasters, in the direction of his father's vicarage at Emminster, carrying, as well as he could, a little basket which contained some black-puddings and a bottle of mead, sent by Mrs Crick, with her kind respects, to his parents. The white lane stretched before him, and his eyes were upon it; but they were staring into next year, and not at the lane. He loved her; ought he to marry her? Dared he to marry her? What would his mother and his brothers say? What would he himself say a couple of years after the event? That would depend upon whether the germs of staunch comradeship underlay the temporary emotion, or whether it were a sensuous joy in her form only, with no substratum of everlastingness.

His father's hill-surrounded little town, the Tudor church-tower of red stone, the clump of trees near the vicarage, came at last into view beneath him, and he rode down towards the well-known gate. Casting a glance in the direction of the church before entering his home, he beheld standing by the vestry-door a group of girls, of ages between twelve and sixteen, apparently awaiting the arrival of some other one, who in a moment became visible; a figure somewhat older than the school-girls, wearing a broad-brimmed hat and highly-starched cambric morning-gown, with a couple of books in her hand.

Clare knew her well. He could not be sure that she observed him; he hoped she did not, so as to render it unnecessary that he should go and speak to her, blameless creature that she was. An overpowering reluctance to greet her made him decide that she had not seen him. The young lady was Miss Mercy Chant, the only daughter of his father's neighbour and friend, whom it was his parents' quiet hope that he might wed some day. She was great at Antinomianism and Bible-classes, and was plainly going to hold a class now. Clare's mind flew to the impassioned, summer-steeped heathens in the Var Vale, their rosy faces court-patched with cow-droppings; and to one the most impassioned of them all.

It was on the impulse of the moment that he had resolved to trot over to Emminster, and hence had not written to apprise his mother and father, aiming, however, to arrive about the breakfast hour, before they should have gone out to their parish duties. He was a little late, and they had already sat down to the morning meal. The group at table jumped up to welcome him as soon as he entered. They were his father and mother, his brother the Reverend Felix—curate at a town in the adjoining county, home for the inside of a fortnight—and his other brother, the Reverend Cuthbert, the classical scholar, and Fellow and Dean of his College, down from Cambridge for the long vacation. His mother appeared in a cap and silver spectacles, and his father looked what in fact he was—an earnest, God-fearing man, somewhat gaunt, in years about sixty-five, his pale face lined with thought and purpose. Over their heads hung the picture of Angel's sister, the eldest of the family, sixteen years his senior, who had married a missionary and gone out to Africa.

Old Mr Clare was a clergyman of a type which, within the last twenty years, has wellnigh dropped out of contemporary life. A spiritual descendant in the direct line of Wycliff, Huss, Luther, Calvin; an Evangelical of the Evangelicals, a Conversionist, a man of Apostolic simplicity in life and thought, he had in his raw youth made up his mind once for all on the deeper questions of existence, and admitted no further reasoning on them thenceforward. He was regarded even by those of his own date and school of thinking as extreme; while, on the other hand, those totally opposed to him were unwillingly won to admiration for his thoroughness, and for the remarkable power he showed in dismissing all question as to principles in his energy for applying them. He loved Paul of Tarsus, liked St John, hated St James as much as he dared, and regarded with mixed feelings Timothy, Titus, and Philemon. The New

Testament was less a Christiad than a Pauliad to his intelligence—less an argument than an intoxication. His creed of determinism was such that it almost amounted to a vice, and quite amounted, on its negative side, to a renunciative philosophy which had cousinship with that of Schopenhauer and Leopardi. He despised the Canons and Rubric, swore by the Articles, and deemed himself consistent through the whole category—which in a way he might have been. One thing he certainly was—sincere.

To the aesthetic, sensuous, pagan pleasure in natural life and lush womanhood which his son Angel had lately been experiencing in Var Vale, his temper would have been antipathetic in a high degree, had he either by inquiry or imagination been able to apprehend it. Once upon a time Angel had been so unlucky as to say to his father, in a moment of irritation, that it might have resulted far better for mankind if Greece had been the source of the religion of modern civilization, and not Palestine; and his father's grief was of that blank description which could not realize that there might lurk a thousandth part of a truth, much less a half truth or a whole truth, in such a proposition. He had simply preached austerely at Angel for some time after. But the kindness of his heart was such that he never resented anything for long, and welcomed his son to-day with a smile which was as candidly sweet as a child's.

Angel sat down, and the place felt like home; yet he did not so much as formerly feel himself one of the family gathered there. Every time that he returned hither he was conscious of this divergence, and since he had last shared in the Vicarage life it had grown even more distinctly foreign to his own than usual. Its transcendental aspirations—still unconsciously based on the geocentric view of things, a zenithal paradise, a nadiral hell—were as foreign to his own as if they had been the dreams of people on another planet. Latterly he had seen only Life, felt only the great passionate pulse of existence, unwarped, uncontorted, untrammelled by those creeds which futilely attempt to check what wisdom would be content to regulate.

On their part they saw a great difference in him, a growing divergence from the Angel Clare of former times. It was chiefly a difference in his manner that they noticed just now, particularly his brothers. He was getting to behave like a farmer; he flung his legs about; the muscles of his face had grown more expressive; his eyes looked as much information as his tongue spoke, and more. The manner of the scholar had nearly disappeared; still more the manner of the drawing-room young man. A prig would have said that he had lost culture, and a prude that he had become coarse. Such was the contagion of domiciliary fellowship with the Talbothays nymphs and swains.

After breakfast he walked with his two brothers, non-evangelical, well-educated, hall-marked young men, correct to their remotest fibre; such unimpeachable models as are turned out yearly by the lathe of a systematic tuition. They were both somewhat short-sighted, and when it was the custom to wear a single eyeglass and string they wore a single eyeglass and string; when it was the custom to wear a double glass they wore a double glass; when it was the custom to wear spectacles they wore spectacles straightway, all without reference to the particular variety of defect in their own vision. When Wordsworth was enthroned they carried pocket copies; and when Shelly was belittled they allowed him to grow dusty on their shelves. When Correggio's Holy Families were admired, they admired Correggio's Holy Families; when he was decried in favour of Velasquez, they sedulously followed suit without any personal objection.

If these two noticed Angel's growing social ineptness, he noticed their growing mental limitations. Felix seemed to him all Church; Cuthbert all College. His Diocesan Synod and Visitations were the mainsprings of the world to the one; Cambridge to the other. Each brother candidly recognized that there were a few unimportant scores of millions of outsiders in civilized society, persons who were neither University men nor churchmen; but they were to be tolerated rather than reckoned with and respected.

They were both dutiful and attentive sons, and were regular in their visits to their parents. Felix, though an offshoot from a far more recent point in the devolution of theology than his father, was less self-sacrificing and disinterested. More tolerant than his father of a contradictory opinion, in its aspect as a danger to its holder, he was less ready than his father to pardon it as a slight to his own teaching. Cuthbert was, upon the whole, the more liberal-minded, though, with greater subtlety, he had not so much heart.

As they walked along the hillside Angel's former feeling revived in him—that whatever their advantages by comparison with himself, neither saw or set forth life as it really was lived. Perhaps, as with many men, their opportunities of observation were not so good as their opportunities of expression. Neither had an adequate conception of the complicated forces at work outside the smooth and gentle current in which they and their associates floated. Neither saw the difference between local truth and universal truth; that what the inner world said in their clerical and academic hearing was quite a different thing from what the outer world was thinking.

'I suppose it is farming or nothing for you now, my dear fellow,' Felix was saying, among other things, to his youngest brother, as he looked through his spectacles at the distant fields with sad austerity. 'And, therefore, we must make the best of it. But I do entreat you to endeavour to keep as much as possible in touch with moral ideals. Farming, of course, means roughing it externally; but high thinking may go with plain living, nevertheless.'

'Of course it may,' said Angel. 'Was it not proved nineteen hundred years ago—if I may trespass upon your domain a little? Why should you think, Felix, that I am likely to drop my high thinking and my moral ideals?'

'Well, I fancied, from the tone of your letters and our conversation—it may be fancy only—that you were somehow losing intellectual grasp. Hasn't it struck you, Cuthbert?'

'Now, Felix,' said Angel drily, 'we are very good friends, you know; each of us treading our allotted circles; but if it comes to intellectual grasp, I think you, as a contented dogmatist, had better leave mine alone, and inquire what has become of yours.'

They returned down the hill to dinner, which was fixed at any time at which their father's and mother's morning work in the parish usually concluded. Convenience as regarded afternoon callers was the last thing to enter into the consideration of unselfish Mr and Mrs Clare; though the three sons were sufficiently in unison on this matter to wish that their parents would conform a little to modern notions.

The walk had made them hungry, Angel in particular, who was now an outdoor man, accustomed to the profuse *dapes inemptae* of the dairyman's somewhat coarsely-laden table. But neither of the old people had arrived, and it was not till the sons were almost tired of waiting that their parents entered. The self-denying pair had been occupied in coaxing the appetites of some of their sick parishioners, whom they, somewhat inconsistently, tried to keep imprisoned in the flesh, their own appetites being quite forgotten.

The family sat down to table, and a frugal meal of cold viands was deposited before them. Angel looked round for Mrs Crick's black-puddings, which he had directed to be nicely grilled, as they did them at the dairy, and of which he wished his father and mother to appreciate the marvellous herbal savours as highly as he did himself.

'Ah! you are looking for the black-puddings, my dear boy,' observed Clare's mother. 'But I am sure you will not mind doing without them, as I am sure your father and I shall not, when you know the reason. I suggested to him that we should take Mrs Crick's kind present to the children of the man who can earn nothing just now because of his attacks of delirium tremens; and he agreed that it would be a great pleasure to them; so we did.'

'Of course,' said Angel cheerfully, looking round for the mead.

'I found the mead so extremely alcoholic,' continued his mother, 'that it was quite unfit for use as a beverage, but as valuable as rum or brandy in an emergency; so I have put it in my medicine-closet.'

'We never drink spirits at this table, on principle,' added his father.

'But what shall I tell the dairyman's wife?' said Angel.

'The truth, of course,' said his father.

'I rather wanted to say we enjoyed the mead and the black-puddings very much. She is a kind, jolly sort of body, and is sure to ask me directly I return.'

'You cannot, if we did not,' Mr Clare answered lucidly.

'Ah—no; though the mead was a drop of pretty tipple.'

'A what?' said Cuthbert and Felix both.

'Oh—'tis an expression they use down at Talbothays,' replied Angel, blushing. He felt that his parents were right in their practice if wrong in their want of sentiment, and said no more.

XXVI

It was not till the evening, after family prayers, that Angel found opportunity of broaching to his father one or two subjects near his heart. He had strung himself up to the purpose while kneeling behind his brothers on the carpet, studying the little nails in the heels of their walking boots. When the service was over they went out of the room with their mother, and Mr Clare and himself were left alone.

The young man first discussed with the elder his plans for the attainment of his position as a farmer on an extensive scale—either in England or in the Colonies. His father then told him that, as he had not been put to the expense of sending Angel up to Cambridge, he had felt it his duty to set by a sum of money every year towards the purchase or lease of land for him some day, that he might not feel himself unduly slighted.

'As far as wordly wealth goes,' continued his father, 'you will no doubt stand far superior to your brothers in a few years.'

This considerateness on old Mr Clare's part led Angel onward to the other and dearer subject. He observed to his father that he was then six-and-twenty, and that when he should start in the farming business he would require eyes in the back of his head to see to all matters—some one would be necessary to superintend the domestic labours of his establishment whilst he was afield. Would it not be well, therefore, for him to marry?

His father seemed to think this idea not unreasonable; and then Angel put the question—

'What kind of wife do you think would be best for me as a thrifty hard-working farmer?'

'A truly Christian woman, who will be a help and a comfort to you in your goings-out and your comings-in. Beyond that, it really matters little. Such an one can be found; indeed, my earnest-minded friend and neighbour, Dr Chant—'

'But ought she not primarily to be able to milk cows, churn good butter, make immense cheeses; know how to sit hens and turkeys, and rear chickens, to direct a field of labourers in an emergency, and estimate the value of sheep and calves?'

'Yes; a farmer's wife; yes, certainly. It would be desirable.' Mr Clare, the elder, had plainly never thought of these points before. 'I was going to add,' he said, 'that for a pure and saintly woman you will not find one more to your true advantage, and certainly not more to your mother's mind and my own, than your friend Mercy, whom you used to show a certain interest in. It is true that my neighbour Chant's daughter has lately caught up the fashion of the younger clergy round about us for decorating the Communion-table—altar, as I was shocked to hear her call it one day—with flowers and other stuff on festival occasions. But her father, who is quite as opposed to such flummery as I, says that can be cured. It is a mere girlish outbreak which, I am sure, will not be permanent.'

'Yes, yes; Mercy is good and devout, I know. But, father, don't you think that a young woman equally pure and virtuous as Miss Chant, but one who, in place of that lady's ecclesiastical accomplishments, understands the duties of farm life as well as a farmer himself, would suit me infinitely better?'

His father persisted in his conviction that a knowledge of a farmer's wife's duties came second to a Pauline view of humanity; and the impulsive Angel, wishing to honour his father's feelings and to advance the cause of his heart at the same time, grew specious. He said that fate or Providence had thrown in his way a woman who possessed every qualification to be the helpmate of an agriculturist, and was decidedly of a serious turn of mind. He would not say whether or not she had attached herself to the sound Low Church School of his father; but she would probably be open to conviction on that point; she was a regular church-goer of simple faith; honest-hearted, receptive, intelligent, graceful to a degree, chaste as a vestal, and, in personal appearance, exceptionally beautiful.

'Is she of a family such as you would care to marry into—a lady, in short?' asked his startled mother, who had come softly into the study during the conversation.

'She is not what in common parlance is called a lady,' said Angel, unflinchingly, 'for she is a cottager's daughter, as I am proud to say. But she *is* a lady, nevertheless—in feeling and nature.'

'Mercy Chant is of a very good family.'

'Pooh!—what's the advantage of that, mother?' said Angel quickly. 'How is family to avail the wife of a man who has to rough it as I have, and shall have to do?'

'Mercy is accomplished. And accomplishments have their charm,' returned his mother, looking at him through her silver spectacles.

'As to external accomplishments, what will be the use of them in the life I am going to lead?—while as to her reading, I can take that in hand. She'll be apt pupil enough, as you would say if you knew her. She's brim full of poetry—actualized poetry, if I may use the expression. She *lives* what paper-poets only write . . . And she is an unimpeachable Christian, I am sure; perhaps of the very tribe, genus, and species you desire to propagate.'

'O Angel, you are mocking!'

'Mother, I beg pardon. But as she really does attend Church almost every Sunday morning, and is a good Christian girl, I am sure you will tolerate any social shortcomings for the sake of that quality, and feel that I may do worse than choose her.' Angel waxed quite earnest on that rather automatic orthodoxy in his beloved Tess which (never dreaming that it might stand him in such good stead) he had been prone to slight when observing it practised by her and the other milkmaids, because of its obvious unreality amid beliefs essentially naturalistic.

In their sad doubts as to whether their son had himself any right whatever to the title he claimed for the unknown young woman, Mr and Mrs Clare began to feel it as an advantage not to be overlooked that she at least was sound in her views; especially as the conjunction of the pair must have arisen by an act of Providence; for Angel never would have made orthodoxy a condition of his choice. They said finally that it was better not to act in a hurry, but that they would not object to see her.

Angel therefore refrained from declaring more particulars now. He felt that, single-minded and self-sacrificing as his parents were, there yet existed certain latent prejudices of theirs, as middle-class people, which it would require some tact to overcome. For though legally at liberty to do as he chose, and though their daughter-in-law's qualifications could make no practical difference to their lives, in the probability of her living far away from them, he wished for affection's sake not to wound their sentiment in the most important decision of his life.

He observed his own inconsistencies in dwelling upon accidents in Tess's life as if they were vital features. It was for herself that he loved Tess; her soul, her heart, her substance—not for her skill in the dairy, her aptness as his scholar, and certainly not for her simple formal faith-professions. Her unsophisticated open-air existence required no varnish of conventionality to make it palatable to him. He held that education had as yet but little affected the beats of emotion and impulse on which domestic happiness depends. It was probable that, in the lapse of ages, improved systems of moral and intellectual training would appreciably, perhaps considerably, elevate the involuntary and even the unconscious instincts of human nature; but up to the present day culture, as far as he could see, might be said to have affected only the mental epiderm of those lives which had been brought under its influence. This belief was confirmed by his experience of women, which, having latterly been extended from the cultivated middle-class into the rural community, had taught him how much less was the intrinsic difference between the good and wise woman of one social stratum and the good and wise woman of another social stratum, than between the good and bad, the wise and the foolish, of the same stratum or class.

It was the morning of his departure. His brothers had already left the vicarage to proceed on a walking tour in the north, whence one was to return to his college, and the other to his curacy. Angel might have accompanied them, but preferred to rejoin his sweetheart at Talbothays. He would have been an awkward member of the party; for, though the most appreciative humanist, the most ideal religionist, even the best-versed Christologist of the three, there was alienation in the standing consciousness that his squareness would not fit the round hole that had been prepared for him. To neither Felix nor Cuthbert had he ventured to mention Tess.

His mother made him sandwiches, and his father accompanied

him, on his own mare, a little way along the road. Having fairly well advanced his own affairs Angel listened in a willing silence, as they jogged on together through the shady lanes, to his father's account of his parish difficulties, and the coldness of brother clergymen whom he loved, because of his strict interpretations of the New Testament by the light of what they deemed a pernicious Calvinistic doctrine.

'Pernicious!' said Mr Clare, with genial scorn; and he proceeded to recount experiences which would show the absurdity of that idea. He told of wondrous conversions of evil livers of which he had been the instrument, not only amongst the poor, but amongst the rich and well-to-do; and he also candidly admitted many failures.

As an instance of the latter, he mentioned the case of a young upstart squire named d'Urberville, living some forty miles off, in the neighbourhood of Trantridge.

'Not one of the ancient d'Urbervilles of Kingsbere and other places?' asked his son. 'That curiously historic worn-out family with its ghostly legend of the coach-and-four?'

'O no. The original d'Urbervilles decayed and disappeared sixty or eighty years ago—at least, I believe so. This seems to be a new family which has taken the name; for the credit of the former knightly line I hope they are spurious, I'm sure. But it is odd to hear you express interest in old families. I thought you set less store by them even than I.'

'You misapprehend me, father; you often do,' said Angel with a little impatience. 'Politically I am sceptical as to the virtue of their being old. Some of the wise even among themselves "exclaim against their own succession", as Hamlet puts it, but lyrically, dramatically, and even historically, I am tenderly attached to them.'

This distinction, though by no means a subtle one, was yet too subtle for Mr Clare the elder, and he went on with the story he had been about to relate; which was that after the death of the senior so-called d'Urberville the young man developed the most culpable passions, though he had a blind mother, whose condition should have made him know better. A knowledge of his career having come to the ears of Mr Clare, when he was in that part of the country preaching missionary sermons, he boldly took occasion to speak to the delinquent on his spiritual state. Though he was a stranger, occupying another's pulpit, he had felt this to be his duty, and took for his text the words from St Luke: 'Thou fool, this night thy soul shall be required of thee!' The young man much resented this directness of attack, and in the war of words which followed when they met he did not scruple publicly to insult Mr Clare, without respect for his gray hairs.

Angel flushed with distress.

'Dear father,' he said sadly, 'I wish you would not expose yourself to such gratuitous pain from scoundrels!'

'Pain?' said his father, his rugged face shining in the ardour of self-abnegation. 'The only pain to me was pain on his account, poor, foolish young man. Do you suppose his incensed words could give me any pain, or even his blows? "Being reviled we bless; being persecuted we suffer it; being defamed we entreat; we are made as the filth of the world, and as the off-scouring of all things unto this day." Those ancient and noble words to the Corinthians are strictly true at this present hour.'

'Not blows, father? He did not proceed to blows?'

'No, he did not. Though I have borne blows from men in a mad state of intoxication.'

'No!'

'A dozen times, my boy. What then? I have saved them from the guilt of murdering their own flesh and blood thereby; and they have lived to thank me, and praise God.'

'May this young man do the same!' said Angel fervently. 'But I fear otherwise, from what you say.'

'We'll hope, nevertheless,' said Mr Clare. 'And I continue to pray for him, though on this side of the grave we shall probably never meet again. But, after all, one of those poor words of mine may spring up in his heart as a good seed some day.'

Now, as always, Clare's father was sanguine as a child; and though the younger could not accept his parent's narrow dogma he revered his practice, and recognized the hero under the pietist. Perhaps he revered his father's practice even more now than ever, seeing that, in the question of making Tessy his wife, his father had not once thought of inquiring whether she were well provided or penniless.

The same unworldliness was what had necessitated Angel's getting a living as a farmer, and would probably keep his brothers in the position of poor parsons for the term of their activities; yet Angel admired it none the less. Indeed, despite his own heterodoxy, Angel often felt that he was nearer to his father on the human side than was either of his brethren.

XXVII

An up-hill and down-dale ride of twenty-odd miles through a garish mid-day atmosphere brought him in the afternoon to a detached knoll a mile or two west of Talbothays, whence he again looked into that green trough of sappiness and humidity, the valley of the Var or Froom. Immediately he began to descend from the upland to the fat alluvial soil below, the atmosphere grew heavier; the languid perfume of the summer fruits, the mists, the hay, the flowers, formed therein a vast pool of odour which at this hour seemed to make the animals, the very bees and butterflies, drowsy. Clare was now so familiar with the spot that he knew the individual cows by their names when, a long distance off, he saw them dotted about the meads. It was with a sense of luxury that he recognized his power of viewing life here from its inner side, in a way that had been quite foreign to him in his student-days; and, much as he loved his parents, he could not help being aware that to come here, as now, after an experience of homelife, affected him like throwing off splints and bandages; even the one customary curb on the humours of English rural societies being absent in this place, Talbothays having no resident landlord.

Not a human being was out of doors at the dairy. The denizens were all enjoying the usual afternoon nap of an hour or so which the exceedingly early hours kept in summer-time rendered a necessity. At the door the wood-hooped pails, sodden and bleached by infinite scrubbings, hung like hats on a stand upon the forked and peeled limb of an oak fixed there for that purpose; all of them ready and dry for the evening milking. Angel entered, and went through the silent passages of the house to the back quarters, where he listened for a moment. Sustained snores came from the cart-house, where some of the men were lying down; the grunt and squeal of sweltering pigs arose from the still further distance. The large-leaved rhubarb and cabbage plants slept too, their broad limp surfaces hanging in the sun like half-closed umbrellas.

He unbridled and fed his horse, and as he re-entered the house the clock struck three. Three was the afternoon skimming-hour; and, with the stroke, Clare heard the creaking of the floor-boards above, and then the touch of a descending foot on the stairs. It was Tess's, who in another moment came down before his eyes.

She had not heard him enter, and hardly realized his presence there. She was yawning, and he saw the red interior of her mouth as if it had been a snake's. She had stretched one arm so high above her coiled-up cable of hair that he could see its satin delicacy above the sunburn; her face was flushed with sleep, and her eyelids hung heavy over their pupils. The brimfulness of her nature breathed from her. It was a moment when a woman's soul is more incarnate than at any other time; when the most spiritual beauty bespeaks itself flesh; and sex takes the outside place in the presentation.

Then those eyes flashed brightly through their filmy heaviness, before the remainder of her face was well awake. With an oddly compounded look of gladness, shyness, and surprise, she exclaimed—

'O Mr Clare! How you frightened me—I—'

There had not at first been time for her to think of the changed relations which his declaration had introduced; but the full sense of the matter rose up in her face when she encountered Clare's tender look as he stepped forward to the bottom stair.

'Dear, darling Tessy!' he whispered, putting his arm round her, and his face to her flushed cheek. 'Don't, for Heaven's sake, Mister me any more. I have hastened back so soon because of you!'

Tess's excitable heart beat against his by way of reply; and there they stood upon the red-brick floor of the entry, the sun slanting in by the window upon his back, as he held her tightly to his breast; upon her inclining face, upon the blue veins of her temple, upon her naked arm, and her neck, and into the depths of her hair. Having been lying down in her clothes she was warm as a sunned cat. At first she would not look straight up at him, but her eyes soon lifted, and his plumbed the deepness of the ever-varying pupils, with their radiating fibrils of blue, and black, and gray, and violet, while she regarded him as Eve at her second waking might have regarded Adam.

'I've got to go a-skimming,' she pleaded, 'and I have on'y old Deb to help me to-day. Mrs Crick is gone to market with Mr Crick, and Retty is not well, and the others are gone out somewhere, and won't be home till milking.'

As they retreated to the milk-house Deborah Fyander appeared on the stairs.

'I have come back, Deborah,' said Mr Clare, upwards. 'So I can help Tess with the skimming; and, as you are very tired, I am sure, you needn't come down till milking-time.'

Possibly the Talbothays milk was not very thoroughly skimmed that afternoon. Tess was in a dream wherein familiar objects appeared as having light and shade and position, but no particular outline. Every time she held the skimmer under the pump to cool it for the work her hand trembled, the ardour of his affection being so palpable that she seemed to flinch under it like a plant in too burning a sun.

Then he pressed her again to his side, and when she had done running her forefinger round the leads to cut off the cream-edge, he cleaned it in nature's way; for the unconstrained manners of Talbothays dairy came convenient now.

'I may as well say it now as later, dearest,' he resumed gently. 'I wish to ask you something of a very practical nature, which I have been thinking of ever since that day last week in the meads. I shall soon want to marry, and, being a farmer, you see I shall require for my wife a woman who knows all about the management of farms. Will you be that woman, Tessy?'

He put it in that way that she might not think he had yielded to an impulse of which his head would disapprove.

She turned quite careworn. She had bowed to the inevitable result of proximity, the necessity of loving him; but she had not calculated upon this sudden corollary, which, indeed, Clare had put before her without quite meaning himself to do it so soon. With pain that was like the bitterness of dissolution she murmured the words of her indispensable and sworn answer as an honourable woman.

'O Mr Clare—I cannot be your wife—I cannot be!'

The sound of her own decision seemed to break Tess's very heart, and she bowed her face in her grief.

'But, Tess!' he said, amazed at her reply, and holding her still more greedily close. 'Do you say no? Surely you love me?'

'O yes, yes! And I would rather be yours than anybody's in the world,' returned the sweet and honest voice of the distressed girl. 'But I *cannot* marry you!'

'Tess,' he said, holding her at arm's length, 'you are engaged to marry some one else!'

'No, no!'

'Then why do you refuse me?'

'I don't want to marry! I have not thought of doing it. I cannot! I only want to love you.'

'But why?'

Driven to subterfuge, she stammered—

'Your father is a parson, and your mother wouldn't like you to marry such as me. She will want you to marry a lady.'

'Nonsense—I have spoken to them both. That was partly why I went home.'

'I feel I cannot—never, never!' she echoed.

'Is it too sudden to be asked thus, my Pretty?'

'Yes—I did not expect it.'

'If you will let it pass, please, Tessy, I will give you time,' he said. 'It was very abrupt to come home and speak to you all at once. I'll not allude to it again for a while.'

She again took up the shining skimmer, held it beneath the pump, and began anew. But she could not, as at other times, hit the exact under-surface of the cream with the delicate dexterity required, try as she might: sometimes she was cutting down into the milk, sometimes in the air. She could hardly see, her eyes having filled with two blurring tears drawn forth by a grief which, to this her best friend and dear advocate, she could never explain.

'I can't skim—I can't!' she said, turning away from him.

Not to agitate and hinder her longer the considerate Clare began talking in a more general way:

'You quite misapprehend my parents. They are the most simple-mannered people alive, and quite unambitious. They are two of the few remaining Evangelical school. Tessy, are you an Evangelical?'

'I don't know.'

'You go to church very regularly, and our parson here is not very High, they tell me.'

Tess's ideas on the views of the parish clergyman, whom she heard every week, seemed to be rather more vague than Clare's, who had never heard him at all.

'I wish I could fix my mind on what I hear there more firmly than I do,' she remarked as a safe generality. 'It is often a great sorrow to me.'

She spoke so unaffected that Angel was sure in his heart that his father could not object to her on religious grounds, even though she did not know whether her principles were High, Low, or Broad. He himself knew that, in reality, the confused beliefs which she held, apparently imbibed in childhood, were, if any thing, Tractarian as to phraseology, and Pantheistic as to essence. Confused or otherwise, to disturb them was his last desire:

> Leave thou thy sister, when she prays,
> Her early Heaven, her happy views;
> Nor thou with shadow'd hint confuse
> A life that leads melodious days.

He had occasionally thought the counsel less honest than musical; but he gladly conformed to it now.

He spoke further of the incidents of his visit, of his father's mode of life, of his zeal for his principles; she grew serener, and the undulations disappeared from her skimming; as she finished one lead after another he followed her, and drew the plugs for letting down the milk.

'I fancied you looked a little downcast when you came in,' she ventured to observe, anxious to keep away from the subject of herself.

'Yes—well, my father has been talking a good deal to me of his troubles and difficulties, and the subject always tends to depress me. He is so zealous that he gets many snubs and buffetings from people of a different way of thinking from himself, and I don't like to hear of such humiliations to a man of his age, the more particularly as I don't think earnestness does any good when carried so far. He has been telling me of a very unpleasant scene in which he took part quite recently. He went as the deputy of some missionary society to preach in the neighbourhood of Trantridge, a place forty miles from here, and made it his business to expostulate with a lax young cynic he met somewhere about there—son of some landowner up that way—and who has a mother afflicted with blindness. My father addressed himself to the gentleman pointblank, and there was quite a disturbance. It was very foolish of my father, I must say, to intrude his conversation upon a stranger when the probabilities were so obvious that it would be useless. But whatever he thinks to be his duty, that he'll do, in season or out of season; and, of course, he makes many enemies, not only among the absolutely vicious, but among the easy-going, who hate being bothered. He says he glories in what happened, and that good may be done indirectly; but I wish he would not so wear himself out now he is getting old, and would leave such pigs to their wallowing.'

Tess's look had grown hard and worn, and her ripe mouth tragical; but she no longer showed any tremulousness. Clare's revived thoughts of his father prevented his noticing her particularly; and so they went on down the white row of liquid rectangles till they had finished and drained them off, when the other maids returned, and took their pails, and Deb came to scald out the leads for the new milk. As Tess withdrew to go afield to the cows he said to her softly—

'And my question, Tessy?'

'O no—no!' replied she with grave hopelessness, as one who had heard anew the turmoil of her own past in the allusion to Alec d'Urberville. 'It *can't* be!'

She went out towards the mead, joining the other milkmaids with a bound, as if trying to make the open air drive away her sad constraint. All the girls drew onward to the spot where the cows were grazing in the farther mead, the bevy advancing with the bold grace of wild animals—the reckless unchastened motion of women accustomed to unlimited space—in which they abandoned themselves to the air as a swimmer to the wave. It seemed natural enough to him now that Tess was again in sight to choose a mate from unconstrained Nature, and not from the abodes of Art.

XXVIII

HER refusal, though unexpected, did not permanently daunt Clare. His experience of women was great enough for him to be aware that the negative often meant nothing more than the preface to the affirmative; and it was little enough for him not to know that in the manner of the present negative there lay a great exception to the dallyings of coyness. That she had already permitted him to make love to her he read as an additional assurance, not fully trowing that in the fields and pastures to 'sigh gratis' is by no means deemed waste; love-making being here more often accepted inconsiderately and for its own sweet sake than in the carking anxious homes of the ambitious, where a girl's craving for an establishment paralyzes her healthy thought of a passion as an end.

'Tess, why did you say "no" in such a positive way?' he asked her in the course of a few days.

She started.

'Don't ask me. I told you why—partly. I am not good enough—not worthy enough.'

'How? Not fine lady enough?'

'Yes—something like that,' murmured she. 'Your friends would scorn me.'

'Indeed, you mistake them—my father and mother. As for my brothers, I don't care—' He clasped his fingers behind her back to keep her from slipping away. 'Now—you did not mean it, sweet?—I am sure you did not! You have made me so restless that I cannot read, or play, or do anything. I am in no hurry, Tess, but I want to know—to hear from your own warm lips—that you will some day be mine—any time you may choose; but some day?'

She could only shake her head and look away from him.

Clare regarded her attentively, conned the characters of her face as if they had been hieroglyphics. The denial seemed real.

'Then I ought not to hold you in this way—ought I? I h right to you—no right to seek out where you are, or to wal you! Honestly, Tess, do you love any other man?'

'How can you ask?' she said, with continued self-suppression.

'I almost know that you do not. But then, why do you repulse me?'

'I don't repulse you. I like you to—tell me you love me; and you may always tell me so as you go about with me—and never offend me.'

'But you will not accept me as a husband?'

'Ah—that's different—it is for your good, indeed my dearest! O, believe me, it is only for your sake! I don't like to give myself the great happiness o' promising to be yours in that way—because—because I am *sure* I ought not to do it.'

'But you will make me happy!'

'Ah—you think so, but you don't know!'

At such times as this, apprehending the grounds of her refusal to be her modest sense of incompetence in matters social and polite, he would say that she was wonderfully well-informed and versatile—which was certainly true, her natural quickness, and her admiration for him, having led her to pick up his vocabulary, his accent, and fragments of his knowledge, to a surprising extent. After these tender contests and her victory she would go away by herself under the remotest cow, if at milking-time, or into the sedge, or into her room, if at a leisure interval, and mourn silently, not a minute after an apparently phlegmatic negative.

The struggle was so fearful; her own heart was so strongly on the side of his—two ardent hearts against one poor little conscience—that she tried to fortify her resolution by every means in her power. She had come to Talbothays with a made-up mind. On no account could she agree to a step which might afterwards cause bitter rueing to her husband for his blindness in wedding her. And she held that what her conscience had decided for her when her mind was unbiassed ought not to be overruled now.

'Why don't somebody tell him all about me?' she said. 'It was only forty miles off—why hasn't it reached here? Somebody must know!'

Yet nobody seemed to know; nobody told him.

For two or three days no more was said. She guessed from the sad countenances of her chamber companions that they regarded her not only as the favourite, but as the chosen; but they could see for themselves that she did not put herself in his way.

Tess had never before known a time in which the thread of her life was so distinctly twisted of two strands, positive pleasure and positive pain. At the next cheese-making the pair were again left alone together. The dairyman himself had been lending a hand; but Mr Crick, as well as his wife, seemed latterly to have acquired a suspicion of mutual interest between these two; though they walked so circumspectly that suspicion was but of the faintest. Anyhow, the dairyman left them to themselves.

They were breaking up the masses of curd before putting them into the vats. The operation resembled the act of crumbling bread on a large scale; and amid the immaculate whiteness of the curds Tess Durbeyfield's hands showed themselves of the pinkness of the rose. Angel, who was filling the vats with his handfuls, suddenly ceased, and laid his hands flat upon hers. Her sleeves were rolled far above the elbow, and bending lower he kissed the inside vein of her soft arm.

Although the early September weather was sultry, her arm, from her dabbling in the curds, was as cold and damp to his mouth as a new-gathered mushroom, and tasted of the whey. But she was such a sheaf of susceptibilities that her pulse was accelerated by the touch, her blood driven to her finger-ends, and the cool arms flushed hot. Then, as though her heart had said, 'Is coyness longer necessary? Truth is truth between man and woman, as between man and man,' she lifted her eyes, and they beamed devotedly into his, as her lip rose in a tender half-smile.

'Do you know why I did that, Tess?' he said.

'Because you love me very much!'

'Yes, and as a preliminary to a new entreaty.'

'Not *again*!'

She looked a sudden fear that her resistance might break down under her own desire.

'O, Tessy!' he went on, 'I *cannot* think why you are so tantalizing.

Why do you disappoint me so? You seem almost like a coquette, upon my life you do—a coquette of the first urban water! They blow hot and blow cold, just as you do; and it is the very last sort of thing to expect to find in a retreat like Talbothays . . . And yet, dearest,' he quickly added, observing how the remark had cut her, 'I know you to be the most honest, spotless creature that ever lived. So how can I suppose you a flirt? Tess, why don't you like the idea of being my wife, if you love me as you seem to do?'

'I have never said I don't like the idea, and I never could say it; because—it isn't true!'

The stress now getting beyond endurance her lip quivered, and she was obliged to go away. Clare was so pained and perplexed that he ran after and caught her in the passage.

'Tell me, tell me!' he said, passionately clasping her, in forgetfulness of his curdy hands: 'do tell me that you won't belong to anybody but me!'

'I will, I will tell you!' she exclaimed. 'And I will give you a complete answer, if you will let me go now. I will tell you my experiences—all about myself—all!'

'Your experiences, dear; yes, certainly; any number.' He expressed assent in loving satire, looking into her face. 'My Tess has, no doubt, almost as many experiences as that wild convolvulus out there on the garden hedge, that opened itself this morning for the first time. Tell me anything, but don't use that wretched expression any more about not being worthy of me.'

'I will try—not! And I'll give you my reasons to-morrow—next week.'

'Say on Sunday?'

'Yes, on Sunday.'

At last she got away, and did not stop in her retreat till she was in the thicket of pollard willows at the lower side of the barton, where she could be quite unseen. Here Tess flung herself down upon the rustling undergrowth of speargrass, as upon a bed, and remained crouching in palpitating misery broken by momentary shoots of joy, which her fears about the ending could not altogether suppress.

In reality, she was drifting into acquiescence. Every see-saw of her breath, every wave of her blood, every pulse singing in her ears, was a voice that joined with nature in revolt against her scrupulousness. Reckless, inconsiderate acceptance of him; to close with him at the altar, revealing nothing, and chancing discovery; to snatch ripe pleasure before the iron teeth of pain could have time to shut upon her: that was what love counselled; and in almost a terror of ecstasy Tess divined that, despite her many months of lonely self-chastisement, wrestlings, communings, schemes to lead a future of austere isolation, love's counsel would prevail.

The afternoon advanced, and still she remained among the willows. She heard the rattle of taking down the pails from the forked stands; the 'waow-waow!' which accompanied the getting together of the cows. But she did not go to the milking. They would see her agitation; and the dairyman, thinking the cause to be love alone, would good-naturedly tease her; and that harassment could not be borne.

Her lover must have guessed her overwrought state, and invented some excuse for her non-appearance, for no inquiries were made or calls given. At half-past six the sun settled down upon the levels, with the aspect of a great forge in the heavens, and presently a monstrous pumpkin-like moon arose on the other hand. The pollard willows, tortured out of their natural shape by incessant choppings, became spiny-haired monsters as they stood up against it. She went in, and upstairs without a light.

It was now Wednesday. Thursday came, and Angel looked thoughtfully at her from a distance, but intruded in no way upon her. The indoor milkmaids, Marian and the rest, seemed to guess that something definite was afoot, for they did not force any remarks upon her in the bedchamber. Friday passed; Saturday. To-morrow was the day.

'I shall give way—I shall say yes—I shall let myself marry him—I cannot help it!' she jealously panted, with her hot face to the pillow that night, on hearing one of the other girls sigh his name in her sleep. 'I can't bear to let anybody have him but me! Yet it is a wrong to him, and may kill him when he knows! O my heart—O—O—O!'

XXIX

'Now, who mid ye think I've heard news o' this morning?' said Dairyman Crick, as he sat down to breakfast next day, with a riddling gaze round upon the munching men and maids. 'Now just who mid ye think?'

One guessed, and another guessed. Mrs Crick did not guess, because she knew already.

'Well,' said the dairyman, ''tis that slack-twisted 'hore's-bird of a fellar, Jack Dollop. He's lately got married to a widow-woman.'

'Not Jack Dollop? A villain—to think o' that!' said a milker.

The name entered quickly into Tess Durbeyfield's consciousness, for it was the name of the lover who had wronged his sweetheart, and had afterwards been so roughly used by the young woman's mother in the butter-churn.

'And has he married the valiant matron's daughter, as he promised?' asked Angel Clare absently, as he turned over the newspaper he was reading at the little table to which he was always banished by Mrs Crick, in her sense of his gentility.

'Not he, sir. Never meant to,' replied the dairyman. 'As I say, 'tis a widow-woman, and she had money, it seems—fifty poun' a year or so; and that was all he was after. They were married in a great hurry; and then she told him that by marrying she had lost her fifty poun' a year. Just fancy the state o' my gentleman's mind at that news! Never such a cat-and-dog life as they've been leading ever since! Serves him well beright. But onluckily the poor woman gets the worst o't.'

'Well, the silly body should have told en sooner that the ghost of her first man would trouble him,' said Mrs Crick.

'Ay; ay,' responded the dairyman indecisively. 'Still, you can see exactly how t'was. She wanted a home, and didn't like to run the risk of losing him. Don't ye think that was something like it, maidens?'

He glanced towards the row of girls.

'She ought to ha' told him just before they went to church, when he could hardly have backed out,' exclaimed Marian.

'Yes, she ought,' agreed Izz.

'She must have seen what he was after, and should ha' refused him,' cried Retty spasmodically.

'And what do you say, my dear?' asked the dairyman of Tess.

'I think she ought—to have told him the true state of things—or else refused him—I don't know,' replied Tess, the bread-and-butter choking her.

'But cust if I'd have done either o't,' said Beck Knibbs, a married helper from one of the cottages. 'All's fair in love and war. I'd ha' married en just as she did, and if he'd said two words to me about not telling him beforehand anything whatsomdever about my first chap that I hadn't chose to tell, I'd ha' knocked him down wi' the rolling-pin—a scram little feller like he! Any woman could do it.'

The laughter which followed this sally was supplemented only by a sorry smile, for form's sake, from Tess. What was comedy to them was tragedy to her; and she could hardly bear their mirth. She soon rose from table, and, with an impression that Clare would follow her, went along a little wriggling path, now stepping to one side of the irrigating channels, and now to the other, till she stood by the main stream of the Var. Men had been cutting the water-weeds higher up the river, and masses of them were floating past her—moving islands of green crow-foot, whereon she might almost have ridden; long locks of which weed had lodged against the piles driven to keep the cows from crossing.

Yes, there was the pain of it. This question of a woman telling her story—the heaviest of crosses to herself—seemed but amusement to others. It was as if people should laugh at martyrdom.

'Tessy!' came from behind her, and Clare sprang across the gully, alighting beside her feet. 'My wife—soon!'

'No, no; I cannot. For your sake, O Mr Clare; for your sake, I say no!'

'Tess!'

'Still I say no!' she repeated.

Not expecting this he had put his arm lightly round her waist the moment after speaking, beneath her hanging tail of hair. (The younger dairymaids, including Tess, breakfasted with their hair loose on Sunday mornings before building it up extra high for attending church, a style they could not adopt when milking with their heads against the cows.) If she had said 'Yes' instead of 'No' he would have kissed her; it had evidently been his intention; but her determined negative deterred his scrupulous heart. Their condition of domiciliary comradeship put her, as the woman, to such disadvantage by its enforced intercourse, that he felt it unfair to her to exercise any pressure of blandishment which he might have honestly employed had she been better able to avoid him. He released her momentarily-imprisoned waist, and withheld the kiss.

It all turned on that release. What had given her strength to refuse him this time was solely the tale of the widow told by the dairyman; and that would have been overcome in another moment. But Angel said no more; his face was perplexed; he went away.

Day after day they met—somewhat less constantly than before; and thus two or three weeks went by. The end of September drew near, and she could see in his eye that he might ask her again.

His plan of procedure was different now—as though he had made up his mind that her negatives were, after all, only coyness and youth startled by the novelty of the proposal. The fitful evasiveness of her manner when the subject was under discussion countenanced the idea. So he played a more coaxing game; and while never going beyond words, or attempting the renewal of caresses, he did his utmost orally.

In this way Clare persistently wooed her in undertones like that of the purling milk—at the cow's side, at skimmings, at butter-makings, at cheese-makings, among broody poultry, and among farrowing pigs—as no milkmaid was ever wooed before by such a man.

Tess knew that she must break down. Neither a religious sense of a certain moral validity in the previous union nor a conscientious wish for candour could hold out against it much longer. She loved him so passionately, and he was so godlike in her eyes; and being, though untrained, instinctively refined, her nature cried for his tutelary guidance. And thus, though Tess kept repeating to herself,

'I can never be his wife', the words were vain. A proof of her weakness lay in the very utterance of what calm strength would not have taken the trouble to formulate. Every sound of his voice beginning on the old subject stirred her with a terrifying bliss, and she coveted the recantation she feared.

His manner was—what man's is not?—so much that of one who would love and cherish and defend her under any conditions, changes, charges, or revelations, that her gloom lessened as she basked in it. The season meanwhile was drawing onward to the equinox, and though it was still fine, the days were much shorter. The dairy had again worked by morning candle-light for a long time; and a fresh renewal of Clare's pleading occurred one morning between three and four.

She had run up in her bedgown to his door to call him as usual; then had gone back to dress and call the others; and in ten minutes was walking to the head of the stairs with the candle in her hand. At the same moment he came down his steps from above in his shirt-sleeves and put his arm across the stairway.

'Now, Miss Flirt, before you go down,' he said peremptorily. 'It is a fortnight since I spoke, and this won't do any longer. You *must* tell me what you mean, or I shall have to leave this house. My door was ajar just now, and I saw you. For your own safety I must go. You don't know. Well? Is it to be yes at last?'

'I am only just up, Mr Clare, and it is too early to take me to task!' she pouted. 'You need not call me Flirt. 'Tis cruel and untrue. Wait till by and by. Please wait till by and by! I will really think seriously about it between now and then. Let me go downstairs!'

She looked a little like what he said she was as, holding the candle sideways, she tried to smile away the seriousness of her words.

'Call me Angel, then, and not Mr Clare.'

'Angel.'

'Angel dearest—why not?'

''Twould mean that I agree, wouldn't it?'

'It would only mean that you love me, even if you cannot marry me; and you were so good as to own that long ago.'

'Very well, then, "Angel dearest", if I *must*,' she murmured, looking at her candle, a roguish curl coming upon her mouth, notwithstanding her suspense.

Clare had resolved never to kiss her until he had obtained her promise; but somehow, as Tess stood there in her prettily tucked-up milking gown, her hair carelessly heaped upon her head till there should be leisure to arrange it when skimming and milking were done, he broke his resolve, and brought his lips to her cheek for one moment. She passed downstairs very quickly, never looking back at him or saying another word. The other maids were already down, and the subject was not pursued. Except Marian they all looked wistfully and suspiciously at the pair, in the sad yellow rays which the morning candles emitted in contrast with the first cold signals of the dawn without.

When skimming was done—which, as the milk diminished with the approach of autumn, was a lessening process day by day—Retty and the rest went out. The lovers followed them.

'Our tremulous lives are so different from theirs, are they not?' he musingly observed to her, as he regarded the three figures tripping before him through the frigid pallor of opening day.

'Not so very different, I think,' she said.

'Why do you think that?'

'There are very few women's lives that are not—tremulous,' Tess replied, pausing over the new word as if it impressed her. 'There's more in those three than you think.'

'What is in them?'

'Almost either of 'em,' she began, 'would make—perhaps would make—a properer wife than I. And perhaps they love you as well as I—almost.'

'O, Tessy!'

There were signs that it was an exquisite relief to her to hear the impatient exclamation, though she had resolved so intrepidly to let generosity make one bid against herself. That was now done, and she had not the power to attempt self-immolation a second time then. They were joined by a milker from one of the cottages, and no more was said on that which concerned them so deeply. But Tess knew that this day would decide it.

In the afternoon several of the dairyman's household and assistants went down to the meads as usual, a long way from the dairy, where many of the cows were milked without being driven home. The supply was getting less as the animals advanced in calf, and the supernumerary milkers of the lush green season had been dismissed.

The work progressed leisurely. Each pailful was poured into tall cans that stood in a large spring-waggon which had been brought upon the scene; and when they were milked the cows trailed away.

Dairyman Crick, who was there with the rest, his wrapper gleaming miraculously white against a leaden evening sky, suddenly looked at his heavy watch.

'Why, 'tis later than I thought,' he said. 'Begad! We shan't be soon enough with this milk at the station, if we don't mind. There's no time to-day to take it home and mix it with the bulk afore sending off. It must go to station straight from here. Who'll drive it across?'

Mr Clare volunteered to do so, though it was none of his business, asking Tess to accompany him. The evening, though sunless, had been warm and muggy for the season, and Tess had come out with her milking-hood only, naked-armed and jacketless; certainly not dressed for a drive. She therefore replied by glancing over her scant habiliments; but Clare gently urged her. She assented by relinquishing her pail and stool to the dairyman to take home; and mounted the spring-waggon beside Clare.

XXX

In the diminishing daylight they went along the level roadway through the meads, which stretched away into gray miles, and were backed in the extreme edge of distance by the swarthy and abrupt slopes of Edgon Heath. On its summit stood clumps and stretches of fir-trees, whose notched tips appeared like battlemented towers crowning black-fronted castles of enchantment.

They were so absorbed in the sense of being close to each other that they did not begin talking for a long while, the silence being broken only by the clucking of the milk in the tall cans behind them. The lane they followed was so solitary that the hazel nuts had remained on the boughs till they slipped from their shells, and the blackberries hung in heavy clusters. Every now and then Angel would fling the lash of his whip round one of these, pluck it off, and give it to his companion.

The dull sky soon began to tell its meaning by sending down herald-drops of rain, and the stagnant air of the day changed into a fitful breeze which played about their faces. The quick-silvery glaze on the rivers and pools vanished; from broad mirrors of light they changed to lustreless sheets of lead, with a surface like a rasp. But that spectacle did not affect her preoccupation. Her countenance, a natural carnation slightly embrowned by the season, had deepened its tinge with the beating of the rain-drops; and her hair, which the pressure of the cows' flanks had, as usual, caused to tumble down from its fastenings and stray beyond the curtain of her calico bonnet, was made clammy by the moisture, till it hardly was better than seaweed.

'I ought not to have come, I suppose,' she murmured, looking at the sky.

'I am sorry for the rain,' said he. 'But how glad I am to have you here!'

Remote Egdon disappeared by degrees behind the liquid gauze. The evening grew darker, and the roads being crossed by gates it was not safe to drive faster than at a walking pace. The air was rather chill.

'I am so afraid you will get cold, with nothing upon your arms and shoulders,' he said. 'Creep close to me, and perhaps the drizzle won't hurt you much. I should be sorrier still if I did not think that the rain might be helping me.'

She imperceptibly crept closer, and he wrapped round them both a large piece of sail-cloth, which was sometimes used to keep the sun off the milk-cans. Tess held it from slipping off him as well as herself, Clare's hands being occupied.

'Now we are all right again. Ah—no we are not! It runs down into my neck a little, and it must still more into yours. That's better. Your arms are like wet marble, Tess. Wipe them in the cloth. Now, if you stay quiet, you will not get another drop. Well, dear—about that question of mine—that long-standing question?'

The only reply that he could hear for a little while was the smack of the horse's hoofs on the moistening road, and the cluck of the milk in the cans behind them.

'Do you remember what you said?'

'I do,' she replied.

'Before we get home, mind.'

'I'll try.'

He said no more then. As they drove on the fragment of an old manor house of Caroline date rose against the sky, and was in due course passed and left behind.

'That,' he observed, to entertain her, 'is an interesting old place—one of the several seats which belonged to an ancient Norman family formerly of great influence in this county, the d'Urbervilles. I never pass one of their residences without thinking of them. There is something very sad in the extinction of a family of renown, even if it was fierce, domineering, feudal renown.'

'Yes,' said Tess.

They crept along towards a point in the expanse of shade just at hand at which a feeble light was beginning to assert its presence, a spot where, by day, a fitful white streak of steam at intervals upon the dark green background denoted intermittent moments of contact between their secluded world and modern life. Modern life stretched out its steam feeler to this point three or four times a day, touched the native existences, and quickly withdrew its feeler again, as if what it touched had been uncongenial.

They reached the feeble light, which came from the smoky lamp of a little railway station; a poor enough terrestrial star, yet in one sense of more importance to Talbothays Dairy and mankind than the celestial ones to which it stood in such humiliating contrast. The cans of new milk were unladen in the rain, Tess getting a little shelter from a neighbouring holly tree.

Then there was the hissing of a train, which drew up almost silently upon the wet rails, and the milk was rapidly swung can by can into the truck. The light of the engine flashed for a second upon Tess Durbeyfield's figure, motionless under the great holly tree. No object could have looked more foreign to the gleaming cranks and wheels than this unsophisticated girl, with the round bare arms, the rainy face and hair, the suspended attitude of a friendly leopard at pause, the print gown of no date or fashion, and the cotton bonnet drooping on her brow.

She mounted again beside her lover, with a mute obedience characteristic of impassioned natures at times, and when they had wrapped themselves up over head and ears in the sail-cloth again, they plunged back into the now thick night. Tess was so receptive that the few minutes of contact with the whirl of material progress lingered in her thought.

'Londoners will drink it at their breakfasts to-morrow, won't they?' she asked. 'Strange people that we have never seen.'

'Yes—I suppose they will. Though not as we send it. When its strength has been lowered, so that it may not get up into their heads.'

'Noble men and noble women, ambassadors and centurions, ladies and tradeswomen, and babies who have never seen a cow.'

'Well, yes; perhaps; particularly centurions.'

'Who don't know anything of us, and where it comes from; or think how we two drove miles across the moor to-night in the rain that it might reach 'em in time?'

'We did not drive entirely on account of these precious Londoners; we drove a little on our own—on account of that anxious matter which you will, I am sure, set at rest, dear Tess. Now, permit me to put it in this way. You belong to me already, you know; your heart, I mean. Does it not?'

'You know as well as I. O yes—yes!'

'Then, if your heart does, why not your hand?'

'My only reason was on account of you—on account of a question. I have something to tell you –'

'But suppose it to be entirely for my happiness, and my worldly convenience also?'

'O yes; if it is for your happiness and worldly convenience. But my life before I came here—I want –'

'Well, it is for my convenience as well as my happiness. If I have a very large farm, either English or colonial, you will be invaluable as a wife to me; better than a woman out of the largest mansion in the country. So please—please, dear Tessy, disabuse your mind of the feeling that you will stand in my way.'

'But my history. I want you to know it—you must let me tell you—you will not like me so well!'

'Tell it if you wish to, dearest. This previous history then. Yes, I was born at so and so, Anno Domini –'

'I was born at Marlott,' she said, catching at his words as a help, lightly as they were spoken. 'And I grew up there. And I was in the Sixth Standard when I left school, and they said I had great aptness, and should make a good teacher, so it was settled that I should be one. But there was trouble in my family; father was not very industrious, and he drank a little.'

'Yes, yes. Poor child! Nothing new.' He pressed her more closely to his side.

'And then—there is something very unusual about it—about me. I—I was—' Tess's breath quickened.

'Yes, dearest. Never mind.'

'I—I am not a Durbeyfield, but a d'Urberville—a descendant of the same family as those that owned the old house we passed. And—we are all gone to nothing!'

'A d'Urberville!—Indeed! And is that all the trouble, dear Tess?'

'Yes,' she answered faintly.

'Well—why should I love you less after knowing this?'

'I was told by the dairyman that you hated old families.'

He laughed.

'Well, it is true, in one sense. I do hate the aristocratic principle of blood before everything, and do think that as reasoners the only pedigrees we ought to respect are those spiritual ones of the wise and virtuous, without regard to corporeal paternity. But I am extremely interested in this news—you can have no idea how interested I am! Are not you interested yourself in being one of that well-known line?'

'No. I have thought it sad—especially since coming here, and knowing that many of the hills and fields I see once belonged to my father's people. But other hills and fields belonged to Retty's people, and perhaps others to Marian's, so that I don't value it particularly.'

'Yes—it is surprising how many of the present tillers of the soil were once owners of it, and I sometimes wonder that a certain school of politicians don't make capital of the circumstance; but they don't seem to know it . . . I wonder that I did not see the resemblance of your name to d'Urberville, and trace the manifest corruption. And this was the carking secret!'

She had not told. At the last moment her courage had failed her, she feared his blame for not telling him sooner; and her instinct of self-preservation was stronger than her candour.

'Of course,' continued the unwitting Clare, 'I should have been glad to know you to be descended exclusively from the long-suffering, dumb, unrecorded rank and file of the English nation, and not from the self-seeking few who made themselves powerful at the expense of the rest. But I am corrupted away from that by my affection for you, Tess [he laughed as he spoke], and made selfish likewise. For your own sake I rejoice in your descent. Society is hopelessly snobbish, and this fact of your extraction may make an appreciable difference to its acceptance of you as my wife, after I have made you the well-read woman that I mean to make you. My mother too, poor soul, will think so much better of you on account of it. Tess, you must spell your name correctly—d'Urberville—from this very day.'

'I like the other way rather best.'

'But you *must*, dearest! Good heavens, why dozens of mushroom millionaires would jump at such a possession! By the bye, there's one of that kidney who has taken the name—where have I heard of him?—Up in the neighbourhood of The Chase, I think. Why, he is the very man who had that rumpus with my father I told you of. What an odd coincidence!'

'Angel, I think I would rather not take the name! It is unlucky, perhaps!' She was agitated.

'Now then, Mistress Teresa d'Urberville, I have you. Take my name, and so you will escape yours! The secret is out, so why should you any longer refuse me?'

'If it is *sure* to make you happy to have me as your wife, and you feel that you do wish to marry me, *very*, *very* much—'

'I do, dearest, of course!'

'I mean, that it is only your wanting me very much, and being hardly able to keep alive without me, whatever my offences, that would make me feel I ought to say I will.'

'You will—you do say it, I know! You will be mine for ever and ever.'

He clasped her close and kissed her.

'Yes!'

She had no sooner said it than she burst into a dry hard sobbing, so violent that it seemed to rend her. Tess was not a hysterical girl by any means, and he was surprised.

'Why do you cry, dearest?'

'I can't tell—quite!—I am so glad to think—of being yours, and making you happy!'

'But this does not seem very much like gladness, my Tessy!'

'I mean—I cry because I have broken down in my vow! I said I would die unmarried!'

'But, if you love me you would like me to be your husband?'

'Yes, yes, yes! But O, I sometimes wish I had never been born!'

'Now, my dear Tess, if I did not know that you are very much excited, and very inexperienced, I should say that remark was not very complimentary. How came you to wish that if you care for me? Do you care for me? I wish you would prove it in some way.'

'How can I prove it more than I have done?' she cried, in a distraction of tenderness. 'Will this prove it more?'

She clasped his neck, and for the first time Clare learnt what an impassioned woman's kisses were like upon the lips of one whom she loved with all her heart and soul, as Tess loved him.

'There—now do you believe?' she asked, flushed, and wiping her eyes.

'Yes. I never really doubted—never, never!'

So they drove on through the gloom, forming one bundle inside the sail-cloth, the horse going as he would, and the rain driving against them. She had consented. She might as well have agreed at first. The 'appetite for joy' which pervades all creation, that tremendous force which sways humanity to its purpose, as the tide sways the helpless weed, was not to be controlled by vague lucubrations over the social rubric.

'I must write to my mother,' she said. 'You don't mind my doing that?'

'Of course not, dear child. You are a child to me, Tess, not to know how very proper it is to write to your mother at such a time, and how wrong it would be in me to object. Where does she live?'

'At the same place—Marlott. On the further side of Blackmoor Vale.'

'Ah, then I *have* seen you before this summer—'

'Yes; at that dance on the green; but you would not dance with me. O, I hope that is of no ill-omen for us now!'

XXXI

Tess wrote a most touching and urgent letter to her mother the very next day, and by the end of the week a response to her communication had arrived in Joan Durbeyfield's wandering last-century hand.

> Dear Tess,—J write these few lines Hoping they will find you well, as they leave me at Present, thank God for it. Dear Tess, we are all glad to Hear that you are going really to be married soon. But with respect to your question, Tess, J say between ourselves, quite private but very strong, that on no account do you say a word of your Bygone Trouble to him. J did not tell everything to your Father, he being so Proud on account of his Respectability, which, perhaps, your Intended is the same. Many a woman—some of the Highest in the Land—have had a Trouble in their time; and why should you Trumpet yours when others don't Trumpet theirs? No girl would be such a Fool, specially as it is so long ago, and not your Fault at all. J shall answer the same if you ask me fifty times. Besides, you must bear in mind that, knowing it to be your Childish Nature to tell all that's in your heart—so simple!—J made you promise me never to let it out by Word or Deed, having your Welfare in my Mind; and you most solemnly did promise it going from this Door. J have not named either that Question or your coming marriage to your Father, as he would blab it everywhere, poor Simple Man.
>
> Dear Tess, keep up your Spirits, and we mean to send you a Hogshead of Cyder for your Wedding, knowing there is not much in your parts, and thin Sour Stuff what there is. So no more at present, and with kind love to your Young Man.—From your affectte. Mother,
>
> J. Durbeyfield

'O mother, mother!' murmured Tess.

She was recognizing how light was the touch of events the most oppressive upon Mrs Durbeyfield's elastic spirit. Her mother did not see life as Tess saw it. That haunting episode of bygone days was to her mother but a passing accident. But perhaps her mother was right as to the course to be followed, whatever she might be in her reasons. Silence seemed, on the face of it, best for her adored one's happiness: silence it should be.

Thus steadied by a command from the only person in the world who had any shadow of right to control her action, Tess grew calmer. The responsibility was shifted, and her heart was lighter than it had been for weeks. The days of declining autumn which followed her assent, beginning with the month of October, formed a season through which she lived in spiritual altitudes more nearly approaching ecstasy than any other period of her life.

There was hardly a touch of earth in her love for Clare. To her sublime trustfulness he was all that goodness could be—knew all that a guide, philosopher, and friend should know. She thought every line in the contour of his person the perfection of masculine beauty, his soul the soul of a saint, his intellect that of a seer. The wisdom of her love for him, as love, sustained her dignity; she seemed to be wearing a crown. The compassion of his love for her, as she saw it, made her lift up her heart to him in devotion. He would sometimes catch her large, worshipful eyes, that had no bottom to them, looking at him from their depths, as if she saw something immortal before her.

She dismissed the past—trod upon it and put it out, as one treads on a coal that is smouldering and dangerous.

She had not known that men could be so disinterested, chivalrous, protective, in their love for women as he. Angel Clare was far from all that she thought him in this respect; absurdly far, indeed; but he was, in truth, more spiritual than animal; he had himself well in hand, and was singularly free from grossness. Though not cold-natured, he was rather bright than hot—less Byronic than Shelleyan; could love desperately, but with a love more especially inclined to the imaginative and ethereal; it was a fastidious emotion which could jealously guard the loved one against his very self. This amazed and enraptured Tess, whose slight experiences had been so infelicitous till now; and in her reaction from indignation against the male sex she swerved to excess of honour for Clare.

They unaffectedly sought each other's company; in her honest faith she did not disguise her desire to be with him. The sum of her instincts on this matter, if clearly stated, would have been that the elusive quality in her sex which attracts men in general might be distasteful to so perfect a man after an avowal of love, since it must in its very nature carry with it a suspicion of art.

The country custom of unreserved comradeship out of doors during betrothal was the only custom she knew, and to her it had no strangeness; though it seemed oddly anticipative to Clare till he saw how normal a thing she, in common with all the other dairy-folk, regarded it. Thus, during this October month of wonderful afternoons they roved along the meads by creeping paths which followed the brinks of trickling tributary brooks, hopping across by little wooden bridges to the other side, and back again. They were never out of the sound of some purling weir, whose buzz accompanied their own murmuring, while the beams of the sun, almost as horizontal as the mead itself, formed a pollen of radiance over the landscape. They saw tiny blue fogs in the shadows of trees and hedges, all the time that there was bright sunshine elsewhere. The sun was so near the ground, and the sward so flat, that the shadows of Clare and Tess would stretch a quarter of a mile ahead of them, like two long fingers pointing afar to where the green alluvial reaches abutted against the sloping sides of the vale.

Men were at work here and there—for it was the season for 'taking up' the meadows, or digging the little waterways clear for the winter irrigation, and mending their banks where trodden down by the cows. The shovelfuls of loam, black as jet, brought there by the river when it was as wide as the whole valley, were an essence of soils, pounded champaigns of the past, steeped, refined, and subtilized to extraordinary richness, out of which came all the fertility of the mead, and of the cattle grazing there.

Clare hardily kept his arm round her waist in sight of these watermen, with the air of a man who was accustomed to public dalliance, though actually as shy as she who, with lips parted and eyes askance on the labourers, wore the look of a wary animal the while.

'You are not ashamed of owning me as yours before them!' she said gladly.

'O no!'

'But if it should reach the ears of your friends at Emminster that you are walking about like this with me, a milkmaid—'

'The most bewitching milkmaid ever seen.'

'They might feel it a hurt to their dignity.'

'My dear girl—a d'Urberville hurt the dignity of a Clare! It is a grand card to play—that of your belonging to such a family, and I am reserving it for a grand effect when we are married, and have the proofs of your descent from Parson Tringham. Apart from that, my future is to be totally foreign to my family—it will not affect even the surface of their lives. We shall leave this part of England—perhaps England itself—and what does it matter how people regard us here? You will like going, will you not?'

She could answer no more than a bare affirmative, so great was the emotion aroused in her at the thought of going through the world with him as his own familiar friend. Her feelings almost filled her ears like a babble of waves, and surged up to her eyes. She put her hand in his, and thus they went on, to a place where the reflected sun glared up from the river, under a bridge, with a molten-metallic glow that dazzled their eyes, though the sun itself was hidden by the bridge. They stood still, whereupon little furred and feathered heads popped up from the smooth surface of the water; but, finding that the disturbing presences had paused, and not passed by, they disappeared again. Upon this river-brink they lingered till the fog began to close round them—which was very early in the evening at this time of the year—settling on the lashes of her eyes, where it rested like crystals, and on his brows and hair.

They walked later on Sundays, when it was quite dark. Some of the dairy-people, who were also out of doors on the first Sunday evening after their engagement, heard her impulsive speeches, ecstasized to fragments, though they were too far off to hear the words discoursed; noted the spasmodic catch in her remarks, broken into syllables by the leapings of her heart, as she walked leaning on his arm; her contented pauses, the occasional little laugh upon which her soul seemed to ride—the laugh of a woman in company with the man she loves and has won from all other women—unlike anything else in nature. They marked the buoyancy of her tread, like the skim of a bird which has not quite alighted.

Her affection for him was now the breath and life of Tess's being; it enveloped her as a photosphere, irradiated her into forgetfulness of her past sorrows, keeping back the gloomy spectres that would persist in their attempts to touch her—doubt, fear, moodiness, care, shame. She knew that they were waiting like wolves just outside the circumscribing light, but she had long spells of power to keep them in hungry subjection there.

A spiritual forgetfulness co-existed with an intellectual remembrance. She walked in brightness, but she knew that in the background those shapes of darkness were always spread. They might be receding, or they might be approaching, one or the other, a little every day.

One evening Tess and Clare were obliged to sit indoors keeping house, all the other occupants of the domicile being away. As they talked she looked thoughtfully up at him, and met his two appreciative eyes.

'I am not worthy of you—no, I am not!' she burst out, jumping up from her low stool as though appalled at his homage, and the fulness of her own joy thereat.

Clare, deeming the whole basis of her excitement to be that which was only the smaller part of it, said—

'I won't have you speak like it, dear Tess! Distinction does not consist in the facile use of a contemptible set of conventions, but in being numbered among those who are true, and honest, and just, and pure, and lovely, and of good report—as you are, my Tess.'

She struggled with the sob in her throat. How often had that string of excellences made her young heart ache in church of late years, and how strange that he should have cited them now.

'Why didn't you stay and love me when I—was sixteen; living with my little sisters and brothers, and you danced on the green?

O, why didn't you, why didn't you!' she said, impetuously clasping her hands.

Angel began to comfort and reassure her, thinking to himself, truly enough, what a creature of moods she was, and how careful he would have to be of her when she depended for her happiness entirely on him.

'Ah—why didn't I stay!' he said. 'That is just what I feel. If I had only known! But you must not be so bitter in your regret—why should you be?'

With the woman's instinct to hide she diverged hastily—

'I should have had four years more of your heart than I can ever have now. Then I should not have wasted my time as I have done—I should have had so much longer happiness!'

It was no mature woman with a long dark vista of intrigue behind her who was tormented thus; but a girl of simple life, not yet one-and-twenty, who had been caught during her days of immaturity like a bird in a springe. To calm herself the more completely she rose from her little stool and left the room, overturning the stool with her skirts as she went.

He sat on by the cheerful firelight thrown from a bundle of green ash-sticks laid across the dogs; the sticks snapped pleasantly, and hissed out bubbles of sap from their ends. When she came back she was herself again.

'Do you not think you are just a wee bit capricious, fitful, Tess?' he said, good humouredly, as he spread a cushion for her on the stool, and seated himself in the settle beside her. 'I wanted to ask you something, and just then you ran away.'

'Yes, perhaps I am capricious,' she murmured. She suddenly approached him, and put a hand upon each of his arms. 'No, Angel, I am not really so—by Nature, I mean!' The more particularly to assure him that she was not, she placed herself close to him in the settle, and allowed her head to find a resting place against Clare's shoulder. 'What did you want to ask me—I am sure I will answer it,' she continued humbly.

'Well, you love me, and have agreed to marry me, and hence there follows a thirdly, "When shall the day be?" '

'I like living like this.'

'But I must think of starting in business on my own hook with the new year, or a little later. And before I get involved in the multifarious details of my new position, I should like to have secured my partner.'

'But,' she timidly answered, 'to talk quite practically, wouldn't it be best not to marry till after all that?—Though I can't bear the thought o' your going away and leaving me here!'

'Of course you cannot—and it is not best in this case. I want you to help me in many ways in making my start. When shall it be? Why not a fortnight from now?'

'No,' she said, becoming grave; 'I have so many things to think of first.'

'But—'

He drew her gently nearer to him.

The reality of marriage was startling when it loomed so near. Before discussion of the question had proceeded further there walked round the corner of the settle into the full firelight of the apartment Mr Dairyman Crick, Mrs Crick, and two of the milkmaids.

Tess sprang like an elastic ball from his side to her feet, while her face flushed and her eyes shone in the firelight.

'I knew how it would be if I sat so close to him!' she cried, with vexation. 'I said to myself, they are sure to come and catch us! But I wasn't really sitting on his knee, though it might ha' seemed as if I was almost!'

'Well—if so be you hadn't told us, I am sure we shouldn't ha' noticed that ye had been sitting anywhere at all in this light,' replied the dairyman. He continued to his wife, with the stolid mien of a man who understood nothing of the emotions relating to matrimony—'Now, Christianer, that shows that folks should never fancy other folks be supposing things when they bain't. O no, I should never ha' thought a word of where she was a sitting to, if she hadn't told me—not I.'

'We are going to be married soon,' said Clare, with improvised phlegm.

'Ah—and be ye! Well, I am truly glad to hear it, sir. I've thought you mid do such a thing for some time. She's too good for a dairymaid—I said so the very first day I zid her—and a prize for any man; and what's more, a wonderful woman for a gentleman-farmer's wife; he won't be at the mercy of his baily wi'her at his side.'

Somehow Tess disappeared. She had been even more struck with the look of the girls who followed Crick than abashed by Crick's blunt praise.

After supper, when she reached her bedroom, they were all present. A light was burning, and each damsel was sitting up whitely in her bed, awaiting Tess, the whole like a row of avenging ghosts.

But she saw in a few moments that there was no malice in their mood. They could scarcely feel as a loss what they had never expected to have. Their condition was objective, contemplative.

'He's going to marry her!' murmured Retty, never taking eyes off Tess. 'How her face do show it!'

'You *be* going to marry him?' asked Marian.

'Yes,' said Tess.

'When?'

'Some day.'

They thought that this was evasiveness only.

'*Yes*—going to *marry* him—a gentleman!' repeated Izz Huett.

And by a sort of fascination the three girls, one after another, crept out of their beds, and came and stood barefooted round Tess. Retty put her hands upon Tess's shoulders, as if to realize her friend's corporeality after such a miracle, and the other two laid their arms round her waist, all looking into her face.

'How it do seem! Almost more than I can think of!' said Izz Huett.

Marian kissed Tess. 'Yes,' she murmured as she withdrew her lips.

'Was that because of love for her, or because other lips have touched there by now?' continued Izz drily to Marian.

'I wasn't thinking o' that,' said Marian simply. 'I was on'y feeling all the strangeness o't—that she is to be his wife, and nobody else. I don't say nay to it, nor either of us, because we did not think of it—only loved him. Still, nobody else is to marry'n in the world—no fine lady, nobody in silks and satins; but she who do live like we.'

'Are you sure you don't dislike me for it?' said Tess in a low voice.

They hung about her in their white nightgowns before replying, as if they considered their answer might lie in her look.

'I don't know—I don't know,' murmured Retty Priddle. 'I want to hate 'ee; but I cannot!'

'That's how I feel,' echoed Izz and Marian. 'I can't hate her. Somehow she hinders me!'

'He ought to marry one of you,' murmured Tess.

'Why?'

'You are all better than I.'

'We better than you?' said the girls in a low, slow whisper. 'No, no, dear Tess!'

'You are!' she contradicted impetuously. And suddenly tearing away from their clinging arms she burst into a hysterical fit of tears, bowing herself on the chest of drawers and repeating incessantly, 'O yes, yes, yes!'

Having once given way she could not stop her weeping.

'He ought to have had one of you!' she cried. 'I think I ought to make him even now! You would be better for him than—I don't know what I'm saying! O! O!'

They went up to her and clasped her round, but still her sobs tore her.

'Get some water,' said Marian. 'She's upset by us, poor thing, poor thing!'

They gently led her back to the side of her bed, where they kissed her warmly.

'You are best for'n,' said Marian. 'More ladylike, and a better scholar than we, especially since he has taught 'ee so much. But even you ought to be proud. You *be* proud, I'm sure!'

'Yes, I am,' said she; 'and I am ashamed at so breaking down!'

When they were all in bed, and the light was out, Marian whispered across to her—

'You will think of us when you be his wife, Tess, and of how we told 'ee that we loved him, and how we tried not to hate you, and did not hate you, and could not hate you, because you were his choice, and we never hoped to be chose by him.'

They were not aware that, at these words, salt, stinging tears trickled down upon Tess's pillow anew, and how she resolved, with a bursting heart, to tell all her history to Angel Clare, despite her mother's command—to let him for whom she lived and breathed despise her if he would, and her mother regard her as a fool, rather than preserve a silence which might be deemed a treachery to him, and which somehow seemed a wrong to these.

XXXII

THIS penitential mood kept her from naming the wedding-day. The beginning of November found its date still in abeyance, though he asked her at the most tempting times. But Tess's desire seemed to be for a perpetual betrothal in which everything should remain as it was then.

The meads were changing now; but it was still warm enough in early afternoons before milking to idle there awhile, and the state of dairy-work at this time of year allowed a spare hour for idling. Looking over the damp sod in the direction of the sun, a glistening ripple of gossamer webs was visible to their eyes under the luminary, like the track of moonlight on the sea. Gnats, knowing nothing of their brief glorification, wandered across the shimmer of this pathway, irradiated as if they bore fire within them, then passed out of its line, and were quite extinct. In the presence of these things he would remind her that the date was still the question.

Or he would ask her at night, when he accompanied her on some mission invented by Mrs Crick to give him the opportunity. This was mostly a journey to the farmhouse on the slopes above the vale, to inquire how the advanced cows were getting on in the straw-barton to which they were relegated. For it was a time of the year that brought great changes to the world of kine. Batches of the animals were sent away daily to their lying-in hospital, where they lived on straw till their calves were born, after which event, and as soon as the calf could walk, mother and offspring were driven back to the dairy. In the interval which elapsed before the calves were sold there was, of course, little milking to be done, but as soon as the calf had been taken away the milkmaids would have to set to work as usual.

Returning from one of these dark walks they reached a great gravel-cliff immediately over the levels, where they stood still and listened. The water was now high in the streams, squirting through the weirs, and tinkling under culverts; the smallest gullies were all full; there was no taking short cuts anywhere, and foot-passengers were compelled to follow the permanent ways. From the whole extent of the invisible vale came a multitudinous intonation; it forced upon their fancy that a great city lay below them, and that the murmur was the vociferation of its populace.

'It seems like tens of thousands of them,' said Tess; 'holding public-meetings in their market-places, arguing, preaching, quarrelling, sobbing, groaning, praying, and cursing.'

Clare was not particularly heeding.

'Did Crick speak to you to-day, dear, about his not wanting much assistance during the winter months?'

'No.'

'The cows are going dry rapidly.'

'Yes. Six or seven went to the straw-barton yesterday, and three the day before, making nearly twenty in the straw already. Ah—is it that the farmer don't want my help for the calving? O, I am not wanted here any more! And I have tried so hard to—'

'Crick didn't exactly say that he would no longer require you. But, knowing what our relations were, he said in the most good-natured and respectful manner possible that he supposed on my leaving at Christmas I should take you with me, and on my asking what he would do without you he merely observed that, as a matter of fact, it was a time of year when he could do with a very little female help. I am afraid I was sinner enough to feel rather glad that he was in this way forcing your hand.'

'I don't think you ought to have felt glad, Angel. Because 'tis always mournful not to be wanted, even if at the same time 'tis convenient.'

'Well, it is convenient—you have admitted that.' He put his finger upon her cheek. 'Ah!' he said.

'What?'

'I feel the red rising up at her having been caught! But why should I trifle so! We will not trifle—life is too serious.'

'It is. Perhaps I saw that before you did.'

She was seeing it then. To decline to marry him after all—in obedience to her emotion of last night—and leave the dairy, meant to go to some strange place, not a dairy; for milkmaids were not in request now calving-time was coming on; to go to some arable farm where no divine being like Angel Clare was. She hated the thought, and she hated more the thought of going home.

'So that, seriously, dearest Tess,' he continued, 'since you will probably have to leave at Christmas, it is in every way desirable and convenient that I should carry you off then as my property. Besides, if you were not the most uncalculating girl in the world you would know that we could not go on like this for ever.'

'I wish we could. That it would always be summer and autumn, and you always courting me, and always thinking as much of me as you have done through the past summer-time!'

'I always shall.'

'O, I know you will!' she cried, with a sudden fervour of faith in him. 'Angel, I will fix the day when I will become yours for always!'

Thus at last it was arranged between them, during that dark walk home, amid the myriads of liquid voices on the right and left.

When they reached the dairy Mr and Mrs Crick were promptly told—with injunctions to secrecy; for each of the lovers was desirous that the marriage should be kept as private as possible. The dairyman, though he had thought of dismissing her soon, now made a great concern about losing her. What should he do about his skimming? Who would make the ornamental butter-pats for the Anglebury and Sandbourne ladies? Mrs Crick congratulated Tess on the shilly-shallying having at last come to an end, and said that directly she set eyes on Tess she divined that she was to be the chosen one of somebody who was no common outdoor man; Tess had looked so superior as she walked across the barton on that afternoon of her arrival; that she was of a good family she could have sworn. In point of fact Mrs Crick did remember thinking that Tess was graceful and good-looking as she approached; but the superiority might have been a growth of the imagination aided by subsequent knowledge.

Tess was now carried along upon the wings of the hours, without the sense of a will. The word had been given; the number of the day written down. Her naturally bright intelligence had begun to admit the fatalistic convictions common to field-folk and those who associate more extensively with natural phenomena than with their fellow-creatures; and she accordingly drifted into that passive responsiveness to all things her lover suggested, characteristic of the frame of mind.

But she wrote anew to her mother, ostensibly to notify the wedding-day; really to again implore her advice. It was a gentleman who had chosen her, which perhaps her mother had not sufficiently considered. A post-nuptial explanation, which might be accepted with a light heart by a rougher man, might not be received with the same feeling by him. But this communication brought no reply from Mrs Durbeyfield.

Despite Angel Clare's plausible representations to himself and to Tess of the practical need for their immediate marriage, there was in truth an element of precipitancy in the step, as became apparent at a later date. He loved her dearly, though perhaps rather ideally and fancifully than with the impassioned thoroughness of her feeling for him. He had entertained no notion, when doomed as he had thought to an unintellectual bucolic life, that such charms as he beheld in this idyllic creature would be found behind the scenes. Unsophistication was a thing to talk of; but he had not known how it really struck one until he came here. Yet he was very far from seeing his future track clearly, and it might be a year or two before he would be able to consider himself fairly started in life. The secret lay in the tinge of recklessness imparted to his career and character by the sense that he had been made to miss his true destiny through the prejudices of his family.

'Don't you think 'twould have been better for us to wait till you were quite settled in your midland farm?' she once asked timidly. (A midland farm was the idea just then.)

'To tell the truth, my Tess, I don't like you to be left anywhere away from my protection and sympathy.'

The reason was a good one, so far as it went. His influence over her had been so marked that she had caught his manner and habits, his speech and phrases, his likings and his aversions. And to leave her in farmland would be to let her slip back again out of accord with him. He wished to have her under his charge for another reason. His parents had naturally desired to see her once at least before he carried her off to a distant settlement, English or colonial; and as no opinion of theirs was to be allowed to change his intention, he judged that a couple of months' life with him in lodgings whilst seeking for an advantageous opening would be of some social assistance to her at what she might feel to be a trying ordeal—her presentation to his mother at the Vicarage.

Next, he wished to see a little of the working of a flour-mill, having an idea that he might combine the use of one with corn-growing. The proprietor of a large old water-mill at Wellbridge—once the mill of an Abbey—had offered him the inspection of his time-honoured mode of procedure, and a hand in the operations for a few days, whenever he should choose to come. Clare paid a visit to the place, some few miles distant, one day at this time, to inquire particulars, and returned to Talbothays in the evening. She found him determined to spend a short time at the Wellbridge flour-mills. And what had determined him? Less the opportunity of an insight into grinding and bolting than the casual fact that lodgings were to be obtained in that very farmhouse which, before its mutilation, had been the mansion of a branch of the d'Urberville family. This was always how Clare settled practical questions; by a sentiment which had nothing to do with them. They decided to go immediately after the wedding, and remain for a fortnight, instead of journeying to towns and inns.

'Then we will start off to examine some farms on the other side of London that I have heard of,' he said, 'and by March or April we will pay a visit to my father and mother.'

Questions of procedure such as these arose and passed, and the day, the incredible day, on which she was to become his, loomed large in the near future. The thirty-first of December, New Year's Eve, was the date. His wife, she said to herself. Could it ever be? Their two selves together, nothing to divide them, every incident shared by them; why not? And yet why?

One Sunday morning Izz Huett returned from church, and spoke privately to Tess.

'You was not called home* this morning.'

'What?'

'It should ha' been the first time of asking to-day,' she answered, looking quietly at Tess. 'You meant to be married New Year's Eve, deary?'

The other returned a quick affirmative.

'And there must be three times of asking. And now there be only two Sundays left between.'

Tess felt her cheek paling; Izz was right; of course there must be three. Perhaps he had forgotten! If so, there must be a week's postponement, and that was unlucky. How could she remind her lover? She who had been so backward, was suddenly fired with impatience and alarm lest she should lose her dear prize.

A natural incident relieved her anxiety. Izz mentioned the omission of the banns to Mrs Crick, and Mrs Crick assumed a matron's privilege of speaking to Angel on the point.

'Have ye forgot 'em, Mr Clare? The banns, I mean.'

'No, I have not forgot 'em,' says Clare.

As soon as he caught Tess alone he assured her:

'Don't let them tease you about the banns. A licence will be quieter for us, and I have decided on a licence without consulting you. So if you go to church on Sunday morning you will not hear your own name, if you wished to.'

'I didn't wish to hear it, dearest,' she said proudly.

But to know that things were in train was an immense relief to Tess notwithstanding, who had well-nigh feared that somebody would stand up and forbid the banns on the ground of her history. How events were favouring her!

'I don't quite feel easy,' she said to herself. 'All this good fortune may be scourged out of me afterwards by a lot of ill. That's how Heaven mostly does. I wish I could have had common banns!'

But everything went smoothly. She wondered whether he would like her to be married in her present best white frock, or if she ought to buy a new one. The question was set at rest by his forethought, disclosed by the arrival of some large packages

* 'Called home'—local phrase for publication of banns.

addressed to her. Inside them she found a whole stock of clothing, from bonnet to shoes, including a perfect morning costume, such as would well suit the simple wedding they planned. He entered the house shortly after the arrival of the packages, and heard her upstairs undoing them.

A minute later she came down with a flush on her face and tears in her eyes.

'How thoughtful you've been!' she murmured, her cheek upon his shoulder. 'Even to the gloves and handkerchief! My own love—how good, how kind!'

'No, no, Tess; just an order to a tradeswoman in London—nothing more.'

And to divert her from thinking too highly of him he told her to go upstairs, and take her time, and see if it all fitted; and, if not, to get the village sempstress to make a few alterations.

She did return upstairs, and put on the gown. Alone, she stood for a moment before the glass looking at the effect of her silk attire; and then there came into her head her mother's ballad of the mystic robe—

> That never would become that wife
> That had once done amiss,

which Mrs Durbeyfield had used to sing to her as a child, so blithely and so archly, her foot on the cradle, which she rocked to the tune. Suppose this robe should betray her by changing colour, as her robe had betrayed Queen Guénever. Since she had been at the dairy she had not thought of the lines till now.

XXXIII

Angel felt that he would like to spend a day with her before the wedding, somewhere away from the dairy, as a last jaunt in her company while they were yet mere lover and mistress; a romantic day, in circumstances that would never be repeated; with that other and greater day beaming close ahead of them. During the preceding week, therefore, he suggested making a few purchases in the nearest town, and they started together.

Clare's life at the dairy had been that of a recluse in respect to the world of his own class. For months he had never gone near a town, and, requiring no vehicle, had never kept one, hiring the dairyman's cob or gig if he rode or drove. They went in the gig that day.

And then for the first time in their lives they shopped as partners in one concern. It was Christmas Eve, with its loads of holly and mistletoe, and the town was very full of strangers who had come in from all parts of the country on account of the day. Tess paid the penalty of walking about with happiness superadded to beauty on her countenance by being much stared at as she moved amid them on his arm.

In the evening they returned to the inn at which they had put up, and Tess waited in the entry while Angel went to see the horse and gig brought to the door. The general sitting-room was full of guests, who were continually going in and out. As the door opened and shut each time for the passage of these, the light within the parlour fell full upon Tess's face. Two men came out and passed by her among the rest. One of them had stared her up and down in surprise, and she fancied he was a Trantridge man, though that village lay so many miles off that Trantridge folk were rarities here.

'A comely maid that,' said the other.

'True, comely enough. But unless I make a great mistake—' And he negatived the remainder of the definition forthwith.

Clare had just returned from the stable-yard, and, confronting the man on the threshold, heard the words, and saw the shrinking of Tess. The insult to her stung him to the quick, and before he had considered anything at all he struck the man on the chin with the full force of his fist, sending him staggering backwards into the passage.

The man recovered himself, and seemed inclined to come on, and Clare, stepping outside the door, put himself in a posture of defence. But his opponent began to think better of the matter. He looked anew at Tess as he passed her, and said to Clare—

'I beg pardon, sir; 'twas a complete mistake. I thought she was another woman, forty miles from here.'

Clare, feeling then that he had been too hasty, and that he was, moreover, to blame for leaving her standing in an inn-passage, did what he usually did in such cases, gave the man five shillings to plaster the blow; and thus they parted, bidding each other a pacific good-night. As soon as Clare had taken the reins from the ostler, and the young couple had driven off, the two men went in the other direction.

'And was it a mistake?' said the second one.

'Not a bit of it. But I didn't want to hurt the gentleman's feelings—not I.'

In the meantime the lovers were driving onward.

'Could we put off our wedding till a little later?' Tess asked in a dry dull voice. 'I mean if we wished?'

'No, my love. Calm yourself. Do you mean that the fellow may have time to summon me for assault?' he asked good-humouredly.

'No—I only meant—if it should have to be put off.'

What she meant was not very clear, and he directed her to dismiss such fancies from her mind, which she obediently did as well as she could. But she was grave, very grave, all the way home; till she thought, 'We shall go away, a very long distance, hundreds of miles from these parts, and such as this can never happen again, and no ghost of the past reach there.'

They parted tenderly that night on the landing, and Clare ascended to his attic. Tess sat up getting on with some little requisites, lest the few remaining days should not afford sufficient time.

While she sat she heard a noise in Angel's room overhead, a sound of thumping and struggling. Everybody else in the house was asleep, and in her anxiety lest Clare should be ill she ran up and knocked at his door, and asked him what was the matter.

'Oh, nothing dear,' he said from within. 'I am so sorry I disturbed you! But the reason is rather an amusing one: I fell asleep and dreamt that I was fighting that fellow again who insulted you and the noise you heard was my pummelling away with my fists at my portmanteau, which I pulled out to-day for packing. I am occasionally liable to these freaks in my sleep. Go to bed and think of it no more.'

This was the last drachm required to turn the scale of her indecision. Declare the past to him by word of mouth she could not; but there was another way. She sat down and wrote on the four pages of a note-sheet a succinct narrative of those events of three or four years ago, put it into an envelope, and directed it to Clare. Then, lest the flesh should again be weak, she crept upstairs without any shoes and slipped the note under his door.

Her night was a broken one, as it well might be, and she listened for the first faint noise overhead. It came, as usual; he descended, as usual. She descended. He met her at the bottom of the stairs and kissed her. Surely it was as warmly as ever!

He looked a little disturbed and worn, she thought. But he said not a word to her about her revelation, even when they were alone. Could he have had it? Unless he began the subject she felt that she could say nothing. So the day passed, and it was evident that whatever he thought he meant to keep to himself. Yet he was frank and affectionate as before. Could it be that her doubts were childish? that he forgave her; that he loved her for what she was, just as she was, and smiled at her disquiet as at a foolish nightmare? Had he really received her note? She glanced into his room, and could see nothing of it. It might be that he forgave her. But even if he had not received it she had a sudden enthusiastic trust that he surely would forgive her.

Every morning and night he was the same, and thus New Year's Eve broke—the wedding-day.

The lovers did not rise at milking-time, having through the whole of this last week of their sojourn at the dairy been accorded something of the position of guests, Tess being honoured with a room of her own. When they arrived downstairs at breakfast-time they were surprised to see what effects had been produced in the large kitchen for their glory since they had last beheld it. At some unnatural hour of the morning the dairyman has caused the yawning chimney-corner to be whitened, and the brick hearth reddened, and a blazing yellow damask blower to be hung across the arch in place of the old grimy blue cotton one with a black sprig pattern which had formerly done duty here. This renovated aspect of what was the focus indeed of the room on a dull winter morning, threw a smiling demeanour over the whole apartment.

'I was determined to do summat in honour o't,' said the dairyman. 'And as you wouldn't hear of my gieing a rattling good randy wi' fiddles and bass-viols complete, as we should ha' done in old times, this was all I could think o' as a noiseless thing.'

Tess's friends lived so far off that none could conveniently have been present at the ceremony, even had any been asked; but as a fact nobody was invited from Marlott. As for Angel's family, he had written and duly informed them of the time, and assured them that he would be glad to see one at least of them there for the day if he would like to come. His brothers had not replied at all, seeming to be indignant with him; while his father and mother had written a rather sad letter, deploring his precipitancy in rushing into marriage, but making the best of the matter by saying that, though a dairywoman was the last daughter-in-law they could have expected, their son had arrived at an age at which he might be supposed to be the best judge.

This coolness in his relations distressed Clare less than it would have done had he been without the grand card with which he meant to surprise them ere long. To produce Tess, fresh from the dairy, as a d'Urberville and a lady, he had felt to be temerarious and risky; hence he had concealed her lineage till such time as, familiarized with wordly ways by a few months' travel and reading with him, he could take her on a visit to his parents, and impart the knowledge while triumphantly producing her as worthy of such an ancient line. It was a pretty lover's dream, if no more. Perhaps Tess's lineage had more value for himself than for anybody in the world besides.

Her perception that Angel's bearing towards her still remained in no whit altered by her own communication rendered Tess guiltily doubtful if he could have received it. She rose from breakfast before he had finished, and hastened upstairs. It had occurred to her to look once more into the queer gaunt room which had been Clare's den, or rather eyrie, for so long, and climbing the ladder she stood at the open door of the apartment, regarding and pondering. She stooped to the threshold of the doorway, where she had pushed in the note two or three days earlier in such excitement. The carpet reached close to the sill, and under the edge of the carpet she discerned the faint white margin of the envelope containing her letter to him, which he obviously had never seen, owing to her having in her haste thrust it beneath the carpet as well as beneath the door.

With a feeling of faintness she withdrew the letter. There it was—sealed up, just as it had left her hands. The mountain had not yet been removed. She could not let him read it now, the house being in full bustle of preparation; and descending to her own room she destroyed the letter there.

She was so pale when he saw her again that he felt quite anxious. The incident of the misplaced letter she had jumped at as if it prevented a confession; but she knew in her conscience that it need not; there was still time. Yet everything was in a stir; there was coming and going; all had to dress, the dairyman and Mrs Crick having been asked to accompany them as witnesses; and reflection or deliberate talk was well-nigh impossible. The only minute Tess could get to be alone with Clare was when they met upon the landing.

'I am so anxious to talk to you—I want to confess all my faults and blunders!' she said with attempted lightness.

'No, no—we can't have faults talked of—you must be deemed perfect to-day at least, my Sweet!' he cried. 'We shall have plenty of time, hereafter, I hope, to talk over our failings. I will confess mine at the same time.'

'But it would be better for me to do it now, I think, so that you could not say—'

'Well, my quixotic one, you shall tell me anything—say, as soon as we are settled in our lodging; not now. I, too, will tell you my faults then. But do not let us spoil the day with them; they will be excellent matter for a dull time.'

'Then you don't wish me to, dearest?'

'I do not, Tessy, really.'

The hurry of dressing and starting left no time for more than this. Those words of his seemed to reassure her on further reflection. She was whirled onward through the next couple of critical hours by the mastering tide of her devotion to him, which closed up further meditation. Her one desire, so long resisted, to make herself his, to call him her lord, her own—then, if necessary, to die—had at last lifted her up from her plodding reflective pathway. In dressing, she moved about in a mental cloud of many-coloured idealities, which eclipsed all sinister contingencies by its brightness.

The church was a long way off, and they were obliged to drive, particularly as it was winter. A close carriage was ordered from a roadside inn, a vehicle which had been kept there ever since the old days of post-chaise travelling. It had stout wheel-spokes, and heavy felloes, a great curved bed, immense straps and springs, and a pole like a battering-ram. The postilion was a venerable 'boy' of sixty—a martyr to rheumatic gout, the result of excessive exposure in youth, counteracted by strong liquors—who had stood at inn-doors doing nothing for the whole five-and-twenty years that had elapsed since he had no longer been required to ride professionally, as if expecting the old times to come back again. He had a permanent running wound on the outside of his right leg, originated by the constant bruisings of aristocratic carriage-poles during the many years that he had been in regular employ at the King's Arms, Casterbridge.

Inside this cumbrous and creaking structure, and behind this decayed conductor, the *partie carrée* took their seats—the bride and bridegroom and Mr and Mrs Crick. Angel would have liked one at least of his brothers to be present as groomsman, but their silence after his gentle hint to that effect by letter had signified that they did not care to come. They disapproved of the marriage, and could not be expected to countenance it. Perhaps it was as well that they could not be present. They were not worldly young fellow, but fraternizing with dairy-folk would have struck unpleasantly upon their biassed niceness, apart from their views of the match.

Upheld by the momentum of the time Tess knew nothing of this; did not see anything; did not know the road they were taking to the church. She knew that Angel was close to her; all the rest was a luminous mist. She was a sort of celestial person, who owed her being to poetry—one of those classical divinities Clare was accustomed to talk to her about when they took their walks together.

The marriage being by licence there were only a dozen or so of people in the church; had there been a thousand they would have produced no more effect upon her. They were at stellar distances from her present world. In the ecstatic solemnity with which she swore her faith to him the ordinary sensibilities of sex seemed a flippancy. At a pause in the service, while they were kneeling together, she unconsciously inclined herself towards him, so that her shoulder touched his arm; she had been frightened by a passing thought, and the movement had been automatic, to assure herself that he was really there, and to fortify her belief that his fidelity would be proof against all things.

Clare knew that she loved him—every curve of her form showed that—but he did not know at that time the full depth of her devotion, its single-mindedness, its meekness; what long-suffering it guaranteed, what honesty, what endurance, what good faith.

As they came out of church the ringers swung the bells off their rests, and a modest peal of three notes broke forth—that limited amount of expression having been deemed sufficient by the church builders for the joys of such a small parish. Passing by the tower with her husband on the path to the gate she could feel the vibrant air humming round them from the louvred belfry in a circle of sound, and it matched the highly-charged mental atmosphere in which she was living.

This condition of mind, wherein she felt glorified by an irradiation not her own, like the angel whom St John saw in the sun, lasted till the sound of the church bells had died away, and the emotions of the wedding-service had calmed down. Her eyes could dwell upon details more clearly now, and Mr and Mrs Crick having directed their own gig to be sent for them, to leave the carriage to the young couple, she observed the build and character of that conveyance for the first time. Sitting in silence she regarded it long.

'I fancy you seem oppressed, Tessy,' said Clare.

'Yes,' she answered, putting her hand to her brow. 'I tremble at many things. It is all so serious, Angel. Among other things I seem to have seen this carriage before, to be very well acquainted with it. It is very odd—I must have seen it in a dream.'

'Oh—you have heard the legend of the d'Urberville Coach—that well-known superstition of this county about your family when they were very popular here; and this lumbering old thing reminds you of it.'

'I have never heard of it to my knowledge,' said she. 'What is the legend—may I know it?'

'Well—I would rather not tell it in detail just now. A certain d'Urberville of the sixteenth or seventeenth century committed a dreadful crime in his family coach; and since that time members of the family see or hear the old coach whenever—But I'll tell you another day—it is rather gloomy. Evidently some dim knowledge of it has been brought back to your mind by the sight of this venerable caravan.'

'I don't remember hearing it before,' she murmured. 'Is it when we are going to die, Angel, that members of my family see it, or is it when we have committed a crime?'

'Now, Tess!'

He silenced her by a kiss.

By the time they reached home she was contrite and spiritless. She was Mrs Angel Clare, indeed, but had she any moral right to the name? Was she not more truly Mrs Alexander d'Urberville? Could intensity of love justify what might be considered in upright souls as culpable reticence? She knew not what was expected of women in such cases; and she had no counsellor.

However, when she found herself alone in her room for a few

minutes—the last day this on which she was ever to enter it—she knelt down and prayed. She tried to pray to God, but it was her husband who really had her supplication. Her idolatry of this man was such that she herself almost feared it to be ill-omened. She was conscious of the notion expressed by Friar Laurence: 'These violent delights have violent ends.' It might be too desperate for human conditions—too rank, too wild, too deadly.

'O my love, my love, why do I love you so!' she whispered there alone; 'for she you love is not my real self, but one in my image; the one I might have been!'

Afternoon came, and with it the hour for departure. They had decided to fulfil the plan of going for a few days to the lodgings in the old farmhouse near Wellbridge Mill, at which he meant to reside during his investigation of flour processes. At two o'clock there was nothing left to do but to start. All the servantry of the dairy were standing in the red-brick entry to see them go out, the dairyman and his wife following to the door. Tess saw her three chamber mates in a row against the wall, pensively inclining their heads. She had much questioned if they would appear at the parting moment; but there they were, stoical and staunch to the last. She knew why the delicate Retty looked so fragile, and Izz so tragically sorrowful, and Marian so blank; and she forgot her own dogging shadow for a moment in contemplating theirs.

She impulsively whispered to him—

'Will you kiss 'em all, once, poor things, for the first and last time?'

Clare had not the least objection to such a farewell formality—which was all that it was to him—and as he passed them he kissed them in succession where they stood, saying 'Goodbye' to each as he did so. When they reached the door Tess femininely glanced back to discern the effect of that kiss of charity; there was no triumph in her glance, as there might have been. If there had it would have disappeared when she saw how moved the girls all were. The kiss had obviously done harm by awakening feelings they were trying to subdue.

Of all this Clare was unconscious. Passing on to the wicket-gate he shook hands with the dairyman and his wife, and expressed his last thanks to them for their attentions; after which there was a moment of silence before they had moved off. It was interrupted by the crowing of a cock. The white one with the rose comb had come and settled on the palings in front of the house, within a few yards of them, and his notes thrilled their ears through, dwindling away like echoes down a valley of rocks.

'Oh?' said Mrs Crick. 'An afternoon crow!'

Two men were standing by the yard gate, holding it open.

'That's bad,' one murmured to the other, not thinking that the words could be heard by the group at the door-wicket.

The cock crew again—straight towards Clare.

'Well!' said the dairyman.

'I don't like to hear him!' said Tess to her husband. 'Tell the man to drive on. Good-bye, good-bye!'

The cock crew again.

'Hoosh! Just you be off, sir, or I'll twist your neck!' said the dairyman with some irritation, turning to the bird and driving him away. And to his wife as they went indoors: 'Now, to think o' that just to-day! I've not heard his crow of an afternoon all the year afore.'

'It only means a change in the weather,' said she; 'not what you think: 'tis impossible!'

XXXIV

THEY drove by the level road along the valley to a distance of a few miles, and, reaching Wellbridge, turned away from the village to the left, and over the great Elizabethan bridge which gives the place half its name. Immediately behind it stood the house wherein they had engaged lodgings, whose exterior features are so well known to all travellers through the Froom Valley; once portion of a fine manorial residence, and the property and seat of a d'Urberville, but since its partial demolition a farm-house.

'Welcome to one of your ancestral mansions!' said Clare as he handed her down. But he regretted the pleasantry; it was too near a satire.

On entering they found that, though they had only engaged a couple of rooms, the farmer had taken advantage of their proposed presence during the coming days to pay a New Year's visit to some friends, leaving a woman from a neighbouring cottage to minister to their few wants. The absoluteness of possession pleased them, and they realized it as the first moment of their experience under their own exclusive rooftree.

But he found that the mouldy old habitation somewhat depressed his bride. When the carriage was gone they ascended the stairs to wash their hands, the charwoman showing the way. On the landing Tess stopped and started.

'What's the matter?' said he.

'Those horrid women!' she answered, with a smile. 'How they frightened me.'

He looked up, and perceived two life-size portraits on panels built into the masonry. As all visitors to the mansion are aware, these paintings represent women of middle age, of a date some two hundred years ago, whose lineaments once seen can never be forgotten. The long pointed features, narrow eye, and smirk of the one, so suggestive of merciless treachery; the bill-hook nose, large teeth, and bold eye of the other, suggesting arrogance to the point of ferocity, haunt the beholder afterwards in his dreams.

'Whose portraits are those?' asked Clare of the charwoman.

'I have been told by old folk that they were ladies of the d'Urberville family, the ancient lords of this manor,' she said. 'Owing to their being builded into the wall they can't be moved away.'

The unpleasantness of the matter was that, in addition to their effect upon Tess, her fine features were unquestionably traceable in these exaggerated forms. He said nothing of this, however, and, regretting that he had gone out of his way to choose the house for their bridal time, went on into the adjoining room. The place having been rather hastily prepared for them they washed their hands in one basin. Clare touched hers under the water.

'Which are my fingers and which are yours?' he said, looking up. 'They are very much mixed.'

'They are all yours,' said she, very prettily, and endeavoured to be gayer than she was. He had not been displeased with her thoughtfulness on such an occasion; it was what every sensible woman would show: but Tess knew that she had been thoughtful to excess, and struggled against it.

The sun was so low on that short last afternoon of the year that it shone in through a small opening and formed a golden staff which stretched across to her skirt, where it made a spot like a paint-mark set upon her. They went into the ancient parlour to tea, and here they shared their first common meal alone. Such was their childishness, or rather his, that he found it interesting to use the same bread-and-butter plate as herself, and to brush crumbs from her lips with his own. He wondered a little that she did not enter into these frivolities with his own zest.

Looking at her silently for a long time; 'She is a dear dear Tess,' he thought to himself, as one deciding on the true construction of a difficult passage. 'Do I realize solemnly enough how utterly and irretrievably this little womanly thing is the creature of my good or bad faith and fortune? I think not. I think I could not, unless I were a woman myself. What I am in wordly estate, she is. What I become, she must become. What I cannot be, she cannot be. And shall I ever neglect her, or hurt her, or even forget to consider her? God forbid such a crime!'

They sat on over the tea-table waiting for their luggage, which the dairyman had promised to send before it grew dark. But evening began to close in, and the luggage did not arrive, and they had brought nothing more than they stood in. With the departure of the sun the calm mood of the winter day changed. Out of doors there began noises as of silk smartly rubbed; the restful dead leaves of the preceding autumn were stirred to irritated resurrection, and whirled about unwillingly, and tapped against the shutters. It soon began to rain.

'That cock knew the weather was going to change,' said Clare.

The woman who had attended upon them had gone home for the night, but she had placed candles upon the table, and now they lit them. Each candle-flame drew towards the fireplace.

'These old houses are so draughty,' continued Angel, looking at the flames, and at the grease guttering down the sides. 'I wonder where that luggage is. We haven't even a brush and comb.'

'I don't know,' she answered, absent-minded.

'Tess, you are not a bit cheerful this evening—not at all as you used to be. Those harridans on the panels upstairs have unsettled you. I am sorry I brought you here. I wonder if you really love me, after all?'

He knew that she did, and the words had no serious intent; but she was surcharged with emotion, and winced like a wounded animal. Though she tried not to shed tears she could not help showing one or two.

'I did not mean it!' said he, sorry. 'You are worried at not having your things, I know. I cannot think why old Jonathan has not come with them. Why, it is seven o'clock? Ah, there he is!'

A knock had come to the door, and, there being nobody else to answer it, Clare went out. He returned to the room with a small package in his hand.

'It is not Jonathan, after all,' he said.

'How vexing!' said Tess.

The packet had been brought by a special messenger, who had arrived at Talbothays from Emminster Vicarage immediately after the departure of the married couple, and had followed them hither, being under injunction to deliver it into nobody's hands but theirs. Clare brought it to the light. It was less than a foot long, sewed up in canvas, sealed in red wax with his father's seal, and directed in his father's hand to 'Mrs Angel Clare.'

'It is a little wedding-present for you, Tess,' said he, handing it to her. 'How thoughtful they are!'

Tess looked a little flustered as she took it.

'I think I would rather have you open it, dearest,' said she, turning over the parcel. 'I don't like to break those great seals; they look so serious. Please open it for me!'

He undid the parcel. Inside was a case of morocco leather, on the top of which lay a note and a key.

The note was for Clare, in the following words:

> MY DEAR SON,—Possibly you have forgotten that on the death of your godmother, Mrs Pitney, when you were a lad, she—vain kind woman that she was—left to me a portion of the contents of her jewel-case in trust for your wife, if you should ever have one, as a mark of her affection for you and whomsoever you should choose. This trust I have fulfilled, and the diamonds have been locked up at my banker's ever since. Though I feel it to be a somewhat incongruous act in the circumstances, I am, as you will see, bound to hand over the articles to the woman to whom the use of them for her lifetime will now rightly belong, and they are therefore promptly sent. They become, I believe, heirlooms, strictly speaking, according to the terms of your godmother's will. The precise words of the clause that refers to this matter are enclosed.

'I do remember,' said Clare; 'but I had quite forgotten.'

Unlocking the case, they found it to contain a necklace, with pendant, bracelets, and ear-rings; and also some other small ornaments.

Tess seemed afraid to touch them at first, but her eyes sparkled for a moment as much as the stones when Clare spread out the set.

'Are they mine?' she asked incredulously.

'They are, certainly,' said he.

He looked into the fire. He remembered how, when he was a

lad of fifteen, his godmother, the Squire's wife—the only rich person with whom he had ever come in contact—had pinned her faith to his success; had prophesied a wondrous career for him. There had seemed nothing at all out of keeping with such a conjectured career in the storing up of these showy ornaments for his wife and the wives of her descendants. They gleamed somewhat ironically now. 'Yet why?' he asked himself. It was but a question of vanity throughout; and if that were admitted into one side of the equation it should be admitted into the other. His wife was a d'Urberville: whom could they become better than her?

Suddenly he said with enthusiasm—

'Tess, put them on—put them on!' And he turned from the fire to help her.

But as if by magic she had already donned them—necklace, earrings, bracelets, and all.

'But the gown isn't right, Tess,' said Clare. 'It ought to be a low one for a set of brilliants like that.'

'Ought it?' said Tess.

'Yes,' said he.

He suggested to her how to tuck in the upper edge of her bodice, so as to make it roughly approximate to the cut for evening wear; and when she had done this, and the pendant to the necklace hung isolated amid the whiteness of her throat, as it was designed to do, he stepped back to survey her.

'My heavens,' said Clare, 'how beautiful you are!'

As everybody knows, fine feathers make fine birds; a peasant girl but very moderately prepossessing to the casual observer in her simple condition and attire, will bloom as an amazing beauty if clothed as a woman of fashion with the aids that Art can render; while the beauty of the midnight crush would often cut but a sorry figure if placed inside the fieldwoman's wrapper upon a monotonous acreage of turnips on a dull day. He had never till now estimated the artistic excellence of Tess's limbs and features.

'If you were only to appear in a ball-room!' he said. 'But no—no, dearest; I think I love you best in the wing-bonnet and cotton-frock—yes, better than in this, well as you support these dignities.'

Tess's sense of her striking appearance had given her a flush of excitement, which was yet not happiness.

'I'll take them off,' she said, 'in case Jonathan should see me. They are not fit for me, are they? They must be sold, I suppose?'

'Let them stay a few minutes longer. Sell them? Never. It would be a breach of faith.'

Influenced by a second thought she readily obeyed. She had something to tell, and there might be help in these. She sat down with the jewels upon her; and they again indulged in conjectures as to where Jonathan could possibly be with their baggage. The ale they had poured out for his consumption when he came had gone flat with long standing.

Shortly after this they began supper, which was already laid on a side-table. Ere they had finished there was a jerk in the fire-smoke, the rising skein of which bulged out into the room, as if some giant had laid his hand on the chimney-top for a moment. It had been caused by the opening of the outer door. A heavy step was now heard in the passage, and Angel went out.

'I couldn' make nobody hear at all by knocking,' apologized Jonathan Kail, for it was he at last; 'and as't was raining out I opened the door. I've brought the things, sir.'

'I am very glad to see them. But you are very late.'

'Well, yes, sir.'

There was something subdued in Jonathan Kail's tone which had not been there in the day, and lines of concern were ploughed upon his forehead in addition to the lines of years. He continued—

'We've all been gallied at the dairy at what might ha' been a most terrible affliction since you and your Mis'ess—so to name her now—left us this a'ternoon. Perhaps you ha'nt forgot the cock's afternoon crow?'

'Dear me;—what—'

'Well, some says it do mane one thing, and some another; but what's happened is that poor little Retty Priddle hev tried to drown herself.'

'No! Really! Why, she bade us good-bye with the rest—'

'Yes. Well, sir, when you and your Mis'ess—so to name what she lawful is—when you two drove away, as I say, Retty and Marian put on their bonnets and went out; and as there is not much doing now, being New Year's Eve, and folks mops and brooms from what's inside 'em, nobody took much notice. They went on to Lew-Everard, where they had summut to drink, and then on they vamped to Dree-armed Cross, and there they seemed to have parted, Retty striking across the water-meads as if for home, and Marian going on to the next village, where there's another public-house. Nothing more was zeed or heard o' Retty till the waterman, on his way home, noticed something by the Great Pool; 'twas her bonnet and shawl packed up. In the water he found her. He and another man brought her home, thinking 'a was dead; but she fetched round by degrees.'

Angel, suddenly recollecting that Tess was overhearing this gloomy tale, went to shut the door between the passage and the ante-room to the inner parlour where she was; but his wife, flinging a shawl round her, had come to the outer room and was listening to the man's narrative, her eyes resting absently on the luggage and the drops of rain glistening upon it.

'And, more than this, there's Marian; she's been found dead drunk by the withy-bed—a girl who hev never been known to touch anything before except shilling ale; though, to be sure, 'a was always a good trencher-woman, as her face showed. It seems as if the maids had all gone out o' their minds!'

'And Izz?' asked Tess.

'Izz is about house as usual; but 'a do say 'a can guess how it happened; and she seems to be very low in mind about it, poor maid, as well she mid be. And so you see, sir, as all this happened just when we was packing your few traps and your Mis'ess's night-rail and dressing things into the cart, why, it belated me.'

'Yes. Well, Jonathan, will you get the trunks upstairs, and drink a cup of ale, and hasten back as soon as you can, in case you should be wanted?'

Tess had gone back to the inner parlour, and sat down by the fire, looking wistfully into it. She heard Jonathan Kail's heavy foot-steps up and down the stairs till he had done placing the luggage, and heard him express his thanks for the ale her husband took out to him, and for the gratuity he received. Jonathan's footsteps then died from the door, and his cart creaked away.

Angel slid forward the massive oak bar which secured the door, and coming in to where she sat over the hearth, pressed her cheeks between his hands from behind. He expected her to jump up gaily and unpack the toilet-gear that she had been so anxious about, but as she did not rise he sat down with her in the firelight, the candles on the supper-table being too thin and glimmering to interfere with its glow.

'I am so sorry you should have heard this sad story about the girls,' he said. 'Still, don't let it depress you. Retty was naturally morbid, you know.'

'Without the least cause,' said Tess. 'While they who have cause to be, hide it, and pretend they are not.'

This incident had turned the scale for her. They were simple and innocent girls on whom the unhappiness of unrequited love had fallen; they had deserved better at the hands of Fate. She had deserved worse—yet she was the chosen one. It was wicked of her to take all without paying. She would pay to the uttermost farthing; she would tell, there and then. This final determination she came to when she looked into the fire, he holding her hand.

A steady glare from the now flameless embers painted the sides and back of the fireplace with its colour, and the well-polished andirons, and the old brass tongs that would not meet. The underside of the mantel-shelf was flushed with the high-coloured light, and the legs of the table nearest the fire. Tess's face and neck reflected the same warmth, which each gem turned into an Aldebaran or a Sirius—a constellation of white, red and green flashes, that interchanged their hues with her every pulsation.

'Do you remember what we said to each other this morning about telling our faults?' he asked abruptly, finding that she still remained immovable. 'We spoke lightly perhaps, and you may well have done so. But for me it was no light promise. I want to make a confession to you, Love.'

This, from him, so unexpectedly apposite, had the effect upon her of a Providential interposition.

'You have to confess something?' she said quickly, and even with gladness and relief.

'You did not expect it? Ah—you thought too highly of me. Now listen. Put your head there, because I want you to forgive me, and not to be indignant with me for not telling you before, as perhaps I ought to have done.'

How strange it was! He seemed to be her double. She did not speak, and Clare went on—

'I did not mention it because I was afraid of endangering my chance of you, darling, the great prize of my life—my Fellowship I call you. My brother's Fellowship was won at his college, mine at Talbothays Dairy. Well, I would not risk it. I was going to tell you a month ago—at the time you agreed to be mine, but I could not; I thought it might frighten you away from me. I put it off; then I thought I would tell you yesterday, to give you a chance at least of escaping me. But I did not. And I did not this morning, when you proposed our confessing our faults on the landing—the sinner that I was! But I must, now I see you sitting there so solemnly. I wonder if you will forgive me?'

'O yes! I am sure that—'

'Well, I hope so. But wait a minute. You don't know. To begin at the beginning. Though I imagine my poor father fears that I am one of the eternally lost for my doctrines, I am of course, a believer in good morals, Tess, as much as you. I used to wish to be a teacher of men, and it was a great disappointment to me when I found I could not enter the Church. I admired spotlessness, even though I could lay no claim to it, and hated impurity, as I hope I do now. Whatever one may think of plenary inspiration, one must heartily subscribe to these words of Paul: "Be thou an example—in word, in conversation, in charity, in spirit, in faith, in purity." It is the only safeguard for us poor human beings. "Integar vitae", says a Roman poet, who is strange company for St Paul –

> The man of upright life, from frailties free,
> Stands not in need of Moorish spear or bow.

Well, a certain place is paved with good intentions, and having felt all that so strongly, you will see what a terrible remorse it bred in me when, in the midst of my fine aims for other people, I myself fell.'

He then told her of that time of his life to which allusion has been made when, tossed about by doubts and difficulties in London, like a cork on the waves, he plunged into eight-and-forty hours' dissipation with a stranger.

'Happily I awoke almost immediately to a sense of my folly,' he continued. 'I would have no more to say to her, and I came home. I have never repeated the offence. But I felt I should like to treat you with perfect frankness and honour, and I could not do so without telling this. Do you forgive me?'

She pressed his hand tightly for an answer.

'Then we will dismiss it at once and for ever!—too painful as it is for the occasion—and talk of something lighter.'

'O, Angel—I am almost glad—because now *you* can forgive *me*! I have not made my confession. I have a confession, too—remember, I said so.'

'Ah, to be sure! Now then for it, wicked little one.'

'Perhaps, although you smile, it is as serious as yours, or more so.'

'It can hardly be more serious, dearest.'

'It cannot—O no, it cannot!' She jumped up joyfully at the hope. 'No, it cannot be more serious, certainly,' she cried, 'because 'tis just the same! I will tell you now.'

She sat down again.

Their hands were still joined. The ashes under the grate were lit by the fire vertically, like a torrid waste. Imagination might have beheld a Last Day luridness in this red-coaled glow, which fell on his face and hand, and on hers, peering into the loose hair about her brow, and firing the delicate skin underneath. A large shadow of her shape rose upon the wall and ceiling. She bent forward, at which each diamond on her neck gave a sinister wink like a toad's; and pressing her forehead against his temple she entered on her story of her acquaintance with Alec d'Urberville and its results, murmuring the words without flinching, and with her eyelids drooping down.

END OF PHASE THE FOURTH

PHASE THE FIFTH

THE WOMAN PAYS

XXXV

HER narrative ended; even its re-assertions and secondary explanations were done. Tess's voice throughout had hardly risen higher than its opening tone; there had been no exculpatory phrase of any kind, and she had not wept.

But the complexion even of external things seemed to suffer transmutation as her announcement progressed. The fire in the grate looked impish—demoniacally funny, as if it did not care in the least about her strait. The fender grinned idly, as if it too did not care. The light from the water-bottle was merely engaged in a chromatic problem. All material objects around announced their irresponsibility with terrible iteration. And yet nothing had changed since the moments when he had been kissing her; or rather, nothing in the substance of things. But the essence of things had changed.

When she ceased the auricular impressions from their previous endearments seemed to hustle away into the corners of their brains, repeating themselves as echoes from a time of supremely purblind foolishness.

Clare performed the irrelevant act of stirring the fire; the intelligence had not even yet got to the bottom of him. After stirring the embers he rose to his feet; all the force of her disclosure had imparted itself now. His face had withered. In the strenuousness of his concentration he treadled fitfully on the floor. He could not, by any contrivance, think closely enough; that was the meaning of his vague movement. When he spoke it was in the most inadequate, commonplace voice of the many varied tones she had heard from him.

'Tess!'

'Yes, dearest.'

'Am I to believe this? From your manner I am to take it as true. O you cannot be out of your mind! You ought to be! Yet you are not . . . My wife, my Tess—nothing in you warrants such a supposition as that?'

'I am not out of my mind,' she said.

'And yet—' He looked vacantly at her, to resume with dazed senses: 'Why didn't you tell me before? Ah, yes, you would have told me, in a way—but I hindered you, I remember!'

These and other of his words were nothing but the perfunctory babble of the surface while the depths remained paralyzed. He turned away, and bent over a chair. Tess followed him to the middle of the room where he was, and stood there staring at him with eyes that did not weep. Presently she slid down upon her knees beside his foot, and from this position she crouched in a heap.

'In the name of our love, forgive me!' she whispered with a dry mouth. 'I have forgiven you for the same!'

And, as he did not answer, she said again—

'Forgive me as you are forgiven! I forgive *you*, Angel.'

'You—yes, you do.'

'But you do not forgive me?'

'O Tess, forgiveness does not apply to the case. You were one person; now you are another. My God—how can forgiveness meet such a grotesque—prestidigitation as that!'

He paused, contemplating this definition; then suddenly broke into horrible laughter—as unnatural and ghastly as a laugh in hell.

'Don't—don't! It kills me quite, that!' she shrieked. 'O have mercy upon me—have mercy!'

He did not answer; and, sickly white, she jumped up.

'Angel, Angel! what do you mean by that laugh?' she cried out. 'Do you know what this is to me?'

He shook his head.

'I have been hoping, longing, praying, to make you happy! I have thought what joy it will be to do it, what an unworthy wife I shall be if I do not! That's what I have felt, Angel!'

'I know that.'

'I thought, Angel, that you loved me—me, my very self! If it is I you do love, O how can it be that you look and speak so? It frightens me! Having begun to love you, I love you for ever—in all changes, in all disgraces, because you are yourself. I ask no more. Then how can you, O my own husband, stop loving me?'

'I repeat, the woman I have been loving is not you.'

'But who?'

'Another woman in your shape.'

She perceived in his words the realization of her own apprehensive foreboding in former times. He looked upon her as a species of impostor; a guilty woman in the guise of an innocent one. Terror was upon her white face as she saw it; her cheek was flaccid, and her mouth had almost the aspect of a round little hole. The horrible sense of his view of her so deadened her that she staggered; and he stepped forward, thinking she was going to fall.

'Sit down, sit down,' he said gently. 'You are ill; and it is natural that you should be.'

She did sit down, without knowing where she was, that strained look still upon her face, and her eyes such as to make his flesh creep.

'I don't belong to you any more, then; do I, Angel?' she asked helplessly. 'It is not me, but another woman like me that he loved, he says.'

The image raised caused her to take pity upon herself as one who was ill-used. Her eyes filled as she regarded her position further; she turned round and burst into a flood of self-sympathetic tears.

Clare was relieved at this change, for the effect on her of what had happened was beginning to be a trouble to him only less than the woe of the disclosure itself. He waited patiently, apathetically, till the violence of her grief had worn itself out, and her rush of weeping had lessened to a catching gasp at intervals.

'Angel,' she said suddenly, in her natural tones, the insane, dry voice of terror having left her now. 'Angel, am I too wicked for you and me to live together?'

'I have not been able to think what we can do.'

'I shan't ask you to let me live with you, Angel, because I have no right to! I shall not write to mother and sisters to say we be married, as I said I would do; and I shan't finish the good-hussif I cut out and meant to make while we were in lodgings.'

'Shan't you?'

'No, I shan't do anything, unless you order me to; and if you go away from me I shall not follow 'ee; and if you never speak to me any more I shall not ask why, unless you tell me I may.'

'And if I do order you to do anything?'

'I will obey you like your wretched slave, even if it is to lie down and die.'

'You are very good. But it strikes me that there is a want of harmony between your present mood of self-sacrifice and your past mood of self-preservation.'

These were the first words of antagonism. To fling elaborate sarcasms at Tess, however, was much like flinging them at a dog or cat. The charms of their subtlety passed by her unappreciated, and she only received them as inimical sounds which meant that anger ruled. She remained mute, not knowing that he was smothering his affection for her. She hardly observed that a tear descended slowly upon his cheek, a tear so large that it magnified the pores of the skin over which it rolled, like the object lens of a microscope. Meanwhile reillumination as to the terrible and total change that her confession had wrought in his life, in his universe, returned to him, and he tried desperately to advance among the new conditions in which he stood. Some consequent action was necessary; yet what?

'Tess,' he said, as gently as he could speak, 'I cannot stay—in this room—just now. I will walk out a little way.'

He quietly left the room, and the two glasses of wine that he had poured out for their supper—one for her, one for him—remained on the table untasted. This was what their *Agape* had come to. At tea, two or three hours earlier, they had, in the freakishness of affection, drunk from one cup.

The closing of the door behind him, gently as it had been pulled to, roused Tess from her stupor. He was gone; she could not stay. Hastily flinging her cloak around her she opened the door and followed, putting out the candles as if she were never coming back. The rain was over and the night was now clear.

She was soon close at his heels, for Clare walked slowly and without purpose. His form beside her light gray figure looked black, sinister, and forbidding, and she felt as sarcasm the touch of the jewels of which she had been momentarily so proud. Clare turned at hearing her footsteps, but his recognition of her presence seemed to make no difference in him, and he went on over the five yawning arches of the great bridge in front of the house.

The cow and horse tracks in the road were full of water, the rain having been enough to charge them, but not enough to wash them away. Across these minute pools the reflected stars flitted in a quick transit as she passed; she would not have known they were shining overhead if she had not seen them there—the vastest things of the universe imaged in objects so mean.

The place to which they had travelled to-day was in the same valley as Talbothays, but some miles lower down the river; and the surroundings being open she kept easily in sight of him. Away from the house the road wound through the meads, and along these she followed Clare without any attempt to come up with him or to attract him, but with dumb and vacant fidelity.

At last, however, her listless walk brought her up alongside him, and still he said nothing. The cruelty of fooled honesty is often great after enlightenment, and it was mighty in Clare now. The outdoor air had apparently taken away from him all tendency to act on impulse; she knew that he saw her without irradiation—in all her bareness; that Time was chanting his satiric psalm at her then—

> Behold, when thy face is made bare, he that loved thee shall hate;
> Thy face shall be no more fair at the fall of thy fate.
> For thy life shall fall as a leaf and be shed as the rain;
> And the veil of thine head shall be grief, and the crown shall be
>   pain.

He was still intently thinking, and her companionship had now insufficient power to break or divert the strain of thought. What a weak thing her presence must have become to him! She could not help addressing Clare.

'What have I done—what *have* I done! I have not told of anything that interferes with or belies my love for you. You don't think I planned it, do you? It is in your own mind what you are angry at, Angel: it is not in me. O, it is not in me, and I am not that deceitful woman you think me!'

'H'm—well. Not deceitful, my wife; but not the same. No, not the same. But do not make me reproach you. I have sworn that I will not; and I will do everything to avoid it.'

But she went on pleading in her distraction; and perhaps said things that would have been better left to silence.

'Angel!—Angel! I was a child—a child when it happened! I knew nothing of men.'

'You were more sinned against than sinning, that I admit.'

'Then you will not forgive me?'

'I do forgive you, but forgiveness is not all.'

'And love me?'

To this question he did not answer.

'O Angel—my mother says that it sometimes happens so!—she knows several cases where they were worse than I, and the husband has not minded it much—has got over it at least. And yet the woman has not loved him as I do you!'

'Don't, Tess; don't argue. Different societies, different manners. You almost make me say you are an unapprehending peasant woman, who have never been initiated into the proportions of social things. You don't know what you say.'

'I am only a peasant by position, not by nature!'

She spoke with an impulse to anger, but it went as it came.

'So much the worse for you. I think that parson who unearthed your pedigree would have done better if he had held his tongue. I cannot help associating your decline as a family with this other fact—of your want of firmness. Decrepit families imply decrepit wills, decrepit conduct. Heaven, why did you give me a handle for despising you more by informing me of your descent! Here was I thinking you a new-sprung child of nature; there were you, the belated seedling of an effete aristocracy!'

'Lots of families are as bad as mine in that! Retty's family were once large landowners, and so were Dairyman Billett's. And the Debbyhouses, who now are carters, were once the De Bayeux family. You find such as I everywhere; 'tis a feature of our county, and I can't help it.'

'So much the worse for the county.'

She took these reproaches in their bulk simply, not in their particulars; he did not love her as he had loved her hitherto, and to all else she was indifferent.

They wandered on again in silence. It was said afterwards that a cottager of Wellbridge, who went out late that night for a doctor, met two lovers in the pastures, walking very slowly, without converse, one behind the other, as in a funeral procession, and the glimpse that he obtained of their faces seemed to denote that they were anxious and sad. Returning later, he passed them again in the same field, progressing just as slowly, and as regardless of the hour and of the cheerless night as before. It was only on account of his preoccupation with his own affairs, and the illness in his house, that he did not bear in mind the curious incident, which, however, he recalled a long while after.

During the interval of the cottager's going and coming, she had said to her husband—

'I don't see how I can help being the cause of much misery to you all your life. The river is down there. I can put an end to myself in it. I am not afraid.'

'I don't wish to add murder to my other follies,' he said.

'I will leave something to show that I did it myself—on account of my shame. They will not blame you then.'

'Don't speak so absurdly—I wish not to hear it. It is nonsense to have such thoughts in this kind of case, which is rather one for satirical laughter than for tragedy. You don't in the least understand the quality of the mishap. It would be viewed in the light of a joke by nine-tenths of the world if it were known. Please oblige me by returning to the house, and going to bed.'

'I will,' said she dutifully.

They had rambled round by a road which led to the well-known ruins of the Cistercian abbey behind the mill, the latter having, in centuries past, been attached to the monastic establishment. The mill still worked on, food being a perennial necessity; the abbey had perished, creeds being transient. One continually sees the ministration of the temporary outlasting the ministration of the eternal. Their walk having been circuitous they were still not far from the house, and in obeying his direction she only had to reach the large stone bridge across the main river, and follow the road for a few yards. When she got back everything remained as she had left it, the fire being still burning. She did not stay downstairs for more than a minute, but proceeded to her chamber, whither the luggage had been taken. Here she sat down on the edge of the bed, looking blankly around, and presently began to undress. In removing the light towards the bedstead its rays fell upon the tester of white dimity; something was hanging beneath it, and she lifted the candle to see what it was. A bough of mistletoe. Angel had put it there; she knew that in an instant. This was the explanation of that mysterious parcel which it had been so difficult to pack and bring; whose contents he would not explain to her, saying that time would soon show her the purpose thereof. In his zest and his gaiety he had hung it there. How foolish and inopportune that mistletoe looked now.

Having nothing more to fear, having scarce anything to hope, for that he would relent there seemed no promise whatever, she lay down dully. When sorrow ceases to be speculative sleep sees her opportunity. Among so many happier moods which forbid repose this was a mood which welcomed it, and in a few minutes the lonely Tess forgot existence, surrounded by the aromatic stillness of the chamber that had once, possibly, been the bride-chamber of her own ancestry.

Later on that night Clare also retraced his steps to the house. Entering softly to the sitting-room he obtained a light, and with the manner of one who had considered his course he spread his rugs upon the old horse-hair sofa which stood there, and roughly shaped it to a sleeping-couch. Before lying down he crept shoeless upstairs, and listened at the door of her apartment. Her measured breathing told that she was sleeping profoundly.

'Thank God!' murmured Clare; and yet he was conscious of a pang of bitterness at the thought—approximately true, though not wholly so—that having shifted the burden of her life to his shoulders she was now reposing without care.

He turned away to descend; then, irresolute, faced round to her door again. In the act he caught sight of one of the d'Urberville dames, whose portrait was immediately over the entrance to Tess's bedchamber. In the candlelight the painting was more than unpleasant. Sinister design lurked in the woman's features, a concentrated purpose of revenge on the other sex—so it seemed to him then. The Caroline bodice of the portrait was low—precisely as Tess's had been when he tucked it in to show the necklace; and again he experienced the distressing sensation of a resemblance between them.

The check was sufficient. He resumed his retreat and descended.

His air remained calm and cold, his small compressed mouth indexing his powers of self-control, his face wearing still that terribly sterile expression which had spread thereon since her disclosure. It was the face of a man who was no longer passion's slave, yet who found no advantage in his enfranchisement. He was simply regarding the harrowing contingencies of human experience, the unexpectedness of things. Nothing so pure, so sweet, so virginal as Tess had seemed possible all the long while that he had adored her, up to an hour ago; but

The little less, and what worlds away!

He argued erroneously when he said to himself that her heart was not indexed in the honest freshness of her face; but Tess had no advocate to set him right. Could it be possible, he continued, that eyes which as they gazed never expressed any divergence from what the tongue was telling, were yet ever seeing another world behind her ostensible one, discordant and contrasting.

He reclined on his couch in the sitting-room, and extinguished the light. The night came in, and took up its place there, unconcerned and indifferent; the night which had already swallowed up his happiness, and was now digesting it listlessly; and was ready to swallow up the happiness of a thousand other people with as little disturbance or change of mien.

XXXVI

CLARE arose in the light of a dawn that was ashy and furtive, as though associated with crime. The fireplace confronted him with its extinct embers; the spread supper-table, whereon stood the two full glasses of untasted wine, now flat and filmy; her vacated seat and his own; the other articles of furniture, with their eternal look of not being able to help it, their intolerable inquiry what was to be done? From above there was no sound; but in a few minutes there came a knock at the door. He remembered that it would be the neighbouring cottager's wife, who was to minister to their wants while they remained here.

The presence of a third person in the house would be extremely awkward just now, and, being already dressed, he opened the window and informed her that they could manage to shift for themselves that morning. She had a milk-can in her hand, which he told her to leave at the door. When the dame had gone away he searched in the back quarters of the house for fuel, and speedily lit a fire. There was plenty of eggs, butter, bread, and so on in the larder, and Clare soon had breakfast laid, his experiences at the dairy having rendered him facile in domestic preparations. The smoke of the kindled wood rose from the chimney without like a lotus-headed column; local people who were passing by saw it, and thought of the newly-married couple, and envied their happiness.

Angel cast a final glance round, and then going to the foot of the stairs, called in a conventional voice—

'Breakfast is ready!'

He opened the front door, and took a few steps in the morning air. When, after a short space, he came back she was already in the sitting-room, mechanically readjusting the breakfast things. As she was fully attired, and the interval since his calling her had been but two or three minutes, she must have been dressed or nearly so before he went to summon her. Her hair was twisted up in a large round mass at the back of her head, and she had put on one of the new frocks—a pale blue woollen garment with neck-frillings of white. Her hands and face appeared to be cold, and she had possibly been sitting dressed in the bedroom a long time without any fire. The marked civility of Clare's tone in calling her seemed to have inspired her, for the moment, with a new glimmer of hope. But it soon died when she looked at him.

The pair were, in truth, but the ashes of their former fires. To the hot sorrow of the previous night had succeeded heaviness; it seemed as if nothing could kindle either of them to fervour of sensation any more.

He spoke gently to her, and she replied with a like undemonstrativeness. At last she came up to him, looking in his sharply-defined face as one who had no consciousness that her own formed a visible object also.

'Angel!' she said, and paused, touching him with her fingers lightly as a breeze, as though she could hardly believe to be there in the flesh the man who was once her lover. Her eyes were bright, her pale cheek still showed its wonted roundness, though half-dried tears had left glistening traces thereon; and the usually ripe red mouth was almost as pale as her cheek. Throbbingly alive as she was still, under the stress of her mental grief the life beat so brokenly, that a little further pull upon it would cause real illness, dull her characteristic eyes, and make her mouth thin.

She looked absolutely pure. Nature, in her fantastic trickery, had set such a seal of maidenhood upon Tess's countenance that he gazed at her with a stupefied air.

'Tess! Say it is not true! No, it is not true!'

'It is true.'

'Every word?'

'Every word.'

He looked at her imploringly, as if he would willingly have taken a lie from her lips, knowing it to be one, and have made of it, by some sort of sophistry, a valid denial. However, she only repeated—

'It is true.'

'Is he living?' Angel then asked.

'The baby died.'

'But the man?'

'He is alive.'

A last despair passed over Clare's face.

'Is he in England?'

'Yes.'

He took a few vague steps.

'My position—is this,' he said abruptly. 'I thought—any man would have thought—that by giving up all ambition to win a wife with social standing, with fortune, with knowledge of the world, I should secure rustic innocence as surely as I should secure pink cheeks; but—However, I am no man to reproach you, and I will not.'

Tess felt his position so entirely that the remainder had not been needed. Therein lay just the distress of it; she saw that he had lost all round.

'Angel—I should not have let it go on to marriage with you if I had not known that, after all, there was a last way out of it for you; though I hoped you would never—'

Her voice grew husky.

'A last way?'

'I mean, to get rid of me. You *can* get rid of me.'

'How?'

'By divorçing me.'

'Good heavens—how can you be so simple! How can I divorce you?'

'Can't you—now I have told you? I thought my confession would give you grounds for that.'

'O Tess—you are too, too—childish—unformed—crude, I suppose! I don't know what you are. You don't understand the law—you don't understand!'

'What—you cannot?'

'Indeed I cannot.'

A quick shame mixed with the misery upon his listener's face.

'I thought—I thought,' she whispered. 'O, now I see how wicked I seem to you! Believe me—believe me, on my soul, I never thought but that you could! I hoped you would not; yet I believed, without a doubt, that you could cast me off if you were determined, and didn't love me at—at—all!'

'You were mistaken,' he said.

'O, then I ought to have done it, to have done it last night! But I hadn't the courage. That's just like me!'

'The courage to do what?'

As she did not answer he took her by the hand.

'What were you thinking of doing?' he inquired.

'Of putting an end to myself.'

'When?'

She writhed under this inquisitorial manner of his. 'Last night,' she answered.

'Where?'

'Under your mistletoe.'

'My good—! How?' he asked sternly.

'I'll tell you, if you won't be angry with me!' she said, shrinking. 'It was with the cord of my box. But I could not—do the last thing! I was afraid that it might cause a scandal to your name.'

The unexpected quality of this confession, wrung from her, and not volunteered, shook him perceptibly. But he still held her, and, letting his glance fall from her face downwards, he said,

'Now, listen to this. You must not dare to think of such a horrible thing! How could you! You will promise me as your husband to attempt that no more.'

'I am ready to promise. I saw how wicked it was.'

'Wicked! The idea was unworthy of you beyond description.'

'But, Angel,' she pleaded, enlarging her eyes in calm unconcern upon him, 'it was thought of entirely on your account—to set you free without the scandal of the divorce that I thought you would have to get. I should never have dreamt of doing it on mine. However, to do it with my own hand is too good for me, after all. It is you, my ruined husband, who ought to strike the blow. I think I should love you more, if that were possible, if you could bring yourself to do it, since there's no other way of escape for 'ee. I feel I am so utterly worthless! So very greatly in the way!'

'Ssh!'

'Well, since you say no, I won't. I have no wish opposed to yours.'

He knew this to be true enough. Since the desperation of the night her activities had dropped to zero, and there was no further rashness to be feared.

Tess tried to busy herself again over the breakfast-table with more or less success, and they sat down both on the same side, so that their glances did not meet. There was at first something awkward in hearing each other eat and drink, but this could not be escaped; moreover, the amount of eating done was small on both sides. Breakfast over he rose, and telling her the hour at which he might be expected to dinner, went off to the miller's in a mechanical pursuance of the plan of studying that business, which had been his only practical reason for coming here.

When he was gone Tess stood at the window, and presently saw his form crossing the great stone bridge which conducted to the mill premises. He sank behind it, crossed the railway beyond, and disappeared. Then, without a sigh, she turned her attention to the room, and began clearing the table and setting it in order.

The charwoman soon came. Her presence was at first a strain upon Tess, but afterwards an alleviation. At half-past twelve she left her assistant alone in the kitchen, and, returning to the sitting-room, waited for the reappearance of Angel's form behind the bridge.

About one he showed himself. Her face flushed, although he was a quarter of a mile off. She ran to the kitchen to get the dinner served by the time he should enter. He went first to the room where they had washed their hands together the day before, and as he entered the sitting-room the dish-covers rose from the dishes as if by his own motion.

'How punctual!' he said.

'Yes. I saw you coming over the bridge,' said she.

The meal was passed in commonplace talk of what he had been doing during the morning at the Abbey Mill, of the methods of bolting and the old-fashioned machinery, which he feared would not enlighten him greatly on modern improved methods, some of it seeming to have been in use ever since the days it ground for the monks in the adjoining conventual buildings—now a heap of ruins. He left the house again in the course of an hour, coming home at dusk, and occupying himself through the evening with his papers. She feared she was in the way, and, when the old woman was gone, retired to the kitchen, where she made herself busy as well as she could for more than an hour.

Clare's shape appeared at the door.

'You must not work like this,' he said. 'You are not my servant; you are my wife.'

She raised her eyes, and brightened somewhat. 'I may think myself that—indeed?' she murmured, in piteous raillery. 'You mean in name! Well, I don't want to be anything more.'

'You *may* think so, Tess! You are. What do you mean?'

'I don't know,' she said hastily, with tears in her accents. 'I thought I—because I am not respectable, I mean. I told you I thought I was not respectable enough long ago—and on that account I didn't want to marry you, only—only you urged me!'

She broke into sobs, and turned her back to him. It would almost have won round any man but Angel Clare. Within the remote depths of his constitution, so gentle and affectionate as he was in general, there lay hidden a hard logical deposit, like a vein of metal in a soft loam, which turned the edge of everything that attempted to traverse it. It had blocked his acceptance of the Church; it blocked his acceptance of Tess. Moreover, his affection itself was less fire than radiance, and, with regard to the other sex, when he ceased to believe he ceased to follow: contrasting in this with many impressionable natures, who remain sensuously infatuated with what they intellectually despise. He waited till her sobbing ceased.

'I wish half the women in England were as respectable as you,' he said, in an ebullition of bitterness against womankind in general. 'It isn't a question of respectability, but one of principle!'

He spoke such things as these and more of a kindred sort to her, being still swayed by the antipathetic wave which warps direct souls with such persistence when once their vision finds itself mocked by appearances. There was, it is true, underneath, a back current of sympathy through which a woman of the world might have conquered him. But Tess did not think of this; she took everything as her deserts, and hardly opened her mouth. The firmness of her devotion to him was indeed almost pitiful; quick-tempered as she naturally was, nothing that he could say made her unseemly; she sought not her own; was not provoked; thought no evil of his treatment of her. She might just now have been Apostolic Charity herself returned to a self-seeking modern world.

This evening, night, and morning were passed precisely as the preceding ones had been passed. On one, and only one, occasion did she—the formerly free and independent Tess—venture to make any advances. It was on the third occasion of his starting after a meal to go out to the flour-mill. As he was leaving the table he said 'Good-bye', and she replied in the same words, at the same time inclining her mouth in the way of his. He did not avail himself of the invitation, saying, as he turned hastily aside—

'I shall be home punctually.'

Tess shrank into herself as if she had been struck. Often enough had he tried to reach those lips against her consent—often had he said gaily that her mouth and breath tasted of the butter and eggs and milk and honey on which she mainly lived, that he drew sustenance from them, and other follies of that sort. But he did not care for them now. He observed her sudden shrinking, and said gently—

'You know, I have to think of a course. It was imperative that we should stay together a little while, to avoid the scandal to you that would have resulted from our immediate parting. But you must see it is only for form's sake.'

'Yes,' said Tess absently.

He went out, and on his way to the mill stood still, and wished for a moment that he had responded yet more kindly, and kissed her once at least.

Thus they lived through this despairing day or two; in the same house, truly; but more widely apart than before they were lovers. It was evident to her that he was, as he had said, living with paralyzed activities, in his endeavour to think of a plan of procedure. She was awe-stricken to discover such determination under such apparent flexibility. His consistency was, indeed, too cruel. She no longer expected forgiveness now. More than once she thought of going away from him during his absence at the mill; but she feared that this, instead of benefiting him, might be the means of hampering and humiliating him yet more if it should become known.

Meanwhile Clare was meditating, verily. His thought had been unsuspended; he was becoming ill with thinking; eaten out with thinking, withered by thinking; scourged out of all his former pulsating flexuous domesticity. He walked about saying to himself, 'What's to be done—what's to be done?' and by chance she overheard him. It caused her to break the reserve about their future which had hitherto prevailed.

'I suppose—you are not going to live with me—long, are you, Angel?' she asked, the sunk corners of her mouth betraying how purely mechanical were the means by which she retained that expression of chastened calm upon her face.

'I cannot,' he said, 'without despising myself, and what is worse, perhaps, despising you. I mean, of course, cannot live with you in the ordinary sense. At present, whatever I feel, I do not despise you. And, let me speak plainly, or you may not see all my difficulties. How can we live together while that man lives?—he being your husband in Nature, and not I. If he were dead it might be different . . . Besides, that's not all the difficulty; it lies in another consideration—one bearing upon the future of other people than ourselves. Think of years to come and children being born to us, and this past matter getting known—for it must get known. There is not an uttermost part of the earth but somebody comes from it or goes to it from elsewhere. Well, think of wretches of our flesh and blood growing up under a taunt which they will gradually get to feel the full force of with their expanding years. What an awakening for them! What a prospect! Can you honestly say Remain, after contemplating this contingency? Don't you think we had better endure the ills we have than fly to others?'

Her eyelids, weighted with trouble, continued drooping as before.

'I cannot say Remain,' she answered. 'I cannot; I had not thought so far.'

Tess's feminine hope—shall we confess it—had been so obstinately recuperative as to revive in her surreptitious visions of a domiciliary intimacy continued long enough to break down his coldness even against his judgment. Though unsophisticated in the usual sense, she was not incomplete; and it would have denoted deficiency of womanhood if she had not instinctively known what an argument lies in propinquity. Nothing else would serve her, she knew, if this failed. It was wrong to hope in what was of the nature of strategy, she said to herself: yet that sort of hope she could not extinguish. His last representation had now been made, and it was, as she said, a new view. She had truly never thought so far as that, and his lucid picture of possible offspring who would scorn her was one that brought deadly conviction to an honest heart which was humanitarian to its centre. Sheer experience had already taught her that, in some circumstances, there was one thing better than to lead a good life, and that was to be saved from leading any life whatever. Like all who have been previsioned by suffering, she could, in the words of M. Sully-Prudhomme, hear a penal sentence in the fiat, 'You shall be born,' particularly if addressed to potential issue of hers.

Yet such is the vulpine slyness of Dame Nature, that, till now, Tess had been hoodwinked by her love for Clare into forgetting it might result in vitalizations that would inflict upon others what she had bewailed as a misfortune to herself.

She therefore could not withstand his argument. But with the self-combating proclivity of the super-sensitive, an answer thereto arose in Clare's own mind, and he almost feared it. It was based on her exceptional physical nature; and she might have used it promisingly. She might have added besides: 'On an Australian upland or Texan plain, who is to know or care about my misfortunes, or to reproach me or you?' Yet, like the majority of women, she accepted the momentary presentment as if it were the inevitable. And she may have been right. The intuitive heart of woman knoweth not only its own bitterness, but its husband's, and even if these assumed reproaches were not likely to be addressed to him or to his by strangers, they might have reached his ears from his own fastidious brain.

It was the third day of the estrangement. Some might risk the odd paradox that with more animalism he would have been the nobler man. We do not say it. Yet Clare's love was doubtless ethereal to a fault, imaginative to impracticability. With these natures, corporeal presence is sometimes less appealing than corporeal absence; the latter creating an ideal presence that conveniently drops the defects of the real. She found that her personality did not plead her cause so forcibly as she had anticipated. The figurative phrase was true: she was another woman than the one who had excited his desire.

'I have thought over what you say,' she remarked to him, moving her forefinger over the tablecloth, her other hand, which bore the ring that mocked them both, supporting her forehead. 'It is quite true all of it; it must be. You must go away from me.'

'But what can you do?'

'I can go home.'

Clare had not thought of that.

'Are you sure?' he inquired.

'Quite sure. We ought to part, and we may as well get it past and done. You once said that I was apt to win men against their better judgment; and if I am constantly before your eyes I may cause you to change your plans in opposition to your reason and wish; and afterwards your repentance and my sorrow will be terrible.'

'And you would like to go home?' he asked.

'I want to leave you, and go home.'

'Then it shall be so.'

Though she did not look up at him, she started. There was a difference between the proposition and the covenant, which she had felt only too quickly.

'I feared it would come to this,' she murmured, her countenance meekly fixed. 'I don't complain, Angel. I—I think it best. What you said has quite convinced me. Yes, though nobody else should reproach me if we should stay together, yet somewhen, years hence, you might get angry with me for any ordinary matter, and knowing what you do of my bygones you yourself might be tempted to say words, and they might be overheard, perhaps by my own children. O, what only hurts me now would torture and kill me then! I will go—to-morrow.'

'And I shall not stay here. Though I didn't like to initiate it, I have seen that it was advisable we should part—at least for a while, till I can better see the shape that things have taken, and can write to you.'

Tess stole a glance at her husband. He was pale, even tremulous; but, as before, she was appalled by the determination revealed in the depths of this gentle being she had married—the will to subdue the grosser to the subtler emotion, the substance to the conception, the flesh to the spirit. Propensities, tendencies, habits, were as dead as leaves upon the tyrannous wind of his imaginative ascendency.

He may have observed her look, for he explained—

'I think of people more kindly when I am away from them'; adding cynically, 'God knows; perhaps we shall shake down together some day, for weariness; thousands have done it!'

That day he began to pack up, and she went upstairs and began to pack also. Both knew that it was in their two minds that they might part the next morning for ever, despite the gloss of assuaging conjectures thrown over their proceeding because they were of the sort to whom any parting which has an air of finality is a torture. He knew, and she knew, that, though the fascination which each had exercised over the other—on her part independently of accomplishments—would probably in the first days of their separation be even more potent than ever, time must attenuate that effect; the practical arguments against accepting her as a housemate might pronounce themselves more strongly in the boreal light of a remoter view. Moreover, when two people are once parted—have abandoned a common domicile and a common environment—new growths insensibly bud upward to fill each vacated place; unforeseen accidents hinder intentions, and old plans are forgotten.

XXXVII

MIDNIGHT came and passed silently, for there was nothing to announce it in the Valley of the Froom.

Not long after one o'clock there was a slight creak in the darkened farmhouse once the mansion of the d'Urbervilles. Tess, who used the upper chamber, heard it and awoke. It had come from the corner step of the staircase, which, as usual, was loosely nailed. She saw the door of her bedroom open, and the figure of her husband crossed the stream of moonlight with a curiously careful tread. He was in his shirt and trousers only, and her first flush of joy died when she perceived that his eyes were fixed in an unnatural stare on vacancy. When he reached the middle of the room he stood still and murmured, in tones of indescribable sadness—

'Dead! dead! dead!'

Under the influence of any strongly-disturbing force Clare would occasionally walk in his sleep, and even perform strange feats, such as he had done on the night of their return from market just before their marriage, when he re-enacted in his bedroom his combat with the man who had insulted her. Tess saw that continued mental distress had wrought him into that somnambulistic state now.

Her loyal confidence in him lay so deep down in her heart that, awake or asleep, he inspired her with no sort of personal fear. If he had entered with a pistol in his hand he would scarcely have disturbed her trust in his protectiveness.

Clare came close, and bent over her. 'Dead, dead, dead!' he murmured.

After fixedly regarding her for some moments with the same gaze of unmeasurable woe he bent lower, enclosed her in his arms, and rolled her in the sheet as in a shroud. Then lifting her from the bed with as much respect as one would show to a dead body, he carried her across the room, murmuring—

'My poor, poor Tess—my dearest, darling Tess! So sweet, so good, so true!'

The words of endearment, withheld so severely in his waking hours, were inexpressibly sweet to her forlorn and hungry heart. If it had been to save her weary life she would not, by moving or struggling, have put an end to the position she found herself in. Thus she lay in absolute stillness, scarcely venturing to breathe, and, wondering what he was going to do with her, suffered herself to be borne out upon the landing.

'My wife—dead, dead!' he said.

He paused in his labours for a moment to lean with her against the banister. Was he going to throw her down? Self-solicitude was near extinction in her, and in the knowledge that he had planned to depart on the morrow, possibly for always, she lay in his arms in this precarious position with a sense rather of luxury than of terror. If they could only fall together, and both be dashed to pieces, how fit, how desirable.

However, he did not let her fall, but took advantage of the support of the handrail to imprint a kiss upon her lips—lips in the daytime scorned. Then he clasped her with a renewed firmness of hold, and descended the staircase. The creak of the loose stair did not awaken him, and they reached the ground-floor safely. Freeing one of his hands from his grasp of her for a moment, he slid back the door-bar and passed out, slightly striking his stockinged toe against the edge of the door. But this he seemed not to mind, and, having room for extension in the open air, he lifted her against his shoulder, so that he could carry her with ease, the absence of clothes taking much from his burden. Thus he bore her off the premises in the direction of the river a few yards distant.

His ultimate intention, if he had any, she had not yet divined; and she found herself conjecturing on the matter as a third person might have done. So easefully had she delivered her whole being up to him that it pleased her to think he was regarding her as his absolute possession, to dispose of as he should choose. It was consoling, under the hovering terror of to-morrow's separation, to feel that he really recognized her now as his wife Tess, and did not cast her off, even if in that recognition he went so far as to arrogate to himself the right of harming her.

Ah! now she knew what he was dreaming of—that Sunday morning when he had borne her along through the water with the other dairymaids, who had loved him nearly as much as she, if that were possible, which Tess could hardly admit. Clare did not cross the bridge with her, but proceeding several paces on the same side towards the adjoining mill, at length stood still on the brink of the river.

Its waters, in creeping down these miles of meadowland, frequently divided, serpentining in purposeless curves, looping themselves around little islands that had no name, returning and re-embodying themselves as a broad main stream further on. Opposite the spot to which he had brought her was such a general confluence, and the river was proportionately voluminous and deep. Across it was a narrow foot-bridge; but now the autumn flood had washed the handrail away, leaving the bare plank only, which, lying a few inches above the speeding current, formed a giddy pathway for even steady heads; and Tess had noticed from the window of the house in the daytime young men walking across upon it as a feat in balancing. Her husband had possibly observed the same performance; anyhow, he now mounted the plank, and sliding one foot forward, advanced along it.

Was he going to drown her? Probably he was. The spot was lonely, the river deep and wide enough to make such a purpose easy of accomplishment. He might drown her if he would; it would be better than parting to-morrow to lead severed lives.

The swift stream raced and gyrated under them, tossing, distorting, and splitting the moon's reflected face. Spots of froth travelled past, and intercepted weeds waved behind the piles. If they could both fall together into the current now, their arms would be so tightly clasped together that they could not be saved; they would go out of the world almost painlessly, and there would be no more reproach to her, or to him for marrying her. His last half-hour with her would have been a loving one, while if they lived till he awoke his daytime aversion would return, and this hour would remain to be contemplated only as a transient dream.

The impulse stirred in her, yet she dared not indulge it, to make a movement that would have precipitated them both into the gulf. How she valued her own life had been proved; but his—she had no right to tamper with it. He reached the other side with her in safety.

Here they were within a plantation which formed the Abbey grounds, and taking a new hold of her he went onward a few steps till they reached the ruined choir of the Abbey-church. Against the north wall was the empty stone coffin of an abbot, in which every tourist with a turn for grim humour was accustomed to stretch himself. In this Clare carefully laid Tess. Having kissed her lips a second time he breathed deeply, as if a greatly desired end were attained. Clare then lay down on the ground alongside, when he immediately fell into the deep dead slumber of exhaustion, and remained motionless as a log. The spurt of mental excitement which had produced the effort was now over.

Tess sat up in the coffin. The night, though dry and mild for the season, was more than sufficiently cold to make it dangerous for him to remain here long, in his half-clothed state. If he were left to himself he would in all probability stay there till the morning, and be chilled to certain death. She had heard of such deaths after sleep-walking. But how could she dare to awaken him, and let him know what he had been doing, when it would mortify him to discover his folly in respect of her? Tess, however, stepping out of her stone confine, shook him slightly, but was unable to arouse him without being violent. It was indispensable to do something, for she was beginning to shiver, the sheet being but a poor protection. Her excitement had in a measure kept her warm during the few minutes' adventure; but that beatific interval was over.

It suddenly occurred to her to try persuasion; and accordingly she whispered in his ear, with as much firmness and decision as she could summon—

'Let us walk on, darling,' at the same time taking him suggestively by the arm. To her relief, he unresistingly acquiesced; her words had apparently thrown him back into his dream, which thenceforward seemed to enter on a new phase, wherein he fancied she had risen as a spirit, and was leading him to Heaven. Thus she conducted him by the arm to the stone bridge in front of their residence, crossing which they stood at the manor-house door. Tess's feet were quite bare, and the stones hurt her, and chilled her to the bone; but Clare was in his woollen stockings, and appeared to feel no discomfort.

There was no further difficulty. She induced him to lie down on his own sofa bed, and covered him up warmly, lighting a temporary fire of wood, to dry any dampness out of him. The noise of these attentions she thought might awaken him, and secretly wished that they might. But the exhaustion of his mind and body was such that he remained undisturbed.

As soon as they met the next morning Tess divined that Angel knew little or nothing of how far she had been concerned in the night's excursion, though, as regarded himself he may have been aware that he had not lain still. In truth, he had awakened that morning from a sleep deep as annihilation; and during those first few moments in which the brain, like a Samson shaking himself, is trying its strength, he had some dim notion of an unusual nocturnal proceeding. But the realities of his situation soon displaced conjecture on the other subject.

He waited in expectancy to discern some mental pointing; he knew that if any intention of his, concluded over-night, did not vanish in the light of morning, it stood on a basis approximating to one of pure reason, even if initiated by impulse of feeling, that it was so far, therefore, to be trusted. He thus beheld in the pale morning light the resolve to separate from her; not as a hot and indignant instinct, but denuded of the passionateness which had made it scorch and burn; standing in its bones; nothing but a skeleton, but none the less there. Clare no longer hesitated.

At breakfast, and while they were packing the few remaining articles, he showed his weariness from the night's effort so unmistakably that Tess was on the point of revealing all that had happened; but the reflection that it would anger him, grieve him, stultify him, to know that he had instinctively manifested a fondness for her of which his common-sense did not approve; that his inclination had compromised his dignity when reason slept, again deterred her. It was too much like laughing at a man when sober for his erratic deeds during intoxication.

It just crossed her mind, too, that he might have a faint recollection of his tender vagary, and was disinclined to allude to it from a conviction that she would take amatory advantage of the opportunity it gave her of appealing to him anew not to go.

He had ordered by letter a vehicle from the nearest town, and soon after breakfast it arrived. She saw in it the beginning of the end—the temporary end, at least, for the revelation of his tenderness by the incident of the night raised dreams of a possible future with him. The luggage was put on the top, and the man drove them off, the miller and the old waiting-woman expressing some surprise at their precipitate departure, which Clare attributed to his discovery that the mill-work was not of the modern kind which he wished to investigate, a statement that was true so far as it went. Beyond this there was nothing in the manner of their leaving to suggest a *fiasco*, or that they were not going together to visit friends.

Their route lay near the dairy from which they had started with such solemn joy in each other a few days back, and, as Clare wished to wind up his business with Mr Crick, Tess could hardly avoid paying Mrs Crick a call at the same time, unless she would excite suspicion of their unhappy state.

To make the call as unobtrusive as possible they left the carriage by the wicket leading down from the high road to the dairy-house, and descended the track on foot, side by side. The withy-bed had been cut, and they could see over the stumps the spot to which Clare had followed her when he pressed her to be his wife; to the left the enclosure in which she had been fascinated by his harp; and far away behind the cowstalls the mead which had been the scene of their first embrace. The gold of the summer picture was now gray, the colours mean, the rich soil mud, and the river cold.

Over the barton-gate the dairyman saw them, and came forward, throwing into his face the kind of jocularity deemed appropriate in Talbothays and its vicinity on the re-appearance of the newly-married. Then Mrs Crick emerged from the house, and several others of their old acquaintance, though Marian and Retty did not seem to be there.

Tess valiantly bore their sly attacks and friendly humours, which affected her far otherwise than they supposed. In the tacit agreement of husband and wife to keep their estrangement a secret they behaved as would have been ordinary. And then, although she would rather there had been no word spoken on the subject, Tess had to hear in detail the story of Marian and Retty. The latter had gone home to her father's, and Marian had left to look for employment elsewhere. They feared she would come to no good.

To dissipate the sadness of this recital Tess went and bade all her favourite cows good-bye, touching each of them with her hand, and as she and Clare stood side by side at leaving, as if united body and soul, there would have been something peculiarly sorry in their aspect to one who should have seen it truly; two limbs of one life, as they outwardly were, his arm touching hers, her skirts touching him, facing one way, as against all the dairy facing the other, speaking in their adieux as 'we', and yet sundered like the poles. Perhaps something unusually stiff and embarrassed in their attitude, some awkwardness in acting up to their profession of unity, different from the natural shyness of young couples, may have been apparent, for when they were gone Mrs Crick said to her husband—

'How onnatural the brightness of her eyes did seem, and how they stood like waxen images and talked as if they were in a dream! Didn't it strike 'ee that 'twas so? Tess had always sommat strange in her, and she's not now quite like the proud young bride of a well-be-doing man.'

They re-entered the vehicle, and were driven along the roads towards Weatherbury and Stagfoot Lane, till they reached the Lane inn, where Clare dismissed the fly and man. They rested here a while, and entering the Vale were next driven onward towards her home by a stranger who did not know their relations. At a midway point, when Nuttlebury had been passed, and where there were cross-roads, Clare stopped the conveyance and said to Tess that if she meant to return to her mother's house it was here that he would leave her. As they could not talk with freedom in the driver's presence he asked her to accompany him for a few steps on foot along one of the branch roads; she assented, and directing the man to wait a few minutes they strolled away.

'Now, let us understand each other,' he said gently. 'There is no anger between us, though there is that which I cannot endure at present. I will try to bring myself to endure it. I will let you know where I go to as soon as I know myself. And if I can bring myself to bear it—if it is desirable, possible—I will come to you. But until I come to you it will be better that you should not try to come to me.'

The severity of the decree seemed deadly to Tess; she saw his view of her clearly enough; he could regard her in no other light than that of one who had practised gross deceit upon him. Yet could a woman who had done even what she had done deserve all this? But she could contest the point with him no further. She simply repeated after him his own words.

'Until you come to me I must not try to come to you?'

'Just so.'

'May I write to you?'

'O yes—if you are ill, or want anything at all. I hope that will not be the case; so that it may happen that I write first to you.'

'I agree to the conditions, Angel; because you know best what my punishment ought to be; only—only—don't make it more than I can bear!'

That was all she said on the matter. If Tess had been artful, had she made a scene, fainted, wept hysterically, in that lonely lane, notwithstanding the fury of fastidiousness with which he was possessed, he would probably not have withstood her. But her mood of long-suffering made his way easy for him, and she herself was his best advocate. Pride, too, entered into her submission—which perhaps was a symptom of that reckless acquiescence in chance too apparent in the whole d'Urberville family—and the many effective chords which she could have stirred by an appeal were left untouched.

The remainder of their discourse was on practical matters only. He now handed her a packet containing a fairly good sum of money, which he had obtained from his bankers for the purpose. The brilliants, the interest in which seemed to be Tess's for her life only (if he understood the wording of the will), he advised her to let him send to a bank for safety; and to this she readily agreed.

These things arranged he walked with Tess back to the carriage, and handed her in. The coachman was paid and told where to drive her. Taking next his own bag and umbrella—the sole articles he had brought with him hitherwards—he bade her good-bye, and they parted there and then.

The fly moved creepingly up a hill, and Clare watched it go with an unpremeditated hope that Tess would look out of the window for one moment. But that she never thought of doing, would not have ventured to do, lying in a half-dead faint inside. Thus he beheld her recede, and in the anguish of his heart quoted a line from a poet, with peculiar emendations of his own—

> God's *not* in his heaven: all's *wrong* with the world!

When Tess had passed over the crest of the hill he turned to go his own way, and hardly knew that he loved her still.

XXXVIII

As she drove on through Blackmoor Vale, and the landscape of her youth began to open around her, Tess aroused herself from her stupor. Her first thought was how would she be able to face her parents?

She reached a turnpike-gate which stood upon the highway to the village. It was thrown open by a stranger, not by the old man who had kept it for many years, and to whom she had been known; he had probably left on New Year's Day, the date when such changes were made. Having received no intelligence lately from her home, she asked the turnpike-keeper for news.

'Oh—nothing, miss,' he answered. 'Marlott is Marlott still. Folks have died and that. John Durbeyfield, too, hev had a daughter married this week to a gentleman-farmer; not from John's own house, you know; they was married elsewhere; the gentleman being of that high standing that John's own folk was not considered well-be-doing enough to have any part in it, the bridegroom seeming not to know how't have been discovered that John is a old and ancient nobleman himself by blood, with family skillentons in their own vaults to this day, but done out of his property in the time o' the Romans. However, Sir John, as we call 'n now, kept up the wedding-day as well as he could, and stood treat to everybody in the parish; and John's wife sung songs at The Pure Drop till past eleven o'clock.'

Hearing this, Tess felt so sick at heart that she could not decide to go home publicly in the fly with her luggage and belongings. She asked the turnpike-keeper if she might deposit her things at his house for a while, and, on his offering no objection, she dismissed her carriage, and went on to the village alone by a back lane.

At sight of her father's chimney she asked herself how she could possibly enter the house? Inside that cottage her relations were calmly supposing her far away on a wedding-tour with a comparatively rich man, who was to conduct her to bouncing prosperity; while here she was, friendless, creeping up to the old door quite by herself, with no better place to go to in the world.

She did not reach the house unobserved. Just by the garden-hedge she was met by a girl who knew her—one of the two or three with whom she had been intimate at school. After making a few inquiries as to how Tess came there, her friend, unheeding her tragic look, interrupted with—

'But where's thy gentleman, Tess?'

Tess hastily explained that he had been called away on business, and, leaving her interlocutor, clambered over the garden-hedge, and thus made her way to the house.

As she went up the garden-path she heard her mother singing by the back door, coming in sight of which she perceived Mrs Durbeyfield on the doorstep in the act of wringing a sheet. Having performed this without observing Tess, she went indoors, and her daughter followed her.

The washing-tub stood in the same old place on the same old quarter-hogshead, and her mother, having thrown the sheet aside, was about to plunge her arms in anew.

'Why—Tess!—my chil'—I thought you was married!—married really and truly this time—we sent the cider—'

'Yes, mother; so I am.'

'Going to be?'

'No—I am married.'

'Married! Then where's thy husband?'

'Oh, he's gone away for a time.'

'Gone away! When was you married, then? The day you said?'

'Yes, Tuesday, mother.'

'And now 'tis on'y Saturday, and he gone away?'

'Yes; he's gone.'

'What's the meaning o' that? 'Nation seize such husbands as you seem to get, say I!'

'Mother!' Tess went across to Joan Durbeyfield, laid her face upon the matron's bosom, and burst into sobs. 'I don't know how to tell 'ee, mother! You said to me, and wrote to me, that I was not to tell him. But I did tell him—I couldn't help it—and he went away!'

'O you little fool—you little fool!' burst out Mrs Durbeyfield, splashing Tess and herself in her agitation. 'My good God! that ever I should ha' lived to say it, but I say it again, you little fool!'

Tess was convulsed with weeping, the tension of so many days having relaxed at last.

'I know it—I know—I know!' she gasped through her sobs. 'But, O my mother, I could not help it! He was so good—and I felt the wickedness of trying to blind him as to what had happened! If—if—it were to be done again—I should do the same. I could not—I dared not—so sin—against him!'

'But you sinned enough to marry him first!'

'Yes, yes; that's where my misery do lie! But I thought he could get rid o' me by law if he were determined not to overlook it. And O, if you knew—if you could only half know how I loved him—how anxious I was to have him—and how wrung I was between caring so much for him and my wish to be fair to him!'

Tess was so shaken that she could get no further, and sank a helpless thing into a chair.

'Well, well; what's done can't be undone! I'm sure I don't know why children o' my bringing forth should all be bigger simpletons than other people's—not to know better than to blab such a thing as that, when he couldn't ha' found it out till too late!' Here Mrs Durbeyfield began shedding tears on her own account as a mother to be pitied. 'What your father will say I don't know,' she continued; 'for he's been talking about the wedding up at Rolliver's and The Pure Drop every day since, and about his family getting back to their rightful position through you—poor silly man!—and now you've made this mess of it! The Lord-a-Lord!'

As if to bring matters to a focus, Tess's father was heard approaching at that moment. He did not, however, enter immediately, and Mrs Durbeyfield said that she would break the bad news to him herself, Tess keeping out of sight for the present. After her first burst of disappointment Joan began to take the mishap as she had taken Tess's original trouble, as she would have taken a wet holiday or failure in the potato-crop; as a thing which had come upon them irrespective of desert or folly; a chance external impingement to be borne with; not a lesson.

Tess retreated upstairs, and beheld casually that the beds had been shifted, and new arrangements made. Her old bed had been adapted for two younger children. There was no place here for her now.

The room below being unceiled she could hear most of what went on there. Presently her father entered, apparently carrying a live hen. He was a foot-haggler now, having been obliged to sell his second horse, and he travelled with his basket on his arm. The hen had been carried about this morning as it was often carried, to show people that he was in his work, though it had lain, with its legs tied, under the table at Rolliver's for more than an hour.

'We've just had up a story about—' Durbeyfield began, and thereupon related in detail to his wife a discussion which had arisen at the inn about the clergy, originated by the fact of his daughter having married into a clerical family. 'They was formerly styled "sir", like my own ancestry,' he said, 'though nowadays their true style, strictly speaking, is "clerk" only.' As Tess had wished that no great publicity should be given to the event, he had mentioned no particulars. He hoped she would remove that prohibition soon. He proposed that the couple should take Tess's own name, d'Urberville, as uncorrupted. It was better than her husband's. He asked if any letter had come from her that day.

Then Mrs Durbeyfield informed him that no letter had come, but Tess unfortunately had come herself.

When at length the collapse was explained to him a sullen mortification, not usual with Durbeyfield, overpowered the influence of the cheering glass. Yet the intrinsic quality of the event moved his touchy sensitiveness less than its conjectured effect upon the minds of others.

'To think, now, that this was to be the end o't!' said Sir John. 'And I with a family vault under that there church of Kingsbere as big as Squire Jollard's ale-cellar, and my folk lying there in sixes and sevens, as genuine county bones and marrow as any recorded in history. And now to be sure what they fellers at Rolliver's and

The Pure Drop will say to me! How they'll squint and glane, and say, "This is yer mighty match is it; this is yer getting back to the true level of yer forefathers in King Norman's time!" I feel this is too much, Joan; I shall put an end to myself, title and all—I can bear it no longer! . . . But she can make him keep her if he's married her?'

'Why, yes. But she won't think o' doing that.'

'D'ye think he really have married her?—or is it like the first—'

Poor Tess, who had heard as far as this, could not bear to hear more. The perception that her word could be doubted even here, in her own parental house, set her mind against the spot as nothing else could have done. How unexpected were the attacks of destiny! And if her father doubted her a little, would not neighbours and acquaintance doubt her much? O, she could not live long at home!

A few days, accordingly, were all that she allowed herself here, at the end of which time she received a short note from Clare, informing her that he had gone to the North of England to look at a farm. In her craving for the lustre of her true position as his wife, and to hide from her parents the vast extent of the division between them, she made use of this letter as her reason for again departing, leaving them under the impression that she was setting out to join him. Still further to screen her husband from any imputation of unkindness to her, she took twenty-five pounds of the fifty pounds Clare had given her, and handed the sum over to her mother, as if the wife of a man like Angel Clare could well afford it, saying that it was a slight return for the trouble and humiliation she had brought upon them in years past. With this assertion of her dignity she bade them farewell; and after that there were lively doings in the Durbeyfield household for some time on the strength of Tess's bounty, her mother saying, and, indeed, believing, that the rupture which had arisen between the young husband and wife had adjusted itself under their strong feeling that they could not live apart from each other.

XXXIX

It was three weeks after the marriage that Clare found himself descending the hill which led to the well-known parsonage of his father. With his downward course the tower of the church rose into the evening sky in a manner of inquiry as to why he had come; and no living person in the twilighted town seemed to notice him, still less to expect him. He was arriving like a ghost, and the sound of his own footsteps was almost an encumbrance to be got rid of.

The picture of life had changed for him. Before this time he had known it but speculatively; now he thought he knew it as a practical man; though perhaps he did not, even yet. Nevertheless humanity stood before him no longer in the pensive sweetness of Italian art, but in the staring and ghastly attitudes of a Wiertz Museum, and with the leer of a study by Van Beers.

His conduct during these first weeks had been desultory beyond description. After mechanically attempting to pursue his agricultural plans as though nothing unusual had happened, in the manner recommended by the great and wise men of all ages, he concluded that very few of those great and wise men had ever gone so far outside themselves as to test the feasibility of their counsel. 'This is the chief thing: be not perturbed,' said the Pagan moralist. That was just Clare's own opinion. But he was perturbed. 'Let not your heart be troubled, neither let it be afraid,' said the Nazarene. Clare chimed in cordially; but his heart was troubled all the same. How he would have liked to confront those two great thinkers, and earnestly appeal to them as fellow-man to fellow-men, and ask them to tell him their method!

His mood transmuted itself into a dogged indifference till at length he fancied he was looking on his own existence with the passive interest of an outsider.

He was embittered by the conviction that all this desolation had been brought about by the accident of her being a d'Urberville. When he found that Tess came of that exhausted ancient line, and was not of the new tribes from below, as he had fondly dreamed, why had he not stoically abandoned her, in fidelity to his principles? This was what he had got by apostasy, and his punishment was deserved.

Then he became weary and anxious, and his anxiety increased. He wondered if he had treated her unfairly. He ate without knowing that he ate, and drank without tasting. As the hours dropped past, as the motive of each act in the long series of bygone days presented itself to his view, he perceived how intimately the notion of having Tess as a dear possession was mixed up with all his schemes and words and ways.

In going hither and thither he observed in the outskirts of a small town a red-and-blue placard setting forth the great advantages of the Empire of Brazil as a field for the emigrating agriculturalist. Land was offered there on exceptionally advantageous terms. Brazil somewhat attracted him as a new idea. Tess could eventually join him there, and perhaps in that country of contrasting scenes and notions and habits the conventions would not be so operative which made life with her seem impracticable to him here. In brief he was strongly inclined to try Brazil, especially as the season for going thither was just at hand.

With this view he was returning to Emminster to disclose his plan to his parents, and to make the best explanation he could make of arriving without Tess, short of revealing what had actually separated them. As he reached the door the new moon shone upon his face, just as the old one had done in the small hours of that morning when he had carried his wife in his arms across the river to the graveyard of the monks; but his face was thinner now.

Clare had given his parents no warning of his visit, and his arrival stirred the atmosphere of the Vicarage as the dive of the kingfisher stirs a quiet pool. His father and mother were both in the drawing-room, but neither of his brothers was now at home. Angel entered, and closed the door quietly behind him.

'But—where's your wife, dear Angel?' cried his mother. 'How you surprise us!'

'She is at her mother's—temporarily. I have come home rather in a hurry because I've decided to go to Brazil.'

'Brazil! Why they are all Roman Catholics there surely!'

'Are they? I hadn't thought of that.'

But even the novelty and painfulness of his going to a Papistical land could not displace for long Mr and Mrs Clare's natural interest in their son's marriage.

'We had your brief note three weeks ago announcing that it had taken place,' said Mrs Clare, 'and your father sent your godmother's gift to her, as you know. Of course it was best that none of us should be present, especially as you preferred to marry her from the dairy, and not at her home, wherever that may be. It would have embarrassed you, and given us no pleasure. Your brothers felt that very strongly. Now it is done we do not complain, particularly if she suits you for the business you have chosen to follow instead of the ministry of the Gospel . . . Yet I wish I could have seen her first, Angel, or have known a little more about her. We sent her no present of our own, not knowing what would best give her pleasure, but you must suppose it only delayed. Angel, there is no irritation in my mind or your father's against you for this marriage; but we have thought it much better to reserve our liking for your wife till we could see her. And now you have not brought her. It seems strange. What has happened?'

He replied that it had been thought best by them that she should go to her parents' home for the present, whilst he came there.

'I don't mind telling you, dear mother,' he said, 'that I always meant to keep her away from this house till I should feel she could come with credit to you. But this idea of Brazil is quite a recent one. If I do go it will be unadvisable for me to take her on this my first journey. She will remain at her mother's till I come back.'

'And I shall not see her before you start?'

He was afraid they would not. His original plan had been, as he had said, to refrain from bringing her there for some little while—not to wound their prejudices—feelings—in any way; and for other reasons he had adhered to it. He would have to visit home in the course of a year, if he went out at once; and it would be possible for them to see her before he started a second time—with her.

A hastily prepared supper was brought in, and Clare made further exposition of his plans. His mother's disappointment at not seeing the bride still remained with her. Clare's late enthusiasm for Tess had infected her through her maternal sympathies, till she had almost fancied that a good thing could come out of Nazareth—a charming woman out of Talbothays Dairy. She watched her son as he ate.

'Cannot you describe her? I am sure she is very pretty, Angel.'

'Of that there can be no question!' he said, with a zest which covered its bitterness.

'And that she is pure and virtuous goes without question?'

'Pure and virtuous, of course, she is.'

'I can see her quite distinctly. You said the other day that she was fine in figure; roundly built; had deep red lips like Cupid's bow; dark eyelashes and brows, an immense rope of hair like a ship's cable; and large eyes violety-bluey-blackish.'

'I did, mother.'

'I quite see her. And living in such seclusion she naturally had scarce ever seen any young man from the world without till she saw you.'

'Scarcely.'

'You were her first love?'

'Of course.'

'There are worse wives than these simple, rosy-mouthed, robust girls of the farm. Certainly I could have wished—well, since my son is to be an agriculturist, it is perhaps but proper that his wife should have been accustomed to an outdoor life.'

His father was less inquisitive; but when the time came for the chapter from the Bible which was always read before evening prayers, the Vicar observed to Mrs Clare—

'I think, since Angel has come, that it will be more appropriate to read the thirty-first of Proverbs than the chapter which we should have had in the usual course of our reading?'

'Yes, certainly,' said Mrs Clare. 'The words of King Lemuel' (she could cite chapter and verse as well as her husband). 'My dear son, your father has decided to read us the chapter in Proverbs in praise of a virtuous wife. We shall not need to be reminded to apply the words to the absent one. May Heaven shield her in all her ways!'

A lump rose in Clare's throat. The portable lectern was taken out from the corner and set in the middle of the fireplace, the two old servants came in, and Angel's father began to read at the tenth verse of the aforesaid chapter—' "Who can find a virtuous woman? for her price is far above rubies. She riseth while it is yet night, and giveth meat to her household. She girdeth her loins with strength and strengtheneth her arms. She perceiveth that her merchandise is good; her candle goeth not out by night. She looketh well to the ways of her household, and eateth not the bread of idleness. Her children arise up and call her blessed; her husband also, and he praiseth her. Many daughters have done virtuously, but thou excellest them all." '

When prayers were over, his mother said—

'I could not help thinking how very aptly that chapter your dear father read applied, in some of its particulars, to the woman you have chosen. The perfect woman, you see, was a working woman; not an idler; not a fine lady; but one who used her hands and her head and her heart for the good of others. "Her children arise up and call her blessed; her husband also, and he praiseth her. Many daughters have done virtuously, but she excelleth them all." Well, I wish I could have seen her, Angel. Since she is pure and chaste she would have been refined enough for me.'

Clare could bear this no longer. His eyes were full of tears, which seemed like drops of molten lead. He bade a quick good-night to these sincere simple souls whom he loved so well; who knew neither the world, the flesh, nor the devil in their own hearts; only as something vague and external to themselves. He went to his own chamber.

His mother followed him, and tapped at his door. Clare opened it to discover her standing without, with anxious eyes.

'Angel,' she asked, 'is there something wrong that you go away so soon? I am quite sure you are not yourself.'

'I am not, quite, mother,' he said.

'About her? Now, my son, I know it is that—I know it is about her! Have you quarrelled in these three weeks?'

'We have not exactly quarrelled,' he said. 'But we have had a difference—'

'Angel—is she a young woman whose history will bear investigation?'

With a mother's instinct Mrs Clare had put her finger on the kind of trouble that would cause such a disquiet as seemed to agitate her son.

'She is spotless!' he replied; and felt that if it had sent him to eternal hell there and then he would have told that lie.

'Then never mind the rest. After all, there are few purer things in nature than an unsullied country maid. Any crudeness of manner which may offend your more educated sense at first, will, I am sure, disappear under the influence of your companionship and tuition.'

Such terrible sarcasm of blind magnanimity brought home to Clare the secondary perception that he had utterly wrecked his career by his marriage, which had not been among his early thoughts after the disclosure. True, on his own account he cared very little about his career; but he had wished to make it at least a respectable one on account of his parents and brothers. And now as he looked into the candle its flame dumbly expressed to him that it was made to shine on sensible people, and that it abhorred lighting the face of a dupe and a failure.

When his agitation had cooled he would be at moments incensed with his poor wife for causing a situation in which he was obliged to practise deception on his parents. He almost talked to her in his anger, as if she had been in the room. And then her cooing voice, plaintive in expostulation, disturbed the darkness, the velvet touch of her lips passed over his brow, and he could distinguish in the air the warmth of her breath.

This night the woman of his belittling deprecations was thinking how great and good her husband was. But over them both there hung a deeper shade than the shade which Angel Clare perceived, namely, the shade of his own limitations. With all his attempted independence of judgment this advanced and well-meaning young man, a sample product of the last five-and-twenty years, was yet the slave to custom and conventionality when surprised back into his early teachings. No prophet had told him, and he was not prophet enough to tell himself, that essentially this young wife of his was as deserving of the praise of King Lemuel as any other woman endowed with the same dislike of evil, her moral value having to be reckoned not by achievement but by tendency. Moreover, the figure near at hand suffers on such occasions, because it shows up its sorriness without shade; while vague figures afar off are honoured, in that their distance makes artistic virtues of their stains. In considering what Tess was not, he overlooked what she was, and forgot that the defective can be more than the entire.

XL

At breakfast Brazil was the topic, and all endeavoured to take a hopeful view of Clare's proposed experiment with that country's soil, notwithstanding the discouraging reports of some farm-labourers who had emigrated thither and returned home within the twelve months. After breakfast Clare went into the little town to wind up such trifling matters as he was concerned with there, and to get from the local bank all the money he possessed. On his way back he encountered Miss Mercy Chant by the church, from whose walls she seemed to be a sort of emanation. She was carrying an armful of Bibles for her class, and such was her view of life that events which produced heartache in others wrought beatific smiles upon her—an enviable result, although, in the opinion of Angel, it was obtained by a curiously unnatural sacrifice of humanity to mysticism.

She had learnt that he was about to leave England, and observed what an excellent and promising scheme it seemed to be.

'Yes; it is a likely scheme enough in a commercial sense, no doubt,' he replied. 'But, my dear Mercy, it snaps the continuity of existence. Perhaps a cloister would be preferable.'

'A cloister! O, Angel Clare!'

'Well.'

'Why, you wicked man, a cloister implies a monk, and a monk Roman Catholicism.'

'And Roman Catholicism sin, and sin damnation. Thou art in a parlous state, Angel Clare.'

'*I* glory in my Protestantism!' she said severely.

Then Clare, thrown by sheer misery into one of the demoniacal moods in which a man does despite to his true principles, called her close to him, and fiendishly whispered in her ear the most heterodox ideas he could think of. His momentary laughter at the horror which appeared on her fair face ceased when it merged in pain and anxiety for his welfare.

'Dear Mercy,' he said, 'you must forgive me. I think I am going crazy!'

She thought that he was; and thus the interview ended, and Clare re-entered the Vicarage. With the local banker he deposited the jewels till happier days should arise. He also paid into the bank thirty pounds—to be sent to Tess in a few months, as she might require; and wrote to her at her parents' home in Blackmoor Vale to inform her of what he had done. This amount, with the sum he had already placed in her hands—about fifty pounds—he hoped would be amply sufficient for her wants just at present, particularly as in an emergency she had been directed to apply to his father.

He deemed it best not to put his parents into communication with her by informing them of her address; and, being unaware of what had really happened to estrange the two, neither his father nor his mother suggested that he should do so. During the day he left the parsonage, for what he had to complete he wished to get done quickly.

As the last duty before leaving this part of England it was necessary for him to call at the Wellbridge farmhouse, in which he had spent with Tess the first three days of their marriage, the trifle of rent having to be paid, the key given up of the rooms they had occupied, and two or three small articles fetched away that they had left behind. It was under this roof that the deepest shadow ever thrown upon his life had stretched its gloom over him. Yet when he had unlocked the door of the sitting-room and looked into it, the memory which returned first upon him was that of their happy arrival on a similar afternoon, the first fresh sense of sharing a habitation conjointly, the first meal together, the chatting by the fire with joined hands.

The farmer and his wife were in the fields at the moment of his visit, and Clare was in the rooms alone for some time. Inwardly swollen with a renewal of sentiments that he had not quite reckoned with, he went upstairs to her chamber, which had never been his. The bed was smooth as she had made it with her own hands on the morning of leaving. The mistletoe hung under the tester just as he had placed it. Having been there three or four weeks it was turning colour, and the leaves and berries were wrinkled. Angel took it down and crushed it into the grate. Standing there he for the first time doubted whether his course in this conjuncture had been a wise, much less a generous, one. But had he not been cruelly blinded? In the incoherent multitude of his emotions he knelt down at the bedside wet-eyed. 'O Tess! If you had only told me sooner, I would have forgiven you!' he mourned.

Hearing a footstep below he rose and went to the top of the stairs. At the bottom of the flight he saw a woman standing, and on her turning up her face recognized the pale, dark-eyed Izz Huett.

'Mr Clare,' she said, 'I've called to see you and Mrs Clare, and to inquire if ye be well. I thought you might be back here again.'

This was a girl whose secret he had guessed, but who had not yet guessed his; an honest girl who loved him—one who would have made as good, or nearly as good, a practical farmer's wife as Tess.

'I am here alone,' he said; 'we are not living here now.' Explaining why he had come, he asked, 'Which way are you going home, Izz?'

'I have no home at Talbothays Dairy now, sir,' she said.

'Why is that?'

Izz looked down.

'It was so dismal there that I left! I am staying out this way.' She pointed in a contrary direction, the direction in which he was journeying.

'Well—are you going there now? I can take you if you wish for a lift.'

Her olive complexion grew richer in hue.

'Thank 'ee, Mr Clare,' she said.

He soon found the farmer, and settled the account for his rent and the few other items which had to be considered by reason of the sudden abandonment of the lodgings. On Clare's return to his horse and gig Izz jumped up beside him.

'I am going to leave England, Izz,' he said, as they drove on. 'Going to Brazil.'

'And do Mrs Clare like the notion of such a journey?' she asked.

'She is not going at present—say for a year or so. I am going out to reconnoitre—to see what life there is like.'

They sped along eastward for some considerable distance, Izz making no observation.

'How are the others?' he inquired. 'How is Retty?'

'She was in a sort of nervous state when I zid her last; and so thin and hollow-cheeked that 'a do seem in a decline. Nobody will ever fall in love wi' her any more,' said Izz absently.

'And Marian?'

Izz lowered her voice.

'Marian drinks.'

'Indeed!'

'Yes. The dairyman has got rid of her.'

'And you!'

'I don't drink, and I bain't in a decline. But—I am no great things at singing afore breakfast now!'

'How is that? Do you remember how neatly you used to turn " 'Twas down in Cupid's Gardens" and "The Tailor's Breeches" at morning milking?'

'Ah, yes! When you first came, sir, that was. Not when you had been there a bit.'

'Why was that falling-off?'

Her black eyes flashed up to his face for one moment by way of answer.

'Izz!—how weak of you—for such as I!' he said, and fell into reverie. 'Then—suppose I had asked *you* to marry me?'

'If you had I should have said "Yes", and you would have married a woman who loved 'ee!'

'Really!'

'Down to the ground!' she whispered vehemently. 'O my God! did you never guess it till now!'

By-and-by they reached a branch road to a village.

'I must get down. I live out there,' said Izz abruptly, never having spoken since her avowal.

Clare slowed the horse. He was incensed against his fate, bitterly disposed towards social ordinances; for they had cooped him up in a corner, out of which there was no legitimate pathway. Why not be revenged on society by shaping his future domesticities loosely, instead of kissing the pedagogic rod of convention in this ensnaring manner.

'I am going to Brazil alone, Izz,' said he. 'I have separated from my wife for personal, not voyaging, reasons. I may never live with her again. I may not be able to love you; but—will you go with me instead of her?'

'You truly wish me to go?'

'I do. I have been badly used enough to wish for relief. And you at least love me disinterestedly.'

'Yes—I will go,' said Izz, after a pause.

'You will? You know what it means, Izz?'

'It means that I shall live with you for the time you are over there—that's good enough for me.'

'Remember, you are not to trust me in morals now. But I ought to remind you that it will be wrong-doing in the eyes of civilization—Western civilization, that is to say.'

'I don't mind that; no woman do when it comes to agony-point, and there's no other way!'

'Then don't get down, but sit where you are.'

He drove past the cross-roads, one mile, two miles, without showing any signs of affection.

'You love me very, very much, Izz?' he suddenly asked.

'I do—I have said I do! I loved you all the time we was at the dairy together!'

'More than Tess?'

She shook her head.

'No,' she murmured, 'not more than she.'

'How's that?'

'Because nobody could love 'ee more than Tess did! . . . She would have laid down her life for 'ee. I could do no more.'

Like the prophet on the top of Peor Izz Huett would fain have spoken perversely at such a moment, but the fascination exercised over her rougher nature by Tess's character compelled her to grace.

Clare was silent; his heart had risen at these straightforward words from such an unexpected unimpeachable quarter. In his throat was something as if a sob had solidified there. His ears repeated. '*She would have laid down her life for 'ee. I could do no more!*'

'Forget our idle talk, Izz,' he said, turning the horse's head suddenly. 'I don't know what I've been saying! I will now drive you back to where your lane branches off.'

'So much for honesty towards 'ee! O—how can I bear it—how can I—how can I!'

Izz Huett burst into wild tears, and beat her forehead as she saw what she had done.

'Do you regret that poor little act of justice to an absent one? O, Izz, don't spoil it by regret!'

She stilled herself by degrees.

'Very well, sir. Perhaps I didn't know what I was saying, either, wh—when I agreed to go! I wish—what cannot be!'

'Because I have a loving wife already.'

'Yes, yes! You have.'

They reached the corner of the lane which they had passed half an hour earlier, and she hopped down.

'Izz—please, please forget my momentary levity!' he cried. 'It was so ill-considered, so ill-advised!'

'Forget it? Never, never! O, it was no levity to me!'

He felt how richly he deserved the reproach that the wounded cry conveyed, and, in a sorrow that was inexpressible, leapt down and took her hand.

'Well, but, Izz, we'll part friends, anyhow? You don't know what I've had to bear!'

She was a really generous girl, and allowed no further bitterness to mar their adieux.

'I forgive 'ee, sir!' she said.

'Now Izz,' he said, while she stood beside him there, forcing himself to the mentor's part he was far from feeling; 'I want you to tell Marian when you see her that she is to be a good woman, and not to give way to folly. Promise that, and tell Retty that there are more worthy men than I in the world, that for my sake she is to act wisely and well—remember the words—wisely and well—for my sake. I send this message to them as a dying man to the dying;

for I shall never see them again. And you, Izzy, you have saved me by your honest words about my wife from an incredible impulse towards folly and treachery. Women may be bad, but they are not so bad as men in these things! On that one account I can never forget you. Be always the good and sincere girl you have hitherto been; and think of me as a worthless lover, but a faithful friend. Promise.'

She gave the promise.

'Heaven bless and keep you, sir. Good-bye!'

He drove on; but no sooner had Izz turned into the lane, and Clare was out of sight, than she flung herself down on the bank in a fit of racking anguish; and it was with a strained unnatural face that she entered her mother's cottage late that night. Nobody ever was told how Izz spent the dark hours that intervened between Angel Clare's parting from her and her arrival home.

Clare, too, after bidding the girl farewell, was wrought to aching thoughts and quivering lips. But his sorrow was not for Izz. That evening he was within a feather-weight's turn of abandoning his road to the nearest station, and driving across that elevated dorsal line of South Wessex which divided him from his Tess's home. It was neither a contempt for her nature, nor the probable state of her heart, which deterred him.

No; it was a sense that, despite her love, as corroborated by Izz's admission, the facts had not changed. If he was right at first, he was right now. And the momentum of the course on which he had embarked tended to keep him going in it, unless diverted by a stronger, more sustained force than had played upon him this afternoon. He could soon come back to her. He took the train that night for London, and five days after shook hands in farewell of his brothers at the port of embarkation.

XLI

From the foregoing events of the winter-time let us press on to an October day, more than eight months subsequent to the parting of Clare and Tess. We discover the latter in changed conditions; instead of a bride with boxes and trunks which others bore, we see her a lonely woman with a basket and a bundle in her own porterage, as at an earlier time when she was no bride; instead of the ample means that were projected by her husband for her comfort through this probationary period, she can produce only a flattened purse.

After again leaving Marlott, her home, she had got through the spring and summer without any great stress upon her physical powers, the time being mainly spent in rendering light irregular service at dairy-work near Port-Bredy to the west of the Blackmoor Valley, equally remote from her native place and from Talbothays. She preferred this to living on his allowance. Mentally she remained in utter stagnation, a condition which the mechanical occupation rather fostered than checked. Her consciousness was at that other dairy, at that other season, in the presence of the tender lover who had confronted her there—he who, the moment she had grasped him to keep for her own, had disappeared like a shape in a vision.

The dairy-work lasted only till the milk began to lessen, for she had not met with a second regular engagement as at Talbothays, but had done duty as a supernumerary only. However, as harvest was now beginning, she had simply to remove from the pasture to the stubble to find plenty of further occupation, and this continued till harvest was done.

Of the five-and-twenty pounds which had remained to her of Clare's allowance, after deducting the other half of the fifty as a contribution to her parents for the trouble and expense to which she had put them, she had as yet spent but little. But there now followed an unfortunate interval of wet weather, during which she was obliged to fall back upon her sovereigns.

She could not bear to let them go. Angel had put them into her hand, had obtained them bright and new from his bank for her; his touch had consecrated them to souvenirs of himself—they appeared to have had as yet no other history than such as was created by his and her own experiences—and to disperse them was like giving away relics. But she had to do it, and one by one they left her hands.

She had been compelled to send her mother her address from time to time, but she concealed her circumstances. When her money had almost gone a letter from her mother reached her. Joan stated that they were in dreadful difficulty; the autumn rains had gone through the thatch of the house, which required entire renewal; but this could not be done because the previous thatching had never been paid for. New rafters and a new ceiling upstairs also were required, which, with the previous bill, would amount to a sum of twenty pounds. As her husband was a man of means, and had doubtless returned by this time, could she not send them the money?

Tess had thirty pounds coming to her almost immediately from Angel's bankers, and, the case being so deplorable, as soon as the sum was received she sent the twenty as requested. Part of the remainder she was obliged to expend in winter clothing, leaving only a nominal sum for the whole inclement season at hand. When the last pound had gone, a remark of Angel's that whenever she required further resources she was to apply to his father, remained to be considered.

But the more Tess thought of the step the more reluctant was she to take it. The same delicacy, pride, false shame, whatever it may be called, on Clare's account, which had led her to hide from her own parents the prolongation of the estrangement, hindered her in owning to his that she was in want after the fair allowance he had left her. They probably despised her already; how much more they would despise her in the character of a mendicant! The consequence was that by no effort could the parson's daughter-in-law bring herself to let him know her state.

Her reluctance to communicate with her husband's parents might, she thought, lessen with the lapse of time; but with her own the reverse obtained. On her leaving their house after the short visit subsequent to her marriage they were under the impression that she was ultimately going to join her husband; and from that time to the present she had done nothing to disturb their belief that she was awaiting his return in comfort, hoping against hope that his journey to Brazil would result in a short stay only, after which he would come to fetch her, or that he would write for her to join him; in any case that they would soon present a united front to their families and the world. This hope she still fostered. To let her parents know that she was a deserted wife, dependent, now that she had relieved their necessities, on her own hands for a living, after the *éclat* of a marriage which was to nullify the collapse of the first attempt, would be too much indeed.

The set of brilliants returned to her mind. Where Clare had deposited them she did not know, and it mattered little, if it were true that she could only use and not sell them. Even were they absolutely hers it would be passing mean to enrich herself by a legal title to them which was not essentially hers at all.

Meanwhile her husband's days had been by no means free from trial. At this moment he was lying ill of fever in the clay lands near Curitiba in Brazil, having been drenched with thunder-storms and persecuted by other hardships, in common with all the English farmers and farm-labourers who, just at this time, were deluded into going thither by the promises of the Brazilian Government, and by the baseless assumption that those frames which, ploughing and sowing on English uplands, had resisted all the weathers to whose moods they had been born, could resist equally well all the weathers by which they were surprised on Brazilian plains.

To return. Thus it happened that when the last of Tess's sovereigns had been spent she was unprovided with others to take their place, while on account of the season she found it increasingly difficult to get employment. Not being aware of the rarity of intelligence, energy, health, and willingness in any sphere of life, she refrained from seeking an indoor occupation; fearing towns, large houses, people of means and social sophistication, and of manners other than rural. From that direction of gentility Black Care had come. Society might be better than she supposed from her slight experience of it. But she had no proof of this, and her instinct in the circumstances was to avoid its purlieus.

The small dairies to the west, beyond Port-Bredy, in which she had served as supernumerary milkmaid during the spring and summer required no further aid. Room would probably have been made for her at Talbothays, if only out of sheer compassion; but comfortable as her life had been there she could not go back. The anti-climax would be too intolerable; and her return might bring reproach upon her idolized husband. She could not have borne their pity, and their whispered remarks to one another upon her strange situation; though she would almost have faced a knowledge of her circumstances by every individual there, so long as her story had remained isolated in the mind of each. It was the interchange of ideas about her that made her sensitiveness wince. Tess could not account for this distinction; she simply knew that she felt it.

She was now on her way to an upland farm in the centre of the county, to which she had been recommended by a wandering letter which had reached her from Marian. Marian has somehow heard that Tess was separated from her husband—probably through Izz Huett—and the good-natured and now tippling girl, deeming Tess in trouble, had hastened to notify to her former friend that she herself had gone to this upland spot after leaving the dairy, and would like to see her there, where there was room for other hands, if it was really true that she worked again as of old.

With the shortening of the days all hope of obtaining her husband's forgiveness began to leave her; and there was something of the habitude of the wild animal in the unreflecting instinct with which she rambled on—disconnecting herself by littles from her eventful past at every step, obliterating her identity, giving no thought to accidents or contingencies which might make a quick discovery of her whereabouts by others of importance to her own happiness, if not to theirs.

Among the difficulties of her lonely position not the least was the attention she excited by her appearance, a certain bearing of distinction, which she had caught from Clare, being superadded to her natural attractiveness. Whilst the clothes lasted which had been prepared for her marriage, these casual glances of interest caused her no inconvenience, but as soon as she was compelled to don the wrapper of a fieldwoman, rude words were addressed to her more than once; but nothing occurred to cause her bodily fear till a particular November afternoon.

She had preferred the country west of the River Brit to the upland farm for which she was now bound, because, for one thing, it was nearer to the home of her husband's father; and to hover about that region unrecognized, with the notion that she might decide to call at the Vicarage some day, gave her pleasure. But having once decided to try the higher and drier levels, she pressed back eastward, marching afoot towards the village of Chalk-Newton, where she meant to pass the night.

The lane was long and unvaried, and, owing to the rapid shortening of the days, dusk came upon her before she was aware. She had reached the top of a hill down which the lane stretched its serpentine length in glimpses, when she heard footsteps behind her back, and in a few moments she was overtaken by a man. He stepped up alongside Tess and said—

'Good-night, my pretty maid': to which she civilly replied.

The light still remaining in the sky lit up her face, though the landscape was nearly dark. The man turned and stared hard at her.

'Why, surely, it is the young wench who was at Trantridge awhile—young Squire d'Urberville's friend? I was there at that time, though I don't live there now.'

She recognized in him the well-to-do boor whom Angel had knocked down at the inn for addressing her coarsely. A spasm of anguish shot through her, and she returned him no answer.

'Be honest enough to own it, and that what I said in the town was true, though your fancy-man was so up about it—hey, my sly one? You ought to beg my pardon for that blow of his, considering.'

Still no answer came from Tess. There seemed only one escape for her hunted soul. She suddenly took to her heels with the speed of the wind, and, without looking behind her, ran along the road till she came to a gate which opened directly into a plantation. Into this she plunged, and did not pause till she was deep enough in its shade to be safe against any possibility of discovery.

Under foot the leaves were dry, and the foliage of some holly bushes which grew among the deciduous trees was dense enough to keep off draughts. She scraped together the dead leaves till she had formed them into a large heap, making a sort of nest in the middle. Into this Tess crept.

Such sleep as she got was naturally fitful; she fancied she heard strange noises, but persuaded herself that they were caused by the breeze. She thought of her husband in some vague warm clime on the other side of the globe, while she was here in the cold. Was there another such a wretched being as she in the world? Tess asked herself; and, thinking of her wasted life, said, 'All is vanity.' She repeated the words mechanically, till she reflected that this was a most inadequate thought for modern days. Solomon had thought as far as that more than two thousand years ago; she herself, though not in the van of thinkers, had got much further. If all were only vanity, who would mind it? All was, alas, worse than vanity—injustice, punishment, exaction, death. The wife of Angel Clare put her hand to her brow, and felt its curve, and the edges of her eye-sockets perceptible under the soft skin, and thought as she did so that a time would come when that bone would be bare. 'I wish it were now,' she said.

In the midst of these whimsical fancies she heard a new strange sound among the leaves. It might be the wind; yet there was scarcely any wind. Sometimes it was a palpitation, sometimes a flutter; sometimes it was a sort of gasp or gurgle. Soon she was certain that the noises came from wild creatures of some kind, the more so when, originating in the boughs overhead, they were followed by the fall of a heavy body upon the ground. Had she been ensconced here under other and more pleasant conditions she would have become alarmed; but, outside humanity, she had at present no fear.

Day at length broke in the sky. When it had been day aloft for some little while it became day in the wood.

Directly the assuring and prosaic light of the world's active hours had grown strong she crept from under her hillock of leaves, and looked around boldly. Then she perceived what had been going on to disturb her. The plantation wherein she had taken shelter ran down at this spot into a peak, which ended it hitherward, outside the hedge being arable ground. Under the trees several pheasants lay about, their rich plumage dabbled with blood; some were dead, some feebly twitching a wing, some staring up at the sky, some pulsating quickly, some contorted, some stretched out—all of them writhing in agony, except the fortunate ones whose tortures had ended during the night by the inability of nature to bear more.

Tess guessed at once the meaning of this. The birds had been driven down into this corner the day before by some shooting-party; and while those that had dropped dead under the shot, or had died before nightfall, had been searched for and carried off, many badly wounded birds had escaped and hidden themselves away, or risen among the thick boughs, where they had maintained their position till they grew weaker with loss of blood in the night-time, when they had fallen one by one as she had heard them.

She had occasionally caught glimpses of these men in girlhood, looking over hedges, or peering through bushes, and pointing their guns, strangely accoutred, a bloodthirsty light in their eyes. She had been told that, rough and brutal as they seemed just then, they were not like this all the year round, but were, in fact, quite civil persons save during certain weeks of autumn and winter, when, like the inhabitants of the Malay Peninsula, they ran amuck, and made it their purpose to destroy life—in this case harmless feathered creatures, brought into being by artificial means solely to gratify these propensities—at once so unmannerly and so unchivalrous towards their weaker fellows in Nature's teeming family.

With the impulse of a soul who could feel for kindred sufferers as much as for herself, Tess's first thought was to put the still living birds out of their torture, and to this end with her own hands she broke the necks of as many as she could find, leaving them to lie where she had found them till the gamekeepers should come—as they probably would come—to look for them a second time.

'Poor darlings—to suppose myself the most miserable being on earth in the sight o' such misery as yours!' she exclaimed, her tears running down as she killed the birds tenderly. 'And not a twinge of bodily pain about me! I be not mangled, and I be not bleeding; and I have two hands to feed and clothe me.' She was ashamed of herself for her gloom of the night, based on nothing more tangible than a sense of condemnation under an arbitrary law of society which had no foundation in Nature.

XLII

It was now broad day, and she started again, emerging cautiously upon the highway. But there was no need for caution; not a soul was at hand, and Tess went onward with fortitude, her recollection of the birds' silent endurance of their night of agony impressing upon her the relativity of sorrows and the tolerable nature of her own, if she could once rise high enough to despise opinion. But that she could not do so long as it was held by Clare.

She reached Chalk-Newton, and breakfasted at an inn, where several young men were troublesomely complimentary to her good looks. Somehow she felt hopeful, for was it not possible that her husband also might say these same things to her even yet? She was bound to take care of herself on the chance of it, and keep off these casual lovers. To this end Tess resolved to run no further risks from her appearance. As soon as she got out of the village she entered a thicket and took from her basket one of the oldest field-gowns, which she had never put on even at the dairy—never since she had worked among the stubble at Marlott. She also, by a felicitous thought, took a handkerchief from her bundle and tied it round her face under her bonnet, covering her chin and half her cheeks and temples, as if she were suffering from toothache. Then with her little scissors, by the aid of a pocket looking-glass, she mercilessly nipped her eyebrows off, and thus insured against aggressive admiration she went on her uneven way.

'What a mommet of a maid!' said the next man who met her to a companion.

Tears came into her eyes for very pity of herself as she heard him.

'But I don't care!' she said. 'O no—I don't care! I'll always be ugly now, because Angel is not here, and I have nobody to take care of me. My husband that was is gone away, and never will love me any more; but I love him just the same, and hate all other men, and like to make 'em think scornfully of me!'

Thus Tess walks on; a figure which is part of the landscape; a fieldwoman pure and simple, in winter guise; a gray serge cape, a red woollen cravat, a stuff skirt covered by a whitey-brown rough wrapper, and buff-leather gloves. Every thread of that old attire has become faded and thin under the stroke of raindrops, the burn of sunbeams, and the stress of winds. There is no sign of young passion in her now—

> The maiden's mouth is cold
> . . . . .
> Fold over simple fold
> Binding her head.

Inside this exterior, over which the eye might have roved as over a thing scarcely percipient, almost inorganic, there was the record of a pulsing life which had learnt too well, for its years, of the dust and ashes of things, of the cruelty of lust and the fragility of love.

Next day the weather was bad, but she trudged on, the honesty, directness, and impartiality of elemental enmity disconcerting her but little. Her object being a winter's occupation and a winter's home, there was no time to lose. Her experience of short hirings had been such that she was determined to accept no more.

Thus she went forward from farm to farm in the direction of the place whence Marian had written to her, which she determined to make use of as a last shift only, its rumoured stringencies being the reverse of tempting. First she inquired for the lighter kinds of employment, and, as acceptance in any variety of these grew hopeless, applied next for the less light, till, beginning with the dairy and poultry tendance that she liked best, she ended with the heavy and coarse pursuits which she liked least—work on arable land: work of such roughness, indeed, as she would never have deliberately volunteered for.

Towards the second evening she reached the irregular chalk table-land or plateau, bosomed with semi-globular tumuli—as if

Cybele the Many-breasted were supinely extended there—which stretched between the valley of her birth and the valley of her love.

Here the air was dry and cold, and the long cart-roads were blown white and dusty within a few hours after rain. There were few trees, or none, those that would have grown in the hedges being mercilessly plashed down with the quickset by the tenant-farmers, the natural enemies of tree, bush, and brake. In the middle distance ahead of her she could see the summits of Bulbarrow and of Nettlecombe Tout, and they seemed friendly. They had a low and unassuming aspect from this upland, though as approached on the other side from Blackmoor in her childhood they were as lofty bastions against the sky. Southerly, at many miles' distance, and over the hills and ridges coastward, she could discern a surface like polished steel: it was the English Channel at a point far out towards France.

Before her, in a slight depression, were the remains of a village. She had, in fact, reached Flintcomb-Ash, the place of Marian's sojourn. There seemed to be no help for it; hither she was doomed to come. The stubborn soil around her showed plainly enough that the kind of labour in demand here was of the roughest kind; but it was time to rest from searching, and she resolved to stay, particularly as it began to rain. At the entrance to the village was a cottage whose gable jutted into the road, and before applying for a lodging she stood under its shelter, and watched the evening close in.

'Who would think I was Mrs Angel Clare!' she said.

The wall felt warm to her back and shoulders, and she found that immediately within the gable was the cottage fireplace, the heat of which came through the bricks. She warmed her hands upon them, and also put her cheek—red and moist with the drizzle—against their comforting surface. The wall seemed to be the only friend she had. She had so little wish to leave it that she could have stayed there all night.

Tess could hear the occupants of the cottage—gathered together after their day's labour—talking to each other within, and the rattle of their supper-plates was also audible. But in the village-street she had seen no soul as yet. The solitude was at last broken by the approach of one feminine figure, who, though the evening was cold, wore the print gown and the tilt-bonnet of summer time. Tess instinctively thought it might be Marian, and when she came near enough to be distinguishable in the gloom surely enough it was she. Marian was even stouter and redder in the face than formerly, and decidedly shabbier in attire. At any previous period of her existence Tess would hardly have cared to renew the acquaintance in such conditions; but her loneliness was excessive, and she responded readily to Marian's greeting.

Marian was quite respectful in her inquiries, but seemed much moved by the fact that Tess should still continue in no better condition than at first; though she had dimly heard of the separation.

'Tess—Mrs Clare—the dear wife of dear he! And is it really so bad as this, my child? Why is your cwomely face tied up in such a way? Anybody been beating 'ee? Not *he*?'

'No, no, no! I merely did it not to be clipsed or colled, Marian.'

She pulled off in disgust a bandage which could suggest such wild thoughts.

'And you've got no collar on' (Tess had been accustomed to wear a little white collar at the dairy).

'I know it, Marian.'

'You've lost it travelling.'

'I've not lost it. The truth is, I don't care anything about my looks; and so I didn't put it on.'

'And you don't wear your wedding-ring?'

'Yes, I do; but not in public. I wear it round my neck on a ribbon. I don't wish people to think who I am by marriage, or that I am married at all; it would be so awkward while I lead my present life.'

Marian paused.

'But you *be* a gentleman's wife; and it seems hardly fair that you should live like this!'

'O yes it is, quite fair; though I am very unhappy.'

'Well, well. *He* married you—and you can be unhappy!'

'Wives are unhappy sometimes; from no fault of their husbands—from their own.'

'You've no faults, deary; that I'm sure of. And he's none. So it must be something outside ye both.'

'Marian, dear Marian, will you do me a good turn without asking questions? My husband has gone abroad, and somehow I have overrun my allowance, so that I have to fall back upon my old work for a time. Do not call me Mrs Clare, but Tess, as before. Do they want a hand here?'

'O yes; they'll take one always, because few care to come. 'Tis a starve-acre place. Corn and swedes are all they grow. Though I be here myself, I feel 'tis a pity for such as you to come.'

'But you used to be as good a dairywoman as I.'

'Yes; but I've got out o' that since I took to drink. Lord, that's the only comfort I've got now! If you engage, you'll be set swede-hacking. That's what I be doing; but you won't like it.'

'O—anything! Will you speak for me?'

'You will do better by speaking for yourself.'

'Very well. Now, Marian, remember—nothing about *him*, if I get the place. I don't wish to bring his name down to the dirt.'

Marian, who was really a trustworthy girl though of coarser grain than Tess, promised anything she asked.

'This is pay-night,' she said, 'and if you were to come with me you would know at once. I be real sorry that you are not happy; but 'tis because he's away, I know. You couldn't be unhappy if he were here, even if he gie'd ye no money—even if he used you like a drudge.'

'That's true; I could not!'

They walked on together, and soon reached the farmhouse, which was almost sublime in its dreariness. There was not a tree within sight; there was not, at this season, a green pasture—nothing but fallow and turnips everywhere; in large fields divided by hedges plashed to unrelieved levels.

Tess waited outside the door of the farmhouse till the group of workfolk had received their wages, and then Marian introduced her. The farmer himself, it appeared, was not at home, but his wife, who represented him this evening, made no objection to hiring Tess, on her agreeing to remain till Old Lady-Day. Female field-labour was seldom offered now, and its cheapness made it profitable for tasks which women could perform as readily as men.

Having signed the agreement, there was nothing more for Tess to do at present than to get a lodging, and she found one in the house at whose gable-wall she had warmed herself. It was a poor subsistence that she had ensured, but it would afford a shelter for the winter at any rate.

That night she wrote to inform her parents of her new address, in case a letter should arrive at Marlott from her husband. But she did not tell them of the sorriness of her situation: it might have brought reproach upon him.

XLIII

THERE was no exaggeration in Marian's definition of Flintcomb-Ash farm as a starve-acre place. The single fat thing on the soil was Marian herself; and she was an importation. Of the three classes of village, the village cared for by its lord, the village cared for by itself, and the village uncared for either by itself or by its lord (in other words, the village of a resident squire's tenantry, the village of free or copy-holders, and the absentee-owner's village, farmed with the land) this place, Flintcomb-Ash, was the third.

But Tess set to work. Patience, that blending of moral courage with physical timidity, was now no longer a minor feature in Mrs Angel Clare; and it sustained her.

The swede-field in which she and her companion were set hacking was a stretch of a hundred odd acres, in one patch, on the highest ground of the farm, rising above stony lanchets or lynchets—the outcrop of siliceous veins in the chalk formation, composed of myriads of loose white flints in bulbous, cusped, and phallic shapes. The upper half of each turnip had been eaten off by the livestock, and it was the business of the two women to grub up the lower or earthy half of the root with a hooked fork called a hacker, that it might be eaten also. Each leaf of the vegetable having already been consumed, the whole field was in colour a desolate drab; it was a complexion without features, as if a face, from chin to brow, should be only an expanse of skin. The sky wore, in another colour, the same likeness; a white vacuity of countenance with the lineaments gone. So these two upper and nether visages confronted each other all day long, the white face looking down on the brown face, and the brown face looking up at the white face, without anything standing between them but the two girls crawling over the surface of the former like flies.

Nobody came near them, and their movements showed a mechanical regularity; their forms standing enshrouded in Hessian 'wroppers'—sleeved brown pinafores, tied behind to the bottom, to keep their gowns from blowing about—scant skirts revealing boots that reached high up the ankles, and yellow sheepskin gloves with gauntlets. The pensive character which the curtained hood lent to their bent heads would have reminded the observer of some early Italian conception of the two Marys.

They worked on hour after hour, unconscious of the forlorn aspect they bore in the landscape, not thinking of the justice or injustice of their lot. Even in such a position as theirs it was possible to exist in a dream. In the afternoon the rain came on again, and Marian said that they need not work any more. But if they did not work they would not be paid; so they worked on. It was so high a situation, this field, that the rain had no occasion to fall, but raced along horizontally upon the yelling wind, sticking into them like glass splinters till they were wet through. Tess had not known till now what was really meant by that. There are degrees of dampness, and a very little is called being wet through in common talk. But to stand working slowly in a field, and feel the creep of rain-water, first in legs and shoulders, then on hips and head, then at back, front, and sides, and yet to work on till the leaden light diminishes and marks that the sun is down, demands a distinct modicum of stoicism, even of valour.

Yet they did not feel the wetness so much as might be supposed. They were both young, and they were talking of the time when they lived and loved together at Talbothays Dairy, that happy green tract of land where summer had been liberal in her gifts; in substance to all, emotionally to these. Tess would fain not have conversed with Marian of the man who was legally, if not actually, her husband; but the irresistible fascination of the subject betrayed her into reciprocating Marian's remarks. And thus, as has been said, though the damp curtains of their bonnets flapped smartly into their faces, and their wrappers clung about them to wearisomeness, they lived all this afternoon in memories of green, sunny, romantic Talbothays.

'You can see a gleam of a hill within a few miles o' Froom Valley from here when 'tis fine,' said Marian.

'Ah! Can you?' said Tess, awake to the new value of this locality.

So the two forces were at work here as everywhere, the inherent will to enjoy, and the circumstantial will against enjoyment. Marian's will had a method of assisting itself by taking from her pocket as the afternoon wore on a pint bottle corked with white rag, from which she invited Tess to drink. Tess's unassisted power of dreaming, however, being enough for her sublimation at present, she declined except the merest sip, and then Marian took a pull herself from the spirits.

'I've got used to it,' she said, 'and can't leave it off now. 'Tis my only comfort—You see I lost him: you didn't; and you can do without it perhaps.'

Tess thought her loss as great as Marian's, but upheld by the dignity of being Angel's wife, in the letter at least, she accepted Marian's differentiation.

Amid this scene Tess slaved in the morning frosts and in the afternoon rains. When it was not swede-grubbing it was swede-trimming, in which process they sliced off the earth and the fibres with a bill-hook before storing the roots for future use. At this occupation they could shelter themselves by a thatched hurdle if it rained; but if it was frosty even their thick leather gloves could not prevent the frozen masses they handled from biting their fingers. Still Tess hoped. She had a conviction that sooner or later the magnanimity which she persisted in reckoning as a chief ingredient of Clare's character would lead him to rejoin her.

Marian, primed to a humorous mood, would discover the queer-shaped flints aforesaid, and shriek with laughter, Tess remaining severely obtuse. They often looked across the country to where the Var or Froom was known to stretch, even though they might not be able to see it; and, fixing their eyes on the cloaking gray mist, imagined the old times they had spent out there.

'Ah,' said Marian, 'how I should like another or two of our old set to come here! Then we could bring up Talbothays every day here afield, and talk of he, and of what nice times we had there, and o' the old things we used to know, and make it all come back again a'most, in seeming!' Marian's eyes softened, and her voice grew vague as the visions returned. 'I'll write to Izz Huett,' she said. 'She's biding at home doing nothing now, I know, and I'll tell her we be here, and ask her to come; and perhaps Retty is well enough now.'

Tess had nothing to say against the proposal, and the next she heard of this plan for importing old Talbothays' joys was two or three days later, when Marian informed her that Izz had replied to her inquiry, and had promised to come if she could.

There had not been such a winter for years. It came on in stealthy and measured glides, like the moves of a chess-player. One morning the few lonely trees and the thorns of the hedgerows appeared as if they had put off a vegetable for an animal integument. Every twig was covered with a white nap as of fur grown from the rind during the night, giving it four times its usual stoutness; the whole bush or tree forming a staring sketch in white lines on the mournful gray of the sky and horizon. Cobwebs revealed their presence on sheds and walls where none had ever been observed till brought out into visibility by the crystallizing atmosphere, hanging like loops of white worsted from salient points of the out-houses, posts, and gates.

After this season of congealed dampness came a spell of dry frost, when strange birds from behind the North Pole began to arrive silently on the upland of Flintcomb-Ash; gaunt spectral creatures with tragical eyes—eyes which had witnessed scenes of cataclysmal horror in inaccessible polar regions of a magnitude such as no human being had ever conceived, in curdling temperatures that no man could endure; which had beheld the crash of icebergs and the slide of snow-hills by the shooting light of the Aurora; been half blinded by the whirl of colossal storms and terraqueous distortions; and retained the expression of feature that such scenes had engendered. These nameless birds came quite near to Tess and Marian, but of all they had seen which humanity would never see, they brought no account. The traveller's ambition to tell was not theirs, and, with dumb impassivity, they dismissed experiences which they did not value for the immediate incidents of this homely upland—the trivial movements of the two girls in disturbing the clods with their hackers so as to uncover something or other that these visitants relished as food.

Then one day a peculiar quality invaded the air of this open country. There came a moisture which was not of rain, and a cold which was not of frost. It chilled the eyeballs of the twain, made their brows ache, penetrated to their skeletons, affecting the surface of the body less than its core. They knew that it meant snow, and in the night the snow came. Tess, who continued to live at the cottage with the warm gable that cheered any lonely pedestrian who paused beside it, awoke in the night, and heard above the thatch noises which seemed to signify that the roof had turned itself into a gymnasium of all the winds. When she lit her lamp to get up in the morning she found that the snow had blown through a chink in the casement, forming a white cone of the finest powder against the inside, and had also come down the chimney, so that it lay sole-deep upon the floor, on which her shoes left tracks when she moved about. Without, the storm drove so fast as to create a snow-mist in the kitchen; but as yet it was too dark out-of-doors to see anything.

Tess knew that it was impossible to go on with the swedes; and by the time she had finished breakfast beside the solitary little lamp, Marian arrived to tell her that they were to join the rest of the women at reed-drawing in the barn till the weather changed. As soon, therefore, as the uniform cloak of darkness without began to turn to a disordered medley of grays, they blew out the lamp, wrapped themselves up in their thickest pinners, tied their woollen cravats round their necks and across their chests, and started for the barn. The snow had followed the birds from the polar basin as a white pillar of a cloud, and individual flakes could not be seen. The blast smelt of icebergs, arctic seas, whales, and white bears, carrying the snow so that it licked the land but did not deepen on it. They trudged onwards with slanted bodies through the flossy fields, keeping as well as they could in the shelter of hedges, which, however, acted as strainers rather than screens. The air, afflicted to pallor with the hoary multitudes that infested it, twisted and spun them eccentrically, suggesting an achromatic chaos of things. But both the young women were fairly cheerful; such weather on a dry upland is not in itself dispiriting.

'Ha-ha! the cunning northern birds knew this was coming,' said

Marian. 'Depend upon't, they keep just in front o't all the way from the North Star. Your husband, my dear, is, I make no doubt, having scorching weather all this time. Lord, if he could only see his pretty wife now! Not that this weather hurts your beauty at all—in fact, it rather does it good.'

'You mustn't talk about him to me, Marian,' said Tess severely.

'Well, but—surely you care for 'n! Do you?'

Instead of answering, Tess, with tears in her eyes, impulsively faced in the direction in which she imagined South America to lie, and, putting up her lips, blew out a passionate kiss upon the snowy wind.

'Well, well, I know you do. But 'pon my body, it is a rum life for a married couple! There—I won't say another word! Well, as for the weather, it won't hurt us in the wheat-barn; but reed-drawing is fearful hard work—worse than swede-hacking. I can stand it because I'm stout; but you be slimmer than I. I can't think why maister should have set 'ee at it.'

They reached the wheat-barn and entered it. One end of the long structure was full of corn; the middle was where the reed-drawing was carried on, and there had already been placed in the reed-press the evening before as many sheaves of wheat as would be sufficient for the women to draw from during the day.

'Why, here's Izz!' said Marian.

Izz it was, and she came forward. She had walked all the way from her mother's home on the previous afternoon, and, not deeming the distance so great, had been belated, arriving, however, just before the snow began, and sleeping at the ale-house. The farmer had agreed with her mother at market to take her on if she came to-day, and she had been afraid to disappoint him by delay.

In addition to Tess, Marian, and Izz, there were two women from a neighbouring village; two Amazonian sisters, whom Tess with a start remembered as Dark Car the Queen of Spades and her junior the Queen of Diamonds—those who had tried to fight with her in the midnight quarrel at Trantridge. They showed no recognition of her, and possibly had none, for they had been under the influence of liquor on that occasion, and were only temporary sojourners there as here. They did all kinds of men's work by preference, including well-sinking, hedging, ditching, and excavating, without any sense of fatigue. Noted reed-drawers were they too, and looked round upon the other three with some superciliousness.

Putting on their gloves all set to work in a row in front of the press, an erection formed of two posts connected by a cross-beam, under which the sheaves to be drawn from were laid ears outward, the beam being pegged down by pins in the uprights, and lowered as the sheaves diminished.

The day hardened in colour, the light coming in at the barn-door upwards from the snow instead of downwards from the sky. The girls pulled handful after handful from the press; but by reason of the presence of the strange women, who were recounting scandals, Marian and Izz could not at first talk of old times as they wished to do. Presently they heard the muffled tread of a horse, and the farmer rode up to the barn-door. When he had dismounted he came close to Tess, and remained looking musingly at the side of her face. She had not turned at first, but his fixed attitude led her to look round, when she perceived that her employer was the native of Trantridge from whom she had taken flight on the high-road because of his allusion to her history.

He waited till she had carried the drawn bundles to the pile outside, when he said, 'So you be the young woman who took my civility in such ill part? Be drowned if I didn't think you might be as soon as I heard of your being hired! Well, you thought you had got the better of me the first time at the inn with your fancy-man, and the second time on the road, when you bolted; but now I think I've got the better of you.' He concluded with a hard laugh.

Tess, between the Amazons and the farmer like a bird caught in a clap-net, returned no answer, continuing to pull the straw. She could read character sufficiently well to know by this time that she had nothing to fear from her employer's gallantry; it was rather the tyranny induced by his mortification at Clare's treatment of him. Upon the whole she preferred that sentiment in man and felt brave enough to endure it.

'You thought I was in love with 'ee I suppose? Some women are such fools, to take every look as serious earnest. But there's nothing like a winter afield for taking that nonsense out o' young wenches' heads; and you've signed and agreed till Lady-Day. Now, are you going to beg my pardon?'

'I think you ought to beg mine.'

'Very well—as you like. But we'll see which is master here. Be they all the sheaves you've done to-day?'

'Yes, sir.'

''Tis a very poor show. Just see what they've done over there' (pointing to the two stalwart women). 'The rest, too, have done better than you.'

'They've all practised it before, and I have not. And I thought it made no difference to you as it is task work, and we are only paid for what we do.'

'Oh, but it does. I want the barn cleared.'

'I am going to work all the afternoon instead of leaving at two as the others will do.'

He looked sullenly at her and went away. Tess felt that she could not have come to a much worse place; but anything was better than gallantry. When two o'clock arrived the professional reed-drawers tossed off the last half-pint in their flagon, put down their hooks, tied their last sheaves, and went away. Marian and Izz would have done likewise, but on hearing that Tess meant to stay, to make up by longer hours for her lack of skill, they would not leave her. Looking out at the snow, which still fell, Marian exclaimed, 'Now we've got it all to ourselves.' And so at last the conversation turned to their old experiences at the dairy; and, of course, the incidents of their affection for Angel Clare.

'Izz and Marian,' said Mrs Angel Clare, with a dignity which was extremely touching, seeing how very little of a wife she was: 'I can't join in talk with you now, as I used to do, about Mr Clare; you will see that I cannot; because, although he is gone away from me for the present, he is my husband.'

Izz was by nature the sauciest and most caustic of all the four girls who had loved Clare. 'He was a very splendid lover, no doubt,' she said; 'but I don't think he is a too fond husband to go away from you so soon.'

'He had to go—he was obliged to go, to see about the land over there!' pleaded Tess.

'He might have tided 'ee over the winter.'

'Ah—that's owing to an accident—a misunderstanding; and we won't argue it,' Tess answered, with tearfulness in her words. 'Perhaps there's a good deal to be said for him! He did not go away, like some husbands, without telling me; and I can always find out where he is.'

After this they continued for some long time in a reverie, as they went on seizing the ears of corn, drawing out the straw, gathering it under their arms, and cutting off the ears with their bill-hooks, nothing sounding in the barn but the swish of the straw and the crunch of the hook. Then Tess suddenly flagged, and sank down upon the heap of wheat-ears at her feet.

'I knew you wouldn't be able to stand it!' cried Marian. 'It wants harder flesh than yours for this work.'

Just then the farmer entered. 'Oh, that's how you get on when I am away,' he said to her.

'But it is my own loss,' she pleaded. 'Not yours.'

'I want it finished,' he said doggedly, as he crossed the barn and went out at the other door.

'Don't 'ee mind him, there's a dear,' said Marian. 'I've worked here before. Now you go and lie down there, and Izz and I will make up your number.'

'I don't like to let you do that. I'm taller than you, too.'

However, she was so overcome that she consented to lie down awhile, and reclined on a heap of pull-tails—the refuse after the straight straw had been drawn—thrown up at the further side of the barn. Her succumbing had been as largely owing to agitation at re-opening the subject of her separation from her husband as to the hard work. She lay in a state of percipience without volition, and the rustle of the straw and the cutting of the ears by the others had the weight of bodily touches.

She could hear from her corner, in addition to these noises, the murmur of their voices. She felt certain that they were continuing the subject already broached, but their voices were so low that she could not catch the words. At last Tess grew more and more anxious to know what they were saying, and, persuading herself that she felt better, she got up and resumed work.

Then Izz Huett broke down. She had walked more than a dozen miles the previous evening, had gone to bed at midnight, and had risen again at five o'clock. Marian alone, thanks to her bottle of liquor and her stoutness of build, stood the strain upon back and arms without suffering. Tess urged Izz to leave off, agreeing, as she felt better, to finish the day without her, and make equal division of the number of sheaves.

Izz accepted the offer gratefully, and disappeared through the great door into the snowy track to her lodging. Marian, as was the case every afternoon at this time on account of the bottle, began to feel in a romantic vein.

'I should not have thought it of him—never!' she said in a dreamy tone. 'And I loved him so! I didn't mind his having *you*. But this about Izz is too bad!'

Tess, in her start at the words, narrowly missed cutting off a finger with the bill-hook.

'Is it about my husband?' she stammered.

'Well, yes. Izz said, "Don't 'ee tell her;" but I am sure I can't help it! It was what he wanted Izz to do. He wanted her to go off to Brazil with him.'

Tess's face faded as white as the scene without, and its curves straightened. 'And did Izz refuse to go?' she asked.

'I don't know. Anyhow he changed his mind.'

'Pooh—then he didn't mean it! 'Twas just a man's jest!'

'Yes he did; for he drove her a good-ways towards the station.'

'He didn't take her!'

They pulled on in silence till Tess, without any premonitory symptoms, burst out crying.

'There!' said Marian. 'Now I wish I hadn't told 'ee!'

'No. It is a very good thing that you have done! I have been living on in a thirtover, lackaday way, and have not seen what it may lead to! I ought to have sent him a letter oftener. He said I could not go to him, but he didn't say I was not to write as often as I liked. I won't dally like this any longer! I have been very wrong and neglectful in leaving everything to be done by him!'

The dim light in the barn grew dimmer, and they could see to work no longer. When Tess had reached home that evening, and had entered into the privacy of her little white-washed chamber, she began impetuously writing a letter to Clare. But falling into doubt she could not finish it. Afterwards she took the ring from the ribbon on which she wore it next her heart, and retained it on her finger all night, as if to fortify herself in the sensation that she was really the wife of this elusive lover of hers, who could propose that Izz should go with him abroad, so shortly after he had left her. Knowing that, how could she write entreaties to him, or show that she cared for him any more?

XLIV

By the disclosure in the barn her thoughts were led anew in the direction which they had taken more than once of late—to the distant Emminster Vicarage. It was through her husband's parents that she had been charged to send a letter to Clare if she desired; and to write to them direct if in difficulty. But that sense of her having morally no claim upon him had always led Tess to suspend her impulse to send these notes; and to the family at the Vicarage, therefore, as to her own parents since her marriage, she was virtually non-existent. This self-effacement in both directions had been quite in consonance with her independent character of desiring nothing by way of favour or pity to which she was not entitled on a fair consideration of her deserts. She had set herself to stand or fall by her qualities, and to waive such merely technical claims upon a strange family as had been established for her by the flimsy fact of a member of that family, in a season of impulse, writing his name in a church-book beside hers.

But now that she was stung to a fever by Izz's tale there was a limit to her powers of renunciation. Why had her husband not written to her? He had distinctly implied that he would at least let her know of the locality to which he had journeyed; but he had not sent a line to notify his address. Was he really indifferent? But was he ill? Was it for her to make some advance? Surely she might summon the courage of solicitude, call at the Vicarage for intelligence, and express her grief at his silence. If Angel's father were the good man she had heard him represented to be, he would be able to enter into her heart-starved situation. Her social hardships she could conceal.

To leave the farm on a week-day was not in her power; Sunday was the only possible opportunity. Flintcomb-Ash being in the middle of the cretaceous tableland over which no railway had climbed as yet, it would be necessary to walk. And the distance being fifteen miles each way she would have to allow herself a long day for the undertaking by rising early.

A fortnight later, when the snow had gone, and had been followed by a hard black frost, she took advantage of the state of the roads to try the experiment. At four o'clock that Sunday morning she came downstairs and stepped out into the starlight. The weather was still favourable, the ground ringing under her feet like an anvil.

Marian and Izz were much interested in her excursion, knowing that the journey concerned her husband. Their lodgings were in a cottage a little further along the lane, but they came and assisted Tess in her departure, and argued that she should dress up in her very prettiest guise to captivate the hearts of her parents-in-law; though she, knowing of the austere and Calvinistic tenets of old Mr Clare, was indifferent, and even doubtful. A year had now elapsed since her sad marriage, but she had preserved sufficient draperies from the wreck of her then full wardrobe to clothe her very charmingly as a simple country girl with no pretensions to recent fashion; a soft gray woollen gown, with white crape quilling against the pink skin of her face and neck, and a black velvet jacket and hat.

''Tis a thousand pities your husband can't see 'ee now—you do look a real beauty!' said Izz Huett, regarding Tess as she stood on the threshold between the steely starlight without and the yellow candlelight within. Izz spoke with a magnanimous abandonment of herself to the situation; she could not be—no woman with a heart bigger than a hazel-nut could be—antagonistic to Tess in her presence, the influence which she exercised over those of her own sex being of a warmth and strength quite unusual, curiously overpowering the less worthy feminine feelings of spite and rivalry.

With a final tug and touch here, and a slight brush there, they let her go; and she was absorbed into the pearly air of the foredawn. They heard her footsteps tap along the hard road as she stepped out to her full pace. Even Izz hoped she would win, and, though without any particular respect for her own virtue, felt glad that she had been prevented wronging her friend when momentarily tempted by Clare.

It was a year ago, all but a day, that Clare had married Tess, and only a few days less than a year that he had been absent from her. Still, to start on a brisk walk, and on such an errand as hers, on a dry clear wintry morning, through the rarefied air of these chalky hogs'-backs, was not depressing; and there is no doubt that her dream at starting was to win the heart of her mother-in-law, tell her whole history to that lady, enlist her on her side, and so gain back the truant.

In time she reached the edge of the vast escarpment below which stretched the loamy Vale of Blackmoor, now lying misty and still in the dawn. Instead of the colourless air of the uplands the atmosphere down there was a deep blue. Instead of the great enclosures of a hundred acres in which she was now accustomed to toil there were little fields below her of less than half-a-dozen acres, so numerous that they looked from this height like the meshes of a net. Here the landscape was whitey-brown; down there, as in Froom Valley, it was always green. Yet it was in that vale that her sorrow had taken shape, and she did not love it as formerly. Beauty to her, as to all who have felt, lay not in the thing, but in what the thing symbolized.

Keeping the Vale on her right she steered steadily westward; passing above the Hintocks, crossing at right-angles the high-road from Sherton-Abbas to Casterbridge, and skirting Dogbury Hill and High-Stoy, with the dell between them called 'The Devil's Kitchen'. Still following the elevated way she reached Cross-in-Hand, where the stone pillar stands desolate and silent, to mark the site of a miracle, or murder, or both. Three miles further she cut across the straight and deserted Roman road called Long-Ash Lane; leaving which as soon as she reached it she dipped down a hill by a transverse lane into the small town or village of Evershead, being now about half-way over the distance. She made a halt here, and breakfasted a second time, heartily enough—not at the Sow-and-Acorn, for she avoided inns, but at a cottage by the church.

The second half of her journey was through a more gentle country, by way of Benvill Lane. But as the mileage lessened between her and the spot of her pilgrimage, so did Tess's confidence decrease, and her enterprise loom out more formidably. She saw her purpose in such staring lines, and the landscape so faintly, that she was sometimes in danger of losing her way. However, about noon she paused by a gate on the edge of the basin in which Emminster and its Vicarage lay.

The square tower, beneath which she knew that at that moment the Vicar and his congregation were gathered, had a severe look in her eyes. She wished that she had somehow contrived to come on a week-day. Such a good man might be prejudiced against a woman who had chosen Sunday, never realizing the necessities of her case. But it was incumbent upon her to go on now. She took off the thick boots in which she had walked thus far, put on her pretty thin ones of patent leather, and, stuffing the former into the hedge by the gate-post where she might readily find them again, descended the hill; the freshness of colour she had derived from the keen air thinning away in spite of her as she drew near the parsonage.

Tess hoped for some accident that might favour her, but nothing favoured her. The shrubs on the Vicarage lawn rustled uncomfortably in the frosty breeze; she could not feel by any stretch of imagination, dressed to her highest as she was, that the house was the residence of near relations; and yet nothing essential, in nature or emotion, divided her from them: in pains, pleasures, thoughts, birth, death, and after-death, they were the same.

She nerved herself by an effort, entered the swing-gate, and rang the door-bell. The thing was done; there could be no retreat. No; the thing was not done. Nobody answered to her ringing. The effort had to be risen to and made again. She rang a second time, and the agitation of the act, coupled with her weariness after the fifteen miles' walk, led her to support herself while she waited by resting her hand on her hip, and her elbow against the wall of the porch. The wind was so nipping that the ivy-leaves had become wizened and gray, each tapping incessantly upon its neighbour with a disquieting stir of her nerves. A piece of blood-stained paper, caught up from some meatbuyer's dust-heap, beat up and down the road without the gate; too flimsy to rest, too heavy to fly away; and a few straws kept it company.

The second peal had been louder, and still nobody came. Then she walked out of the porch, opened the gate, and passed through. And though she looked dubiously at the house-front as if inclined to return, it was with a breath of relief that she closed the gate. A feeling haunted her that she might have been recognized (though how she could not tell), and orders been given not to admit her.

Tess went as far as the corner. She had done all she could do; but determined not to escape present trepidation at the expense of future distress, she walked back again quite past the house, looking up at all the windows.

Ah—the explanation was that they were all at church, every one. She remembered her husband saying that his father always insisted upon the household, servants included, going to morning-service, and, as a consequence, eating cold food when they came home. It was, therefore, only necessary to wait till the service was over. She would not make herself conspicuous by waiting on the spot, and she started to get past the church into the lane. But as she reached the churchyard-gate the people began pouring out, and Tess found herself in the midst of them.

The Emminster congregation looked at her as only a congregation of small country-townsfolk walking home at its leisure can look at a woman out of the common whom it perceives to be a stranger. She quickened her pace, and ascended the road by which she had come, to find a retreat between its hedges till the Vicar's family should have lunched, and it might be convenient for them to receive her. She soon distanced the churchgoers, except two youngish men, who, linked arm-in-arm, were beating up behind her at a quick step.

As they drew nearer she could hear their voices engaged in earnest discourse, and, with the natural quickness of a woman in her situation, did not fail to recognize in those voices the quality of her husband's tones. The pedestrians were his two brothers. Forgetting all her plans, Tess's one dread was lest they should overtake her now, in her disorganized condition, before she was prepared to confront them; for though she felt that they could not identify her she instinctively dreaded their scrutiny. The more briskly they walked the more briskly walked she. They were plainly bent upon taking a short quick stroll before going indoors to lunch or dinner, to restore warmth to limbs chilled with sitting through a long service.

Only one person had preceded Tess up the hill—a ladylike young woman, somewhat interesting, though, perhaps, a trifle *guindée* and prudish. Tess had nearly overtaken her when the speed of her brothers-in-law brought them so nearly behind her back that she could hear every word of their conversation. They said nothing, however, which particularly interested her till, observing the young lady still further in front, one of them remarked, 'There is Mercy Chant. Let us overtake her.'

Tess knew the name. It was the woman who had been destined for Angel's life-companion by his and her parents, and whom he probably would have married but for her intrusive self. She would have known as much without previous information if she had waited a moment, for one of the brothers proceeded to say: 'Ah! poor Angel, poor Angel! I never see that nice girl without more and more regretting his precipitancy in throwing himself away upon a dairymaid, or whatever she may be. It is a queer business, apparently. Whether she has joined him yet or not I don't know; but she had not done so some months ago when I heard from him.'

'I can't say. He never tells me anything nowadays. His ill-considered marriage seems to have completed that estrangement from me which was begun by his extraordinary opinions.'

Tess beat up the long hill still faster; but she could not outwalk them without exciting notice. At last they outsped her altogether, and passed her by. The young lady still further ahead heard their footsteps and turned. Then there was a greeting and a shaking of hands, and the three went on together.

They soon reached the summit of the hill, and, evidently intending this point to be the limit of their promenade, slackened pace and turned all three aside to the gate whereat Tess had paused an hour before that time to reconnoitre the town before descending into it. During their discourse one of the clerical brothers probed the hedge carefully with his umbrella, and dragged something to light.

'Here's a pair of old boots,' he said. 'Thrown away, I suppose, by some tramp or other.'

'Some impostor who wished to come into the town barefoot, perhaps, and so excite our sympathies,' said Miss Chant. 'Yes, it must have been, for they are excellent walking-boots—by no means worn out. What a wicked thing to do! I'll carry them home for some poor person.'

Cuthbert Clare, who had been the one to find them, picked them up for her with the crook of his stick; and Tess's boots were appropriated.

She, who had heard this, walked past under the screen of her woollen veil, till, presently looking back, she perceived that the church party had left the gate with her boots and retreated down the hill.

Thereupon our heroine resumed her walk. Tears, blinding tears, were running down her face. She knew that it was all sentiment, all baseless impressibility, which had caused her to read the scene as her own condemnation; nevertheless she could not get over it; she could not contravene in her own defenceless person all these untoward omens. It was impossible to think of returning to the Vicarage. Angel's wife felt almost as if she had been hounded up that hill like a scorned thing by those—to her—super-fine clerics. Innocently as the slight had been inflicted, it was somewhat unfortunate that she had encountered the son and not the father, who, despite his narrowness, was far less starched and ironed than they, and had to the full the gift of charity. As she again thought of her dusty boots she almost pitied those habiliments for the quizzing to which they had been subjected, and felt how hopeless life was for their owner.

'Ah!' she said, still sighing in pity of herself, '*they* didn't know that I wore those over the roughest part of the road to save these pretty ones *he* bought for me—no—they did not know it! And they didn't think that *he* chose the colour o' my pretty frock—no—how could they? If they had known perhaps they would not have cared, for they don't care much for him, poor thing!'

Then she grieved for the beloved man whose conventional standard of judgment had caused her all these latter sorrows; and she went her way without knowing that the greatest misfortune of her life was this feminine loss of courage at the last and critical moment through her estimating her father-in-law by his sons. Her present condition was precisely one which would have enlisted the sympathies of old Mr and Mrs Clare. Their hearts went out of them at a bound towards extreme cases, when the subtle mental troubles of the less desperate among mankind failed to win their interest or regard. In jumping at Publicans and Sinners they would forget that a word might be said for the worries of Scribes and Pharisees; and this defect or limitation might have recommended their own daughter-in-law to them at this moment as a fairly choice sort of lost person for their love.

Thereupon she began to plod back along the road by which she had come not altogether full of hope, but full of a conviction that a crisis in her life was approaching. No crisis, apparently, had supervened; and there was nothing left for her to do but to continue upon that starve-acre farm till she could again summon courage to face the vicarage. She did, indeed, take sufficient interest in herself to throw up her veil on this return journey, as if to let the world see that she could at least exhibit a face such as Mercy Chant could not show. But it was done with a sorry shake of the head. 'It is nothing—it is nothing!' she said. 'Nobody loves it; nobody sees it. Who cares about the looks of a castaway like me!'

Her journey back was rather a meander than a march. It had no sprightliness, no purpose; only a tendency. Along the tedious length of Benvill Lane she began to grow tired, and she leant upon gates and paused by milestones.

She did not enter any house till, at the seventh or eight mile, she descended the steep long hill below which lay the village or townlet of Evershead, where in the morning she had breakfasted with such contrasting expectations. The cottage by the church, in which she again sat down, was almost the first at that end of the village, and while the woman fetched her some milk from the pantry, Tess, looking down the street, perceived that the place seemed quite deserted.

'The people are gone to afternoon service, I suppose?' she said.

'No, my dear,' said the old woman. ''Tis too soon for that; the bells hain't strook out yet. They be all gone to hear the preaching in yonder barn. A ranter preaches there between the services—an excellent, fiery, Christian man, they say. But, Lord, I don't go to hear'n! What comes in the regular way over the pulpit is hot enough for I.'

Tess soon went onward into the village, her footsteps echoing against the houses as though it were a place of the dead. Nearing the central part her echoes were intruded on by other sounds; and seeing the barn not far off the road, she guessed these to be the utterances of the preacher.

His voice became so distinct in the still clear air that she could soon catch his sentences, though she was on the closed side of the barn. The sermon, as might be expected, was of the extremest antinomian type; on justification by faith, as expounded in the theology of St Paul. This fixed idea of the rhapsodist was delivered with animated enthusiasm, in a manner entirely declamatory, for he had plainly no skill as a dialectician. Although Tess had not heard the beginning of the address, she learnt what the text had been from its constant iteration—

> 'O foolish Galatians, who hath bewitched you, that ye should not obey the truth, before whose eyes Jesus Christ hath been evidently set forth, crucified among you?'

Tess was all the more interested, as she stood listening behind, in finding that the preacher's doctrine was a vehement form of the views of Angel's father, and her interest intensified when the speaker began to detail his own spiritual experiences of how he had come by those views. He had, he said, been the greatest of sinners. He had scoffed; he had wantonly associated with the reckless and the lewd. But a day of awakening had come, and, in a human sense, it had been brought about mainly by the influence of a certain clergyman, whom he had at first grossly insulted; but whose parting words had sunk into his heart, and had remained there, till by the grace of Heaven they had worked this change in him, and made him what they saw him.

But more startling to Tess than the doctrine had been the voice, which, impossible as it seemed, was precisely that of Alec d'Urberville. Her face fixed in painful suspense she came round to the front of the barn, and passed before it. The low winter sun beamed directly upon the great double-doored entrance on this side; one of the doors being open, so that the rays stretched far in over the threshing-floor to the preacher and his audience, all snugly sheltered from the northern breeze. The listeners were entirely villagers, among them being the man whom she had seen carrying the red paint-pot on a former memorable occasion. But her attention was given to the central figure, who stood upon some sacks of corn, facing the people and the door. The three o'clock sun shone full upon him, and the strange enervating conviction that her seducer confronted her, which had been gaining ground in Tess ever since she had heard his words distinctly, was at last established as a fact indeed.

END OF PHASE THE FIFTH

PHASE THE SIXTH

THE CONVERT

XLV

Till this moment she had never seen or heard from d'Urberville since her departure from Trantridge.

The rencounter came at a heavy moment, one of all moments calculated to permit its impact with the least emotional shock. But such was unreasoning memory that, though he stood there openly and palpably a converted man, who was sorrowing for his past irregularities, a fear overcame her, paralyzing her movement so that she neither retreated nor advanced.

To think of what emanated from that countenance when she saw it last, and to behold it now! . . . There was the same handsome unpleasantness of mien, but now he wore neatly trimmed, old-fashioned whiskers, the sable moustache having disappeared; and his dress was half-clerical, a modification which had changed his expression sufficiently to abstract the dandyism from his features, and to hinder for a second her belief in his identity.

To Tess's sense there was, just at first, a ghastly *bizarrerie*, a grim incongruity, in the march of these solemn words of Scripture out of such a mouth. This too familiar intonation, less than four years earlier, had brought to her ears expressions of such divergent purpose that her heart became quite sick at the irony of the contrast.

It was less a reform than a transfiguration. The former curves of sensuousness were now modulated to lines of devotional passion. The lip-shapes that had meant seductiveness were now made to express supplication; the glow on the cheek that yesterday could be translated as riotousness was evangelized to-day into the splendour of pious rhetoric; animalism had become fanaticism; Paganism Paulinism; the bold rolling eye that had flashed upon her form in the old time with such mastery now beamed with the rude energy of a theolatry that was almost ferocious. Those black angularities which his face had used to put on when his wishes were thwarted now did duty in picturing the incorrigible backslider who would insist upon turning again to his wallowing in the mire.

The lineaments, as such, seemed to complain. They had been diverted from their hereditary connotation to signify impressions for which nature did not intend them. Strange that their very elevation was a misapplication, that to raise seemed to falsify.

Yet could it be so? She would admit the ungenerous sentiment no longer. D'Urberville was not the first wicked man who had turned away from his wickedness to save his soul alive, and why should she deem it unnatural in him? It was but the usage of thought which had been jarred in her at hearing good new words in bad old notes. The greater the sinner the greater the saint; it was not necessary to dive far into Christian history to discover that.

Such impressions as these moved her vaguely, and without strict definiteness. As soon as the nerveless pause of her surprise would allow her to stir, her impulse was to pass on out of his sight. He had obviously not discerned her yet in her position against the sun.

But the moment that she moved again he recognized her. The effect upon her old lover was electric, far stronger than the effect of his presence upon her. His fire, the tumultuous ring of his eloquence, seemed to go out of him. His lip struggled and trembled under the words that lay upon it; but deliver them it could not as long as she faced him. His eyes, after their first glance upon her face, hung confusedly in every other direction but hers, but came back in a desperate leap every few seconds. This paralysis lasted, however, but a short time; for Tess's energies returned with the atrophy of his, and she walked as fast as she was able past the barn and onward.

As soon as she could reflect it appalled her, this change in their relative platforms. He who had wrought her undoing was now on the side of the Spirit, while she remained unregenerate. And, as in the legend, it had resulted that her Cyprian image had suddenly appeared upon his altar, whereby the fire of the priest has been wellnigh extinguished.

She went on without turning her head. Her back seemed to be endowed with a sensitiveness to ocular beams—even her clothing—so alive was she to a fancied gaze which might be resting upon her from the outside of that barn. All the way along to this point her heart had been heavy with an inactive sorrow; now there was a change in the quality of its trouble. That hunger for affection too long withheld was for the time displaced by an almost physical sense of an implacable past which still engirdled her. It intensified her consciousness of error to a practical despair; the break of continuity between her earlier and present existence, which she had hoped for, had not, after all, taken place. Bygones would never be complete bygones till she was a bygone herself.

Thus absorbed she recrossed the northern part of Long-Ash Lane at right angles, and presently saw before her the road ascending whitely to the upland along whose margin the remainder of her journey lay. Its dry pale surface stretched severely onward, unbroken by a single figure, vehicle, or mark, save some occasional brown horse-droppings which dotted its cold aridity here and there. While slowly breasting this ascent Tess became conscious of footsteps behind her, and turning she saw approaching that well-known form—so strangely accoutred as the Methodist—the one personage in all the world she wished not to encounter alone on this side of the grave.

There was not much time, however, for thought or elusion, and she yielded as calmly as she could to the necessity of letting him overtake her. She saw that he was excited, less by the speed of his walk than by the feelings within him.

'Tess!' he said.

She slackened speed without looking round.

'Tess!' he repeated. 'It is I—Alec d'Urberville.'

She then looked back at him, and he came up.

'I see it is,' she answered coldly.

'Well—is that all? Yet I deserve no more! Of course,' he added, with a slight laugh, 'there is something of the ridiculous to your eyes in seeing me like this. But—I must put up with that . . . I heard you had gone away, nobody knew where. Tess, you wonder why I have followed you?'

'I do, rather; and I would that you had not, with all my heart!'

'Yes—you may well say it,' he returned grimly, as they moved onward together, she with unwilling tread. 'But don't mistake me;

I beg this because you may have been led to do so in noticing—if you did notice it—how your sudden appearance unnerved me down there. It was but a momentary faltering; and considering what you had been to me, it was natural enough. But will helped me through it—though perhaps you think me a humbug for saying it—and immediately afterwards I felt that, of all persons in the world whom it was my duty and desire to save from the wrath to come—sneer if you like—the woman whom I had so grievously wronged was that person. I have come with that sole purpose in view—nothing more.'

There was the smallest vein of scorn in her words of rejoinder: 'Have you saved yourself? Charity begins at home, they say.'

'*I* have done nothing!' said he indifferently. 'Heaven, as I have been telling my hearers, has done all. No amount of contempt that you can pour on me, Tess, will equal what I have poured upon myself—the old Adam of my former years! Well, it is a strange story; believe it or not; but I can tell you the means by which my conversion was brought about, and I hope you will be interested enough at least to listen. Have you ever heard the name of the parson of Emminster—you must have done so?—old Mr Clare; one of the most earnest of his school; one of the few intense men left in the Church; not so intense as the extreme wing of Christian believers with which I have thrown in my lot, but quite an exception among the Established clergy, the younger of whom are gradually attenuating the true doctrines by their sophistries, till they are but the shadow of what they were. I only differ from him on the question of Church and State—the interpretation of the text, "Come out from among them and be ye separate, saith the Lord"—that's all. He is one who, I firmly believe, has been the humble means of saving more souls in this country than any other man you can name. You have heard of him?'

'I have,' she said.

'He came to Trantridge two or three years ago to preach on behalf of some missionary society; and I, wretched fellow that I was, insulted him when, in his disinterestedness, he tried to reason with me and show me the way. He did not resent my conduct, he simply said that some day I should receive the first-fruits of the

Spirit—that those who came to scoff sometimes remained to pray. There was a strange magic in his words. They sank into my mind. But the loss of my mother hit me most; and by degrees I was brought to see daylight. Since then my one desire has been to hand on the true view to others, and that is what I was trying to do to-day; though it is only lately that I have preached hereabout. The first months of my ministry have been spent in the North of England among strangers, where I preferred to make my earliest clumsy attempts, so as to acquire courage before undergoing that severest of all tests of one's sincerity, addressing those who have known one, and have been one's companions in the days of darkness. If you could only know, Tess, the pleasure of having a good slap at yourself, I am sure—'

'Don't go on with it!' she cried passionately, as she turned away from him to a stile by the wayside, on which she bent herself. 'I can't believe in such sudden things! I feel indignant with you for talking to me like this, when you know—when you know what harm you've done me! You, and those like you, take your fill of pleasure on earth by making the life of such as me bitter and black with sorrow; and then it is a fine thing, when you have had enough of that, to think of securing your pleasure in heaven by becoming converted! Out upon such—I don't believe in you—I hate it!'

'Tess,' he insisted; 'don't speak so! It came to me like a jolly new idea! And you don't believe me? What don't you believe?'

'Your conversion. Your scheme of religion.'

'Why?'

She dropped her voice. 'Because a better man than you does not believe in such.'

'What a woman's reason! Who is this better man?'

'I cannot tell you.'

'Well,' he declared, a resentment beneath his words seeming ready to spring out at a moment's notice. 'God forbid that I should say I am a good man—and you know I don't say any such thing. I am new to goodness, truly; but new comers see furthest sometimes.'

'Yes,' she replied sadly. 'But I cannot believe in your conversion to a new spirit. Such flashes as you feel, Alec, I fear don't last!'

Thus speaking she turned from the stile over which she had

been leaning, and faced him; whereupon his eyes, falling casually upon the familiar countenance and form, remained contemplating her. The inferior man was quiet in him now; but it was surely not extracted, nor even entirely subdued.

'Don't look at me like that!' he said abruptly.

Tess, who had been quite unconscious of her action and mien, instantly withdrew the large dark gaze of her eyes, stammering with a flush, 'I beg your pardon!' And there was revived in her the wretched sentiment which had often come to her before, that in inhabiting the fleshly tabernacle with which nature had endowed her she was somehow doing wrong.

'No, no! Don't beg my pardon. But since you wear a veil to hide your good looks, why don't you keep it down?'

She pulled down the veil, saying hastily, 'It was mostly to keep off the wind.'

'It may seem harsh of me to dictate like this,' he went on; 'but it is better that I should not look too often on you. It might be dangerous.'

'Ssh!' said Tess.

'Well, women's faces have had too much power over me already for me not to fear them! An evangelist has nothing to do with such as they; and it reminds me of the old times that I would forget!'

After this their conversation dwindled to a casual remark now and then as they rambled onward, Tess inwardly wondering how far he was going with her, and not liking to send him back by positive mandate. Frequently when they came to a gate or stile they found painted thereon in red or blue letters some text of Scripture, and she asked him if he knew who had been at the pains to blazon these announcements. He told her that the man was employed by himself and others who were working with him in that district, to paint these reminders that no means might be left untried which might move the hearts of a wicked generation.

At length the road touched the spot called 'Cross-in-Hand'. Of all spots on the bleached and desolate upland this was the most forlorn. It was so far removed from the charm which is sought in landscape by artists and view-lovers as to reach a new kind of beauty, a negative beauty of tragic tone. The place took its name from a stone pillar which stood there, a strange rude monolith, from a stratum unknown in any local quarry, on which was roughly carved a human hand. Differing accounts were given of its history and purport. Some authorities stated that a devotional cross had once formed the complete erection thereon, of which the present relic was but the stump; others that the stone as it stood was entire, and that it had been fixed there to mark a boundary or place of meeting. Anyhow, whatever the origin of the relic, there was and is something sinister, or solemn, according to mood, in the scene amid which it stands; something tending to impress the most phlegmatic passer-by.

'I think I must leave you now,' he remarked, as they drew near to this spot. 'I have to preach at Abbot's-Cernel at six this evening, and my way lies across to the right from here. And you upset me somewhat too, Tessy—I cannot, will not, say why. I must go away and get strength . . . How is it that you speak so fluently now? Who has taught you such good English?'

'I have learnt things in my troubles,' she said evasively.

'What troubles have you had?'

She told him of the first one—the only one that related to him.

D'Urberville was struck mute. 'I knew nothing of this till now!' he next murmured. 'Why didn't you write to me when you felt your trouble coming on?'

She did not reply; and he broke the silence by adding: 'Well—you will see me again.'

'No,' she answered. 'Do not again come near me!'

'I will think. But before we part come here.' He stepped up to the pillar. 'This was once a Holy Cross. Relics are not in my creed; but I fear you at moments—far more than you need fear me at present; and to lessen my fear, put your hand upon that stone hand, and swear that you will never tempt me—by your charms or ways.'

'Good God—how can you ask what is so unnecessary! All that is furthest from my thought!'

'Yes—but swear it.'

Tess, half frightened, gave way to his importunity; placed her hand upon the stone and swore.

'I am sorry you are not a believer,' he continued; 'that some unbeliever should have got hold of you and unsettled your mind. But no more now. At home at least I can pray for you; and I will; and who knows what may not happen? I'm off. Good-bye!'

He turned to a hunting-gate in the hedge, and without letting his eyes again rest upon her leapt over, and struck out across the down in the direction of Abbot's-Cernel. As he walked his pace showed perturbation, and by-and-by, as if instigated by a former thought, he drew from his pocket a small book, between the leaves of which was folded a letter, worn and soiled, as from much re-reading. D'Urberville opened the letter. It was dated several months before this time, and was signed by Parson Clare.

The letter began by expressing the writer's unfeigned joy at d'Urberville's conversion, and thanked him for his kindness in communicating with the parson on the subject. It expressed Mr Clare's warm assurance of forgiveness for d'Urberville's former conduct, and his interest in the young man's plans for the future. He, Mr Clare, would much have liked to see d'Urberville in the Church to whose ministry he had devoted so many years of his own life, and would have helped him to enter a theological college to that end; but since his correspondent had possibly not cared to do this on account of the delay it would have entailed, he was not the man to insist upon its paramount importance. Every man must work as he could best work, and in the method towards which he felt impelled by the Spirit.

D'Urberville read and re-read this letter, and seemed to quiz himself cynically. He also read some passages from memoranda as he walked till his face assumed a calm, and apparently the image of Tess no longer troubled his mind.

She meanwhile had kept along the edge of the hill by which lay her nearest way home. Within the distance of a mile she met a solitary shepherd.

'What is the meaning of that old stone I have passed?' she asked of him. 'Was it ever a Holy Cross?'

'Cross—no; 'twer not a cross! 'Tis a thing of ill-omen, Miss. It was put up in wuld times by the relations of a malefactor who was tortured there by nailing his hand to a post and afterwards hung.

The bones lie underneath. They say he sold his soul to the devil, and that he walks at times.'

She felt the *petite mort* at this unexpectedly gruesome information, and left the solitary man behind her. It was dusk when she drew near to Flintcomb-Ash, and in the lane at the entrance to the hamlet she approached a girl and her lover without their observing her. They were talking no secrets, and the clear unconcerned voice of the young woman, in response to the warmer accents of the man, spread into the chilly air as the one soothing thing within the dusky horizon, full of a stagnant obscurity upon which nothing else intruded. For a moment the voices cheered the heart of Tess, till she reasoned that this interview had its origin, on one side or the other, in the same attraction which had been the prelude to her own tribulation. When she came close the girl turned serenely and recognized her, the young man walking off in embarrassment. The woman was Izz Huett, whose interest in Tess's excursion immediately superseded her own proceedings. Tess did not explain very clearly its results, and Izz, who was a girl of tact, began to speak of her own little affair, a phase of which Tess had just witnessed.

'He is Amby Seedling, the chap who used to sometimes come and help at Talbothays,' she explained indifferently. 'He actually inquired and found out that I had come here, and has followed me. He says he's been in love wi' me these two years. But I've hardly answered him.'

XLVI

Several days had passed since her futile journey, and Tess was afield. The dry winter wind still blew, but a screen of thatched hurdles erected in the eye of the blast kept its force away from her. On the sheltered side was a turnip-slicing machine, whose bright blue hue of new paint seemed almost vocal in the otherwise subdued scene. Opposite its front was a long mound or 'grave', in which the roots had been preserved since early winter. Tess was standing at the uncovered end, chopping off with a bill-hook the fibres and earth from each root, and throwing it after the operation into the slicer. A man was turning the handle of the machine, and from its trough came the newly-cut swedes, the fresh smell of whose yellow chips was accompanied by the sounds of the snuffling wind, the smart swish of the slicing-blades, and the choppings of the hook in Tess's leather-gloved hand.

The wide acreage of blank agricultural brownness, apparent where the swedes had been pulled, was beginning to be striped in wales of darker brown, gradually broadening to ribands. Along the edge of each of these something crept upon ten legs, moving without haste and without rest up and down the whole length of the field; it was two horses and a man, the plough going between them, turning up the cleared ground for a spring sowing.

For hours nothing relieved the joyless monotony of things. Then, far beyond the ploughing-teams, a black speck was seen. It had come from the corner of a fence, where there was a gap, and its tendency was up the incline, towards the swede-cutters. From the proportions of a mere point it advanced to the shape of a ninepin, and was soon perceived to be a man in black, arriving from the direction of Flintcomb-Ash. The man at the slicer, having nothing else to do with his eyes, continually observed the comer, but Tess, who was occupied, did not perceive him till her companion directed her attention to his approach.

It was not her hard taskmaster, Farmer Groby; it was one in a semi-clerical costume, who now represented what had once been the free-and-easy Alec d'Urberville. Not being hot at his preaching there was less enthusiasm about him now, and the presence of the grinder seemed to embarrass him. A pale distress was already on Tess's face, and she pulled her curtained hood further over it.

D'Urberville came up and said quietly—

'I want to speak to you, Tess.'

'You have refused my last request, not to come near me!' said she.

'Yes, but I have a good reason.'

'Well, tell it.'

'It is more serious than you may think.'

He glanced round to see if he were overheard. They were at some distance from the man who turned the slicer, and the movement of the machine, too, sufficiently prevented Alec's words reaching other ears. D'Urberville placed himself so as to screen Tess from the labourer, turning his back to the latter.

'It is this,' he continued, with capricious compunction. 'In thinking of your soul and mine when we last met, I neglected to inquire as to your worldly condition. You were well dressed, and I did not think of it. But I see now that it is hard—harder than it used to be when I—knew you—harder than you deserve. Perhaps a good deal of it is owing to me!'

She did not answer, and he watched her inquiringly, as, with bent head, her face completely screened by the hood, she resumed her trimming of the swedes. By going on with her work she felt better able to keep him outside her emotions.

'Tess,' he added, with a sigh of discontent,—'yours was the very worst case I ever was concerned in! I had no idea of what had resulted till you told me. Scamp that I was to foul that innocent life! The whole blame was mine—the whole unconventional business of our time at Trantridge. You, too, the real blood of which I am but the base imitation, what a blind young thing you were as to possibilities! I say in all earnestness that it is a shame for parents to bring up their girls in such dangerous ignorance of the gins and nets that the wicked may set for them, whether their motive be a good one or the result of simple indifference.'

Tess still did no more than listen, throwing down one globular root and taking up another with automatic regularity, the pensive contour of the mere fieldwoman alone marking her.

'But it is not that I came to say,' d'Urberville went on. 'My circumstances are these. I have lost my mother since you were at Trantridge, and the place is my own. But I intend to sell it, and devote myself to missionary work in Africa. A devil of a poor hand I shall make at the trade, no doubt. However, what I want to ask you is, will you put it in my power to do my duty—to make the only reparation I can make for the trick played you: that is, will you be my wife, and go with me? . . . I have already obtained this precious document. It was my mother's dying wish.'

He drew a piece of parchment from his pocket, with a slight fumbling of embarrassment.

'What is it?' said she.

'A marriage licence.'

'O no, sir—no!' she said quickly, starting back.

'You will not? Why is that?'

And as he asked the question a disappointment which was not entirely the disappointment of thwarted duty crossed d'Urberville's face. It was unmistakably a sympton that something of his old passion for her had been revived; duty and desire ran hand-in-hand.

'Surely,' he began again, in more impetuous tones, and then looked round at the labourer who turned the slicer.

Tess, too, felt that the argument could not be ended there. Informing the man that a gentleman had come to see her, with whom she wished to walk a little way, she moved off with d'Urberville across the zebra-striped field. When they reached the first newly-ploughed section he held out his hand to help her over it; but she stepped forward on the summits of the earth-rolls as if she did not see him.

'You will not marry me, Tess, and make me a self-respecting man?' he repeated, as soon as they were over the furrows.

'I cannot.'

'But why?'

'You know I have no affection for you.'

'But you would get to feel that in time, perhaps—as soon as you really could forgive me?'

'Never!'

'Why so positive?'

'I love somebody else.'

The words seemed to astonish him.

'You do?' he cried. 'Somebody else? But has not a sense of what is morally right and proper any weight with you?'

'No, no, no—don't say that!'

'Anyhow, then, your love for this other man may be only a passing feeling which you will overcome—'

'No—no.'

'Yes, yes! Why not?'

'I cannot tell you.'

'You must in honour!'

'Well then . . . I have married him.'

'Ah!' he exclaimed; and he stopped dead and gazed at her.

'I did not wish to tell—I did not mean to!' she pleaded. 'It is a secret here, or at any rate but dimly known. So will you, *please* will you, keep from questioning me? You must remember that we are now strangers.'

'Strangers—are we? Strangers!'

For a moment a flash of his old irony marked his face; but he determinedly chastened it down.

'Is that man your husband?' he asked mechanically, denoting by a sign the labourer who turned the machine.

'That man!' she said proudly. 'I should think not!'

'Who, then?'

'Do not ask what I do not wish to tell!' she begged, and flashed her appeal to him from her upturned face and lash-shadowed eyes.

D'Urberville was disturbed.

'But I only asked for your sake!' he retorted hotly. 'Angels of heaven!—God forgive me for such an expression—I came here, I swear, as I thought for your good. Tess—don't look at me so—I cannot stand your looks! There never were such eyes, surely, before Christianity or since! There—I won't lose my head; I dare not. I own that the sight of you has waked up my love for you, which, I believed, was extinguished with all such feelings. But I thought that our marriage might be a sanctification for us both. "The unbelieving husband is sanctified by the wife, and the unbelieving wife is sanctified by the husband," I said to myself. But my plan is dashed from me; and I must bear the disappointment!'

He moodily reflected with his eyes on the ground.

'Married. Married! . . . Well, that being so,' he added, quite calmly, tearing the licence slowly into halves and putting them in his pocket; 'that being prevented, I should like to do some good to you and your husband, whoever he may be. There are many questions that I am tempted to ask but I will not do so, of course, in opposition to your wishes. Though, if I could know your husband, I might more easily benefit him and you. Is he on this farm?'

'No,' she murmured. 'He is far away.'

'Far away? From *you*? What sort of husband can he be?'

'O, do not speak against him! It was through you! He found out—'

'Ah, is it so! . . . That's sad, Tess!'

'Yes.'

'But to stay away from you—to leave you to work like this!'

'He does not leave me to work!' she cried, springing to the defence of the absent one with all her fervour. 'He don't know it! It is by my own arrangement.'

'Then, does he write?'

'I—I cannot tell you. There are things which are private to ourselves.'

'Of course that means that he does not. You are a deserted wife, my fair Tess!'

In an impulse he turned suddenly to take her hand; the buff-glove was on it, and he seized only the rough leather fingers which did not express the life or shape of those within.

'You must not—you must not!' she cried fearfully, slipping her hand from the glove as from a pocket, and leaving it in his grasp. 'O, will you go away—for the sake of me and my husband—go, in the name of your own Christianity!'

'Yes, yes; I will,' he said abruptly, and thrusting the glove back to her turned to leave. Facing round, however, he said 'Tess, as God is my judge, I meant no humbug in taking your hand!'

A pattering of hoofs on the soil of the field, which they had not noticed in their preoccupation, ceased close behind them; and a voice reached her ear:

'What the devil are you doing away from your work at this time o'day?'

Farmer Groby had espied the two figures from the distance, and had inquisitively ridden across, to learn what was their business in his field.

'Don't speak like that to her!' said d'Urberville, his face blackening with something that was not Christianity.

'Indeed, Mister! And what mid Methodist pa'sons have to do with she?'

'Who is the fellow?' asked d'Urberville, turning to Tess.

She went close up to him.

'Go—I do beg you!' she said.

'What! And leave you to that tyrant? I can see in his face what a churl he is.'

'He won't hurt me. *He's* not in love with me. I can leave at Lady-Day.'

'Well, I have no right but to obey, I suppose. But—well, goodbye!'

Her defender, whom she dreaded more than her assailant, having reluctantly disappeared, the farmer continued his reprimand, which Tess took with the greatest coolness, that sort of attack being independent of sex. To have as a master this man of stone, who would have cuffed her if he had dared, was almost a relief after her former experiences. She silently walked back towards the summit of the field that was the scene of her labour, so absorbed in the interview which had just taken place that she was hardly aware that the nose of Groby's horse almost touched her shoulders.

'If so be you make an agreement to work for me till Lady-Day, I'll see that you carry it out,' he growled. ''Od rot the women—now 'tis one thing, and then 'tis another. But I'll put up with it no longer!'

Knowing very well that he did not harass the other women of the farm as he harassed her out of spite for the flooring he had once received, she did for one moment picture what might have been the result if she had been free to accept the offer just made her of being the monied Alec's wife. It would have lifted her completely out of subjection, not only to her present oppressive employer, but to a whole world who seemed to despise her. 'But no, no!' she said breathlessly; 'I could not have married him now! He is so unpleasant to me.'

That very night she began an appealing letter to Clare, concealing from him her hardships, and assuring him of her undying affection. Any one who had been in a position to read between the lines would have seen that at the back of her great love was some monstrous fear—almost a desperation—as to some secret contingencies which were not disclosed. But again she did not finish her effusion; he had asked Izz to go with him, and perhaps he did not care for her at all. She put the letter in her box, and wondered if it would ever reach Angel's hands.

After this her daily tasks were gone through heavily enough, and brought on the day which was of great import to agriculturists—the day of the Candlemas Fair. It was at this fair that new engagements were entered into for the twelve months following the ensuing Lady-Day, and those of the farming population who thought of changing their places duly attended at the county-town where the fair was held. Nearly all the labourers on Flintcomb-Ash Farm intended flight, and early in the morning there was a general exodus in the direction of the town, which lay at a distance of from ten to a dozen miles over hilly country. Though Tess also meant to leave at the quarter-day she was one of the few who did not go to the fair, having a vaguely-shaped hope that something would happen to render another outdoor engagement unnecessary.

It was a peaceful February day, of wonderful softness for the time, and one would almost have thought that winter was over. She had hardly finished her dinner when d'Urberville's figure darkened the window of the cottage wherein she was a lodger, which she had all to herself to-day.

Tess jumped up, but her visitor had knocked at the door, and she could hardly in reason run away. D'Urberville's knock, his walk up to the door, had some indescribable quality of difference from his air when she last saw him. They seemed to be acts of which the doer was ashamed. She thought that she would not open the door; but, as there was no sense in that either, she arose, and having lifted the latch stepped back quickly. He came in, saw her, and flung himself down into a chair before speaking.

'Tess—I couldn't help it!' he began desperately, as he wiped his heated face, which had also a superimposed flush of excitement. 'I felt that I must call at least to ask how you are. I assure you I had not been thinking of you at all till I saw you that Sunday; now I cannot get rid of your image, try how I may! It is hard that a good woman should do harm to a bad man; yet so it is. If you would only pray for me, Tess!'

The suppressed discontent of his manner was almost pitiable, and yet Tess did not pity him.

'How can I pray for you,' she said, 'when I am forbidden to believe that the great Power who moves the world would alter His plans on my account?'

'You really think that?'

'Yes. I have been cured of the presumption of thinking otherwise.'

'Cured? By whom?'

'By my husband, if I must tell.'

'Ah—your husband—your husband! How strange it seems! I remember you hinted something of the sort the other day. What do you really believe in these matters, Tess?' he asked. 'You seem to have no religion—perhaps owing to me.'

'But I have. Though I don't believe in anything supernatural.'

D'Urberville looked at her with misgiving.

'Then do you think that the line I take is all wrong?'

'A good deal of it.'

'H'm—and yet I've felt so sure about it,' he said uneasily.

'I believe in the *spirit* of the Sermon on the Mount, and so did my dear husband . . . But I don't believe—'

Here she gave her negations.

'The fact is,' said d'Urberville drily, 'whatever your dear husband believed you accept, and whatever he rejected you reject, without the least inquiry or reasoning on your own part. That's just like you women. Your mind is enslaved to his.'

'Ah, because he knew everything!' said she, with a triumphant simplicity of faith in Angel Clare that the most perfect man could hardly have deserved, much less her husband.

'Yes, but you should not take negative opinions wholesale from another person like that. A pretty fellow he must be to teach you such scepticism!'

'He never forced my judgment! He would never argue on the subject with me! But I looked at it in this way; what he believed, after inquiring deep into doctrines, was much more likely to be right than what I might believe, who hadn't looked into doctrines at all.'

'What used he to say? He must have said something?'

She reflected; and with her acute memory for the letter of Angel Clare's remarks, even when she did not comprehend their spirit, she recalled a merciless polemical syllogism that she had heard him use when, as it occasionally happened, he indulged in a species of thinking aloud with her at his side. In delivering it she gave also Clare's accent and manner with reverential faithfulness.

'Say that again,' asked d'Urberville, who has listened with the greatest attention.

She repeated the argument, and d'Urberville thoughtfully murmured the words after her.

'Anything else?' he presently asked.

'He said at another time something like this'; and she gave another, which might possibly have been paralleled in many a work of the pedigree ranging from the *Dictionnaire Philosophique* to Huxley's *Essays*.

'Ah—ha! How do you remember them?'

'I wanted to believe what he believed, though he didn't wish me to; and I managed to coax him to tell me a few of his thoughts. I can't say I quite understand that one; but I know it is right.'

'H'm. Fancy your being able to teach me what you don't know yourself!'

He fell into thought.

'And so I threw in my spiritual lot with his,' she resumed. 'I didn't wish it to be different. What's good enough for him is good enough for me.'

'Does he know that you are as big an infidel as he?'

'No—I never told him—if I am an infidel.'

'Well—you are better off to-day than I am, Tess, after all! You don't believe that you ought to preach my doctrine, and, therefore, do no despite to your conscience in abstaining. I do believe I ought to preach it, but like the devils I believe and tremble, for I suddenly leave off preaching it, and give way to my passion for you.'

'How?'

'Why,' he said aridly; 'I have come all the way here to see you to-day! But I started from home to go to Casterbridge Fair, where I have undertaken to preach the Word from a waggon at half-past two this afternoon, and where all the brethren are expecting me this minute. Here's the announcement.'

He drew from his breast-pocket a poster whereon was printed the day, hour, and the place of meeting, at which he, d'Urberville, would preach the Gospel as aforesaid.

'But how can you get there?' said Tess, looking at the clock.

'I cannot get there! I have come here.'

'What, you have really arranged to preach, and—'

'I have arranged to preach, and I shall not be there—by reason of my burning desire to see a woman whom I once despised!—No, by my word and truth, I never despised you; if I had I should not love you now! Why I did not despise you was on account of your being unsmirched in spite of all; you withdrew yourself from me so quickly and resolutely when you saw the situation; you did not remain at my pleasure; so there was one petticoat in the world for whom I had no contempt, and you are she. But you may well despise me now! I thought I worshipped on the mountains, but I find I still serve in the groves! Ha! ha!'

'O Alec d'Urberville! what does this mean? What have I done!'

'Done?' he said, with a soulless sneer in the word. 'Nothing intentionally. But you have been the means—the innocent means—of my backsliding, as they call it. I ask myself, am I, indeed, one of those "servants of corruption" who, "after they have escaped the pollutions of the world, are again entangled therein and overcome"—whose latter end is worse than their beginning?' He laid his hand on her shoulder. 'Tess, my girl, I was on the way to, at least, social salvation till I saw you again!' he said freakishly shaking her, as if she were a child. 'And why then have you tempted me? I was firm as a man could be till I saw those eyes and that mouth again—surely there never was such a maddening mouth since Eve's!' His voice sank, and a hot archness shot from his own black eyes. 'You temptress, Tess; you dear damned witch of Babylon—I could not resist you as soon as I met you again!'

'I couldn't help your seeing me again!' said Tess, recoiling.

'I know it—I repeat that I do not blame you. But the fact remains. When I saw you ill-used on the farm that day I was nearly mad to think that I had no legal right to protect you—that I could not have it; whilst he who has it seems to neglect you utterly!'

'Don't speak against him—he is absent!' she cried in much excitement. 'Treat him honourably—he has never wronged you! O leave his wife before any scandal spreads that may do harm to his honest name!'

'I will—I will,' he said, like a man awakening from a luring dream. 'I have broken my engagement to preach to those poor drunken boobies at the fair—it is the first time I have played such a practical joke. A month ago I should have been horrified at such a possibility. I'll go away—to swear—and—ah, can I! to keep away.' Then, suddenly: 'One clasp, Tessy—one! Only for old friendship—'

'I am without defence, Alec! A good man's honour is in my keeping—think—be ashamed!'

'Pooh! Well yes—yes!'

He clenched his lips, mortified with himself for his weakness. His eyes were equally barren of worldly and religious faith. The corpses of those old fitful passions which had lain inanimate amid the lines of his face ever since his reformation seemed to wake and come together as in a resurrection. He went out indeterminately.

Though d'Urberville had declared that this breach of his engagement to-day was the simple backsliding of a believer, Tess's words, as echoed from Angel Clare, had made a deep impression upon him, and continued to do so after he had left her. He moved on in silence, as if his energies were benumbed by the hitherto undreamt-of possibility that his position was untenable. Reason had had nothing to do with his whimsical conversion, which was perhaps the mere freak of a careless man in search of a new sensation, and temporarily impressed by his mother's death.

The drops of logic Tess had let fall into the sea of his enthusiasm served to chill its effervescence to stagnation. He said to himself, as he pondered again and again over the crystallized phrases that she had handed on to him, 'That clever fellow little thought that, by telling her those things, he might be paving my way back to her!'

XLVII

It is the threshing of the last wheat-rick at Flintcomb-Ash Farm. The dawn of the March morning is singularly inexpressive, and there is nothing to show where the eastern horizon lies. Against the twilight rises the trapezoidal top of the stack, which has stood forlornly here through the washing and bleaching of the wintry weather.

When Izz Huett and Tess arrived at the scene of operations only a rustling denoted that others had preceded them; to which, as the light increased, there were presently added the silhouettes of two men on the summit. They were busily 'unhaling' the rick, that is, stripping off the thatch before beginning to throw down the sheaves; and while this was in progress Izz and Tess, with the other women-workers, in their whitey-brown pinners, stood waiting and shivering, Farmer Groby having insisted upon their being on the spot thus early to get the job over if possible by the end of the day. Close under the eaves of the stack, and as yet barely visible, was the red tyrant that the women had come to serve—a timber-framed construction, with straps and wheels appertaining—the threshing-machine which, whilst it was going, kept up a despotic demand upon the endurance of their muscles and nerves.

A little way off there was another indistinct figure; this one black, with a sustained hiss that spoke of strength very much in reserve. The long chimney running up beside an ash-tree, and the warmth which radiated from the spot, explained without the necessity of much daylight that here was the engine which was to act as the *primum mobile* of this little world. By the engine stood a dark motionless being, a sooty and grimy embodiment of tallness, in a sort of trance, with a heap of coals by his side: it was the engine-man. The isolation of his manner and colour lent him the appearance of a creature from Tophet, who had strayed into the pellucid smokelessness of this region of yellow grain and pale soil, with which he had nothing in common, to amaze and to discompose its aborigines.

What he looked he felt. He was in the agricultural world, but not of it. He served fire and smoke; these denizens of the fields served weather, vegetation, frost, and sun. He travelled with his engine from farm to farm, from county to county, for as yet the steam threshing-machine was itinerant in this part of Wessex. He spoke in a strange northern accent; his thoughts being turned inwards upon himself, his eye on his iron charge, hardly perceiving the scenes around him, and caring for them not at all: holding only strictly necessary intercourse with the natives, as if some ancient doom compelled him to wander here against his will in the service of his Plutonic master. The long strap which ran from the driving-wheel of his engine to the red thresher under the rick was the sole tie-line between agriculture and him.

While they uncovered the sheaves he stood apathetic beside his portable repository of force, round whose hot blackness the morning air quivered. He had nothing to do with preparatory labour. His fire was waiting incandescent, his steam was at high pressure, in a few seconds he could make the long strap move at an invisible velocity. Beyond its extent the environment might be corn, straw, or chaos; it was all the same to him. If any of the autochthonous idlers asked him what he called himself, he replied shortly, 'an engineer'.

The rick was unhaled by full daylight; the men then took their places, the women mounted, and the work began. Farmer Groby—or, as they called him, 'he'—had arrived ere this, and by his orders Tess was placed on the platform of the machine, close to the man who fed it, her business being to untie every sheaf of corn handed on to her by Izz Huett, who stood next, but on the rick; so that the feeder could seize it and spread it over the revolving drum, which whisked out every grain in one moment.

They were soon in full progress, after a preparatory hitch or two, which rejoiced the hearts of those who hated machinery. The work sped on till breakfast-time, when the thresher was stopped for half an hour; and on starting again after the meal the whole supplementary strength of the farm was thrown into the labour of constructing the straw-rick, which began to grow beside the stack of corn. A hasty lunch was eaten as they stood, without leaving their positions, and then another couple of hours brought them near to dinner-time; the inexorable wheels continuing to spin, and the penetrating hum of the thresher to thrill to the very marrow all who were near the revolving wire-cage.

The old men on the rising straw-rick talked of the past days when they had been accustomed to thresh with flails on the oaken barn-floor; when everything, even to winnowing, was effected by hand-labour, which, to their thinking, though slow, produced better results. Those, too, on the corn-rick talked a little; but the perspiring ones at the machine, including Tess, could not lighten their duties by the exchange of many words. It was the ceaselessness of the work which tried her so severely, and began to make her wish that she had never come to Flintcomb-Ash. The women on the corn-rick—Marian, who was one of them, in particular—could stop to drink ale or cold tea from the flagon now and then, or to exchange a few gossiping remarks while they wiped their faces or cleared the fragments of straw and husk from their clothing; but for Tess there was no respite; for, as the drum never stopped, the man who fed it could not stop, and she, who had to supply the man with untied sheaves, could not stop either, unless Marian changed places with her, which she sometimes did for half an hour in spite of Groby's objection that she was too slow-handed for a feeder.

For some probably economical reason it was usually a woman who was chosen for this particular duty, and Groby gave as his motive in selecting Tess that she was one of those who best combined strength with quickness in untying, and both with staying power, and this may have been true. The hum of the thresher, which prevented speech, increased to a raving whenever the supply of corn fell short of the regular quantity. As Tess and the man who fed could never turn their heads she did not know that just before the dinner-hour a person had come silently into the field by the gate, and had been standing under a second rick watching the scene, and Tess in particular. He was dressed in a tweed suit of fashionable pattern, and he twirled a gay walking-cane.

'Who is that?' said Izz Huett to Marian. She had at first addressed the inquiry to Tess, but the latter could not hear it.

'Somebody's fancy-man, I s'pose,' said Marian laconically.

'I'll lay a guinea he's after Tess.'

'O no. 'Tis a ranter pa'son who's been sniffing after her lately; not a dandy like this.'

'Well—this is the same man.'

'The same man as the preacher? But he's quite different!'

'He hev left off his black coat and white neckercher, and hev cut off his whiskers; but he's the same man for all that.'

'D'ye really think so? Then I'll tell her,' said Marian.

'Don't. She'll see him soon enough, good-now.'

'Well, I don't think it at all right for him to join his preaching to courting a married woman, even though her husband mid be abroad, and she, in a sense, a widow.'

'Oh—he can do her no harm,' said Izz drily. 'Her mind can no more be heaved from that one place where it do bide than a stooded waggon from the hole he's in. Lord love 'ee, neither court-paying, nor preaching, nor the seven thunders themselves, can wean a woman when 'twould be better for her that she should be weaned.'

Dinner-time came, and the whirling ceased; whereupon Tess left her post, her knees trembling so wretchedly with the shaking of the machine that she could scarcely walk.

'You ought to het a quart o' drink into 'ee, as I've done,' said Marian. 'You wouldn't look so white then. Why, souls above us, your face is as if you'd been hagrode!'

It occurred to the good-natured Marian that, as Tess was so tired, her discovery of her visitor's presence might have the bad effect of taking away her appetite; and Marian was thinking of inducing Tess to descend by a ladder on the further side of the stack when the gentleman came forward and looked up.

Tess uttered a short little 'Oh!' And a moment after she said, quickly, 'I shall eat my dinner here—right on the rick.'

Sometimes, when they were so far from their cottages, they all did this; but as there was rather a keen wind going to-day, Marian and the rest descended, and sat under the straw-stack.

The new-comer was, indeed, Alec d'Urberville, the late Evangelist, despite his changed attire and aspect. It was obvious at a glance that the original *Weltlust* had come back; that he had restored himself, as nearly as a man could do who had grown three or four years older, to the old jaunty, slap-dash guise under which Tess had first known her admirer, and cousin so-called. Having decided to remain where she was, Tess sat down among the bundles, out of sight of the ground, and began her meal; till, by-and-by, she heard footsteps on the ladder, and immediately after Alec appeared upon the stack—now an oblong and level platform of sheaves. He strode across them, and sat down opposite to her without a word.

Tess continued to eat her modest dinner, a slice of thick pancake which she had brought with her. The other workfolk were by this time all gathered under the rick, where the loose straw formed a comfortable retreat.

'I am here again, as you see,' said d'Urberville.

'Why do you trouble me so!' she cried, reproach flashing from her very finger-ends.

'*I* trouble *you*? I think I may ask, why do you trouble me?'

'Sure, I don't trouble you any-when!'

'You say you don't? But you do! You haunt me. Those very eyes that you turned upon me with such a bitter flash a moment ago, they come to me just as you showed them then, in the night and in the day! Tess, ever since you told me of that child of ours, it is just as if my feelings, which have been flowing in a strong puritanical stream, had suddenly found a way open in the direction of you, and had all at once gushed through. The religious channel is left dry forthwith; and it is you who have done it!'

She gazed in silence.

'What—you have given up your preaching entirely?' she asked.

She had gathered from Angel sufficient of the incredulity of modern thought to despise flash enthusiasms; but, as a woman, she was somewhat appalled.

In affected severity d'Urberville continued –

'Entirely. I have broken every engagement since that afternoon I was to address the drunkards at Casterbridge Fair. The deuce only knows what I am thought of by the brethren. Ah-ha! The brethren! No doubt they pray for me—weep for me; for they are kind people in their way. But what do I care? How could I go on with the thing when I had lost my faith in it?—it would have been hypocrisy of the basest kind! Among them I should have stood like Hymenaeus and Alexander, who were delivered over to Satan that they might learn not to blaspheme. What a grand revenge you have taken! I saw you innocent, and I deceived you. Four years after, you find me a Christian enthusiast; you then work upon me, perhaps to my complete perdition! But Tess, my coz, as I used to call you, this is only my way of talking, and you must not look so horribly concerned. Of course you have done nothing except retain your pretty face and shapely figure. I saw it on the rick before you saw me—that tight pinafore-thing sets it off, and that wing-bonnet—you field-girls should never wear those bonnets if you wish to keep out of danger.' He regarded her silently for a few moments, and with a short cynical laugh resumed: 'I believe that if the bachelor-apostle, whose deputy I thought I was, had been tempted by such a pretty face, he would have let go the plough for her sake as I do!'

Tess attempted to expostulate, but at this juncture all her fluency failed her, and without heeding he added:

'Well, this paradise that you supply is perhaps as good as any other, after all. But to speak seriously, Tess.' D'Urberville rose and came nearer, reclining sideways amid the sheaves, and resting upon his elbow. 'Since I last saw you, I have been thinking of what you said that *he* said. I have come to the conclusion that there does seem rather a want of common-sense in these threadbare old propositions; how I could have been so fired by poor Parson Clare's enthusiasm, and have gone so madly to work, transcending even him, I cannot make out! As for what you said last time, on the strength of your wonderful husband's intelligence—whose name you have never told me—about having what they call an ethical system without any dogma, I don't see my way to that at all.'

'Why, you have the religion of loving-kindness and purity at least, if you can't have—what do you call it—dogma.'

'O no! I'm a different sort of fellow from that! If there's nobody to say, "Do this, and it will be a good thing for you after you are dead; do that, and it will be a bad thing for you," I can't warm up. Hang it, I am not going to feel responsible for my deeds and passions if there's nobody to be responsible to; and if I were you, my dear, I wouldn't either!'

She tried to argue, and tell him that he had mixed in his dull brain two matters, theology and morals, which in the primitive days of mankind had been quite distinct. But owing to Angel Clare's reticence, to her absolute want of training, and to her being a vessel of emotions rather than reasons, she could not get on.

'Well, never mind,' he resumed. 'Here I am, my love, as in the old times!'

'Not as then—never as then—'tis different!' she entreated. 'And there was never warmth with me! O why didn't you keep your faith, if the loss of it has brought you to speak to me like this!'

'Because you've knocked it out of me; so the evil be upon your sweet head! Your husband little thought how his teaching would recoil upon him! Ha-ha—I'm awfully glad you have made an apostate of me all the same! Tess, I am more taken with you than ever, and I pity you too. For all your closeness, I see you are in a bad way—neglected by one who ought to cherish you.'

She could not get her morsels of food down her throat; her lips were dry, and she was ready to choke. The voices and laughs of the workfolk eating and drinking under the rick came to her as if they were a quarter of a mile off.

'It is cruelty to me!' she said. 'How—how can you treat me to this talk, if you care ever so little for me?'

'True, true,' he said, wincing a little. 'I did not come to reproach you for my deeds. I came, Tess, to say that I don't like you to be working like this, and I have come on purpose for you. You say you have a husband who is not I. Well, perhaps you have; but I've never seen him, and you've not told me his name; and altogether he seems rather a mythological personage. However, even if you have one, I think I am nearer to you than he is. I, at any rate, try to help you out of trouble, but he does not, bless his invisible face! The words of the stern prophet Hosea that I used to read come back to me. Don't you know them, Tess?—"And she shall follow after her lover, but she shall not overtake him; and she shall seek him, but shall not find him; then shall she say, I will go and return to my first husband; for then was it better with me than now!" . . .

Tess, my trap is waiting just under the hill, and—darling mine, not his!—you know the rest.'

Her face had been rising to a dull crimson fire while he spoke; but she did not answer.

'You have been the cause of my backsliding,' he continued, stretching his arm towards her waist; 'you should be willing to share it, and leave that mule you call husband for ever.'

One of her leather gloves, which she had taken off to eat her skimmer-cake, lay in her lap, and without the slightest warning she passionately swung the glove by the gauntlet directly in his face. It was heavy and thick as a warrior's, and it struck him flat on the mouth. Fancy might have regarded the act as the recrudescence of a trick in which her armed progenitors were not unpractised. Alec fiercely started up from his reclining position. A scarlet oozing appeared where her blow had alighted, and in a moment the blood began dropping from his mouth upon the straw. But he soon controlled himself, calmly drew his handkerchief from his pocket, and mopped his bleeding lips.

She too had sprung up, but she sank down again.

'Now, punish me!' she said, turning up her eyes to him with the hopeless defiance of the sparrow's gaze before its captor twists its neck. 'Whip me, crush me; you need not mind those people under the rick! I shall not cry out. Once victim, always victim—that's the law!'

'O no, no, Tess,' he said blandly. 'I can make full allowance for this. Yet you most unjustly forget one thing, that I would have married you if you have not put it out of my power to do so. Did I not ask you flatly to be my wife—hey? Answer me.'

'You did.'

'And you cannot be. But remember one thing!' His voice hardened as his temper got the better of him with the recollection of his sincerity in asking her and her present ingratitude, and he stepped across to her side and held her by the shoulders, so that she shook under his grasp. 'Remember, my lady, I was your master once! I will be your master again. If you are any man's wife you are mine!'

The threshers now began to stir below.

'So much for our quarrel,' he said, letting her go. 'Now I shall leave you, and shall come again for your answer during the afternoon. You don't know me yet! But I know you.'

She had not spoken again, remaining as if stunned. D'Urberville retreated over the sheaves, and descended the ladder, while the workers below rose and stretched their arms, and shook down the beer they had drunk. Then the threshing-machine started afresh; and amid the renewed rustle of the straw Tess resumed her position by the buzzing drum as one in a dream, untying sheaf after sheaf in endless succession.

XLVIII

In the afternoon the farmer made it known that the rick was to be finished that night, since there was a moon by which they could see to work, and the man with the engine was engaged for another farm on the morrow. Hence the twanging and humming and rustling proceeded with even less intermission than usual.

It was not till 'nammet'-time, about three o'clock, that Tess raised her eyes and gave a momentary glance round. She felt but little surprise at seeing that Alec d'Urberville had come back, and was standing under the hedge by the gate. He had seen her lift her eyes, and waved his hand urbanely to her, while he blew her a kiss. It meant that their quarrel was over. Tess looked down again, and carefully abstained from gazing in that direction.

Thus the afternoon dragged on. The wheat-rick shrank lower, and the straw-rick grew higher, and the corn-sacks were carted away. At six o'clock the wheat-rick was about shoulder-high from the ground. But the unthreshed sheaves remaining untouched seemed countless still, notwithstanding the enormous numbers that had been gulped down by the insatiable swallower, fed by the man and Tess, through whose two young hands the greater part of them had passed. And the immense stack of straw where in the morning there had been nothing, appeared as the *faeces* of the same buzzing red glutton. From the west sky a wrathful shine—all that wild March could afford in the way of sunset—had burst forth after the cloudy day, flooding the tired and sticky faces of the threshers, and dyeing them with a coppery light, as also the flapping garments of the women, which clung to them like dull flames.

A panting ache ran through the rick. The man who fed was weary, and Tess could see that the red nape of his neck was encrusted with dirt and husks. She still stood at her post, her flushed and perspiring face coated with the corn-dust, and her white bonnet embrowned by it. She was the only woman whose place was upon the machine so as to be shaken bodily by its spinning, and the decrease of the stack now separated her from Marian and Izz, and prevented their changing duties with her as they had done. The incessant quivering, in which every fibre of her frame participated, had thrown her into a stupefied reverie in which her arms worked on independently of her consciousness. She hardly knew where she was, and did not hear Izz Huett tell her from below that her hair was tumbling down.

By degress the freshest among them began to grow cadaverous and saucer-eyed. Whenever Tess lifted her head she beheld always the great upgrown strawstack, with the men in shirtsleeves upon it, against the gray north sky; in front of it the long red elevator like a Jacob's ladder, on which a perpetual stream of threshed straw ascended, a yellow river running up-hill, and spouting out on the top of the rick.

She knew that Alec d'Urberville was still on the scene, observing her from some point or other, though she could not say where. There was an excuse for his remaining, for when the threshed rick drew near its final sheaves a little ratting was always done, and men unconnected with the threshing sometimes dropped in for that performance—sporting characters of all descriptions, gents with terriers and facetious pipes, roughs with sticks and stones.

But there was another hour's work before the layer of live rats at the base of the stack would be reached; and as the evening light in the direction of the Giant's Hill by Abbot's-Cernel dissolved away, the white-faced moon of the season arose from the horizon that lay towards Middleton Abbey and Shottsford on the other side. For the last hour or two Marian had felt uneasy about Tess, whom she could not get near enough to speak to, the other women having kept up their strength by drinking ale, and Tess having done without it through traditionary dread, owing to its results at her home in childhood. But Tess still kept going: if she could not fill her part she would have to leave; and this contingency, which she would have regarded with equanimity and even with relief a month or two earlier, had become a terror since d'Urberville had begun to hover round her.

The sheaf-pitchers and feeders had now worked the rick so low that people on the ground could talk to them. To Tess's surprise Farmer Groby came up on the machine to her, and said that if she desired to join her friend he did not wish her to keep on any longer, and would send somebody else to take her place. The 'friend' was d'Urberville, she knew, and also that this concession had been granted in obedience to the request of that friend, or enemy. She shook her head and toiled on.

The time for the rat-catching arrived at last, and the hunt began. The creatures had crept downwards with the subsidence of the rick till they were all together at the bottom, and being now uncovered from their last refuge they ran across the open ground in all directions, a loud shriek from the by-this-time half-tipsy Marian informing her companions that one of the rats had invaded her person—a terror which the rest of the women had guarded against by various schemes of skirt-tucking and self-elevation. The rat was at last dislodged, and, amid the barking of dogs, masculine shouts, feminine screams, oaths, stampings, and confusion as of Pandemonium, Tess untied her last sheaf; the drum slowed, the whizzing ceased, and she stepped from the machine to the ground.

Her lover, who had only looked on at the rat-catching, was promptly at her side.

'What—after all—my insulting slap too!' said she in an under-breath. She was so utterly exhausted that she had not strength to speak louder.

'I should indeed be foolish to feel offended at anything you say or do,' he answered, in the seductive voice of the Trantridge time. 'How the little limbs tremble! You are as weak as a bled calf, you know you are; and yet you need have done nothing since I arrived. How could you be so obstinate? However, I have told the farmer that he has no right to employ women at steam-threshing. It is not proper work for them; and on all the better class of farms it has been given up, as he knows very well. I will walk with you as far as your home.'

'O yes,' she answered with a jaded gait. 'Walk wi' me if you will! I do bear in mind that you came to marry me before you knew o' my state. Perhaps—perhaps you are a little better and kinder than

I have been thinking you were. Whatever is meant as kindness I am grateful for; whatever is meant in any other way I am angered at. I cannot sense your meaning sometimes.'

'If I cannot legitimize our former relations at least I can assist you. And I will do it with much more regard for your feelings than I formerly showed. My religious mania, or whatever it was, is over. But I retain a little good nature; I hope I do. Now Tess, by all that's tender and strong between man and woman, trust me! I have enough and more than enough to put you out of anxiety, both for yourself and your parents and sisters. I can make them all comfortable if you will only show confidence in me.'

'Have you seen 'em lately?' she quickly inquired.

'Yes. They didn't know where you were. It was only by chance that I found you here.'

The cold moon looked aslant upon Tess's fagged face between the twigs of the garden-hedge as she paused outside the cottage which was her temporary home, d'Urberville pausing beside her.

'Don't mention my little brothers and sisters—don't make me break down quite!' she said. 'If you want to help them—God knows they need it—do it without telling me. But no, no!' she cried. 'I will take nothing from you, either for them or for me!'

He did not accompany her further, since, as she lived with the household, all was public indoors. No sooner had she herself entered, laved herself in a washing-tub, and shared supper with the family than she fell into thought, and withdrawing to the table under the wall, by the light of her own little lamp wrote in a passionate mood—

> My own Husband,—Let me call you so—I must—even if it makes you angry to think of such an unworthy wife as I. I must cry to you in my trouble—I have no one else! I am so exposed to temptation, Angel. I fear to say who it is, and I do not like to write about it at all. But I cling to you in a way you cannot think! Can you not come to me now, at once, before anything terrible happens? O, I know you cannot, because you are so far away! I think I must die if you do not come soon, or tell me to come to you. The punishment you have measured out to me is deserved—

I do know that—well deserved—and you are right and just to be angry with me. But, Angel, please, please, not to be just—only a little kind to me, even if I do not deserve it, and come to me! If you would come, I could die in your arms! I would be well content to do that if so be you had forgiven me!

Angel, I live entirely for you. I love you too much to blame you for going away, and I know it was necessary you should find a farm. Do not think I shall say a word of sting or bitterness. Only come back to me. I am desolate without you, my darling, O, so desolate! I do not mind having to work: but if you will send me one little line and say, '*I am coming soon*', I will bide on, Angel—O, so cheerfully!

It has been so much my religion ever since we were married to be faithful to you in every thought and look, that even when a man speaks a compliment to me before I am aware, it seems wronging you. Have you never felt one little bit of what you used to feel when we were at the dairy? If you have, how can you keep away from me? I am the same woman, Angel, as you fell in love with; yes, the very same!—not the one you disliked but never saw. What was the past to me as soon as I met you? It was a dead thing altogether. I became another woman, filled full of new life from you. How could I be the early one? Why do you not see this? Dear, if you would only be a little more conceited, and believe in yourself so far as to see that you were strong enough to work this change in me, you would perhaps be in a mind to come to me, your poor wife.

How silly I was in my happiness when I thought I could trust you always to love me! I ought to have known that such as that was not for poor me. But I am sick at heart, not only for old times, but for the present. Think—think how it do hurt my heart not to see you ever—ever! Ah, if I could only make your dear heart ache one little minute of each day as mine does every day and all day long, it might lead you to show pity to your poor lonely one.

People still say that I am rather pretty, Angel (handsome is the word they use, since I wish to be truthful). Perhaps I am what they say. But I do not value my good looks; I only like to have them because they belong to you, my dear, and that there may be at least one thing about me worth your having. So much have I felt this, that when I met with annoyance on account of the same I tied up my face in a bandage as long as people would believe in it. O Angel, I tell you all this not from vanity—you will certainly know I do not—but only that you may come to me!

If you really cannot come to me will you let me come to you! I am, as I say, worried, pressed to do what I will not do. It cannot be that I shall yield one inch, yet I am in terror as to what an accident might lead to, and I so defenceless on account of my first error. I cannot say more about this—it makes me too miserable. But if I break down by falling into some fearful snare, my last state will be worse than my first. O God, I cannot think of it! Let me come at once, or at once come to me!

I would be content, ay, glad, to live with you as your servant, if I may not as your wife; so that I could only be near you, and get glimpses of you, and think of you as mine.

The daylight has nothing to show me, since you are not here, and I don't like to see the rooks and starlings in the fields, because I grieve and grieve to miss you who used to see them with me. I long for only one thing in heaven or earth or under the earth, to meet you, my own dear! Come to me—come to me, and save me from what threatens me!—Your faithful heartbroken

TESS.

XLIX

The appeal duly found its way to the breakfast-table of the quiet Vicarage to the westward, in that valley where the air is so soft and the soil so rich that the effort of growth requires but superficial aid by comparison with the tillage at Flintcomb-Ash, and where to Tess the human world seemed so different (though it was much the same). It was purely for security that she had been requested by Angel to send her communications through his father, whom he kept pretty well informed of his changing addresses in the country he had gone to exploit for himself with a heavy heart.

'Now,' said old Mr Clare to his wife, when he had read the envelope, 'if Angel proposes leaving Rio for a visit home at the end of next month, as he told us that he hoped to do, I think this may hasten his plans; for I believe it to be from his wife.' He breathed deeply at the thought of her; and the letter was redirected to be promptly sent on to Angel.

'Dear fellow, I hope he will get home safely,' murmured Mrs Clare. 'To my dying day I shall feel that he has been ill-used. You should have sent him to Cambridge in spite of his want of faith, and given him the same chance as the other boys had. He would have grown out of it under proper influence, and perhaps would have taken Orders after all. Church or no Church, it would have been fairer to him.'

This was the only wail with which Mrs Clare ever disturbed her husband's peace in respect of their sons. And she did not vent this often; for she was as considerate as she was devout, and knew that his mind too was troubled by doubts as to his justice in this matter. Only too often had she heard him lying awake at night, stifling sighs for Angel with prayers. But the uncompromising Evangelical did not even now hold that he would have been justified in giving his son, an unbeliever, the same academic advantages that he had given to the two others, when it was possible, if not probable, that those very advantages might have been used to decry the doctrines which he had made it his life's mission and desire to propagate, and the mission of his ordained sons likewise. To put with one hand a pedestal under the feet of the two faithful ones, and with the other to exalt the unfaithful by the same artificial means, he deemed to be alike inconsistent with his convictions, his position, and his hopes. Nevertheless, he loved his misnamed Angel, and in secret mourned over this treatment of him as Abraham might have mourned over the doomed Isaac while they went up the hill together. His silent self-generated regrets were far bitterer than the reproaches which his wife rendered audible.

They blamed themselves for this unlucky marriage. If Angel had never been destined for a farmer he would never have been thrown with agricultural girls. They did not distinctly know what had separated him and his wife, nor the date on which the separation had taken place. At first they had supposed it must be something of the nature of a serious aversion. But in his later letters he occasionally alluded to the intention of coming home to fetch her; from which expressions they hoped the division might not owe its origin to anything so hopelessly permanent as that. He had told them that she was with her relatives, and in their doubts they had decided not to intrude into a situation which they knew no way of bettering.

The eyes for which Tess's letter was intended were gazing at this time on a limitless expanse of country from the back of a mule which was bearing him from the interior of the South-American Continent towards the coast. His experiences of this strange land had been sad. The severe illness from which he had suffered shortly after his arrival had never wholly left him, and he had by degrees almost decided to relinquish his hope of farming here, though, as long as the bare possibility existed of his remaining, he kept this change of view a secret from his parents.

The crowds of agricultural labourers who had come out to the country in his wake, dazzled by representations of easy independence, had suffered, died, and wasted away. He would see mothers from English farms trudging along with their infants in their arms, when the child would be stricken with fever and would die; the mother would pause to dig a hole in the loose earth with her bare hands, would bury the babe therein with the same natural grave-tools, shed one tear, and again trudge on.

Angel's original intention had not been emigration to Brazil, but a northern or eastern farm in his own country. He had come to this place in a fit of desperation, the Brazil movement among the English agriculturists having by chance coincided with his desire to escape from his past existence.

During this time of absence he had mentally aged a dozen years. What arrested him now as of value in life was less its beauty that its pathos. Having long discredited the old systems of mysticism, he now began to discredit the old appraisements of morality. He thought they wanted readjusting. Who was the moral man? Still more pertinently, who was the moral woman? The beauty or ugliness of a character lay not only in its achievements, but in its aims and impulses; its true history lay, not among things done, but among things willed.

How, then, about Tess?

Viewing her in these lights, a regret for his hasty judgment began to oppress him. Did he reject her eternally, or did he not? He could no longer say that he would always reject her, and not to say that was in spirit to accept her now.

This growing fondness of her memory coincided in point of time with her residence at Flintcomb-Ash, but it was before she had felt herself at liberty to trouble him with a word about her circumstances or her feelings. He was greatly perplexed; and in his perplexity as to her motives in withholding intelligence he did not inquire. Thus her silence of docility was misinterpreted. How much it really said if he had understood!—that she adhered with literal exactness to orders which he had given and forgotten; that despite her natural fearlessness she asserted no rights, admitted his judgment to be in every respect the true one, and bent her head dumbly thereto.

In the before-mentioned journey by mules through the interior of the country, another man rode beside him. Angel's companion was also an Englishman, bent on the same errand, though he came from another part of the island. They were both in a state of mental depression, and they spoke of home affairs. Confidence begat confidence. With that curious tendency evinced by men, more especially when in distant lands, to entrust to strangers details of their lives which they would on no account mention to friends, Angel admitted to this man as they rode along the sorrowful facts of his marriage.

The stranger had sojourned in many more lands and among many more peoples than Angel; to his cosmopolitan mind such deviations from the social norm, so immense to domesticity, were no more than are the irregularities of vale and mountain-chain to the whole terrestrial curve. He viewed the matter in quite a different light from Angel; thought that what Tess had been was of no importance beside what she would be, and plainly told Clare that he was wrong in coming away from her.

The next day they were drenched in a thunderstorm. Angel's companion was struck down with fever, and died by the week's end. Clare waited a few hours to bury him, and then went on his way.

The cursory remarks of the large-minded stranger, of whom he knew absolutely nothing beyond a commonplace name, were sublimed by his death, and influenced Clare more than all the reasoned ethics of the philosophers. His own parochialism made him ashamed by its contrast. His inconsistencies rushed upon him in a flood. He had persistently elevated Hellenic Paganism at the expense of Christianity; yet in that civilization an illegal surrender was not certain disesteem. Surely then he might have regarded that abhorrence of the un-intact state, which he had inherited with the creed of mysticism, as at least open to correction when the result was due to treachery. A remorse struck into him. The words of Izz Huett, never quite stilled in his memory, came back to him. He had asked Izz if she loved him, and she had replied in the affirmative. Did she love him more than Tess did? No, she had replied; Tess would lay down her life for him, and she herself could do no more.

He thought of Tess as she had appeared on the day of the wedding. How her eyes had lingered upon him; how she had hung upon his words as if they were a god's! And during the terrible evening over the hearth, when her simple soul uncovered itself to his, how pitiful her face had looked by the rays of the fire, in her inability to realize that his love and protection could possibly be withdrawn.

Thus from being her critic he grew to be her advocate. Cynical things he had uttered to himself about her; but no man can be always a cynic and live; and he withdrew them. The mistake of expressing them had arisen from his allowing himself to be influenced by general principles to the disregard of the particular instance.

But the reasoning is somewhat musty; lovers and husbands have gone over the ground before to-day. Clare had been harsh towards her; there is no doubt of it. Men are too often harsh with women they love or have loved; women with men. And yet these harshnesses are tenderness itself when compared with the universal harshness out of which they grow; the harshness of the position towards the temperament, of the means towards the aims, of to-day towards yesterday, of hereafter towards to-day.

The historic interest of her family—the masterful line of d'Urbervilles—whom he had despised as a spent force, touched his sentiments now. Why had he not known the difference between the political value and the imaginative value of these things? In the latter aspect her d'Urberville descent was a fact of great dimensions; worthless to economics, it was a most useful ingredient to the dreamer, to the moralizer on declines and falls. It was a fact that would soon be forgotten—that bit of distinction in poor Tess's blood and name, and oblivion would fall upon her hereditary link with the marble monuments and leaded skeletons at Kingsbere. So does Time ruthlessly destroy his own romances. In recalling her face again and again, he thought now that he could see therein a flash of the dignity which must have graced her grand-dames; and the vision sent that *aura* through his veins which he had formerly felt, and which left behind it a sense of sickness.

Despite her not inviolate past, what still abode in such a woman as Tess outvalued the freshness of her fellows. Was not the gleaming of the grapes of Ephraim better than the vintage of Abi-ezer?

So spoke love renascent, preparing the way for Tess's devoted outpouring, which was then just being forwarded to him by his father; though owing to his distance inland it was to be a long time in reaching him.

Meanwhile the writer's expectation that Angel would come in response to the entreaty was alternately great and small. What lessened it was that the facts of her life which had led to the parting had not changed—could never change; and that, if her presence had not attenuated them, her absence could not. Nevertheless she addressed her mind to the tender question of what she could do to please him best if he should arrive. Sighs were expended on the wish that she had taken more notice of the tunes he played on his harp, that she had inquired more curiously of him which were his favourite ballads among those the country-girls sang. She indirectly inquired of Amby Seedling, who had followed Izz from Talbothays, and by chance Amby remembered that, amongst the snatches of melody in which they had indulged at the dairyman's, to induce the cows to let down their milk, Clare had seemed to like 'Cupid's Gardens', 'I have parks, I have hounds', and 'The break o' the day'; and had seemed not to care for 'The Tailor's Breeches', and 'Such a beauty I did grow', excellent ditties as they were.

To perfect the ballads was now her whimsical desire. She practised them privately at odd moments, especially 'The break o' the day':

> Arise, arise, arise!
> And pick your love a posy,
> All o' the sweetest flowers
> That in the garden grow.
> The turtle doves and sma' birds
> In every bough a-building,
> So early in the May-time,
> At the break o' the day!

It would have melted the heart of a stone to hear her singing these ditties, whenever she worked apart from the rest of the girls in this cold dry time; the tears running down her cheeks all the while at the thought that perhaps he would not, after all, come to hear her, and the simple silly words of the songs resounding in painful mockery of the aching heart of the singer.

Tess was so wrapt up in this fanciful dream that she seemed not to know how the season was advancing; that the days had lengthened, that Lady-Day was at hand, and would soon be followed by Old Lady-Day, the end of her term here.

But before the quarter-day had quite come something happened which made Tess think of far different matters. She was at her lodging as usual one evening, sitting in the downstairs room with the rest of the family, when somebody knocked at the door and inquired for Tess. Through the doorway she saw against the declining light a figure with the height of a woman and the breadth of a child, a tall, thin, girlish creature whom she did not recognize in the twilight till the girl said 'Tess!'

'What—is it 'Liza-Lu?' asked Tess, in startled accents. Her sister, whom a little over a year ago she had left at home as a child, had sprung up by a sudden shoot to a form of this presentation, of which as yet Lu seemed herself scarce able to understand the meaning. Her thin legs, visible below her once long frock, now short by her growing, and her uncomfortable hands and arms, revealed her youth and inexperience.

'Yes, I have been traipsing about all day, Tess,' said Lu, with unemotional gravity, 'a-trying to find 'ee; and I'm very tired.'

'What is the matter at home?'

'Mother is took very bad, and the doctor says she's dying, and as father is not very well neither, and says 'tis wrong for a man of such a high family as his to slave and drave at common labouring work, we don't know what to do.'

Tess stood in reverie a long time before she thought of asking 'Liza-Lu to come in and sit down. When she had done so, and 'Liza-Lu was having some tea, she came to a decision. It was imperative that she should go home. Her agreement did not end till Old Lady-Day, the sixth of April, but as the interval thereto was not a long one she resolved to run the risk of starting at once.

To go that night would be a gain of twelve hours; but her sister was too tired to undertake such a distance till the morrow. Tess ran down to where Marian and Izz lived, informed them of what had happened, and begged them to make the best of her case to the farmer. Returning, she got Lu a supper, and after that, having tucked the younger into her own bed, packed up as many of her belongings as would go into a withy basket, and started, directing Lu to follow her next morning.

L

She plunged into the chilly equinoctial darkness as the clock struck ten, for her fifteen miles' walk under the steely stars. In lonely districts night is a protection rather than a danger to a noiseless pedestrian, and knowing this Tess pursued the nearest course along by-lanes that she would almost have feared in the day time; but marauders were wanting now, and spectral fears were driven out of her mind by thoughts of her mother. Thus she proceeded mile after mile, ascending and descending till she came to Bulbarrow, and about midnight looked from that height into the abyss of chaotic shade which was all that revealed itself of the vale on whose further side she was born. Having already traversed about five miles on the upland she had now some ten or eleven in the lowland before her journey would be finished. The winding road downwards became just visible to her under the wan starlight as she followed it, and soon she paced a soil so contrasting with that above it that the difference was perceptible to the tread and to the smell. It was the heavy clay land of Blackmoor Vale, and a part of the Vale to which turnpike-roads had never penetrated. Superstitions linger longest on these heavy soils. Having once been forest, at this shadowy time it seemed to assert something of its old character, the far and the near being blended, and every tree and tall hedge making the most of its presence. The harts that had been hunted here, the witches that had been pricked and ducked, the green-spangled fairies that 'whickered' at you as you passed;—the place teemed with beliefs in them still, and they formed an impish multitude now.

At Nuttlebury she passed the village inn, whose sign creaked in response to the greeting of her footsteps, which not a human soul heard but herself. Under the thatched roofs her mind's eye beheld relaxed tendons and flaccid muscles, spread out in the darkness beneath coverlets made of little purple patchwork squares, and undergoing a bracing process at the hands of sleep for renewed labour on the morrow, as soon as a hint of pink nebulosity appeared on Hambledon Hill.

At three she turned the last corner of the maze of lanes she had threaded, and entered Marlott, passing the field in which, as a club-girl, she had first seen Angel Clare, when he had not danced with her; the sense of disappointment remained with her yet. In the direction of her mother's house she saw a light. It came from the bedroom window, and a branch waved in front of it and made it wink at her. As soon as she could discern the outline of the house—newly thatched with her money—it had all its old effect upon Tess's imagination. Part of her body and life it ever seemed to be; the slope of its dormers, the finish of its gables, the broken courses of brick which topped the chimney, all had something in common with her personal character. A stupefaction had come into these features, to her regard; it meant the illness of her mother.

She opened the door so softly as to disturb nobody; the lower room was vacant, but the neighbour who was sitting up with her mother came to the top of the stairs, and whispered that Mrs Durbeyfield was no better, though she was sleeping just then. Tess prepared herself a breakfast, and then took her place as nurse in her mother's chamber.

In the morning, when she contemplated the children, they had all a curiously elongated look; although she had been away little more than a year their growth was astounding; and the necessity of applying herself heart and soul to their needs took her out of her own cares.

Her father's ill-health was of the same indefinite kind, and he sat in his chair as usual. But the day after her arrival he was unusually bright. He had a rational scheme for living, and Tess asked him what it was.

'I'm thinking of sending round to all the old antiqueerians in this part of England,' he said, 'asking them to subscribe to a fund to maintain me. I'm sure they'd see it as a romantical, artistical, and proper thing to do. They spend lots o' money in keeping up old ruins, and finding the bones o' things, and such like; and living remains must be more interesting to 'em still, if they only knowed of me. Would that somebody would go round and tell 'em what there is living among 'em, and they thinking nothing of him! If Pa'son Tringham, who discovered me, had lived, he'd ha' done it, I'm sure.'

Tess postponed her arguments on this high project till she had grappled with pressing matters in hand, which seemed little improved by her remittances. When indoor necessities had been eased she turned her attention to external things. It was now the season for planting and sowing; many gardens and allotments of the villagers had already received their spring tillage; but the garden and the allotment of the Durbeyfields were behindhand. She found, to her dismay, that this was owing to their having eaten all the seed potatoes,—that last lapse of the improvident. At the earliest moment she obtained what others she could procure, and in a few days her father was well enough to see to the garden, under Tess's persuasive efforts: while she herself undertook the allotment-plot which they rented in a field a couple of hundred yards out of the village.

She liked doing it after the confinement of the sick chamber, where she was not now required by reason of her mother's improvement. Violent motion relieved thought. The plot of ground was in a high, dry, open enclosure, where there were forty or fifty such pieces, and where labour was at its briskest when the hired labour of the day had ended. Digging began usually at six o'clock, and extended indefinitely into the dusk or moonlight. Just now heaps of dead weeds and refuse were burning on many of the plots, the dry weather favouring their combustion.

One fine day Tess and 'Liza-Lu worked on here with their neighbours till the last rays of the sun smote flat upon the white pegs that divided the plots. As soon as twilight succeeded to sunset the flare of the couch-grass and cabbage-stalk fires began to light up the allotments fitfully, their outlines appearing and disappearing under the dense smoke as wafted by the wind. When a fire glowed, banks of smoke, blown level along the ground, would themselves become illuminated to an opaque lustre, screening the workpeople from one another; and the meaning of the 'pillar of a cloud', which was a wall by day and a light by night, could be understood.

As evening thickened some of the gardening men and women gave over for the night, but the greater number remained to get their planting done, Tess being among them, though she sent her sister home. It was on one of the couch-burning plots that she laboured with her fork, its four shining prongs resounding against the stones and dry clods in little clicks. Sometimes she was completely involved in the smoke of her fire; then it would leave her figure free, irradiated by the brassy glare from the heap. She was oddly dressed to-night, and presented a somewhat staring aspect, her attire being a gown bleached by many washings, with a short black jacket over it, the effect of the whole being that of a wedding and funeral guest in one. The women further back wore white aprons, which, with their pale faces, were all that could be seen of them in the gloom, except when at moments they caught a flash from the flames.

Westward, the wiry boughs of the bare thorn hedge which formed the boundary of the field rose against the pale opalescence of the lower sky. Above, Jupiter hung like a full-blown jonquil, so bright as almost to throw a shade. A few small nondescript stars were appearing elsewhere. In the distance a dog barked, and wheels occasionally rattled along the dry road.

Still the prongs continued to click assiduously, for it was not late; and though the air was fresh and keen there was a whisper of spring in it that cheered the workers on. Something in the place, the hour, the crackling fires, the fantastic mysteries of light and shade, made others as well as Tess enjoy being there. Nightfall, which in the frost of winter comes as a fiend and in the warmth of summer as a lover, came as a tranquillizer on this March day.

Nobody looked at his or her companions. The eyes of all were on the soil as its turned surface was revealed by the fires. Hence as Tess stirred the clods, and sang her foolish little songs with scarce now a hope that Clare would ever hear them, she did not for a long time notice the person who worked nearest to her—a man in a long smockfrock who, she found, was forking the same plot as herself, and whom she supposed her father had sent there to advance the work. She became more conscious of him when the direction of his digging brought him closer. Sometimes the smoke divided them; then it swerved, and the two were visible to each other but divided from all the rest.

Tess did not speak to her fellow-worker, nor did he speak to her. Nor did she think of him further than to recollect that he had not been there when it was broad daylight, and that she did not know him as any one of the Marlott labourers, which was no wonder, her absences having been so long and frequent of late years. By-and-by he dug so close to her that the fire-beams were reflected as distinctly from the steel prongs of his fork as from her own. On going up to the fire to throw a pitch of dead weeds upon it, she found that he did the same on the other side. The fire flared up, and she beheld the face of d'Urberville.

The unexpectedness of his presence, the grotesqueness of his appearance in a gathered smockfrock, such as was now worn only by the most old-fashioned of the labourers, had a ghastly comicality that chilled her as to its bearing. D'Urberville emitted a low long laugh.

'If I were inclined to joke I should say, How much this seems like Paradise!' he remarked whimsically, looking at her with an inclined head.

'What do you say?' she weakly asked.

'A jester might say this is just like Paradise. You are Eve, and I am the old Other One come to tempt you in the disguise of an inferior animal. I used to be quite up in that scene of Milton's when I was theological. Some of it goes—

> "Empress, the way is ready, and not long,
> Beyond a row of myrtles . . .
> . . . If thou accept
> My conduct, I can bring thee thither soon."
> "Lead then," said Eve.

And so on. My dear, dear Tess, I am only putting this to you as a thing that you might have supposed or said quite untruly, because you think so badly of me.'

'I never said you were Satan, or thought it. I don't think of you in that way at all. My thoughts of you are quite cold, except when you affront me. What, did you come digging here entirely because of me?'

'Entirely. To see you; nothing more. The smockfrock, which I saw hanging for sale as I came along, was an after-thought, that I mightn't be noticed. I come to protest against your working like this.'

'But I like doing it—it is for my father.'

'Your engagement at the other place is ended?'

'Yes.'

'Where are you going to next? To join your dear husband?'

She could not bear the humiliating reminder.

'O—I don't know!' she said bitterly. 'I have no husband!'

'It is quite true—in the sense you mean. But you have a friend, and I have determined that you shall be comfortable in spite of yourself. When you get down to your house you will see what I have sent there for you.'

'O, Alec, I wish you wouldn't give me anything at all! I cannot take it from you! I don't like—it is not right!'

'It is right!' he cried lightly. 'I am not going to see a woman whom I feel so tenderly for as I do for you, in trouble without trying to help her.'

'But I am very well off! I am only in trouble about—about—not about living at all!'

She turned, and desperately resumed her digging, tears dripping upon the fork-handle and upon the clods.

'About the children—your brothers and sisters,' he resumed. 'I've been thinking of them.'

Tess's heart quivered—he was touching her in a weak place. He had divined her chief anxiety. Since returning home her soul had gone out to those children with an affection that was passionate.

'If your mother does not recover, somebody ought to do something for them; since your father will not be able to do much, I suppose?'

'He can with my assistance. He must!'

'And with mine.'

'No, sir!'

'How damned foolish this is!' burst out d'Urberville. 'Why, he thinks we are the same family; and will be quite satisfied!'

'He don't. I've undeceived him.'

'The more fool you!'

D'Urberville in anger retreated from her to the hedge, where he pulled off the long smockfrock which had disguised him; and rolling it up and pushing it into the couch-fire, went away.

Tess could not get on with her digging after this; she felt restless; she wondered if he had gone back to her father's house; and taking the fork in her hand proceeded homewards.

Some twenty yards from the house she was met by one of her sisters.

'O, Tessy—what do you think! 'Liza-Lu is a-crying, and there's a lot of folk in the house, and mother is a good deal better, but they think father is dead!'

The child realized the grandeur of the news; but not as yet its sadness; and stood looking at Tess with round-eyed importance, till, beholding the effect produced upon her, she said—

'What, Tess, shan't we talk to father never no more?'

'But father was only a little bit ill!' exclaimed Tess distractedly.

'Liza-Lu came up.

'He dropped down just now, and the doctor who was there for mother said there was no chance for him, because his heart was growed in.'

Yes; the Durbeyfield couple had changed places; the dying one was out of danger, and the indisposed one was dead. The news meant even more than it sounded. Her father's life had a value apart from his personal achievements, or perhaps it would not have had much. It was the last of the three lives for whose duration the house and premises were held under a lease; and it had long been coveted by the tenant-farmer for his regular labourers, who were stinted in cottage accommodation. Moreover, 'liviers' were disapproved of in villages almost as much as little freeholders, because of their independence of manner, and when a lease determined it was never renewed.

Thus the Durbeyfields, once d'Urbervilles, saw descending upon them the destiny which, no doubt, when they were among the Olympians of the county, they had caused to descend many a time, and severely enough, upon the heads of such landless ones as they themselves were now. So do flux and reflux—the rhythm of change—alternate and persist in everything under the sky.

LI

At length it was the eve of Old Lady-Day, and the agricultural world was in a fever of mobility such as only occurs at that particular date of the year. It is a day of fulfilment; agreements for outdoor service during the ensuing year, entered into at Candlemas, are to be now carried out. The labourers—or 'work-folk', as they used to call themselves immemorially till the other word was introduced from without—who wish to remain no longer in old places are removing to the new farms.

These annual migrations from farm to farm were on the increase here. When Tess's mother was a child the majority of the field-folk about Marlott had remained all their lives on one farm, which had been the home also of their fathers and grandfathers; but latterly the desire for yearly removal had risen to a high pitch. With the younger families it was a pleasant excitement which might possibly be an advantage. The Egypt of one family was the Land of Promise to the family who saw it from a distance, till by residence there it became in turn their Egypt also; and so they changed and changed.

However, all the mutations so increasingly discernible in village life did not originate entirely in the agricultural unrest. A depopulation was also going on. The village had formerly contained, side by side with the agricultural labourers, an interesting and better-informed class, ranking distinctly above the former—the class to which Tess's father and mother had belonged—and including the carpenter, the smith, the shoemaker, the huckster, together with nondescript workers other than farm-labourers; a set of people who owed a certain stability of aim and conduct to the fact of their being life-holders like Tess's father, or copyholders, or, occasionally, small freeholders. But as the long holdings fell in they were seldom again let to similar tenants, and were mostly pulled down, if not absolutely required by the farmer for his hands. Cottagers who were not directly employed on the land were looked upon with disfavour, and the banishment of some starved the trade of others, who were thus obliged to follow. These families, who had formed the backbone of the village life in the past, who were the depositaries of the village traditions, had to seek refuge in the large centres; the process, humorously designated by statisticians as 'the tendency of the rural population towards the large towns', being really the tendency of water to flow uphill when forced by machinery.

The cottage accommodation at Marlott having been in this manner considerably curtailed by demolitions, every house which remained standing was required by the agriculturist for his work-people. Ever since the occurrence of the event which had cast such a shadow over Tess's life, the Durbeyfield family (whose descent was not credited) had been tacitly looked on as one which would have to go when their lease ended, if only in the interests of morality. It was, indeed, quite true that the household had not been shining examples either of temperance, soberness, or chastity. The father, and even the mother, had got drunk at times, the younger children seldom had gone to church, and the eldest daughter had made queer unions. By some means the village had to be kept pure. So on this, the first Lady-Day on which the Durbeyfields were expellable, the house, being roomy, was required for a carter with a large family; and Widow Joan, her daughters Tess and 'Liza-Lu, the boy Abraham and the younger children, had to go elsewhere.

On the evening preceding their removal it was getting dark betimes by reason of a drizzling rain which blurred the sky. As it was the last night they would spend in the village which had been their home and birthplace, Mrs Durbeyfield, 'Liza-Lu, and Abraham had gone out to bid some friends good-bye, and Tess was keeping house till they should return.

She was kneeling in the window-bench, her face close to the casement, where an outer pane of rain-water was sliding down the inner pane of glass. Her eyes rested on the web of a spider, probably starved long ago, which had been mistakenly placed in a corner where no flies ever came, and shivered in the slight draught through the casement. Tess was reflecting on the position of the household, in which she perceived her own evil influence. Had she not come home her mother and the children might probably have been allowed to stay on as weekly tenants. But she had been observed almost immediately on her return by some people of scrupulous character and great influence: they had seen her idling in the churchyard, restoring as well as she could with a little trowel a baby's obliterated grave. By this means they had found that she was living here again; her mother was scolded for 'harbouring' her; sharp retorts had ensued from Joan who had independently offered to leave at once; she had been taken at her word; and here was the result.

'I ought never to have come home,' said Tess to herself, bitterly.

She was so intent upon these thoughts that she hardly at first took note of a man in a white mackintosh whom she saw riding down the street. Possibly it was owing to her face being near to the pane that he saw her so quickly, and directed his horse so close to the cottage-front that his hoofs were almost upon the narrow border for plants growing under the wall. It was not till he touched the window with his riding-crop that she observed him. The rain had nearly ceased, and she opened the casement in obedience to his gesture.

'Didn't you see me?' asked d'Urberville.

'I was not attending,' she said. 'I heard you, I believe, though I fancied it was a carriage and horses. I was in a sort of dream.'

'Ah! you heard the d'Urberville Coach, perhaps. You know the legend, I suppose?'

'No. My—somebody was going to tell it me once, but didn't.'

'If you are a genuine d'Urberville I ought not to tell you either, I suppose. As for me, I'm a sham one, so it doesn't matter. It is rather dismal. It is that this sound of a non-existent coach can only be heard by one of d'Urberville blood, and it is held to be of ill-omen to the one who hears it. It has to do with a murder, committed by one of the family, centuries ago.'

'Now you have begun it, finish it.'

'Very well. One of the family is said to have abducted some beautiful woman, who tried to escape from the coach in which he was carrying her off, and in the struggle he killed her—or she killed him—I forget which. Such is one version of the tale . . . I see that your tubs and buckets are packed. Going away, aren't you?'

'Yes, to-morrow—Old Lady-Day.'

'I heard you were, but could hardly believe it; it seems so sudden. Why is it?'

'Father's was the last life on the property, and when that dropped we had no further right to stay. Though we might, perhaps, have stayed as weekly tenants—if it had not been for me.'

'What about you?'

'I am not a—proper woman.'

D'Urberville's face flushed.

'What a blasted shame! Miserable snobs! May their dirty souls be burnt to cinders!' he exclaimed in tones of ironic resentment. 'That's why you are going, is it? Turned out?'

'We are not turned out exactly; but as they said we should have to go soon, it was best to go now everybody was moving, because there are better chances.'

'Where are you going to?'

'Kingsbere. We have taken rooms there. Mother is so foolish about father's people that she will go there.'

'But your mother's family are not fit for lodgings, and in a little hole of a town like that. Now why not come to my garden-house at Trantridge? There are hardly any poultry now, since my mother's death; but there's the house, as you know it, and the garden. It can be whitewashed in a day, and your mother can live there quite comfortably; and I will put the children to a good school. Really I ought to do something for you!'

'But we have already taken the rooms at Kingsbere!' she declared. 'And we can wait there—'

'Wait—what for? For that nice husband, no doubt. Now look here, Tess, I know what men are, and, bearing in mind the *grounds* of your separation, I am quite positive he will never make it up with you. Now, though I have been your enemy, I am your friend, even if you won't believe it. Come to this cottage of mine. We'll get up a regular colony of fowls, and your mother can attend to them excellently; and the children can go to school.'

Tess breathed more and more quickly, and at length she said—

'How do I know that you would do all this? Your views may change—and then—we should be—my mother would be—homeless again.'

'Oh no—no. I would guarantee you against such as that in writing, if necessary. Think it over.'

Tess shook her head. But d'Urberville persisted; she had seldom seen him so determined; he would not take a negative.

'Please just tell your mother,' he said, in emphatic tones. 'It is her business to judge—not yours. I shall get the house swept out and whitened to-morrow morning, and fires lit; and it will be dry by the evening, so that you can come straight there. Now mind, I shall expect you.'

Tess again shook her head; her throat swelling with complicated emotion. She could not look up at d'Urberville.

'I owe you something for the past, you know,' he resumed. 'And you cured me, too, of that craze; so I am glad—'

'I would rather you had kept the craze, so that you had kept the practice which went with it!'

'I am glad of this opportunity of repaying you a little. Tomorrow I shall expect to hear your mother's goods unloading . . . Give me your hand on it now—dear, beautiful Tess!'

With the last sentence he had dropped his voice to a murmur, and put his hand in at the half-open casement. With stormy eyes she pulled the stay-bar quickly, and, in doing so, caught his arm between the casement and the stone mullion.

'Damnation—you are very cruel!' he said, snatching out his arm. 'No, no!—I know you didn't do it on purpose. Well, I shall expect you, or your mother and the children at least.'

'I shall not come—I have plenty of money!' she cried.

'Where?'

'At my father-in-law's, if I ask for it.'

'*If* you ask for it. But you won't, Tess; I know you; you'll never ask for it—you'll starve first!'

With these words he rode off. Just at the corner of the street he met the man with the paint-pot, who asked him if he had deserted the brethren.

'You go to the devil!' said d'Urberville.

Tess remained where she was a long while, till a sudden rebellious sense of injustice caused the region of her eyes to swell with the rush of hot tears thither. Her husband, Angel Clare himself, had, like others, dealt out hard measure to her, surely he had! She had never before admitted such a thought; but he had surely! Never in her life—she could swear it from the bottom of her soul—had she ever intended to do wrong; yet these hard judgments had come. Whatever her sins, they were not sins of intention, but of inadvertence, and why should she have been punished so persistently?

She passionately seized the first piece of paper that came to hand, and scribbled the following lines:

> O why have you treated me so monstrously, Angel! I do not deserve it. I have thought it all over carefully, and I can never, never forgive you! You know that I did not intend to wrong you—why have you so wronged me? You are cruel, cruel indeed! I will try to forget you. It is all injustice I have received at your hands!
>
> T.

She watched till the postman passed by, ran out to him with her epistle, and then again took her listless place inside the window-panes.

It was just as well to write like that as to write tenderly. How could he give way to entreaty? The facts had not changed: there was no new event to alter his opinion.

It grew darker, the fire-light shining over the room. The two biggest of the younger children had gone out with their mother; the four smallest, their ages ranging from three-and-a-half years to eleven, all in black frocks, were gathered round the hearth babbling their own little subjects. Tess at length joined them, without lighting a candle.

'This is the last night that we shall sleep here, dears, in the house where we were born,' she said quickly. 'We ought to think of it, oughtn't we?'

They all became silent; with the impressibility of their age they were ready to burst into tears at the picture of finality she had conjured up, though all the day hitherto they had been rejoicing in the idea of a new place. Tess changed the subject.

'Sing to me, dears,' she said.

'What shall we sing?'

'Anything you know; I don't mind.'

There was a momentary pause; it was broken, first, by one little tentative note; then a second voice strengthened it, and a third and a fourth chimed in in unison, with words they had learnt at the Sunday-school—

Here we suffer grief and pain,
Here we meet to part again;
In Heaven we part no more.

The four sang on with the phlegmatic passivity of persons who had long ago settled the question, and there being no mistake about it, felt that further thought was not required. With features strained hard to enunciate the syllabes they continued to regard the centre of the flickering fire, the notes of the youngest straying over into the pauses of the rest.

Tess turned from them, and went to the window again. Darkness had now fallen without, but she put her face to the pane as though to peer into the gloom. It was really to hide her tears. If she could only believe what the children were singing; if she were only sure, how different all would now be; how confidently she would leave them to Providence and their future kingdom! But, in default of that, it behoved her to do something; to be their Providence; for to Tess, as to not a few millions of others, there was ghastly satire in the poet's lines—

Not in utter nakedness
But trailing clouds of glory do we come.

To her and her like, birth itself was an ordeal of degrading personal compulsion, whose gratuitousness nothing in the result seemed to justify, and at best could only palliate.

In the shades of the wet road she soon discerned her mother with tall 'Liza-Lu and Abraham. Mrs Durbeyfield's pattens clicked up to the door, and Tess opened it.

'I see the tracks of a horse outside the window,' said Joan. 'Hev somebody called?'

'No,' said Tess.

The children by the fire looked gravely at her, and one murmured—

'Why, Tess, the gentleman a-horseback!'

'He didn't call,' said Tess. 'He spoke to me in passing.'

'Who was the gentleman?' asked her mother. 'Your husband?'

'No. He'll never, never come,' answered Tess in stony hopelessness.

'Then who was it?'

'Oh, you needn't ask. You've seen him before, and so have I.'

'Ah! What did he say?' said Joan curiously.

'I will tell you when we are settled in our lodgings at Kingsbere to-morrow—every word.'

It was not her husband, she had said. Yet a consciousness that in a physical sense this man alone was her husband seemed to weigh on her more and more.

LII

DURING the small hours of the next morning, while it was still dark, dwellers near the highways were conscious of a disturbance of their night's rest by rumbling noises, intermittently continuing till daylight—noises as certain to recur in this particular first week of the month as the voice of the cuckoo in the third week of the same. They were the preliminaries of the general removal, the passing of the empty waggons and teams to fetch the goods of the migrating families; for it was always by the vehicle of the farmer who required his services that the hired man was conveyed to his destination. That this might be accomplished within the day was the explanation of the reverberation occurring so soon after midnight, the aim of the carters being to reach the door of the outgoing households by six o'clock, when the loading of their movables at once began.

But to Tess and her mother's household no such anxious farmer sent his team. They were only women; they were not regular labourers; they were not particularly required anywhere; hence they had to hire a waggon at their own expense, and got nothing sent gratuitously.

It was a relief to Tess, when she looked out of the window that morning, to find that though the weather was windy and louring, it did not rain, and that the waggon had come. A wet Lady-Day was a spectre which removing families never forgot; damp furniture, damp bedding, damp clothing accompanied it, and left a train of ills.

Her mother, 'Liza-Lu, and Abraham were also awake, but the younger children were let sleep on. The four breakfasted by the thin light, and the 'house-ridding' was taken in hand.

It proceeded with some cheerfulness, a friendly neighbour or two assisting. When the large articles of furniture had been packed in position a circular nest was made of the beds and bedding, in which Joan Durbeyfield and the young children were to sit through the journey. After loading there was a long delay before the horses were brought, these having been unharnessed during the ridding; but at length, about two o'clock, the whole was under way, the cooking-pot swinging from the axle of the waggon, Mrs Durbeyfield and family at the top, the matron having in her lap, to prevent injury to its works, the head of the clock, which, at any exceptional lurch of the waggon, struck one, or one-and-a-half, in hurt tones. Tess and the next eldest girl walked alongside till they were out of the village.

They had called on a few neighbours that morning and the previous evening, and some came to see them off, all wishing them well, though, in their secret hearts, hardly expecting welfare possible to such a family, harmless as the Durbeyfields were to all except themselves. Soon the equipage began to ascend to higher ground, and the wind grew keener with the change of level and soil.

The day being the sixth of April, the Durbeyfield waggon met many other waggons with families on the summit of the load, which was built on a wellnigh unvarying principle, as peculiar, probably, to the rural labourer as the hexagon to the bee. The groundwork of the arrangement was the family dresser, which, with its shining handles, and finger-marks, and domestic evidences thick upon it, stood importantly in front, over the tails of the shaft-horses, in its erect and natural position, like some Ark of the Covenant that they were bound to carry reverently.

Some of the households were lively, some mournful; some were stopping at the doors of wayside inns; where, in due time, the Durbeyfield menagerie also drew up to bait horses and refresh the travellers.

During the halt Tess's eyes fell upon a three-pint blue mug, which was ascending and descending through the air to and from the feminine section of a household, sitting on the summit of a load that had also drawn up at a little distance from the same inn. She followed one of the mug's journeys upward, and perceived it to be clasped by hands whose owner she well knew. Tess went towards the waggon.

'Marian and Izz!' she cried to the girls, for it was they, sitting with the moving family at whose house they had lodged. 'Are you house-ridding to-day, like everybody else?'

They were, they said. It had been too rough a life for them at Flintcomb-Ash, and they had come away, almost without notice, leaving Groby to prosecute them if he chose. They told Tess their destination, and Tess told them hers.

Marian leant over the load, and lowered her voice. 'Do you know that the gentleman who follows 'ee—you'll guess who I mean—came to ask for 'ee at Flintcomb after you had gone? We didn't tell'n where you was, knowing you wouldn't wish to see him.'

'Ah—but I did see him!' Tess murmured. 'He found me.'

'And do he know where you be going?'

'I think so.'

'Husband come back?'

'No.'

She bade her acquaintance good-bye—for the respective carters had now come out from the inn—and the two waggons resumed their journey in opposite directions; the vehicle whereon sat Marian, Izz, and the ploughman's family with whom they had thrown in their lot, being brightly painted, and drawn by three powerful horses with shining brass ornaments on their harness; while the waggon on which Mrs Durbeyfield and her family rode was a creaking erection that would scarcely bear the weight of the superincumbent load; one which had known no paint since it was made, and drawn by two horses only. The contrast well marked the difference between being fetched by a thriving farmer and conveying oneself whither no hirer waited one's coming.

The distance was great—too great for a day's journey—and it was with the utmost difficulty that the horses performed it. Though they had started so early it was quite late in the afternoon when they turned the flank of an eminence which formed part of the upland called Greenhill. While the horses stood to stale and breathe themselves Tess looked around. Under the hill, and just ahead of them, was the half-dead townlet of their pilgrimage, Kingsbere, where lay those ancestors of whom her father had spoken and sung to painfulness: Kingsbere, the spot of all spots in the world which could be considered the d'Urbervilles' home, since they had resided there for full five hundred years.

A man could be seen advancing from the outskirts towards them, and when he beheld the nature of their waggon-load he quickened his steps.

'You be the woman they call Mrs Durbeyfield, I reckon?' he said to Tess's mother, who had descended to walk the remainder of the way.

She nodded. 'Though widow of the late Sir John d'Urberville, poor nobleman, if I cared for my rights; and returning to the domain of his forefathers.'

'Oh? Well, I know nothing about that; but if you be Mrs Durbeyfield, I am sent to tell 'ee that the rooms you wanted be let. We didn't know you was coming till we got your letter this morning—when 'twas too late. But no doubt you can get other lodgings somewhere.'

The man had noticed the face of Tess, which had become ash-pale at his intelligence. Her mother looked hopelessly at fault. 'What shall we do now, Tess?' she said bitterly. 'Here's a welcome to your ancestors' lands! However, let's try further.'

They moved on into the town, and tried with all their might, Tess remaining with the waggon to take care of the children whilst her mother and 'Liza-Lu made inquiries. At the last return of Joan to the vehicle, an hour later, when her search for accommodation had still been fruitless, the driver of the waggon said the goods must be unloaded, as the horses were half-dead, and he was bound to return part of the way at least that night.

'Very well—unload it here,' said Joan recklessly. 'I'll get shelter somewhere.'

The waggon had drawn up under the churchyard wall, in a spot screened from view, and the driver, nothing loth, soon hauled down the poor heap of household goods. This done she paid him, reducing herself to almost her last shilling thereby, and he moved off and left them, only too glad to get out of further dealings with such a family. It was a dry night, and he guessed that they would come to no harm.

Tess gazed desperately at the pile of furniture. The cold sunlight of this spring evening peered invidiously upon the crocks and kettles, upon the bunches of dried herbs shivering in the breeze, upon the brass handles of the dresser, upon the wicker-cradle they had all been rocked in, and upon the well-rubbed clock-case, all of which gave out the reproachful gleam of indoor articles abandoned to the vicissitudes of a roofless exposure for which they were never made. Round about were deparked hills and slopes—now cut up into little paddocks—and the green foundations that showed where the d'Urberville mansion once had stood; also an outlying stretch of Egdon Heath that had always belonged to the estate. Hard by, the aisle of the church called the d'Urberville Aisle looked on imperturbably.

'Isn't your family vault your own freehold?' said Tess's mother, as she returned from a reconnoitre of the church and graveyard. 'Why of course 'tis, and that's where we will camp, girls, till the place of your ancestors finds us a roof! Now Tess and 'Liza and Abraham, you help me. We'll make a nest for these children, and then we'll have another look round.'

Tess listlessly lent a hand, and in a quarter of an hour the old four-post bedstead was dissociated from the heap of goods, and erected under the south wall of the church, the part of the building known as the d'Urberville Aisle, beneath which the huge vaults lay. Over the tester of the bedstead was a beautifully traceried window, of many lights, its date being the fifteenth century. It was called the d'Urberville Window, and in the upper part could be discerned heraldic emblems like those on Durbeyfield's old seal and spoon.

Joan drew the curtains round the bed so as to make an excellent tent of it, and put the smaller children inside. 'If it comes to the worst we can sleep there too, for one night,' she said. 'But let us try further on, and get something for the dears to eat! O, Tess, what's the use of your playing at marrying gentlemen, if it leaves us like this!'

Accompanied by 'Liza-Lu and the boy she again ascended the little lane which secluded the church from the townlet. As soon as they got into the street they beheld a man on horseback gazing up and down. 'Ah—I'm looking for you!' he said, riding up to them. 'This is indeed a family gathering on the historic spot!'

It was Alec d'Urberville. 'Where is Tess?' he asked.

Personally Joan had no liking for Alec. She cursorily signified that direction of the church, and went on, d'Urberville saying that he would see them again, in case they should be still unsuccessful in their search for shelter, of which he had just heard. When they had gone d'Urberville rode to the inn, and shortly after came out on foot.

In the interim Tess, left with the children inside the bedstead, remained talking with them awhile, till, seeing that no more could be done to make them comfortable just then, she walked about the churchyard, now beginning to be embrowned by the shades of nightfall. The door of the church was unfastened, and she entered it for the first time in her life.

Within the window under which the bedstead stood were the tombs of the family, covering in their dates several centuries. They were canopied, altar-shaped, and plain; their carvings being defaced and broken; their brasses torn from the matrices, the rivet-holes remaining like marten-holes in a sand-cliff. Of all the reminders that she had ever received that her people were socially extinct there was none so forcible as this spoliation.

She drew near to a dark stone on which was inscribed:

Ostium sepulchri antiquae familiae d'Urberville

Tess did not read Church-Latin like a Cardinal, but she knew that this was the door of her ancestral sepulchre, and that the tall knights of whom her father had chanted in his cups lay inside.

She musingly turned to withdraw, passing near an altar-tomb, the oldest of them all, on which was a recumbent figure. In the dusk she had not noticed it before, and would hardly have noticed it now but for an odd fancy that the effigy moved. As soon as she drew close to it she discovered all in a moment that the figure was a living person; and the shock to her sense of not having been alone was so violent that she was quite overcome, and sank down nigh to fainting, not however till she had recognized Alec d'Urberville in the form.

He leapt off the slab and supported her.

'I saw you come in,' he said smiling, 'and got up there not to interrupt your meditations. A family gathering, is it not, with these old fellows under us here? Listen.'

He stamped with his heel heavily on the floor; whereupon there arose a hollow echo from below.

'That shook them a bit, I'll warrant!' he continued. 'And you thought I was the mere stone reproduction of one of them. But no. The old order changeth. The little finger of the sham d'Urberville can do more for you than the whole dynasty of the real underneath . . . Now command me. What shall I do?'

'Go away!' she murmured.

'I will—I'll look for your mother,' said he blandly. But in passing her he whispered: 'Mind this; you'll be civil yet!'

When he was gone she bent down upon the entrance to the vaults, and said—

'Why am I on the wrong side of this door!'

In the meantime Marian and Izz Huett had journeyed onward with the chattels of the ploughman in the direction of their land of Canaan—the Egypt of some other family who had left it only that morning. But the girls did not for a long time think of where they were going. Their talk was of Angel Clare and Tess, and Tess's persistent lover, whose connection with her previous history they had partly heard and partly guessed ere this.

''Tisn't as though she had never known him afore,' said Marian. 'His having won her once makes all the difference in the world. 'Twould be a thousand pities if he were to tole her away again. Mr Clare can never be anything to us, Izz; and why should we grudge him to her, and not try to mend this quarrel? If he could on'y know what straits she's put to, and what's hovering round, he might come to take care of his own.'

'Could we let him know?'

They thought of this all the way to their destination; but the bustle of re-establishment in their new place took up all their attention then. But when they were settled, a month later, they heard of Clare's approaching return, though they had learnt nothing more of Tess. Upon that, agitated anew by their attachment to him, yet honourably disposed to her, Marian uncorked the penny ink-bottle they shared, and a few lines were concocted between the two girls.

> Honour'd Sir—Look to your Wife if you do love her as much as she do love you. For she is sore put to by an Enemy in the shape of a Friend. Sir, there is one near her who ought to be Away. A woman should not be try'd beyond her Strength, and continual dropping will wear away a Stone—ay, more—a Diamond.
>
> From Two Well-Wishers.

This they addressed to Angel Clare at the only place they had ever heard him to be connected with, Emminster Vicarage; after which they continued in a mood of emotional exaltation at their own generosity, which made them sing in hysterical snatches and weep at the same time.

END OF PHASE THE SIXTH

PHASE THE SEVENTH

FULFILMENT

LIII

It was evening at Emminster Vicarage. The two customary candles were burning under their green shades in the Vicar's study, but he had not been sitting there. Occasionally he came in, stirred the small fire which sufficed for the increasing mildness of the spring, and went out again; sometimes pausing at the front door, going on to the drawing-room, then returning again to the front door.

It faced westward, and though gloom prevailed inside, there was still light enough without to see with distinctness. Mrs Clare, who had been sitting in the drawing-room, followed him hither.

'Plenty of time yet,' said the Vicar. 'He doesn't reach Chalk-Newton till six, even if the train should be punctual, and ten miles of country-road, five of them in Crimmercrock Lane, are not jogged over in a hurry by our old horse.'

'But he has done it in an hour with us, my dear.'

'Years ago.'

Thus they passed the minutes, each well knowing that this was only waste of breath, the one essential being simply to wait.

At length there was a slight noise in the lane, and the old pony-chaise appeared indeed outside the railings. They saw alight therefrom a form which they affected to recognize, but would actually have passed by in the street without identifying had he not got out of their carriage at the particular moment when a particular person was due.

Mrs Clare rushed through the dark passage to the door, and her husband came more slowly after her.

The new arrival, who was just about to enter, saw their anxious faces in the doorway and the gleam of the west in their spectacles because they confronted the last rays of day; but they could only see his shape against the light.

'O, my boy, my boy—home again at last!' cried Mrs Clare, who cared no more at that moment for the stains of heterodoxy which had caused all this separation than for the dust upon his clothes. What woman, indeed, among the most faithful adherents of the truth, believes the promises and threats of the Word in the sense in which she believes in her own children, or would not throw her theology to the wind if weighed against their happiness? As soon as they reached the room where the candles were lighted she looked at his face.

'O, it is not Angel—not my son—the Angel who went away!' she cried in all the irony of sorrow, as she turned herself aside.

His father, too, was shocked to see him, so reduced was that figure from its former contours by worry and the bad season that Clare had experienced, in the climate to which he had so rashly hurried in his first aversion to the mockery of events at home. You could see the skeleton behind the man, and almost the ghost behind the skeleton. He matched Crivelli's dead *Christus*. His sunken eye-pits were of morbid hue, and the light in his eyes had waned. The angular hollows and lines of his aged ancestors had succeeded to their reign in his face twenty years before their time.

'I was ill over there, you know,' he said. 'I am all right now.'

As if, however, to falsify this assertion, his legs seemed to give way, and he suddenly sat down to save himself from falling. It was only a slight attack of faintness, resulting from the tedious day's journey, and the excitement of arrival.

'Has any letter come for me lately?' he asked. 'I received the last you sent on by the merest chance, and after considerable delay through being inland; or I might have come sooner.'

'It was from your wife, we supposed?'

'It was.'

Only one other had recently come. They had not sent it on to him, knowing he would start for home so soon.

He hastily opened the letter produced, and was much disturbed to read in Tess's handwriting the sentiments expressed in her last hurried scrawl to him.

O why have you treated me so monstrously, Angel! I do not deserve it. I have thought it all over carefully, and I can never, never forgive you! You know that I did not intend to wrong you—why have you so wronged me? You are cruel, cruel indeed! I will try to forget you. It is all injustice I have received at your hands! T.

'It is quite true!' said Angel, throwing down the letter. 'Perhaps she will never be reconciled to me!'

'Don't, Angel, be so anxious about a mere child of the soil!' said his mother.

'Child of the soil! Well, we all are children of the soil. I wish she were so in the sense you mean; but let me now explain to you what I have never explained before, that her father is a descendant in the male line of one of the oldest Norman houses, like a good many others who lead obscure agricultural lives in our villages, and are dubbed "sons of the soil!".'

He soon retired to bed; and the next morning, feeling exceedingly unwell, he remained in his room pondering. The circumstances amid which he had left Tess were such that though, while on the south of the Equator and just in receipt of her loving epistle, it had seemed the easiest thing in the world to rush back to her arms the moment he chose to forgive her, now that he had arrived it was not so easy as it had seemed. She was passionate, and her present letter, showing that her estimate of him had changed under his delay—too justly changed, he sadly owned,—made him ask himself if it would be wise to confront her unannounced in the presence of her parents. Supposing that her love had indeed turned to dislike during the last weeks of separation, a sudden meeting might lead to bitter words.

Clare therefore thought it would be best to prepare Tess and her family by sending a line to Marlott announcing his return, and his hope that she was still living with them there, as he had arranged for her to do when he left England. He despatched the inquiry that very day, and before the week was out there came a short reply from Mrs Durbeyfield which did not remove his embarrassment, for it bore no address, though to his surprise it was not written from Marlott.

SIR—J write these few lines to say that my Daughter is away

> from me at present, and J am not sure when she will return, but J will let you know as Soon as she do. J do not feel at liberty to tell you Where she is temperly biding. J should say that me and my Family have left Marlott for some Time.—Yours,
>
> J. Durbeyfield.

It was such a relief to Clare to learn that Tess was at least apparently well that her mother's still reticence as to her whereabouts did not long distress him. They were all angry with him, evidently. He would wait till Mrs Durbeyfield could inform him of Tess's return, which her letter implied to be soon. He deserved no more. His had been a love 'which alters when it alteration finds'. He had undergone some strange experiences in his absence; he had seen the virtual Faustina in the literal Cornelia, a spiritual Lucretia in a corporeal Phryne; he had thought of the women taken and set in the midst as one deserving to be stoned, and the wife of Uriah being made a queen; and he had asked himself why he had not judged Tess constructively rather than biographically, by the will rather than by the deed?

A day or two passed while he waited at his father's house for the promised second note from Joan Durbeyfield, and indirectly to recover a little more strength. The strength showed signs of coming back, but there was no sign of Joan's letter. Then he hunted up the old letter sent to him in Brazil, which Tess had written from Flintcomb-Ash, and re-read it. The sentences touched him now as much as when he had first perused them.

> I must cry to you in my trouble—I have no one else . . . I think I must die if you do not come soon, or tell me to come to you . . . Please, please not to be just; only a little kind to me! . . . If you would come I could die in your arms! I would be well content to do that if so be you had forgiven me! . . . If you will send me one little line and say, *I am coming soon*, I will bide on, Angel, I so cheerfully! . . . Think how it do hurt my heart not to see you ever, ever! Ah, if I could only make your dear heart ache one little minute of each day as mine does every day and all day

long, it might lead you to show pity to your poor lonely one . . . I would be content, ay, glad, to live with you as your servant, if I may not as your wife; so that I could only be near you, and get glimpses of you, and think of you as mine . . . I long for only one thing in heaven, or earth, or under the earth, to meet you, my own dear! Come to me, come to me, and save me from what threatens me.

Clare determined that he would no longer believe in her more recent and severer regard of him; but would go and find her immediately. He asked his father if she had applied for any money during his absence. His father returned a negative, and then for the first time it occurred to Angel that her pride had stood in her way, and that she had suffered privation. From his remarks his parents now gathered the real reason of the separation; and their Christianity was such that, reprobates being their especial care, the tenderness towards Tess which her blood, her simplicity, even her poverty, had not engendered, was instantly excited by her sin.

Whilst he was hastily packing together a few articles for his journey he glanced over a poor plain missive also lately come to hand—the one from Marian and Izz Huett, beginning—

'Honour'd Sir—Look to your wife if you do love her as much as she do you,' and signed, 'From Two Well-Wishers.'

LIV

In a quarter of an hour Clare was leaving the house, whence his mother watched his thin figure as it disappeared into the street. He had declined to borrow his father's old mare, well knowing of its necessity to the household. He went to the inn, where he hired a trap, and could hardly wait during the harnessing. In a very few minutes after he was driving up the hill out of the town which, three or four months earlier in the year, Tess had descended with such hopes and ascended with such shattered purposes.

Benvill Lane soon stretched before him, its hedges and trees purple with buds; but he was looking at other things, and only recalled himself to the scene sufficiently to enable him to keep the way. In something less than an hour-and-a-half he had skirted the south of the King's Hintock estates and ascended to the untoward solitude of Cross-in-Hand, the unholy stone whereon Tess had been compelled by Alec d'Urberville, in his whim of reformation, to swear the strange oath that she would never wilfully tempt him again. The pale and blasted nettle-stems of the preceding year even now lingered nakedly in the banks, young green nettles of the present spring growing from their roots.

Thence he went along the verge of the upland overhanging the other Hintocks, and, turning to the right, plunged into the bracing calcareous region of Flintcomb-Ash, the address from which she had written to him in one of the letters, and which he supposed to be the place of sojourn referred to by her mother. Here, of course, he did not find her; and what added to his depression was the discovery that no 'Mrs Clare' had ever been heard of by the cottagers or by the farmer himself, though Tess was remembered well enough by her Christian name. His name she had obviously never used during their separation, and her dignified sense of their total severance was shown not much less by this abstention than by the hardships she had chosen to undergo (of which he now learnt for the first time) rather than apply to his father for more funds.

From this place they told him Tess Durbeyfield had gone, without due notice, to the home of her parents on the other side of Blackmoor, and it therefore became necessary to find Mrs Durbeyfield. She had told him she was not now at Marlott, but had been curiously reticent as to her actual address, and the only course was to go to Marlott and inquire for it. The farmer who had been so churlish with Tess was quite smooth-tongued to Clare, and lent him a horse and man to drive him towards Marlott, the gig he had arrived in being sent back to Emminster; for the limit of a day's journey with that horse was reached.

Clare would not accept the loan of the farmer's vehicle for a further distance than to the outskirts of the Vale, and, sending it back with the man who had driven him, he put up at an inn, and next day entered on foot the region wherein was the spot of his dear Tess's birth. It was as yet too early in the year for much colour to appear in the gardens and foliage; the so-called spring was but winter overlaid with a thin coat of greenness, and it was of a parcel with his expectations.

The house in which Tess had passed the years of her childhood was now inhabited by another family who had never known her. The new residents were in the garden, taking as much interest in their own doings as if the homestead had never passed its primal time in conjunction with the histories of others, beside which the histories of these were but as a tale told by an idiot. They walked about the garden paths with thoughts of their own concerns entirely uppermost, bringing their actions at every moment into jarring collision with the dim ghosts behind them, talking as though the time when Tess lived there were not one whit intenser in story than now. Even the spring birds sang over their heads as if they thought there was nobody missing in particular.

On inquiry of these precious innocents, to whom even the name of their predecessors was a failing memory, Clare learned that John Durbeyfield was dead; that his widow and children had left Marlott, declaring that they were going to live at Kingsbere, but instead of doing so had gone on to another place they mentioned. By this time Clare abhorred the house for ceasing to contain Tess, and hastened away from its hated presence without once looking back.

His way was by the field in which he had first beheld her at the dance. It was as bad as the house—even worse. He passed on through the churchyard, where, amongst the new headstones, he saw one of a somewhat superior design to the rest. The inscription ran thus:

> In memory of John Durbeyfield, rightly d'Urberville, of the once powerful family of that Name, and Direct Descendant through an Illustrious Line from Sir Pagan d'Urberville, one of the Knights of the Conqueror. Died March 10th, 18—
>
> How are the Mighty Fallen.

Some man, apparently the sexton, had observed Clare standing there, and drew nigh. 'Ah, sir, now that's a man who didn't want to lie here, but wished to be carried to Kingsbere, where his ancestors be.'

'And why didn't they respect his wish?'

'Oh—no money. Bless your soul, sir, why—there, I wouldn't wish to say it everywhere, but—even this headstone, for all the flourish wrote upon en, is not paid for.'

'Ah, who put it up?'

The man told the name of a mason in the village, and, on leaving the churchyard, Clare called at the mason's house. He found that the statement was true, and paid the bill. This done he turned in the direction of the migrants.

The distance was too long for a walk, but Clare felt such a strong desire for isolation that at first he would neither hire a conveyance nor go to a circuitous line of railway by which he might eventually reach the place. At Shaston, however, he found he must hire; but the way was such that he did not enter Joan's place till about seven o'clock in the evening, having traversed a distance of over twenty miles since leaving Marlott.

The village being small he had little difficulty in finding Mrs Durbeyfield's tenement, which was a house in a walled garden, remote from the main road, where she had stowed away her clumsy old furniture as best she could. It was plain that for some reason or other she had not wished him to visit her, and he felt his call to be somewhat of an intrusion. She came to the door herself, and the light from the evening sky fell upon her face.

This was the first time that Clare had ever met her, but he was too preoccupied to observe more than that she was still a handsome woman, in the garb of a respectable widow. He was obliged to explain that he was Tess's husband, and his object in coming there, and he did it awkwardly enough. 'I want to see her at once,' he added. 'You said you would write to me again, but you have not done so.'

'Because she've not come home,' said Joan.

'Do you know if she is well?'

'I don't. But you ought to, sir,' said she.

'I admit it. Where is she staying?'

From the beginning of the interview Joan had disclosed her embarrassment by keeping her hand to the side of her cheek.

'I—don't know exactly where she is staying,' she answered. 'She was—but—'

'Where was she?'

'Well, she is not there now.'

In her evasiveness she paused again, and the younger children had by this time crept to the door, where, pulling at his mother's skirts, the youngest murmured—

'In this the gentleman who is going to marry Tess?'

'He has married her,' Joan whispered. 'Go inside.'

Clare saw her efforts for reticence, and asked—

'Do you think Tess would wish me to try and find her? If not, of course – '

'I don't think she would.'

'Are you sure?'

'I am sure she wouldn't.'

He was turning away; and then he thought of Tess's tender letter.

'I am sure she would!' he retorted passionately. 'I know her better than you do.'

'That's very likely, sir; for I have never really known her.'

'Please tell me her address, Mrs Durbeyfield, in kindness to a lonely wretched man!'

Tess's mother again restlessly swept her cheek with her vertical hand, and seeing that he suffered, she at last said, in a low voice—

'She is at Sandbourne.'

'Ah—where there? Sandbourne has become a large place, they say.'

'I don't know more particularly than I have said—Sandbourne. For myself, I was never there.'

It was apparent that Joan spoke the truth in this, and he pressed her no further.

'Are you in want of anything?' he said gently.

'No, sir,' she replied. 'We are fairly well provided for.'

Without entering the house Clare turned away. There was a station three miles ahead, and paying off his coachman, he walked thither. The last train to Sandbourne left shortly after, and it bore Clare on its wheels.

LV

At eleven o'clock that night, having secured a bed at one of the hotels and telegraphed his address to his father immediately on his arrival, he walked out into the streets of Sandbourne. It was too late to call on or inquire for any one, and he reluctantly postponed his purpose till the morning. But he could not retire to rest just yet.

This fashionable watering-place, with its eastern and its western stations, its piers, its groves of pines, its promenades, and its covered gardens, was, to Angel Clare, like a fairy place suddenly created by the stroke of a wand, and allowed to get a littly dusty. An outlying eastern tract of the enormous Egdon Waste was close at hand, yet on the very verge of that tawny piece of antiquity such a glittering novelty as this pleasure city had chosen to spring up. Within the space of a mile from its outskirts every irregularity of the soil was prehistoric, every channel an undisturbed British trackway; not a sod having been turned there since the days of the Caesars. Yet the exotic had grown here, suddenly as the prophet's gourd; and had drawn hither Tess.

By the midnight lamps he went up and down the winding ways of this new world in an old one, and could discern between the trees and against the stars the lofty roofs, chimneys, gazebos, and towers of the numerous fanciful residences of which the place was composed. It was a city of detached mansions; a Mediterranean lounging-place on the English Channel; and as seen now by night it seemed even more imposing than it was.

The sea was near at hand, but not intrusive; it murmured, and he thought it was the pines; the pines murmured in precisely the same tones, and he thought they were the sea.

Where could Tess possibly be, a cottage-girl, his young wife, amidst all this wealth and fashion? The more he pondered the more was he puzzled. Were there any cows to milk here? There certainly were no fields to till. She was most probably engaged to do something in one of these large houses; and he sauntered along, looking at the chamber-windows and their lights going out one by one; and wondered which of them might be hers.

Conjecture was useless, and just after twelve o'clock he entered and went to bed. Before putting out his light he re-read Tess's impassioned letter. Sleep, however, he could not,—so near her, yet so far from her—and he continually lifted the window-blind and regarded the backs of the opposite houses, and wondered behind which of the sashes she reposed at that moment.

He might almost as well have sat up all night. In the morning he arose at seven, and shortly after went out, taking the direction of the chief post-office. At the door he met an intelligent postman coming out with letters for the morning delivery.

'Do you know the address of a Mrs Clare?' asked Angel.

The postman shook his head.

Then, remembering that she would have been likely to continue the use of her name, Clare said—

'Or a Miss Durbeyfield?'

'Durbeyfield?'

This also was strange to the postman addressed.

'There's visitors coming and going every day, as you know sir,' he said; 'and without the name of the house 'tis impossible to find 'em.'

One of his comrades hastening out at that moment, the name was repeated to him.

'I know no name of Durbeyfield; but there is the name of d'Urberville at The Herons,' said the second.

'That's it!' cried Clare, pleased to think that she had reverted to the real pronunciation. 'What place is The Herons?'

'A stylish lodging-house. 'Tis all lodging-houses here, bless 'ee.'

Clare received directions how to find the house, and hastened thither, arriving with the milkman. The Herons, though an ordinary villa, stood in its own grounds, and was certainly the last place in which one would have expected to find lodgings, so private was its appearance. If poor Tess was a servant here, as he feared, she would go to the back-door to that milkman, and he was inclined to go thither also. However, in his doubts he turned to the front, and rang.

The hour being early the landlady herself opened the door. Clare inquired for Teresa d'Urberville or Durbeyfield.

'Mrs d'Urberville?'

'Yes.'

Tess, then, passed as a married woman, and he felt glad even though she had not adopted his name.

'Will you kindly tell her that a relative is anxious to see her?'

'It is rather early. What name shall I give, sir?'

'Angel.'

'Mr Angel?'

'No; Angel. It is my Christian name. She'll understand.'

'I'll see if she is awake.'

He was shown into the front room—the dining-room—and looked out through the spring curtains at the little lawn, and the rhododendrons and other shrubs upon it. Obviously her position was by no means so bad as he had feared, and it crossed his mind that she must somehow have claimed and sold the jewels to attain it. He did not blame her for one moment. Soon his sharpened ear detected footsteps upon the stairs, at which his heart thumped so painfully that he could hardly stand firm. 'Dear me! what will she think of me, so altered as I am!' he said to himself; and the door opened.

Tess appeared on the threshold—not at all as he had expected to see her—bewilderingly otherwise, indeed. Her great natural beauty was, if not heightened, rendered more obvious by her attire. She was loosely wrapped in a cashmere dressing-gown of gray-white, embroidered in half-mourning tints, and she wore slippers of the same hue. Her neck rose out of a frill of down, and her well-remembered cable of dark-brown hair was partially coiled up in a mass at the back of her head and partly hanging on her shoulder—the evident result of haste.

He had held out his arms, but they had fallen again to his side; for she had not come forward, remaining still in the opening of the doorway. Mere yellow skeleton that he was now he felt the contrast between them, and thought his appearance distasteful to her.

'Tess!' he said huskily, 'can you forgive me for going away? Can't you—come to me? How do you get to be—like this?'

'It is too late,' said she, her voice sounding hard through the room, her eyes shining unnaturally.

'I did not think rightly of you—I did not see you as you were!' he continued to plead. 'I have learnt to since, dearest Tessy mine!'

'Too late, too late!' she said, waving her hand in the impatience of a person whose tortures cause every instant to seem an hour. 'Don't come close to me, Angel! No—you must not. Keep away.'

'But don't you love me, my dear wife, because I have been so pulled down by illness? You are not so fickle—I am come on purpose for you—my mother and father will welcome you now!'

'Yes—O, yes, yes! But I say, I say it is too late.'

She seemed to feel like a fugitive in a dream, who tries to move away, but cannot. 'Don't you know all—don't you know it? Yet how do you come here if you do not know?'

'I inquired here and there, and I found the way.'

'I waited and waited for you,' she went on, her tones suddenly resuming their old fluty pathos. 'But you did not come! And I wrote to you, and you did not come! He kept on saying you would never come any more, and that I was a foolish woman. He was very kind to me, and to mother, and to all of us after father's death. He—'

'I don't understand.'

'He has won me back to him.'

Clare looked at her keenly, then, gathering her meaning, flagged like one plague-stricken, and his glance sank; it fell on her hands, which, once rosy, were now white and more delicate.

She continued—

'He is upstairs. I hate him now, because he told me a lie—that you would not come again; and you *have* come! These clothes are what he's put upon me: I didn't care what he did wi' me! But—will you go away, Angel, please, and never come any more?'

They stood fixed, their baffled hearts looking out of their eyes with a joylessness pitiful to see. Both seemed to implore something to shelter them from reality.

'Ah—it is my fault!' said Clare.

But he could not get on. Speech was as inexpressive as silence.

But he had a vague consciousness of one thing, though it was not clear to him till later; that his original Tess had spiritually ceased to recognize the body before him as hers—allowing it to drift, like a corpse upon the current, in a direction dissociated from its living will.

A few instants passed, and he found that Tess was gone. His face grew colder and more shrunken as he stood concentrated on the moment, and a minute or two after he found himself in the street, walking along he did not know whither.

LVI

Mrs Brooks, the lady who was the householder at The Herons, and owner of all the handsome furniture, was not a person of an unusually curious turn of mind. She was too deeply materialized, poor woman, by her long and enforced bondage to that arithmetical demon Profit-and-Loss, to retain much curiosity for its own sake, and apart from possible lodgers' pockets. Nevertheless, the visit of Angel Clare to her well-paying tenants, Mr and Mrs d'Urberville, as she deemed them, was sufficiently exceptional in point of time and manner to reinvigorate the feminine proclivity which had been stifled down as useless save in its bearings on the letting trade.

Tess had spoken to her husband from the doorway, without entering the dining-room, and Mrs Brooks, who stood with the partly-closed door of her own sitting-room at the back of the passage, could hear fragments of the conversation—if conversation it could be called—between those two wretched souls. She heard Tess re-ascend the stairs to the first floor, and the departure of Clare, and the closing of the front door behind him. Then the door of the room above was shut, and Mrs Brooks knew that Tess had re-entered her apartment. As the young lady was not fully dressed Mrs Brooks knew that she would not emerge again for some time.

She accordingly ascended the stairs softly, and stood at the door of the front room—a drawing-room, connected with the room immediately behind it (which was a bedroom) by folding-doors in the common manner. This first floor, containing Mrs Brooks's best apartments, had been taken by the week by the d'Urbervilles. The back room was now in silence; but from the drawing-room there came sounds.

All that she could at first distinguish of them was one syllable, continually repeated in a low note of moaning, as if it came from a soul bound to some Ixionian wheel—

'O—O—O!'

Then a silence, then a heavy sigh, and again—

'O—O—O!'

The landlady looked through the keyhole. Only a small space of the room inside was visible, but within that space came a corner of the breakfast table, which was already spread for the meal, and also a chair beside. Over the seat of the chair Tess's face was bowed, her posture being a kneeling one in front of it; her hands were clasped over her head, the skirts of her dressing-gown and the embroidery of her night-gown flowed upon the floor behind her, and her stockingless feet, from which the slippers had fallen, protruded upon the carpet. It was from her lips that came the murmur of unspeakable despair.

Then a man's voice from the adjoining bedroom—

'What's the matter?'

She did not answer, but went on, in a tone which was a soliloquy rather than an exclamation, and a dirge rather than a soliloquy. Mrs Brooks could only catch a portion:

'And then my dear, dear husband came home to me . . . and I did not know it! . . . And you had used your cruel persuasion upon me . . . you did not stop using it—no—you did not stop! My little sisters and brothers and my mother's needs—they were the things you moved me by . . . and you said my husband would never come back—never; and you taunted me, and said what a simpleton I was to expect him! . . . And at last I believed you and gave way! . . . And then he came back! Now he is gone. Gone a second time, and I have lost him now for ever . . . and he will not love me the littlest bit ever any more—only hate me! . . . O yes, I have lost him now—again because of—you!' In writhing, with her head on the chair, she turned her face towards the door, and Mrs Brooks could see the pain upon it; and that her lips were bleeding from the clench of her teeth upon them, and that the long lashes of her closed eyes stuck in wet tags to her cheeks. She continued: 'And he is dying—he looks as if he is dying! . . . And my sin will kill him and not kill me! . . . O, you have torn my life all to pieces . . . made me be what I prayed you in pity not to make me be again! . . . My own true husband will never, never—O God—I can't bear this!—I cannot!'

There were more and sharper words from the man; then a sudden rustle; she had sprung to her feet. Mrs Brooks, thinking that the speaker was coming to rush out of the door, hastily retreated down the stairs.

She need not have done so, however, for the door of the sitting-room was not opened. But Mrs Brooks felt it unsafe to watch on the landing again, and entered her own parlour below.

She could hear nothing through the floor, although she listened intently, and thereupon went to the kitchen to finish her interrupted breakfast. Coming up presently to the front room on the ground floor she took up some sewing, waiting for her lodgers to ring that she might take away the breakfast, which she meant to do herself, to discover what was the matter if possible. Overhead, as she sat, she could now hear the floorboards slightly creak, as if some one were walking about, and presently the movement was explained by the rustle of garments against the banisters, the opening and the closing of the front door, and the form of Tess passing to the gate on her way into the street. She was fully dressed now in the walking costume of a well-to-do young lady in which she had arrived, with the sole addition that over her hat and black feathers a veil was drawn.

Mrs Brooks had not been able to catch any word of farewell, temporary or otherwise, between her tenants at the door above. They might have quarrelled, or Mr d'Urberville might still be asleep, for he was not an early riser.

She went into the back room which was more especially her own apartment, and continued her sewing there. The lady lodger did not return, nor did the gentleman ring his bell. Mrs Brooks pondered on the delay, and on what probable relation the visitor who had called so early bore to the couple upstairs. In reflecting she leant back in her chair.

As she did so her eyes glanced casually over the ceiling till they were arrested by a spot in the middle of its white surface which she had never noticed there before. It was about the size of a wafer when she first observed it, but it speedily grew as large as the palm of her hand, and then she could perceive that it was red. The oblong white ceiling, with this scarlet blot in the midst, had the appearance of a gigantic ace of hearts.

Mrs Brooks had strange qualms of misgiving. She got upon the table, and touched the spot in the ceiling with her fingers. It was damp, and she fancied that it was a blood stain.

Descending from the table, she left the parlour, and went upstairs, intending to enter the room overhead, which was the bedchamber at the back of the drawing-room. But, nerveless woman as she had now become, she could not bring herself to attempt the handle. She listened. The dead silence within was broken only by a regular beat.

Drip, drip, drip.

Mrs Brooks hastened downstairs, opened the front door, and ran into the street. A man she knew, one of the workmen employed at an adjoining villa, was passing by, and she begged him to come in and go upstairs with her; she feared something had happened to one of her lodgers. The workman assented, and followed her to the landing.

She opened the door of the drawing-room, and stood back for him to pass in, entering herself behind him. The room was empty; the breakfast—a substantial repast of coffee, eggs, and a cold ham—lay spread upon the table untouched, as when she had taken it up, excepting that the carving knife was missing. She asked the man to go through the folding-doors into the adjoining room.

He opened the doors, entered a step or two, and came back almost instantly with a rigid face. 'My good God, the gentleman in bed is dead! I think he has been hurt with a knife—a lot of blood has run down upon the floor!'

The alarm was soon given, and the house which had lately been so quiet resounded with the tramp of many footsteps, a surgeon among the rest. The wound was small, but the point of the blade had touched the heart of the victim, who lay on his back, pale, fixed, dead, as if he had scarcely moved after the infliction of the blow. In a quarter of an hour the news that a gentleman who was a temporary visitor to the town had been stabbed in his bed, spread through every street and villa of the popular watering-place.

LVII

Meanwhile Angel Clare had walked automatically along the way by which he had come, and, entering his hotel, sat down over the breakfast, staring at nothingness. He went on eating and drinking unconsciously till on a sudden he demanded his bill; having paid which he took his dressing-bag in his hand, the only luggage he had brought with him, and went out.

At the moment of his departure a telegram was handed to him—a few words from his mother, starting that they were glad to know his address, and informing him that his brother Cuthbert had proposed to and been accepted by Mercy Chant.

Clare crumpled up the paper, and followed the route to the station; reaching it, he found that there would be no train leaving for an hour and more. He sat down to wait, and having waited a quarter of an hour felt that he could wait there no longer. Broken in heart and numbed, he had nothing to hurry for; but he wished to get out of a town which had been the scene of such an experience, and turned to walk to the first station onward, and let the train pick him up there.

The highway that he followed was open, and at a little distance dipped into a valley, across which it could be seen running from edge to edge. He had traversed the greater part of this depression, and was climbing the western acclivity, when, pausing for breath, he unconsciously looked back. Why he did so he could not say, but something seemed to impel him to the act. The tape-like surface of the road diminished in his rear as far as he could see, and as he gazed a moving spot intruded on the white vacuity of its perspective.

It was a human figure running. Clare waited with a dim sense that somebody was trying to overtake him.

The form descending the incline was a woman's, yet so entirely was his mind blinded to the idea of his wife's following him that even when she came nearer he did not recognize her under the totally changed attire in which he now beheld her. It was not till she was quite close that he could believe her to be Tess.

'I saw you—turn away from the station—just before I got there—and I have been following you all this way!'

She was so pale, so breathless, so quivering in every muscle, that he did not ask her a single question, but seizing her hand, and pulling it within his arm, he led her along. To avoid meeting any possible wayfarers he left the high road, and took a footpath under some fir-trees. When they were deep among the moaning boughs he stopped and looked at her inquiringly.

'Angel,' she said, as if waiting for this, 'do you know what I have been running after you for? To tell you that I have killed him!' A pitiful white smile lit her face as she spoke.

'What!' said he, thinking from the strangeness of her manner that she was in some delirium.

'I have done it—I don't know how,' she continued. 'Still, I owed it to you, and to myself, Angel. I feared long ago, when I struck him on the mouth with my glove, that I might do it some day for the trap he set for me in my simple youth, and his wrong to you through me. He has come between us and ruined us, and now he can never do it any more. I never loved him at all, Angel, as I loved you. You know it, don't you? You believe it? You didn't come back to me, and I was obliged to go back to him. Why did you go away—why did you—when I loved you so? I can't think why you did it. But I don't blame you; only, Angel, will you forgive me my sin against you, now I have killed him? I thought as I ran along that you would be sure to forgive me now I have done that. It came to me as a shining light that I should get you back that way. I could not bear the loss of you any longer—you don't know how entirely I was unable to bear your not loving me! Say you do now, dear, dear husband; say you do, now I have killed him!'

'I do love you, Tess—O, I do—it is all come back!' he said, tightening his arms round her with fervid pressure. 'But how do you mean—you have killed him?'

'I mean that I have,' she murmured in a reverie.

'What, bodily? Is he dead?'

'Yes. He heard me crying about you, and he bitterly taunted me; and called you by a foul name; and then I did it. My heart could not bear it. He had nagged me about you before. And then I dressed myself and came away to find you.'

By degrees he was inclined to believe that she had faintly attempted, at least, what she said she had done; and his horror at her impulse was mixed with amazement at the strength of her affection for himself, and at the strangeness of its quality, which had apparently extinguished her moral sense altogether. Unable to realize the gravity of her conduct she seemed at last content; and he looked at her as she lay upon his shoulder, weeping with happiness, and wondered what obscure strain in the d'Urberville blood had led to this aberration—if it were an aberration. There momentarily flashed through his mind that the family tradition of the coach and murder might have arisen because the d'Urbervilles had been known to do these things. As well as his confused and excited ideas could reason, he supposed that in the moment of mad grief of which she spoke her mind had lost its balance, and plunged her into this abyss.

It was very terrible if true; if a temporary hallucination, sad. But, anyhow, here was this deserted wife of his, this passionately-fond woman, clinging to him without a suspicion that he would be anything to her but a protector. He saw that for him to be otherwise was not, in her mind, within the region of the possible. Tenderness was absolutely dominant in Clare at last. He kissed her endlessly with his white lips, and held her hand, and said—

'I will not desert you! I will protect you by every means in my power, dearest love, whatever you may have done or not have done!'

They then walked on under the trees, Tess turning her head every now and then to look at him. Worn and unhandsome as he had become, it was plain that she did not discern the least fault in his appearance. To her he was, as of old, all that was perfection, personally and mentally. He was still her Antinous, her Apollo even; his sickly face was beautiful as the morning to her affectionate regard on this day no less than when she first beheld him; for was it not the face of the one man on earth who had loved her purely, and who had believed in her as pure.

With an instinct as to possibilities he did not now, as he had intended, make for the first station beyond the town, but plunged still farther under the firs, which here abounded for miles. Each clasping the other round the waist they promenaded over the dry bed of fir-needles, thrown into a vague intoxicating atmosphere at the consciousness of being together at last, with no living soul between them; ignoring that there was a corpse. Thus they proceeded for several miles till Tess, arousing herself, looked about her, and said, timidly—

'Are we going anywhere in particular?'

'I don't know, dearest. Why?'

'I don't know.'

'Well, we might walk a few miles further, and when it is evening find lodgings somewhere or other—in a lonely cottage, perhaps. Can you walk well, Tessy?'

'O yes! I could walk for ever and ever with your arm round me!'

Upon the whole it seemed a good thing to do. Thereupon they quickened their pace, avoiding high roads, and following obscure paths tending more or less northward. But there was an unpractical vagueness in their movements throughout the day; neither one of them seemed to consider any question of effectual escape, disguise, or long concealment. Their every idea was temporary and unforefending, like the plans of two children.

At mid-day they drew near to a roadside inn, and Tess would have entered it with him to get something to eat, but he persuaded her to remain among the trees and bushes of this half-woodland, half-moorland part of the country, till he should come back. Her clothes were of recent fashion; even the ivory-handled parasol that she carried was of a shape unknown in the retired spot to which they had now wandered; and the cut of such articles would have attracted attention in the settle of a tavern. He soon returned, with food enough for half-a-dozen people and two bottles of wine—enough to last them for a day or more, should any emergency arise.

They sat down upon some dead boughs and shared their meal. Between one and two o'clock they packed up the remainder and went on again.

'I feel strong enough to walk any distance,' said she.

'I think we may as well steer in a general way towards the interior of the country, where we can hide for a time, and are less likely to be looked for than anywhere near the coast,' Clare remarked. 'Later on, when they have forgotten us, we can make for some port.'

She made no reply to this beyond that of grasping him more tightly, and straight inland they went. Though the season was an English May the weather was serenely bright, and during the afternoon it was quite warm. Through the latter miles of their walk their footpath had taken them into the depths of the New Forest, and towards evening, turning the corner of a lane, they perceived behind a brook and bridge a large board on which was painted in white letters, 'This desirable Mansion to be Let Furnished'; particulars following, with directions to apply to some London agents. Passing through the gate they could see the house, an old brick building of regular design and large accommodation.

'I know it,' said Clare. 'It is Bramshurst Court. You can see that it is shut up, and grass is growing on the drive.'

'Some of the windows are open,' said Tess.

'Just to air the rooms, I suppose.'

'All these rooms empty, and we without a roof to our heads!'

'You are getting tired, my Tess!' he said. 'We'll stop soon.' And kissing her sad mouth he again led her onwards.

He was growing weary likewise, for they had wandered a dozen or fifteen miles, and it became necessary to consider what they should do for rest. They looked from afar at isolated cottages and little inns, and were inclined to approach one of the latter, when their hearts failed them, and they sheered off. At length their gait dragged, and they stood still.

'Could we sleep under the trees?' she asked.

He thought the season insufficiently advanced.

'I have been thinking of that empty mansion we passed,' he said. 'Let us go back towards it again.'

They retraced their steps, but it was half an hour before they stood without the entrance-gate as earlier. He then requested her to stay where she was, whilst he went to see who was within.

She sat down among the bushes within the gate, and Clare crept towards the house. His absence lasted some considerable time, and when he returned Tess was wildly anxious, not for herself, but for him. He had found out from a boy that there was only an old woman in charge as caretaker, and she only came there on fine days, from the hamlet near, to open and shut the windows. She would come to shut them at sunset. 'Now, we can get in through one of the lower windows, and rest there,' said he.

Under his escort she went tardily forward to the main front, whose shuttered windows, like sightless eyeballs, excluded the possibility of watchers. The door was reached a few steps further, and one of the windows beside it was open. Clare clambered in, and pulled Tess in after him.

Except the hall the rooms were all in darkness, and they ascended the staircase. Up here also the shutters were tightly closed, the ventilation being perfunctorily done, for this day at least, by opening the hall-window in front and an upper window behind. Clare unlatched the door of a large chamber, felt his way across it, and parted the shutters to the width of two or three inches. A shaft of dazzling sunlight glanced into the room, revealing heavy, old-fashioned furniture, crimson damask hangings, and an enormous four-post bedstead, along the head of which were carved running figures, apparently Atalanta's race.

'Rest at last!' said he, setting down his bag and the parcel of viands.

They remained in great quietness till the caretaker should have come to shut the windows: as a precaution, putting themselves in total darkness by barring the shutters as before, lest the woman should open the door of their chamber for any casual reason. Between six and seven o'clock she came, but did not approach the wing they were in. The heard her close the windows, fasten them, lock the door, and go away. Then Clare again stole a chink of light from the window, and they shared another meal, till by-and-by they were enveloped in the shades of night which they had no candle to disperse.

LVIII

The night was strangely solemn and still. In the small hours she whispered to him the whole story of how he had walked in his sleep with her in his arms across the Froom stream, at the imminent risk of both their lives, and laid her down in the stone coffin at the ruined abbey. He had never known of that till now.

'Why didn't you tell me next day?' he said. 'It might have prevented much misunderstanding and woe.'

'Don't think of what's past!' said she. 'I am not going to think outside of now. Why should we! Who knows what tomorrow has in store?'

But it apparently had no sorrow. The morning was wet and foggy, and Clare, rightly informed that the caretaker only opened the windows on fine days, ventured to creep out of their chamber, and explore the house, leaving Tess asleep. There was no food on the premises, but there was water, and he took advantage of the fog to emerge from the mansion, and fetch tea, bread, and butter from a shop in a little place two miles beyond, as also a small tin kettle and spirit-lamp, that they might get fire without smoke. His re-entry awoke her; and they breakfasted on what he had brought.

They were indisposed to stir abroad, and the day passed, and the night following, and the next, and next; till, almost without their being aware, five days had slipped by in absolute seclusion, not a sight or sound of a human being disturbing their peacefulness, such as it was. The changes of the weather were their only events, the birds of the New Forest their only company. By tacit consent they hardly once spoke of any incident of the past subsequent to their wedding-day. The gloomy intervening time seemed to sink into chaos, over which the present and prior times closed as if it never had been. Whenever he suggested that they should leave their shelter, and go forwards towards Southampton or London, she showed a strange unwillingness to move.

'Why should we put an end to all that's sweet and lovely!' she deprecated. 'What must come will come.' And, looking through the shutter-chink: 'All is trouble outside there; inside here content.'

He peeped out also. It was quite true; within was affection, union, error forgiven; outside was the inexorable.

'And—and,' she said, pressing her cheek against his; 'I fear that what you think of me now may not last. I do not wish to outlive your present feeling for me. I would rather not. I would rather be dead and buried when the times comes for you to despise me, so that it may never be known to me that you despised me.'

'I cannot ever despise you.'

'I also hope that. But considering what my life has been I cannot see why any man should, sooner or later, be able to help despising me . . . How wickedly mad I was! Yet formerly I never could bear to hurt a fly or a worm, and the sight of a bird in a cage used often to make me cry.'

They remained yet another day. In the night the dull sky cleared, and the result was that the old caretaker at the cottage awoke early. The brilliant sunrise made her unusually brisk; she decided to open the contiguous mansion immediately, and to air it thoroughly on such a day. Thus it occurred that, having arrived and opened the lower rooms before six o'clock, she ascended to the bedchambers, and was about to turn the handle of the one wherein they lay. At that moment she fancied she could hear the breathing of persons within. Her slippers and her antiquity had rendered her progress a noiseless one so far, and she made for instant retreat; then, deeming that her hearing might have deceived her, she turned anew to the door and softly tried the handle. The lock was out of order, but a piece of furniture had been moved forward on the inside, which prevented her opening the door more than an inch or two. A stream of morning light through the shutter-chink fell upon the faces of the pair, wrapped in profound slumber, Tess's lips being parted like a half-opened flower near his cheek. The caretaker was so struck with their innocent appearance, and with the elegance of Tess's gown hanging across a chair, her silk stockings beside it, the pretty parasol, and the other habits in which she had arrived because she had none else, that her first indignation at the effrontery of tramps and vagabonds gave way to a momentary sentimentality over this genteel elopement, as it seemed. She closed the door, and withdrew as softly as she had come, to go and consult with her neighbours on the odd discovery.

Not more than a minute had elapsed after her withdrawal when Tess woke, and then Clare. Both had a sense that something had disturbed them, though they could not say what; and the uneasy feeling which it engendered grew stronger. As soon as he was dressed he narrowly scanned the lawn through the two or three inches of shutter-chink.

'I think we will leave at once,' said he. 'It is a fine day. And I cannot help fancying somebody is about the house. At any rate, the woman will be sure to come to-day.'

She passively assented, and putting the room in order they took up the few articles that belonged to them, and departed noiselessly. When they had got into the Forest she turned to take a last look at the house.

'Ah, happy house—good-bye!' she said. 'My life can only be a question of a few weeks. Why should we not have stayed there?'

'Don't say it, Tess! We shall soon get out of this district altogether. We'll continue our course as we've begun it, and keep straight north. Nobody will think of looking for us there. We shall be looked for at the Wessex ports if we are sought at all. When we are in the north we will get to a port and away.'

Having thus persuaded her the plan was pursued, and they kept a bee line northward. Their long repose at the manor-house lent them walking power now; and towards mid-day they found that they were approaching the steepled city of Melchester, which lay directly in their way. He decided to rest her in a clump of trees during the afternoon, and push onward under cover of darkness. At dusk Clare purchased food as usual, and their night march began, the boundary between Upper and Mid-Wessex being crossed about eight o'clock.

To walk across country without much regard to roads was not new to Tess, and she showed her old agility in the performance.

The intercepting city, ancient Melchester, they were obliged to pass through in order to take advantage of the town bridge for crossing a large river that obstructed them. It was about midnight when they went along the deserted streets, lighted fitfully by the few lamps, keeping off the pavement that it might not echo their footsteps. The graceful pile of cathedral architecture rose dimly on their left hand, but it was lost upon them now. Once out of the town they followed the turnpike-road, which after a few miles plunged across an open plain.

Though the sky was dense with cloud a diffused light from some fragment of a moon had hitherto helped them a little. But the moon had now sunk, the clouds seemed to settle almost on their heads, and the night grew as dark as a cave. However, they found their way along, keeping as much on the turf as possible that their tread might not resound, which it was easy to do, there being no hedge or fence of any kind. All around was open loneliness and black solitude, over which a stiff breeze blew.

They had proceeded thus gropingly two or three miles further when on a sudden Clare became conscious of some vast erection close in his front, rising sheer from the grass. They had almost struck themselves against it.

'What monstrous place is this?' said Angel.

'It hums,' said she. 'Hearken!'

He listened. The wind, playing upon the edifice, produced a booming tune, like the note of some gigantic one-stringed harp. No other sound came from it, and lifting his hand and advancing a step or two, Clare felt the vertical surface of the structure. It seemed to be of solid stone, without joint or moulding. Carrying his fingers onward he found that what he had come in contact with was a colossal rectangular pillar; by stretching out his left hand he could feel a similar one adjoining. At an indefinite height overhead something made the black sky blacker, which had the semblance of a vast architrave uniting the pillars horizontally. They carefully entered beneath and between; the surfaces echoed their soft rustle; but they seemed to be still out of doors. The place was roofless. Tess drew her breath fearfully, and Angel, perplexed, said—

'What can it be?'

Feeling sideways they encountered another tower-like pillar, square and uncompromising as the first; beyond it another and another. The place was all doors and pillars, some connected above by continuous architraves.

'A very Temple of the Winds,' he said.

The next pillar was isolated; others composed a trilithon; others were prostrate, their flanks forming a causeway wide enough for a carriage; and it was soon obvious that they made up a forest of monoliths grouped upon the grassy expanse of the plain. The couple advanced further into this pavilion of the night till they stood in its midst.

'It is Stonehenge!' said Clare.

'The heathen temple, you mean?'

'Yes. Older than the centuries; older than the d'Urbervilles! Well, what shall we do, darling? We may find shelter further on.'

But Tess, really tired by this time, flung herself upon an oblong slab that lay close at hand, and was sheltered from the wind by a pillar. Owing to the action of the sun during the preceding day the stone was warm and dry, in comforting contrast to the rough and chill grass around, which had damped her skirts and shoes.

'I don't want to go any further, Angel,' she said stretching out her hand for his. 'Can't we bide here?'

'I fear not. This spot is visible for miles by day, although it does not seem so now.'

'One of my mother's people was a shepherd hereabouts, now I think of it. And you used to say at Talbothays that I was a heathen. So now I am at home.'

He knelt down beside her outstretched form, and put his lips upon hers.

'Sleepy are you, dear? I think you are lying on an altar.'

'I like very much to be here,' she murmured. 'It is so solemn and lonely—after my great happiness—with nothing but the sky above my face. It seems as if there were no folk in the world but we two; and I wish there were not—except 'Liza-Lu.'

Clare thought she might as well rest here till it should get a little lighter, and he flung his overcoat upon her, and sat down by her side.

'Angel, if anything happens to me, will you watch over 'Liza-Lu for my sake?' she asked, when they had listened a long time to the wind among the pillars.

'I will.'

'She is so good and simple and pure. O, Angel—I wish you would marry her if you lose me, as you will do shortly. O, if you would!'

'If I lose you I lose all! And she is my sister-in-law.'

'That's nothing, dearest. People marry sister-laws continually about Marlott; and 'Liza-Lu is so gentle and sweet, and she is growing so beautiful. O I could share you with her willingly when we are spirits! If you would train her and teach her, Angel, and bring her up for your own self! . . . She has all the best of me without the bad of me; and if she were to become yours it would almost seem as if death had not divided us . . . Well, I have said it: I won't mention it again.'

She ceased, and he fell into thought. In the far north-east sky he could see between the pillars a level streak of light. The uniform concavity of black cloud was lifting bodily like the lid of a pot, letting in at the earth's edge the coming day, against which the towering monoliths and trilithons began to be blackly defined.

'Did they sacrifice to God here?' asked she.

'No,' said he.

'Who to?'

'I believe to the sun. That lofty stone set away by itself is in the direction of the sun, which will presently rise behind it.'

'This reminds me, dear,' she said. 'You remember you never would interfere with any belief of mine before we were married? But I knew your mind all the same, and I thought as you thought—not from any reasons of my own, but because you thought so. Tell me now, Angel, do you think we shall meet again after we are dead? I want to know.'

He kissed her to avoid a reply at such a time.

'O, Angel—I fear that means no!' said she, with a suppressed sob. 'And I wanted so to see you again—so much, so much! What—not even you and I, Angel, who love each other so well?'

Like a greater than himself, to the critical question at the critical time he did not answer; and they were again silent. In a minute or two her breathing became more regular, her clasp of his hand relaxed, and she fell asleep. The band of silver paleness along the east horizon made even the distant parts of the Great Plain appear dark and near; and the whole enormous landscape bore that impress of reserve, taciturnity, and hesitation which is usual just before day. The eastward pillars and their architraves stood up blackly against the light, and the great flame-shaped Sun-stone beyond them; and the Stone of Sacrifice midway. Presently the night wind died out, and the quivering little pools in the cup-like hollows of the stones lay still. At the same time something seemed to move on the verge of the dip eastward—a mere dot. It was the head of a man approaching them from the hollow beyond the Sun-stone. Clare wished they had gone onward, but in the circumstances decided to remain quiet. The figure came straight towards the circle of pillars in which they were.

He heard something behind him, the brush of feet. Turning, he saw over the prostrate columns another figure; then before he was aware, another was at hand on the right, under a trilithon, and another on the left. The dawn shone full on the front of the man westward, and Clare could discern from this that he was tall, and walked as if trained. They all closed in with evident purpose. Her story then was true! Springing to his feet, he looked around for a weapon, loose stone, means of escape, anything. By this time the nearest man was upon him.

'It is no use, sir,' he said. 'There are sixteen of us on the Plain, and the whole country is reared.'

'Let her finish her sleep!' he implored in a whisper of the men as they gathered round.

When they saw where she lay, which they had not done till then, they showed no objection, and stood watching her, as still as the pillars around. He went to the stone and bent over her, holding one poor little hand; her breathing now was quick and small, like that of a lesser creature than a woman. All waited in the growing light, their faces and hands as if they were silvered, the remainder of their figures dark, the stones glistening green-gray, the Plain still a mass of shade. Soon the light was strong, and a ray shone upon her unconscious form, peering under her eyelids and waking her.

'What is it, Angel?' she said, starting up. 'Have they come for me?'

'Yes, dearest,' he said. 'They have come.'

'It is as it should be,' she murmured. 'Angel, I am almost glad—yes, glad! This happiness could not have lasted. It was too much. I have had enough; and now I shall not live for you to despise me!'

She stood up, shook herself, and went forward, neither of the men having moved.

'I am ready,' she said quietly.

LIX

The city of Wintoncester, that fine old city, aforetime capital of Wessex, lay amidst its convex and concave downlands in all the brightness and warmth of a July morning. The gabled brick, tile, and freestone houses had almost dried off for the season their integument of lichen, the streams in the meadows were low, and in the sloping High Street, from the West Gateway to the mediaeval cross, and from the mediaeval cross to the bridge, that leisurely dusting and sweeping was in progress which usually ushers in an old-fashioned market-day.

From the western gate aforesaid the highway, as every Wintoncestrian knows, ascends a long and regular incline of the exact length of a measured mile, leaving the houses gradually behind. Up this road from the precincts of the city two persons were walking rapidly, as if unconscious of the trying ascent—unconscious through preoccupation and not through buoyancy. They had emerged upon this road through a narrow barred wicket in a high wall a little lower down. They seemed anxious to get out of the sight of the houses and of their kind, and this road appeared to offer the quickest means of doing so. Though they were young they walked with bowed heads, which gait of grief the sun's rays smiled on pitilessly.

One of the pair was Angel Clare, the other a tall budding creature—half girl, half woman—a spiritualized image of Tess, slighter than she, but with the same beautiful eyes—Clare's sister-in-law, 'Liza-Lu. Their pale faces seemed to have shrunk to half their natural size. They moved on hand in hand, and never spoke a word, the drooping of their heads being that of Giotto's 'Two Apostles'.

When they had nearly reached the top of the great West Hill the clocks in the town struck eight. Each gave a start at the notes, and, walking onward yet a few steps, they reached the first milestone, standing whitely on the green margin of the grass, and backed by the down, which here was open to the road. They entered upon the turf, and, impelled by a force that seemed to overrule their will, suddenly stood still, turned, and waited in paralyzed suspense beside the stone.

The prospect from this summit was almost unlimited. In the valley beneath lay the city they had just left, its more prominent buildings showing as in an isometric drawing—among them the broad cathedral tower, with its Norman windows and immense length of aisle and nave, the spires of St Thomas's, the pinnacled tower of the College, and, more to the right, the tower and gables of the ancient hospice, where to this day the pilgrim may receive his dole of bread and ale. Behind the city swept the rotund upland of St Catherine's Hill; further off, landscape beyond landscape, till the horizon was lost in the radiance of the sun hanging above it.

Against these far stretches of country rose, in front of the other city edifices, a large red-brick building, with level gray roofs, and rows of short barred windows bespeaking captivity, the whole contrasting greatly by its formalism with the quaint irregularities of the Gothic erections. It was somewhat disguised from the road in passing it by yews and evergreen oaks, but it was visible enough up here. The wicket from which the pair had lately emerged was in the wall of this structure. From the middle of the building an ugly flat-topped octagonal tower ascended against the east horizon, and viewed from this spot, on its shady side and against the light, it seemed the one blot in the city's beauty. Yet it was with this blot, and not with the beauty, that the two gazers were concerned.

Upon the cornice of the tower a tall staff was fixed. Their eyes were riveted on it. A few minutes after the hour had struck something moved slowly up the staff, and extended itself upon the breeze. It was a black flag.

'Justice' was done, and the President of the Immortals, in Aeschylean phrase, had ended his sport with Tess. And the d'Urberville knights and dames slept on in their tombs unknowing. The two speechless gazers bent themselves down to the earth, as if in prayer, and remained thus a long time, absolutely motionless: the flag continued to wave silently. As soon as they had strength they arose, joined hands again, and went on.

Jude the Obscure

'The letter killeth'

Contents

Preface to the First Edition

The history of this novel (whose birth in its present shape has been much retarded by the necessities of periodical publication) is briefly as follows. The scheme was jotted down in 1890, from notes made in 1887 and onwards, some of the circumstances being suggested by the death of a woman in the former year. The scenes were revisited in October 1892; the narrative written in outline in 1892 and the spring of 1893, and at full length, as it now appears, from August 1893 onwards into the next year; the whole, with the exception of a few chapters, being in the hands of the publisher by the end of 1894. It was begun as a serial story in *Harper's Magazine* at the end of November 1894, and was continued in monthly parts.

But, as in the case of *Tess of the d'Urbervilles*, the magazine version was for various reasons an abridged and modified one, the present edition being the first in which the whole appears as originally written. And in the difficulty of coming to an early decision in the matter of a title, the tale was issued under a provisional name, two such titles having, in fact, been successively adopted. The present and final title, deemed on the whole the best, was the one earliest thought of.

For a novel addressed by a man to men and women of full age; which attempts to deal unaffectedly with the fret and fever, derision and disaster, that may press in the wake of the strongest passion known to humanity; to tell, without a mincing of words, of a deadly war raged between flesh and spirit; and to point the tragedy of unfulfilled aims, I am not aware that there is anything in the handling to which exception can be taken.

Like former productions of this pen, *Jude the Obscure* is simply an endeavour to give shape and coherence to a series of seemings, or personal impressions, the questions of their consistency or their discordance, of their permanence or their transitoriness, being regarded as not of the first moment.

August, 1895

Postcript

The issue of this book sixteen years ago, with the explanatory Preface given above, was followed by unexpected incidents, and one can now look back for a moment at what happened. Within a day or two of its publication the reviewers pronounced upon it in tones to which the reception of *Tess of the d'Urbervilles* bore no comparison, though there were two or three dissentients from the chorus. This salutation of the story in England was instantly cabled to America, and the music was reinforced on that side of the Atlantic in a shrill crescendo.

In my own eyes the sad feature of the attack was that the greater part of the story—that which presented the shattered ideals of the two chief characters, and had been more especially, and indeed almost exclusively, the part of interest to myself—was practically ignored by the adverse press of the two countries; the while that some twenty or thirty pages of sorry detail deemed necessary to complete the narrative, and show the antithesis in Jude's life, were almost the sole portions read and regarded. And curiously enough, a reprint the next year of a fantastic tale that had been published in a family paper some time before, drew down upon my head a continuation of the same sort of invective from several quarters.

So much for the unhappy beginning of *Jude*'s career as a book. After these verdicts from the press its next misfortune was to be burnt by a bishop—probably in his despair at not being able to burn me.

Then somebody discovered that Jude was a moral work—austere in its treatment of a difficult subject—as if the writer had not all the time said in the Preface that it was meant to be so. Thereupon many uncursed me, and the matter ended, the only effect of it on human conduct that I could discover being its effect on myself—

the experience completely curing me of further interest in novel-writing.

One incident among many arising from the storm of words was that an American man of letters, who did not whitewash his own morals, informed me that, having bought a copy of the book on the strength of the shocked criticisms, he read on and on, wondering when the harmfulness was going to begin, and at last flung it across the room with execrations at having been induced by the rascally reviewers to waste a dollar-and-a-half on what he was pleased to call 'a religious and ethical treatise'.

I sympathized with him, and assured him honestly that the misrepresentations had been no collusive trick of mine to increase my circulation among the subscribers to the papers in question.

Then there was the case of the lady who having shuddered at the book in an influential article bearing intermediate headlines of horror, and printed in a world-read journal, wrote to me shortly afterwards that it was her desire to make my acquaintance.

To return, however, to the book itself. The marriage laws being used in great part as the tragic machinery of the tale, and its general drift on the domestic side tending to show that, in Diderot's words, the civil law should be only the enunciation of the law of nature (a statement that requires some qualification, by the way), I have been charged since 1895 with a large responsibility in this country for the present 'shop-soiled' condition of the marriage theme (as a learned writer characterized it the other day). I do not know. My opinion at that time, if I remember rightly, was what it is now, that a marriage should be dissolvable as soon as it becomes a cruelty to either of the parties—being then essentially and morally no marriage—and it seemed a good foundation for the fable of a tragedy, told for its own sake as a presentation of particulars containing a good deal that was universal, and not without a hope that certain cathartic, Aristotelian qualities might be found therein.

The difficulties down to twenty or thirty years back of acquiring knowledge in letters without pecuniary means were used in the same way; though I was informed that some readers thought these episodes an attack on venerable institutions, and that when Ruskin

College was subsequently founded it should have been called the College of Jude the Obscure.

Artistic effort always pays heavily for finding its tragedies in the forced adaptation of human instincts to rusty and irksome moulds that do not fit them. To do Bludyer and the conflagatory bishop justice, what they meant seems to have been only this 'We Britons hate ideas, and we are going to live up to that privilege of our native country. Your picture may not show the untrue, or the uncommon, or even be contrary to the canons of art; but it is not the view of life that we who thrive on conventions can permit to be painted.'

But what did it matter. As for the matrimonial scenes, in spite of their 'touching the spot', and the screaming of a poor lady in *Blackwood* that there was an unholy anti-marriage league afoot, the famous contract—sacrament I mean—is doing fairly well still, and people marry and give in what may or may not be true marriage as light-heartedly as ever. The author has even been reproached by some earnest correspondents that he has left the question where he found it, and has not pointed the way to a much-needed reform.

After the issue of *Jude the Obscure* as a serial story in Germany, an experienced reviewer of that country informed the writer that Sue Bridehead, the heroine, was the first delineation in fiction of the woman who was coming into notice in her thousands every year—the slight, pale 'bachelor' girl—the intellectualized, emancipated bundle of nerves that modern conditions were producing, mainly in cities as yet; who does not recognize the necessity for most of her sex to follow marriage as a profession, and boast themselves as superior people because they are licensed to be loved on the premises. The regret of this critic was that the portrait of the newcomer had been left to be drawn by a man, and was not done by one of her own sex, who would never have allowed her to break down at the end.

Whether this assurance is borne out by dates I cannot say. Nor am I able, across the gap of years since the production of the novel, to exercise more criticism upon it of a general kind than extends to a few verbal corrections, whatever, good or bad, it may contain.

And no doubt there can be more in a book than the author consciously put there, which will help either to its profit or to its disadvantage as the case may be.

April 1912 T.H.

PART FIRST

AT MARYGREEN

'Yea, many there be that have run out of their wits for women, and become servants for their sakes. Many also have perished, have erred, and sinned, for women. . . . O ye men, how can it be but women should be strong, seeing they do thus?'

—Esdras

I

THE schoolmaster was leaving the village, and everybody seemed sorry. The miller at Cresscombe lent him the small white tilted cart and horse to carry his goods to the city of his destination, about twenty miles off, such a vehicle proving of quite sufficient size for the departing teacher's effects. For the school-house had been partly furnished by the managers, and the only cumbersome article possessed by the master, in addition to the packing-case of books, was a cottage piano that he had bought at an auction during the year in which he thought of learning instrumental music. But the enthusiasm having waned he had never acquired any skill in playing, and the purchased article had been a perpetual trouble to him ever since in moving house.

The rector had gone away for the day, being a man who disliked the sight of changes. He did not mean to return till the evening, when the new school-teacher would have arrived and settled in, and everything would be smooth again.

The blacksmith, the farm bailiff, and the schoolmaster himself were standing in perplexed attitudes in the parlour before the instrument. The master had remarked that even if he got it into the cart he should not know what to do with it on his arrival at Christminster, the city he was bound for, since he was only going into temporary lodgings just at first.

A little boy of eleven, who had been thoughtfully assisting in the packing, joined the group of men, and as they rubbed their chins he spoke up, blushing at the sound of his own voice: 'Aunt have got a great fuel-house, and it could be put there, perhaps, till you've found a place to settle in, sir.'

'A proper good notion,' said the blacksmith.

It was decided that a deputation should wait on the boy's aunt—an old maiden resident—and ask her if she would house the piano till Mr Phillotson should send for it. The smith and the bailiff started to see the practicability of the suggested shelter, and the boy and the schoolmaster were left standing alone.

'Sorry I am going, Jude?' asked the latter kindly.

Tears rose into the boy's eyes, for he was not among the regular day scholars, who came unromantically close to the schoolmaster's life, but one who had attended the night school only during the present teacher's term of office. The regular scholars, if the truth must be told, stood at the present moment afar off, like certain historic disciples, indisposed to any enthusiastic volunteering of aid.

The boy awkwardly opened the book he held in his hand, which Mr Phillotson had bestowed on him as a parting gift, and admitted that he was sorry.

'So am I,' said Mr Phillotson.

'Why do you go, sir?' asked the boy.

'Ah—that would be a long story. You wouldn't understand my reasons, Jude. You will, perhaps, when you are older.'

'I think I should now, sir.'

'Well—don't speak of this everywhere. You know what a university is, and a university degree? It is the necessary hallmark of a man who wants to do anything in teaching. My scheme, or dream, is to be a university graduate, and then to be ordained. By going to live at Christminster, or near it, I shall be at headquarters, so to speak, and if my scheme is practicable at all, I consider that being on the spot will afford me a better chance of carrying it out than I should have elsewhere.'

The smith and his companion returned. Old Miss Fawley's fuel-house was dry, and eminently practicable; and she seemed willing to give the instrument standing-room there. It was accordingly left in the school till the evening, when more hands would be available for removing it; and the schoolmaster gave a final glance round.

The boy Jude assisted in loading some small articles, and at nine o'clock Mr Phillotson mounted beside his box of books and other *impedimenta*, and bade his friends good-bye.

'I shan't forget you, Jude,' he said, smiling, as the cart moved off. 'Be a good boy, remember; and be kind to animals and birds, and read all you can. And if ever you come to Christminster remember you hunt me out for old aquaintance' sake.'

The cart creaked across the green, and disappeared round the corner by the rectory-house. The boy returned to the draw-well at the edge of the greensward, where he had left his buckets when he went to help his patron and teacher in the loading. There was a quiver in his lip now, and after opening the well-cover to begin lowering the bucket he paused and leant with his forehead and arms against the frame-work, his face wearing the fixity of a thoughtful child's who has felt the pricks of life somewhat before his time. The well into which he was looking was as ancient as the village itself, and from his present position appeared as a long circular perspective ending in a shining disk of quivering water at a distance of a hundred feet down. There was a lining of green moss near the top, and nearer still the hart's-tongue fern.

He said to himself, in the melodramatic tones of a whimsical boy, that the schoolmaster had drawn at that well scores of times on a morning like this, and would never draw there any more. 'I've seen him look down into it, when he was tired with his drawing, just as I do now, and when he rested a bit before carrying the buckets home! But he was too clever to bide here any longer—a small sleepy place like this!'

A tear rolled from his eye into the depths of the well. The morning was a little foggy, and the boy's breathing unfurled itself as a thicker fog upon the still and heavy air. His thoughts were interrupted by a sudden outcry:

'Bring on that water, will ye, you idle young harlican!'

It came from an old woman who had emerged from her door towards the garden gate of a green-thatched cottage not far off. The boy quickly waved a signal of assent, drew the water with what was a great effort for one of his stature, landed and emptied the big bucket into his own pair of smaller ones, and pausing a moment for breath, started with them across the patch of clammy greensward whereon the well stood—nearly in the centre of the little village, or rather hamlet of Marygreen.

It was as old-fashioned as it was small, and it rested in the lap of an undulating upland adjoining the North Wessex downs. Old as it was, however, the well-shaft was probably the only relic of the local history that remained absolutely unchanged. Many of the thatched and dormered dwelling-houses had been pulled down of late years, and many trees felled on the green. Above all, the original church, humpbacked, wood-turreted, and quaintly hipped, had been taken down, and either cracked up into heaps of road-metal in the lane, or utilized as pig-sty walls, garden seats, guard-stones to fences, and rockeries in the flower-beds of the neighbourhood. In place of it a tall new building of modern Gothic design, unfamiliar to English eyes, had been erected on a new piece of ground by a certain obliterator of historic records who had run down from London and back in a day. The site whereon so long had stood the ancient temple to the Christian divinities was not even recorded on the green and level grass-plot that had immemorially been the churchyard, the obliterated graves being commemorated by eighteenpenny cast-iron crosses warranted to last five years.

II

SLENDER as was Jude Fawley's frame he bore the two brimming house-buckets of water to the cottage without resting. Over the door was a little rectangular piece of blue board, on which was painted in yellow letters, 'Drusilla Fawley, Baker'. Within the little lead panes of the window—this being one of the few old houses left—were five bottles of sweets, and three buns on a plate of the willow pattern.

While emptying the buckets at the back of the house he could hear an animated conversation in progress within-doors between his great-aunt, the Drusilla of the signboard, and some other villagers. Having seen the schoolmaster depart, they were summing up particulars of the event, and indulging in predictions of his future.

'And who's he?' asked one, comparatively a stranger, when the boy entered.

'Well ye med ask it, Mrs Williams. He's my great-nephew—come since you was last this way.' The old inhabitant who answered was a tall, gaunt woman, who spoke tragically on the most trivial subject, and gave a phrase of her conversation to each auditor in turn. 'He come from Mellstock, down in South Wessex, about a year ago—wọrse luck for 'n, Belinda' (turning to the right) 'where his father was living, and was took wi' the shakings for death, and died in two days, as you know, Caroline' (turning to the left). 'It would ha' been a blessing if Goddy-mighty had took thee too, wi' thy mother and father, poor useless boy! But I've got him here to stay with me till I can see what's to be done with un, though I am obliged to let him earn any penny he can. Just now he's a-scaring of birds for Farmer Troutham. It keeps him out of mischty. Why do ye turn away, Jude?' she continued, as the boy, feeling the impact of their glances like slaps upon his face, moved aside.

The local washerwoman replied that it was perhaps a very good plan of Miss or Mrs Fawley's (as they called her indifferently) to have him with her—'to kip 'ee company in your loneliness, fetch water, shet the winder-shetters o' nights, and help in the bit o' baking.'

Miss Fawley doubted it. . . . 'Why didn't ye get the schoolmaster to take 'ee to Christminster wi' un, and make a scholar of 'ee,' she continued, in frowning pleasantry. 'I'm sure he couldn't ha' took a better one. The boy is crazy for books, that he is. It runs in our family rather. His cousin Sue is just the same—so I've heard; but I have not seen the child for years, though she was born in this place, within these four walls, as it happened. My niece and her husband, after they were married, didn' get a house of their own for some year or more; and then they only had one till—Well, I won't go into that. Jude my child, don't *you* ever marry. 'Tisn't for the Fawleys to take that step any more. She, their only one, was like a child o' my own, Belinda, till the split come! Ah, that a little maid should know such changes!'

Jude, finding the general attention again centering on himself, went out to the bakehouse, where he ate the cake provided for his breakfast. The end of his spare time had now arrived, and emerging from the garden by getting over the hedge at the back he pursued a path northward, till he came to a wide and lonely depression in the general level of the upland, which was sown as a corn-field. This vast concave was the scene of his labours for Mr Troutham the farmer, and he descended into the midst of it.

The brown surface of the field went right up towards the sky all round, where it was lost by degrees in the mist that shut out the actual verge and accentuated the solitude. The only marks on the uniformity of the scene were a rick of last year's produce standing in the midst of the arable, the rooks that rose at his approach, and the path athwart the fallow by which he had come, trodden now by he hardly knew whom, though once by many of his own dead family.

'How ugly it is here!' he murmured.

The fresh harrow-lines seemed to stretch like the channellings in a piece of new corduroy, lending a meanly utilitarian air to the expanse, taking away its gradations, and depriving it of all history beyond that of the few recent months, though to every clod and stone there really attached associations enough and to spare—echoes of songs from ancient harvest-days, of spoken words, and of sturdy deeds. Every inch of the ground had been the site, first or last, of energy, gaiety, horseplay, bickerings, weariness. Groups of gleaners had squatted in the sun on every square yard. Love-matches that had populated the adjoining hamlet had been made up there between reaping and carrying. Under the hedge which divided the field from a distant plantation girls had given themselves to lovers who would not turn their heads to look at them by the next harvest; and in that ancient cornfield many a man had made love-promises to a woman at whose voice he had trembled by the next seed-time after fulfilling them in the church adjoining. But this neither Jude nor the rooks around him considered. For them it was a lonely place, possessing, in the one view, only the quality of a work-ground, and in the other that of a granary good to feed in.

The boy stood under the rick before mentioned, and every few seconds used his clacker or rattle briskly. At each clack the rooks left off pecking, and rose and went away on their leisurely wings, burnished like tassets of mail, afterwards wheeling back and regarding him warily, and descending to feed at a more respectful distance.

He sounded the clacker till his arm ached, and at length his heart grew sympathetic with the birds' thwarted desires. They seemed, like himself, to be living in a world which did not want them. Why should he frighten them away? They took upon them more and more the aspect of gentle friends and pensioners—the only friends he could claim as being in the least degree interested in him, for his aunt had often told him that she was not. He ceased his rattling, and they alighted anew.

'Poor little dears!' said Jude, aloud. 'You *shall* have some dinner—you shall. There is enough for us all. Farmer Troutham can afford to let you have some. Eat, then, my dear little birdies, and make a good meal!'

They stayed and ate, inky spots on the nut-brown soil, and Jude enjoyed their appetite. A magic thread of fellow-feeling united his own life with theirs. Puny and sorry as those lives were, they much resembled his own.

His clacker he had by this time thrown away from him, as being a mean and sordid instrument, offensive both to the birds and to himself as their friend. All at once he became conscious of a smart blow upon his buttock, followed by a loud clack, which announced to his surprised senses that the clacker had been the instrument of offence used. The birds and Jude started up simultaneously, and he dazed eyes of the latter beheld the farmer in person, the great Troutham himself, his red face glaring down upon Jude's cowering frame, the clacker swinging in his hand.

'So it's "Eat, my dear birdies," is it, young man? "Eat, dear birdies," indeed! I'll tickle your breeches, and see if you say, "Eat, dear birdies," again in a hurry! And you've been idling at the schoolmaster's too, instead of coming here, ha'n't ye, hey? That's how you earn your sixpence a day for keeping the rooks off my corn!'

Whilst saluting Jude's ears with his impassioned rhetoric, Troutham had seized his left hand with his own left, and swinging his slim frame round him at arm's-length, again struck Jude on the hind parts with the flat side of Jude's own rattle, till the field echoed with the blows, which were delivered once or twice at each revolution.

'Don't 'ee, sir—please don't 'ee!' cried the whirling child, as helpless under the centrifugal tendency of his person as a hooked fish swinging to land, and beholding the hill, the rick, the plantation, the path and the rooks going round and round him in an amazing circular race. 'I—I—sir—only meant that—there was a good crop in the ground—I saw 'em sow it—and the rooks could have a little bit for dinner—and you wouldn't miss it, sir—and Mr Phillotson said I was to be kind to 'em—O, O, O!'

This truthful explanation seemed to exasperate the farmer even more than if Jude had stoutly denied saying anything at all; and he still smacked the whirling urchin, the clacks of the instrument continuing to resound all across the field and as far as the ears of distant workers—who gathered thereupon that Jude was pursuing his business of clacking with great assiduity—and echoing from the brand-new church tower just behind the mist, towards the building of which structure the farmer had largely subscribed, to testify his love for God and man.

Presently Troutham grew tired of his punitive task, and depositing the quivering boy on his legs, took a sixpence from his pocket and gave it him in payment for his day's work, telling him to go home and never let him see him in one of those fields again.

Jude leaped out of arm's reach, and walked along the track-way weeping—not from the pain, though that was keen enough; not from the perception of the flaw in the terrestrial scheme, by which what was good for God's birds was bad for God's gardener; but with the awful sense that he had wholly disgraced himself before he had been a year in the parish, and hence might be a burden to his great-aunt for life.

With this shadow on his mind he did not care to show himself in the village, and went homeward by a roundabout track behind a high hedge and across a pasture. Here he beheld scores of coupled earthworms lying half their length on the surface of the damp ground, as they always did in such weather at that time of the year. It was impossible to advance in regular steps without crushing some of them at each tread.

Though Farmer Troutham had just hurt him, he was a boy who could not himself bear to hurt anything. He had never brought home a nest of young birds without lying awake in misery half the night after, and often reinstating them and the nest in their original place the next morning. He could scarcely bear to see trees cut down or lopped, from a fancy that it hurt them; and late pruning, when the sap was up and the tree bled profusely, had been a positive grief to him in his infancy. This weakness of character, as it may be called, suggested that he was the sort of man who was born to ache a good deal before the fall of the curtain upon his unnecessary life should signify that all was well with him again. He carefully picked his way on tiptoe among the earthworms, without killing a single one.

On entering the cottage he found his aunt selling a penny loaf to a little girl, and when the customer was gone she said, 'Well, how do you come to be back here in the middle of the morning like this?'

'I'm turned away.'

'What?'

'Mr Troutham have turned me away because I let the rooks have a few peckings of corn. And there's my wages—the last I shall ever hae!'

He threw sixpence tragically on the table.

'Ah!' said his aunt, suspending her breath. And she opened upon him a lecture on how she would now have him all the spring upon her hands doing nothing. 'If you can't skeer birds, what can ye do? There! don't ye look so deedy! Farmer Troutham is not so much better than myself, come to that. But 'tis as Job said, "Now they that are younger than I have me in derision, whose fathers I would have disdained to have set with the dogs of my flock." His father was my father's journeyman, anyhow, and I must have been a fool to let 'ee go to work for 'n, which I shouldn't ha' done but to keep 'ee out of mischty.'

More angry with Jude for demeaning her by coming there than for dereliction of duty, she rated him primarily from that point of view, and only secondarily from a moral one.

'Not that you should have let the birds eat what Farmer Troutham planted. Of course you was wrong in that. Jude, Jude, why didstn't go off with that schoolmaster of thine to Christminster or somewhere? But, O no—poor or'nary child—there never was any sprawl on thy side of the family, and never will be!'

'Where is this beautiful city, aunt—this place where Mr Phillotson is gone to?' asked the boy, after meditating in silence.

'Lord! you ought to know where the city of Christminster is. Near a score of miles from here. It is a place much too good for you ever to have much to do with, poor boy, I'm a-thinking.'

'And will Mr Phillotson always be there?'

'How can I tell?'

'Couldn't I go to see him?'

'Lord, no! You didn't grow up hereabout, or you wouldn't ask such as that. We've never had anything to do with folk in Christminster, nor folk in Christminster with we.'

Jude went out, and, feeling more than ever his existence to be an undemanded one, he lay down upon his back on a heap of litter near the pig-sty. The fog had by this time become more translucent, and the position of the sun could be seen through it. He pulled his straw hat over his face, and peered through the interstices of the plaiting at the white brightness, vaguely reflecting. Growing up brought responsibilities, he found. Events did not rhyme quite as he had thought. Nature's logic was too horrid for him to care for. That mercy towards one set of creatures was cruelty towards another sickened his sense of harmony. As you got older, and felt yourself to be at the centre of your time, and not at a point in its circumference, as you had felt when you were little, you were seized with a sort of shuddering, he perceived. All around you there seemed to be something glaring, garish, rattling, and the noises and glares hit upon the little cell called your life, and shook it, and warped it.

If he could only prevent himself growing up! He did not want to be a man.

Then, like the natural boy, he forgot his despondency, and sprang up. During the remainder of the morning he helped his aunt, and in the afternoon, when there was nothing more to be done, he went into the village. Here he asked a man whereabouts Christminster lay.

'Christminster? O, well, out by there yonder; though I've never bin there—not I. I've never had any business at such a place.'

The man pointed north-eastward, in the very direction where lay that field in which Jude had so disgraced himself. There was something unpleasant about the coincidence for the moment, but the fearsomeness of this fact rather increased his curiosity about the city. The farmer had said he was never to be seen in that field again; yet Christminster lay across it, and the path was a public one. So, stealing out of the hamlet he descended into the same hollow which had witnessed his punishment in the morning, never swerving an inch from the path, and climbing up the long and tedious ascent on the other side, till the track joined the highway by a little clump of trees. Here the ploughed land ended, and all before him was bleak open down.

III

Not a soul was visible on the hedgeless highway, or on either side of it, and the white road seemed to ascend and diminish till it joined the sky. At the very top it was crossed at right angles by a green 'ridgeway'—the Icknield Street and original Roman road through the district. This ancient track ran east and west for many miles, and down almost to within living memory had been used for driving flocks and herds to fairs and markets. But it was now neglected and overgrown.

The boy had never before strayed so far north as this from the nestling hamlet in which he had been deposited by the carrier from a railway station southward, one dark evening some few months earlier, and till now he had had no suspicion that such a wide, flat, low-lying country lay so near at hand, under the very verge of his upland world. The whole northern semicircle between east and west, to a distance of forty or fifty miles, spread itself before him; a bluer, moister atmosphere, evidently, than that he breathed up here.

Not far from the road stood a weather-beaten old barn of reddish-gray brick and tile. It was known as the Brown House by the people of the locality. He was about to pass it when he perceived a ladder against the eaves; and the reflection that the higher he got, the further he could see, led Jude to stand and regard it. On the slope of the roof two men were repairing the tiling. He turned into the ridgeway and drew towards the barn.

When he had wistfully watched the workmen for some time he took courage, and ascended the ladder till he stood beside them.

'Well, my lad, and what may you want up here?'

'I wanted to know where the city of Christminster is, if you please.'

'Christminster is out across there, by that clump. You can see it—at least you can on a clear day. Ah, no, you can't now.'

The other tiler, glad of any kind of diversion from the monotony of his labour, had also turned to look towards the quarter designated. 'You can't often see it in weather like this,' he said. 'The time I've noticed it is when the sun is going down in a blaze of flame, and it looks like—I don't know what.'

'The heavenly Jerusalem,' suggested the serious urchin.

'Ay—though I should never ha' thought of it myself. . . . But I can't see no Christminster to-day.'

The boy strained his eyes also; yet neither could he see the far-off city. He descended from the barn, and abandoning Christminster with the versatility of his age he walked along the ridge-track, looking for any natural objects of interest that might lie in the banks thereabout. When he repassed the barn to go back to Marygreen he observed that the ladder was still in its place, but the men had finished their day's work and gone away.

It was waning towards evening; there was still a faint mist, but it had cleared a little except in the damper tracts of subjacent country and along the river-courses. He thought again of Christminster, and wished, since he had come two or three miles from his aunt's house on purpose, that he could have seen for once this attractive city of which he had been told. But even if he waited here it was hardly likely that the air would clear before night. Yet he was loth to leave the spot, for the northern expanse became lost to view on retreating towards the village only a few hundred yards.

He ascended the ladder to have one more look at the point the men had designated, and perched himself on the highest rung, overlying the tiles. He might not be able to come so far as this for many days. Perhaps if he prayed, the wish to see Christminster might be forwarded. People said that, if you prayed, things sometimes came to you, even though they sometimes did not. He had read in a tract that a man who had begun to build a church, and had no money to finish it, knelt down and prayed, and the money came in by the next post. Another man tried the same experiment, and the money did not come; but he found afterwards that the breeches he knelt in were made by a wicked Jew. This was not discouraging, and turning on the ladder Jude knelt on the third rung, where, resting against those above it, he prayed that the mist might rise.

He then seated himself again, and waited. In the course of ten or fifteen minutes the thinning mist dissolved altogether from the northern horizon, as it had already done elsewhere, and about a quarter of an hour before the time of sunset the westward clouds parted, the sun's position being partially uncovered, and the beams streaming out in visible lines between the two bars of slaty cloud. The boy immediately looked back in the old direction.

Some way within the limits of the stretch of landscape, points of light like the topaz gleamed. The air increased in transparency with the lapse of minutes, till the topaz points showed themselves to be the vanes, windows, wet roof slates, and other shining spots upon the spires, domes, freestone-work, and varied outlines that were faintly revealed. It was Christminster, unquestionably; either directly seen, or miraged in the peculiar atmosphere.

The spectator gazed on and on till the windows and vanes lost their shine, going out almost suddenly like extinguished candles. The vague city became veiled in mist. Turning to the west, he saw that the sun had disappeared. The foreground of the scene had grown funereally dark, and near objects put on the hues and shapes of chimaeras.

He anxiously descended the ladder, and started homewards at a run, trying not to think of giants, Herne the Hunter. Apollyon lying in wait for Christian, or of the captain with the bleeding hole in his forehead and the corpses round him that remutinied every night on board the bewitched ship. He knew that he had grown out of belief in these horrors, yet he was glad when he saw the church tower and the lights in the cottage windows, even though this was not the home of his birth, and his great-aunt did not care much about him.

Inside and round about that old woman's 'shop' window, with its twenty-four little panes set in lead-work, the glass of some of them oxidized with age, so that you could hardly see the poor penny articles exhibited within, and forming part of a stock which a strong man could have carried, Jude had his outer being for some long tideless time. But his dreams were as gigantic as his surroundings were small.

Through the solid barrier of cold cretaceous upland to the northward he was always beholding a gorgeous city—the fancied place he had likened to the new Jerusalem, though there was perhaps more of the painter's imagination and less of the diamond merchant's in his dreams thereof than in those of the Apocalyptic writer. And the city acquired a tangibility, a permanence, a hold on his life, mainly from the one nucleus of fact that the man for whose knowledge and purposes he had so much reverence was actually living there; not only so, but living among the more thoughtful and mentally shining ones therein.

In sad wet seasons, though he knew it must rain at Christminster too, he could hardly believe that it rained so drearily there. Whenever he could get away from the confines of the hamlet for an hour or two, which was not often, he would steal off to the Brown House on the hill and strain his eyes persistently; sometimes to be rewarded by the sight of a dome or spire, at other times by a little smoke, which in his estimate had some of the mysticism of incense.

Then the day came when it suddenly occurred to him that if he ascended to the point of view after dark, or possibly went a mile or two further, he would see the night lights of the city. It would be necessary to come back alone, but even that consideration did not deter him, for he could throw a little manliness into his mood, no doubt.

The project was duly executed. It was not late when he arrived at the place of outlook, only just after dusk; but a black north-east sky, accompanied by a wind from the same quarter, made the occasion dark enough. He was rewarded; but what he saw was not the lamps in rows, as he had half expected. No individual light was visible, only a halo or glow-fog over-arching the place against the black heavens behind it, making the light and the city seem distant but a mile or so.

He set himself to wonder on the exact point in the glow where the schoolmaster might be—he who never communicated with anybody at Marygreen now; who was as if dead to them here. In the glow he seemed to see Phillotson promenading at ease, like one of the forms in Nebuchadnezzar's furnace.

He had heard that breezes travelled at the rate of ten miles an hour, and the fact now came into his mind. He parted his lips as he faced the north-east, and drew in the wind as if it were a sweet liquor.

'You,' he said, addressing the breeze caressingly, 'were in Christminster city between one and two hours ago, floating along the streets, pulling round the weather-cocks, touching Mr Phillotson's face, being breathed by him; and now you are here, breathed by me—you, the very same.'

Suddenly there came along this wind something towards him—a message from the place—from some soul residing there, it seemed. Surely it was the sound of bells, the voice of the city, faint and musical, calling to him, 'We are happy here!'

He had become entirely lost to his bodily situation during this mental leap, and only got back to it by a rough recalling. A few yards below the brow of the hill on which he paused a team of horses made its appearance, having reached the place by dint of half an hour's serpentine progress from the bottom of the immense declivity. They had a load of coals behind them—a fuel that could only be got into the upland by this particular route. They were accompanied by a carter, a second man, and a boy, who now kicked a large stone behind one of the wheels, and allowed the panting animals to have a long rest, while those in charge took a flagon off the load and indulged in a drink round.

They were elderly men, and had genial voices. Jude addressed them, inquiring if they had come from Christminster.

'Heaven forbid, with this load!' said they.

'The place I mean is that one yonder.' He was getting so romantically attached to Christminster that, like a young lover alluding to his mistress, he felt bashful at mentioning its name again. He pointed to the light in the sky—hardly perceptible to their older eyes.

'Yes. There do seem a spot a bit brighter in the nor'-east than elsewhere, though I shouldn't ha' noticed it myself, and no doubt it med be Christminster.'

Here a little book of tales which Jude had tucked up under his arm, having brought them to read on his way hither before it grew dark, slipped and fell into the road. The carter eyed him while he picked it up and straightened the leaves.

'Ah, young man,' he observed, 'you'd have to get your head screwed on t'other way before you could read what they read there.'

'Why?' asked the boy.

'O, they never look at anything that folks like we can understand,' the carter continued, by way of passing the time. 'On'y foreign tongues used in the days of the Tower of Babel, when no two families spoke alike. They read that sort of thing as fast as a night-hawk will whir. 'Tis all learning there—nothing but learning, except religion. And that's learning too, for I never could understand it. Yes, 'tis a serious-minded place. Not but there's wenches in the streets o'nights. . . . You know, I suppose, that they raise pa'sons there like radishes in a bed? And though it do take—how many years, Bob?—five years to turn a lirruping hobble-de-hoy chap into a solemn preaching man with no corrupt passions, they'll do it, if it can be done, and polish un off like the workmen they be, and turn un out wi' a long face, and a long black coat and waist-coat, and a religious collar and hat, same as they used to wear in the Scriptures, so that his own mother wouldn't know un sometimes. . . . There, 'tis their business, like anybody else's.'

'But how should you know—'

'Now don't you interrupt, my boy. Never interrupt your senyers. Move the fore hoss aside, Bobby; here's som'at coming. . . . You must mind that I be a-talking of the college life. 'Em lives on a lofty level; there's no gainsaying it, though I myself med not think much of 'em. As we be here in our bodies on this high ground, so be they in their minds—noble-minded men enough, no doubt—some on 'em—able to earn hundreds by thinking out loud. And some on 'em be strong young fellows that can earn a'most as much in silver cups. As for music, there's beautiful music everywhere in Christminster. You med be religious, or you med not, but you can't help striking in your homely note with the rest. And there's a street in the place—the main street—that had'nt another like it in the world. I should think I did know a little about Christminster!'

By this time the horses had recovered breath and bent to their collars again. Jude, throwing a last adoring look at the distant halo, turned and walked beside his remarkably well-informed friend, who had no objection to tell him as they moved on more yet of the city—its towers and halls and churches. The waggon turned into a cross-road, whereupon Jude thanked the carter warmly for his information, and said he only wished he could talk half as well about Christminster as he.

'Well, 'tis oonly what has come in my way,' said the carter unboastfully. 'I've never been there, no more than you; but I've picked up the knowledge here and there, and you be welcome to it. A-getting about the world as I do, and mixing with all classes of society, one can't help hearing of things. A friend o'mine, that used to clane the boots at the Crozier Hotel in Christminster when he was in his prime, why, I knowed un as well as my own brother in his later years.'

Jude continued his walk homeward alone, pondering so deeply that he forgot to feel timid. He suddenly grew older. It had been the yearning of his heart to find something to anchor on, to cling to—for some place which he could call admirable. Should he find that place in this city if he could get there? Would it be a spot in which, without fear of farmers, or hindrance, or ridicule, he could watch and wait, and set himself to some mighty undertaking like the men of old of whom he had heard? As the halo had been to his eyes when gazing at it a quarter of an hour earlier, so was the spot mentally to him as he pursued his dark way.

'It is a city of light,' he said to himself.

'The tree of knowledge grows there,' he added a few steps further on.

'It is a place that teachers of men spring from and go to.'

'It is what you may call a castle, manned by scholarship and religion.'

After this figure he was silent a long while, till he added:

'It would just suit me.'

IV

Walking somewhat slowly by reason of his concentration, the boy—an ancient man in some phases of thought, much younger than his years in others—was overtaken by a light-footed pedestrian, whom, notwithstanding the gloom, he could perceive to be wearing an extraordinarily tall hat, a swallow-tailed coat, and a watch-chain that danced madly and threw around scintillations of sky-light as its owner swung along upon a pair of thin legs and noiseless boots. Jude, beginning to feel lonely, endeavoured to keep up with him.

'Well, my man! I'm in a hurry, so you'll have to walk pretty fast if you keep alongside of me. Do you know who I am?'

'Yes, I think. Physician Vilbert?'

'Ah—I'm known everywhere, I see. That comes of being a public benefactor.'

Vilbert was an itinerant quack-doctor, well known to the rustic population, and absolutely unknown to anybody else, as he, indeed, took care to be, to avoid inconvenient investigations. Cottagers formed his only patients, and his Wessex-wide repute was among them alone. His position was humbler and his field more obscure than those of the quacks with capital and an organized system of advertising. He was, in fact, a survival. The distances he traversed on foot were enormous, and extended nearly the whole length and breadth of Wessex. Jude had one day seen him selling a pot of coloured lard to an old woman as a certain cure for a bad leg, the woman arranging to pay a guinea, in instalments of a shilling a fortnight, for the precious salve, which, according to the physician, could only be obtained from a particular animal which grazed on Mount Sinai, and was to be captured only at great risk to life and limb. Jude, though he already had his doubts about this gentleman's medicines, felt him to be unquestionably a travelled personage, and one who might be a trustworthy source of information on matters not strictly professional.

'I s'pose you've been to Christminster, Physician?'

'I have—many times,' replied the long thin man. 'That's one of my centres.'

'It's a wonderful city for scholarship and religion?'

'You'd say so, my boy, if you'd seen it. Why, the very sons of the old women who do the washing of the colleges can talk in Latin—not good Latin, that I admit, as a critic: dog-Latin—cat-Latin, as we used to call it in my undergraduate days.'

'And Greek?'

'Well—that's more for the men who are in training for bishops, that they may be able to read the New Testament in the original.'

'I want to learn Latin and Greek myself.'

'A lofty desire. You must get a grammar of each tongue.'

'I mean to go to Christminster some day.'

'Whenever you do, you say that Physician Vilbert is the only proprietor of those celebrated pills that infallibly cure all disorders of the alimentary system, as well as asthma and shortness of breath. Two and threepence a box—specially licensed by the government stamp.'

'Can you get me the grammars if I promise to say it here-about?'

'I'll sell you mine with pleasure—those I used as a student.'

'O, thank you, sir!' said Jude gratefully, but in gasps, for the amazing speed of the physician's walk kept him in a dog-trot which was giving him a stitch in the side.

'I think you'd better drop behind, my young man. Now I'll tell you what I'll do. I'll get you the grammars, and give you a first lesson, if you'll remember at every house in the village, to recommend Physician Vilbert's golden ointment, life-drops, and female pills.'

'Where will you be with the grammars?'

'I shall be passing here this day fortnight at precisely this hour of five-and-twenty minutes past seven. My movements are as truly timed as those of the planets in their courses.'

'Here I'll be to meet you,' said Jude.

'With orders for my medicines?'

'Yes, Physician.'

Jude then dropped behind, waited a few minutes to recover breath, and went home with a consciousness of having struck a blow for Christminster.

Through the intervening fortnight he ran about and smiled outwardly at his inward thoughts, as if they were people meeting and nodding to him—smiled with that singularly beautiful irradiation which is seen to spread on young faces at the inception of some glorious idea, as if a supernatural lamp were held inside their transparent natures, giving rise to the flattering fancy that heaven lies about them then.

He honestly performed his promise to the man of many cures, in whom he now sincerely believed, walking miles hither and thither among the surrounding hamlets as the physician's agent in advance. On the evening appointed he stood motionless on the plateau, at the place where he had parted from Vilbert, and there awaited his approach. The road-physician was fairly up to time; but, to the surprise of Jude on striking into his pace, which the pedestrian did not diminish by a single unit of force, the latter seemed hardly to recognize his young companion, though with the lapse of the fortnight the evenings had grown light. Jude thought it might perhaps be owing to his wearing another hat, and he saluted the physician with dignity.

'Well, my boy?' said the latter abstractedly.

'I've come,' said Jude.

'You? who are you? O yes—to be sure? Got any orders, lad?'

'Yes.' And Jude told him the names and addresses of the cottagers who were willing to test the virtues of the world-renowned pills and salve. The quack mentally registered these with great care.

'And the Latin and Greek grammars?' Jude's voice trembled with anxiety.

'What about them?'

'You were to bring me yours, that you used before you took your degree.'

'Ah, yes, yes! Forgot all about it—all! So many lives depending on my attention, you see, my man, that I can't give so much thought as I would like to other things.'

Jude controlled himself sufficiently long to make sure of the truth: and he repeated, in a voice of dry misery, 'You haven't brought 'em!'

'No. But you must get me some more orders from sick people, and I'll bring the grammars next time.'

Jude dropped behind. He was an unsophisticated boy, but the gift of sudden insight which is sometimes vouchsafed to children showed him all at once what shoddy humanity the quack was made of. There was to be no intellectual light from this source. The leaves dropped from his imaginary crown of laurel; he turned to a gate, leant against it, and cried bitterly.

The disappointment was followed by an interval of blankness. He might, perhaps, have obtained grammars from Alfredston, but to do that required money, and a knowledge of what books to order; and though physically comfortable, he was in such absolute dependence as to be without a farthing of his own.

At this date Mr Phillotson sent for his pianoforte, and it gave Jude a lead. Why should he not write to the schoolmaster, and ask him to be so kind as to get him the grammars in Christminster? He might slip a letter inside the case of the instrument, and it would be sure to reach the desired eyes. Why not ask him to send any old second-hand copies, which would have the charm of being mellowed by the university atmosphere?

To tell his aunt of his intention would be to defeat it. It was necessary to act alone.

After a further consideration of a few days he did act, and on the day of the piano's departure, which happened to be his next birthday, clandestinely placed the letter inside the packing-case, directed to his much-admired friend; being afraid to reveal the operation to his aunt Drusilla, lest she should discover his motive, and compel him to abandon his scheme.

The piano was despatched, and Jude waited days and weeks, calling every morning at the cottage post-office before his great-aunt was stirring. At last a packet did indeed arrive at the village, and he saw from the ends of it that it contained two thin books. He took it away into a lonely place, and sat down on a felled elm to open it.

Ever since his first ecstasy or vision of Christminster and its possibilities, Jude had meditated much and curiously on the probable sort of process that was involved in turning the expressions of one language into those of another. He concluded that a grammar of the required tongue would contain, primarily, a rule, prescription, or clue of the nature of a secret cipher, which, once known, would enable him, by merely applying it, to change at will all words of his own speech into those of the foreign one. His childish idea was, in fact, a pushing to the extremity of mathematical precision what is everywhere known as Grimm's Law—an aggrandizement of rough rules to ideal completeness. Thus he assumed that the words of the required language were always to be found somewhere latent in the words of the given language by those who had the art to uncover them, such art being furnished by the books aforesaid.

When, therefore, having noted that the packet bore the postmark of Christminster, he cut the string, opened the volumes, and turned to the Latin grammar, which chanced to come uppermost, he could scarcely believe his eyes.

The book was an old one—thirty years old, soiled, scribbled wantonly over with a strange name in every variety of enmity to the letterpress, and marked at random with dates twenty years earlier than his own day. But this was not the cause of Jude's amazement. He learnt for the first time that there was no law of transmutation, as in his innocence he had supposed (there was, in some degree, but the grammarian did not recognize it), but that every word in both Latin and Greek was to be individually committed to memory at the cost of years of plodding.

Jude flung down the books, lay backward along the broad trunk of the elm, and was an utterly miserable boy for the space of a quarter of an hour. As he had often done before, he pulled his hat over his face and watched the sun peering insidiously at him through the interstices of the straw. This was Latin and Greek, then, was it, this grand delusion! The charm he had supposed in store for him was really a labour like that of Israel in Egypt.

What brains they must have in Christminster and the great schools, he presently thought, to learn words one by one up to tens of thousands! There were no brains in his head equal to this business; and as the little sun-rays continued to stream in through his hat at him, he wished he had never seen a book, that he might never see another, that he had never been born.

Somebody might have come along that way who would have asked him his trouble, and might have cheered him by saying that his notions were further advanced than those of his grammarian. But nobody did come, because nobody does; and under the crushing recognition of his gigantic error Jude continued to wish himself out of the world.

V

During the three or four succeeding years a quaint and singular vehicle might have been discerned moving along the lanes and by-roads near Marygreen, driven in a quaint and singular way.

In the course of a month or two after the receipt of the books Jude had grown callous to the shabby trick played him by the dead languages. In fact, his disappointment at the nature of those tongues had, after a while, been the means of still further glorifying the erudition of Christminster. To acquire languages, departed or living, in spite of such obstinacies as he now knew them inherently to possess, was a herculean performance which gradually led him on to a greater interest in it than in the presupposed patent process. The mountain-weight of material under which the idea lay in those dusty volumes called the classics piqued him into a dogged, mouse-like subtlety of attempt to move it piecemeal.

He had endeavoured to make his presence tolerable to his crusty maiden aunt by assisting her to the best of his ability, and the business of the little cottage bakery had grown in consequence. An aged horse with a hanging head had been purchased for eight pounds at a sale, a creaking cart with a whity-brown tilt obtained for a few pounds more, and in this turn-out it became Jude's business thrice a week to carry loaves of bread to the villagers and solitary cotters immediately around Marygreen.

The singularity aforesaid lay, after all, less in the conveyance itself than in Jude's manner of conducting it along its route. Its interior was the scene of most of Jude's education by 'private study'. As soon as the horse had learnt the road and the houses at which he was to pause awhile, the boy, seated in front, would slip the reins over his arm, ingeniously fix open, by means of a strap attached to the tilt, the volume he was reading, spread the dictionary on his knees, and plunge into the simpler passages from Caesar, Virgil, or

Horace, as the case might be, in his purblind stumbling way, and with an expenditure of labour that would have made a tender-hearted pedagogue shed tears; yet somehow getting at the meaning of what he read, and divining rather than beholding the spirit of the original, which often to his mind was something else than that which he was taught to look for.

The only copies he had been able to lay hands on were old Delphin editions, because they were superseded, and therefore cheap. But, bad for idle school-boys, it did so happen that they were passably good for him. The hampered and lonely itinerant conscientiously covered up the marginal readings, and used them merely on points of construction, as he would have used a comrade or tutor who should have happened to be passing by. And though Jude may have had little chance of becoming a scholar by these rough and ready means, he was in the way of getting into the groove he wished to follow.

While he was busied with these ancient pages, which had already been thumbed by hands possibly in the grave, digging out the thoughts of these minds so remote yet so near, the bony old horse pursued his rounds, and Jude would be aroused from the woes of Dido by the stoppage of his cart and the voice of some old woman crying, 'Two to-day, baker, and I return this stale one.'

He was frequently met in the lanes by pedestrians and others without his seeing them, and by degrees the people of the neighbourhood began to talk about his method of combining work and play (such they considered his reading to be), which, though probably convenient enough to himself, was not altogether a safe proceeding for other travellers along the same roads. There were murmurs. Then a private resident of an adjoining place informed the local policeman that the baker's boy should not be allowed to read while driving, and insisted that it was the constable's duty to catch him in the act, and take him to the police court at Alfredston, and get him fined for dangerous practices on the highway. The policeman thereupon lay in wait for Jude, and one day accosted him and cautioned him.

As Jude had to get up at three o'clock in the morning to heat the oven, and mix and set in the bread that he distributed later in the day, he was obliged to go to bed at night immediately after laying the sponge; so that if he could not read his classics on the highways he could hardly study at all. The only thing to be done was, therefore, to keep a sharp eye ahead and around him as well as he could in the circumstances, and slip away his books as soon as anybody loomed in the distance, the policeman in particular. To do that official justice, he did not put himself much in the way of Jude's bread-cart, considering that in such a lonely district the chief danger was to Jude himself, and often on seeing the white tilt over the hedges he would move in another direction.

On a day when Fawley was getting quite advanced, being now about sixteen, and had been stumbling through the 'Carmen Saeculare', on his way home, he found himself to be passing over the high edge of the plateau by the Brown House. The light had changed, and it was the sense of this which had caused him to look up. The sun was going down, and the full moon was rising simultaneously behind the woods in the opposite quarter. His mind had become so impregnated with the poem that, in a moment of the same impulsive emotion which years before had caused him to kneel on the ladder, he stopped the horse, alighted, and glancing round to see that nobody was in sight, knelt down on the roadside bank with open book. He turned first to the shiny goddess, who seemed to look so softly and critically at his doings, then to the disappearing luminary on the other hand, as he began:

'Phoebe silvarumque potens Diana!'

The horse stood still till he had finished the hymn, which Jude repeated under the sway of a polytheistic fancy that he would never have thought of humouring in broad daylight.

Reaching home, he mused over his curious superstition, innate or acquired, in doing this, and the strange forgetfulness which had led to such a lapse from common-sense and custom in one who wished, next to being a scholar, to be a Christian divine. It had all come of reading heathen works exclusively. The more he thought of it the more convinced he was of his inconsistency. He began to wonder whether he could be reading quite the right books for his object in life. Certainly there seemed little harmony between this pagan literature and the mediaeval colleges at Christminster, that ecclesiastical romance in stone.

Ultimately he decided that in his sheer love of reading he had taken up a wrong emotion for a Christian young man. He had dabbled in Clarke's Homer, but had never yet worked much at the New Testament in the Greek, though he possessed a copy, obtained by post from a second-hand bookseller. He abandoned the now familiar Ionic for a new dialect, and for a long time onward limited his reading almost entirely to the Gospels and Epistles in Griesbach's text. Moreover, on going into Alfredston one day, he was introduced to patristic literature by finding at the bookseller's some volumes of the Fathers which had been left behind by an insolvent clergyman of the neighbourhood.

As another outcome of this change of groove he visited on Sundays all the churches within a walk, and deciphered the Latin inscriptions on fifteenth-century brasses and tombs. On one of these pilgrimages he met with a hunchbacked old woman of great intelligence, who read everything she could lay her hands on, and she told him more yet of the romantic charms of the city of light and lore. Thither he resolved as firmly as ever to go.

But how live in that city? At present he had no income at all. He had no trade or calling of any dignity or stability whatever on which he could subsist while carrying out an intellectual labour which might spread over many years.

What was most required by citizens? Food, clothing, and shelter. An income from any work in preparing the first would be too meagre; for making the second he felt a distaste; the preparation of the third requisite he inclined to. They built in a city; therefore he would learn to build. He thought of his unknown uncle, his cousin Susanna's father, an ecclesiastical worker in metal, and somehow mediaeval art in any material was a trade for which he had rather a fancy. He could not go far wrong in following his uncle's footsteps, and engaging himself awhile with the carcasses that contained the scholar souls.

As a preliminary he obtained some small blocks of freestone, metal not being available, and suspending his studies awhile, occupied his spare half-hours in copying the heads and capitals in his parish church.

There was a stone-mason of a humble kind in Alfredston, and as soon as he had found a substitute for himself in his aunt's little business, he offered his services to this man for a trifling wage. Here Jude had the opportunity of learning at least the rudiments of freestone-working. Some time later he went to a church-builder in the same place, and under the architect's direction became handy at restoring the dilapidated masonries of several village churches round about.

Not forgetting that he was only following up this handicraft as a prop to lean on while he prepared those greater engines which he flattered himself would be better fitted for him, he yet was interested in his pursuit on its own account. He now had lodgings during the week in the little town, whence he returned to Marygreen village every Saturday evening. And thus he reached and passed his nineteenth year.

VI

At this memorable date of his life he was, one Saturday, returning from Alfredston to Marygreen about three o'clock in the afternoon. It was fine, warm, and soft summer weather, and he walked with his tools at his back, his little chisels clinking faintly against the larger ones in his basket. It being the end of the week he had left work early, and he had come out of the town by a roundabout route which he did not usually frequent, having promised to call at a flour-mill near Cresscombe to execute a commission for his aunt.

He was in an enthusiastic mood. He seemed to see his way to living comfortably in Christminster in the course of a year or two, and knocking at the doors of one of those strongholds of learning of which he had dreamed so much. He might, of course, have gone there now, in some capacity or other, but he preferred to enter the city with a little more assurance as to means than he could be said to feel at present. A warm self-content suffused him when he considered what he had already done. Now and then as he went along he turned to face the peeps of country on either side of him. But he hardly saw them; the act was an automatic repetition of what he had been accustomed to do when less occupied; and the one matter which really engaged him was the mental estimate of his progress thus far.

'I have acquired quite an average student's power to read the common ancient classics, Latin in particular.' This was true, Jude possessing a facility in that language which enabled him with great ease to himself to beguile his lonely walks by imaginary conversations therein.

'I have read two books of the Iliad, besides being pretty familiar with passages such as the speech of Phoenix in the ninth book, the fight of Hector and Ajax in the fourteenth, the appearance of Achilles unarmed and his heavenly armour in the eighteenth, and the funeral games in the twenty-third. I have also done some Hesiod, a little scrap of Thucydides, and a lot of the Greek Testament. . . . I wish there was only one dialect, all the same.

'I have done some mathematics, including the first six and the eleventh and twelfth books of Euclid; and algebra as far as simple questions.

'I know something of the Fathers, and something of Roman and English history.

'These things are only a beginning. But I shall not make much further advance here, from the difficulty of getting books. Hence I must next concentrate all my energies on settling in Christminster. Once there I shall so advance, with the assistance I shall there get, that my present knowledge will appear to me but as childish ignorance. I must save money, and I will; and one of those colleges shall open its doors to me—shall welcome whom now it would spurn, if I wait twenty years for the welcome.

'I'll be D.D. before I have done!'

And then he continued to dream, and thought he might become even a bishop by leading a pure, energetic, wise, Christian life. And what an example he would set! If his income were £5000 a year, he would give away £4500 in one form and another, and live sumptuously (for him) on the remainder. Well, on second thoughts, a bishop was absurd. He would draw the line at an archdeacon. Perhaps a man could be as good and as learned and as useful in the capacity of archdeacon as in that of bishop. Yet he thought of the bishop again.

'Meanwhile I will read, as soon as I am settled in Christminster, the books I have not been able to get hold of here: Livy, Tacitus, Herodotus, Aeschylus, Sophocles, Aristophanes—'

'Ha, ha, ha! Hoity-toity!' The sounds were expressed in light voices on the other side of the hedge, but he did not notice them. His thoughts went on:

'—Euripides, Plato, Aristotle, Lucretius, Epictetus, Seneca, Antoninus. Then I must master other things: the Fathers thoroughly; Bede and ecclesiastical history generally; a smattering of Hebrew—I only know the letters as yet—'

'Hoity-toity!'

'—but I can work hard. I have staying power in abundance, thank God! and it is that which tells. . . . Yes, Christminster shall be my Alma Mater; and I'll be her beloved son, in whom she shall be well pleased.'

In his deep concentration on these transactions of the future Jude's walk had slackened, and he was now standing quite still, looking at the ground as though the future were thrown thereon by a magic lantern. On a sudden something smacked him sharply in the ear, and he became aware that a soft cold substance had been flung at him, and had fallen at his feet.

A glance told him what it was—a piece of flesh, the characteristic part of a barrow-pig, which the countrymen used for greasing their boots, as it was useless for any other purpose. Pigs were rather plentiful hereabout, being bred and fattened in large numbers in certain parts of North Wessex.

On the other side of the hedge was a stream, whence, as he now for the first time realized, had come the slight sounds of voices and laughter that had mingled with his dreams. He mounted the bank and looked over the fence. On the further side of the stream stood a small homestead, having a garden and pig-sties attached; in front of it, beside the brook, three young women were kneeling, with buckets and platters beside them containing heaps of pigs' chitterlings, which they were washing in the running water. One or two pairs of eyes slyly glanced up, and perceiving that his attention had at last been attracted, and that he was watching them, they braced themselves for inspection by putting their mouths demurely into shape and recommencing their rinsing operations with assiduity.

'Thank you!' said Jude severely.

'I *didn't* throw it, I tell you!' asserted one girl to her neighbour, as if unconscious of the young man's presence.

'Nor I,' the second answered.

'O, Anny, how can you!' said the third.

'If I had thrown anything at all, it shouldn't have been *that*!'

'Pooh! I don't care for him!' And they laughed and continued their work, without looking up, still ostentatiously accusing each other.

Jude grew sarcastic as he wiped his face, and caught their remarks.

'*You* didn't do it—O no!' he said to the up-stream one of the three.

She whom he addressed was a fine dark-eyed girl, not exactly handsome, but capable of passing as such at a little distance, despite some coarseness of skin and fibre. She had a round and prominent bosom, full lips, perfect teeth, and the rich complexion of a Cochin hen's egg. She was a complete and substantial female animal—no more, no less; and Jude was almost certain that to her was attributable the enterprise of attracting his attention from dreams of the humaner letters to what was simmering in the minds around him.

'That you'll never be told,' said she deedily.

'Whoever did it was wasteful of other people's property.'

'Oh, that's nothing.'

'But you want to speak to me, I suppose?'

'O yes; if you like to.'

'Shall I clamber across, or will you come to the plank above here?'

Perhaps she foresaw an opportunity; for somehow or other the eyes of the brown girl rested in his own when he had said the words, and there was a momentary flash of intelligence, a dumb announcement of affinity *in posse*, between herself and him, which, so far as Jude Fawley was concerned, had no sort of premeditation in it. She saw that he had singled her out from the three, as a woman is singled out in such cases, for no reasoned purpose of further acquaintance, but in commonplace obedience to conjunctive orders from headquarters, unconsciously received by unfortunate men when the last intention of their lives is to be occupied with the feminine.

Springing to her feet, she said: 'Bring back what is lying there.'

Jude was now aware that no message on any matter connected with her father's business had prompted her signal to him. He set down his basket of tools, picked up the scrap of offal, beat a pathway for himself with his stick, and got over the hedge. They walked in parallel lines, one on each bank of the stream, towards the small plank bridge. As the girl drew nearer to it, she gave, without Jude perceiving it, an adroit little suck to the interior of each of her cheeks in succession, by which curious and original manoeuvre she brought as by magic upon its smooth and rotund surface a perfect dimple, which she was able to retain there as long as she continued to smile. This production of dimples at will was a not unknown operation, which many attempted, but only a few succeeded in accomplishing.

They met in the middle of the plank, and Jude, tossing back her missile, seemed to expect her to explain why she had audaciously stopped him by this novel artillery instead of by hailing him.

But she, slyly looking in another direction, swayed herself backwards and forwards on her hand as it clutched the rail of the bridge; till, moved by amatory curiosity, she turned her eyes critically upon him.

'You don't think *I* would shy things at you?'

'O no.'

'We are doing this for my father, who naturally doesn't want anything thrown away. He makes that into dubbin.' She nodded towards the fragment on the grass.

'What made either of the others throw it, I wonder?' Jude asked, politely accepting her assertion, though he had very large doubts as to its truth.

'Impudence. Don't tell folk it was I, mind!'

'How can I? I don't know your name.'

'Ah, no. Shall I tell it to you?'

'Do!'

'Arabella Donn. I'm living here.'

'I must have known it if I had often come this way. But I mostly go straight along the high-road.'

'My father is a pig-breeder, and these girls are helping me wash the innerds for black-puddings and such like.'

They talked a little more and a little more, as they stood regarding each other and leaning against the hand-rail of the bridge. The unvoiced call of woman to man, which was uttered very distinctly by Arabella's personality, held Jude to the spot against his intention—almost against his will, and in a way new to his experience.

It is scarcely an exaggeration to say that till this moment Jude had never looked at a woman to consider her as such, but had vaguely regarded the sex as beings outside his life and purposes. He gazed from her eyes to her mouth, thence to her bosom, and to her full round naked arms, wet, mottled with the chill of the water, and firm as marble.

'What a nice-looking girl you are!' he murmured, though the words had not been necessary to express his sense of her magnetism.

'Ah, you should see me Sundays!' she said piquantly.

'I don't suppose I could?' he answered.

'That's for you to think on. There's nobody after me just now, though there med be in a week or two.' She had spoken this without a smile, and the dimples disappeared.

Jude felt himself drifting strangely, but could not help it. 'Will you let me?'

'I don't mind.'

By this time she had managed to get back one dimple by turning her face aside for a moment and repeating the odd little sucking operation before mentioned, Jude being still unconscious of more than a general impression of her appearance. 'Next Sunday?' he hazarded. 'To-morrow, that is?'

'Yes.'

'Shall I call?'

'Yes.'

She brightened with a little glow of triumph, swept him almost tenderly with her eyes in turning, and retracing her steps down the brookside grass rejoined her companions.

Jude Fawley shouldered his tool-basket and resumed his lonely way, filled with an ardour at which he mentally stood at gaze. He had just inhaled a single breath from a new atmosphere, which had evidently been hanging round him everywhere he went, for he knew not how long, but had somehow been divided from his actual breathing as by a sheet of glass. The intentions as to reading, working, and learning, which he had so precisely formulated only a few minutes earlier, were suffering a curious collapse into a corner, he knew not how.

'Well, it's only a bit of fun,' he said to himself, faintly conscious that to common-sense there was something lacking, and still more obviously something redundant, in the nature of this girl who had drawn him to her, which made it necessary that he should assert mere sportiveness on his part as his reason in seeking her—something in her quite antipathetic to that side of him which had been occupied with literary study and the magnificent Christminster dream. It had been no vestal who chose *that* missile for opening her attack on him. He saw this with his intellectual eye, just for a short fleeting while, as by the light of a falling lamp one might momentarily see an inscription on a wall before being enshrouded in darkness. And then this passing discriminative power was withdrawn, and Jude was lost to all conditions of things in the advent of a fresh and wild pleasure, that of having found a new channel for emotional interest hitherto unsuspected, though it had lain close beside him. He was to meet this enkindling one of the other sex on the following Sunday.

Meanwhile the girl had joined her companions, and she silently resumed her flicking and sousing of the chitterlings in the pellucid stream.

'Catched un, my dear?' laconically asked the girl called Anny.

'I don't know. I wish I had thrown something else than that!' regretfully murmured Arabella.

'Lord! he's nobody, though you med think so. He used to drive old Drusilla Fawley's bread-cart out at Marygreen, till he 'prenticed himself at Alfredston. Since then he's been very stuck up, and always reading. He wants to be a scholar, they say.'

'O, I don't care what he is, or anything about 'n. Don't you think it, my child!'

'O, don't ye! You needn't try to deceive us! What did you stay talking to him for, if you didn't want un? Whether you do or whether you don't, he's as simple as a child. I could see it as you courted on the bridge, when he looked at 'ee as if he had never seen a woman before in his born days. Well, he's to be had by any woman who can get him to care for her a bit, if she likes to set herself to catch him the right way.'

VII

THE next day Jude Fawley was pausing in his bedroom with the sloping ceiling, looking at the books on the table, and then at the black mark on the plaster above them, made by the smoke of his lamp in past months.

It was Sunday afternoon, four-and-twenty hours after his meeting with Arabella Donn. During the whole bygone week he had been resolving to set this afternoon apart for a special purpose—the re-reading of his Greek Testament—his new one, with better type than his old copy, following Griesbach's text as amended by numerous correctors, and with variorum readings in the margin. He was proud of the book, having obtained it by boldly writing to its London publisher, a thing he had never done before.

He had anticipated much pleasure in this afternoon's reading, under the quiet roof of his great-aunt's house as formerly, where he now slept only two nights a week. But a new thing, a great hitch, had happened yesterday in the gliding and noiseless current of his life, and he felt as a snake must feel who has sloughed off its winter skin, and cannot understand the brightness and sensitiveness of its new one.

He would not go out to meet her, after all. He sat down, opened the book, and with his elbows firmly planted on the table, and his hands to his temples, began at the beginning:

Η ΚΑΙΝΗ ΔΙΑΘΗΚΗ.

Had he promised to call for her? Surely he had! She would wait indoors, poor girl, and waste all her afternoon on account of him. There was a something in her, too, which was very winning, apart from promises. He ought not to break faith with her. Even though he had only Sundays and week-day evenings for reading he could afford one afternoon, seeing that other young men afforded so many. After to-day he would never probably see her again. Indeed, it would be impossible, considering what his plans were.

In short, as if materially, a compelling arm of extraordinary muscular power seized hold of him—something which had nothing in common with the spirits and influences that had moved him hitherto. This seemed to care little for his reason and his will, nothing for his so-called elevated intentions, and moved him along, as a violent schoolmaster a schoolboy he has seized by the collar, in a direction which tended towards the embrace of a woman for whom he had no respect, and whose life had nothing in common with his own except locality.

Η ΚΑΙΝΗ ΔΙΑΘΗΚΗ was no more heeded, and the predestinate Jude sprang up and across the room. Foreseeing such an event he had already arrayed himself in his best clothes. In three minutes he was out of the house and descending by the path across the wide vacant hollow of corn-ground which lay between the village and the isolated house of Arabella in the dip beyond the upland.

As he walked he looked at his watch. He could be back in two hours, easily, and a good long time would still remain to him for reading after tea.

Passing the few unhealthy fir-trees and cottage where the path joined the highway he hastened along, and struck away to the left, descending the steep side of the country to the west of the Brown House. Here at the base of the chalk formation he neared the brook that oozed from it, and followed the stream till he reached her dwelling. A smell of piggeries came from the back, and the grunting of the originators of that smell. He entered the garden, and knocked at the door with the knob of his stick.

Somebody had seen him through the window, for a male voice on the inside said:

'Arabella! Here's your young man come coorting! Mizzel, my girl!'

Jude winced at the words. Courting in such a business-like aspect as it evidently wore to the speaker was the last thing he was thinking of. He was going to walk with her, perhaps kiss her; but 'courting' was too coolly purposeful to be anything but repugnant to his ideas. The door was opened and he entered, just as Arabella came downstairs in radiant walking attire.

'Take a chair, Mr What's-your-name?' said her father, an energetic, black-whiskered man, in the same business-like tones Jude had heard from outside.

'I'd rather go out at once, wouldn't you?' she whispered to Jude.

'Yes,' said he. 'We'll walk up to the Brown House and back, we can do it in half-an-hour.'

Arabella looked so handsome amid her untidy surroundings that he felt glad he had come, and all the misgivings vanished that had hitherto haunted him.

First they clambered to the top of the great down, during which ascent he had occasionally to take her hand to assist her. Then they bore off to the left along the crest into the ridgeway, which they followed till it intersected the high-road at the Brown House aforesaid, the spot of his former fervid desires to behold Christminster. But he forgot them now. He talked the commonest local twaddle to Arabella with greater zest than he would have felt in discussing all the philosophies with all the Dons in the recently adored University, and passed the spot where he had knelt to Diana and Phoebus without remembering that there were any such people in the mythology, or that the Sun was anything else than a useful lamp for illuminating Arabella's face. An indescribable lightness of heel served to lift him along; and Jude, the incipient scholar, prospective D.D., Professor, Bishop, or what not, felt himself honoured and glorified by the condescension of this handsome country wench in agreeing to take a walk with him in her Sunday frock and ribbons.

They reached the Brown House barn—the point at which he had planned to turn back. While looking over the vast northern landscape from this spot they were struck by the rising of a dense volume of smoke from the neighbourhood of the little town which lay beneath them at a distance of a couple of miles.

'It is a fire,' said Arabella. 'Let's run and see it—do! It is not far!'

The tenderness which had grown up in Jude's bosom left him no will to thwart her inclination now—which pleased him in affording him excuse for a longer time with her. They started off down the hill almost at a trot; but on gaining level ground at the bottom, and walking a mile, they found that the spot of the fire was much further off than it had seemed.

Having begun their journey, however, they pushed on; but it was not till five o'clock that they found themselves on the scene—the distance being altogether about half-a-dozen miles from Marygreen, and three from Arabella's. The conflagration had been got under by the time they reached it, and after a short inspection of the melancholy ruins they retraced their steps—their course lying through the town of Alfredston.

Arabella said she would like some tea, and they entered an inn of an inferior class, and gave their order. As it was not for beer they had a long time to wait. The maid-servant recognized Jude, and whispered her surprise to her mistress in the background, that he, the student, 'who kept hisself up so particular', should have suddenly descended so low as to keep company with Arabella. The latter guessed what was being said, and laughed as she met the serious and tender gaze of her lover—the low and triumphant laugh of a careless woman who sees she is winning her game.

They sat and looked round the room, and at the picture of Samson and Delilah which hung on the wall, and the circular beer-stains on the table, and at the spittoons underfoot filled with sawdust. The whole aspect of the scene had that depressing effect on Jude which few places can produce like a taproom on a Sunday evening when the setting sun is slanting in, and no liquor is going, and the unfortunate wayfarer finds himself with no other haven of rest.

It began to grow dusk. They could not wait longer, really, for the tea, they said. 'Yet what else can we do?' asked Jude. 'It is a three-mile walk for you.'

'I suppose we can have some beer,' said Arabella.

'Beer, O yes. I had forgotten that. Somehow it seems odd to come to a public-house for beer on a Sunday evening.'

'But we didn't.'

'No, we didn't.' Jude by this time wished he was out of such an uncongenial atmosphere; but he ordered the beer, which was promptly brought.

Arabella tasted it. 'Ugh!' she said.

Jude tasted. 'What's the matter with it?' he asked. 'I don't understand beer very much now, it is true. I like it well enough, but it is bad to read on, and I find coffee better. But this seems all right.'

'Adulterated—I can't touch it!' She mentioned three or four ingredients that she detected in the liquor beyond malt and hops, much to Jude's surprise.

'How much you know!' he said good-humouredly.

Nevertheless she returned to the beer and drank her share, and they went on their way. It was now nearly dark, and as soon as they had withdrawn from the lights of the town they walked closer together, till they touched each other. She wondered why he did not put his arm around her waist, but he did not: he merely said what to himself seemed a quite bold enough thing: 'Take my arm.'

She took it, thoroughly, up to the shoulder. He felt the warmth of her body against his, and putting his stick under his other arm held with his right hand her right as it rested in its place.

'Now we are well together, dear, aren't we?' he observed.

'Yes,' said she; adding to herself: 'Rather mild!'

'How fast I have become!' he was thinking.

Thus they walked till they reached the foot of the upland, where they could see the white highway ascending before them in the gloom. From this point the only way of getting to Arabella's was by going up the incline, and dipping again into her valley on the right. Before they had climbed far they were nearly run into by two men who had been walking on the grass unseen.

'These lovers—you find 'em out o'doors in all seasons and weathers—lovers and homeless dogs only,' said one of the men as they vanished down the hill.

Arabella tittered lightly.

'Are we lovers?' asked Jude.

'You know best.'

'But you can tell me?'

For answer she inclined her head upon his shoulder. Jude took the hint, and encircling her waist with his arm, pulled her to him and kissed her.

They walked now no longer arm in arm but, as she had desired, clasped together. After all, what did it matter since it was dark, said Jude to himself. When they were half way up the long hill they paused as by arrangement, and he kissed her again. They reached the top, and he kissed her once more.

'You can keep your arm there, if you would like to,' she said gently.

He did so, thinking how trusting she was.

Thus they slowly went towards her home. He had left his cottage at half-past three, intending to be sitting down again to the New Testament by half-past five. It was nine o'clock when, with another embrace, he stood to deliver her up at her father's door.

She asked him to come in, if only for a minute, as it would seem so odd otherwise, and as if she had been out alone in the dark. He gave way, and followed her in. Immediately that the door was opened he found, in addition to her parents, several neighbours sitting round. They all spoke in a congratulatory manner, and took him seriously as Arabella's intended partner.

They did not belong to his set or circle, and he felt out of place and embarrassed. He had not meant this: a mere afternoon of pleasant walking with Arabella, that was all he had meant. He did not stay longer than to speak to her stepmother, a simple, quiet woman without features or character; and bidding them all good night plunged with a sense of relief into the track over the down.

But that sense was only temporary: Arabella soon reasserted her sway in his soul. He walked as if he felt himself to be another man from the Jude of yesterday. What were his books to him? what were his intentions, hitherto adhered to so strictly, as to not wasting a single minute of time day by day? 'Wasting!' It depended on your point of view to define that: he was just living for the first time: not wasting life. It was better to love a woman than to be a graduate, or a parson; ay, or a pope!

When he got back to the house his aunt had gone to bed, and a general consciousness of his neglect seemed written on the face of all things confronting him. He went upstairs without a light, and the dim interior of his room accosted him with sad inquiry. There lay his book open, just as he had left it, and the capital letters on the title-page regarded him with fixed reproach in the grey starlight, like the unclosed eyes of a dead man:

Η ΚΑΙΝΗ ΔΙΑΘΗΚΗ.

Jude had to leave early next morning for his usual week of absence at lodgings; and it was with a sense of futility that he threw into his basket upon his tools and other necessaries the unread book he had brought with him.

He kept his impassioned doings a secret almost from himself. Arabella, on the contrary, made them public among all her friends and acquaintance.

Retracing by the light of dawn the road he had followed a few hours earlier under cover of darkness, with his sweetheart by his side, he reached the bottom of the hill, where he walked slowly, and stood still. He was on the spot where he had given her the first kiss. As the sun had only just risen it was possible that nobody had passed there since. Jude looked on the ground and sighed. He looked closely, and could just discern in the damp dust the imprints of their feet as they had stood locked in each other's arms. She was not there now, and 'the embroidery of imagination upon the stuff of nature' so depicted her past presence that a void was in his heart which nothing could fill. A pollard willow stood close to the place, and that willow was different from all other willows in the world. Utter annihilation of the six days which must elapse before he could see her again as he had promised would have been his intensest wish if he had had only the week to live.

An hour and half later Arabella came along the same way with her two companions of the Saturday. She passed unheedingly the scene of the kiss, and the willow that marked it, though chattering freely on the subject to the other two.

'And what did he tell 'ee next?'

'Then he said—' And she related almost word for word some of his tenderest speeches. If Jude had been behind the fence he would have felt not a little surprised at learning how very few of his sayings and doings on the previous evening were private.

'You've got him to care for 'ee a bit, 'nation if you han't!' murmured Anny judicially. 'It's well to be you!'

In a few moments Arabella replied in a curiously low, hungry tone of latent sensuousness: 'I've got him to care for me: yes! But I want him to more than care for me; I want him to have me—to marry me! I must have him. I can't do without him. He's the sort of man I long for. I shall go mad if I can't give myself to him altogether! I felt I should when I first saw him!'

'As he is a romancing, straightfor'ard, honest chap, he's to be had, and as a husband, if you set about catching him in the right way.'

Arabella remained thinking awhile. 'What med be the right way?' she asked.

'O you don't know—you don't!' said Sarah, the third girl.

'On my word I don't!—No further, that is, than by plain courting, and taking care he don't go too far!'

The third girl looked at the second. 'She *don't* know!'

''Tis clear she don't!' said Anny.

'And having lived in a town, too, as one may say! Well, we can teach 'ee some'at then, as well as you us.'

'Yes. And how do you mean—a sure way to gain a man? Take me for an innocent, and have done wi'it!'

'As a husband.'

'A countryman that's honourable and serious-minded such as he; God forbid that I should say a sojer, or sailor, or commercial gent from the towns, or any of them that be slippery with poor women! I'd do no friend that harm!'

'Well, such as he, of course!'

Arabella's companions looked at each other, and turning up their eyes in drollery began smirking. Then one went up close to Arabella, and, although nobody was near, imparted some information in a low tone, the other observing curiously the effect upon Arabella.

'Ah!' said the last-named slowly. 'I own I didn't think of that way! . . . But suppose he *isn't* honourable? A woman had better not have tried it!'

'Nothing venture nothing have! Besides, you make sure that he's honourable before you begin. You'd be safe enough with yours. I wish I had the chance! Lots of girls do it; or do you think they'd get married at all?'

Arabella pursued her way in silent thought. 'I'll try it!' she whispered; but not to them.

VIII

One week's end Jude was as usual walking out to his aunt's at Marygreen from his lodging in Alfredston, a walk which now had large attractions for him quite other than his desire to see his aged and morose relative. He diverged to the right before ascending the hill with the single purpose of gaining, on his way, a glimpse of Arabella that should not come into the reckoning of regular appointments. Before quite reaching the homestead his alert eye perceived the top of her head moving quickly hither and thither over the garden hedge. Entering the gate he found that three young unfattened pigs had escaped from their sty by leaping clean over the top, and that she was endeavouring unassisted to drive them in through the door which she had set open. The lines of her countenance changed from the rigidity of business to the softness of love when she saw Jude, and she bent her eyes languishingly upon him. The animals took advantage of the pause by doubling and bolting out of the way.

'They were only put in this morning!' she cried, stimulated to pursue in spite of her lover's presence. 'They were drove from Spaddleholt Farm only yesterday, where father bought 'em at a stiff price enough. They were wanting to get home again, the stupid toads! Will you shut the garden gate, dear, and help me to get 'em in? There are no men-folk at home, only mother, and they'll be lost if we don't mind.'

He set himself to assist, and dodged this way and that over the potato rows and the cabbages. Every now and then they ran together, when he caught her for a moment and kissed her. The first pig was got back promptly; the second with some difficulty; the third, a long-legged creature, was more obstinate and agile. He plunged through a hole in the garden hedge, and into the lane.

'He'll be lost if I don't follow 'n!' said she. 'Come along with me!'

She rushed in full pursuit out of the garden. Jude alongside her, barely contriving to keep the fugitive in sight. Occasionally they would shout to some boy to stop the animal, but he always wriggled past and ran on as before.

'Let me take your hand, darling,' said Jude. 'You are getting out of breath.' She gave him her now hot hand with apparent willingness, and they trotted along together.

'This comes of driving 'em home,' she remarked. 'They always know the way back if you do that. They ought to have been carted over.'

By this time the pig had reached an unfastened gate admitting to the open down, across which he sped with all the agility his little legs afforded. As soon as the pursuers had entered and ascended to the top of the high ground it became apparent that they would have to run all the way to the farmer's if they wished to get at him. From this summit he could be seen as a minute speck, following an unerring line towards his old home.

'It is no good!' cried Arabella. 'He'll be there long before we get there. It don't matter now we know he's not lost or stolen on the way. They'll see it is ours, and send un back. O dear, how hot I be!'

Without relinquishing her hold of Jude's hand she swerved aside and flung herself down on the sod under a stunted thorn, precipitately pulling Jude on to his knees at the same time.

'O, I ask pardon—I nearly threw you down, didn't I! But I am so tired!'

She lay supine, and straight as an arrow, on the sloping sod of this hill-top, gazing up into the blue miles of the sky, and still retaining her warm hold of Jude's hand. He reclined on his elbow near her.

'We've run all this way for nothing,' she went on, her form heaving and falling in quick pants, her face flushed, her full red lips parted, and a fine dew of perspiration on her skin. 'Well—why don't you speak, deary?'

'I'm blown too. It was all up hill.'

They were in absolute solitude—the most apparent of all solitudes, that of empty surrounding space. Nobody could be nearer than a mile to them without their seeing them. They were, in fact, on one of the summits of the county, and the distant landscape around Christminster could be discerned from where they lay. But Jude did not think of that then.

'O, I can see such a pretty thing up this tree,' said Arabella. 'A sort of a—caterpillar, of the most loveliest green and yellow you ever came across!'

'Where?' said Jude, sitting up.

'You can't see him there—you must come here,' said she.

He bent nearer and put his head in front of hers. 'No—I can't see it,' he said.

'Why, on the limb there where it branches off—close to the moving leaf—there!' She gently pulled him down beside her.

'I don't see it,' he repeated, the back of his head against her cheek. 'But I can, perhaps, standing up.' He stood accordingly, placing himself in the direct line of her gaze.

'How stupid you are!' she said crossly, turning away her face.

'I don't care to see it, dear: why should I?' he replied, looking down upon her. 'Get up, Abby.'

'Why?'

'I want you to let me kiss you. I've been waiting to ever so long!'

She rolled round her face, remained a moment looking deedily aslant at him; then with a slight curl of the lip sprang to her feet, and exclaiming abruptly 'I must mizzel!' walked off quickly homeward. Jude followed and rejoined her.

'Just one!' he coaxed.

'Shan't!' she said.

He, surprised: 'What's the matter?'

She kept her two lips resentfully together, and Jude followed her like a pet lamb till she slackened her pace and walked beside him, talking calmly on indifferent subjects, and always checking him if he tried to take her hand or clasp her waist. Thus they descended to the precincts of her father's homestead, and Arabella went in, nodding good-bye to him with a supercilious, affronted air.

'I expect I took too much liberty with her, somehow,' Jude said to himself, as he withdrew with a sigh and went on to Marygreen.

On Sunday morning the interior of Arabella's home was, as usual, the scene of a grand weekly cooking, the preparation of the special

Sunday dinner. Her father was shaving before a little glass hung on the mullion of the window, and her mother and Arabella herself were shelling beans hard by. A neighbour passed on her way home from morning service at the nearest church, and seeing Donn engaged at the window with the razor, nodded and came in.

She at once spoke playfully to Arabella: 'I zeed 'ee running with 'un—hee-hee! I hope 'tis coming to something?'

Arabella merely threw a look of consciousness into her face without raising her eyes.

'He's for Christminster, I hear, as soon as he can get there.'

'Have you heard that lately—quite lately?' asked Arabella with a jealous, tigerish indrawing of breath.

'O no! But it has been known a long time that it is his plan. He's on'y waiting here for an opening. Ah well: he must walk about with somebody I s'pose. Young men don't mean much now-a-days. 'Tis a sip here and a sip there with 'em. 'Twas different in my time.'

When the gossip had departed Arabella said suddenly to her mother: 'I want you and father to go and inquire how the Edlins be, this evening after tea. Or no—there's evening service at Fensworth—you can walk to that.'

'Oh? What's up to-night, then?'

'Nothing. Only I want the house to myself. He's shy; and I can't get un to come in when you are here. I shall let him slip through my fingers if I don't mind, much as I care for 'n!'

'If it is fine we med as well go, since you wish.'

In the afternoon Arabella met and walked with Jude, who had now for weeks ceased to look into a book of Greek, Latin, or any other tongue. They wandered up the slopes till they reached the green track along the ridge, which they followed to the circular British earth-bank adjoining, Jude thinking of the great age of the trackway, and of the drovers who had frequented it, probably before the Romans knew the country. Up from the level lands below them floated the chime of church bells. Presently they were reduced to one note, which quickened, and stopped.

'Now we'll go back,' said Arabella, who had attended to the sounds.

Jude assented. So long as he was near her he minded little where he was. When they arrived at her house he said lingeringly: 'I won't come in. Why are you in such a hurry to go in to-night? It is not near dark.'

'Wait a moment,' said she. She tried the handle of the door and found it locked.

'Ah—they are gone to church,' she added. And searching behind the scraper she found the key and unlocked the door. 'Now, you'll come in a moment?' she asked lightly. 'We shall be all alone.'

'Certainly,' said Jude with alacrity, the case being unexpectedly altered.

Indoors they went. Did he want any tea? No, it was too late: he would rather sit and talk to her. She took off her jacket and hat, and they sat down—naturally enough close together.

'Don't touch me, please,' she said softly. 'I am part egg-shell. Or perhaps I had better put it in a safe place.' She began unfastening the collar of her gown.

'What is it?' said her lover.

'An egg—a cochin's egg. I am hatching a very rare sort. I carry it about everywhere with me, and it will get hatched in less than three weeks.'

'Where do you carry it?'

'Just here.' She put her hand into her bosom and drew out the egg, which was wrapped in wool, outside it being a piece of pig's bladder, in case of accidents. Having exhibited it to him she put it back. 'Now mind you don't come near me. I don't want to get it broke, and have to begin another.'

'Why do you do such a strange thing?'

'It's an old custom. I suppose it is natural for a woman to want to bring live things into the world.'

'It is very awkward for me just now,' he said, laughing.

'It serves you right. There—that's all you can have of me.'

She had turned round her chair, and, reaching over the back of it, presented her cheek to him gingerly.

'That's very shabby of you!'

'You should have catched me a minute ago when I had put the egg down! There!' she said defiantly, 'I am without it now!' She had quickly withdrawn the egg a second time; but before he could quite reach her she had put it back as quickly, laughing with the excitement of her strategy. Then there was a little struggle, Jude making a plunge for it and capturing it triumphantly. Her face flushed; and becoming suddenly conscious he flushed also.

They looked at each other, panting; till he rose and said: 'One kiss, now I can do it without damage to property; and I'll go!'

But she had jumped up too. 'You must find me first!' she cried.

Her lover followed her as she withdrew. It was now dark inside the room, and the window being small he could not discover for a long time what had become of her, till a laugh revealed her to have rushed up the stairs, whither Jude rushed at her heels.

IX

It was some two months later in the year, and the pair had met constantly during the interval. Arabella seemed dissatisfied; she was always imagining, and waiting, and wondering.

One day she met the itinerant Vilbert. She, like all the cottagers thereabout, knew the quack well, and she began telling him of her experiences. Arabella had been gloomy, but before he left her she had grown brighter. That evening she kept an appointment with Jude, who seemed sad.

'I'm going away,' he said to her. 'I think I ought to go. I think it will be better both for you and me. I wish some things had never begun! I was much to blame, I know. But it is never too late to mend.'

Arabella began to cry. 'How do you know it is not too late?' she said. 'That's all very well to say! I haven't told you yet!' and she looked into his face with streaming eyes.

'What?' he asked, turning pale. 'Not . . . ?'

'Yes! And what shall I do if you desert me?'

'O Arabella—how can you say that, my dear. You *know* I wouldn't desert you!'

'Well then—'

'I have next to no wages as yet, you know; or perhaps I should have thought of this before. . . . But, of course, if that's the case, we must marry! What other thing do you think I could dream of doing?'

'I thought—I thought, deary, perhaps you would go away all the more for that, and leave me to face it alone!'

'You knew better! Of course I never dreamt six months ago, or even three, of marrying. It is a complete smashing up of my plans—I mean my plans before I knew you, my dear. But what are they, after all! Dreams about books, and degrees, and impossible fellowships, and all that. Certainly we'll marry: we must!'

That night he went out alone, and walked in the dark, self-communing. He knew well, too well, in the secret centre of his brain, that Arabella was not worth a great deal as a specimen of womankind. Yet, such being the custom of the rural districts among honourable young men who had drifted so far into intimacy with a woman as he unfortunately had done, he was ready to abide by what he had said, and take the consequences. For his own soothing he kept up a factitious belief in her. His idea of her was the thing of most consequence, not Arabella herself, he sometimes said laconically.

The banns were put in and published the very next Sunday. The people of the parish all said what a simple fool young Fawley was. All his reading had only come to this, that he would have to sell his books to buy saucepans. Those who guessed the probable state of affairs, Arabella's parents being among them, declared that it was the sort of conduct they would have expected of such an honest young man as Jude in reparation of the wrong he had done his innocent sweetheart. The parson who married them seemed to think it satisfactory too.

And so, standing before the aforesaid officiator, the two swore that at every other time of their lives till death took them, they would assuredly believe, feel, and desire precisely as they had believed, felt, and desired during the few preceding weeks. What was as remarkable as the undertaking itself was the fact that nobody seemed at all surprised at what they swore.

Fawley's aunt being a baker she made him a bride-cake, saying bitterly that it was the last thing she could do for him, poor silly fellow; and that it would have been far better if, instead of his living to trouble her, he had gone underground years before with his father and mother. Of this cake Arabella took some slices, wrapped them up in white note-paper, and sent them to her companions in the pork-dressing business, Anny and Sarah, labelling each packet '*In remembrance of good advice*'.

The prospects of the newly married couple were certainly not very brilliant even to the most sanguine mind. He, a stonemason's apprentice, nineteen years of age, was working for half wages till he should be out of his time. His wife was absolutely useless in a town-lodging, where he at first had considered it would be necessary for them to live. But the urgent need of adding to income in ever so little a degree caused him to take a lonely roadside cottage between the Brown House and Marygreen, that he might have the profits of a vegetable garden, and utilize her past experiences by letting her keep a pig. But it was not the sort of life he had bargained for, and it was a long way to walk to and from Alfredston every day. Arabella, however, felt that all these makeshifts were temporary: she had gained a husband; that was the thing—a husband with a lot of earning power in him for buying her frocks and hats when he should begin to get frightened a bit, and stick to his trade, and throw aside those stupid books for practical undertakings.

So to the cottage he took her on the evening of the marriage, giving up his old room at his aunt's—where so much of the hard labour at Greek and Latin had been carried on.

A little chill overspread him at her first unrobing. A long tail of hair, which Arabella wore twisted up in an enormous knob at the back of her head, was deliberately unfastened, stroked out, and hung upon the looking-glass which he had bought her.

'What—it wasn't your own?' he said, with a sudden distaste for her.

'O no—it never is nowadays with the better class.'

'Nonsense! Perhaps not in towns. But in the country it is supposed to be different. Besides, you've enough of your own, surely?'

'Yes, enough as country notions go. But in towns the men expect more, and when I was barmaid at Aldbrickham—'

'Barmaid at Aldbrickham?'

'Well, not exactly barmaid—I used to draw the drink at a public-house there—just for a little time; that was all. Some people put me up to getting this, and I bought it just for a fancy. The more you have the better in Aldbrickham, which is a finer town than all your Christminsters. Every lady of position wears false hair—the barber's assistant told me so.'

Jude thought with a feeling of sickness that though this might be true to some extent, for all that he knew, many unsophisticated girls would and did go to towns and remain there for years without losing their simplicity of life and embellishments. Others, alas, had an instinct towards artificiality in their very blood, and became adepts in counterfeiting at the first glimpse of it. However, perhaps there was no great sin in a woman adding to her hair, and he resolved to think no more of it.

A new-made wife can usually manage to excite interest for a few weeks, even though the prospects of the household ways and means are cloudy. There is a certain piquancy about her situation, and her manner to her acquaintance at the sense of it, which carries off the gloom of facts, and renders even the humblest bride independent awhile of the real. Mrs Jude Fawley was walking in the streets of Alfredston one market-day with this quality in her carriage when she met Anny her former friend, whom she had not seen since the wedding.

As usual they laughed before talking; the world seemed funny to them without saying it.

'So it turned out a good plan you see!' remarked the girl to the wife. 'I knew it would with such as him. He's a dear good fellow, and you ought to be proud of un.'

'I am,' said Mrs Fawley quietly.

'And when do you expect—?'

'Ssh! Not at all.'

'What!'

'I was mistaken.'

'O Arabella, Arabella; you be a deep one! Mistaken! well, that's clever—it's a real stroke of genius! It is a thing I never thought o', wi' all my experience! I never thought beyond bringing about the real thing—not that one could sham it!'

'Don't you be too quick to cry sham! 'Twasn't sham. I didn't know.'

'My word—won't he be in a taking! He'll give it to 'ee o' Saturday nights! Whatever it was, he'll say it was a trick—a double one, by the Lord!'

'I'll own to the first, but not to the second. . . . Pooh—he won't care! He'll be glad I was wrong in what I said. He'll shake down, bless 'ee—men always do. What can 'em do otherwise? Married is married.'

Nevertheless it was with a little uneasiness that Arabella approached the time when in the natural course of things she would have to reveal that the alarm she had raised had been without foundation. The occasion was one evening at bed-time, and they were in their chamber in the lonely cottage by the wayside to which Jude walked home from his work every day. He had worked hard the whole twelve hours, and had retired to rest before his wife. When she came into the room he was between sleeping and waking, and was barely conscious of her undressing before the little looking-glass as he lay.

One action of hers, however, brought him to full cognition. Her face being reflected towards him as she sat, he could perceive that she was amusing herself by artificially producing in each cheek the dimple before alluded to, a curious accomplishment of which she was mistress, effecting it by a momentary suction. It seemed to him for the first time that the dimples were far oftener absent from her face during his intercourse with her nowadays than they had been in the earlier weeks of their acquaintance.

'Don't do that, Arabella!' he said suddenly. 'There is no harm in it, but—I don't like to see you.'

She turned and laughed. 'Lord, I didn't know you were awake!' she said. 'How countrified you are! That's nothing.'

'Where did you learn it?'

'Nowhere that I know of. They used to stay without any trouble when I was at the public-house; but now they won't. My face was fatter then.'

'I don't care about dimples. I don't think they improve a woman—particularly a married woman, and of full-sized figure like you.'

'Most men think otherwise.'

'I don't care what most men think, if they do. How do you know?'

'I used to be told so when I was serving in the tap-room.'

'Ah—that public-house experience accounts for your knowing about the adulteration of the ale when we went and had some that Sunday evening. I thought when I married you that you had always lived in your father's house.'

'You ought to have known better than that, and seen I was a

little more finished than I could have been by staying where I was born. There was not much to do at home, and I was eating my head off, so I went away for three months.'

'You'll soon have plenty to do now, dear, won't you?'

'How do you mean?'

'Why, of course—little things to make.'

'Oh.'

'When will it be? Can't you tell me exactly, instead of in such general terms as you have used?'

'Tell you?'

'Yes—the date.'

'There's nothing to tell. I made a mistake.'

'What?'

'It was a mistake.'

He sat bolt upright in bed and looked at her. 'How can that be?'

'Women fancy wrong things sometimes.'

'But—! Why, of course, so unprepared as I was, without a stick of furniture, and hardly a shilling, I shouldn't have hurried on our affair, and brought you to a half-furnished hut before I was ready, if it had not been for the news you gave me, which made it necessary to save you, ready or no. . . . Good God!'

'Don't take on, dear. What's done can't be undone.'

'I have no more to say!'

He gave the answer simply, and lay down; and there was silence between them.

When Jude awoke the next morning he seemed to see the world with a different eye. As to the point in question he was compelled to accept her word; in the circumstances he could not have acted otherwise while ordinary notions prevailed. But how came they to prevail?

There seemed to him, vaguely and dimly, something wrong in a social ritual which made necessary a cancelling of well-formed schemes involving years of thought and labour, of fore-going a man's one opportunity of showing himself superior to the lower animals, and of contributing his units of work to the general progress of his generation, because of a momentary surprise by a new and transitory instinct which had nothing in it of the nature of vice, and could be only at the most called weakness. He was inclined to inquire what he had done, or she lost, for that matter, that he deserved to be caught in a gin which would cripple him, if not her also, for the rest of a lifetime? There was perhaps something fortunate in the fact that the immediate reason of his marriage had proved to be non-existent. But the marriage remained.

X

THE time arrived for killing the pig which Jude and his wife had fattened in their sty during the autumn months, and the butchering was timed to take place as soon as it was light in the morning, so that Jude might get to Alfredston without losing more than a quarter of a day.

The night had seemed strangely silent. Jude looked out of the window long before dawn, and perceived that the ground was covered with snow—snow rather deep for the season, it seemed, a few flakes still falling.

'I'm afraid the pig-killer won't be able to come,' he said to Arabella.

'Oh, he'll come. You must get up and make the water hot, if you want Challow to scald him. Though I like singing best.'

'I'll get up,' said Jude. 'I like the way of my own county.'

He went downstairs, lit the fire under the copper, and began feeding it with bean-stalks, all the time without a candle, the blaze flinging a cheerful shine into the room: though for him the sense of cheerfulness was lessened by thoughts on the reason of that blaze—to heat water to scale the bristles from the body of an animal that as yet lived, and whose voice could be continually heard from a corner of the garden. At half-past six, the time of appointment with the butcher, the water boiled, and Jude's wife came downstairs.

'Is Challow come?' she asked.

'No.'

They waited, and it grew lighter, with the dreary light of a snowy dawn. She went out, gazed along the road, and returning said, 'He's not coming. Drunk last night, I expect. The snow is not enough to hinder him, surely!'

'Then we must put it off. It is only the water boiled for nothing. The snow may be deep in the valley.'

'Can't be put off. There's no more victuals for the pig. He ate the last mixing o'barleymeal yesterday morning.'

'Yesterday morning? What has he lived on since?'

'Nothing.'

'What—he has been starving?'

'Yes. We always do it the last day or two, to save bother with the innerds. What ignorance, not to know that!'

'That accounts for his crying so. Poor creature!'

'Well—you must do the sticking—there's no help for it. I'll show you how. Or I'll do it myself—I think I could. Though as it is such a big pig I had rather Challow had done it. However, his basket o'knives and things have been already sent on here, and we can use 'em.'

'Of course you shan't do it,' said Jude. 'I'll do it, since it must be done.'

He went out to the sty, shovelled away the snow for the space of a couple of yards or more, and placed the stool in front, with the knives and ropes at hand. A robin peered down at the preparations from the nearest tree, and, not liking the sinister look of the scene, flew away, though hungry. By this time Arabella had joined her husband, and Jude, rope in hand, got into the sty, and noosed the affrighted animal, who, beginning with a squeak of surprise, rose to repeated cries of rage. Arabella opened the sty-door, and together they hoisted the victim on to the stool, legs upward, and while Jude held him Arabella bound him down, looping the cord over his legs to keep him from struggling.

The animal's note changed its quality. It was not now rage, but the cry of despair; long drawn, slow and hopeless.

'Upon my soul I would sooner have gone without the pig than have had this to do!' said Jude. 'A creature I have fed with my own hands.'

'Don't be such a tender-hearted fool! There's the sticking-knife—the one with the point. Now whatever you do, don't stick un too deep.'

'I'll stick him effectually, so as to make short work of it. That's the chief thing.'

'You must not!' she cried. 'The meat must be well bled, and to do that he must die slow. We shall lose a shilling a score if the meat is red and bloody! Just touch the vein, that's all. I was brought up to it, and I know. Every good butcher keeps un bleeding long. He ought to be eight or ten minutes dying, at least.'

'He shall not be half a minute if I can help it, however the meat may look,' said Jude determinedly. Scraping the bristles from the pig's upturned throat, as he had seen the butchers do, he slit the fat; then plunged in the knife with all his might.

''Od damn it all!' she cried, 'that ever I should say it! You've over-stuck un! And I telling you all the time—'

'Do be quiet, Arabella, and have a little pity on the creature!'

'Hold up the pail to catch the blood, and don't talk!'

However unworkmanlike the deed, it had been mercifully done. The blood flowed out in a torrent instead of in the trickling stream she had desired. The dying animal's cry assumed its third and final tone, the shriek of agony; his glazing eyes riveting themselves on Arabella with the eloquently keen reproach of a creature recognizing at last the treachery of those who had seemed his only friends.

'Make un stop that!' said Arabella. 'Such a noise will bring somebody or other up here, and I don't want people to know we are doing it ourselves.' Picking up the knife from the ground whereon Jude had flung it, she slipped it into the gash, and slit the windpipe. The pig was instantly silent, his dying breath coming through the hole.

'That's better,' she said.

'It is a hateful business!' said he.

'Pigs must be killed.'

The animal heaved in a final convulsion, and, despite the rope, kicked out with all his last strength. A tablespoonful of black clot came forth, the trickling of red blood having ceased for some seconds.

'That's it: now he'll go,' said she. 'Artful creatures—they always keep back a drop like that as long as they can!'

The last plunge had come so unexpectedly as to make Jude stagger, and in recovering himself he kicked over the vessel in which the blood had been caught.

'There!' she cried, thoroughly in a passion. 'Now I can't make any blackpot. There's a waste, all through you!'

Jude put the pail upright, but only about a third of the whole steaming liquid was left in it, the main part being splashed over the snow, and forming a dismal, sordid, ugly spectacle—to those who saw it as other than an ordinary obtaining of meat. The lips and nostrils of the animal turned livid, then white, and the muscles of his limbs relaxed.

'Thank God!' Jude said. 'He's dead.'

'What's God got to do with such a messy job as a pig-killing, I should like to know!' she said scornfully. 'Poor folks must live.'

'I know, I know,' said he. 'I don't scold you.'

Suddenly they became aware of a voice at hand.

'Well done, young married volk! I couldn't have carried it out much better myself, cuss me if I could!' The voice, which was husky, came from the garden-gate, and looking up from the scene of slaughter they saw the burly form of Mr Challow leaning over the gate, critically surveying their performance.

''Tis well for 'ee to stand there and glane!' said Arabella. 'Owing to your being late the meat is bloodied and half spoiled! 'Twon't fetch so much by a shilling a score!'

Challow expressed his contrition. 'You should have waited a bit,' he said, shaking his head, 'and not have done this—in the delicate state, too, that you be in at present, ma'am. 'Tis risking yourself too much.'

'You needn't be concerned about that,' said Arabella, laughing. Jude too laughed, but there was a strong flavour of bitterness in his amusement.

Challow made up for his neglect of the killing by zeal in the scalding and scraping. Jude felt dissatisfied with himself as a man at what he had done, though aware of his lack of common-sense, and that the deed would have amounted to the same thing if carried out by deputy. The white snow, stained with the blood of his fellow-mortal, wore an illogical look to him as a lover of justice, not to say a Christian; but he could not see how the matter was to be mended. No doubt he was, as his wife had called him, a tender-hearted fool.

He did not like the road to Alfredston now. It stared him cynically in the face. The wayside objects reminded him so much of his courtship of his wife that, to keep them out of his eyes, he read whenever he could as he walked to and from his work. Yet he sometimes felt that by caring for books he was not escaping commonplace nor gaining rare ideas, every working-man being of that taste now. When passing near the spot by the stream on which he had first made her acquaintance he one day heard voices just as he had done at that earlier time. One of the girls who had been Arabella's companions was talking to a friend in a shed, himself being the subject of discourse, possibly because they had seen him in the distance. They were quite unaware that the shed-walls were so thin that he could hear their words as he passed.

'Howsomever, 'twas I put her up to it! "Nothing venture nothing have," I said. If I hadn't she'd no more have been his mis'ess than I.'

''Tis my belief she knew there was nothing the matter when she told him she was . . .'

What had Arabella been put up to by this woman, so that he should make her his 'mis'ess', otherwise wife? The suggestion was horridly unpleasant, and it rankled in his mind so much that instead of entering his own cottage when he reached it he flung his basket inside the garden-gate and passed on, determined to go and see his old aunt and get some supper there.

This made his arrival home rather late. Arabella, however, was busy melting down lard from fat of the deceased pig, for she had been out on a jaunt all day, and so delayed her work. Dreading lest what he had heard should lead him to say something regrettable to her he spoke little. But Arabella was very talkative, and said among other things that she wanted some money. Seeing the book sticking out of his pocket she added that he ought to earn more.

'An apprentice's wages are not meant to be enough to keep a wife on, as a rule, my dear.'

'Then you shouldn't have had one.'

'Come, Arabella! That's too bad, when you know how it came about.'

'I'll declare afore Heaven that I thought what I told you was true. Doctor Vilbert thought so. It was a good job for you that it wasn't so!'

'I don't mean that,' he said hastily. 'I mean before that time. I know it was not your fault; but those women friends of yours gave you bad advice. If they hadn't, or you hadn't taken it, we should at this moment have been free from a bond which, not to mince matters, galls both of us devilishly. It may be very sad, but it is true.'

'Who's been telling you about my friends? What advice? I insist upon your telling me.'

'Pooh—I'd rather not.'

'But you shall—you ought to. It is mean of 'ee not to!'

'Very well.' And he hinted gently what had been revealed to him. 'But I don't wish to dwell upon it. Let us say no more about it.'

Her defensive manner collapsed. 'That was nothing,' she said, laughing coldly. 'Every woman has a right to do such as that. The risk is hers.'

'I quite deny it, Bella. She might if no life-long penalty attached to it for the man, or, in his default, for herself; if the weakness of the moment could end with the moment, or even with the year. But when effects stretch so far she should not go and do that which entraps a man if he is honest, or herself if he is otherwise.'

'What ought I to have done?'

'Given me time. . . . Why do you fuss yourself about melting down that pig's fat to-night? Please put it away!'

'Then I must do it to-morrow morning. It won't keep.'

'Very well—do.'

XI

Next morning, which was Sunday, she resumed operations about ten o'clock: and the renewed work recalled the conversation which had accompanied it the night before, and put her back into the same intractable temper.

'That's the story about me in Marygreen, is it—that I entrapped 'ee? Much of a catch you were, Lord send!' As she warmed she saw some of Jude's dear ancient classics on a table where they ought not to have been laid. 'I won't have them books here in the way!' she cried petulantly; and seizing them one by one she began throwing them upon the floor.

'Leave my books alone!' he said. 'You might have thrown them aside if you had liked, but as to soiling them like that, it is disgusting!' In the operation of making lard Arabella's hands had become smeared with the hot grease, and her fingers consequently left very perceptible imprints on the book-covers. She continued deliberately to toss the books severally upon the floor, till Jude, incensed beyond bearing, caught her by the arms to make her leave off. Somehow, in doing so, he loosened the fastening of her hair, and it rolled about her ears.

'Let me go!' she said.

'Promise to leave the books alone.'

She hesitated. 'Let me go!' she repeated.

'Promise!'

After a pause: 'I do.'

Jude relinquished his hold, and she crossed the room to the door, out of which she went with a set face, and into the highway. Here she began to saunter up and down, perversely pulling her hair into a worse disorder than he had caused, and unfastening several buttons of her gown. It was a fine Sunday morning, dry, clear and frosty, and the bells of Alfredston Church could be heard on the breeze from the north. People were going along the road, dressed in their holiday clothes; they were mainly lovers—such pairs as Jude and Arabella had been when they sported along the same track some months earlier. These pedestrians turned to stare at the extraordinary spectacle she now presented, bonnetless, her dishevelled hair blowing in the wind, her bodice apart, her sleeves rolled above her elbows for her work, and her hands reeking with melted fat. One of the passers said in mock terror: 'Good Lord deliver us!'

'See how he's served me!' she cried. 'Making me work Sunday mornings when I ought to be going to my church, and tearing my hair off my head, and my gown off my back!'

Jude was exasperated, and went out to drag her in by main force. Then he suddenly lost his heat. Illuminated with the sense that all was over between them, and that it mattered not what she did, or he, her husband stood still, regarding her. Their lives were ruined, he thought; ruined by the fundamental error of their matrimonial union: that of having based a permanent contract on a temporary feeling which had no necessary connection with affinities that alone render a life-long comradeship tolerable.

'Going to ill-use me on principle, as your father ill-used your mother, and your father's sister ill-used her husband?' she asked. 'All you be a queer lot as husbands and wives!'

Jude fixed an arrested, surprised look on her. But she said no more, and continued her saunter till she was tired. He left the spot, and, after wandering vaguely a little while, walked in the direction of Marygreen. Here he called upon his great-aunt, whose infirmities daily increased.

'Aunt—did my father ill-use my mother, and my aunt her husband?' said Jude abruptly, sitting down by the fire.

She raised her ancient eyes under the rim of the bygone bonnet that she always wore. 'Who's been telling you that?' she said.

'I have heard it spoken of, and want to know all.'

'You med so well, I s'pose; though your wife—I reckon 'twas she—must have been a fool to open up that! There isn't much to know after all. Your father and mother couldn't get on together, and they parted. It was coming home from Alfredston market, when you were a baby—on the hill by the Brown House barn—that they had their last difference, and took leave of one another for the last time. Your mother soon afterwards died—she drowned herself, in short, and your father went away with you to South Wessex, and never came here any more.'

Jude recalled his father's silence about North Wessex and Jude's mother, never speaking of either till his dying day.

'It was the same with your father's sister. Her husband offended her, and she so disliked living with him afterwards that she went away to London with her little maid. The Fawleys were not made for wedlock: it never seemed to sit well upon us. There's sommat in our blood that won't take kindly to the notion of being bound to do what we do readily enough if not bound. That's why you ought to have hearkened to me, and not ha' married.'

'Where did father and mother part—by the Brown House, did you say?'

'A little further on—where the road to Fenworth branches off, and the handpost stands. A gibbet once stood there not unconnected with our history. But let that be.'

In the dusk of that evening Jude walked away from his old aunt's as if to go home. But as soon as he reached the open down he struck out upon it till he came to a large round pond. The frost continued, though it was not particularly sharp, and the larger stars overhead came out slow and flickering. Jude put one foot on the edge of the ice, and then the other; it cracked under his weight; but this did not deter him. He ploughed his way inward to the centre, the ice making sharp noises as he went. When just about the middle he looked around him and gave a jump. The cracking repeated itself; but he did not go down. He jumped again, but the cracking had ceased. Jude went back to the edge, and stepped upon the ground.

It was curious, he thought. What was he reserved for? He supposed he was not a sufficiently dignified person for suicide. Peaceful death abhorred him as a subject, and would not take him.

What could he do of a lower kind than self-extermination; what was there less noble, more in keeping with his present degraded position? He could get drunk. Of course that was it; he had forgotten. Drinking was the regular, stereotyped resource of the despairing worthless. He began to see now why some men boozed at inns. He struck down the hill northwards and came to an obscure public-house. On entering and sitting down the sight of the picture of Samson and Delilah on the wall caused him to recognize the place as that he had visited with Arabella on that first Sunday evening of their courtship. He called for liquor and drank briskly for an hour or more.

Staggering homeward late that night, with all his sense of depression gone, and his head fairly clear still, he began to laugh boisterously, and to wonder how Arabella would receive him in his new aspect. The house was in darkness when he entered, and in his stumbling state it was some time before he could get a light. Then he found that, though the marks of pig-dressing, of fats and scallops, were visible, the materials themselves had been taken away. A line written by his wife on the inside of an old envelope was pinned to the cotton blower of the fireplace:

'*Have gone to my friends. Shall not return.*'

All the next day he remained at home, and sent off the carcase of the pig to Alfredston. He then cleaned up the premises, locked the door, put the key in a place she would know if she came back, and returned to his masonry at Alfredston.

At night when he again plodded home he found she had not visited the house. The next day went in the same way, and the next. Then there came a letter from her.

That she had grown tired of him she frankly admitted. He was such a slow old coach and she did not care for the sort of life he led. There was no prospect of his ever bettering himself or her. She further went on to say that her parents had, as he knew, for some time considered the question of emigrating to Australia, the pig-jobbing business being a poor one nowadays. They had at last decided to go, and she proposed to go with them, if he had no objection. A woman of her sort would have more chance over there than in this stupid country.

Jude replied that he had not the least objection to her going. He thought it a wise course, since she wished to go, and one that might be to the advantage of both. He enclosed in the packet containing the letter the money that had been realized by the sale of the pig, with all he had besides, which was not much.

From that day he heard no more of her except indirectly, though her father and his household did not immediately leave, but waited till his goods and other effects had been sold off. When Jude learnt that there was to be an auction at the house of the Donns he packed his own household goods into a waggon, and sent them to her at the aforesaid homestead, that she might sell them with the rest, or as many of them as she should choose.

He then went into lodgings at Alfredston, and saw in a shop-window the little handbill announcing the sale of his father-in-law's furniture. He noted its date, which came and passed without Jude's going near the place, or perceiving that the traffic out of Alfredston by the southern road was materially increased by the auction. A few days later he entered a dingy broker's shop in the main street of the town, and amid a heterogeneous collection of saucepans, a clothes-horse, rolling pin, brass candlestick, swing looking-glass, and other things at the back of the shop, evidently just brought in from a sale, he perceived a framed photograph, which turned out to be his own portrait.

It was one which he had had specially taken and framed by a local man in bird's-eye maple, as a present for Arabella, and had duly given her on their wedding-day. On the back was still to be read, '*Jude to Arabella*', with the date. She must have thrown it in with the rest of her property at the auction.

'Oh,' said the broker, seeing him look at this and the other articles in the heap, and not perceiving that the portrait was of himself: 'It is a small lot of stuff that was knocked down to me at a cottage sale out on the road to Marygreen. The frame is a very useful one, if you take out the likeness. You shall have it for a shilling.'

The utter death of every tender sentiment in his wife, as brought home to him by this mute and undesigned evidence of her sale of his portrait and gift, was the conclusive little stroke required to demolish all sentiment in him. He paid the shilling, took the photograph away with him, and burnt it, frame and all, when he reached his lodging.

Two or three days later he heard that Arabella and her parents had departed. He had sent a message offering to see her for a formal leave-taking, but she had said that it would be better otherwise, since she was bent on going, which perhaps was true. On the evening following their emigration, when his day's work was done, he came out of doors after supper, and strolled in the starlight along the too familiar road towards the upland whereon had been experienced the chief emotions of his life. It seemed to be his own again.

He could not realize himself. On the old track he seemed to be a boy still, hardly a day older than when he had stood dreaming at the top of that hill, inwardly fired for the first time with ardours for Christminster and scholarship. 'Yet I am a man,' he said. 'I have a wife. More, I have arrived at the still riper stage of having disagreed with her, disliked her, had a scuffle with her, and parted from her.'

He remembered then he was standing not far from the spot at which the parting between his father and his mother was said to have occurred.

A little further on was the summit whence Christminster, or what he had taken for that city, had seemed to be visible. A milestone, now as always, stood at the roadside hard by. Jude drew near it, and felt rather than read the mileage to the city. He remembered that once on his way home he had proudly cut with his keen new chisel an inscription on the back of that milestone, embodying his aspirations. It had been done in the first week of his apprenticeship, before he had been diverted from his purposes by an unsuitable woman. He wondered if the inscription were legible still, and going to the back of the milestone brushed away the nettles. By the light of a match he could still discern what he had cut so enthusiastically so long ago:

THITHER ☞
J. F.

The sight of it, unimpaired, within its screen of grass and nettles, lit in his soul a spark of the old fire. Surely his plan should be to move onward through good and ill—to avoid morbid sorrow even though he did see ugliness in the world? *Bene agere et laetari*—to do good cheerfully—which he had heard to be the philosophy of one Spinoza, might be his own even now.

He might battle with his evil star, and follow out his original intention.

By moving to a spot a little way off he uncovered the horizon in a north-easterly direction. There actually rose the faint halo, a small dim nebulousness, hardly recognizable save by the eye of faith. It was enough for him. He would go to Christminster as soon as the term of his apprenticeship expired.

He returned to his lodgings in a better mood, and said his prayers.

PART SECOND

AT CHRISTMINSTER

'Save his own soul he hath no star.'

—SWINBURNE

'Notitiam primosque gradus vicinia fecit;
Tempore crevit amor.'

—OVID

I

The next noteworthy move in Jude's life was that in which he appeared gliding steadily onward through a dusky landscape of some three years' later leafage than had graced his courtship of Arabella, and the disruption of his coarse conjugal life with her. He was walking towards Christminster City, at a point a mile or two to the south-west of it.

He had at last found himself clear of Marygreen and Alfredston: he was out of his apprenticeship, and with his tools at his back seemed to be in the way of making a new start—the start to which, barring the interruption involved in his intimacy and married experience with Arabella, he had been looking forward for about ten years.

Jude would now have been described as a young man with a forcible, meditative, and earnest rather than handsome cast of countenance. He was of dark complexion, with dark harmonizing eyes, and he wore a closely trimmed black beard of more advanced growth than usual at his age; this, with his great mass of black curly hair, was some trouble to him in combing and washing out the stone-dust that settled on it in the pursuit of his trade. His capabilities in the latter, having been acquired in the country, were of an all-round sort, including monumental stone-cutting, gothic free-stone work for the restoration of churches, and carving of a general kind. In London he would probably have become specialized and have made himself a 'moulding mason', a 'foliage sculptor'—perhaps a 'statuary'.

He had that afternoon driven in a cart from Alfredston to the village nearest the city in this direction, and was now walking the remaining four miles rather from choice than from necessity, having always fancied himself arriving thus.

The ultimate impulse to come had had a curious origin—one

more nearly related to the emotional side of him than to the intellectual, as is often the case with young men. One day while in lodgings at Alfredston he had gone to Marygreen to see his old aunt, and had observed between the brass candlesticks on her mantelpiece the photograph of a pretty girlish face, in a broad hat with radiating folds under the brim like the rays of a halo. He had asked who she was. His grand-aunt had gruffly replied that she was his cousin Sue Bridehead, of the inimical branch of the family; and on further questioning the old woman had replied that the girl lived in Christminster, though she did not know where, or what she was doing.

His aunt would not give him the photograph. But it haunted him; and ultimately formed a quickening ingredient in his latent intent of following his friend the schoolmaster thither.

He now paused at the top of a crooked and gentle declivity, and obtained his first near view of the city. Grey stoned and dun-roofed, it stood within hail of the Wessex border, and almost with the tip of one small toe within it, at the northern-most point of the crinkled line along which the leisurely Thames strokes the fields of that ancient kingdom. The buildings now lay quiet in the sunset, a vane here and there on their many spires and domes giving sparkle to a picture of sober secondary and tertiary hues.

Reaching the bottom he moved along the level way between pollard willows growing indistinct in the twilight, and soon confronted the outmost lamps of the town—some of those lamps which had sent into the sky the gleam and glory that caught his strained gaze in his days of dreaming, so many years ago. They winked their yellow eyes at him dubiously, and as if, though they had been awaiting him all these years in disappointment at his tarrying, they did not much want him now.

He was a species of Dick Whittington whose spirit was touched to finer issues than a mere material gain. He went along the outlying streets with the cautious tread of an explorer. He saw nothing of the real city in the suburbs on this side. His first want being a lodging he scrutinized carefully such localities as seemed to offer on inexpensive terms the modest type of accommodation he demanded; and after inquiry took a room in a suburb nick-named

'Beersheba', though he did not know this at the time. Here he installed himself, and having had some tea sallied forth.

It was a windy, whispering, moonless night. To guide himself he opened under a lamp a map he had brought. The breeze ruffled and fluttered it, but he could see enough to decide on the direction he should take to reach the heart of the place.

After many turnings he came up to the first ancient mediaeval pile that he had encountered. It was a college, as he could see by the gateway. He entered it, walked round, and penetrated to dark corners which no lamplight reached. Close to this college was another; and a little further on another; and then he began to be encircled as it were with the breath and sentiment of the venerable city. When he passed objects out of harmony with its general expression he allowed his eyes to slip over them as if he did not see them.

A bell began clanging, and he listened till a hundred-and-one strokes had sounded. He must have made a mistake, he thought: it was meant for a hundred.

When the gates were shut, and he could no longer get into the quadrangles, he rambled under the walls and doorways, feeling with his fingers the contours of their mouldings and carving. The minutes passed, fewer and fewer people were visible, and still he serpentined among the shadows, for had he not imagined these scenes through ten bygone years, and what mattered a night's rest for once? High against the black sky the flash of a lamp would show crocketed pinnacles and indented battlements. Down obscure alleys, apparently never trodden now by the foot of man, and whose very existence seemed to be forgotten, there would jut into the path porticoes, oriels, doorways of enriched and florid middle-age design, their extinct air being accentuated by the rottenness of the stones. It seemed impossible that modern thought could house itself in such decrepit and superseded chambers.

Knowing not a human being here, Jude began to be impressed with the isolation of his own personality, as with a self-spectre, the sensation being that of one who walked but could not make himself seen or heard. He drew his breath pensively, and, seeming thus almost his own ghost, gave his thoughts to the other ghostly presences with which the nooks were haunted.

During the interval of preparation for this venture, since his wife and furniture's uncompromising disappearance into space, he had read and learnt almost all that could be read and learnt by one in his position, of the worthies who had spent their youth within these reverend walls, and whose souls had haunted them in their maturer age. Some of them, by the accidents of his reading, loomed out in his fancy disproportionately large by comparison with the rest. The brushing of the wind against the angles, buttresses, and door-jambs were as the passing of these only other inhabitants, the tappings of each ivy leaf on its neighbour were as the mutterings of their mournful souls, the shadows as their thin shapes in nervous movement, making him comrades in his solitude. In the gloom it was as if he ran against them without feeling their bodily frames.

The streets were now deserted, but on account of these things he could not go in. There were poets abroad, of early date and of late, from the friend and eulogist of Shakespeare down to him who has recently passed into silence, and that musical one of the tribe who is still among us. Speculative philosophers drew along, not always with wrinkled foreheads and hoary hair as in framed portraits, but pink-faced, slim, and active as in youth; modern divines sheeted in their surplices, among whom the most real to Jude Fawley were the founders of the religious school called Tractarian; the well-known three, the enthusiast, the poet, and the formularist, the echoes of whose teachings had influenced him even in his obscure home. A start of aversion appeared in his fancy to move them at sight of those other sons of the place, the form in the full-bottomed wig, statesman, rake, reasoner, and sceptic; the smoothly shaven historian so ironically civil to Christianity; with others of the same incredulous temper, who knew each quad as well as the faithful, and took equal freedom in haunting its cloisters.

He regarded the statesmen in their various types, men of firmer movement and less dreamy air; the scholar, the speaker, the plodder; the man whose mind grew with his growth in years, and the man whose mind contracted with the same.

The scientists and philologists followed on in his mind-sight in an odd impossible combination, men of meditative faces, strained foreheads, and weak-eyed as bats with constant research: then official characters—such men as Governor-Generals and Lord-Lieutenants, in whom he took little interest; Chief-Justices and Lord Chancellors, silent thin-lipped figures of whom he knew barely the names. A keener regard attached to the prelates, by reason of his own former hopes. Of them he had an ample band—some men of heart, others rather men of head; he who apologized for the Church in Latin; the saintly author of the Evening Hymn; and near them the great itinerant preacher, hymn-writer, and zealot, shadowed like Jude by his matrimonial difficulties.

Jude found himself speaking out loud, holding conversations with them as it were, like an actor in a melodrama who apostrophizes the audience on the other side of the footlights; till he suddenly ceased with a start at his absurdity. Perhaps those incoherent words of the wanderer were heard within the walls by some student or thinker over his lamp; and he may have raised his head, and wondered what voice it was, and what it betokened. Jude now perceived that, so far as solid flesh went, he had the whole aged city to himself with the exception of a belated townsman here and there, and that he seemed to be catching a cold.

A voice reached him out of the shade; a real and local voice:

'You've been a-settin' a long time on that plinth-stone, young man. What med you be up to?'

It came from a policeman who had been observing Jude without the latter observing him.

Jude went home and to bed, after reading up a little about these men and their several messages to the world from a book or two that he had brought with him concerning the sons of the University. As he drew towards sleep various memorable words of theirs that he had just been conning seemed spoken by them in muttering utterances; some audible, some unintelligible to him. One of the spectres (who afterwards mourned Christminster as 'the home of lost causes', though Jude did not remember this) was now apostrophizing her thus:

'Beautiful city! so venerable, so lovely, so unravaged by the fierce intellectual life of our century, so serene! . . . Her ineffable charm keeps ever calling us to the true goal of all of us, to the ideal, to perfection.'

Another voice was that of the Corn Law convert, whose phantom he had just seen in the quadrangle with a great bell. Jude thought his soul might have been shaping the historic words of his master-speech:

'Sir, I may be wrong, but my impression is that my duty towards a country threatened with famine requires that that which has been the ordinary remedy under all similar circumstances should be resorted to now, namely, that there should be free access to the food of man from whatever quarter it may come. . . . Deprive me of office to-morrow, you can never deprive me of the consciousness that I have exercised the powers committed to me from no corrupt or interested motives, from no desire to gratify ambition, for no personal gain.'

Then the sly author of the immortal Chapter on Christianity: 'How shall we excuse the supine inattention of the Pagan and philosophic world, to those evidences [miracles] which were presented by Omnipotence? . . . The sages of Greece and Rome turned aside from the awful spectacle, and appeared unconscious of any alterations in the moral or physical government of the world.'

Then the shade of the poet, the last of the optimists:

> 'How the world is made for each of us!
> . . . .
> And each of the Many helps to recruit
> The life of the race by a general plan.'

Then one of the three enthusiasts he had seen just now, the author of the *Apologia*:

'My argument was . . . that absolute certitude as to the truth of natural theology was the result of an assemblage of concurring and converging probabilities . . . that probabilities which did not reach to logical certainty might create a mental certitude.'

The second of them, no polemic, murmured quieter things:

> 'Why should we faint, and fear to live alone,
> Since all alone, so Heaven has will'd, we die?'

He likewise heard some phrases spoken by the phantom with the short face, the genial Spectator:

'When I look upon the tombs of the great, every motion of envy dies in me: when I read the epitaphs of the beautiful, every inordinate desire goes out; when I meet with the grief of parents upon a tombstone, my heart melts with compassion; when I see the tombs of the parents themselves, I consider the vanity of grieving for those whom we must quickly follow.'

And lastly a gentle-voiced prelate spoke, during whose meek, familiar rhyme, endeared to him from earliest childhood, Jude fell asleep:

> 'Teach me to live, that I may dread
> The grave as little as my bed.
> Teach me to die . . .'

He did not wake till morning. The ghostly past seemed to have gone, and everything spoke of to-day. He started up in bed, thinking he had overslept himself, and then said:

'By Jove—I had quite forgotten my sweet-faced cousin, and that she's here all the time! . . . and my old schoolmaster, too.' His words about his schoolmaster had, perhaps, less zest in them than his words concerning his cousin.

II

Necessary mediations on the actual, including the mean bread-and-cheese question, dissipated the phantasmal for a while, and compelled Jude to smother high thinkings under immediate needs. He had to get up, and seek for work, manual work; the only kind deemed by many of its professors to be work at all.

Passing out into the streets on this errand he found that the colleges had treacherously changed their sympathetic countenances: some were pompous; some had put on the look of family vaults above ground; something barbaric loomed in the masonries of all. The spirits of the great men had disappeared.

The numberless architectural pages around him he read, naturally, less as an artist-critic of their forms than as an artizan and comrade of the dead handicraftsmen whose muscles had actually executed those forms. He examined the mouldings, stroked them as one who knew their beginning, said they were difficult or easy in the working, had taken little or much time, were trying to the arm, or convenient to the tool.

What at night had been perfect and ideal was by day the more or less defective real. Cruelties, insults, had, he perceived, been inflicted on the aged erections. The condition of several moved him as he would have been moved by maimed sentient beings. They were wounded, broken, sloughing off their outer shape in the deadly struggle against years, weather, and man.

The rottenness of these historical documents reminded him that he was not, after all, hastening on to begin the morning practically as he had intended. He had come to work, and to live by work, and the morning had nearly gone. It was, in one sense, encouraging to think that in a place of crumbling stones there must be plenty for one of his trade to do in the business of renovation. He asked his way to the workyard of the stonemason whose name had been given him at Alfredston; and soon heard the familiar sound of the rubbers and chisels.

The yard was a little centre of regeneration. Here, with keen edges and smooth curves, were forms in the exact likeness of those he had seen abraded and time-eaten on the walls. These were the ideas in modern prose which the lichened colleges presented in old poetry. Even some of those antiques might have been called prose when they were new. They had done nothing but wait, and had become poetical. How easy to the smallest building; how impossible to most men.

He asked for the foreman, and looked round among the new traceries, mullions, transoms, shafts, pinnacles, and battlements standing on the bankers half worked, or waiting to be removed. They were marked by precision, mathematical straightness, smoothness, exactitude: there in the old walls were the broken lines of the original idea; jagged curves, disdain of precision, irregularity, disarray.

For a moment there fell on Jude a true illumination; that here in the stone yard was a centre of effort as worthy as that dignified by the name of scholarly study within the noblest of the colleges. But he lost it under stress of his old idea. He would accept any employment which might be offered him on the strength of his late employer's recommendation; but he would accept it as a provisional thing only. This was his form of the modern vice of unrest.

Moreover he perceived that at best only copying, patching and imitating went on here; which he fancied to be owing to some temporary and local cause. He did not at that time see that mediaevalism was as dead as a fern-leaf in a lump of coal; that other developments were shaping in the world around him, in which Gothic architecture and its associations had no place. The deadly animosity of contemporary logic and vision towards so much of what he held in reverence was not yet revealed to him.

Having failed to obtain work here as yet he went away, and thought again of his cousin, whose presence somewhere at hand he seemed to feel in wavelets of interest, if not of emotion. How he wished he had that pretty portrait of her! At last he wrote to his aunt to send it. She did so, with a request, however, that he was not to bring disturbance into the family by going to see the girl or her relations. Jude, a ridiculously affectionate fellow, promised nothing, put the photograph on the mantelpiece, kissed it—he did not know why—and felt more at home. She seemed to look down and preside over his tea. It was cheering—the one thing uniting him to the emotions of the living city.

There remained the schoolmaster—probably now a reverend parson. But he could not possibly hunt up such a respectable man just yet; so raw and unpolished was his condition, so precarious were his fortunes. Thus he still remained in loneliness. Although people moved round him he virtually saw none. Not as yet having mingled with the active life of the place it was largely non-existent to him. But the saints and prophets in the window-tracery, the paintings in the galleries, the statues, the busts, the gurgoyles, the corbel-heads—these seemed to breathe his atmosphere. Like all new comers to a spot on which the past is deeply graven he heard that past announcing itself with an emphasis altogether unsuspected by, and even incredible to, the habitual residents.

For many days he haunted the cloisters and quadrangles of the colleges at odd minutes in passing them, surprised by impish echoes of his own footsteps, smart as the blows of a mallet. The Christminster 'sentiment', as it had been called, ate further and further into him; till he probably knew more about those buildings materially, artistically, and historically, than any one of their inmates.

It was not till now, when he found himself actually on the spot of his enthusiasm, that Jude perceived how far away from the object of that enthusiasm he really was. Only a wall divided him from those happy young contemporaries of his with whom he shared a common mental life; men who had nothing to do from morning till night but to read, mark, learn, and inwardly digest. Only a wall—but what a wall!

Every day, every hour, as he went in search of labour, he saw them going and coming also, rubbed shoulders with them, heard their voices, marked their movements. The conversation of some of the more thoughtful among them seemed often-times, owing to his long and persistent preparation for this place, to be peculiarly akin to his own thoughts. Yet he was as far from them as if he had been at the antipodes. Of course he was. He was a young workman in a white blouse, and with stone-dust in the creases of his clothes; and in passing him they did not even see him, or hear him, rather saw through him as through a pane of glass at their familiars beyond. Whatever they were to him, he to them was not on the spot at all; and yet he had fancied he would be close to their lives by coming there.

But the future lay ahead after all; and if he could only be so fortunate as to get into good employment he would put up with the inevitable. So he thanked God for his health and strength, and took courage. For the present he was outside the gates of everything, colleges included: perhaps some day he would be inside. Those palaces of light and leading; he might some day look down on the world through their panes.

At length he did receive a message from the stonemason's yard—that a job was waiting for him. It was his first encouragement, and he closed with the offer promptly.

He was young and strong, or he never could have executed with such zest the undertakings to which he now applied himself, since they involved reading most of the night after working all the day. First he bought a shaded lamp for four and sixpence, and obtained a good light. Then he got pens, paper, and such other necessary books as he had been unable to obtain elsewhere. Then, to the consternation of his landlady, he shifted all the furniture of his room—a single one for living and sleeping—rigged up a curtain on a rope across the middle, to make a double chamber out of one, hung up a thick blind that nobody should know how he was curtailing the hours of sleep, laid out his books, and sat down.

Having been deeply encumbered by marrying, getting a cottage, and buying the furniture which had disappeared in the wake of his wife, he had never been able to save any money since the time of those disastrous ventures, and till his wages began to come in he was obliged to live in the narrowest way. After buying a book or two he could not even afford himself a fire; and when the nights reeked with the raw and cold air from the Meadows he sat over his lamp in a greatcoat, and woollen gloves.

From his window he could perceive the spire of the Cathedral, and the ogee dome under which resounded the great bell of the city. The tall tower, tall belfry windows, and tall pinnacles of the college by the bridge he could also get a glimpse of by going to the staircase. These objects he used as stimulants when his faith in the future was dim.

Like enthusiasts in general he made no inquiries into details of procedure. Picking up general notions from casual acquaintance, he never dwelt upon them. For the present, he said to himself, the one thing necessary was to get ready by accumulating money and knowledge, and await whatever chances were afforded to such a one of becoming a son of the University. 'For wisdom is a defence, and money is a defence; but the excellency of knowledge is, that wisdom giveth life to them that have it.' His desire absorbed him, and left no part of him to weigh its practicability.

At this time he received a nervously anxious letter from his poor old aunt, on the subject which had previously distressed her—a fear that Jude would not be strong-minded enough to keep away from his cousin Sue Bridehead and her relations. Sue's father, his aunt believed, had gone back to London, but the girl remained at Christminster. To make her still more objectionable she was an artist or designer of some sort in what was called an ecclesiastical warehouse, which was a perfect seed-bed of idolatry, and she was no doubt abandoned to mummeries on that account—if not quite a Papist. (Miss Drusilla Fawley was of her date, Evangelical.)

As Jude was rather on an intellectual track than a theological, this news of Sue's probable opinions did not much influence him one way or the other, but the clue to her whereabouts was decidedly interesting. With an altogether singular pleasure he walked at his earliest spare minutes past the shops answering to his great-aunt's description; and beheld in one of them a young girl sitting behind a desk, who was suspiciously like the original of the portrait. He ventured to enter on a trivial errand, and having made his purchase lingered on the scene. The shop seemed to be kept entirely by women. It contained Anglican books, stationery, texts, and fancy goods: little plaster angels on brackets, Gothic-framed pictures of saints, ebony crosses that were almost crucifixes, prayer-books that were almost missals. He felt very shy of looking at the girl in the desk; she was so pretty that he could not believe it possible that she should belong to him. Then she spoke to one of the two older women behind the counter; and he recognized in the accents certain qualities of his own voice; softened and sweetened, but his own. What was she doing? He stole a glance round. Before her lay a piece of zinc, cut to the shape of a scroll three or four feet long, and coated with a dead-surface paint on one side. Hereon she was designing or illuminating, in characters of Church text, the single word

ALLELUJA

'A sweet, saintly, Christian business, hers!' thought he.

Her presence here was now fairly enough explained, her skill in work of this sort having no doubt been acquired from her father's occupation as an ecclesiastical worker in metal. The lettering on which she was engaged was clearly intended to be fixed up in some chancel to assist devotion.

He came out. It would have been easy to speak to her there and then, but it seemed scarcely honourable towards his aunt to disregard her request so incontinently. She had used him roughly, but she had brought him up; and the fact of her being powerless to control him lent a pathetic force to a wish that would have been inoperative as an argument.

So Jude gave no sign. He would not call upon Sue just yet. He had other reasons against doing so when he had walked away. She seemed so dainty beside himself in his rough working-jacket and dusty trousers that he felt he was as yet unready to encounter her, as he had felt about Mr Phillotson. And how possible it was that she had inherited the antipathies of her family, and would scorn him, as far as a Christian could, particularly when he had told her that unpleasant part of his history which had resulted in his becoming enchained to one of her own sex whom she would certainly not admire.

Thus he kept watch over her, and liked to feel she was there.

The consciousness of her living presence stimulated him. But she remained more or less an ideal character, about whose form he began to weave curious and fantastic day-dreams.

Between two and three weeks afterwards Jude was engaged with some more men, outside Crozier College in Old-time Street, in getting a block of worked freestone from a waggon across the pavement, before hoisting it to the parapet which they were repairing. Standing in position the head man said, 'Spaik when ye heave! He-ho!' And they heaved.

All of a sudden, as he lifted, his cousin stood close to his elbow, pausing a moment on the bend of her foot till the obstructing object should have been removed. She looked right into his face with liquid, untranslatable eyes, that combined, or seemed to him to combine, keenness with tenderness, and mystery with both, their expression, as well as that of her lips, taking its life from some words just spoken to a companion, and being carried on into his face quite unconsciously. She no more observed his presence than that of the dustmotes which his manipulations raised into the sunbeams.

His closeness to her was so suggestive that he trembled, and turned his face away with a shy instinct to prevent her recognizing him, though as she had never once seen him she could not possibly do so; and might very well never have heard even his name. He could perceive that though she was a country-girl at bottom, a latter girlhood of some years in London, and a womanhood here, had taken all rawness out of her.

When she was gone he continued his work, reflecting on her. He had been so caught by her influence that he had taken no count of her general mould and build. He remembered now that she was not a large figure, that she was light and slight, of the type dubbed elegant. That was about all he had seen. There was nothing statuesque in her; all was nervous motion. She was mobile, living, yet a painter might not have called her handsome or beautiful. But the much that she was surprised him. She was quite a long way removed from the rusticity that was his. How could one of his cross-grained, unfortunate, almost accursed stock, have contrived to reach this pitch of niceness? London had done it, he supposed.

From this moment the emotion which had been accumulating in his breast as the bottled-up effect of solitude and the poetized locality he dwelt in, insensibly began to precipitate itself on this half-visionary form; and he perceived that, whatever his obedient wish in a contrary direction, he would soon be unable to resist the desire to make himself known to her.

He affected to think of her quite in a family way, since there were crushing reasons why he should not and could not think of her in any other.

The first reason was that he was married, and it would be wrong. The second was that they were cousins. It was not well for cousins to fall in love even when circumstances seemed to favour the passion. The third: even were he free, in a family like his own where marriage usually meant a tragic sadness, marriage with a blood-relation would duplicate the adverse conditions, and a tragic sadness might be intensified to a tragic horror.

Therefore, again, he would have to think of Sue with only a relation's mutual interest in one belonging to him; regard her in a practical way as some one to be proud of; to talk and nod to; later on, to be invited to tea by, the emotion spent on her being rigorously that of a kinsman and well-wisher. So would she be to him a kindly star, an elevating power, a companion in Anglican worship, a tender friend.

III

But under the various deterrent influences Jude's instinct was to approach her timidly, and the next Sunday he went to the morning service in the Cathedral-church of Cardinal College to gain a further view of her, for he had found that she frequently attended there.

She did not come, and he awaited her in the afternoon, which was finer. He knew that if she came at all she would approach the building along the eastern side of the great green quadrangle from which it was accessible and he stood in a corner while the bell was going. A few minutes before the hour for service she appeared as one of the figures walking along under the College walls, and at sight of her he advanced up the side opposite, and followed her into the building, more than ever glad that he had not as yet revealed himself. To see her, and to be himself unseen and unknown, was enough for him at present.

He lingered awhile in the vestibule, and the service was some way advanced when he was put into a seat. It was a louring, mournful, still afternoon, when a religion of some sort seems a necessity to ordinary practical men, and not only a luxury of the emotional and leisured classes. In the dim light and the baffling glare of the clerestory windows he could discern the opposite worshippers indistinctly only, but he saw that Sue was among them. He had not long discovered the exact seat that she occupied when the chanting of the 119th Psalm in which the choir was engaged reached its second part, *In quo corriget*, the organ changing to a pathetic Gregorian tune as the singers gave forth:

'Wherewithal shall a young man cleanse his way?'

It was the very question that was engaging Jude's attention at this moment. What a wicked worthless fellow he had been to give vent as he had done to an animal passion for a woman, and allow it to lead to such disastrous consequences; then to think of putting an end to himself; then to go recklessly and get drunk. The great waves of pedal music tumbled round the choir, and, nursed on the supernatural as he had been, it is not wonderful that he could hardly believe that the psalm was not specifically set by some regardful Providence for this moment of his first entry into the solemn building. And yet it was the ordinary psalm for the twenty-fourth evening of the month.

The girl for whom he was beginning to nourish an extra-ordinary tenderness, was at this time ensphered by the same harmonies as those which floated into his ears; and the thought was a delight to him. She was probably a frequenter of this place, and, steeped body and soul in church sentiment as she must be by occupation and habit, had, no doubt, much in common with him. To an impressionable and lonely young man the consciousness of having at last found anchorage for his thoughts, which promised to supply both social and spiritual possibilities, was like the dew of Hermon, and he remained throughout the service in a sustaining atmosphere of ecstasy.

Though he was loth to suspect it, some people might have said to him that the atmosphere blew as distinctly from Cyprus as from Galilee.

Jude waited till she had left her seat and passed under the screen before he himself moved. She did not look towards him, and by the time he reached the door she was half way down the broad path. Being dressed up in his Sunday suit he was inclined to follow her and reveal himself. But he was not quite ready; and, alas, ought he to do so with the kind of feeling that was awakening in him?

For though it had seemed to have an ecclesiastical basis during the service, and he had persuaded himself that such was the case, he could not altogether be blind to the real nature of the magnetism. She was such a stranger that the kinship was affectation, and he said, 'It can't be! I, a man with a wife, must not know her!' Still Sue *was* his own kin, and the fact of his having a wife, even though she was not in evidence in this hemisphere, might be a help in one sense. It would put all thought of a tender wish on his part out of Sue's mind, and make her intercourse with him free and fearless. It was with some heartache that he saw how little he cared for the freedom and fearlessness that would result in her from such knowledge.

Some little time before the date of this service in the cathedral the pretty, liquid-eyed, light-footed young woman Sue Bridehead had n afternoon's holiday, and leaving the ecclesiastical establishment in which she not only assisted but lodged, took a walk into the country with a book in her hand. It was one of those cloudless days which sometimes occur in Wessex and elsewhere between days of cold and wet, as if intercalated by caprice of the weather-god. She went along for a mile or two until she came to much higher ground than that of the city she had left behind her. The road passed between green fields, and coming to a stile Sue paused there, to finish the page she was reading, and then looked back at the towers and domes and pinnacles new and old.

On the other side of the stile, in the footpath, she beheld a foreigner with black hair and a sallow face, sitting on the grass beside a large square board whereon were fixed, as closely as they could stand, a number of plaster statuettes, some of them bronzed, which he was re-arranging before proceeding with them on his way. They were in the main reduced copies of ancient marbles, and comprised divinities of a very different character from those the girl was accustomed to see portrayed, among them being a Venus of standard pattern, a Diana, and, of the other sex, Apollo, Bacchus, and Mars. Though the figures were many yards away from her the south-west sun brought them out so brilliantly against the green herbage that she could discern their contours with luminous distinctness; and being almost in a line between herself and the church towers of the city they awoke in her an oddly foreign and contrasting set of ideas by comparison. The man rose, and seeing her, politely took off his cap, and cried 'I-i-i-mages!' in an accent that agreed with his appearance. In a moment he dexterously lifted upon his knee the great board with its assembled notabilities divine and human, and raised it to the top of his head, bringing them on to her and resting the board on the stile. First he offered her his smaller wares—the busts of kings and queens, then a minstrel, then a winged Cupid. She shook her head.

'How much are these two?' she said, touching with her fingers the Venus and the Apollo—the largest figures on the tray.

He said she could have them for ten shillings.

'I cannot afford that,' said Sue. She offered considerably less, and to her surprise the image-man drew them from their wire stay and handed them over the stile. She clasped them as treasures.

When they were paid for, and the man had gone, she began to be concerned as to what she should do with them. They seemed so very large now that they were in her possession, and so very naked. Being of a nervous temperament she trembled at her enterprise. When she handled them the white pipeclay came off on her gloves and jacket. After carrying them along a little way openly an idea came to her, and, pulling some huge burdock leaves, parsley, and other rank growths from the hedge, she wrapped up her burden as well as she could in these, so that what she carried appeared to be an enormous armful of green stuff gathered by a zealous lover of nature.

'Well, anything is better than those everlasting church fal-lals!' she said. But she was still in a trembling state, and seemed almost to wish she had not bought the figures.

Occasionally peeping inside the leaves to see that Venus's arm was not broken, she entered her heathen load into the most Christian city in the country by an obscure street running parallel to the main one, and round a corner to the side door of the establishment to which she was attached. Her purchases were taken straight up to her own chamber, and she at once attempted to lock them in a box that was her very own property; but finding them too cumbersome she wrapped them in large sheets of brown paper, and stood them on the floor in a corner.

The mistress of the house, Miss Fontover, was an elderly lady in spectacles, dressed almost like an abbess; a dab at Ritual, as became one of her business, and a worshipper at the ceremonial church of St Silas, in the suburb of Beersheba before-mentioned, which Jude also had begun to attend. She was the daughter of a clergyman in reduced circumstances, and at his death, which had occurred several years before this date, she boldly avoided penury by taking over a little shop of church requisites and developing it to its present creditable proportions. She wore a cross and beads round her neck as her only ornament, and knew the Christian Year by heart.

She now came to call Sue to tea, and, finding that the girl did not respond for a moment, entered the room just as the other was hastily putting a string round each parcel.

'Something you have been buying, Miss Bridehead?' she asked, regarding the enwrapped objects.

'Yes—just something to ornament my room,' said Sue.

'Well, I should have thought I had put enough here already,' said Miss Fontover, looking round at the Gothic-framed prints of saints, the Church-text scrolls, and other articles which, having become too stale to sell, had been used to furnish this obscure hamber. 'What is it? How bulky!' She tore a little hole, about as big as a wafer, in the brown paper, and tried to peep in. 'Why, statuary? Two figures? Where did you get them?'

'O—I bought them of a travelling man who sells casts—'

'Two saints?'

'Yes.'

'What ones?'

'St Peter and St—St Mary Magdalen.'

'Well—now come down to tea, and go and finish that organ-text, if there's light enough afterwards.'

These little obstacles to the indulgence of what had been the merest passing fancy, created in Sue a great zest for unpacking her objects and looking at them, and at bedtime, when she was sure of being undisturbed, she unrobed the divinities in comfort. Placing the pair of figures on the chest of drawers, a candle on each side of them, she withdrew to the bed, flung herself down thereon, and began reading a book she had taken from her box, which Miss Fontover knew nothing of. It was a volume of Gibbon, and she read the chapter dealing with the reign of Julian the Apostate. Occasionally she looked up at the statuettes, which appeared strange and out of place, there happening to be a Calvary print hanging between them, and, as if the scene suggested the action, she at length jumped up and withdrew another book from her box—a volume of verse—and turned to the familiar poem—

> Thou hast conquered, O pale Galilean:
> The world has grown grey from thy breath!

which she read to the end. Presently she put out the candles, undressed, and finally extinguished her own light.

She was of an age which usually sleeps soundly, yet to-night she kept waking up, and every time she opened her eyes there was enough diffused light from the street to show her the white plaster figures, standing on the chest of drawers in odd contrast to their environment of text and martyr, and the Gothic-framed Crucifix-picture that was only discernible now as a Latin cross, the figure thereon being obscured by the shades.

On one of these occasions the church clocks struck some small hour. It fell upon the ears of another person who sat bending over his books at a not very distant spot in the same city. Being Saturday night the morrow was one on which Jude had not set his alarm-clock to call him at his usually early time, hence he had stayed up, as was his custom, two or three hours later than he could afford to do on any other day of the week. Just then he was earnestly reading from his Griesbach's text. At the very time that Sue was tossing and staring at her figures, the policeman and belated citizens passing along under his window might have heard, if they had stood still, strange syllables mumbled with fervour within—words that had for Jude an indescribable enchantment: inexplicable sounds something like these:

'All hemin heis Theos ho Pater, ex hou ta panta, kai hemeis eis auton:'

Till the sounds rolled with reverent loudness, as a book was heard to close:

'Kai heis Kurios Iesous Christos, di hou ta panta kai hemeis di autou!'

IV

He was a handy man at his trade, an all-round man, as artizans in country-towns are apt to be. In London the man who carves the boss or knob of leafage declines to cut the fragment of moulding which merges in that leafage, as if it were a degradation to do the second half of one whole. When there was not much Gothic moulding for Jude to run, or much window-tracery on the bankers, he would go out lettering monuments or tombstones, and take a pleasure in the change of handiwork.

The next time that he saw her was when he was on a ladder executing a job of this sort inside one of the churches. There was a short morning service, and when the parson entered Jude came down from his ladder, and sat with the half-dozen people forming the congregation, till the prayers should be ended, and he could resume his tapping. He did not observe till the service was half over that one of the women was Sue, who had perforce accompanied the elderly Miss Fontover thither.

Jude sat watching her pretty shoulders, her easy, curiously nonchalant risings and sittings, and her perfunctory genuflexions, and thought what a help such an Anglican would have been to him in happier circumstances. It was not so much his anxiety to get on with his work that made him go up to it immediately the worshippers began to take their leave: it was that he dared not, in this holy spot, confront the woman who was beginning to influence him in such an indescribable manner. Those three enormous reasons why he must not attempt to intimate acquaintance with Sue Bridehead now that his interest in her had shown itself to be unmistakably of a sexual kind, loomed as stubbornly as ever. But it was also obvious that man could not live by work alone; that the particular man Jude, at any rate, wanted something to love. Some men would have rushed incontinently to her, snatched the pleasure of easy friendship which she could hardly refuse, and have left the rest to chance. Not so Jude—at first.

But as the days, and still more particularly the lonely evenings, dragged along, he found himself, to his moral consternation, to be thinking more of her instead of thinking less of her, and experiencing a fearful bliss in doing what was erratic, informal, and unexpected. Surrounded by her influence all day, walking past the spots she frequented, he was always thinking of her, and was obliged to own to himself that his conscience was likely to be the loser in this battle.

To be sure she was almost an ideality to him still. Perhaps to know her would be to cure himself of this unexpected and unauthorized passion. A voice whispered that, though he desired to know her, he did not desire to be cured.

There was not the least doubt that from his own orthodox point of view the situation was growing immoral. For Sue to be the loved one of a man who was licensed by the laws of his country to love Arabella and none other unto his life's end, was a pretty bad second beginning when the man was bent on such a course as Jude purposed. This conviction was so real with him that one day when, as was frequent, he was at work in a neighbouring village church alone, he felt it to be his duty to pray against his weakness. But much as he wished to be an exemplar in these things he could not get on. It was quite impossible, he found, to ask to be delivered from temptation when your heart's desire was to be tempted unto seventy times seven. So he excused himself. 'After all,' he said, 'it is not altogether an *erotolepsy* that is the matter with me, as at that first time. I can see that she is exceptionally bright; and it is partly a wish for intellectual sympathy, and a craving for loving-kindness in my solitude.' Thus he went on adoring her, fearing to realize that it was human perversity. For whatever Sue's virtues, talents, or ecclesiastical saturation, it was certain that those items were not at all the cause of his affection for her.

On an afternoon at this time a young girl entered the stone-mason's yard with some hesitation, and, lifting her skirts to avoid dragging them in the white dust, crossed towards the office.

'That's a nice girl,' said one of the men known as Uncle Joe.

'Who is she?' asked another.

'I don't know—I've seen her about here and there. Why, yes, she's the daughter of that clever chap Bridehead who did all the wrought ironwork at St Silas' ten years ago, and went away to London afterwards. I don't know what he's doing now—not much I fancy—as she's come back here.'

Meanwhile the young woman had knocked at the office door and asked if Mr Jude Fawley was at work in the yard. It so happened that Jude had gone out somewhere or other that afternoon, which information she received with a look of disappointment, and went away immediately. When Jude returned they told him, and described her, whereupon he exclaimed, 'Why—that's my cousin Sue!'

He looked along the street after her, but she was out of sight. He had no longer any thought of a conscientious avoidance of her, and resolved to call upon her that very evening. And when he reached his lodging he found a note from her—a first note—one of those documents which, simple and commonplace in themselves, are seen retrospectively to have been pregnant with impassioned consequences. The very unconsciousness of a looming drama which is shown in such innocent first epistles from women to men, or *vice versa*, makes them, when such a drama follows, and they are read over by the purple or lurid light of it, all the more impressive, solemn, and in cases, terrible.

Sue's was of the most artless and natural kind. She addressed him as her dear cousin Jude; said she had only just learnt by the merest accident that he was living in Christminster, and reproached him with not letting her know. They might have had such nice times together, she said, for she was thrown much upon herself, and had hardly any congenial friend. But now there was every probability of her soon going away, so that the chance of companionship would be lost perhaps for ever.

A cold sweat overspread Jude at the news that she was going away. That was a contingency he had never thought of, and it spurred him to write all the more quickly to her. He would meet her that very evening, he said, one hour from the time of writing, at the cross in the pavement which marked the spot of Martyrdoms.

When he had despatched the note by a boy he regretted that in his hurry he should have suggested to her to meet him out of doors, when he might have said he would call upon her. It was, in fact, the country custom to meet thus, and nothing else had occurred to him. Arabella had been met in the same way, unfortunately, and it might not seem respectable to a dear girl like Sue. However, it could not be helped now, and he moved towards the point a few minutes before the hour, under the glimmer of the newly lighted lamps.

The broad street was silent, and almost deserted, although it was not late. He saw a figure on the other side, which turned out to be hers, and they both converged towards the cross-mark at the same moment. Before either had reached it she called out to him:

'I am not going to meet you just there, for the first time in my life! Come further on.'

The voice, though positive and silvery, had been tremulous. They walked on in parallel lines, and, waiting her pleasure, Jude watched till she showed signs of closing in, when he did likewise, the place being where the carriers' carts stood in the daytime, though there was none on the spot then.

'I am sorry that I asked you to meet me, and didn't call,' began Jude with the bashfulness of a lover. 'But I thought it would save time if we were going to walk.'

'O—I don't mind that,' she said with the freedom of a friend. 'I have really no place to ask anybody in to. What I meant was that the place you chose was so horrid—I suppose I ought not to say horrid,—I mean gloomy and inauspicious in its associations. . . . But isn't it funny to begin like this, when I don't know you yet?' She looked him up and down curiously, though Jude did not look much at her.

'You seem to know me more than I know you,' she added.

'Yes—I have seen you now and then.'

'And you knew who I was, and didn't speak? And now I am going away!'

'Yes. That's unfortunate. I have hardly any other friend. I have, indeed, one very old friend here somewhere, but I don't quite like to call on him just yet. I wonder if you know anything of him—Mr Phillotson? A parson somewhere about the county I think he is.'

'No—I only know of one Mr Phillotson. He lives a little way out in the country, at Lumsdom. He's a village schoolmaster.'

'Ah! I wonder if he's the same. Surely it is impossible! Only a schoolmaster still! Do you know his Christian name—is it Richard?'

'Yes—it is; I've directed books to him, though I've never seen him.'

'Then he couldn't do it!'

Jude's countenance fell, for how could he succeed in an enterprise wherein the great Phillotson had failed? He would have had a day of despair if the news had not arrived during his sweet Sue's presence, but even at this moment he had visions of how Phillotson's failure in the grand University scheme would depress him when she had gone.

'As we are going to take a walk, suppose we go and call upon him?' said Jude suddenly. 'It is not late.'

She agreed, and they went along up a hill, and through some prettily wooden country. Presently the embattled tower and square turret of the church rose into the sky, and then the schoolhouse. They inquired of a person in the street if Mr Phillotson was likely to be at home, and were informed that he was always at home. A knock brought him to the schoolhouse door, with a candle in his hand and a look of inquiry on his face, which had grown thin and careworn since Jude last set eyes on him.

That after all these years the meeting with Mr Phillotson should be of this homely complexion destroyed at one stroke the halo which had surrounded the schoolmaster's figure in Jude's imagination ever since their parting. It created in him at the same time a sympathy with Phillotson as an obviously much chastened and disappointed man. Jude told him his name, and said he had come to see him as an old friend who had been kind to him in his youthful days.

'I don't remember you in the least,' said the schoolmaster thoughtfully. 'You were one of my pupils you say? Yes, no doubt; but they number so many thousands by this time of my life, and have naturally changed so much, that I remember very few except the quite recent ones.'

'It was out at Marygreen,' said Jude, wishing he had not come.

'Yes. I was there a short time. And is this an old pupil, too?'

'No—that's my cousin. . . . I wrote to you for some grammars, if you recollect, and you sent them?'

'Ah—yes!—I do dimly recall that incident.'

'It was very kind of you to do it. And it was you who first started me on that course. On the morning you left Marygreen, when your goods were on the waggon, you wished me good-bye, and said your scheme was to be a University man and enter the church—that a degree was the necessary hall-mark of one who wanted to do anything as a theologian or teacher.'

'I remember I thought all that privately; but I wonder I did not keep my own counsel. The idea was given up years ago.'

'I have never forgotten it. It was that which brought me to this part of the country, and out here to see you to-night.'

'Come in,' said Phillotson. 'And your cousin, too.'

They entered the parlour of the schoolhouse, where there was a lamp with a paper shade, which threw light down on three or four books. Phillotson took it off, so that they could see each other better, and the rays fell on the nervous little face and vivacious dark eyes and hair of Sue, on the earnest features of her cousin, and on the schoolmaster's own maturer face and figure, showing him to be a spare and thoughtful personage of five-and-forty, with a thin-lipped, somewhat refined mouth, a slightly stooping habit, and a black frock coat, which from continued frictions shone a little at the shoulder-blades, the middle of the back, and the elbows.

The old friendship was imperceptibly renewed, the schoolmaster speaking of his experiences, and the cousins of theirs. He told them that he still thought of the church sometimes, and that though he could not enter it as he had intended to do in former years he might enter it as a licentiate. Meanwhile, he said, he was comfortable in his present position, though he was in want of a pupil-teacher.

They did not stay to supper. Sue having to be indoors before it grew late, and the road was retraced to Christminster. Though they had talked of nothing more than general subjects Jude was surprised to find what a revelation of woman his cousin was to him. She was so vibrant that everything she did seemed to have its source in feeling. An exciting thought would make her walk ahead so fast that he could hardly keep up with her; and her sensitiveness on some points was such that it might have been misread as vanity. It was with heartsickness he perceived that, while her sentiments towards him were those of the frankest friendliness only, he loved her more than before becoming acquainted with her; and the gloom of the walk home lay not in the night overhead, but in the thought of her departure.

'Why must you leave Christminster?' he said regretfully. 'How can you do otherwise than cling to a city in whose history such men as Newman, Pusey, Ward, Keble, loom so large!'

'Yes—they do. Though how large do they loom in the history of the world? . . . What a funny reason for caring to stay! I should never have thought of it!' She laughed.

'Well—I must go,' she continued. 'Miss Fontover, one of the partners whom I serve, is offended with me, and I with her; and it is best to go.'

'How did that happen?'

'She broke some statuary of mine.'

'Oh? Wilfully?'

'Yes. She found it in my room, and though it was my property she threw it on the floor and stamped on it, because it was not according to her taste, and ground the arms and the head of one of the figures all to bits with her heel—a horrid thing!'

'Too Catholic-Apostolic for her, I suppose? No doubt she called them Popish images and talked of the invocation of saints.'

'No. . . . No, she didn't do that. She saw the matter quite differently.'

'Ah! Then I am surprised!'

'Yes. It was for quite some other reason that she didn't like my patron-saints. So I was led to retort upon her; and the end of it was that I resolved not to stay, but to get into an occupation in which I shall be more independent.'

'Why don't you try teaching again? You once did, I heard.'

'I never thought of resuming it; for I was getting on as an art-designer.'

'*Do* let me ask Mr Phillotson to let you try your hand in his school? If you like it, and go to a Training College, and become a first-class certificated mistress, you get twice as large an income as any designer or church artist, and twice as much freedom.'

'Well—ask him. Now I must go in. Good-bye, dear Jude! I am so glad we have met at last. We needn't quarrel because our parents did, need we?'

Jude did not like to let her see quite how much he agreed with her, and went his way to the remote street in which he had his lodging.

To keep Sue Bridehead near him was now a desire which operated without regard of consequences, and the next evening he again set out for Lumsdon, fearing to trust to the persuasive effects of a note only. The schoolmaster was unprepared for such a proposal.

'What I rather wanted was a second year's transfer, as it is called,' he said. 'Of course your cousin would do, personally; but she has had no experience. O—she has, has she? Does she really think of adopting teaching as a profession?'

Jude said she was disposed to do so, he thought, and his ingenious arguments on her natural fitness for assisting Mr Phillotson, of which Jude knew nothing whatever, so influenced the schoolmaster that he said he would engage her, assuring Jude as a friend that unless his cousin really meant to follow on in the same course, and regarded this step as the first stage of an apprenticeship, of which her training in a normal school would be the second stage, her time would be wasted quite, the salary being merely nominal.

The day after this visit Phillotson received a letter from Jude, containing the information that he had again consulted his cousin, who took more and more warmly to the idea of tuition; and that she had agreed to come. It did not occur for a moment to the schoolmaster and recluse that Jude's ardour in promoting the arrangement arose from any other feelings towards Sue than the instinct of co-operation common among members of the same family.

V

The schoolmaster sat in his homely dwelling attached to the school, both being modern erections; and he looked across the way at the old house in which his teacher Sue had taken a lodging. The arrangement had been concluded very quickly. A pupil-teacher who was to have been transferred to Mr Phillotson's school had failed him, and Sue had been taken as stop-gap. All such provisional arrangements as these could only last till the next annual visit of H.M. Inspector, whose approval was necessary to make them permanent. Having taught for some two years in London, though she had abandoned that vocation of late, Miss Bridehead was not exactly a novice, and Phillotson thought there would be no difficulty in retaining her services, which he already wished to do, though she had only been with him three or four weeks. He had found her quite as bright as Jude had described her; and what master-tradesman does not wish to keep an apprentice who saves him half his labour?

It was a little over half-past eight o'clock in the morning, and he was waiting to see her cross the road to the school, when he would follow. At twenty minutes to nine she did cross, a light hat tossed on her head; and he watched her as a curiosity. A new emanation, which had nothing to do with her skill as a teacher, seemed to surround her this morning. He went to the school also, and Sue remained governing her class at the other end of the room, all day under his eye. She certainly was an excellent teacher.

It was part of his duty to give her private lessons in the evening, and some article in the Code made it necessary that a respectable, elderly woman should be present at these lessons when the teacher and the taught were of different sexes. Richard Phillotson thought of the absurdity of the regulation in this case, when he was old enough to be the girl's father; but he faithfully acted up to it; and sat down with her in a room where Mrs Hawes, the widow at whose house Sue lodged, occupied herself with sewing. The regulation was, indeed, not easy to evade, for there was no other sitting-room in the dwelling.

Sometimes as she figured—it was arithmetic that they were working at—she would involuntarily glance up with a little inquiring smile at him, as if she assumed that, being the master, he must perceive all that was passing in her brain, as right or wrong. Phillotson was not really thinking of the arithmetic at all, but of her, in a novel way which somehow seemed strange to him as preceptor. Perhaps she knew that he was thinking of her thus.

For a few weeks their work had gone on with a monotony which in itself was a delight to him. Then it happened that the children were to be taken to Christminster to see an itinerant exhibition, in the shape of a model of Jerusalem, to which schools were admitted at a penny a head in the interests of education. They marched along the road two and two, she beside her class with her simple cotton sunshade, her little thumb cocked up against its stem; and Phillotson behind in his long dangling coat, handling his walking-stick genteelly, in the musing mood which had come over him since her arrival. The afternoon was one of sun and dust, and when they entered the exhibition room few people were present but themselves.

The model of the ancient city stood in the middle of the apartment, and the proprietor, with a fine religious philanthropy written on his features, walked round it with a pointer in his hand, showing the young people the various quarters and places known to them by name from reading their Bibles; Mount Moriah, the Valley of Jehoshaphat, the City of Zion, the walls and the gates, outside one of which there was a large mound like a tumulus, and on the mound a little white cross. The spot, he said, was Calvary.

'I think,' said Sue to the schoolmaster, as she stood with him a little in the background, 'that this model, elaborate as it is, is a very imaginary production. How does anybody know that Jerusalem was like this in the time of Christ? I am sure this man doesn't.'

'It is made after the best conjectural maps, based on actual visits to the city as it now exists.'

'I fancy we have had enough of Jerusalem,' she said, 'considering we are not descended from the Jews. There was nothing first-rate about the place, or people, after all—as there was about Athens, Rome, Alexandria, and other old cities.'

'But my dear girl, consider what it is to us!'

She was silent, for she was easily repressed; and then perceived behind the group of children clustered round the model a young man in a white flannel jacket, his form being bent so low in his intent inspection of the Valley of Jehoshaphat that his face was almost hidden from view by the Mount of Olives. 'Look at your cousin Jude,' continued the schoolmaster. 'He doesn't think we have had enough of Jerusalem!'

'Ah—I didn't see him!' she cried in her quick light voice. 'Jude—how seriously you are going into it!'

Jude started up from his reverie, and saw her. 'O—Sue!' he said, with a glad flush of embarrassment. 'These are your school-children, of course! I saw that schools were admitted in the afternoons, and thought you might come; but I got so deeply interested that I didn't remember where I was. How it carries one back, doesn't it! I could examine it for hours, but I have only a few minutes, unfortunately; for I am in the middle of a job out here.'

'Your cousin is so terribly clever that she criticizes it unmercifully,' said Phillotson, with good-humoured satire. 'She is quite sceptical as to its correctness.'

'No, Mr Phillotson, I am not—altogether! I hate to be what is called a clever girl—there are too many of that sort now!' answered Sue sensitively. 'I only meant—I don't know what I meant—except that it was what you don't understand!'

'*I* know your meaning,' said Jude ardently (although he did not). 'And I think you are quite right.'

'That's a good Jude—I know *you* believe in me!' She impulsively seized his hand, and leaving a reproachful look on the schoolmaster turned away to Jude, her voice revealing a tremor which she herself felt to be absurdly uncalled for by sarcasm so gentle. She had not the least conception how the hearts of the twain went out to her at this momentary revelation of feeling, and what a complication she was building up thereby in the futures of both.

The model wore too much of an educational aspect for the children not to tire of it soon, and a little later in the afternoon they were all marched back to Lumsdon, Jude returning to his work. He watched the juvenile flock in their clean frocks and pinafores, filing down the street towards the country beside Phillotson and Sue, and a sad, dissatisfied sense of being out of the scheme of the latters' lives had possession of him. Phillotson had invited him to walk out and see them on Friday evening, when there would be no lessons to give to Sue, and Jude had eagerly promised to avail himself of the opportunity.

Meanwhile the scholars and teachers moved homewards, and the next day, on looking on the black-board in Sue's class, Phillotson was surprised to find upon it, skilfully drawn in chalk, a perspective view of Jerusalem, with every building shown in its place.

'I thought you took no interest in the model, and hardly looked at it?' he said.

'I hardly did,' she said, 'but I remembered that much of it.'

'It is more than I had remembered myself.'

Her Majesty's school-inspector was at that time paying 'surprise-visits' in this neighbourhood to test the teaching unawares; and two days later, in the middle of the morning lessons, the latch of the door was softly lifted, and in walked my gentleman, the king of terrors—to pupil-teachers.

To Mr Phillotson the surprise was not great; like the lady in the story he had been played that trick too many times to be unprepared. But Sue's class was at the further end of the room, and her back was towards the entrance; the inspector therefore came and stood behind her and watched her teaching some half-minute before she became aware of his presence. She turned, and realized that an oft-dreaded moment had come. The effect upon her timidity was such that she uttered a cry of fright. Phillotson, with a strange instinct of solicitude quite beyond his control, was at her side just in time to prevent her falling from faintness. She soon recovered herself, and laughed; but when the inspector had gone there was a reaction, and she was so white that Phillotson took her into his room, and gave her some brandy to bring her round. She found him holding her hand.

'You ought to have told me,' she gasped petulantly, 'that one of the Inspector's surprise-visits was imminent! O what shall I do! Now he'll write and tell the managers that I am no good, and I shall be disgraced for ever!'

'He won't do that, my dear little girl. You are the best teacher ever I had!'

He looked so gently at her that she was moved, and regretted that she had upbraided him. When she was better she went home.

Jude in the meantime had been waiting impatiently for Friday. On both Wednesday and Thursday he had been so much under the influence of his desire to see her that he walked after dark some distance along the road in the direction of the village, and, on returning to his room to read, found himself quite unable to concentrate his mind on the page. On Friday, as soon as he had got himself up as he thought Sue would like to see him, and made a hasty tea, he set out, notwithstanding that the evening was wet. The trees overhead deepened the gloom of the hour, and they dripped sadly upon him, impressing him with forebodings—illogical forebodings; for though he knew that he loved her he also knew that he could not be more to her than he was.

On turning the corner and entering the village the first sight that greeted his eyes was that of two figures under one umbrella coming out of the vicarage gate. He was too far back for them to notice him, but he knew in a moment that they were Sue and Phillotson. The latter was holding the umbrella over her head, and they had evidently been paying a visit to the vicar—probably on some business connected with the school work. And as they walked along the wet and deserted lane Jude saw Phillotson place his arm round the girl's waist; whereupon she gently removed it; but he replaced it; and she let it remain, looking quickly round her with an air of misgiving. She did not look absolutely behind her, and therefore did not see Jude, who sank into the hedge like one struck with a blight. There he remained hidden till they had reached Sue's cottage and she had passed in, Phillotson going on to the school hard by.

'O, he's too old for her—too old!' cried Jude in all the terrible sickness of hopeless, handicapped love.

He could not interfere. Was he not Arabella's? He was unable to go on further, and retraced his steps towards Christminster. Every tread of his feet seemed to say to him that he must on no account stand in the schoolmaster's way with Sue. Phillotson was perhaps twenty years her senior, but many a happy marriage had been made in such conditions of age. The ironical clinch to his sorrow was given by the thought that the intimacy between his cousin and the schoolmaster had been brought about entirely by himself.

VI

Jude's old and embittered aunt lay unwell at Marygreen, and on the following Sunday he went to see her—a visit which was the result of a victorious struggle against his inclination to turn aside to the village of Lumsdon and obtain a miserable interview with his cousin, in which the word nearest his heart could not be spoken, and the sight which had tortured him could not be revealed.

His aunt was now unable to leave her bed, and a great part of Jude's short day was occupied in making arrangements for her comfort. The little bakery business had been sold to a neighbour, and with the proceeds of this and her savings she was comfortably supplied with necessaries and more, a widow of the same village living with her and ministering to her wants. It was not till the time had nearly come for him to leave that he obtained a quiet talk with her, and his words tended insensibly towards his cousin.

'Was Sue born here?'

'She was—in this room. They were living here at that time. What made 'ee ask that?'

'O—I wanted to know.'

'Now you've been seeing her!' said the harsh old woman. 'And what did I tell 'ee?'

'Well—that I was not to see her.'

'Have you gossiped with her?'

'Yes.'

'Then don't keep it up. She was brought up by her father to hate her mother's family; and she'll look with no favour upon a working chap like you—a townish girl as she's become by now. I never cared much about her. A pert little thing, that's what she was too often, with her tight-strained nerves. Many's the time I've smacked her for her impertinence. Why, one day when she was walking into the pond with her shoes and stockings off, and her petticoats pulled above her knees, afore I could cry out for shame, she said: "Move on, aunty! This is no sight for modest eyes!" '

'She was a little child then.'

'She was twelve if a day.'

'Well—of course. But now she's older, she's of a thoughtful, quivering, tender nature, and as sensitive as—'

'Jude!' cried his aunt, springing up in bed. 'Don't you be a fool about her!'

'No, no, of course not.'

'Your marrying that woman Arabella was about as bad a thing as a man could possibly do for himself by trying hard. But she's gone to the other side of the world, and med never trouble you again. And there'll be a worse thing if you, tied and bound as you are, should have a fancy for Sue. If your cousin is civil to you, take her civility for what it is worth. But anything more than a relation's good wishes it is stark madness for 'ee to give her. If she's townish and wanton it med bring 'ee to ruin.'

'Don't say anything against her, aunt! Don't, please!'

A relief was afforded to him by the entry of the companion and nurse of his aunt, who must have been listening to the conversation, for she began a commentary on past years, introducing Sue Bridehead as a character in her recollections. She described what an odd little maid Sue had been when a pupil at the village school across the green opposite, before her father went to London—how, when the vicar arranged readings and recitations, she appeared on the platform, the smallest of them all, 'in her little white frock, and shoes, and pink sash'; how she recited 'Excelsior', 'There was a sound of revelry by night', and 'The Raven'; how during the delivery she would knit her little brows and glare round tragically, and say to the empty air, as if some real creature stood there—

'Ghastly, grim, and ancient Raven, wandering from the Nightly
shore,
Tell me what thy lordly name is on the Night's Plutonian shore!'

'She'd bring up the nasty carrion bird that clear,' corroborated the sick woman reluctantly, 'as she stood there in her little sash and things, that you could see un a'most before your very eyes. You too, Jude, had the same trick as a child of seeming to see things in the air.'

The neighbour told also of Sue's accomplishments in other kinds: 'She was not exactly a tomboy, you know; but she could do things that only boys do, as a rule. I've seen her hit in and steer down the long slide on yonder pond, with her little curls blowing, one of a file of twenty moving along against the sky like shapes painted on glass, and up the back slide without stopping. All boys except herself; and then they'd cheer her, and then she'd say, "Don't be saucy, boys," and suddenly run indoors. They'd try to coax her out again. But 'a wouldn't come.'

These retrospective visions of Sue only made Jude the more miserable that he was unable to woo her, and he left the cottage of his aunt that day with a heavy heart. He would fain have glanced into the school to see the room in which Sue's little figure had so glorified itself; but he checked his desire and went on.

It being Sunday evening some villagers who had known him during his residence here were standing in a group in their best clothes. Jude was startled by a salute from one of them:

'Ye've got there right enough, then!'

Jude showed that he did not understand.

'Why, to the seat of l'arning—the "City of Light" you used to talk to us about as a little boy! Is it all you expected of it?'

'Yes; more!' cried Jude.

'When I was there once for an hour I didn't see much in it for my part; auld crumbling buildings, half church, half almshouse, and not much going on at that.'

'You are wrong, John; there is more going on than meets the eye of a man walking through the streets. It is a unique centre of thought and religion—the intellectual and spiritual granary of this country. All that silence and absence of goings-on is the stillness of infinite motion—the sleep of the spinning-top, to borrow the simile of a well-known writer.'

'O, well, it med be all that, or it med not. As I say, I didn't see nothing of it the hour or two I was there; so I went in and had a pot o' beer, and a penny loaf, and a ha'porth o' cheese, and waited till it was time to come along home. You've j'ined a College by this time, I suppose?'

'Ah, no!' said Jude. 'I am almost as far off that as ever.'

'How so?'

Jude slapped his pocket.

'Just what we thought! Such places be not for such as you—only for them with plenty o' money.'

'There you are wrong,' said Jude, with some bitterness. 'They are for such ones!'

Still, the remark was sufficient to withdraw Jude's attention from the imaginative world he had lately inhabited, in which an abstract figure, more or less himself, was steeping his mind in a sublimation of the arts and sciences, and making his calling and election sure to a seat in the paradise of the learned. He was set regarding his prospects in a cold northern light. He had lately felt that he could not quite satisfy himself in his Greek—in the Greek of the dramatists particularly. So fatigued was he sometimes after his day's work that he could not maintain the critical attention necessary for thorough application. He felt that he wanted a coach—a friend at his elbow to tell him in a moment what sometimes would occupy him a weary month in extracting from unanticipative, clumsy books.

It was decidedly necessary to consider facts a little more closely than he had done of late. What was the good, after all, of using up his spare hours in a vague labour called 'private study' without giving an outlook on practicabilities?

'I ought to have thought of this before,' he said, as he journeyed back. 'It would have been better never to have embarked in the scheme at all than to do it without seeing clearly where I am going, or what I am aiming at. . . . This hovering outside the walls of the colleges, as if expecting some arm to be stretched out from them to lift me inside, won't do! I must get special information.'

The next week accordingly he sought it. What at first seemed an opportunity occurred one afternoon when he saw an elderly gentleman, who had been pointed out as the Head of a particular College, walking in the public path of a park-like enclosure near the spot at which Jude chanced to be sitting. The gentleman came nearer, and Jude looked anxiously at his face. It seemed benign, considerate, yet rather reserved. On second thoughts Jude felt that he could not go up and address him; but he was sufficiently influenced by the incident to think what a wise thing it would be for him to state his difficulties by letter to some of the best and most judicious of those old masters, and obtain their advice.

During the next week or two he accordingly placed himself in such positions about the city as would afford him glimpses of several of the most distinguished among the Provosts, Wardens, and other Heads of Houses; and from those he ultimately selected five whose physiognomies seemed to say to him that they were appreciative and far-seeing men. To these five he addressed letters, briefly stating his difficulties, and asking their opinion on his stranded situation.

When the letters were posted Jude mentally began to criticize them; he wished they had not been sent. 'It is just one of those intrusive, vulgar, pushing, applications which are so common in these days,' he thought. 'Why couldn't I know better than address utter strangers in such a way? I may be an impostor, an idle scamp, a man with a bad character, for all that they know to the contrary. . . . Perhaps that's what I am!'

Nevertheless, he found himself clinging to the hope of some reply as to his one last chance of redemption. He waited day after day, saying that it was perfectly absurd to expect, yet expecting. While he waited he was suddenly stirred by news about Phillotson. Phillotson was giving up the school near Christminster, for a larger one further south, in Mid-Wessex. What this meant; how it would affect his cousin; whether, as seemed possible, it was a practical move of the schoolmaster's towards a larger income, in view of a provision for two instead of one, he would not allow himself to say. And the tender relations between Phillotson and the young girl of whom Jude was passionately enamoured effectually made it repugnant to Jude's tastes to apply to Phillotson for advice on his own scheme.

Meanwhile the academic dignitaries to whom Jude had written vouchsafed no answer, and the young man was thus thrown back entirely on himself, as formerly, with the added gloom of a weakened hope. By indirect inquiries he soon perceived clearly, what he had long uneasily suspected, that to qualify himself for certain open scholarships and exhibitions was the only brilliant course. But to do this a good deal of coaching would be necessary, and much natural ability. It was next to impossible that a man reading on his own system, however widely and thoroughly, even over the prolonged period of ten years, should be able to compete with those who had passed their lives under trained teachers and had worked to ordained lines.

The other course, that of buying himself in, so to speak, seemed the only one really open to men like him, the difficulty being simply of a material kind. With the help of his information he began to reckon the extent of this material obstacle, and ascertained, to his dismay, that, at the rate at which, with the best of fortune, he would be able to save money, fifteen years must elapse before he could be in a position to forward testimonials to the Head of a College and advance to a matriculation examination. The undertaking was hopeless.

He saw what a curious and cunning glamour the neighbourhood of the place had exercised over him. To get there and live there, to move along the churches and halls and become imbued with the *genius loci*, had seemed to his dreaming youth, as the spot shaped its charms to him from its halo on the horizon, the obvious and ideal thing to do. 'Let me only get there,' he had said with the fatuousness of Crusoe over his big boat, 'and the rest is but a matter of time and energy.' It would have been far better for him in every way if he had never come within sight and sound of the delusive precincts, had gone to some busy commercial town with the sole object of making money by his wits, and thence surveyed his plan in true perspective. Well, all that was clear to him amounted to this, that the whole scheme had burst up, like an iridescent soap-bubble, under the touch of a reasoned inquiry. He looked back at himself along the vista of his past years, and his thought was akin to Heine's:

> Above the youth's inspired and flashing eyes
> I see the motley mocking fool's-cap rise!

Fortunately he had not been allowed to bring his disappointment into his dear Sue's life by involving her in this collapse. And the painful details of his awakening to a sense of his limitations should now be spared her as far as possible. After all, she had only known a little part of the miserable struggle in which he had been engaged thus unequipped, poor, and unforeseeing.

He always remembered the appearance of the afternoon on which he awoke from his dream. Not quite knowing what to do with himself, he went up to an octagonal chamber in the lantern of a singularly built theatre that was set amidst this quaint and singular city. It had windows all round, from which an outlook over the whole town and its edifices could be gained. Jude's eyes swept all the views in succession, meditatively, mournfully, yet sturdily. Those buildings and their associations and privileges were not for him. From the looming roof of the great library, into which he hardly ever had time to enter, his gaze travelled on to the varied spires, halls, gables, streets, chapels, gardens, quadrangles, which composed the *ensemble* of this unrivalled panorama. He saw that his destiny lay not with these, but among the manual toilers in the shabby purlieu which he himself occupied, unrecognized as part of the city at all by its visitors and panegyrists, yet without whose denizens the hard readers could not read nor the high thinkers live.

He looked over the town into the country beyond, to the trees which screened her whose presence had at first been the support of his heart, and whose loss was now a maddening torture. But for this blow he might have borne with his fate. With Sue as companion he could have renounced his ambitions with a smile. Without her it was inevitable that the reaction from the long strain to which he had subjected himself should affect him disastrously. Phillotson had no doubt passed through a similar intellectual disappointment to that which now enveloped him. But the schoolmaster had been since blest with the consolation of sweet Sue, while for him there was no consoler.

Descending to the streets, he went listlessly along till he arrived at an inn, and entered it. Here he drank several glasses of beer in rapid succession, and when he came out it was night. By the light of the flickering lamps he rambled home to supper, and had not long been sitting at table when his landlady brought up a letter that had just arrived for him. She laid it down as if impressed with a sense of its possible importance, and on looking at it Jude perceived that it bore the embossed stamp of one of the Colleges whose heads he had addressed. '*One*—at last!' cried Jude.

The communication was brief, and not exactly what he had expected; though it really was from the Master in person. It ran thus:

BIBLIOLL COLLEGE

SIR,—I have read your letter with interest; and, judging from your description of yourself as a working-man, I venture to think that you will have a much better chance of success in life by remaining in your own sphere and sticking to your trade than by adopting any other course. That, therefore, is what I advise you to do. Yours faithfully,

T. TETUPHENAY

To Mr J. FAWLEY, Stone-mason

This terribly sensible advice exasperated Jude. He had known all that before. He knew it was true. Yet it seemed a hard slap after ten years of labour, and its effect upon him just now was to make him rise recklessly from the table, and, instead of reading as usual, to go downstairs and into the street. He stood at a bar and tossed off two or three glasses, then unconsciously sauntered along till he came to a spot called The Fourways in the middle of the city, gazing abstractedly at the groups of people like one in a trance, till, coming to himself, he began talking to the policeman fixed there.

That officer yawned, stretched out his elbows, elevated himself an inch and a half on the balls of his toes, smiled, and looking humorously at Jude, said, 'You've had a wet, young man.'

'No; I've only begun,' he replied cynically.

Whatever his wetness, his brains were dry enough. He only heard in part the policeman's further remarks, having fallen into thought on what struggling people like himself had stood at that Crossway, whom nobody ever thought of now. It had more history than the oldest college in the city. It was literally teeming, stratified, with the shades of human groups, who had met there for tragedy, comedy, farce; real enactments of the intensest kind. At Fourways men had stood and talked of Napoleon, the loss of America, the execution of King Charles, the burning of the Martyrs, the Crusades, the Norman Conquest, possibly of the arrival of Caesar. Here the two sexes had met for loving, hating, coupling, parting; had waited, had suffered, for each other; had triumphed over each other; cursed each other in jealousy, blessed each other in forgiveness.

He began to see that the town life was a book of humanity infinitely more palpitating, varied, and compendious that the gown life. These struggling men and women before him were the reality of Christminster, though they knew little of Christ or Minster. That was one of the humours of things. The floating population of students and teachers, who did know both in a way, were not Christminster in a local sense at all.

He looked at his watch, and, in pursuit of this idea, he went on till he came to a public hall, where a promenade concert was in progress. Jude entered, and found the room full of shop youths and girls, soldiers, apprentices, boys of eleven smoking cigarettes, and light women of the more respectable and amateur class. He has tapped the real Christminster life. A band was playing, and the crowd walked about and jostled each other, and every now and then a man got upon a platform and sang a comic song.

The spirit of Sue seemed to hover round him and prevent his flirting and drinking with the frolicsome girls who made advances—wistful to gain a little joy. At ten o'clock he came away, choosing a circuitous route homeward to pass the gates of the College whose Head had just sent him the note.

The gates were shut, and, by an impulse, he took from his pocket the lump of chalk which as a workman he usually carried there, and wrote along the wall:

'I have understanding as well as you; I am not inferior to you: yea, who knoweth not such things as these?' —Job xii. 3.

VII

The stroke of scorn relieved his mind, and the next morning he laughed at his self-conceit. But the laugh was not a healthy one. He re-read the letter from the Master, and the wisdom in its lines, which had at first exasperated him, chilled and depressed him now. He saw himself as a fool indeed.

Deprived of the objects of both intellect and emotion, he could not proceed to his work. Whenever he felt reconciled to his fate as a student, there came to disturb his calm his hopeless relations with Sue. That the one affined soul he had ever met was lost to him through his marriage returned upon him with cruel persistency, till, unable to bear it longer, he again rushed for distraction to the real Christminster life. He now sought it out in an obscure and low-ceiled tavern up a court which was well known to certain worthies of the place, and in brighter times would have interested him simply by its quaintness. Here he sat more or less all the day, convinced that he was at bottom a vicious character, of whom it was hopeless to expect anything.

In the evening the frequenters of the house dropped in one by one, Jude still retaining his seat in the corner, though his money was all spent, and he had not eaten anything the whole day except a biscuit. He surveyed his gathering companions with all the equanimity and philosophy of a man who has been drinking long and slowly, and made friends with several: to wit, Tinker Taylor, a decayed church-ironmonger who appeared to have been of a religious turn in earlier years, but was somewhat blasphemous now; also a red-nosed auctioneer; also two Gothic masons like himself, called Uncle Jim and Uncle Joe. There were present, too, some clerks, and a gown- and surplice-maker's assistant; two ladies who sported moral characters of various depths of shade, according to their company, nicknamed 'Bower o' Bliss' and 'Freckles'; some horsey men 'in the know' of betting circles; a travelling actor from the theatre, and two devil-may-care young men who proved to be gownless undergraduates; they had slipped in by stealth to meet a man about bull-pups, and stayed to drink and smoke short pipes with the racing gents aforesaid, looking at their watches every now and then.

The conversation waxed general. Christminster society was criticized, the Dons, magistrates, and other people in authority being sincerely pitied for their shortcomings, while opinions on how they ought to conduct themselves and their affairs to be properly respected, were exchanged in a large-minded and disinterested manner.

Jude Fawley, with the self-conceit, effrontery, and *aplomb* of a strong-brained fellow in liquor, threw in his remarks somewhat peremptorily; and his aims having been what they were for so many years, everything the others said turned upon his tongue, by a sort of mechanical craze, to the subject of scholarship and study, the extent of his own learning being dwelt upon with an insistence that would have appeared pitiable to himself in his sane hours.

'I don't care a damn,' he was saying, 'for any Provost, Warden, Principal, Fellow, or cursed Master of Arts in the University! What I know is that I'd lick 'em on their own ground if they'd give me a chance, and show 'em a few things they are not up to yet!'

'Hear, hear!' said the undergraduates from the corner, where they were talking privately about the pups.

'You always was fond o' books, I've heard,' said Tinker Taylor, 'and I don't doubt what you state. Now with me 'twas different. I always saw there was more to be learnt outside a book than in; and I took my steps accordingly, or I shouldn't have been the man I am.'

'You aim at the Church, I believe?' said Uncle Joe. 'If you are such a scholar as to pitch yer hopes so high as that, why not give us a specimen of your scholarship? Canst say the Creed in Latin, man? That was how they once put it to a chap down in my country.'

'I should think so!' said Jude haughtily.

'Not he! Like his conceit!' screamed one of the ladies.

'Just you shut up, Bower o' Bliss!' said one of the undergraduates.

'Silence!' He drank off the spirits in his tumbler, rapped with it on the counter, and announced, 'The gentleman in the corner is going to rehearse the Articles of his Belief, in the Latin tongue, for the edification of the company.'

'I won't!' said Jude.

'Yes—have a try!' said the surplice-maker.

'You can't!' said Uncle Joe.

'Yes, he can!' said Tinker Taylor.

'I'll swear I can!' said Jude. 'Well, come now, stand me a small Scotch cold, and I'll do it straight off.'

'That's a fair offer,' said the undergraduate, throwing down the money for the whisky.

The barmaid concocted the mixture with the bearing of a person compelled to live amongst animals of inferior species, and the glass was handed across to Jude, who, having drunk the contents, stood up and began rhetorically, without hesitation:

'Credo in unum Deum, Patrem omnipotentem, Factorem coeli et terrae, visibilium omnium et invisibilium.'

'Good! Excellent Latin!' cried one of the undergraduates, who, however, had not the slightest conception of a single word.

A silence reigned among the rest in the bar, and the maid stood still, Jude's voice echoing sonorously into the inner parlour, where the landlord was dozing, and bringing him out to see what was gong on. Jude had declaimed steadily ahead, and was continuing:

'Crucifixus etiam pro nobis: sub Pontio Pilato passus, et sepultus est. Et resurrexit tertia die, secundum Scripturas.'

'That's the Nicene,' sneered the second undergraduate. 'And we wanted the Apostles'!'

'You didn't say so! And every fool knows, except you, that the Nicene is the most historic creed!'

'Let un go on, let un go on!' said the auctioneer.

But Jude's mind seemed to grow confused soon, and he could not get on. He put his hand to his forehead, and his face assumed an expression of pain.

'Give him another glass—then he'll fetch up and get through it,' said Tinker Taylor.

Somebody threw down threepence, the glass was handed, Jude

stretched out his arm for it without looking, and having swallowed the liquor, went on in a moment in a revived voice, raising it as he neared the end with the manner of a priest leading a congregation:

'Et in Spiritum Sanctum, Dominum et vivificantem, qui ex Patre Filioque procedit. Qui cum Patre et Filio simul adoratur et conglorificatur. Qui locutus est per prophetas.

'Et unam Catholicam et Apostolicam Ecclesiam. Confiteor unum Baptisma in remissionem peccatorum. Et expecto Ressurectionem mortuorum. Et vitam venturi saeculi. Amen.'

'Well done!' said several, enjoying the last word, as being the first and only one they had recognized.

Then Jude seemed to shake the fumes from his brain, as he stared round upon them.

'You pack of fools!' he cried. 'Which one of you knows whether I have said it or no? It might have been the Rat-catcher's Daughter in double Dutch for all that your besotted heads can tell! See what I have brought myself to—the crew I have come among!'

The landlord, who had already had his license endorsed for harbouring queer characters, feared a riot, and came outside the counter; but Jude, in his sudden flash of reason, had turned in disgust and left the scene, the door slamming with a dull thud behind him.

He hastened down the lane and round into the straight broad street, which he followed till it merged in the highway, and all sound of his late companions had been left behind. Onward he still went, under the influence of a childlike yearning for the one being in the world to whom it seemed possible to fly—an unreasoning desire, whose ill judgment was not apparent to him now. In the course of an hour, when it was between ten and eleven o'clock, he entered the village of Lumsdon, and reaching the cottage, saw that a light was burning in a downstairs room, which he assumed, rightly as it happened, to be hers.

Jude stepped close to the wall, and tapped with his finger on the pane, saying impatiently, 'Sue. Sue!'

She must have recognized his voice, for the light disappeared from the apartment, and in a second or two the door was unlocked and opened, and Sue appeared with a candle in her hand.

'Is it Jude? Yes, it is! My dear, dear cousin, what's the matter?'

'Oh, I am—I couldn't help coming, Sue!' he said, sinking down upon the doorstep. 'I am so wicked, Sue—my heart is nearly broken, and I could not bear my life as it was! So I have been drinking, and blaspheming, or next door to it, and saying holy things in disreputable quarters—repeating in idle bravado words which ought never to be uttered but reverently! O, do anything with me, Sue—kill me—I don't care! Only don't hate me and despise me like all the rest of the world!'

'You are ill, poor dear! No, I won't despise you; of course I won't! Come in and rest, and let me see what I can do for you. Now lean on me, and don't mind.' With one hand holding the candle and the other supporting him, she led him indoors, and placed him in the only easy-chair the meagrely furnished house afforded, stretching his feet upon another, and pulling off his boots. Jude, now getting towards his sober senses, could only say, 'Dear, dear Sue!' in a voice broken by grief and contrition.

She asked him if he wanted anything to eat, but he shook his head. Then telling him to go to sleep, and that she would come down early in the morning and get him some breakfast, she bade him good-night and ascended the stairs.

Almost immediately he fell into a heavy slumber, and did not wake till dawn. At first he did not know where he was, but by degrees his situation cleared to him, and he beheld it in all the ghastliness of a right mind. She knew the worst of him—the very worst. How could he face her now? She would soon be coming down to see about breakfast, as she had said, and there would he be in all his shame confronting her. He could not bear the thought, and softly drawing on his boots, and taking his hat from the nail on which she had hung it, he slipped noiselessly out of the house.

His fixed idea was to get away to some obscure spot and hide, and perhaps pray; and the only spot which occurred to him was Marygreen. He called at his lodging in Christminster, where he found awaiting him a note of dismissal from his employer; and having packed up he turned his back upon the city that had been such a thorn in his side, and struck southward into Wessex. He had no money left in his pocket, his small savings, deposited at one of the banks in Christminster, having fortunately been left untouched. To get to Marygreen, therefore, his only course was walking; and the distance being nearly twenty miles, he had ample time to complete on the way the sobering process begun in him.

At some hour of the evening he reached Alfredston. Here he pawned his waistcoat, and having gone out of the town a mile or two, slept under a rick that night. At dawn he rose, shook off the hayseeds and stems from his clothes, and started again, breasting the long white road up the hill to the downs, which had been visible to him a long way off, and passing the milestone at the top, whereupon he had carved his hopes years ago.

He reached the ancient hamlet while the people were at breakfast. Weary and mud-bespattered, but quite possessed of his ordinary clearness of brain, he sat down by the well, thinking as he did so what a poor Christ he made. Seeing a trough of water near he bathed his face, and went on to the cottage of his great-aunt, whom he found breakfasting in bed, attended by the woman who lived with her.

'What—out o' work?' asked his relative, regarding him through eyes sunken deep, under lids heavy as pot-covers, no other cause for his tumbled appearance suggesting itself to one whose whole life had been a struggle with material things.

'Yes,' said Jude heavily. 'I think I must have a little rest.'

Refreshed by some breakfast, he went up to his old room and lay down in his shirt-sleeves, after the manner of the artizan. He fell asleep for a short while, and when he awoke it was as if he had awakened in hell. It *was* hell—'the hell of conscious failure', both in ambition and in love. He thought of that previous abyss into which he had fallen before leaving this part of the country; the deepest deep he had supposed it then; but it was not so deep as this. That had been the breaking of the outer bulwarks of his hope: this was of his second line.

If he had been a woman he must have screamed under the nervous tension which he was now undergoing. But that relief being denied to his virility, he clenched his teeth in misery, bringing lines about his mouth like those in the Laocoon, and corrugations between his brows.

A mournful wind blew through the trees, and sounded in the chimney like the pedal notes of an organ. Each ivy leaf overgrowing the wall of the churchless churchyard hard by, now abandoned, pecked its neighbour smartly, and the vane on the new Victorian-Gothic church in the new spot had already begun to creak. Yet apparently it was not always the outdoor wind that made the deep murmurs; it was a voice. He guessed its origin in a moment or two; the curate was praying with his aunt in the adjoining room. He remembered her speaking of him. Presently the sounds ceased, and a step seemed to cross the landing. Jude sat up, and shouted 'Hoi!'

The step made for his door, which was open, and a man looked in. It was a young clergyman.

'I think you are Mr Highridge,' said Jude. 'My aunt has mentioned you more than once. Well, here I am, just come home; a fellow gone to the bad; though I had the best intentions in the world at one time. Now I am melancholy mad, what with drinking and one thing and another.'

Slowly Jude unfolded to the curate his late plans and movements, by an unconscious bias dwelling less upon the intellectual and ambitious side of his dream, and more upon the theological, though this had, up till now, been merely a portion of the general plan of advancement.

'Now I know I have been a fool, and that folly is with me,' added Jude in conclusion. 'And I don't regret the collapse of my University hopes one jot. I wouldn't begin again if I were sure to succeed. I don't care for social success any more at all. But I do feel I should like to do some good thing; and I bitterly regret the Church, and the loss of my chance of being her ordained minister.'

The curate, who was a new man to this neighbourhood, had grown deeply interested, and at last he said: 'If you feel a real call to the ministry, and I won't say from your conversation that you do not, for it is that of a thoughtful and educated man, you might enter the Church as a licentiate. Only you must make up your mind to avoid strong drink.'

'I could avoid that easily enough, if I had any kind of hope to support me!'

PART THIRD

AT MELCHESTER

'For there was no other girl, O bridegroom, like her!'

—Sappho (*H. T. Wharton*)

I

It was a new idea—the ecclesiastical and altruistic life as distinct from the intellectual and emulative life. A man could preach and do good to his fellow-creatures without taking double-firsts in the schools of Christminster, or having anything but ordinary knowledge. The old fancy which had led on to the culminating vision of the bishopric had not been an ethical or theological enthusiasm at all, but a mundane ambition masquerading in a surplice. He feared that his whole scheme had degenerated to, even though it might not have originated in, a social unrest which had no foundation in the nobler instincts; which was purely an artificial product of civilization. There were thousands of young men on the same self-seeking track at the present moment. The sensual hind who ate, drank, and lived carelessly with his wife through the days of his vanity was a more likable being than he.

But to enter the Church in such an unscholarly way that he could not in any probability rise to a higher grade through all his career than that of the humble curate wearing his life out in an obscure village or city slum—that might have a touch of goodness and greatness in it; that might be true religion, and a purgatorial course worthy of being followed by a remorseful man.

The favourable light in which this new thought showed itself by contrast with his foregone intentions cheered Jude, as he sat there, shabby and lonely; and it may be said to have given, during the next few days, the *coup de grâce* to his intellectual career—a career which had extended over the greater part of a dozen years. He did nothing, however, for some long stagnant time to advance his new desire, occupying himself with little local jobs in putting up and lettering headstones about the neighbouring villages, and submitting to be regarded as a social failure, a returned purchase, by the half-dozen or so of farmers and other country-people who condescended to nod to him.

The human interest of the new intention—and a human interest is indispensable to the most spiritual and self-sacrificing—was created by a letter from Sue, bearing a fresh postmark. She evidently wrote with anxiety, and told very little about her own doings, more than that she had passed some sort of examination for a Queen's Scholarship, and was going to enter a Training College at Melchester to complete herself for a vocation she had chosen, partly by his influence. There was a Theological College at Melchester; Melchester was a quiet and soothing place, almost entirely ecclesiastical in its tone; a spot where worldly learning and intellectual smartness had no establishment; where the altruistic feeling that he did possess would perhaps be more highly estimated than a brilliancy which he did not.

As it would be necessary that he should continue for a time to work at his trade while reading up Divinity, which he had neglected at Christminster for the ordinary classical grind, what better course for him than to get employment at the further city, and pursue this plan of reading? That his excessive human interest in the new place was entirely of Sue's making, while at the same time Sue was to be regarded even less than formerly as proper to create it, had an ethical contradictoriness to which he was not blind. But that much he conceded to human frailty, and hoped to learn to love her only as a friend and kinswoman.

He considered that he might so mark out his coming years as to begin his ministry at the age of thirty—an age which much attracted him as being that of his exemplar when he first began to teach in Galilee. This would allow him plenty of time for deliberate study, and for acquiring capital by his trade to help his aftercourse of keeping the necessary terms at a Theological College.

Christmas had come and passed, and Sue had gone to the Melchester Normal School. The time was just the worst in the year for Jude to get into new employment, and he had written suggesting to her that he should postpone his arrival for a month or so, till the days had lengthened. She had acquiesced so readily that he wished he had not proposed it—she evidently did not much care about him, though she had never once reproached him for his strange conduct in coming to her that night, and his silent disappearance. Neither had she ever said a word about her relations with Mr Phillotson.

Suddenly, however, quite a passionate letter arrived from Sue. She was quite lonely and miserable, she told him. She hated the place she was in; it was worse than the ecclesiastical designer's; worse than anywhere. She felt utterly friendless; could he come immediately?—though when he did come she would only be able to see him at limited times, the rules of the establishment she found herself in being strict to a degree. It was Mr Phillotson who had advised her to come there, and she wished she had never listened to him.

Phillotson's suit was not exactly prospering, evidently; and Jude felt unreasonably glad. He packed up his things and went to Melchester with a lighter heart than he had known for months.

This being the turning over a new leaf he duly looked about for a temperance hotel, and found a little establishment of that description in the street leading from the station. When he had had something to eat he walked out into the dull winter light over the town bridge, and turned the corner towards the Close. The day was foggy, and standing under the walls of the most graceful architectural pile in England he paused and looked up. The lofty building was visible as far as the roof-ridge; above, the dwindling spire rose more and more remotely, till its apex was quite lost in the mist drifting across it.

The lamps now began to be lighted, and turning to the west front he walked round. He took it as a good omen that numerous blocks of stone were lying about, which signified that the cathedral was undergoing restoration or repair to a considerable extent. It seemed to him, full of the superstitions of his beliefs, that this was an exercise of forethought on the part of a ruling Power, that he might find plenty to do in the art he practised while waiting for a call to higher labours.

Then a wave of warmth came over him as he thought how near he stood to the bright-eyed vivacious girl with the broad forehead and pile of dark hair above it; the girl with the kindling glance, daringly soft at times—something like that of the girls he had seen in engravings from paintings of the Spanish school. She was here—actually in this Close—in one of the houses confronting this very west façade.

He went down the broad gravel path towards the building. It was an ancient edifice of the fifteenth century, once a palace, now a training-school, with mullioned and transomed windows, and a courtyard in front shut in from the road by a wall. Jude opened the gate and went up to the door through which, on inquiring for his cousin, he was gingerly admitted to a waiting-room, and in a few minutes she came.

Though she had been here such a short while, she was not as he had seen her last. All her bounding manner was gone; her curves of motion had become subdued lines. The screens and subtleties of convention had likewise disappeared. Yet neither was she quite the woman who had written the letter that summoned him. That had plainly been dashed off in an impulse which second thoughts had somewhat regretted; thoughts that were possibly of his recent self-disgrace. Jude was quite overcome with emotion.

'You don't—think me a demoralized wretch—for coming to you as I was—and going so shamefully, Sue?'

'O, I have tried not to! You said enough to let me know what had caused it. I hope I shall never have any doubt of your worthiness, my poor Jude! And I am glad you have come!'

She wore a mulberry-coloured gown with a little lace collar. It was made quite plain, and hung about her slight figure with clinging gracefulness. Her hair, which formerly she had worn according to the custom of the day, was now twisted up tightly, and she had altogether the air of a woman clipped and pruned by severe discipline, an under-brightness shining through from the depths which that discipline had not yet been able to reach.

She had come forward prettily; but Jude felt that she had hardly expected him to kiss her, as he was burning to do, under other colours than those of cousinship. He could not perceive the least sign that Sue regarded him as a lover, or ever would do so, now that she knew the worst of him, even if he had the right to behave as one; and this helped on his growing resolve to tell her of his matrimonial entanglement, which he had put off doing from time to time in sheer dread of losing the bliss of her company.

Sue came out into the town with him, and they walked and talked with tongues centred only on the passing moments. Jude said he would like to buy her a little present of some sort, and then she confessed, with something of shame, that she was dreadfully hungry. They were kept on very short allowances in the College, and a dinner, tea, and supper all in one was the present she most desired in the world. Jude thereupon took her to an inn and ordered whatever the house afforded, which was not much. The place, however, gave them a delightful opportunity for a *tête-à-tête*, nobody else being in the room, and they talked freely.

She told him about the school as it was at that date, and the rough living, and the mixed character of her fellow-students, gathered together from all parts of the diocese, and how she had to get up and work by gas-light in the early morning, with all the bitterness of a young person to whom restraint was new. To all this he listened; but it was not what he wanted especially to know—her relations with Phillotson. That was what she did not tell. When they had sat and eaten, Jude impulsively placed his hand upon hers; she looked up and smiled, and took his quite freely into her own little soft one, dividing his fingers and coolly examining them, as if they were the fingers of a glove she was purchasing.

'Your hands are rather rough, Jude, aren't they?' she said.

'Yes. So would yours be if they held a mallet and chisel all day.'

'I don't dislike it, you know. I think it is noble to see a man's hands subdued to what he works in. . . . Well, I'm rather glad I came to this Training-School, after all. See how independent I shall be after the two years' training! I shall pass pretty high, I expect, and Mr Phillotson will use his influence to get me a big school.'

She had touched the subject at last. 'I had a suspicion, a fear,' said Jude, 'that he—cared about you rather warmly, and perhaps wanted to marry you.'

'Now don't be such a silly boy!'

'He has said something about it, I expect.'

'If he had, what would it matter? An old man like him!'

'O, come, Sue; he's not so very old. And I know what I saw him doing—'

'Not kissing me—that I'm certain!'

'No. But putting his arm round your waist.'

'Ah—I remember. But I didn't know he was going to.'

'You are wriggling out of it, Sue, and it isn't quite kind!'

Her ever-sensitive lip began to quiver, and her eye to blink, at something this reproof was deciding her to say.

'I know you'll be angry if I tell you everything, and that's why I don't want to!'

'Very well, then, dear,' he said soothingly. 'I have no real right to ask you, and I don't wish to know.'

'I shall tell you!' said she, with the perverseness that was part of her. 'This is what I have done: I have promised—I have promised—that I will marry him when I come out of the Training-School two years hence, and have got my Certificate; his plan being that we shall then take a large double school in a great town—he the boys' and I the girls'—as married school-teachers often do, and make a good income between us.'

'O, Sue! . . . But of course it is right—you couldn't have done better!'

He glanced at her and their eyes met, the reproach in his own belying his words. Then he drew his hand quite away from hers, and turned his face in estrangement from her to the window. Sue regarded him passively without moving.

'I knew you would be angry!' she said with an air of no emotion whatever. 'Very well—I am wrong, I suppose! I ought not to have let you come to see me! We had better not meet again; and we'll only correspond at long intervals, on purely business matters!'

This was just the one thing he would not be able to bear, as she probably knew, and it brought him round at once. 'O yes, we will,' he said quickly. 'Your being engaged can make no difference to me whatever. I have a perfect right to see you when I want to; and I shall!'

'Then don't let us talk of it any more. It is quite spoiling our evening together. What does it matter about what one is going to do two years hence!'

She was something of a riddle to him, and he let the subject drift away. 'Shall we go and sit in the Cathedral?' he asked, when their meal was finished.

'Cathedral? Yes. Though I think I'd rather sit in the railway station,' she answered, a remnant of vexation still in her voice. 'That's the centre of the town life now. The Cathedral has had its day!'

'How modern you are!'

'So would you be if you had lived so much in the Middle Ages as I have done these last few years! The Cathedral was a very good place four or five centuries ago; but it is played out now . . . I am not modern, either. I am more ancient than mediaevalism, if you only knew.'

Jude looked distressed.

'There—I won't say any more of that!' she cried. 'Only you don't know how bad I am, from your point of view, or you wouldn't think so much of me, or care whether I was engaged or not. Now there's just time for us to walk round the Close, then I must go in, or I shall be locked out for the night.'

He took her to the gate and they parted. Jude had a conviction that his unhappy visit to her on that sad night had precipitated this marriage engagement, and it did anything but add to his happiness. Her reproach had taken that shape, then, and not the shape of words. However, next day he set about seeking employment, which was not so easy to get as at Christminster, there being, as a rule, less stone-cutting in progress in this quiet city, and hands being mostly permanent. But he edged himself in by degrees. His first work was some carving at the cemetery on the hill; and ultimately he became engaged on the labour he most desired—the Cathedral repairs, which were very extensive, the whole interior stonework having been overhauled, to be largely replaced by new.

It might be a labour of years to get it all done, and he had confidence enough in his own skill with the mallet and chisel to feel that it would be a matter of choice with himself how long he would stay.

The lodgings he took near the Close Gate would not have disgraced a curate, the rent representing a higher percentage on his wages than mechanics of any sort usually care to pay. His combined bed and sitting room was furnished with framed photographs of the rectories and deaneries at which his landlady had lived as trusted servant in her time, and the parlour downstairs bore a clock on the mantelpiece inscribed to the effect that it was presented to the same serious-minded woman by her fellow-servants on the occasion of her marriage. Jude added to the furniture of his room by unpacking photographs of the ecclesiastical carvings and monuments that he had executed with his own hands; and he was deemed a satisfactory acquisition as tenant of the vacant apartment.

He found an ample supply of theological books in the city bookshops, and with these his studies were recommenced in a different spirit and direction from his former course. As a relaxation from the Fathers, and such stock works as Paley and Butler, he read Newman, Pusey, and many other modern lights. He hired a harmonium, set it up in his lodging, and practised chants thereon, single and double.

II

'To-morrow is our grand day, you know. Where shall we go?'

'I have leave from three till nine. Wherever we can get to and come back from in that time. Not ruins, Jude—I don't care for them.'

'Well—Wardour Castle. And then we can do Fonthill if we like—all in the same afternoon.'

'Wardour is Gothic ruins—and I hate Gothic!'

'No. Quite otherwise. It is a classic building—Corinthian, I think; with a lot of pictures.'

'Ah—that will do. I like the sound of Corinthian. We'll go.'

Their conversation had run thus some few weeks later, and next morning they prepared to start. Every detail of the outing was a facet reflecting a sparkle to Jude, and he did not venture to meditate on the life of inconsistency he was leading. His Sue's conduct was one lovely conundrum to him; he could say no more.

There duly came the charm of calling at the College door for her; her emergence in a nunlike simplicity of costume that was rather enforced than desired; the traipsing along to the station, the porters' 'B'your leave!' the screaming of the trains—everything formed the basis of a beautiful crystallization. Nobody stared at Sue, because she was so plainly dressed, which comforted Jude in the thought that only himself knew the charms those habiliments subdued. A matter of ten pounds spent in a drapery-shop, which had no connection with her real life or her real self, would have set all Melchester staring. The guard of the train thought they were lovers, and put them into a compartment all by themselves.

'That's a good intention wasted!' said she.

Jude did not respond. He thought the remark unnecessarily cruel, and partly untrue.

They reached the Park and Castle and wandered through the

picture-galleries, Jude stopping by preference in front of the devotional pictures of Del Sarto, Guido Reni, Spagnoletto, Sassoferrato, Carlo Dolci, and others. Sue paused patiently beside him, and stole critical looks into his face as, regarding the Virgins, Holy Families, and Saints, it grew reverent and abstracted. When she had thoroughly estimated him at this, she would move on and wait for him before a Lely or Reynolds. It was evident that her cousin deeply interested her, as one might be interested in a man puzzling out his way along a labyrinth from which one had one's self escaped.

When they came out a long time still remained to them, and Jude proposed that as soon as they had had something to eat they should walk across the high country to the north of their present position, and intercept the train of another railway leading back to Melchester, at a station about seven miles off. Sue, who was inclined for any adventure that would intensify the sense of her day's freedom, readily agreed; and away they went, leaving the adjoining station behind them.

It was indeed open country, wide and high. They talked and bounded on, Jude cutting from a little covert a long walking-stick for Sue as tall as herself, with a great crook, which made her look like a shepherdess. About half-way on their journey they crossed a main road running due east and west—the old road from London to Land's End. They paused, and looked up and down it for a moment, and remarked upon the desolation which had come over this once lively thoroughfare, while the wind dipped to earth and scooped straws and hay-stems from the ground.

They crossed the road and passed on, but during the next half-mile Sue seemed to grow tired, and Jude began to be distressed for her. They had walked a good distance altogether, and if they could not reach the other station it would be rather awkward. For a long time there was no cottage visible on the wide expanse of down and turnip-land; but presently they came to a sheepfold, and next to the shepherd, pitching hurdles. He told them that the only house near was his mother's and his, pointing to a little dip ahead from which a faint blue smoke arose, and recommended them to go on and rest there.

This they did, and entered the house, admitted by an old woman without a single tooth, to whom they were as civil as strangers can be when their only chance of rest and shelter lies in the favour of the householder.

'A nice little cottage,' said Jude.

'O, I don't know about the niceness. I shall have to thatch it soon, and where the thatch is to come from I can't tell, for straw do get that dear, that 'twill soon be cheaper to cover your house wi' chainey plates than thatch.'

They sat resting, and the shepherd came in. 'Don't 'ee mind I,' he said with a deprecating wave of the hand; 'bide here as long as ye will. But mid you be thinking o' getting back to Melchester tonight by train? Because you'll never do it in this world, since you don't know the lie of the country. I don't mind going with ye some o' the ways, but even then the train mid be gone.'

They started up.

'You can bide here, you know, over the night—can't 'em, mother? The place is welcome to ye. 'Tis hard lying, rather, but volk may do worse.' He turned to Jude and asked privately: 'Be you a married couple?'

'Hsh—no!' said Jude.

'O—I meant nothing ba'dy—not I! Well then, she can go into mother's room, and you and I can lie in the outer chimmer after they've gone through. I can call ye soon enough to catch the first train back. You've lost this one now.'

On consideration they decided to close with this offer, and drew up and shared with the shepherd and his mother the boiled bacon and greens for supper.

'I rather like this,' said Sue, while their entertainers were clearing away the dishes. 'Outside all laws except gravitation and germination.'

'You only think you like it; you don't: you are quite a product of civilization,' said Jude, a recollection of her engagement reviving his soreness a little.

'Indeed I am not, Jude. I like reading and all that, but I crave to get back to the life of my infancy and its freedom.'

'Do you remember it so well? You seem to me to have nothing unconventional at all about you.'

'O, haven't I! You don't know what's inside me.'

'What?'

'The Ishmaelite.'

'An urban miss is what you are.'

She looked severe disagreement, and turned away.

The shepherd aroused them the next morning, as he had said. It was bright and clear, and the four miles to the train were accomplished pleasantly. When they had reached Melchester, and walked to the Close, and the gables of the old building in which she was again to be immured rose before Sue's eyes, she looked a little scared. 'I expect I shall catch it!' she murmured.

They rang the great bell and waited.

'O, I bought something for you, which I had nearly forgotten,' she said quickly, searching her pocket. 'It is a new little photograph of me. Would you like it!'

'*Would* I!' He took it gladly, and the porter came. There seemed to be an ominous glance on his face when he opened the gate. She passed in, looking back at Jude, and waving her hand.

III

The seventy young women, of ages varying in the main from nineteen to one-and-twenty, though several were older, who at this date filled the species of nunnery known as the Training-School at Melchester, formed a very mixed community, which included the daughters of mechanics, curates, surgeons, shopkeepers, farmers, dairymen, soldiers, sailors, and villagers. They sat in the large school-room of the establishment on the evening previously described, and word was passed round that Sue Bridehead had not come in at closing-time.

'She went out with her young man,' said a second-year's student, who knew about young men. 'And Miss Traceley saw her at the station with him. She'll have it hot when she does come.'

'She said he was her cousin,' observed a youthful new girl.

'That excuse has been made a little too often in this school to be effectual in saving our souls,' said the head girl of the year, drily.

The fact was that, only twelve months before, there had occurred a lamentable seduction of one of the pupils, who had made the same statement in order to gain meetings with her lover. The affair had created a scandal, and the management had consequently been rough on cousins ever since.

At nine o'clock the names were called, Sue's being pronounced three times sonorously by Miss Traceley without eliciting an answer.

At a quarter past nine the seventy stood up to sing the 'Evening Hymn', and then knelt down to prayers. After prayers they went in to supper, and every girl's thought was, Where is Sue Bridehead? Some of the students, who had seen Jude from the window, felt that they would not mind risking her punishment for the pleasure of being kissed by such a friendly-faced young man. Hardly one among them believed in cousinship.

Half-an-hour later they all lay in their cubicles, their tender feminine faces upturned to the flaring gas-jets which at intervals stretched down the long dormitories, every face bearing the legend 'The Weaker' upon it, as the penalty of the sex wherein they were moulded, which by no possible exertion of their willing hearts and abilities could be made strong while the inexorable laws of nature remain what they are. They formed a pretty, suggestive, pathetic sight, of whose pathos and beauty they were themselves unconscious, and would not discover till, amid the storms and strains of after-years, with their injustice, loneliness, child-bearing, and bereavement, their minds would revert to this experience as to something which had been allowed to slip past them insufficiently regarded.

One of the mistresses came in to turn out the lights, and before doing so gave a final glance at Sue's cot, which remained empty, and her little dressing-table at the foot, which, like all the rest, was ornamented with various girlish trifles, framed photographs being not the least conspicuous among them. Sue's table had a moderate show, two men in their filigree and velvet frames standing together beside her looking-glass.

'Who are these men—did she ever say?' asked the mistress. 'Strictly speaking, relations' portraits only are allowed on these tables, you know.'

'One—the middle-aged man,' said a student in the next bed—'is the schoolmaster she served under—Mr Phillotson.'

'And the other—this undergraduate in cap and gown—who is he?'

'He is a friend, or was. She has never told his name.'

'Was it either of these two who came for her?'

'No.'

'You are sure 'twas not the undergraduate?'

'Quite. He was a young man with a black beard.'

The lights were promptly extinguished, and till they fell asleep the girls indulged in conjectures about Sue, and wondered what games she had carried on in London and at Christminster before she came here, some of the more restless ones getting out of bed and looking from the mullioned windows at the vast west front of the Cathedral opposite, and the spire rising behind it.

When they awoke the next morning they glanced into Sue's nook, to find it still without a tenant. After the early lessons by gas-light, in half-toilet, and when they had come up to dress for breakfast, the bell of the entrance gate was heard to ring loudly. The mistress of the dormitory went away, and presently came back to say that the Principal's orders were that nobody was to speak to Bridehead without permission.

When, accordingly, Sue came into the dormitory to hastily tidy herself, looking flushed and tired, she went to her cubicle in silence, none of them coming out to greet her or to make inquiry. When they had gone downstairs they found that she did not follow them into the dining-hall to breakfast, and they then learnt that she had been severely reprimanded, and ordered to a solitary room for a week, there to be confined, and take her meals, and do all her reading.

At this the seventy murmured, the sentence being, they thought, too severe. A round robin was prepared and sent in to the Principal, asking for a remission of Sue's punishment. No notice was taken. Towards evening, when the geography mistress began dictating her subject, the girls in the class sat with folded arms.

'You mean that you are not going to work?' said the mistress at last. 'I may as well tell you that it has been ascertained that the young man Bridehead stayed out with was not her cousin, for the very good reason that she has no such relative. We have written to Christminster to ascertain.'

'We are willing to take her word,' said the head girl.

'This young man was discharged from his work at Christminster for drunkenness and blasphemy in public-houses, and he has come here to live, entirely to be near her.'

However, they remained stolid and motionless, and the mistress left the room to inquire from her superiors what was to be done.

Presently, towards dusk, the pupils, as they sat, heard exclamations from the first-year's girls in an adjoining classroom, and one rushed in to say that Sue Bridehead had got out of the back window of the room in which she had been confined, escaped in the dark across the lawn, and disappeared. How she had managed to get out of the garden nobody could tell, as it was bounded by the river at the bottom, and the side door was locked.

They went and looked at the empty room, the casement between the middle mullions of which stood open. The lawn was again searched with a lantern, every bush and shrub being examined, but she was nowhere hidden. Then the porter of the front gate was interrogated, and on reflection he said that he remembered hearing a sort of splashing in the stream at the back, but he had taken no notice, thinking some ducks had come down the river from above.

'She must have walked through the river!' said a mistress.

'Or drounded herself,' said the porter.

The mind of the matron was horrified—not so much at the possible death of Sue as at the possible half-column detailing that event in all the newspapers, which, added to the scandal of the year before, would give the College an unenviable notoriety for many months to come.

More lanterns were procured, and the river examined; and then, at last, on the opposite shore, which was open to the fields, some little boot-tracks were discerned in the mud, which left no doubt that the too excitable girl had waded through a depth of water reaching nearly to her shoulders—for this was the chief river of the county, and was mentioned in all the geography books with respect. As Sue had not brought disgrace upon the school by drowning herself, the matron began to speak superciliously of her, and to express gladness that she was gone.

On the self-same evening Jude sat in his lodgings by the Close Gate. Often at this hour after dusk he would enter the silent Close, and stand opposite the house that contained Sue, and watch the shadows of the girls' heads passing to and fro upon the blinds, and wish he had nothing else to do but to sit reading and learning all day what many of the thoughtless inmates despised. But to-night, having finished tea and brushed himself up, he was deep in the perusal of the Twenty-ninth Volume of Pusey's Library of the Fathers, a set of books which he had purchased of a second-hand dealer at a price that seemed to him to be one of miraculous cheapness for that invaluable work. He fancied he heard something rattle lightly against his window; then he heard it again. Certainly somebody had thrown gravel. He rose and gently lifted the sash.

'Jude!' (from below).

'Sue!'

'Yes—it is! Can I come up without being seen?'

'O yes!'

'Then don't come down. Shut the window.'

Jude waited, knowing that she could enter easily enough, the front door being opened merely by a knob which anybody could turn, as in most old country towns. He palpitated at the thought that she had fled to him in her trouble as he had fled to her in his. What counterparts they were! He unlatched the door of his room, heard a stealthy rustle on the dark stairs, and in a moment she appeared in the light of his lamp. He went up to seize her hand, and found she was clammy as a marine deity, and that her clothes clung to her like the robes upon the figures in the Parthenon frieze.

'I'm so cold!' she said through her chattering teeth. 'Can I come by your fire, Jude?'

She crossed to his little grate and very little fire, but as the water dripped from her as she moved, the idea of drying herself was absurd. 'Whatever have you done, darling?' he asked, with alarm, the tender epithet slipping out unawares.

'Walked through the largest river in the county—that's what I've done! They locked me up for being out with you; and it seemed so unjust that I couldn't bear it, so I got out of the window and escaped across the stream!' She had begun the explanation in her usual slightly independent tones, but before she had finished the thin pink lips trembled, and she could hardly refrain from crying.

'Dear Sue!' he said. 'You must take off all your things! And let me see—you must borrow some from the landlady. I'll ask her.'

'No, no! Don't let her know, for God's sake! We are so near the school that they'll come after me!'

'Then you must put on mine. You don't mind?'

'O no.'

'My Sunday suit, you know. It is close here.' In fact, everything was close and handy in Jude's single chamber, because there was not room for it to be otherwise. He opened a drawer, took out his best dark suit, and giving the garments a shake, said, 'Now, how long shall I give you?'

'Ten minutes.'

Jude left the room and went into the street, where he walked up and down. A clock struck half-past seven, and he returned. Sitting in his only arm-chair he saw a slim and fragile being masquerading as himself on a Sunday, so pathetic in her defencelessness that his heart felt big with the sense of it. On two other chairs before the fire were her wet garments. She blushed as he sat down beside her, but only for a moment.

'I suppose, Jude, it is odd that you should see me like this and all my things hanging there? Yet what nonsense! They are only a woman's clothes—sexless cloth and linen. . . . I wish I didn't feel so ill and sick! Will you dry my clothes now? Please do, Jude, and I'll get a lodging by and by. It is not late yet.'

'No, you shan't, if you are ill. You must stay here. Dear, dear Sue, what can I get for you?'

'I don't know! I can't help shivering. I wish I could get warm.' Jude put on her his great-coat in addition, and then ran to the nearest public-house, whence he returned with a little bottle in his hand. 'Here's six of best brandy,' he said. 'Now you drink it, dear; all of it.'

'I can't out of the bottle, can I?' Jude fetched the glass from the dressing-table, and administered the spirit in some water. She gasped a little, but gulped it down, and lay back in the arm-chair.

She then began to relate circumstantially her experiences since they had parted; but in the middle of her story her voice faltered, her head nodded, and she ceased. She was in a sound sleep. Jude, dying of anxiety lest she should have caught a chill which might permanently injure her, was glad to hear the regular breathing. He softly went nearer to her, and observed that a warm flush now rosed her hitherto blue cheeks, and felt that her hanging hand was no longer cold. Then he stood with his back to the fire regarding her, and saw in her almost a divinity.

IV

Jude's reverie was interrupted by the creak of footsteps ascending the stairs.

He whisked Sue's clothing from the chair where it was drying, thrust it under the bed, and sat down to his book. Somebody knocked and opened the door immediately. It was the landlady.

'O, I didn't know whether you was in or not, Mr Fawley. I wanted to know if you would require supper. I see you've a young gentleman—'

'Yes, ma'am. But I think I won't come down tonight. Will you bring supper up on a tray, and I'll have a cup of tea as well.'

It was Jude's custom to go downstairs to the kitchen, and eat his meals with the family, to save trouble. His landlady brought up the supper, however, on this occasion, and he took it from her at the door.

When she had descended he set the teapot on the hob, and drew out Sue's clothes anew; but they were far from dry. A thick woollen gown, he found, held a deal of water. So he hung them up again, and enlarged his fire and mused as the steam from the garments went up the chimney.

Suddenly she said, 'Jude!'

'Yes. All right. How do you feel now?'

'Better. Quite well. Why, I fell asleep, didn't I? What time is it? Not late surely?'

'It is past ten.'

'Is it really? What *shall* I do!' she said, starting up.

'Stay where you are.'

'Yes; that's what I want to do. But I don't know what they would say! And what will you do?'

'I am going to sit here by the fire all night, and read. Tomorrow is Sunday, and I haven't to go out anywhere. Perhaps you will be saved a severe illness by resting there. Don't be frightened. I'm all right. Look here, what I have got for you. Some supper.'

When she had sat upright she breathed plaintively and said, 'I do feel rather weak still. I thought I was well; and I ought not to be here, ought I?' But the supper fortified her somewhat, and when she had had some tea and had lain back again she was bright and cheerful.

The tea must have been green, or too long drawn, for she seemed preternaturally wakeful afterwards, though Jude, who had not taken any, began to feel heavy; till her conversation fixed his attention.

'You called me a creature of civilization, or something, didn't you?' she said, breaking a silence. 'It was very odd you should have done that.'

'Why?'

'Well, because it is provokingly wrong. I am a sort of negation of it.'

'You are very philosophical. "A negation" is profound talking.'

'Is it? Do I strike you as being learned?' she asked, with a touch of raillery.

'No—not learned. Only you don't talk quite like a girl—well, a girl who has had no advantages.'

'I have had advantages. I don't know Latin and Greek, though I know the grammars of those tongues. But I know most of the Greek and Latin classics through translations, and other books too. I read Lemprière, Catullus, Martial, Juvenal, Lucian, Beaumont and Fletcher, Boccaccio, Scarron, De Brantôme, Stern, De Foe, Smollet, Fielding, Shakespeare, the Bible, and other such; and found that all interest in the unwholesome part of those books ended with its mystery.'

'You have read more than I,' he said with a sigh. 'How came you to read some of those queerer ones?'

'Well,' she said thoughtfully, 'it was by accident. My life has been entirely shaped by what people call a peculiarity in me. I have no fear of men, as such, nor of their books. I have mixed with them—one or two of them particularly—almost as one of their own sex. I mean I have not felt them as most women are taught to feel—to be on their guard against attacks on their virtue; for no average man—no man short of a sensual savage—will molest a woman by day or night, at home or abroad, unless she invites him. Until she says by a look "Come on" he is always afraid to, and if you never say it, or look it, he never comes. However, what I was going to say is that when I was eighteen I formed a friendly intimacy with an undergraduate at Christminster, and he taught me a great deal, and lent me books which I should never have got hold of otherwise.'

'Is your friendship broken off?'

'O yes. He died, poor fellow, two or three years after he had taken his degree and left Christminster.'

'You saw a good deal of him, I suppose?'

'Yes. We used to go about together—on walking tours, reading tours, and things of that sort—like two men almost. He asked me to live with him, and I agreed to by letter. But when I joined him in London I found he meant a different thing from what I meant. He wanted me to be his mistress, in fact, but I wasn't in love with him—and on my saying I should go away if he didn't agree to *my* plan, he did so. We shared a sitting-room for fifteen months; and he became a leader-writer for one of the great London dailies; till he was taken ill, and had to go abroad. He said I was breaking his heart by holding out against him so long at such close quarters; he could never have believed it of woman. I might play that game once too often, he said. He came home merely to die. His death caused a terrible remorse in me for my cruelty—though I hope he died of consumption and not of me entirely. I went down to Sandbourne to his funeral, and was his only mourner. He left me a little money—because I broke his heart, I suppose. That's how men are—so much better than women!'

'Good heavens!—what did you do then?'

'Ah—now you are angry with me!' she said, a contralto note of tragedy coming suddenly into her silvery voice. 'I wouldn't have told you if I had known!'

'No, I am not. Tell me all.'

'Well, I invested his money, poor fellow, in a bubble scheme, and lost it. I lived about London by myself for some time, and then I returned to Christminster, as my father—who was also in London, and had started as an art metal-worker near Long-Acre—wouldn't have me back; and I got that occupation in the artist-shop where you found me . . . I said you didn't know how bad I was!'

Jude looked round upon the arm-chair and its occupant, as if to read more carefully the creature he had given shelter to. His voice trembled as he said: 'However you have lived, Sue, I believe you are as innocent as you are unconventional!'

'I am not particularly innocent, as you see, now that I have

twitched the robe
From that blank lay-figure your fancy draped,

said she, with an ostensible sneer, though he could hear that she was brimming with tears. 'But I have never yielded myself to any lover, if that's what you meant! I have remained as I began.'

'I quite believe you. But some women would not have remained as they began.'

'Perhaps not. Better women would not. People say I must be cold-natured,—sexless—on account of it. But I won't have it! Some of the most passionately erotic poets have been the most self-contained in their daily lives.'

'Have you told Mr Phillotson about this University-scholar-friend?'

'Yes—long ago. I have never made any secret of it to anybody.'

'What did he say?'

'He did not pass any criticism—only said I was everything to him, whatever I did; and things like that.'

Jude felt much depressed; she seemed to get further and further away from him with her strange ways and curious unconsciousness of gender.

'Aren't you *really* vexed with me, dear Jude?' she suddenly asked, in a voice of such extraordinary tenderness that it hardly seemed to come from the same woman who had just told her story so lightly. 'I would rather offend anybody in the world than you, I think!'

'I don't know whether I am vexed or not. I know I care very much about you!'

'I care as much for you as for anybody I ever met.'

'You don't care *more*! There, I ought not to say that. Don't answer it!'

There was another long silence. He felt that she was treating him cruelly, though he could not quite say in what way. Her very helplessness seemed to make her so much stronger than he.

'I am awfully ignorant on general matters, although I have worked so hard,' he said, to turn the subject. 'I am absorbed in Theology, you know. And what do you think I should be doing just about now, if you weren't here? I should be saying my evening prayers. I suppose you wouldn't like—'

'O no, no,' she answered, 'I would rather not, if you don't mind. I should seem so—such a hypocrite.'

'I thought you wouldn't join, so I didn't propose it. You must remember that I hope to be a useful minister some day.'

'To be ordained, I think you said?'

'Yes.'

'Then you haven't given up the idea?—I thought that perhaps you had by this time.'

'Of course not. I fondly thought at first that you felt as I do about that, as you were so mixed up in Christminster Anglicanism. And Mr Phillotson—'

'I have no respect for Christminster whatever, except, in a qualified degree, on its intellectual side,' said Sue Bridehead earnestly. 'My friend I spoke of took that out of me. He was the most irreligious man I ever knew, and the most moral. And intellect at Christminster is new wine in old bottles. The mediaevalism of Christminster must go, be sloughed off, or Christminster itself will have to go. To be sure, at times one couldn't help having a sneaking liking for the traditions of the old faith, as preserved by a section of the thinkers there in touching and simple sincerity; but when I was in my saddest, rightest mind I always felt,

> O ghastly glories of saints, dead limbs of gibbeted Gods!

'Sue, you are not a good friend of mine to talk like that!'

'Then I won't, dear Jude!' The emotional throat-note had come back, and she turned her face away.

'I still think Christminster has much that is glorious; though I was resentful because I couldn't get there.' He spoke gently, and resisted his impulse to pique her on to tears.

'It is an ignorant place, except as to the townspeople, artizans, drunkards, and paupers,' she said, perverse still at his differing from her. '*They* see life as it is, of course; but few of the people in the college do. You prove it in your own person. You are one of the very men Christminster was intended for when the colleges were founded; a man with a passion for learning, but no money, or opportunities, or friends. But you were elbowed off the pavement by the millionaires' sons.'

'Well, I can do without what it confers. I care for something higher.'

'And I for something broader, truer,' she insisted. 'At present intellect in Christminster is pushing one way, and religion the other: and so they stand stock-still, like two rams butting each other.'

'What would Mr Phillotson—'

'It is a place full of fetichists and ghost-seers!'

He noticed that whenever he tried to speak of the schoolmaster she turned the conversation to some generalizations about the offending University. Jude was extremely, morbidly, curious about her life as Phillotson's *protégée* and betrothed; yet she would not enlighten him.

'Well, that's just what I am, too,' he said. 'I am fearful of life, spectre-seeing always.'

'But you are good and dear!' she murmured.

His heart bumped, and he made no reply.

'You are in the Tractarian stage just now, are you not?' she added, putting on flippancy to hide real feeling, a common trick with her. 'Let me see—when was I there?—In the year eighteen hundred and—'

'There's a sarcasm in that which is rather unpleasant to me, Sue. Now will you do what I want you to? And this time I read a chapter, and then say prayers, as I told you. Now will you concentrate your attention on any book of these you like, and sit with your back to me, and leave me to my custom? You are sure you won't join me?'

'I'll look at you.'

'No. Don't tease, Sue!'

'Very well—I'll do just as you bid me, and I won't vex you, Jude,' she replied, in the tone of a child who was going to be good for ever after, turning her back upon him accordingly. A small Bible other than the one he was using lay near her, and during his retreat she took it up, and turned over the leaves.

'Jude,' she said brightly, when he had finished and come back to her; 'will you let me make you a *new* New Testament, like the one I made for myself at Christminster?'

'O yes. How was that made?'

'I altered my old one by cutting up all the Epistles and Gospels into separate *brochures*, and re-arranging them in chronological order as written, beginning the book with Thessalonians, following on with the Epistles, and putting the Gospels much further on. Then I had the volume rebound. My University friend Mr—but never mind his name, poor boy—said it was an excellent idea. I know that reading it afterwards made it twice as interesting as before, and twice as understandable.'

'H'm!' said Jude, with a sense of sacrilege.

'And what a literary enormity this is,' she said, as she glanced into the pages of Solomon's Song. 'I mean the synopsis at the head of each chapter, explaining away the real nature of that rhapsody. You needn't be alarmed: nobody claims inspiration for the chapter headings. Indeed, many divines treat them with contempt. It seems the drollest thing to think of the four-and-twenty elders, or bishops, or whatever number they were, sitting with long faces and writing down such stuff.'

Jude looked pained. 'You are quite Voltairean!' he murmured.

'Indeed? Then I won't say any more, except that people have no right to falsify the Bible! I *hate* such humbug as could attempt to plaster over with ecclesiastical abstractions such ecstatic, natural, human love as lies in that great and passionate song!' Her speech had grown spirited, and almost petulant at his rebuke, and her eyes moist. 'I *wish* I had a friend here to support me; but nobody is ever on my side!'

'But, my dear Sue, my very dear Sue, I am not against you!' he said, taking her hand, and surprised at her introducing personal feeling into mere argument.

'Yes you are, yes you are!' she cried, turning away her face that he might not see her brimming eyes. 'You are on the side of the people in the Training School—at least you seem almost to be! What I insist on is, that to explain such verses as this: "Whither is thy beloved gone, O thou fairest among women?" by the note: "*The Church professeth her faith*" is supremely ridiculous!'

'Well then, let it be! You make such a personal matter of everything! I am—only too inclined just now to apply the words profanely. You know *you* are fairest among women to me, come to that!'

'But you are not to say it now!' Sue replied, her voice changing to its softest note of severity. Then their eyes met, and they shook hands like cronies in a tavern, and Jude saw the absurdity of quarrelling on such a hypothetical subject, and she the silliness of crying about what was written in an old book like the Bible.

'I won't disturb your convictions—I really won't!' she went on soothingly, for now he was rather more ruffled than she. 'But I did want and long to ennoble some man to high aims; and when I saw you, and knew you wanted to be my comrade, I—shall I confess it?—thought that man might be you. But you take so much tradition on trust that I don't know what to say.'

'Well, dear; I suppose one must take some things on trust. Life isn't long enough to work out everything in Euclid problems before you believe it. I take Christianity.'

'Well, perhaps you might take something worse.'

'Indeed I might. Perhaps I have done so!' He thought of Arabella.

'I won't ask what, because we are going to be *very* nice with each other, aren't we, and never, never, vex each other any more?' She looked up trustfully, and her voice seemed trying to nestle in his breast.

'I shall always care for you!' said Jude.

'And I for you. Because you are single-hearted, and forgiving to your faulty and tiresome little Sue!'

He looked away, for that epicene tenderness of hers was too harrowing. Was it that which had broken the heart of the poor leader-writer; and was he to be the next one? . . . But Sue was so dear! . . . If he could only get over the sense of her sex, as she seemed to be able to do so easily of his, what a comrade she would make; for their difference of opinion on conjectural subjects only drew them closer together on matters of daily human experience. She was nearer to him than any other woman he had ever met, and he could scarcely believe that time, creed, or absence, would ever divide him from her.

But his grief at her incredulities returned. They sat on till she fell asleep again, and he nodded in his chair likewise. Whenever he aroused himself he turned her things, and made up the fire anew. About six o'clock he awoke completely, and lighting a candle, found that her clothes were dry. Her chair being a far more comfortable one than his she still slept on inside his great-coat, looking warm as a new bun and boyish as a Ganymedes. Placing the garments by her and touching her on the shoulder he went downstairs, and washed himself by starlight in the yard.

V

When he returned she was dressed as usual.

'Now could I get out without anybody seeing me?' she asked. 'The town is not yet astir.'

'But you have had no breakfast.'

'O, I don't want any! I fear I ought not to have run away from that school! Things seem so different in the cold light of morning, don't they? What Mr Phillotson will say I don't know! It was quite by his wish that I went there. He is the only man in the world for whom I have any respect or fear. I hope he'll forgive me; but he'll scold me dreadfully, I expect!'

'I'll go to him and explain—' began Jude.

'O no, you shan't. I don't care for him! He may think what he likes—I shall do just as I choose!'

'But you just this moment said—'

'Well, if I did, I shall do as I like for all him! I have thought of what I shall do—go to the sister of one of my fellow-students in the Training School, who has asked me to visit her. She has a school near Shaston, about eighteen miles from here—and I shall stay there till this has blown over, and I get back to the Training School again.'

At the last moment he persuaded her to let him make her a cup of coffee, in a portable apparatus he kept in his room for use on rising to go to his work every day before the household was astir.

'Now a dew-bit to eat with it,' he said; 'and off we go. You can have a regular breakfast when you get there.'

They went quietly out of the house, Jude accompanying her to the station. As they departed along the street a head was thrust out of an upper window of his lodging and quickly withdrawn. Sue still seemed sorry for her rashness, and to wish she had not rebelled; telling him at parting that she would let him know as soon as she got re-admitted to the Training School. They stood rather miserably together on the platform; and it was apparent that he wanted to say more.

'I want to tell you something—two things,' he said hurriedly as the train came up. 'One is a warm one, the other a cold one!'

'Jude,' she said. 'I know one of them. And you mustn't!'

'What?'

'You mustn't love me. You are to like me—that's all!'

Jude's face became so full of complicated glooms that hers was agitated in sympathy as she bade him adieu through the carriage window. And then the train moved on, and waving her pretty hand to him she vanished away.

Melchester was a dismal place enough for Jude that Sunday of her departure, and that Close so hateful that he did not go once to the Cathedral services. The next morning there came a letter from her, which, with her usual promptitude, she had written directly she had reached the friend's house. She told him of her safe arrival and comfortable quarters, and then added:—

> What I really write about, dear Jude, is something I said to you at parting. You had been so very good and kind to me that when you were out of sight I felt what a cruel and ungrateful woman I was to say it, and it has reproached me ever since. *If you want to love me, Jude, you may*: I don't mind at all; and I'll never say again that you mustn't!
>
> Now I won't write any more about that. You do forgive your thoughtless friend for her cruelty? and won't make her miserable by saying you don't?—Ever,
>
> SUE

It would be superfluous to say what his answer was; and how he thought what he would have done had he been free, which should have rendered a long residence with a female friend quite unnecessary for Sue. He felt he might have been pretty sure of his own victory if it had come to a conflict between Phillotson and himself for the possession of her.

Yet Jude was in danger of attaching more meaning to Sue's impulsive note than it really was intended to bear.

After the lapse of a few days he found himself hoping that she would write again. But he received no further communication; and in the intensity of his solicitude he sent another note, suggesting that he should pay her a visit some Sunday, the distance being under eighteen miles.

He expected a reply on the second morning after despatching his missive; but none came. The third morning arrived; the postman did not stop. This was Saturday, and in a feverish state of anxiety about her he sent off three brief lines stating that he was coming the following day, for he felt sure something had happened.

His first and natural thought had been that she was ill from her immersion; but it soon occurred to him that somebody would have written for her in such a case. Conjectures were put an end to by his arrival at the village school-house near Shaston on the bright morning of Sunday, between eleven and twelve o'clock, when the parish was as vacant as a desert, most of the inhabitants having gathered inside the church, whence their voices could occasionally be heard in unison.

A little girl opened the door. 'Miss Bridehead is upstairs,' she said. 'And will you please walk up to her?'

'Is she ill?' asked Jude hastily.

'Only a little—not very.'

Jude entered and ascended. On reaching the landing a voice told him which way to turn—the voice of Sue calling his name. He passed the doorway, and found her lying in a little bed in a room a dozen feet square.

'O Sue!' he cried, sitting down beside her and taking her hand. 'How is this! You couldn't write?'

'No—it wasn't that!' she answered. 'I did catch a bad cold—but I could have written. Only I wouldn't!'

'Why not?—frightening me like this!'

'Yes—that was what I was afraid of! But I had decided not to write to you any more. They won't have me back at the school—that's why I couldn't write. Not the fact, but the reason!'

'Well?'

'They not only won't have me, but they gave me a parting piece of advice—'

'What?'

She did not answer directly. 'I vowed I never would tell you, Jude—it is so vulgar and distressing!'

'Is it about us?'

'Yes.'

'But do tell me!'

'Well—somebody has sent them baseless reports about us, and they say you and I ought to marry as soon as possible, for the sake of my reputation! . . . There—now I have told you, and I wish I hadn't!'

'O poor Sue!'

'I don't think of you like that means! It did just *occur* to me to regard you in the way they think I do, but I hadn't begun to. I *have* recognized that the cousinship was merely nominal, since we met as total strangers. But my marrying you, dear Jude—why, of course, if I had reckoned upon marrying you I shouldn't have come to you so often! And I never supposed you thought of such a thing as marrying me till the other evening; when I began to fancy you did love me a little. Perhaps I ought not to have been so intimate with you. It is all my fault. Everything is my fault always!'

The speech seemed a little forced and unreal, and they regarded each other with a mutual distress.

'I was so blind at first!' she went on. 'I didn't see what you felt at all. O you have been unkind to me—you have—to look upon me as a sweetheart without saying a word, and leaving me to discover it myself! Your attitude to me has become known; and naturally they think we've been doing wrong! I'll never trust you again!'

'Yes, Sue,' he said simply; 'I am to blame—more than you think. I was quite aware that you did not suspect till within the last meeting or two what I was feeling about you. I admit that our meeting as strangers prevented a sense of relationship, and that it was a sort of subterfuge to avail myself of it. But don't you think I deserve a little consideration for concealing my wrong, very wrong, sentiments, since I couldn't help having them?'

She turned her eyes doubtfully towards him, and then looked away as if afraid she might forgive him.

By every law of nature and sex a kiss was the only rejoinder that fitted the mood and the moment, under the suasion of which Sue's undemonstrative regard of him might not inconceivably have changed its temperature. Some men would have cast scruples to the winds, and ventured it, oblivious both of Sue's declaration of her neutral feelings, and of the pair of autographs in the vestry chest of Arabella's parish church. Jude did not. He had, in fact, come in part to tell his own fatal story. It was upon his lips; yet at the hour of this distress he could not disclose it. He preferred to dwell upon the recognized barriers between them.

'Of course—I know you don't—care about me in any particular way,' he sorrowed. 'You ought not, and you are right. You belong to—Mr Phillotson. I suppose he has been to see you?'

'Yes,' she said shortly, her face changing a little. 'Though I didn't ask him to come. You are glad, of course, that he has been! But I shouldn't care if he didn't come any more!'

It was very perplexing to her lover that she should be piqued at his honest acquiescence in his rival, if Jude's feelings of love were deprecated by her. He went on to something else.

'This will blow over, dear Sue,' he said. 'The Training School authorities are not all the world. You can get to be a student in some other, no doubt.'

'I'll ask Mr Phillotson,' she said decisively.

Sue's kind hostess now returned from church, and there was no more intimate conversation. Jude left in the afternoon, hopelessly unhappy. But he had seen her, and sat with her. Such intercourse as that would have to content him for the remainder of his life. The lesson of renunciation it was necessary and proper that he, as a parish priest, should learn.

But the next morning when he awoke he felt rather vexed with her, and decided that she was rather unreasonable, not to say capricious. Then, in illustration of what he had begun to discern as one of her redeeming characteristics there came promptly a note, which she must have written almost immediately he had gone from her:

Forgive me for my petulance yesterday! I was horrid to you; I know it, and I feel perfectly miserable at my horridness. It was so dear of you not to be angry! Jude, please still keep me as your friend and associate, with all my faults. I'll try not to be like it again.

I am coming to Melchester on Saturday, to get my things away from the T. S., &c. I could walk with you for half-an-hour, if you would like?—Your repentant,

SUE

Jude forgave her straightaway, and asked her to call for him at the Cathedral works when she came.

VI

Meanwhile a middle-aged man was dreaming a dream of great beauty concerning the writer of the above letter. He was Richard Phillotson, who had recently removed from the mixed village school at Lumsdon near Christminster, to undertake a large boys' school in his native town of Shaston, which stood on a hill sixty miles to the south-west as the crow flies.

A glance at the place and its accessories was almost enough to reveal that the schoolmaster's plans and dreams so long indulged in had been abandoned for some new dream with which neither the Church nor literature had much in common. Essentially an unpractical man, he was now bent on making and saving money for a practical purpose—that of keeping a wife, who, if she chose, might conduct one of the girls' schools adjoining his own; for which purpose he had advised her to go into training, since she would not marry him off-hand.

About the time that Jude was removing from Marygreen to Melchester, and entering on adventures at the latter place with Sue, the schoolmaster was settling down in the new schoolhouse at Shaston. All the furniture being fixed, the books shelved, and the nails driven, he had begun to sit in his parlour during the dark winter nights and re-attempt some of his old studies—one branch of which had included Roman-Britannic antiquities—an unremunerative labour for a National school-master but a subject, that, after his abandonment of the University scheme, had interested him as being a comparatively unworked mine; practicable to those who, like himself, had lived in lonely spots where these remains were abundant, and were seen to compel inferences in startling contrast to accepted views on civilization of that time.

A resumption of this investigation was the outward and apparent hobby of Phillotson at present—his ostensible reason for going alone into fields where causeways, dykes, and tumuli abounded, or shutting himself up in his house with a few urns, tiles, and mosaics he had collected, instead of calling round upon his neighbours, who for their part had showed themselves willing enough to be friendly with him. But it was not the real, or the whole, reason, after all. Thus on a particular evening in the month, when it had grown quite late—to near midnight, indeed—and the light of his lamp, shining from his window at a salient angle of the hill-top town over infinite miles of valley westward, announced as by words a place and person given over to study, he was not exactly studying.

The interior of the room—the books, the furniture, the schoolmaster's loose coat, his attitude at the table, even the flickering of the fire, bespoke the same dignified tale of undistracted research—more than creditable to a man who had had no advantages beyond those of his own making. And yet the tale, true enough till latterly, was not true now. What he was regarding was not history. They were historic notes, written in a bold womanly hand at his dictation some months before, and it was the clerical rendering of word after word that absorbed him.

He presently took from a drawer a carefully tied bundle of letters, few, very few, as correspondence counts nowadays. Each was in its envelope just as it had arrived, and the handwriting was of the same womanly character as the historic notes. He unfolded them one by one and read them musingly. At first sight there seemed in these small documents to be absolutely nothing to muse over. They were straightforward, frank letters, signed 'Sue B—'; just such ones as would be written during short absences, with no other thought than their speedy destruction, and chiefly concerning books in reading and other experiences of a Training School, forgotten doubtless by the writer with the passing of the day of their inditing. In one of them—quite a recent one—the young woman said that she had received his considerate letter, and that it was honourable and generous of him to say he would not come to see her oftener than she desired (the school being such an awkward place for callers, and because of her strong wish that her engagement to him should not be known, which it would infallibly be if he visited her often). Over these phrases the schoolmaster pored. What precise shade of satisfaction was to be gathered from a woman's gratitude that the man who loved her had not been often to see her? The problem occupied him, distracted him.

He opened another drawer, and found therein an envelope, from which he drew a photograph of Sue as a child, long before he had known her, standing under trellis-work with a little basket in her hand. There was another of her as a young woman, her dark eyes and hair making a very distinct and attractive picture of her, which just disclosed, too, the thoughtfulness that lay behind her lighter moods. It was a duplicate of the one she had given Jude, and would have given to any man. Phillotson brought it half-way to his lips, but withdrew it in doubt at her perplexing phrases: ultimately kissing the dead pasteboard with all the passionateness, and more than all the devotion, of a young man of eighteen.

The schoolmaster's was an unhealthy-looking, old-fashioned face, rendered more old-fashioned by his style of shaving. A certain gentlemanliness had been imparted to it by nature, suggesting an inherent wish to do rightly by all. His speech was a little slow, but his tones were sincere enough to make his hesitation no defect. His greying hair was curly, and radiated from a point in the middle of his crown. There were four lines across his forehead, and he only wore spectacles when reading at night. It was almost certainly a renunciation forced upon him by his academic purpose, rather than a distaste for women, which had hitherto kept him from closing with one of the sex in matrimony.

Such silent proceedings as those of this evening were repeated many and oft times when he was not under the eye of the boys, whose quick and penetrating regard would frequently become almost intolerable to the self-conscious master in his present anxious care for Sue, making him, in the grey hours of morning, dread to meet anew the gimlet glances, lest they should read what the dream within him was.

He had honourably acquiesced in Sue's announced wish that he was not often to visit her at the Training School; but at length, his patience being sorely tried, he set out one Saturday afternoon to pay her an unexpected call. There the news of her departure—expulsion as it might almost have been considered—was flashed upon him without warning or mitigation as he stood at the door expecting in a few minutes to behold her face; and when he turned away he could hardly see the road before him.

Sue had, in fact, never written a line to her suitor on the subject, although it was fourteen days old. A short reflection told him that this proved nothing, a natural delicacy being as ample a reason for silence as any degree of blameworthiness.

They had informed him at the school where she was living, and having no immediate anxiety about her comfort his thoughts took the direction of a burning indignation against the Training School Committee. In his bewilderment Phillotson entered the adjacent cathedral, just now in a direly dismantled state by reason of the repairs. He sat down on a block of freestone, regardless of the dusty imprint it made on his breeches; and his listless eyes following the movements of the workmen he presently became aware that the reputed culprit, Sue's lover Jude, was one amongst them.

Jude had never spoken to his former hero since the meeting by the model of Jerusalem. Having inadvertently witnessed Phillotson's tentative courtship of Sue in the lane there had grown up in the younger man's mind a curious dislike to think of the elder, to meet him, to communicate in any way with him; and since Phillotson's success in obtaining at least her promise had become known to Jude, he had frankly recognized that he did not wish to see or hear of his senior any more, learn anything of his pursuits, or even imagine again what excellencies might appertain to his character. On this very day of the schoolmaster's visit Jude was expecting Sue, as she had promised; and when therefore he saw the schoolmaster in the nave of the building, saw, moreover, that he was coming to speak to him, he felt no little embarrassment; which Phillotson's own embarrassment prevented his observing.

Jude joined him, and they both withdrew from the other workmen to the spot where Phillotson had been sitting. Jude offered him a piece of sackcloth for a cushion, and told him it was dangerous to sit on the bare block.

'Yes; yes,' said Phillotson abstractedly, as he re-seated himself, his eyes resting on the ground as if he were trying to remember where he was. 'I won't keep you long. It was merely that I have heard that you have seen my little friend Sue recently. It occurred to me to speak to you on that account. I merely want to ask—about her.'

'I think I know what!' Jude hurriedly said. 'About her escaping from the Training School, and her coming to me?'

'Yes.'

'Well'—Jude for a moment felt an unprincipled and fiendish wish to annihilate his rival at all cost. By the exercise of that treachery which love for the same woman renders possible to men the most honourable in every other relation of life, he could send off Phillotson in agony and defeat by saying that the scandal was true, and that Sue had irretrievably committed herself with him. But his action did not respond for a moment to his animal instinct; and what he said was, 'I am glad of your kindness in coming to talk plainly to me about it. You know what they say?—that I ought to marry her.'

'What!'

'And I wish with all my soul I could!'

Phillotson trembled, and his naturally pale face acquired a corpse-like sharpness in its lines. 'I had no idea that it was of this nature! God forbid!'

'No, no!' said Jude aghast. 'I thought you understood? I mean that were I in a position to marry her, or some one, and settle down, instead of living in lodgings here and there, I should be glad!'

What he had really meant was simply that he loved her.

'But—since this painful matter has been opened up—what really happened?' asked Phillotson, with the firmness of a man who felt that a sharp smart now was better than a long agony of suspense hereafter. 'Cases arise, and this is one, when even ungenerous questions must be put to make false assumptions impossible, and to kill scandal.'

Jude explained readily; giving the whole series of adventures, including the night at the shepherd's, her wet arrival at his lodging, her indisposition from her immersion, their vigil of discussion, and his seeing her off next morning.

'Well now,' said Phillotson at the conclusion, 'I take it as your final word, and I know I can believe you, that the suspicion which led to her rustication is an absolutely baseless one?'

'It is,' said Jude solemnly. 'Absolutely. So help me God!'

The schoolmaster rose. Each of the twain felt that the interview could not comfortably merge in a friendly discussion of their recent experiences, after the manner of friends; and when Jude had taken him round, and shown him some features of the renovation which the old cathedral was undergoing, Phillotson bade the young man good-day and went away.

This visit took place about eleven o'clock in the morning; but no Sue appeared. When Jude went to his dinner at one he saw his beloved ahead of him in the street leading up from the North Gate, walking as if in no way looking for him. Speedily overtaking her he remarked that he had asked her to come to him at the Cathedral, and she had promised.

'I have been to get my things from the College,' she said—an observation which he was expected to take as an answer, though it was not one. Finding her to be in this evasive mood he felt inclined to give her the information so long withheld.

'You have not seen Mr Phillotson to-day?' he ventured to inquire.

'I have not. But I am not going to be cross-examined about him; and if you ask anything more I won't answer!'

'It is very odd that—' He stopped, regarding her.

'What?'

'That you are often not so nice in your real presence as you are in your letters!'

'Does it really seem so to you?' said she, smiling with quick curiosity. 'Well, that's strange; but I feel just the same about you, Jude. When you are gone away I seem such a cold-hearted—'

As she knew his sentiment towards her Jude saw that they were getting upon dangerous ground. It was now, he thought, that he must speak as an honest man.

But he did not speak, and she continued: 'It was that which made me write and say—I didn't mind your loving me,—if you wanted to, much!'

The exultation he might have felt at what that implied, or seemed to imply, was nullified by his intention, and he rested rigid till he began: 'I have never told you—'

'Yes you have,' murmured she.

'I mean, I have never told you my history—all of it.'

'But I guess it. I know nearly.'

Jude looked up. Could she possibly know of that morning performance of his with Arabella: which in a few months had ceased to be a marriage more completely than by death? He saw that she did not.

'I can't quite tell you here in the street,' he went on with a gloomy tongue. 'And you had better not come to my lodgings. Let us go in here.'

The building by which they stood was the market-house; it was the only place available; and they entered, the market being over, and the stalls and areas empty. He would have preferred a more congenial spot, but, as usually happens, in place of a romantic field or solemn aisle for his tale, it was told while they walked up and down over a floor littered with rotten cabbage-leaves, and amid all the usual squalors of decayed vegetable matter and unsaleable refuse. He began and finished his brief narrative, which merely led up to the information that he had married a wife some years earlier, and that his wife was living still. Almost before her countenance had time to change she hurried out the words.

'Why didn't you tell me before!'

'I couldn't. It seemed so cruel to tell it.'

'To yourself, Jude. So it was better to be cruel to me!'

'No, dear darling!' cried Jude passionately. He tried to take her hand, but she withdrew it. Their old relations of confidence seemed suddenly to have ended, and the antagonisms of sex to sex were left without any counterpoising predilections. She was his comrade, friend, unconscious sweetheart no longer; and her eyes regarded him in estranged silence.

'I was ashamed of the episode in my life which brought about the marriage,' he continued. 'I can't explain it precisely now. I could have done it if you had taken it differently!'

'But how can I?' she burst out. 'Here I have been saying, or writing, that—that you might love me, or something of the sort!—just out of charity—and all the time—O it is perfectly damnable how things are!' she said, stamping her foot in a nervous quiver.

'You take me wrong, Sue! I never thought you cared for me at all, till quite lately; so I felt it did not matter! Do you care for me, Sue?—you know how I mean?—I don't like "out of charity" at all!'

It was a question which in the circumstances Sue did not choose to answer.

'I suppose she—your wife—is—a very pretty woman, even if she's wicked?' she asked quickly.

'She's pretty enough, as far as that goes.'

'Prettier than I am, no doubt!'

'You are not the least alike. And I have never seen her for years. . . . But she's sure to come back—they always do!'

'How strange of you to stay apart from her like this!' said Sue, her trembling lip and lumpy throat belying her irony. 'You, such a religious man. How will the demi-gods in your Pantheon—I mean those legendary persons you call Saints—intercede for you after this? Now if I had done such a thing it would have been different, and not remarkable, for I at least don't regard marriage as a Sacrament. Your theories are not so advanced as your practice!'

'Sue, you are terribly cutting when you like to be—a perfect Voltaire! But you must treat me as you will!'

When she saw how wretched he was she softened, and trying to blink away her sympathetic tears said with all the winning reproachfulness of a heart-hurt woman: 'Ah—you should have told me before you gave me that idea that you wanted to be allowed to love me! I had no feeling before that moment at the railway-station, except—' For once Sue was as miserable as he, in her attempts to keep herself free from emotion, and her less than half-success.

'Don't cry, dear!' he implored.

'I am—not crying—because I meant to—love you; but because of your want of—confidence!'

They were quite screened from the Market-square without, and he could not help putting out his arm towards her waist. His momentary desire was the means of her rallying. 'No, no!' she said, drawing back stringently, and wiping her eyes. 'Of course not! It would be hypocrisy to pretend that it would be meant as from my cousin; and it can't be in any other way.'

They moved on a dozen paces, and she showed herself recovered. It was distracting to Jude, and his heart would have ached less had she appeared anyhow but as she did appear; essentially large-minded and generous on reflection, despite a previous exercise of those narrow womanly humours on impulse that were necessary to give her sex.

'I don't blame you for what you couldn't help,' she said smiling. 'How should I be so foolish! I do blame you a little bit for not telling me before. But after all it doesn't matter. We should have had to keep apart, you see, even if this had not been in your life.'

'No, we shouldn't, Sue! This is the only obstacle!'

'You forget that I must have loved you, and wanted to be your wife, even if there had been no obstacle,' said Sue, with a gentle seriousness which did not reveal her mind. 'And then we are cousins, and it is bad for cousins to marry. And—I am engaged to somebody else. As to our going on together as we were going, in a sort of friendly way, the people round us would have made it unable to continue. Their views of the relations of man and woman are limited, as is proved by their expelling me from the school. Their philosophy only recognizes relations based on animal desire. The wide field of strong attachment where desire plays, at least, only a secondary part, is ignored by them—the part of—who is it?—Venus Urania.'

Her being able to talk learnedly showed that she was mistress of herself again; and before they parted she had almost regained her vivacious glance, her reciprocity of tone, her gay manner, and her second-thought attitude of critical largeness towards others of her age and sex.

He could speak more freely now. 'There were several reasons against my telling you rashly. One was what I have said; another, that it was always impressed upon me that I ought not to marry—that I belonged to an odd and peculiar family—the wrong breed for marriage.'

'Ah—who used to say that to you?'

'My great-aunt. She said it always ended badly with us Fawleys.'

'That's strange. My father used to say the same to me!'

They stood possessed by the same thought, ugly enough, even as an assumption: that a union between them, had such been possible, would have meant a terrible intensification—two bitters in one dish.

'O but there can't be anything in it!' she said with nervous lightness. 'Our family have been unlucky of late years in choosing mates—that's all.'

And then they pretended to persuade themselves that all that had happened was of no consequence, and that they could still be cousins and friends and warm correspondents, and have happy genial times when they met, even if they met less frequently than before. Their parting was in good friendship, and yet Jude's last look into her eyes was tinged with inquiry, for he felt that he did not even now quite know her mind.

VII

Tidings from Sue a day or two after passed across Jude like a withering blast.

Before reading the letter he was led to suspect that its contents were of a somewhat serious kind by catching sight of the signature—which was in her full name, never used in her correspondence with him since her first note:

> My dear Jude,—I have something to tell you which perhaps you will not be surprised to hear, though certainly it may strike you as being accelerated (as the railway companies say of their trains). Mr Phillotson and I are to be married quite soon—in three or four weeks. We had intended, as you know, to wait till I had gone through my course of training and obtained my certificate, so as to assist him, if necessary, in the teaching. But he generously says he does not see any object in waiting, now I am not at the Training School. It is so good of him, because the awkwardness of my situation has really come about by my fault in getting expelled.
>
> Wish me joy. Remember I say you are to, and you mustn't refuse!—Your affectionate cousin,
>
> Susanna Florence Mary Bridehead

Jude staggered under the news; could eat no breakfast; and kept on drinking tea because his mouth was so dry. Then presently he went to his work and laughed the usual bitter laugh of a man so confronted. Everything seemed turning to satire. And yet, what could the poor girl do? he asked himself: and felt worse than shedding tears.

'O Susanna Florence Mary!' he said as he worked. 'You don't know what marriage means!'

Could it be possible that his announcement of his own marriage had pricked her on to this, just as his visit to her when in liquor may have pricked her on to her engagement? To be sure, there seemed to exist these other and sufficient reasons, practical and social, for her decision; but Sue was not a very practical or calculating person; and he was compelled to think that a pique at having his secret sprung upon her had moved her to give way to Phillotson's probable representations, that the best course to prove how unfounded were the suspicions of the school authorities would be to marry him offhand, as in fulfilment of an ordinary engagement. Sue had, in fact, been placed in an awkward corner. Poor Sue!

He determined to play the Spartan; to make the best of it, and support her; but he could not write the requested good wishes for a day or two. Meanwhile there came another note from his impatient little dear:

> Jude, will you give me away? I have nobody else who could do it so conveniently as you, being the only married relation I have here on the spot, even if my father were friendly enough to be willing, which he isn't. I hope you won't think it a trouble? I have been looking at the marriage service in the Prayer-book, and it seems to me very humiliating that a giver-away should be required at all. According to the ceremony as there printed, my bridegroom chooses me of his own will and pleasure; but I don't choose him. Somebody *gives* me to him, like a she-ass or she-goat, or any other domestic animal. Bless your exalted views of woman, O Churchman! But I forget: I am no longer privileged to tease you.—Ever,
>
> SUSANNA FLORENCE MARY BRIDEHEAD

Jude screwed himself up to heroic key; and replied:

> MY DEAR SUE,—Of course I wish you joy! And also of course I will give you away. What I suggest is that, as you have no house of your own, you do not marry from your school friend's, but

from mine. It would be more proper. I think, since I am, as you say, the person nearest related to you in this part of the world.

I don't see why you sign your letter in such a new and terribly formal way? Surely you care a bit about me still!—Ever your affectionate,

JUDE

What had jarred on him even more than the signature was a little sting he had been silent on—the phrase 'married relation'—What an idiot it made him seem as her lover! If Sue had written that in satire, he could hardly forgive her; if in suffering—ah, that was another thing!

His offer of his lodging must have commended itself to Phillotson at any rate, for the schoolmaster sent him a line of warm thanks, accepting the convenience. Sue also thanked him. Jude immediately moved into more commodious quarters, as much to escape the espionage of the suspicious landlady who had been one cause of Sue's unpleasant experience as for the sake of room.

Then Sue wrote to tell him the day fixed for the wedding; and Jude decided, after inquiry, that she should come into residence on the following Saturday, which would allow of a ten day's stay in the city prior to the ceremony, sufficiently representing a nominal residence of fifteen.

She arrived by the ten o'clock train on the day aforesaid, Jude not going to meet her at the station, by her special request, that he should not lose a morning's work and pay, she said (if this were her true reason). But so well by this time did he know Sue that the remembrance of their mutual sensitiveness at emotional crises might, he thought, have weighed with her in this. When he came home to dinner she had taken possession of her apartment.

She lived in the same house with him, but on a different floor, and they saw each other little, an occasional supper being the only meal they took together, when Sue's manner was something that of a scared child. What she felt he did not know; their conversation was mechanical, though she did not look pale or ill. Phillotson came frequently, but mostly when Jude was absent. On the morning of the wedding, when Jude had given himself a holiday, Sue and her cousin had breakfast together for the first and last time during this curious interval; in his room—the parlour—which he had hired for the period of Sue's residence. Seeing, as women do, how helpless he was in making the place comfortable, she bustled about.

'What's the matter, Jude?' she said suddenly.

He was leaning with his elbows on the table and his chin on his hands, looking into a futurity which seemed to be sketched out on the tablecloth.

'O—nothing!'

'You are "father", you know. That's what they call the man who gives you away.'

Jude could have said 'Phillotson's age entitles him to be called that!' But he would not annoy her by such a cheap retort.

She talked incessantly, as if she dreaded his indulgence in reflection, and before the meal was over both he and she wished they had not put such confidence in their new view of things, and had taken breakfast apart. What oppressed Jude was the thought that, having done a wrong thing of this sort himself, he was aiding and abetting the woman he loved in doing a like wrong thing, instead of imploring and warning her against it. It was on his tongue to say, 'You have quite made up your mind?'

After breakfast they went out on an errand together moved by a mutual thought that it was the last opportunity they would have of indulging in unceremonious companionship. By the irony of fate, and the curious trick in Sue's nature of tempting Providence at critical times, she took his arm as they walked through the muddy street—a thing she had never done before in her life—and on turning the corner they found themselves close to a grey Perpendicular church with a low-pitched roof—the church of St Thomas.

'That's the church,' said Jude.

'Where I am going to be married?'

'Yes.'

'Indeed!' she exclaimed with curiosity. 'How I should like to go in and see what the spot is like where I am soon to kneel and do it.'

Again he said to himself, 'She does not realize what marriage means!'

He passively acquiesced in her wish to go in, and they entered by the western door. The only person inside the gloomy building was a charwoman cleaning. Sue still held Jude's arm, almost as if she loved him. Cruelly sweet, indeed, she had been to him that morning; but his thoughts of a penance in store for her were tempered by an ache:

> . . . I can find no way
> How a blow should fall, such as falls on men
> Nor prove too much for your womanhood!

They strolled undemonstratively up the nave towards the altar railing, which they stood against in silence, turning then and walking down the nave again, her hand still on his arm, precisely like a couple just married. The too suggestive incident, entirely of her making, nearly broke down Jude.

'I like to do things like this,' she said in the delicate voice of an epicure in emotions, which left no doubt that she spoke the truth.

'I know you do!' said Jude.

'They are interesting, because they have probably never been done before. I shall walk down the church like this with my husband in about two hours, shan't I!'

'No doubt you will!'

'Was it like this when you were married?'

'Good God, Sue—don't be so awfully merciless! . . . There, dear one, I didn't mean it!'

Ah—you are vexed!' she said regretfully, as she blinked away an access of eye moisture. 'And I promised never to vex you! . . . I suppose I ought not to have asked you to bring me in here. O I oughtn't! I see it now. My curiosity to hunt up a new sensation always leads me into these scrapes. Forgive me! . . . You will, won't you, Jude?'

The appeal was so remorseful that Jude's eyes were even wetter than hers as he pressed her hand for Yes.

'Now we'll hurry away, and I won't do it any more!' she continued humbly; and they came out of the building, Sue intending to go on to the station to meet Phillotson. But the first person they encountered on entering the main street was the schoolmaster himself, whose train had arrived sooner than Sue expected. There was nothing really to demur to in her leaning on Jude's arm; but she withdrew her hand; and Jude thought that Phillotson had looked surprised.

'We have been doing such a funny thing!' said she, smiling candidly. 'We've been to the church, rehearsing as it were. Haven't we, Jude?'

'How?' said Phillotson curiously.

Jude inwardly deplored what he thought to be unnecessary frankness; but she had gone too far not to explain all, which she accordingly did, telling him how they had marched up to the altar.

Seeing how puzzled Phillotson seemed, Jude said as cheerfully as he could, 'I am going to buy her another little present. Will you both come to the shop with me?'

'No,' said Sue, 'I'll go on to the house with him;' and requesting her lover not to be a long time she departed with the schoolmaster.

Jude soon joined them at his rooms, and shortly after they prepared for the ceremony. Phillotson's hair was brushed to a painful extent, and his shirt collar appeared stiffer than it had been for the previous twenty years. Beyond this he looked dignified and thoughtful, and altogether a man of whom it was not unsafe to predict that he would make a kind and considerate husband. That he adored Sue was obvious; and she could almost be seen to feel that she was undeserving his adoration.

Although the distance was so short he had hired a fly from the Red Lion, and six or seven women and children had gathered by the door when they came out. The schoolmaster and Sue were unknown, though Jude was getting to be recognized as a citizen; and the couple were judged to be some relations of his from a distance, nobody supposing Sue to have been a recent pupil at the Training School.

In the carriage Jude took from his pocket his extra little wedding-present, which turned out to be two or three yards of white tulle, which he threw over her bonnet and all, as a veil.

'It looks so odd over a bonnet,' she said. 'I'll take the bonnet off.'

'O no—let it stay,' said Phillotson. And she obeyed.

When they had passed up the church and were standing in their places Jude found that the antecedent visit had certainly taken off the edge of this performance, but by the time they were half way on with the service he wished from his heart that he had not undertaken the business of giving her away. How could Sue have had the temerity to ask him to do it—a cruelty possibly to herself as well as to him? Women were different from men in such matters. Was it that they were, instead of more sensitive, as reputed, more callous, and less romantic; or were they more heroic? Or was Sue simply so perverse that she wilfully gave herself and him pain for the odd and mournful luxury of practising long-suffering in her own person, and of being touched with tender pity for him at having made him practise it? He could perceive that her face was nervously set, and when they reached the trying ordeal of Jude giving her to Phillotson she could hardly command herself; rather, however, as it seemed, from her knowledge of what her cousin must feel, whom she need not have had there at all, than from self-consideration. Possibly she would go on inflicting such pains again and again, and grieving for the sufferer again and again, in all her colossal inconsistency.

Phillotson seemed not to notice, to be surrounded by a mist which prevented his seeing the emotions of others. As soon as they had signed their names and come away, and the suspense was over, Jude felt relieved.

The meal at his lodging was a very simple affair, and at two o'clock they went off. In crossing the pavement to the fly she looked back; and there was a frightened light in her eyes. Could it be that Sue had acted with such unusual foolishness as to plunge into she knew not what for the sake of asserting her independence of him, of retaliating on him for his secrecy? Perhaps Sue was thus venturesome with men because she was childishly ignorant of that side of their natures which wore out women's hearts and lives.

When her foot was on the carriage-step she turned round, saying that she had forgotten something. Jude and the landlady offered to get it.

'No,' she said, running back. 'It is my handkerchief. I know where I left it.'

Jude followed her back. She had found it, and came holding it in her hand. She looked into his eyes with her own tearful ones, and her lips suddenly parted as if she were going to avow something. But she went on; and whatever she had meant to say remained unspoken.

VIII

Jude wondered if she had really left her handkerchief behind; or whether it were that she had miserably wished to tell him of a love that at the last moment she could not bring herself to express.

He could not stay in his silent lodging when they were gone, and fearing that he might be tempted to drown his misery in alcohol he went upstairs, changed his dark clothes for his white, his thin boots for this thick, and proceeded to his customary work for the afternoon.

But in the cathedral he seemed to hear a voice behind him, and to be possessed with an idea that she would come back. She could not possibly go home with Phillotson, he fancied. The feeling grew and stirred. The moment that the clock struck the last of his working hours he threw down his tools and rushed homeward. 'Has anybody been for me?' he asked.

Nobody had been there.

As he could claim the downstairs sitting-room till twelve o'clock that night he sat in it all the evening; and even when the clock had struck eleven, and the family had retired, he could not shake off the feeling that she would come back and sleep in the little room adjoining his own, in which she had slept so many previous days. Her actions were always unpredictable: why should she not come? Gladly would he have compounded for the denial of her as a sweetheart and wife by having her live thus as a fellow-lodger and friend, even on the most distant terms. His supper still remained spread; and going to the front door, and softly setting it open, he returned to the room and sat as watchers sit on Old-Midsummer eves, expecting the phantom of the Beloved. But she did not come.

Having indulged in this wild hope he went upstairs, and looked out of the window, and pictured her through the evening journey to London, whither she and Phillotson had gone for their holiday;

their rattling along through the damp night to their hotel, under the same sky of ribbed cloud as that he beheld, through which the moon showed its position rather than its shape, and one or two of the larger stars made themselves visible as faint nebulae only. It was a new beginning of Sue's history. He projected his mind into the future, and saw her with children more or less in her own likeness around her. But the consolation of regarding them as a continuation of her identity was denied to him, as to all such dreamers, by the wilfulness of Nature in not allowing issue from one parent alone. Every desired renewal of an existence is debased by being half alloy. 'If at the estrangement or death of my lost love, I could go and see her child—hers solely—there would be comfort in it!' said Jude. And then he again uneasily saw, as he had latterly seen with more and more frequency, the scorn of Nature for man's finer emotions, and her lack of interest in his aspirations.

The oppressive strength of his affection for Sue showed itself on the morrow and following days yet more clearly. He could no longer endure the light of the Melchester lamps; the sunshine was as drab paint; and the blue sky as zinc. Then he received news that his old aunt was dangerously ill at Marygreen, which intelligence almost coincided with a letter from his former employer at Christminster, who offered him permanent work of a good class if he would come back. The letters were almost a relief to him. He started to visit Aunt Drusilla, and resolved to go onward to Christminster to see what worth there might be in the builder's offer.

Jude found his aunt even worse than the communication from the Widow Edlin had led him to expect. There was every possibility of her lingering on for weeks or months, though little likelihood. He wrote to Sue informing her of the state of her aunt, and suggesting that she might like to see her aged relative alive. He would meet her at Alfredston Road, the following evening, Monday, on his way back from Christminster, if she could come by the up-train which crossed the down-train at that station. Next morning, accordingly, he went on to Christminster, intending to return to Alfredston soon enough to keep the suggested appointment with Sue.

The City of learning wore an estranged look, and he had lost all feeling for its associations. Yet as the sun made vivid lights and shades of the mullioned architecture of the façades, and drew patterns of the crinkled battlements on the young turf of the quadrangles, Jude thought he had never seen the place look so beautiful. He came to the street in which he had first beheld Sue. The chair she had occupied when, leaning over her ecclesiastical scrolls, a hog-hair brush in her hand, her girlish figure had arrested the gaze of his inquiring eyes, stood precisely in its former spot, empty. It was as if she were dead, and nobody had been found capable of succeeding her in that artistic pursuit. Hers was now the City phantom, while those of the intellectual and devotional worthies who had once moved him to emotion were no longer able to assert their presence there.

However, here he was; and in fulfilment of his intention he went on to his former lodging in 'Beersheba', near the ritualistic church of St Silas. The old landlady who opened the door seemed glad to see him again, and bringing some lunch informed him that the builder who had employed him had called to inquire his address.

Jude went on to the stone-yard where he had worked. But the old sheds and bankers were distasteful to him; he felt it impossible to engage himself to return and stay in this place of vanished dreams. He longed for the hour of the homeward train to Alfredston, where he might probably meet Sue.

Then, for one ghastly half-hour of depression caused by these scenes, there returned upon him that feeling which had been his undoing more than once—that he was not worth the trouble of being taken care of either by himself or others; and during this half-hour he met Tinker Taylor, the bankrupt ecclesiastical ironmonger, at Fourways, who proposed that they should adjourn to a bar and drink together. They walked along the street till they stood before one of the great palpitating centres of Christminster life, the inn wherein he formerly had responded to the challenge to rehearse the Creed in Latin—now a popular tavern with a spacious and inviting entrance, which gave admittance to a bar that had been entirely renovated and refitted in modern style since Jude's residence here.

Tinker Taylor drank off his glass and departed, saying it was too stylish a place now for him to feel at home in, unless he was drunker than he had money to be just then. Jude was longer finishing his, and stood abstractedly silent in the, for the minute, almost empty place. The bar had been gutted and newly arranged throughout, mahogany fixtures having taken the place of the old painted ones, while at the back of the standing-space there were stuffed sofa-benches. The room was divided into compartments in the approved manner, between which were scenes of ground glass in mahogany framing, to prevent topers in one compartment being put to the blush by the recognitions of those in the next. On the inside of the counter two barmaids leant over the white-handled beer-engines, and the row of little silvered taps inside, dripping into a pewter trough.

Feeling tired, and having nothing more to do till the train left, Jude sat down on one of the sofas. At the back of the barmaids rose bevel-edged mirrors, with glass shelves running along their front, on which stood precious liquids that Jude did not know the name of, in bottles of topaz, sapphire, ruby and amethyst. The moment was enlivened by the entrance of some customers into the next compartment, and the starting of the mechanical tell-tale of monies received, which emitted a ting-ting every time a coin was put in.

The barmaid attending to this compartment was invisible to Jude's direct glance, though a reflection of her back in the glass behind her was occasionally caught by his eyes. He had only observed this listlessly, when she turned her face for a moment to the glass to set her hair tidy. Then he was amazed to discover that the face was Arabella's.

If she had come to his compartment she would have seen him. But she did not, this being presided over by the maiden on the other side. Abby was in a black gown, with white linen cuffs and a broad white collar, and her figure, more developed than formerly, was accentuated by a bunch of daffodils that she wore on her left bosom. In the compartment she served stood an electro-plated fountain of water over a spirit-lamp, whose blue flame sent a steam from the top, all this being visible to him only in the mirror behind her; which also reflected the faces of the men she was attending to—one of them a handsome, dissipated young fellow, possibly an undergraduate, who had been relating to her an experience of some humorous sort.

'O, Mr Cockman, now! How can you tell such a tale to me in my innocence!' she cried gaily. 'Mr Cockman, what do you use to make your moustache curl so beautiful?' As the young man was clean shaven the retort provoked a laugh at his expense.

'Come!' said he, 'I'll have a Curaçoa; and a light, please.'

She served the liqueur from one of the lovely bottles, and striking a match held it to his cigarette with ministering archness while he whiffed.

'Well, have you heard from your husband lately, my dear?' he asked.

'Not a sound,' said she.

'Where is he?'

'I left him in Australia; and I suppose he's there still.'

Jude's eyes grew rounder.

'What made you part from him?'

'Don't you ask questions, and you won't hear lies.'

'Come then, give me my change, which you've been keeping from me for the last quarter of an hour; and I'll romantically vanish up the street of this picturesque city.'

She handed the change over the counter, in taking which he caught her fingers and held them. There was a slight struggle and titter, and he bade her good-bye and left.

Jude had looked on with the eye of a dazed philosopher. It was extraordinary how far removed from his life Arabella now seemed to be. He could not realize their nominal closeness. And, this being the case, in his present frame of mind he was indifferent to the fact that Arabella was his wife indeed.

The compartment that she served emptied itself of visitors, and after a brief thought he entered it, and went forward to the counter. Arabella did not recognize him for a moment. Then their glances met. She started; till a humorous impudence sparkled in her eyes, and she spoke.

'Well, I'm blest! I thought you were underground years ago!'

'Oh!'

'I never heard anything of you, or I don't know that I should have come here. But never mind! What shall I treat you to this afternoon? A Scotch and soda? Come, anything that the house will afford, for old acquaintance' sake!'

'Thanks, Arabella,' said Jude without a smile. 'But I don't want anything more than I've had.' The fact was that her unexpected presence there had destroyed at a stroke his momentary taste for strong liquor as completely as if it had whisked him back to his milk-fed infancy.

'That's a pity, now you could get it for nothing.'

'How long have you been here?'

'About six weeks. I returned from Sydney three months ago. I always liked this business, you know.'

'I wonder you came to this place!'

'Well, as I say, I thought you were gone to glory, and being in London I saw the situation in an advertisement. Nobody was likely to know me here, even if I had minded, for I was never in Christminster in my growing up.'

'Why did you return from Australia?'

'Oh, I had my reasons. . . . Then you are not a Don yet?'

'No.'

'Not even a Reverend?'

'No.'

'Nor so much as a Rather Reverend dissenting gentleman?'

'I am as I was.'

'True—you look so.' She idly allowed her fingers to rest on the pull of the beer-engine as she inspected him critically. He observed that her hands were smaller and whiter than when he had lived with her, and that on the hand which pulled the engine she wore an ornamental ring set with what seemed to be real sapphires—which they were, indeed, and were much admired as such by the young men who frequented the bar.

'So you pass as having a living husband,' he continued.

'Yes. I thought it might be awkward if I called myself a widow, as I should have liked.'

'True. I am known here a little.'

'I didn't mean on that account—for as I said I didn't expect you. It was for other reasons.'

'What were they?'

'I don't care to go into them,' she replied evasively. 'I make a very good living, and I don't know that I want your company.'

Here a chappie with no chin, and a moustache like a lady's eyebrow, came and asked for a curiously compounded drink, and Arabella was obliged to go and attend to him. 'We can't talk here,' she said, stepping back a moment. 'Can't you wait till nine? Say yes, and don't be a fool. I can get off duty two hours sooner than usual, if I ask. I am not living in the house at present.'

He reflected and said gloomily, 'I'll come back. I suppose we'd better arrange something.'

'O bother arranging! I'm not going to arrange anything!'

'But I must know a thing or two; and, as you say, we can't talk here. Very well; I'll call for you.'

Depositing his unemptied glass he went out and walked up and down the street. Here was a rude flounce into the pellucid sentimentality of his sad attachment to Sue. Though Arabella's word was absolutely untrustworthy, he thought there might be some truth in her implication that she had not wished to disturb him, and had really supposed him dead. However, there was only one thing now to be done, and that was to play a straightforward part, the law being the law, and the woman between whom and himself there was no more unity than between east and west being in the eye of the Church one person with him.

Having to meet Arabella here, it was impossible to meet Sue at Alfredston as he had promised. At every thought of this a pang had gone through him; but the conjecture could not be helped. Arabella was perhaps an intended intervention to punish him for his unauthorized love. Passing the evening, therefore, in a desultory waiting about the town wherein he avoided the precincts of every Cloister and Hall, because he could not bear to behold them, he repaired to a tavern bar while the hundred and one strokes were resounding from the Great Bell of Cardinal College, a coincidence which seemed to him gratuitous irony. The inn was now brilliantly lighted up, and the scene was altogether more brisk and gay. The faces of the barmaidens had risen in colour, each having a pink flush on her cheek; the manners were still more vivacious than before—more abandoned, more excited, more sensuous, and they expressed their sentiments and desires less euphemistically, laughing in a lackadaisical tone, without reserve.

The bar had been crowded with men of all sorts during the previous hour, and he had heard from without the hubbub of their voices; but the customers were fewer at last. He nodded to Arabella, and told her that she would find him outside the door when she came away.

'But you must have something with me first,' she said with great good-humour. 'Just an early nightcap: I always do. Then you can go out and wait a minute, as it is best we should not be seen going together.' She drew a couple of liqueur glasses of brandy; and though she had evidently, from her countenance, already taken in enough alcohol either by drinking or, more probably, from the atmosphere she had breathed for so many hours, she finished hers quickly. He also drank his, and went outside the house.

In a few minutes she came, in a thick jacket and a hat with a black feather. 'I live quite near,' she said, taking his arm, 'and can let myself in by a latch-key at any time. What arrangement do you want to come to?'

'O—none in particular,' he answered, thoroughly sick and tired, his thoughts again reverting to Alfredston, and the train he did not go by; the probable disappointment of Sue that he was not there when she arrived, and the missed pleasure of her company on the long and lonely climb by starlight up the hills to Marygreen. 'I ought to have gone back really! My aunt is on her deathbed, I fear.'

'I'll go over with you to-morrow. I think I could get a day off.'

There was something particularly uncongenial in the idea of Arabella, who had no more sympathy than a tigress with his relations or him, coming to the bedside of his dying aunt, and meeting Sue. Yet he said, 'Of course, if you'd like to, you can.'

'Well, that we'll consider. . . . Now, until we have come to some agreement it is awkward our being together here—where you are known, and I am getting known, though without any suspicion that I have anything to do with you. As we are going towards the station suppose we take the nine-forty train to Aldbrickham? We shall be there in little more than half-an-hour, and nobody will know us for one night, and we shall be quite free to act as we choose till we have made up our minds whether we'll make anything public or not.'

'As you like.'

'Then wait till I get two or three things. This is my lodging. Sometimes when late I sleep at the hotel where I am engaged, so nobody will think anything of my staying out.'

She speedily returned, and they went on to the railway, and made the half-hour's journey to Aldbrickham, where they entered a third-rate inn near the station in time for a late supper.

IX

On the morrow between nine and half-past they were journeying back to Christminster, the only two occupants of a compartment in a third-class railway-carriage. Having, like Jude, made rather a hasty toilet to catch the train, Arabella looked a little frowsy, and her face was very far from possessing the animation which had characterized it at the bar the night before. When they came out of the station she found that she still had half-an-hour to spare before she was due at the bar. They walked in silence a little way out of the town in the direction of Alfredston. Jude looked up the far highway.

'Ah . . . poor feeble me!' he murmured at last.

'What?' said she.

'This is the very road by which I came into Christminster years ago full of plans!'

'Well, whatever the road is I think my time is nearly up, as I have to be in the bar by eleven o'clock. And as I said, I shan't ask for the day to go with you to see your aunt. So perhaps we had better part here. I'd sooner not walk up Chief Street with you, since we've come to no conclusion at all.'

'Very well. But you said when we were getting up this morning that you had something you wished to tell me before I left?'

'So I had—two things—one in particular. But you wouldn't promise to keep it a secret. I'll tell you now if you promise? As an honest woman I wish you to know it. . . . It was what I began telling you in the night—about the gentleman who managed the Sydney hotel.' Arabella spoke somewhat hurriedly for her. 'You'll keep it close?'

'Yes—yes—I promise!' said Jude impatiently. 'Of course I don't want to reveal your secrets.'

'Whenever I met him out for a walk, he used to say that he was much taken with my looks, and he kept pressing me to marry him. I never thought of coming back to England again; and being out there in Australia, with no home of my own after leaving my father, I at last agreed, and did.'

'What—marry him?'

'Yes.'

'Regularly—legally—in church?'

'Yes. And lived with him till shortly before I left. It was stupid, I know; but I did! There, now I've told you. Don't round upon me! He talks of coming back to England, poor old chap. But if he does, he won't be likely to find me.'

Jude stood pale and fixed.

'Why the devil didn't you tell me last night!' he said.

'Well—I didn't. . . . Won't you make it up with me, then?'

'So in talking of "your husband" to the bar gentlemen you meant him, of course—not me!'

'Of course. . . . Come, don't fuss about it.'

'I have nothing more to say!' replied Jude. 'I have nothing at all to say about the—crime—you've confessed to!'

'Crime! Pooh. They don't think much of such as that over there! Lots of 'em do it. . . . Well, if you take it like that I shall go back to him! He was very fond of me, and we lived honourable enough, and as respectable as any married couple in the Colony! How did I know where you were?'

'I won't go blaming you. I could say a good deal; but perhaps it would be misplaced. What do you wish me to do?'

'Nothing. There was one thing more I wanted to tell you; but I fancy we've seen enough of one another for the present! I shall think over what you said about your circumstances, and let you know.'

Thus they parted. Jude watched her disappear in the direction of the hotel, and entered the railway station close by. Finding that it wanted three-quarters of an hour of the time at which he could get a train back to Alfredston, he strolled mechanically into the city as far as to the Fourways, where he stood as he had so often stood before, and surveyed Chief Street stretching ahead, with its college after college, in picturesqueness unrivalled except by such Continental vistas as the Street of Palaces in Genoa; the lines of the buildings being as distinct in the morning air as in an architectural drawing. But Jude was far from seeing or criticizing these things; they were hidden by an indescribable consciousness of Arabella's midnight contiguity, a sense of degradation at his revived experiences with her, of her appearance as she lay asleep at dawn, which set upon his motionless face a look as of one accurst. If he could only have felt resentment towards her he would have been less unhappy; but he pitied while he condemned her.

Jude turned and retraced his steps. Drawing again towards the station he started at hearing his name pronounced—less at the name than at the voice. To his great surprise no other than Sue stood like a vision before him—her look bodeful and anxious as in a dream, her little mouth nervous, and her strained eyes speaking reproachful inquiry.

'O Jude—I am so glad—to meet you like this!' she said in quick, uneven accents not far from a sob. Then she flushed as she observed his thought that they had not met since her marriage.

They looked away from each other to hide their emotion, took each other's hand without further speech, and went on together awhile, till she glanced at him with furtive solicitude. 'I arrived at Alfredston station last night, as you asked me to, and there was nobody to meet me! But I reached Marygreen alone, and they told me aunt was a trifle better. I sat up with her, and as you did not come all night I was frightened about you—I thought that perhaps, when you found yourself back in the old city, you were upset at—at thinking I was—married, and not there as I used to be; and that you had nobody to speak to; so you had tried to drown your gloom!—as you did at that former time when you were disappointed about entering as a student, and had forgotten your promise to me that you never would again. And this, I thought, was why you hadn't come to meet me!'

'And you came to hunt me up, and deliver me, like a good angel!'

'I thought I would come by the morning train and try to find out—in case—in case—'

'I did think of my promise to you, dear, continually! I shall never break out again as I did, I am sure. I may have been doing nothing better, but I was not doing that—I loathe the thought of it.'

'I am glad your staying had nothing to do with that. But,' she said, the faintest pout entering into her tone, 'you didn't come back last night and meet me, as you engaged to!'

'I didn't—I am sorry to say. I had an appointment at nine o'clock—too late for me to catch the train that would have met yours, or to get home at all.'

Looking at his loved one as she appeared to him now, in his tender thought the sweetest and most disinterested comrade that he had ever had, living largely in vivid imaginings, so ethereal a creature that her spirit could be seen trembling through her limbs, he felt heartily ashamed of his earthliness in spending the hours he had spent in Arabella's company. There was something rude and immoral in thrusting these recent facts of his life upon the mind of one who, to him, was so uncarnate as to seem at times impossible as a human wife to any average man. And yet she was Phillotson's. How she had become such, how she lived as such, passed his comprehension as he regarded her to-day.

'You'll go back with me?' he said. 'There's a train just now. I wonder how my aunt is by this time. . . . And so, Sue, you really came on my account all this way! At what an early time you must have started, poor thing!'

'Yes. Sitting up watching alone made me all nerves for you, and instead of going to bed when it got light I started. And now you won't frighten me like this again about your morals for nothing?'

He was not so sure that she had been frightened about his morals for nothing. He released her hand till they had entered the train,—it seemed the same carriage he had lately got out of with another—where they sat down side by side, Sue between him and the window. He regarded the delicate lines of her profile, and the small, tight, apple-like convexities of her bodice, so different from Arabella's amplitudes. Though she knew he was looking at her she did not turn to him, but kept her eyes forward, as if afraid that by meeting his own some troublous discussion would be initiated.

'Sue—you are married now, you know, like me; and yet we have been in such a hurry that we have not said a word about it!'

'There's no necessity,' she quickly returned.

'O well—perhaps not. . . . But I wish—'

'Jude—don't talk about *me*—I wish you wouldn't!' she entreated. 'It distresses me, rather. Forgive my saying it! . . . Where did you stay last night?'

She asked the question in perfect innocence, to change the topic. He knew that, and said merely, 'At an inn,' though it would have been a relief to tell her of his meeting with an unexpected one. But the latter's final announcement of her marriage in Australia bewildered him lest what he might say should do his ignorant wife an injury.

Their talk proceeded but awkwardly till they reached Alfredston. That Sue was not as she had been, but was labelled 'Phillotson', paralyzed Jude whenever he wanted to commune with her as an individual. Yet she seemed unaltered—he could not say why. There remained the five-mile extra journey into the country, which it was just as easy to walk as to drive, the greater part of it being uphill. Jude had never before in his life gone that road with Sue, though he had with another. It was now as if he carried a bright light which temporarily banished the shady associations of the earlier time.

Sue talked; but Jude noticed that she still kept the conversation from herself. At length he inquired if her husband were well.

'O yes,' she said. 'He is obliged to be in the school all the day, or he would have come with me. He is so good and kind that to accompany me he would have dismissed the school for once, even against his principles—for he is strongly opposed to giving casual holidays—only I wouldn't let him. I felt it would be better to come alone. Aunt Drusilla, I knew, was so very eccentric; and his being almost a stranger to her now would have made it irksome to both. Since it turns out that she is hardly conscious I am glad I did not ask him.'

Jude had walked moodily while this praise of Phillotson was being expressed. 'Mr Phillotson obliges you in everything, as he ought,' he said.

'Of course.'

'You ought to be a happy wife.'

'And of course I am.'

'Bride, I might almost have said, as yet. It is not so many weeks since I gave you to him, and—'

'Yes, I know! I know!' There was something in her face which belied her late assuring words, so strictly proper and so lifelessly spoken that they might have been taken from a list of model speeches in 'The Wife's Guide to Conduct'. Jude knew the quality of every vibration in Sue's voice, could read every symptom of her mental condition; and he was convinced that she was unhappy, although she had not been a month married. But her rushing away thus from home, to see the last of a relative whom she had hardly known in her life, proved nothing; for Sue naturally did such things as those.

'Well, you have my good wishes now as always, Mrs Phillotson.'

She reproached him by a glance.

'No, you are not Mrs Phillotson,' murmured Jude. 'You are dear, free Sue Bridehead, only you don't know it! Wifedom has not yet squashed up and digested you in its vast maw as an atom which has no further individuality.'

Sue put on a look of being offended, till she answered, 'Nor has husbandom you, so far as I can see!'

'But it has!' he said, shaking his head sadly.

When they reached the lone cottage under the firs, between the Brown House and Marygreen, in which Jude and Arabella had lived and quarrelled, he turned to look at it. A squalid family lived there now. He could not help saying to Sue: 'That's the house my wife and I occupied the whole of the time we lived together. I brought her home to that house.'

She looked at it. 'That to you was what the school-house at Shaston is to me.'

'Yes; but I was not very happy there, as you are in yours.'

She closed her lips in retortive silence, and they walked some way till she glanced at him to see how he was taking it. 'Of course I may have exaggerated your happiness—one never knows,' he continued blandly.

'Don't think that, Jude, for a moment, even though you may

have said it to sting me! He's as good to me as a man can be, and gives me perfect liberty—which elderly husbands don't do in general. . . . If you think I am not happy because he's too old for me, you are wrong.'

'I don't think anything against him—to you, dear.'

'And you won't say things to distress me, will you?'

'I will not.'

He said no more, but he knew that, from some cause or other, in taking Phillotson as a husband, Sue felt that she had done what she ought not to have done.

They plunged into the concave field on the other side of which rose the village—the field wherein Jude had received a thrashing from the farmer many years earlier. On ascending to the village and approaching the house they found Mrs Edlin standing at the door, who at sight of them lifted her hands deprecatingly. 'She's downstairs, if you'll believe me!' cried the widow. 'Out 'o bed she got, and nothing could turn her. What will come o't I do not know!'

On entering, there indeed by the fireplace sat the old woman, wrapped in blankets, and turning upon them a countenance like that of Sebastiano's Lazarus. They must have looked their amazement, for she said in a hollow voice:

'Ah—sceered ye, have I! I wasn't going to bide up there no longer, to please nobody! 'Tis more than flesh and blood can bear, to be ordered to do this and that by a feller that don't know half as well as you do yourself! . . . Ah—you'll rue this marrying as well as he!' she added, turning to Sue. 'All our family do,—and nearly all everybody else's. You should have done as I did, you simpleton! And Phillotson the schoolmaster, of all men! What made 'ee marry him?'

'What makes most women marry, aunt?'

'Ah! You mean to say you loved the man!'

'I don't mean to say anything definite.'

'Do ye love un?'

'Don't ask me, aunt.'

'I can mind the man very well. A very civil, honourable liver; but Lord!—I don't want to wownd your feelings, but—there be certain men here and there that no woman of any niceness can stomach. I should have said he was one. I don't say so *now*, since you must ha' known better than I,—but that's what I *should* have said!'

Sue jumped up and went out. Jude followed her, and found her in the outhouse, crying.

'Don't cry, dear!' said Jude in distress. 'She means well, but is very crusty and queer now, you know.'

'O no—it isn't that!' said Sue, trying to dry her eyes. 'I don't mind her roughness one bit.'

'What is it, then?'

'It is that what she says is—is true!'

'God—what—you don't like him?' asked Jude.

'I don't mean that!' she said hastily. 'That I ought—perhaps I ought not to have married!'

He wondered if she had really been going to say that at first. They went back, and the subject was smoothed over, and her aunt took rather kindly to Sue, telling her that not many young women newly married would have come so far to see a sick old crone like her. In the afternoon Sue prepared to depart, Jude hiring a neighbour to drive her to Alfredston.

'I'll go with you to the station, if you'd like?' he said.

She would not let him. The man came round with the trap, and Jude helped her into it, perhaps with unnecessary attention, for she looked at him prohibitively.

'I suppose—I may come to see you some day, when I am back again at Melchester?' he half-crossly observed.

She bent down and said softly: 'No, dear—you are not to come yet. I don't think you are in a good mood.'

'Very well,' said Jude. 'Good-bye!'

'Good-bye!' She waved her hand and was gone.

'She's right! I won't go!' he murmured.

He passed the evening and following days in mortifying by every possible means his wish to see her, nearly starving himself in attempts to extinguish by fasting his passionate tendency to love her. He read sermons on discipline; and hunted up passages in Church history that treated of the Ascetics of the second century. Before he had returned from Marygreen to Melchester there arrived a letter from Arabella. The sight of it revived a stronger feeling of self-condemnation for his brief return to her society than for his attachment to Sue.

The letter, he perceived, bore a London postmark instead of the Christminster one. Arabella informed him that a few days after their parting in the morning at Christminster, she had been surprised by an affectionate letter from her Australian husband, formerly manager of the hotel in Sydney. He had come to England on purpose to find her; and had taken a free, fully-licensed public, in Lambeth, where he wished her to join him in conducting the business, which was likely to be a very thriving one, the house being situated in an excellent, densely populated, gin-drinking neighbourhood, and already doing a trade of £200 a month, which could be easily doubled.

As he had said that he loved her very much still, and implored her to tell him where she was, and as they had only parted in a slight tiff, and as her engagement in Christminster was only temporary, she had just gone to join him as he urged. She could not help feeling that she belonged to him more than to Jude, since she had properly married him, and had lived with him much longer than with her first husband. In thus wishing Jude good-bye she bore him no ill-will, and trusted he would not turn upon her, a weak woman, and inform against her, and bring her to ruin now that she had a chance of improving her circumstances and leading a genteel life.

X

Jude returned to Melchester, which had the questionable recommendation of being only a dozen and a half miles from his Sue's now permanent residence. At first he felt that this nearness was a distinct reason for not going southward at all; but Christminster was too sad a place to bear, while the proximity of Shaston to Melchester might afford him the glory of worsting the Enemy in a close engagement, such as was deliberately sought by the priests and virgins of the early Church, who, disdaining an ignominious flight from temptation, became even chamber-partners with impunity. Jude did not pause to remember that, in the laconic words of the historian, 'insulted Nature sometimes vindicated her rights' in such circumstances.

He now returned with feverish desperation to his study for the priesthood—in the recognition that the single-mindedness of his aims, and his fidelity to the cause, had been more than questionable of late. His passion for Sue troubled his soul; yet his lawful abandonment to the society of Arabella for twelve hours seemed instinctively a worse thing—even though she had not told him of her Sydney husband till afterwards. He had, he verily believed, overcome all tendency to fly to liquor—which, indeed, he had never done from taste, but merely as an escape from intolerable misery of mind. Yet he perceived with despondency that, taken all round, he was a man of too many passions to make a good clergyman; the utmost he could hope for was that in a life of constant internal warfare between flesh and spirit the former might not always be victorious.

As a hobby, auxiliary to his readings in Divinity, he developed his slight skill in church-music and thorough-bass, till he could join in part-singing from notation with some accuracy. A mile or two from Melchester there was a restored village church, to which Jude had originally gone to fix the new columns and capitals. By this means he had become acquainted with the organist, and the ultimate result was that he joined the choir as a bass voice.

He walked out to this parish twice every Sunday, and sometimes in the week. One evening about Easter the choir met for practice, and a new hymn which Jude had heard of as being by a Wessex composer was to be tried and prepared for the following week. It turned out to be a strangely emotional composition. As they all sang it over and over again its harmonies grew upon Jude, and moved him exceedingly.

When they had finished he went round to the organist to make inquiries. The score was in manuscript, the name of the composer being at the head, together with the title of the hymn: 'The Foot of the Cross'.

'Yes,' said the organist. 'He is a local man. He is a professional musician at Kennetbridge—between here and Christminster. The vicar knows him. He was brought up and educated in Christminster traditions, which accounts for the quality of the piece. I think he plays in the large church there, and has a surpliced choir. He comes to Melchester sometimes, and once tried to get the Cathedral organ when the post was vacant. The hymn is getting about everywhere this Easter.'

As he walked humming the air on his way home, Jude fell to musing on its composer, and the reasons why he composed it. What a man of sympathies he must be! Perplexed and harassed as he himself was about Sue and Arabella, and troubled as was his conscience by the complication of his position, how he would like to know that man! 'He of all men would understand my difficulties,' said the impulsive Jude. If there were any person in the world to choose as a confidant, this composer would be the one, for he must have suffered, and throbbed, and yearned.

In brief, ill as he could afford the time and money for the journey, Fawley resolved, like the child that he was, to go to Kennetbridge the very next Sunday. He duly started, early in the morning, for it was only by a series of crooked railways that he could get to the town. About mid-day he reached it, and crossing the bridge into the quaint old borough he inquired for the house of the composer.

They told him it was a red brick building some little way further on. Also that the gentleman himself had just passed along the street not five minutes before.

'Which way?' asked Jude with alacrity.

'Straight along homeward from church.'

Jude hastened on, and soon had the pleasure of observing a man in a black coat and a black slouched felt hat no considerable distance ahead. Stretching out his legs yet more widely he stalked after. 'A hungry soul in pursuit of a full soul!' he said. 'I must speak to that man!'

He could not, however, overtake the musician before he had entered his own house, and then arose the question if this were an expedient time to call. Whether or not he decided to do so there and then, now that he had got here, the distance home being too great for him to wait till late in the afternoon. This man of soul would understand scant ceremony, and might be quite a perfect adviser in a case in which an earthly and illegitimate passion had cunningly obtained entrance into his heart through the opening afforded for religion.

Jude accordingly rang the bell, and was admitted.

The musician came to him in a moment, and being respectably dressed, good-looking, and frank in manner, Jude obtained a favourable reception. He was nevertheless conscious that there would be a certain awkwardness in explaining his errand.

'I have been singing in the choir of a little church near Melchester,' he said. 'And we have this week practised "The Foot of the Cross", which I understand, sir, that you composed?'

'I did—a year or so ago.'

'I—like it. I think it supremely beautiful!'

'Ah well—other people have said so too. Yes, there's money in it, if I could only see about getting it published. I have other compositions to go with it, too; I wish I could bring them out; for I haven't made a five-pound note out of any of them yet. These publishing people—they want the copyright of an obscure composer's work, such as mine is, for almost less than I should have to pay a person for making a fair manuscript copy of the score. The one you speak of I have lent to various friends about here and Melchester, and so it has got to be sung a little. But music is a poor staff to lean on—I am giving it up entirely. You must go into trade if you want to make money nowadays. The wine business is what I am thinking of. This is my forthcoming list—it is not issued yet—but you can take one.'

He handed Jude an advertisement list of several pages in booklet shape, ornamentally margined with a red line, in which were set forth the various clarets, champagnes, ports, sherries, and other wines with which he purposed to initiate his new venture. It took Jude more than by surprise that the man with the soul was thus and thus; and he felt that he could not open up his confidences.

They talked a little longer, but constrainedly, for when the musician found that Jude was a poor man his manner changed from what it had been while Jude's appearance and address deceived him as to his position and pursuits. Jude stammered out something about his feelings in wishing to congratulate the author on such an exalted composition, and took an embarrassed leave.

All the way home by the slow Sunday train, sitting in the fireless waiting-rooms on this cold spring day, he was depressed enough at his simplicity in taking such a journey. But no sooner did he reach his Melchester lodgings than he found awaiting him a letter which had arrived that morning a few minutes after he had left the house. It was a contrite little note from Sue, in which she said, with sweet humility, that she felt she had been horrid in telling him he was not to come to see her; that she despised herself for having been so conventional; and that he was to be sure to come by the eleven-forty-five train that very Sunday, and have dinner with them at half-past one.

Jude almost tore his hair at having missed this letter till it was too late to act upon its contents; but he had chastened himself considerably of late, and at last his chimerical expedition to Kennetbridge really did seem to have been another special intervention of Providence to keep him away from temptation. But a growing impatience of faith, which he had noticed in himself more than once of late, made him pass over in ridicule the idea that God sent people on fools' errands. He longed to see her; he was angry at having missed her; and he wrote instantly, telling her what had happened, and saying he had not enough patience to wait till the following Sunday, but would come any day in the week that she liked to name.

Since he wrote a little over-ardently, Sue, as her manner was, delayed her reply till Thursday before Good Friday, when she said he might come that afternoon if he wished, this being the earliest day on which she could welcome him, for she was now assistant-teacher in her husband's school. Jude therefore got leave from the Cathedral works at the trifling expense of a stoppage of pay, and went.

PART FOURTH

AT SHASTON

'Whoso prefers either Matrimony or other Ordinance before the Good of Man and the plain Exigence of Charity, let him profess Papist, or Protestant, or what he will, he is no better than a Pharisee.'

—J. Milton

I

Shaston, the ancient British Palladour,

> From whose foundation first such strange reports arise

(as Drayton sang it), was, and is, in itself the city of a dream. Vague imaginings of its castle, its three mints, its magnificent apsidal Abbey, the chief glory of South Wessex, its twelve churches, its shrines, chantries, hospitals, its gabled freestone mansions—all now ruthlessly swept away—throw the visitor, even against his will, into a pensive melancholy, which the stimulating atmosphere and limitless landscape around him can scarcely dispel. The spot was the burial-place of a king and a queen, of abbots and abbesses, saints and bishops, knights and squires. The bones of King Edward 'the Martyr', carefully removed hither for holy preservation, brought Shaston a renown which made it the resort of pilgrims from every part of Europe, and enabled it to maintain a reputation extending far beyond English shores. To this fair creation of the great Middle-Age the Dissolution was, as historians tell us, the death-knell. With the destruction of the enormous abbey the whole place collapsed in a general ruin: the Martyr's bones met with the fate of the sacred pile that held them, and not a stone is now left to tell where they lie.

The natural picturesqueness and singularity of the town still remain; but strange to say these qualities, which were noted by many writers in ages when scenic beauty is said to have been unappreciated, are passed over in this, and one of the queerest and quaintest spots in England stands virtually unvisited to-day.

It has a unique position on the summit of a steep and imposing scarp, rising on the north, south, and west sides of the borough out of the deep alluvial Vale of Blackmoor, the view from Castle Green over three counties of verdant pasture—South, Mid, and Nether Wessex—being as sudden a surprise to the unexpectant traveller's eyes as the medicinal air is to his lungs. Impossible to a railway, it can best be reached on foot, next best by light vehicles; and it is hardly accessible to these but by a sort of isthmus on the north-east, that connects it with the high chalk table-land on that side.

Such is, and such was, the now world-forgotten Shaston or Palladour. Its situation rendered water the great want of the town; and within living memory, horses, donkeys and men may have been seen toiling up the winding ways to the top of the height, laden with tubs and barrels filled from the wells beneath the mountain, and hawkers retailing their contents at the price of a halfpenny a bucketful.

This difficulty in the water supply, together with two other odd facts, namely, that the chief graveyard slopes up as steeply as a roof behind the church, and that in former times the town passed through a curious period of corruption, conventual and domestic, gave rise to the saying that Shaston was remarkable for three consolations to man, such as the world afforded not elsewhere. It was a place where the churchyard lay nearer heaven than the church steeple, where beer was more plentiful than water, and where there were more wanton women than honest wives and maids. It is also said that after the middle ages the inhabitants were too poor to pay their priests, and hence were compelled to pull down their churches, and refrain altogether from the public worship of God; a necessity which they bemoaned over their cups in the settles of their inns on Sunday afternoons. In those days the Shastonians were apparently not without a sense of humour.

There was another peculiarity—this a modern one—which Shaston appeared to owe to its site. It was the resting-place and head-quarters of the proprietors of wandering vans, shows, shooting-galleries, and other itinerant concerns, whose business lay largely at fairs and markets. As strange wild birds are seen assembled on some lofty promontory, meditatively pausing for longer flights, or to return by the course they followed thither, so here, in this cliff-town, stood in stultified silence the yellow and green caravans bearing names not local, as if surprised by a change in the landscape so violent as to hinder their further progress; and here they usually remained all the winter till they turned to seek again their old tracks in the following spring.

It was to this breezy and whimsical spot that Jude ascended from the nearest station for the first time in his life about four o'clock one afternoon, and entering on the summit of the peak after a toilsome climb, passed the first houses of the aerial town; and drew towards the school-house. The hour was too early; the pupils were still in school, humming small, like a swarm of gnats; and he withdrew a few steps along Abbey Walk, whence he regarded the spot which fate had made the home of all he loved best in the world. In front of the schools, which were extensive and stone-built, grew two enormous beeches with smooth mouse-coloured trunks, as such trees will only grow on chalk uplands. Within the mullioned and transomed windows he could see the black, brown, and flaxen crowns of the scholars over the sills, and to pass the time away he walked down to the level terrace where the Abbey gardens once had spread, his heart throbbing in spite of him.

Unwilling to enter till the children were dismissed he remained here till young voices could be heard in the open air, and girls in white pinafores over red and blue frocks appeared dancing along the paths which the abbess, prioress, sub-prioress, and fifty nuns had demurely paced three centuries earlier. Retracing his steps he found that he had waited too long, and that Sue had gone out into the town at the heels of the last scholar, Mr Phillotson having been absent all the afternoon at a teachers' meeting at Shottsford.

Jude went into the empty schoolroom and sat down, the girl who was sweeping the floor having informed him that Mrs Phillotson would be back again in a few minutes. A piano stood near—actually the old piano that Phillotson had possessed at Marygreen—and though the dark afternoon almost prevented him seeing the notes Jude touched them in his humble way, and could not help modulating into the hymn which had so affected him in the previous week.

A figure moved behind him, and thinking it was still the girl with the broom Jude took no notice, till the person came close and laid her fingers lightly upon his bass hand. The imposed hand was a little one he seemed to know, and he turned.

'Don't stop,' said Sue. 'I like it. I learnt it before I left Melchester. They used to play it in the Training School.'

'I can't strum before you! Play it for me.'

'O well—I don't mind.'

Sue sat down, and her rendering of the piece, though not remarkable, seemed divine as compared with his own. She, like him, was evidently touched—to her own surprise—by the recalled air; and when she had finished, and he moved his hand towards hers, it met his own half-way. Jude grasped it—just as he had done before her marriage.

'It is odd,' she said, in a voice quite changed, 'that I should care about that air; because—'

'Because what?'

'I am not that sort—quite.'

'Not easily moved?'

'I didn't quite mean that.'

'O, but you *are* one of that sort, for you are just like me at heart!'

'But not at head.'

She played on, and suddenly turned round; and by an unpremeditated instinct each clasped the other's hand again.

She uttered a forced little laugh as she relinquished his quickly. 'How funny!' she said. 'I wonder what we both did that for?'

'I suppose because we are both alike, as I said before.'

'Not in our thoughts! Perhaps a little in our feelings.'

'And they rule thoughts. . . . Isn't it enough to make one blaspheme that the composer of that hymn is one of the most commonplace men I ever met!'

'What—you know him?'

'I went to see him.'

'O you goose—to do just what I should have done! Why did you?'

'Because we are not alike,' he said drily.

'Now we'll have some tea,' said Sue. 'Shall we have it here instead of in my house? It is no trouble to get the kettle and things brought in. We don't live at the school, you know, but in that ancient dwelling across the way called Old-Grove Place. It is so antique and dismal that it depresses me dreadfully. Such houses are very well to visit, but not to live in—I feel crushed into the earth by the weight of so many previous lives there spent. In a new place like these schools there is only your own life to support. Sit down, and I'll tell Ada to bring the tea-things across.'

He waited in the light of the stove, the door of which she flung open before going out, and when she returned, followed by the maiden with tea, they sat down by the same light, assisted by the blue rays of a spirit-lamp under the brass kettle on the stand.

'This is one of your wedding-presents to me,' she said, signifying the latter.

'Yes,' said Jude.

The kettle of his gift sang with some satire in its note, to his mind; and to change the subject he said, 'Do you know of any good readable edition of the uncanonical books of the New Testament? You don't read them in the school, I suppose?'

'O dear no!—'twould alarm the neighbourhood. . . . Yes, there is one. I am not familiar with it now, though I was interested in it when my former friend was alive. Cowper's *Apocryphal Gospels*.'

'That sounds like what I want.' His thoughts, however, reverted with a twinge to the 'former friend'—by whom she meant, as he knew, the University comrade of her earlier days. He wondered if she talked of him to Phillotson.

'The Gospel of Nicodemus is very nice,' she went on, to keep him from his jealous thoughts, which she read clearly, as she always did. Indeed when they talked on an indifferent subject, as now, there was ever a second silent conversation passing between their emotions, so perfect was the reciprocity between them. 'It is quite like the genuine article. All cut up into verses, too; so that it is like one of the other evangelists read in a dream, when things are the same, yet not the same. But, Jude, do you take an interest in those questions still? Are you getting up *Apologetica*?'

'Yes. I am reading Divinity harder than ever.'

She regarded him curiously.

'Why do you look at me like that?' said Jude.

'Oh—why do you want to know?'

'I am sure you can tell me anything I may be ignorant of in that subject. You must have learnt a lot of everything from your dear dead friend!'

'We won't get on to that now!' she coaxed. 'Will you be carving out at that church again next week, where you learnt the pretty hymn?'

'Yes, perhaps.'

'That will be very nice. Shall I come and see you there? It is in this direction, and I could come any afternoon by train for half-an-hour?'

'No. Don't come!'

'What—aren't we going to be friends, then, any longer, as we used to be?'

'No.'

'I didn't know that. I thought you were always going to be kind to me!'

'No, I am not.'

'What have I done, then? I am sure I thought we two—' The *tremelo* in her voice caused her to break off.

'Sue, I sometimes think you are a flirt,' said he abruptly.

There was a momentary pause, till she suddenly jumped up; and to his surprise he saw by the kettle-flame that her face was flushed.

'I can't talk to you any longer, Jude!' she said, the tragic contralto note having come back as of old. 'It is getting too dark to stay together like this, after playing morbid Good Friday tunes that make one feel what one shouldn't! . . . We mustn't sit and talk in this way any more. Yes—you must go away, for you mistake me! I am very much the reverse of what you say so cruelly—O Jude, it *was* cruel to say that! Yet I can't tell you the truth—I should shock you by letting you know how I give way to my impulses, and how much I feel that I shouldn't have been provided with attractiveness unless it were meant to be exercised! Some women's love of being loved is insatiable; and so, often, is their love of loving; and in the last case they may find that they can't give it continuously to the chamber-officer appointed by the bishop's licence to receive it.

But you are so straightforward, Jude, that you can't understand me! . . . Now you must go. I am sorry my husband is not at home.'

'Are you?'

'I perceive I have said that in mere conversation! Honestly I don't think I am sorry. It does not matter, either way, sad to say!'

As they had overdone the grasp of hands some time sooner, she touched his fingers but lightly when he went out now. He had hardly gone from the door when, with a dissatisfied look, she jumped on a form and opened the iron casement of a window beneath which he was passing in the path without. 'When do you leave here to catch your train, Jude?' she asked.

He looked up in some surprise. 'The coach that runs to meet it goes in three-quarters of an hour or so.'

'What will you do with yourself for the time?'

'O—wander about, I suppose. Perhaps I shall go and sit in the old church.'

'It does seem hard of me to pack you off so! You have thought enough of churches, Heaven knows, without going into one in the dark. Stay there.'

'Where?'

'Where you are. I can talk to you better like this than when you were inside. . . . It was so kind and tender of you to give half a day's work to come to see me! . . . You are Joseph the dreamer of dreams, dear Jude. And a tragic Don Quixote. And sometimes you are St Stephen, who, while they were stoning him, could see Heaven opened. O my poor friend and comrade, you'll suffer yet!'

Now that the high window-sill was between them, so that he could not get at her, she seemed not to mind indulging in a frankness she had feared at close quarters. 'I have been thinking,' she continued, still in the tone of one brimful of feeling, 'that the social moulds civilization fits us into have no more relation to our actual shapes than the conventional shapes of the constellations have to the real star-patterns. I am called Mrs Richard Phillotson, living a calm wedded life with my counterpart of that name. But I am not really Mrs Richard Phillotson, but a woman tossed about, all alone, with aberrant passions, and unaccountable antipathies. . . . Now you mustn't wait longer, or you will lose the coach. Come and see me again. You must come to the house then.'

'Yes!' said Jude. 'When shall it be?'

'To-morrow week. Good-bye—good-bye!' She stretched out her hand and stroked his forehead pitifully—just once. Jude said good-bye, and went away into the darkness.

Passing along Bimport Street he thought he heard the wheels of the coach departing, and, truly enough, when he reached the Duke's Arms in the Market Place the coach had gone. It was impossible for him to get to the station on foot in time for this train, and he settled himself perforce to wait for the next—the last to Melchester that night.

He wandered about awhile, obtained something to eat; and then, having another half-hour on his hands, his feet involuntarily took him through the venerable graveyard of Trinity Church, with its avenues of limes, in the direction of the schools again. They were entirely in darkness. She had said she lived over the way at Old-Grove Place, a house which he soon discovered from her description of its antiquity.

A glimmering candle-light shone from a front window, the shutters being yet unclosed. He could see the interior clearly—the floor sinking a couple of steps below the road without, which had become raised during the centuries since the house was built. Sue, evidently just come in, was standing with her hat on in this front parlour or sitting-room, whose walls were lined with wainscoting of panelled oak reaching from floor to ceiling, the latter being crossed by huge moulded beams only a little way above her head. The mantelpiece was of the same heavy description, carved with Jacobean pilasters and scroll-work. The centuries did, indeed, ponderously overhang a young wife who passed her time here.

She had opened a rosewood work-box, and was looking at a photograph. Having contemplated it a little while she pressed it against her bosom, and put it again in its right place.

Then becoming aware that she had not obscured the windows she came forward to do so, candle in hand. It was too dark for her to see Jude without, but he could see her face distinctly, and there was an unmistakable tearfulness about the dark, long-lashed eyes.

She closed the shutters, and Jude turned away to pursue his solitary journey home. 'Whose photograph was she looking at?' he said. He had once given her his; but she had others, he knew. Yet it was his, surely?

He knew he should go to see her again, according to her invitation. Those earnest men he read of, the saints, whom Sue, with gentle irreverence, called his demi-gods, would have shunned such encounters if they doubted their own strength. But he could not. He might fast and pray during the whole interval, but the human was more powerful in him than the Divine.

II

HOWEVER, if God disposed not, woman did. The next morning but one brought him this note from her:

> Don't come next week. On your own account don't! We were too free, under the influence of that morbid hymn and the twilight. Think no more than you can help of
>
> SUSANNA FLORENCE MARY

The disappointment was keen. He knew her mood, the look of her face, when she subscribed herself at length thus. But whatever her mood he could not say she was wrong in her view. He replied:

> I acquiesce. You are right. It is a lesson in renunciation which I suppose I ought to learn at this season.
>
> JUDE

He despatched the note on Easter Eve, and there seemed a finality in their decisions. But other forces and laws than theirs were in operation. On Easter Monday morning he received a message from the Widow Edlin, whom he had directed to telegraph if anything serious happened:

> Your aunt is sinking. Come at once.

He threw down his tools and went. Three and a half hours later he was crossing the downs about Marygreen, and presently plunged into the concave field across which the short cut was made to the village. As he ascended on the other side a labouring man, who had been watching his approach from a gate across the path, moved uneasily, and prepared to speak. 'I can see in his face that she is dead,' said Jude. 'Poor Aunt Drusilla!'

It was as he had supposed, and Mrs Edlin had sent out the man to break the news to him.

'She wouldn't have knowed 'ee. She lay like a doll wi' glass eyes; so it didn't matter that you wasn't here,' said he.

Jude went on to the house, and in the afternoon, when everything was done, and the layers-out had finished their beer, and gone, he sat down alone in the silent place. It was absolutely necessary to communicate with Sue, though two or three days earlier they had agreed to mutual severance. He wrote in the briefest terms:

> Aunt Drusilla is dead, having been taken almost suddenly. The funeral is on Friday afternoon.

He remained in and about Marygreen through the intervening days, went out on Friday morning to see that the grave was finished, and wondered if Sue would come. She had not written, and that seemed to signify rather that she would come than that she would not. Having timed her by her only possible train, he locked the door about mid-day, and crossed the hollow field to the verge of the upland by the Brown House, where he stood and looked over the vast prospect northwards, and over the nearer landscape in which Alfredston stood. Two miles behind it a jet of white steam was travelling from the left to the right of the picture.

There was a long time to wait, even now, till he would know if she had arrived. He did wait, however, and at last a small hired vehicle pulled up at the bottom of the hill, and a person alighted, the conveyance going back, while the passenger began ascending the hill. He knew her; and she looked so slender to-day that it seemed as if she might be crushed in the intensity of a too passionate embrace—such as it was not for him to give. Two-thirds of the way up her head suddenly took a solicitous poise, and he knew that she had at that moment recognized him. Her face soon began a pensive smile, which lasted till, having descended a little way, he met her.

'I thought,' she began with nervous quickness, 'that it would be so sad to let you attend the funeral alone! And so—at the last moment—I came.'

'Dear faithful Sue!' murmured Jude.

With the elusiveness of her curious double nature, however, Sue did not stand still for any further greeting, though it wanted some time to the burial. A pathos so unusually compounded as that which attached to this hour was unlikely to repeat itself for years, if ever, and Jude would have paused, and meditated and conversed. But Sue either saw it not at all, or, seeing it more than he, would not allow herself to feel it.

The sad and simple ceremony was soon over, their progress to the church being almost at a trot, the bustling undertaker having a more important funeral an hour later, three miles off. Drusilla was put into the new ground, quite away from her ancestors. Sue and Jude had gone side by side to the grave, and now sat down to tea in the familiar house; their lives united at least in this last attention to the dead.

'She was opposed to marriage, from first to last, you say?' murmured Sue.

'Yes. Particularly for members of our family.'

Her eyes met his, and remained on him awhile.

'We are rather a sad family, don't you think, Jude?'

'She said we made bad husbands and wives. Certainly we make unhappy ones. At all events, I do, for one!'

Sue was silent. 'Is it wrong, Jude,' she said with a tentative tremor, 'for a husband or wife to tell a third person that they are unhappy in their marriage? If a marriage ceremony is a religious thing, it is possibly wrong; but if it is only a sordid contract based on material convenience in householding, rating, and taxing, and the inheritance of land and money by children, making it necessary that the male parent should be known—which it seems to be—why surely a person may say, even proclaim upon the housetops, that it hurts and grieves him or her?'

'I have said so, anyhow, to you.'

Presently she went on: 'Are there many couples, do you think, where one dislikes the other for no definite fault?'

'Yes, I suppose. If either cares for another person, for instance.'

'But even apart from that? Wouldn't the woman, for example, be very bad-natured if she didn't like to live with her husband; merely'—her voice undulated, and he guessed things—'merely because she had a personal feeling against it—a physical objection—a fastidiousness, or whatever it may be called—although she might respect and be grateful to him? I am merely putting a case. Ought she to try to overcome her pruderies?'

Jude threw a troubled look at her. He said, looking away: 'It would be just one of those cases in which my experiences go contrary to my dogmas. Speaking as an order-loving man—which I hope I am, though I fear I am not—I should say, yes. Speaking from experience and unbiased nature, I should say, no. . . . Sue, I believe you are not happy!'

'Of course I am!' she contradicted. 'How can a woman be unhappy who has only been married eight weeks to a man she chose freely?'

' "Chose freely!" '

'Why do you repeat it? . . . But I have to go back by the six o'clock train. You will be staying on here, I suppose?'

'For a few days to wind up aunt's affairs. This house is gone now. Shall I go to the train with you?'

A little laugh of objection came from Sue. 'I think not. You may come part of the way.'

'But stop—you can't go to-night! That train won't take you to Shaston. You must stay and go back to-morrow. Mrs Edlin has plenty of room, if you don't like to stay here?'

'Very well,' she said dubiously. 'I didn't tell him I would come for certain.'

Jude went to the widow's house adjoining, to let her know; and returning in a few minutes sat down again.

'It is horrible how we are circumstanced, Sue—horrible!' he said abruptly, with his eyes bent to the floor.

'No! Why?'

'I can't tell you all my part of the gloom. Your part is that you ought not to have married him. I saw it before you had done it, but I thought I mustn't interfere. I was wrong. I ought to have!'

'But what makes you assume all this, dear?'

'Because—I can see you through your feathers, my poor little bird!'

Her hand lay on the table, and Jude put his upon it. Sue drew hers away.

'That's absurd, Sue,' cried he, 'after what we've been talking about! I am more strict and formal than you, if it comes to that; and that you should object to such an innocent action shows that you are ridiculously inconsistent!'

'Perhaps it was too prudish,' she said repentantly. 'Only I have fancied it was a sort of trick of ours—too frequent perhaps. There, you may hold it as much as you like. Is that good of me?'

'Yes; very.'

'But I must tell him.'

'Who?'

'Richard.'

'O—of course, if you think it necessary. But as it means nothing it may be bothering him needlessly.'

'Well—are you sure you mean it only as my cousin?'

'Absolutely sure, I have no feeling of love left in me.'

'That's news. How has it come to be?'

'I've seen Arabella.'

She winced at the hit; then said curiously, 'When did you see her?'

'When I was at Christminster.'

'So she's come back; and you never told me! I suppose you will live with her now?'

'Of course—just as you live with your husband.'

She looked at the window pots with the geraniums and cactuses, withered for want of attention, and through them at the outer distance, till her eyes began to grow moist. 'What is it?' said Jude, in a softened tone.

'Why should you be so glad to go back to her if—if—what you used to say to me is still true—I mean if it were true then! Of course it is not now! How could your heart go back to Arabella so soon?'

'A special Providence, I suppose, helped it on its way.'

'Ah—it isn't true!' she said with gentle resentment. 'You are teasing me—that's all—because you think I am not happy!'

'I don't know. I don't wish to know.'

'If I were unhappy it would be my fault, my wickedness; not that I should have a right to dislike him! He is considerate to me in everything; and he is very interesting, from the amount of general knowledge he has acquired by reading everything that comes his way. . . . Do you think, Jude, that a man ought to marry a woman his own age, or one younger than himself—eighteen years—as I am than he?'

'It depends upon what they feel for each other.'

He gave her no opportunity of self-satisfaction, and she had to go on unaided, which she did in a vanquished tone, verging on tears:

'I—I think I must be equally honest with you as you have been with me. Perhaps you have seen what it is I want to say?—that though I like Mr Phillotson as a friend, I don't like him—it is a torture to me to—live with him as a husband!—There, now I have let it out—I couldn't help it, although I have been—pretending I am happy.—Now you'll have a contempt for me for ever, I suppose!' She bent down her face upon her hands as they lay upon the cloth, and silently sobbed in little jerks that made the fragile three-legged table quiver.

'I have only been married a month or two!' she went on, still remaining bent upon the table, and sobbing into her hands. 'And it is said that what a woman shrinks from—in the early days of her marriage—she shakes down to with comfortable indifference in half-a-dozen years. But that is much like saying that the amputation of a limb is no affliction, since a person gets comfortably accustomed to the use of a wooden leg or arm in the course of time!'

Jude could hardly speak, but he said, 'I thought there was something wrong, Sue! O, I thought there was!'

'But it is not as you think!—there is nothing wrong except my own wickedness, I suppose you'd call it—a repugnance on my part, for a reason I cannot disclose, and what would not be admitted as one by the world in general! . . . What tortures me so much is the necessity of being responsive to this man whenever he wishes, good as he is morally!—the dreadful contract to feel in a particular way in a matter whose essence is its voluntariness! . . . I wish he would beat me, or be faithless to me, or do some open thing that I could talk about as a justification for feeling as I do! But he does nothing, except that he has grown a little cold since he has found out how I feel. That's why he didn't come to the funeral. . . . Oh, I am very miserable—I don't know what to do! . . . Don't come near me, Jude, because you mustn't. Don't—don't!'

But he had jumped up and put his face against hers—or rather against her ear, her face being inaccessible.

'I told you not to, Jude!'

'I know you did—I only wish to—console you! It all arose through my being married before we met, didn't it? You would have been my wife, Sue, wouldn't you, if it hadn't been for that?'

Instead of replying she rose quickly, and saying she was going to walk to her aunt's grave in the churchyard to recover herself, went out of the house. Jude did not follow her. Twenty minutes later he saw her cross the village green towards Mrs Edlin's, and soon she sent a little girl to fetch her bag, and tell him she was too tired to see him again that night.

In the lonely room of his aunt's house Jude sat watching the cottage of the Widow Edlin as it disappeared behind the night shade. He knew that Sue was sitting within its walls equally lonely and disheartened; and again questioned his devotional motto that all was for the best.

He retired to rest early, but his sleep was fitful from the sense that Sue was so near at hand. At some time near two o'clock, when he was beginning to sleep more soundly, he was aroused by a shrill squeak that had been familiar enough to him when he lived regularly at Marygreen. It was the cry of a rabbit caught in a gin. As was the little creature's habit, it did not soon repeat its cry; and probably would not do so more than once or twice; but would remain bearing its torture till the morrow, when the trapper would come and knock it on the head.

He who in his childhood had saved the lives of the earthworms now began to picture the agonies of the rabbit from its lacerated leg. If it were a 'bad catch' by the hind-leg, the animal would tug during the ensuing six hours till the iron teeth of the trap had stripped the leg-bone of its flesh, when, should a weak-springed instrument enable it to escape, it would die in the fields from the mortification of the limb. If it were a 'good catch', namely, by the fore-leg, the bone would be broken, and the limb nearly torn in two in attempts at an impossible escape.

Almost half-an-hour passed, and the rabbit repeated its cry. Jude could rest no longer till he had put it out of its pain, so dressing himself quickly he descended, and by the light of the moon went across the green in the direction of the sound. He reached the hedge bordering the widow's garden, when he stood still. The faint click of the trap as dragged about by the writhing animal guided him now, and reaching the spot he struck the rabbit on the back of the neck with the side of his palm, and it stretched itself out dead.

He was turning away when he saw a woman looking out of the open casement at a window on the ground floor of the adjacent cottage. 'Jude!' said a voice timidly—Sue's voice. 'It is you—is it not?'

'Yes, dear!'

'I haven't been able to sleep at all, and then I heard the rabbit, and couldn't help thinking of what it suffered, till I felt I must come down and kill it! But I am so glad you got there first.... They ought not to be allowed to set these steel traps, ought they!'

Jude had reached the window, which was quite a low one, so that she was visible down to her waist. She let go of the casement-stay and put her hand upon his, her moonlit face regarding him wistfully.

'Did it keep you awake?' he said.

'No—I was awake.'

'How was that?'

'O, you know—now! I know you, with your religious doctrines, think that a married woman in trouble of a kind like mine commits a mortal sin in making a man the confidant of it, as I did you. I wish I hadn't, now!'

'Don't wish it, dear,' he said. 'That may have *been* my view; but my doctrines and I begin to part company.'

'I knew it—I knew it! And that's why I vowed I wouldn't disturb your beliefs. But—I am so *glad* to see you!—and, O, I didn't mean to see you again, now the last tie between us, Aunt Drusilla, is dead!'

Jude seized her hand and kissed it. 'There is a stronger one left!' he said. 'I'll never care about my doctrines or my religion any more! Let them go! Let me help you, even if I do love you, and even if you . . .'

'Don't say it!—I know what you mean; but I can't admit so much as that. There! Guess what you like, but don't press me to answer questions!'

'I wish you were happy, whatever I may be!'

'I *can't* be! So few could enter into my feeling—they would say 'twas my fanciful fastidiousness, or something of that sort, and condemn me. . . . It is none of the natural tragedies of love that's love's usual tragedy in civilized life, but a tragedy artificially manufactured for people who in a natural state would find relief in parting! . . . It would have been wrong, perhaps, for me to tell my distress to you, if I had been able to tell it to anybody else. But I have nobody. And I *must* tell somebody! Jude, before I married him I had never thought out fully what marriage meant, even though I knew. It was idiotic of me—there is no excuse. I was old enough, and I thought I was very experienced. So I rushed on, when I had got into that Training School scrape, with all the cock-sureness of the fool that I was! . . . I am certain one ought to be allowed to undo what one has done so ignorantly! I daresay it happens to lots of women; only they submit, and I kick. . . . When people of a later age look back upon the barbarous customs and superstitions of the times that we have the unhappiness to live in, what *will* they say!'

'You are very bitter, darling Sue! How I wish—I wish—'

'You must go in now!'

In a moment of impulse she bent over the sill, and laid her face upon his hair, weeping, and then imprinting a scarcely perceptible little kiss upon the top of his head, withdrawing quickly, so that he could not put his arms round her, as otherwise he unquestionably would have done. She shut the casement, and he returned to his cottage.

III

SUE's distressful confession recurred to Jude's mind all the night as being a sorrow indeed.

The morning after, when it was time for her to go, the neighbours saw her companion and herself disappearing on foot down the hill path which led into the lonely road to Alfredston. An hour passed before he returned along the same route, and in his face there was a look of exaltation not unmixed with recklessness. An incident had occurred.

They had stood parting in the silent highway, and their tense and passionate moods had led to bewildered inquiries of each other on how far their intimacy ought to go; till they had almost quarrelled, and she had said tearfully that it was hardly proper of him as a parson in embryo to think of such a thing as kissing her even in farewell, as he now wished to do. Then she had conceded that the fact of the kiss would be nothing: all would depend upon the spirit of it. If given in the spirit of a cousin and a friend she saw no objection: if in the spirit of a lover she could not permit it. 'Will you swear that it will not be in that spirit?' she had said.

No: he would not. And then they had turned from each other in estrangement, and gone their several ways, till at a distance of twenty or thirty yards both had looked round simultaneously. That look behind was fatal to the reserve hitherto more or less maintained. They had quickly run back, and met, embracing most unpremeditatedly, kissed close and long. When they parted for good it was with flushed cheeks on her side, and a beating heart on his.

The kiss was a turning-point in Jude's career. Back again in the cottage, and left to reflection, he saw one thing: that though his kiss of that aerial being had seemed the purest moment of his faultful life, as long as he nourished his unlicensed tenderness it was glaringly inconsistent for him to pursue the idea of becoming the soldier and servant of a religion in which sexual love was regarded as at its best a frailty, and at its worst damnation. What Sue had said in warmth was really the cold truth. When to defend his affection tooth and nail, to persist with headlong force in impassioned attentions to her, was all he thought of, he was condemned *ipso facto* as a professor of the accepted school of morals. He was as unfit, obviously, by nature, as he had been by social position, to fill the part of a propounder of accredited dogma.

Strange that his aspiration—towards academical proficiency—had been checked by a woman, and that his second aspiration—towards apostleship—had also been checked by a woman. 'Is it,' he said, 'that the women are to blame; or is it the artificial system of things, under which the normal sex-impulses are turned into devilish domestic gins and springes to noose and hold back those who want to progress?'

It had been his standing desire to become a prophet, however humble, to his struggling fellow-creatures, without any thought of personal gain. Yet with a wife living away from him with another husband, and himself in love erratically, the loved one's revolt against her state being possibly on his account, he had sunk to be barely respectable according to regulation views.

It was not for him to consider further: he had only to confront the obvious, which was that he had made himself quite an imposter as a law-abiding religious teacher.

At dusk that evening he went into the garden and dug a shallow hole, to which he brought out all the theological and ethical works that he possessed, and had stored here. He knew that, in this country of true believers, most of them were not saleable at a much higher price than waste-paper value, and preferred to get rid of them in his own way, even if he should sacrifice a little money to the sentiment of thus destroying them. Lighting some loose pamphlets to begin with, he cut the volumes into pieces as well as he could, and with a three-pronged fork shook them over the flames. They kindled, and lighted up the back of the house, the pigsty, and his own face, till they were more or less consumed.

Though he was almost a stranger here now, passing cottagers talked to him over the garden hedge.

'Burning up your awld aunt's rubbidge, I suppose? Ay; a lot gets heaped up in nooks and corners when you've lived eighty years in one house.'

It was nearly one o'clock in the morning before the leaves, covers, and binding of Jeremy Taylor, Butler, Doddridge, Paley, Pusey, Newman and the rest had gone to ashes; but the night was quiet, and as he turned and turned the paper shreds with the fork, the sense of being no longer a hypocrite to himself afforded his mind a relief which gave him calm. He might go on believing as before, but he professed nothing, and no longer owned and exhibited engines of faith which, as their proprietor, he might naturally be supposed to exercise on himself first of all. In his passion for Sue he could now stand as an ordinary sinner, and not as a whited sepulchre.

Meanwhile Sue, after parting from him earlier in the day, had gone along to the station, with tears in her eyes for having run back and let him kiss her. Jude ought not to have pretended that he was not a lover, and made her give way to an impulse to act unconventionally, if not wrongly. She was inclined to call it the latter; Sue's logic was extraordinarily compounded, and seemed to maintain that before a thing was done it might be right to do, but that being done it became wrong; or, in other words, that things which were right in theory were wrong in practice.

'I have been too weak, I think!' she jerked out as she pranced on, shaking down tear-drops now and then. 'It was burning, like a lover's—O it was! And I won't write to him any more, or at least for a long time, to impress him with my dignity! And I hope it will hurt him very much—expecting a letter to-morrow morning, and the next, and the next, and no letter coming. He'll suffer then with suspense—won't he, that's all—and I am very glad of it!'—Tears of pity for Jude's approaching sufferings at her hands mingled with those which had surged up in pity for herself.

Then the slim little wife of a husband whose person was disagreeable to her, the ethereal, fine-nerved, sensitive girl, quite unfitted by temperament and instinct to fulfil the conditions of the matrimonial relation with Phillotson, possibly with scarce any man, walked fitfully along, and panted, and brought weariness into her eyes by gazing and worrying hopelessly.

Phillotson met her at the arrival station, and, seeing that she was troubled, thought it must be owing to the depressing effect of her aunt's death and funeral. He began telling her of his day's doings, and how his friend Gillingham, a neighbouring schoolmaster whom he had not seen for years, had called upon him. While ascending to the town, seated on the top of the omnibus beside him, she said suddenly and with an air of self-chastisement, regarding the white road and its bordering bushes of hazel:

'Richard—I let Mr Fawley hold my hand a long while. I don't know whether you think it wrong?'

He, waking apparently from thoughts of far different mould, said vaguely, 'O, did you? What did you do that for?'

'I don't know. He wanted to, and I let him.'

'I hope it pleased him. I should think it was hardly a novelty.'

They lapsed into silence. Had this been a case in the court of an omniscient judge he might have entered on his notes the curious fact that Sue had placed the minor for the major indiscretion, and had not said a word about the kiss.

After tea that evening Phillotson sat balancing the school registers. She remained in an unusually silent, tense, and ruthless condition, and at last, saying she was tired, went to bed early. When Phillotson arrived upstairs, weary with the drudgery of the attendance-numbers, it was a quarter to twelve o'clock. Entering their chamber, which by day commanded a view of some thirty or forty miles over the Vale of Blackmoor, and even into Outer Wessex, he went to the window, and, pressing his face against the pane, gazed with hard-breathing fixity into the mysterious darkness which now covered the far-reaching scene. He was musing. 'I think,' he said at last, without turning his head, 'that I must get the Committee to change the school-stationer. All the copybooks are sent wrong this time.'

There was no reply. Thinking Sue was dozing he went on:

'And there must be a re-arrangement of that ventilator in the class-room. The wind blows down upon my head unmercifully, and gives me the earache.'

As the silence seemed more absolute than ordinarily he turned round. The heavy, gloomy oak wainscot, which extended over the walls upstairs and down in the dilapidated 'Old-Grove House', and the massive chimney-piece reaching to the ceiling, stood in odd contrast to the new and shining brass bedstead, and the new suite of birch furniture that he had bought for her, the two styles seeming to nod to each other across three centuries upon the shaking floor.

'Soo!' he said (this being the way in which he pronounced her name).

She was not in the bed, though she had apparently been there—the clothes on her side being flung back. Thinking she might have forgotten some kitchen detail and gone downstairs for a moment to see to it, he pulled off his coat and idled quietly enough for a few minutes, when, finding she did not come, he went out upon the landing, candle in hand, and said again 'Soo!'

'Yes!' came back to him in her voice, from the distant kitchen quarter.

'What are you doing down there at midnight—tiring yourself out for nothing!'

'I am not sleepy; I am reading; and there is a larger fire here.'

He went to bed. Some time in the night he awoke. She was not there, even now. Lighting a candle he hastily stepped out upon the landing, and again called her name.

She answered 'Yes!' as before; but the tones were small and confined, and whence they came he could not at first understand. Under the staircase was a large clothes-closet, without a window; they seemed to come from it. The door was shut, but there was no lock or other fastening. Phillotson, alarmed, went towards it, wondering if she had suddenly become deranged.

'What are you doing in there?' he asked.

'Not to disturb you I came here, as it was so late.'

'But there's no bed, is there? And no ventilation! Why, you'll be suffocated if you stay all night!'

'O no, I think not. Don't trouble about me.'

'But—' Phillotson seized the knob and pulled at the door. She had fastened it inside with a piece of string, which broke at his pull. There being no bedstead she had flung down some rugs and made a little nest for herself in the very cramped quarters the closet afforded.

When he looked in upon her she sprang out of her lair, great-eyed and trembling.

'You ought not to have pulled open the door!' she cried excitedly. 'It is not becoming in you! O, will you go away; please will you!'

She looked so pitiful and pleading in her white night-gown against the shadowy lumber-hole that he was quite worried. She continued to beseech him not to disturb her.

He said: 'I've been kind to you, and given you every liberty; and it is monstrous that you should feel in this way!'

'Yes,' said she, weeping. 'I know that! It is wrong and wicked of me, I suppose! I am very sorry. But it is not I altogether that am to blame!'

'Who is then? Am I?'

'No—I don't know! The universe, I suppose—things in general, because they are so horrid and cruel!'

'Well, it is no use talking like that. Making a man's house so unseemly at this time o' night! Eliza will hear, if we don't mind.' (He meant the servant.) 'Just think if either of the parsons in this town was to see us now! I hate such eccentricities, Sue. There's no order or regularity in your sentiments! . . . But I won't intrude on you further; only I would advise you not to shut the door too tight, or I shall find you stifled to-morrow.'

On rising the next morning he immediately looked into the closet, but Sue had already gone downstairs. There was a little nest where she had lain, and spiders' webs hung overhead. 'What must a woman's aversion be when it is stronger than her fear of spiders!' he said bitterly.

He found her sitting at the breakfast-table, and the meal began almost in silence, the burghers walking past upon the pavement—or rather roadway, pavements being scarce here—which was two or three feet above the level of the parlour floor. They nodded down to the happy couple their morning greetings, as they went on.

'Richard,' she said all at once; 'would you mind my living away from you?'

'Away from me? Why, that's what you were doing when I married you. What then was the meaning of marrying at all?'

'You wouldn't like me any the better for telling you.'

'I don't object to know.'

'Because I thought I could do nothing else. You had got my promise a long time before that, remember. Then, as time went on, I regretted I had promised you, and was trying to see an honourable way to break if off. But as I couldn't I became rather reckless and careless about the conventions. Then you know what scandals were spread, and how I was turned out of the Training School you have taken such time and trouble to prepare me for and get me into; and this frightened me, and it seemed then that the one thing I could do would be to let the engagement stand. Of course I, of all people, ought not to have cared what was said, for it was just what I fancied I never did care for. But I was a coward—as so many women are—and my theoretic unconventionality broke down. If that had not entered into the case it would have been better to have hurt your feelings once for all then, than to marry you and hurt them all my life after. . . . And you were so generous in never giving credit for a moment to the rumour.'

'I am bound in honesty to tell you that I weighed its probability, and inquired of your cousin about it.'

'Ah!' she said with pained surprise.

'I didn't doubt you.'

'But you inquired!'

'I took his word.'

Her eyes had filled. '*He* wouldn't have inquired!' she said. 'But you haven't answered me. Will you let me go away? I know how irregular it is of me to ask it—'

'It is irregular.'

'But I do ask it! Domestic laws should be made according to temperaments, which should be classified. If people are at all peculiar in character they have to suffer from the very rules that produce comfort in others! . . . Will you let me?'

'But we married—'

'What is the use of thinking of laws and ordinances,' she burst out, 'if they make you miserable when you know you are committing no sin?'

'But you are committing a sin in not liking me.'

'I *do* like you! But I didn't reflect it would be—that it would be so much more than that.... For a man and woman to live on intimate terms when one feels as I do is adultery, in any circumstances, however legal. There—I've said it!... Will you let me, Richard?'

'You distress me, Susanna, by such importunity!'

'Why can't we agree to free each other? We made the compact, and surely we can cancel it—not legally, of course; but we can morally, especially as no new interests, in the shape of children, have arisen to be looked after. Then we might be friends, and meet without pain to either. O Richard, be my friend and have pity! We shall both be dead in a few years, and then what will it matter to anybody that you relieved me from constraint for a little while? I daresay you think me eccentric, or super-sensitive, or something absurd. Well—why should I suffer for what I was born to be, if it doesn't hurt other people?'

'But it does—it hurts *me*! And you vowed to love me.'

'Yes—that's it! I am in the wrong. I always am! It is as culpable to bind yourself to love always as to believe a creed always, and as silly as to vow always to like a particular food or drink!'

'And do you mean, by living away from me, living by yourself?'

'Well, if you insisted, yes. But I meant living with Jude.'

'As his wife?'

'As I choose.'

Phillotson writhed.

Sue continued: 'She, or he, "who lets the world, or his own portion of it, choose his plan of life for him, has no need of any other faculty than the ape-like one of imitation." J. S. Mill's words, those are. I have been reading it up. Why can't you act upon them? I wish to, always.'

'What do I care about J. S. Mill!' moaned he. 'I only want to lead a quiet life! Do you mind my saying that I have guessed what never once occurred to me before our marriage—that you were in love, and are in love, with Jude Fawley!'

'You may go on guessing that I am, since you have begun. But do you suppose that if I had been I should have asked you to let me go and live with him?'

The ringing of the school bell saved Phillotson from the necessity of replying at present to what apparently did not strike him as being such a convincing *argumentum ad verecundiam* as she, in her loss of courage at the last moment, meant it to appear. She was beginning to be so puzzling and unstateable that he was ready to throw in with her other little peculiarities the extremest request which a wife could make.

They proceeded to the schools that morning as usual, Sue entering the class-room, where he could see the back of her head through the glass partition whenever he turned his eyes that way. As he went on giving and hearing lessons his forehead and eyebrows twitched from concentrated agitation of thought; till at length he tore a scrap from a sheet of scribbling paper and wrote:

> Your request prevents my attending to work at all. I don't know what I am doing! Was it seriously made?

He folded the piece of paper very small, and gave it to a little boy to take to Sue. The child toddled off into the class-room. Phillotson saw his wife turn and take the note, and the bend of her pretty head as she read it, her lips slightly crisped, to prevent undue expression under fire of so many young eyes. He could not see her hands, but she changed her position, and soon the child returned, bringing nothing in reply. In a few minutes, however, one of Sue's class appeared, with a little note similar to his own. These words only were pencilled there-in:

> I am sincerely sorry to say that it was seriously made.

Phillotson looked more disturbed than before, and the meeting-place of his brows twitched again. In ten minutes he called up the child he had just sent to her, and despatched another missive:

God knows I don't want to thwart you in any reasonable way. My whole thought is to make you comfortable and happy. But I cannot agree to such a preposterous notion as your going to live with your lover. You would lose everybody's respect and regard; and so should I!

After an interval a similar part was enacted in the class-room, and an answer came:

I know you mean my good. But I don't want to be respectable! To produce 'Human development in its richest diversity' (to quote your Humboldt) is to my mind far above respectability. No doubt my tastes are low—in your view—hopelessly low! If you won't let me go to him, will you grant me this one request—allow me to live in your house in a separate way?

To this he returned no answer.

She wrote again:

I know what you think. But cannot you have pity on me? I beg you to; I implore you to be merciful! I would not ask if I were not almost compelled by what I can't bear! No poor woman has ever wished more than I that Eve had not fallen, so that (as the primitive Christians believed) some harmless mode of vegetation might have peopled Paradise. But I won't trifle! Be kind to me—even though I have not been kind to you! I will go away, go abroad, anywhere, and never trouble you.

Nearly an hour passed, and then he returned an answer:

I do not wish to pain you. How well you *know* I don't! Give me a little time. I am disposed to agree to your last request.

One line from her:

Thank you from my heart, Richard. I do not deserve your kindness.

All day Phillotson bent a dazed regard upon her through the glazed partition; and he felt as lonely as when he had not known her.

But he was as good as his word, and consented to her living apart in the house. At first, when they met at meals, she had seemed more composed under the new arrangement; but the irksomeness of their position worked on her temperament, and the fibres of her nature seemed strained like harp-strings. She talked vaguely and indiscriminately to prevent his talking pertinently.

IV

PHILLOTSON was sitting up late, as was often his custom, trying to get together the materials for his long-neglected hobby of Roman antiquities. For the first time since reviving the subject he felt a return of his old interest in it. He forgot time and place, and when he remembered himself and ascended to rest it was nearly two o'clock.

His preoccupation was such that, though he now slept on the other side of the house, he mechanically went to the room that he and his wife had occupied when he first became a tenant of Old-Grove Place, which since his differences with Sue had been hers exclusively. He entered, and unconsciously began to undress.

There was a cry from the bed, and a quick movement. Before the schoolmaster had realized where he was he perceived Sue starting up half-awake, staring wildly, and springing out upon the floor on the side away from him, which was towards the window. This was somewhat hidden by the canopy of the bedstead, and in a moment he heard her flinging up the sash. Before he had thought that she meant to do more than get air she had mounted upon the sill and leapt out. She disappeared in the darkness, and he heard her fall below.

Phillotson, horrified, ran downstairs, striking himself sharply against the newel in his haste. Opening the heavy door he ascended the two or three steps to the level of the ground, and there on the gravel before him lay a white heap. Phillotson seized it in his arms, and bringing Sue into the hall seated her on a chair, where he gazed at her by the flapping light of the candle which he had set down in the draught on the bottom stair.

She had certainly not broken her neck. She looked at him with eyes that seemed not to take him in; and though not particularly large in general they appeared so now. She pressed her side and rubbed her arm, as if conscious of pain; then stood up, averting her face, in evident distress at his gaze.

'Thank God—you are not killed! Though it's not for want of trying—not much hurt I hope?'

Her fall, in fact, had not been a serious one, probably owing to the lowness of the old rooms and to the high level of the ground without. Beyond a scraped elbow and a blow in the side she had apparently incurred little harm.

'I was asleep, I think!' she began, her pale face still turned away from him. 'And something frightened me—a terrible dream—I thought I saw you—' The actual circumstances seemed to come back to her, and she was silent.

Her cloak was hanging at the back of the door, and the wretched Phillotson flung it round her. 'Shall I help you upstairs?' he asked drearily; for the significance of all this sickened him of himself and of everything.

'No thank you, Richard. I am very little hurt. I can walk.'

'You ought to lock your door,' he mechanically said, as if lecturing in school. 'Then no one could intrude even by accident.'

'I have tried—it won't lock. All the doors are out of order.'

The aspect of things was not improved by her admission. She ascended the staircase slowly, the waving light of the candle shining on her. Phillotson did not approach her, or attempt to ascend himself till he heard her enter her room. Then he fastened up the front door, and returning sat down on the lower stairs, holding the newel with one hand, and bowing his face into the other. Thus he remained for a long long time—a pitiable object enough to one who had seen him; till, raising his head and sighing a sigh which seemed to say that the business of his life must be carried on, whether he had a wife or no, he took the candle and went upstairs to his lonely room on the other side of the landing.

No further incident touching the matter between them occurred till the following evening, when, immediately school was over, Phillotson walked out of Shaston, saying he required no tea, and not informing Sue where he was going. He descended from the town level by a steep road in a north-westerly direction, and continued to move downwards till the soil changed from its white dryness to a tough brown clay. He was now on the low alluvial beds

> Where Duncliffe is the traveller's mark
> And cloty Stour's a-rolling dark.

More than once he looked back in the increasing obscurity of evening. Against the sky was Shaston, dimly visible

> On the grey-topp'd height
> Of Paladore, as pale day wore
> Away . . .

The new-lit lights from its windows burnt with a steady shine as if watching him, one of which windows was his own. Above it he could just discern the pinnacled tower of Trinity Church. The air down here, tempered by the thick damp bed of tenacious clay, was not as it had been above, but soft and relaxing, so that when he had walked a mile or two he was obliged to wipe his face with his handkerchief.

Leaving Duncliffe Hill on the left he proceeded without hesitation through the shade, as a man goes on, night or day, in a district over which he has played as a boy. He had walked altogether about four and a half miles

> Where Stour receives her strength,
> From six cleere fountains fed,

when he crossed a tributary of the Stour, and reached Leddenton—a little town of three or four thousand inhabitants—where he went on to the boys' school, and knocked at the door of the master's residence.

A boy pupil-teacher opened it, and to Phillotson's inquiry if Mr Gillingham was at home replied that he was, going at once off to his own house, and leaving Phillotson to find his way in as he could. He discovered his friend putting away some books from which he had been giving evening lessons. The light of the paraffin lamp fell on Phillotson's face—pale and wretched by contrast with his friend's, who had a cool, practical look. They had been schoolmates in boyhood, and fellow-students at Wintoncester Training College, many years before this time.

'Glad to see you, Dick! But you don't look well? Nothing the matter?'

Phillotson advanced without replying, and Gillingham closed the cupboard and pulled up beside his visitor.

'Why you haven't been here—let me see—since you were married? I called, you know, but you were out; and upon my word it is such a climb after dark that I have been waiting till the days are longer before lumpering up again. I am glad you didn't wait, however.'

Though well-trained and even proficient masters, they occasionally used a dialect-word of their boyhood to each other in private.

'I've come, George, to explain to you my reasons for taking a step that I am about to take, so that you, at least, will understand my motives if other people question them anywhen—as they may, indeed certainly will. . . . But anything is better than the present condition of things. God forbid that you should ever have such an experience as mine!'

'Sit down. You don't mean—anything wrong between you and Mrs Phillotson?'

'I do. . . . My wretched state is that I've a wife I love, who not only does not love me, but—but—Well, I won't say. I know her feeling! I should prefer hatred from her!'

'Ssh!'

'And the sad part of it is that she is not so much to blame as I. She was a pupil-teacher under me, as you know, and I took advantage of her inexperience, and toled her out for walks, and got her to agree to a long engagement before she well knew her own mind. Afterwards she saw somebody else, but she blindly fulfilled her engagement.'

'Loving the other?'

'Yes; with a curious tender solicitude seemingly; though her exact feeling for him is a riddle to me—and to him too, I think—possibly to herself. She is one of the oddest creatures I ever met. However,

I have been struck with these two facts; the extraordinary sympathy, or similarity, between the pair. He is her cousin, which perhaps accounts for some of it. They seem to be one person split in two! And with her unconquerable aversion to myself as a husband, even though she may like me as a friend, 'tis too much to bear longer. She has conscientiously struggled against it, but to no purpose. I cannot bear it—I cannot! I can't answer her arguments—she has read ten times as much as I. Her intellect sparkles like diamonds, while mine smoulders like brown paper. . . . She's one too many for me!'

'She'll get over it, good-now?'

'Never! It is—but I won't go into it—there are reasons why she never will. At last she calmly and firmly asked if she might leave me and go to him. The climax came last night, when, owing to my entering her room by accident, she jumped out of window—so strong was her dread of me! She pretended it was a dream, but that was to soothe me. Now when a woman jumps out of window without caring whether she breaks her neck or no, she's not to be mistaken; and this being the case I have come to a conclusion: that it is wrong to so torture a fellow-creature any longer; and I won't be the inhuman wretch to do it, cost what it may!'

'What—you'll let her go? And with her lover?'

'Whom with is her matter. I shall let her go; with him certainly, if she wishes. I know I may be wrong—I know I can't logically, or religiously, defend my concession to such a wish of hers; or harmonize it with the doctrines I was brought up in. Only I know one thing: something within me tells me I am doing wrong in refusing her. I, like other men, profess to hold that if a husband gets a so-called preposterous request from his wife, the only course that can possibly be regarded as right and proper and honourable in him is to refuse it, and put her virtuously under lock and key, and murder her lover perhaps. But is that essentially right, and proper, and honourable, or is it contemptibly mean and selfish? I don't profess to decide. I simply am going to act by instinct, and let principles take care of themselves. If a person who has blindly walked into a quagmire cries for help, I am inclined to give it, if possible.'

'But—you see, there's the question of neighbours and society—what will happen if everybody—'

'O, I am not going to be a philosopher any longer! I only see what's under my eyes.'

'Well—I don't agree with your instinct, Dick!' said Gillingham gravely. 'I am quite amazed, to tell the truth, that such a sedate, plodding fellow as you should have entertained such a craze for a moment. You said when I called that she was puzzling and peculiar: I think you are!'

'Have you ever stood before a woman whom you know to be intrinsically a good woman, while she has pleaded for release—been the man she has knelt to and implored indulgence of?'

'I am thankful to say I haven't.'

'Then I don't think you are in a position to give an opinion. I have been that man, and it makes all the difference in the world, if one has any manliness or chivalry in him. I had not the remotest idea—living apart from women as I have done for so many years—that merely taking a woman to church and putting a ring upon her finger could by any possibility involve one in such a daily, continuous tragedy as that now shared by her and me!'

'Well, I could admit some excuse for letting her leave you, provided she kept to herself. But to go attended by a cavalier—that makes a difference.'

'Not a bit. Suppose, as I believe, she would rather endure her present misery than be made to promise to keep apart from him? All that is a question for herself. It is not the same thing at all as the treachery of living on with a husband and playing him false. . . . However, she has not distinctly implied living with him as wife, though I think she means to. . . . And to the best of my understanding it is not an ignoble, merely animal, feeling between the two: that is the worst of it; because it makes me think their affection will be enduring. I did not mean to confess to you that in the first jealous weeks of my marriage, before I had come to my right mind, I hid myself in the school one evening when they were together there, and I heard what they said. I am ashamed of it now, though I suppose I was only exercising a legal right. I found from their manner that an extraordinary affinity, or sympathy, entered into their attachment, which somehow took away all flavour of grossness. Their supreme desire is to be together—to share each other's emotions, and fancies, and dreams.'

'Platonic!'

'Well no. Shelleyan would be nearer to it. They remind me of—what are their names—Laon and Cythna. Also of Paul and Virginia a little. The more I reflect, the more *entirely* I am on their side!'

'But if people did as you want to do, there'd be a general domestic disintegration. The family would no longer be the social unit.'

'Yes—I am all abroad, I suppose!' said Phillotson sadly. 'I was never a very bright reasoner, you remember. . . . And yet, I don't see why the woman and the children should not be the unit without the man.'

'By the Lord Harry!—Matriarchy! . . . Does *she* say all this too?'

'O no. She little thinks I have out-Sued Sue in this—all in the last twelve hours!'

'It will upset all received opinion hereabout. Good God—what will Shaston say!'

'I don't say that it won't. I don't know—I don't know! . . . As I say, I am only a feeler, not a reasoner.'

'Now,' said Gillingham, 'let us take it quietly, and have something to drink over it.' He went under the stairs, and produced a bottle of cider-wine, of which they drank a rummer each. 'I think you are rafted, and not yourself,' he continued. 'Do go back and make up your mind to put up with a few whims. But keep her. I hear on all sides that she's a charming young thing.'

'Ah yes! That's the bitterness of it! Well, I won't stay. I have a long walk before me.'

Gillingham accompanied his friend a mile on his way, and at parting expressed his hope that this consultation, singular as its subject was, would be the renewal of their old comradeship. 'Stick to her!' were his last words, flung into the darkness after Phillotson; from which his friend answered 'Ay, ay!'

But when Phillotson was alone under the clouds of night, and no sound was audible but that of the purling tributaries of the Stour, he said, 'So Gillingham, my friend, you had no stronger arguments against it than those!'

'I think she ought to be smacked, and brought to her senses, that's what I think!' murmured Gillingham, as he walked back alone.

The next morning came, and at breakfast Phillotson told Sue:

'You may go—with whom you will. I absolutely and unconditionally agree.'

Having once come to this conclusion it seemed to Phillotson more and more indubitably the true one. His mild serenity at the sense that he was doing his duty by a woman who was at his mercy almost overpowered his grief at relinquishing her.

Some days passed, and the evening of their last meal together had come—a cloudy evening with wind—which indeed was very seldom absent in this elevated place. How permanently it was imprinted upon his vision; that look of her as she glided into the parlour to tea; a slim flexible figure; a face, strained from its roundness, and marked by the pallors of restless days and nights, suggesting tragic possibilities quite at variance with her times of buoyancy; a trying of this morsel and that, and an inability to eat either. Her nervous manner, begotten of a fear lest he should be injured by her course, might have been interpreted by a stranger as displeasure that Phillotson intruded his presence on her for the few brief minutes that remained.

'You had better have a slice of ham, or an egg, or something with your tea? You can't travel on a mouthful of bread and butter.'

She took the slice he helped her to; and they discussed as they sat trivial questions of housekeeping, such as where he would find the key of this or that cupboard, what little bills were paid, and what not.

'I am a bachelor by nature, as you know, Sue,' he said, in a heroic attempt to put her at her ease. 'So that being without a wife will not really be irksome to me, as it might be to other men who have had one a little while. I have, too, this grand hobby in my head of writing "The Roman Antiquities of Wessex", which will occupy all my spare hours.'

'If you will send me some of the manuscript to copy at any time, as you used to, I will do it with so much pleasure!' she said with amenable gentleness. 'I should much like to be some help to you still—as a—friend.'

Phillotson mused, and said: 'No, I think we ought to be really separate, if we are to be at all. And for this reason, that I don't wish to ask you any questions, and particularly wish you not to give me information as to your movements, or even your address. . . . Now, what money do you want? You must have some, you know.'

'O, of course, Richard, I couldn't think of having any of *your* money to go away from you with! I don't want any either. I have enough of my own to last me for a long while, and Jude will let me have—'

'I would rather not know anything about him, if you don't mind. You are free absolutely, and your course is your own.'

'Very well. But I'll just say that I have packed only a change or two of my own personal clothing and one or two little things besides that are my very own. I wish you would look into my trunk before it is closed. Besides that I have only a small parcel that will go into Jude's portmanteau.'

'Of course I shall do no such thing as examine your luggage! I wish you would take three-quarters of the household furniture. I don't want to be bothered with it. I have a sort of affection for a little of it that belonged to my poor mother and father. But the rest you are welcome to whenever you like to send for it.'

'That I shall never do.'

'You go by the six-thirty train, don't you? It is now a quarter to six.'

'You . . . You don't seem very sorry I am going, Richard!'

'O no—perhaps not.'

'I like you much for how you have behaved. It is a curious thing that directly I have begun to regard you as not my husband, but as my old teacher, I like you. I won't be so affected as to say I love you, because you know I don't, except as a friend. But you do seem that to me!'

Sue was for a few moments a little tearful at these reflections, and then the station omnibus came round to take her up. Phillotson saw her things put on top, handed her in, and was obliged to make an appearance of kissing her as he wished her good-bye, which she quite understood and imitated. From the cheerful manner in which they parted the omnibusman had no other idea than that she was going for a short visit.

When Phillotson got back into the house he went upstairs and opened the window in the direction the omnibus had taken. Soon the noise of its wheels died away. He came down then, his face compressed like that of one bearing pain; he put on his hat and went out, following by the same route for nearly a mile. Suddenly turning round he came home.

He had no sooner entered than the voice of his friend Gillingham greeted him from the front room.

'I could make nobody hear; so finding your door open I walked in, and made myself comfortable. I said I would call, you remember.'

'Yes. I am much obliged to you, Gillingham, particularly for coming to-night.'

'How is Mrs—'

'She is quite well. She is gone—just gone. That's her tea-cup, that she drank out of only an hour ago. And that's the plate she—' Phillotson's throat got choked up, and he could not go on. He turned and pushed the tea-things aside.

'Have you had any tea, by-the-bye?' he asked presently in a renewed voice.

'No—yes—never mind,' said Gillingham, preoccupied. 'Gone, you say she is?'

'Yes. . . . I would have died for her; but I wouldn't be cruel to her in the name of the law. She is, as I understand, gone to join her lover. What they are going to do I cannot say. Whatever it may be she has my full consent to.'

There was a stability, a ballast, in Phillotson's pronouncement which restrained his friend's comment. 'Shall I—leave you?' he asked.

'No, no. It is a mercy to me that you have come. I have some articles to arrange and clear away. Would you help me?'

Gillingham assented; and having gone to the upper rooms the schoolmaster opened drawers, and began taking out all Sue's things that she had left behind, and laying them in a large box. 'She wouldn't take all I wanted her to,' he continued. 'But when I made up my mind to her going to live in her own way I did make up my mind.'

'Some men would have stopped at an agreement to separate.'

'I've gone into all that, and don't wish to argue it. I was, and am, the most old-fashioned man in the world on the question of marriage—in fact I had never thought critically about its ethics at all. But certain facts stared me in the face, and I couldn't go against them.'

They went on with the packing silently. When it was done Phillotson closed the box and turned the key.

'There,' he said. 'To adorn her in somebody's eyes; never again in mine!'

V

Four-and-twenty hours before this time Sue had written the following note to Jude:

> It is as I told you; and I am leaving to-morrow evening. Richard and I thought it could be done with less obtrusiveness after dark. I feel rather frightened, and therefore ask you to be sure you are on the Melchester platform to meet me. I arrive at a little to seven. I know you will, of course, dear Jude; but I feel so timid that I can't help begging you to be punctual. He has been so *very* kind to me through it all!
>
> Now to our meeting!
>
> S.

As she was carried by the omnibus further and further down from the mountain town—the single passenger that evening—she regarded the receding road with a sad face. But no hesitation was apparent therein.

The up-train by which she was departing stopped by signal only. To Sue it seemed strange that such a powerful organization as a railway-train should be brought to a standstill on purpose for her—a fugitive from her lawful home.

The twenty minutes' journey drew towards its close, and Sue began gathering her things together to alight. At the moment that the train came to a standstill by the Melchester platform a hand was laid on the door and she beheld Jude. He entered the compartment promptly. He had a black bag in his hand, and was dressed in the dark suit he wore on Sundays and in the evening after work. Altogether he looked a very handsome young fellow, his ardent affection for her burning in his eyes.

'O Jude!' She clasped his hand with both hers, and her tense state caused her to simmer over in a little succession of dry sobs. 'I—I am so glad! I get out here?'

'No. I get in, dear one! I've packed. Besides this bag I've only a big box which is labelled.'

'But don't I get out? Aren't we going to stay here?'

'We couldn't possibly, don't you see. We are known here—I, at any rate, am well known. I've booked for Aldbrickham; and here's your ticket for the same place, as you have only one to here.'

'I thought we should have stayed here,' she repeated.

'It wouldn't have done at all.'

'Ah!—Perhaps not.'

'There wasn't time for me to write and say the place I had decided on. Aldbrickham is a much bigger town—sixty or seventy thousand inhabitants—and nobody knows anything about us there.'

'And you have given up your Cathedral work here?'

'Yes. It was rather sudden—your message coming unexpectedly. Strictly, I might have been made to finish out the week. But I pleaded urgency and I was let off. I would have deserted any day at your command, dear Sue. I have deserted more than that for you!'

'I fear I am doing you a lot of harm. Ruining your prospects of the Church; ruining your progress in your trade; everything!'

'The Church is no more to me. Let it lie! *I* am not to be one of

The soldier-saints who, row on row,
Burn upward each to his point of bliss,

if any such there be! My point of bliss is not upward, but here.'

'O I seem so bad—upsetting men's courses like this!' said she, taking up in her voice the emotion that had begun in his. But she recovered her equanimity by the time they had travelled a dozen miles.

'He has been so good in letting me go,' she resumed. 'And here's a note I found on my dressing-table, addressed to you.'

'Yes. He's not an unworthy fellow,' said Jude, glancing at the note. 'And I am ashamed of myself for hating him because he married you.'

'According to the rule of women's whims I suppose I ought to suddenly love him, because he has let me go so generously and unexpectedly,' she answered smiling. 'But I am so cold, or devoid of gratitude, or so something, that even this generosity hasn't made me love him, or repent, or want to stay with him as his wife; although I do feel I like his large-mindedness, and respect him more than ever.'

'It may not work so well for us as if he had been less kind, and you had run away against his will,' murmured Jude.

'That I *never* would have done.'

Jude's eyes rested musingly on her face. Then he suddenly kissed her; and was going to kiss her again. 'No—only once now—please, Jude!'

'That's rather cruel,' he answered; but acquiesced. 'Such a strange thing has happened to me,' Jude continued after a silence. 'Arabella has actually written to ask me to get a divorce from her—in kindness to her, she says. She wants to honestly and legally marry that man she has already married virtually; and begs me to enable her to do it.'

'What have you done?'

'I have agreed. I thought at first I couldn't do it without getting her into trouble about that second marriage, and I don't want to injure her in any way. Perhaps she's no worse than I am, after all! But nobody knows about it over here, and I find it will not be a difficult proceeding at all. If she wants to start afresh I have only too obvious reasons for not hindering her.'

'Then you'll be free?'

'Yes. I shall be free.'

'Where are we booked for?' she asked, with the discontinuity that marked her tonight.

'Aldbrickham, as I said.'

'But it will be very late when we get there?'

'Yes. I thought of that, and I wired for a room for us at the Temperance Hotel there.'

'One?'

'Yes—one.'

She looked at him. 'O Jude!' Sue bent her forehead against the corner of the compartment. 'I thought you might do it; and that I was deceiving you. But I didn't mean that!'

In the pause that followed, Jude's eyes fixed themselves with a stultified expression on the opposite seat. 'Well!' he said. . . . 'Well!'

He remained in silence; and seeing how discomfited he was she put her face against his cheek, murmuring, 'Don't be vexed, dear!'

'Oh—there's no harm done,' he said. 'But—I understand it like that. . . . Is this a sudden change of mind?'

'You have no right to ask me such a question; and I shan't answer!' she said, smiling.

'My dear one, your happiness is more to me than anything—although we seem to verge on quarrelling so often!—and your will is law to me. I am something more than a mere—selfish fellow, I hope. Have it as you wish!' On reflection his brow showed perplexity. 'But perhaps it is that you don't love me—not that you have become conventional! Much as, under your teaching, I hate convention, I hope it *is* that, not the other terrible alternative!'

Even at this obvious moment for candour Sue could not be quite candid as to the state of that mystery, her heart. 'Put it down to my timidity,' she said with hurried evasiveness; 'to a woman's natural timidity when the crisis comes. I *may* feel as well as you that I have a perfect right to live with you as you thought—from this moment. I *may* hold the opinion that, in a proper state of society, the father of a woman's child will be as much a private matter of hers as the cut of her under-linen, on whom nobody will have any right to question her. But partly, perhaps, because it is by his generosity that I am now free, I would rather not be other than a little rigid. If there had been a rope-ladder, and he had run after us with pistols, it would have seemed different, and I may have acted otherwise. But don't press me and criticize me, Jude! Assume that I haven't the courage of my opinions. I know I am a poor miserable creature. My nature is not so passionate as yours!'

He repeated simply: 'I thought—what I naturally thought. But if we are not lovers, we are not. Phillotson thought so, I am sure. See, here is what he has written to me.' He opened the letter she had brought, and read:

'I make only one condition—that you are tender and kind to

her. I know you love her. But even love may be cruel at times. You are made for each other; it is obvious, palpable, to any unbiased older person. You were all along "the shadowy third" in my short life with her. I repeat, take care of Sue.'

'He's a good fellow, isn't he!' she said with latent tears. On reconsideration she added, 'He was very resigned to letting me go—too resigned almost! I never was so near being in love with him as when he made such thoughtful arrangements for my being comfortable on my journey, and offering to provide money. Yet I was not. If I loved him ever so little as a wife, I'd go back to him even now.'

'But you don't, do you?'

'It is true—O so terribly true!—I don't.'

'Nor me either, I half fear!' he said pettishly. 'Nor anybody perhaps!—Sue, sometimes, when I am vexed with you, I think you are incapable of real love.'

'That's not good and loyal of you!' she said, and drawing away from him as far as she could, looked severely out into the darkness. She added in hurt tones, without turning round: 'My liking for you is not as some women's perhaps. But it is a delight in being with you, of a supremely delicate kind, and I don't want to go further and risk it by—an attempt to intensify it! I quite realized that, as woman with man, it was a risk to come. But, as *me* with *you*, I resolved to trust you to set my wishes above your gratification. Don't discuss it further, dear Jude!'

'Of course, if it would make you reproach yourself . . . but you do like me very much, Sue? say you do! Say that you do a quarter, a tenth, as much as I do you; and I'll be content!'

'I've let you kiss me, and that tells enough.'

'Just once or so!'

'Well—don't be a greedy boy.'

He leant back, and did not look at her for a long time. That episode in her past history of which she had told him—of the poor Christminster graduate whom she had handled thus, returned to Jude's mind; and he saw himself as a possible second in such a torturing destiny.

'This is a queer elopement!' he murmured. 'Perhaps you are

making a cat's-paw of me with Phillotson all this time. Upon my word it almost seems so—to see you sitting up there so prim!'

'Now you mustn't be angry—I won't let you!' she coaxed, turning and moving nearer to him. 'You did kiss me just now, you know; and I didn't dislike you to, I own it, Jude. Only I don't want to let you do it again, just yet—considering how we are circumstanced, don't you see!'

He could never resist her when she pleaded (as she well knew). And they sat side by side with joined hands, till she aroused herself at some thought.

'I can't possibly go to that Temperance Inn, after your telegraphing that message!'

'Why not?'

'You can see well enough!'

'Very well; there'll be some other one open, no doubt. I have sometimes thought, since your marrying Phillotson because of a stupid scandal, that under the affectation of independent views you are as enslaved to the social code as any woman I know!'

'Not mentally. But I haven't the courage of my views, as I said before. I didn't marry him altogether because of the scandal. But sometimes a woman's *love of being loved* gets the better of her conscience, and though she is agonized at the thought of treating a man cruelly, she encourages him to love her while she doesn't love him at all. Then, when she sees him suffering, her remorse sets in, and she does what she can to repair the wrong.'

'You mean that you flirted outrageously with him, poor old chap, and then repented, and to make reparation, married him, though you tortured yourself to death by doing it.'

'Well—if you will put it brutally!—it was a little like that—that and the scandal together—and your concealing from me what you ought to have told me before!'

He could see that she was distressed and tearful at his criticisms, and soothed her, saying: 'There, dear; don't mind! Crucify me, if you will! You know you are all the world to me, whatever you do!'

'I am very bad and unprincipled—I know you think that!' she said, trying to blink away her tears.

'I think and know you are my dear Sue, from whom neither

length nor breadth, nor things present nor things to come, can divide me!'

Though so sophisticated in many things she was such a child in others that this satisfied her, and they reached the end of their journey on the best of terms. It was about ten o'clock when they arrived at Aldbrickham, the county town of North Wessex. As she would not go to the Temperance Hotel because of the form of his telegram, Jude inquired for another; and a youth who had volunteered to find one wheeled their luggage to The George further on, which proved to be the inn at which Jude had stayed with Arabella on that one occasion of their meeting after their division for years.

Owing, however, to their now entering it by another door, and to his preoccupation, he did not at first recognize the place. When they had engaged their respective rooms they went down to a late supper. During Jude's temporary absence the waiting-maid spoke to Sue.

'I think, ma'am, I remember your relation, or friend, or whatever he is, coming here once before—late, just like this, with his wife—a lady, at any rate, that wasn't you by no manner of means—jest as med be with you now.'

'O do you?' said Sue, with a certain sickness of heart. 'Though I think you must be mistaken! How long ago was it?'

'About a month or two. A handsome, full-figured woman. They had this room.'

When Jude came back and sat down to supper Sue seemed moping and miserable. 'Jude,' she said to him plaintively, at their parting that night upon the landing, 'it is not so nice and pleasant as it used to be with us! I don't like it here—I can't bear the place! And I don't like you so well as I did!'

'How fidgeted you seem, dear! Why do you change like this?'

'Because it was cruel to bring me here!'

'Why?'

'You were lately here with Arabella. There, now I have said it!'

'Dear me, why—' said Jude looking round him. 'Yes—it is the same! I really didn't know it, Sue. Well—it is not cruel, since we have come as we have—two relations staying together.'

'How long ago was it you were here? Tell me, tell me!'

'The day before I met you in Christminster, when we went back to Marygreen together. I told you I had met her.'

'Yes, you said you had met her, but you didn't tell me all. Your story was that you had met as estranged people, who were not husband and wife at all in Heaven's sight—not that you had made it up with her.'

'We didn't make it up,' he said sadly. 'I can't explain, Sue.'

'You've been false to me; you, my last hope! And I shall never forget it, never!'

'But by your own wish, dear Sue, we are only to be friends, not lovers! It is so very inconsistent of you to—'

'Friends can be jealous!'

'I don't see that. You concede nothing to me and I have to concede everything to you. After all, you were on good terms with your husband at that time.'

'No, I wasn't, Jude. O how can you think so! And you have taken me in, even if you didn't intend to.' She was so mortified that he was obliged to take her into her room and close the door lest the people should hear. 'Was it this room? Yes it was—I see by your look it was! I won't have it for mine! O it was treacherous of you to have her again! *I* jumped out of the window!'

'But Sue, she was, after all, my legal wife, if not—'

Slipping down on her knees Sue buried her face in the bed and wept.

'I never knew such an unreasonable—such a dog-in-the-manger feeling,' said Jude. 'I am not to approach you, nor anybody else!'

'O don't you *understand* my feeling! *Why* don't you! Why are you so gross! *I* jumped out of the window!'

'Jumped out of window?'

'I can't explain!'

It was true that he did not understand her feeling very well. But he did a little; and began to love her none the less.

'I—I thought you cared for nobody—desired nobody in the world but me at that time—and ever since!' continued Sue.

'It is true. I did not, and don't now!' said Jude, as distressed as she.

'But you must have thought much of her! Or—'

'No—I need not—you don't understand me either—women never do! Why should you get into such a tantrum about nothing?'

Looking up from the quilt she pouted provokingly: 'If it hadn't been for that, perhaps I would have gone on to the Temperance Hotel, after all, as you proposed; for I was beginning to think I did belong to you!'

'O, it is of no consequence!' said Jude distantly.

'I thought, of course, that she had never been really your wife since she left you of her own accord years and years ago! My sense of it was, that a parting such as yours from her, and mine from him, ended the marriage.'

'I can't say more without speaking against her, and I don't want to do that,' said he. 'Yet I must tell you one thing, which would settle the matter in any case. She has married another man—really married him! I knew nothing about it till after the visit we made here.'

'Married another? . . . It is a crime—as the world treats it, but does not believe.'

'There—now you are yourself again. Yes, it is a crime—as you don't hold, but would fearfully concede. But I shall never inform against her! and it is evidently a prick of conscience in her that has led her to urge me to get a divorce, that she may re-marry this man legally. So you perceive I shall not be likely to see her again.'

'And you didn't really know anything of this when you saw her?' said Sue more gently, as she rose.

'I did not. Considering all things, I don't think you ought to be angry, darling!'

'I am not. But I shan't go to the Temperance Hotel!'

He laughed. 'Never mind!' he said. 'So that I am near you, I am comparatively happy. It is more than this earthly wretch called Me deserves—you spirit, you disembodied creature, you dear, sweet, tantalizing phantom—hardly flesh at all; so that when I put my arms round you I almost expect them to pass through you as through air! Forgive me for being gross, as you call it! Remember that our calling cousins when really strangers was a snare. The enmity of our parents gave a piquancy to you in my eyes that was intenser even than the novelty of ordinary new acquaintance.'

'Say those pretty lines, then, from Shelley's "Epipsychidion" as if they meant me!' she solicited, slanting up closer to him as they stood. 'Don't you know them?'

'I know hardly any poetry,' he replied mournfully.

'Don't you? These are some of them:

> There was a Being whom my spirit oft
> Met on its visioned wanderings far aloft.
> . . . .
> A seraph of Heaven, too gentle to be human,
> Veiling beneath that radiant form of woman. . . .

O it is too flattering, so I won't go on! But say it's me!—say it's me!'

'It *is* you, dear; exactly like you!'

'Now I forgive you! And you shall kiss me just once there—not very long.' She put the tip of her finger gingerly to her cheek; and he did as commanded. 'You do care for me very much, don't you, in spite of my not—you know?'

'Yes, sweet!' he said with a sigh; and bade her good-night.

VI

In returning to his native town of Shaston as schoolmaster Phillotson had won the interest and awakened the memories of the inhabitants, who, though they did not honour him for his miscellaneous acquirements as he would have been honoured elsewhere, retained for him a sincere regard. When, shortly after his arrival, he brought home a pretty wife—awkwardly pretty for him, if he did not take care, they said—they were glad to have her settle among them.

For some time after her flight from that home Sue's absence did not excite comment. Her place as monitor in the school was taken by another young woman within a few days of her vacating it, which substitution also passed without remark, Sue's services having been of a provisional nature only. When, however, a month had passed, and Phillotson casually admitted to acquaintance that he did not know where his wife was staying, curiosity began to be aroused; till, jumping to conclusions, people ventured to affirm that Sue had played him false and run away from him. The schoolmaster's growing languor and listlessness over his work gave countenance to the idea.

Though Phillotson had held his tongue as long as he could, except to his friend Gillingham, his honesty and directness would not allow him to do so when misapprehensions as to Sue's conduct spread abroad. On a Monday morning the chairman of the School Committee called, and after attending to the business of the school drew Phillotson aside out of earshot of the children.

'You'll excuse my asking, Phillotson, since everybody is talking of it; is it true as to your domestic affairs—that your wife's going away was no visit, but a secret elopement with a lover? If so, I condole with you.'

'Don't,' said Phillotson. 'There was no secret about it.'

'She has gone to visit friends?'

'No.'

'Then what has happened?'

'She has gone away under circumstances that usually call for condolence with the husband. But I gave my consent.'

The chairman looked as if he had not apprehended the remark.

'What I say is quite true,' Phillotson continued testily. 'She asked leave to go away with her lover, and I let her. Why shouldn't I? A woman of full age, it was a question for her own conscience—not for me. I was not her gaoler. I can't explain any further. I don't wish to be questioned.'

The children observed that much seriousness marked the faces of the two men, and went home and told their parents that something new had happened about Mrs Phillotson. Then Phillotson's little maidservant, who was a schoolgirl just out of her standards, said that Mr Phillotson had helped in his wife's packing, had offered her what money she required, and had written a friendly letter to her young man, telling him to take care of her. The chairman of committee thought the matter over, and talked to the other managers of the school, till a request came to Phillotson to meet them privately. The meeting lasted a long time, and at the end the schoolmaster came home, looking as usual pale and worn. Gillingham was sitting in his house awaiting him.

'Well; it is as you said,' observed Phillotson, flinging himself down wearily in a chair. 'They have requested me to send in my resignation on account of my scandalous conduct in giving my tortured wife her liberty—or, as they call it, condoning her adultery. But I shan't resign!'

'I think I would.'

'I won't. It is no business of theirs. It doesn't affect me in my public capacity at all. They may expel me if they like.'

'If you make a fuss it will get into the papers, and you'll never get appointed to another school. You see, they have to consider what you did as done by a teacher of youth—and its effects as such upon the morals of the town; and, to ordinary opinion, your position is indefensible. You must let me say that.'

To this good advice, however, Phillotson would not listen.

'I don't care,' he said. 'I don't go unless I am turned out. And for this reason; that by resigning I acknowledge I have acted wrongly by her; when I am more and more convinced every day that in the sight of Heaven and by all natural, straightforward humanity, I have acted rightly.'

Gillingham saw that his rather headstrong friend would not be able to maintain such a position as this; but he said nothing further, and in due time—indeed, in a quarter of an hour—the formal letter of dismissal arrived, the managers having remained behind to write it after Phillotson's withdrawal. The latter replied that he should not accept dismissal; and called a public meeting, which he attended, although he looked so weak and ill that his friend implored him to stay at home. When he stood up to give his reasons for contesting the decision of the managers he advanced them firmly, as he had done to his friend, and contended, moreover, that the matter was a domestic theory which did not concern them. This they overruled, insisting that the private eccentricities of a teacher came quite within their sphere of control, as it touched the morals of those he taught. Phillotson replied that he did not see how an act of natural charity could injure morals.

All the respectable inhabitants and well-to-do fellow-natives of the town were against Phillotson to a man. But, somewhat to his surprise, some dozen or more champions rose up in his defence as from the ground.

It has been stated that Shaston was the anchorage of a curious and interesting group of itinerants, who frequented the numerous fairs and markets held up and down Wessex during the summer and autumn months. Although Phillotson had never spoken to one of these gentlemen they now nobly led the forlorn hope in his defence. The body included two cheap-jacks, a shooting-gallery proprietor and the ladies who loaded the guns, a pair of boxing-masters, a steam-roundabout manager, two travelling broom-makers, who called themselves widows, a gingerbread-stall keeper, a swing-boat owner, and a 'test-your-strength' man.

This generous phalanx of supporters, and a few others of independent judgment, whose own domestic experiences had been not without vicissitude, came up and warmly shook hands with Phillotson; after which they expressed their thoughts so strongly to the meeting that issue was joined, the result being a general scuffle, wherein a blackboard was split, three panes of the school-windows were broken, an ink-bottle was spilled over a town-councillor's shirt-front, a church-warden was dealt such a topper with the map of Palestine that his head went right through Samaria, and many black eyes and bleeding noses were given, one of which, to everybody's horror, was the venerable incumbent's, owing to the zeal of an emancipated chimney-sweep, who took the side of Phillotson's party. When Phillotson saw the blood running down the rector's face he deplored almost in groans the untoward and degrading circumstances, regretted that he had not resigned when called upon, and went home so ill that next morning he could not leave his bed.

The farcical yet melancholy event was the beginning of a serious illness for him; and he lay in his lonely bed in the pathetic state of mind of a middle-aged man who perceives at length that his life, intellectual and domestic, is tending to failure and gloom. Gillingham came to see him in the evenings, and on one occasion mentioned Sue's name.

'She doesn't care anything about me!' said Phillotson. 'Why should she?'

'She doesn't know you are ill.'

'So much the better for both of us.'

'Where are her lover and she living?'

'At Melchester—I suppose; at least he was living there some time ago.'

When Gillingham reached home he sat and reflected, and at last wrote an anonymous line to Sue, on the bare chance of its reaching her, the letter being enclosed in an envelope addressed to Jude at the diocesan capital. Arriving at that place it was forwarded to Marygreen in North Wessex, and thence to Aldbrickham by the only person who knew his present address—the widow who had nursed his aunt.

Three days later, in the evening, when the sun was going down in splendour over the lowlands of Blackmoor, and making the Shaston windows like tongues of fire to the eyes of the rustics in that Vale, the sick man fancied that he heard somebody come to the house, and a few minutes after there was a tap at the bedroom door. Phillotson did not speak; the door was hesitatingly opened, and there entered—Sue.

She was in light spring clothing, and her advent seemed ghostly—like the flitting in of a moth. He turned his eyes upon her, and flushed; but appeared to check his primary impulse to speak.

'I have no business here,' she said, bending her frightened face to him. 'But I heard you were ill—very ill; and—and as I know that you recognize other feelings between man and woman than physical love, I have come.'

'I am not very ill, my dear friend. Only unwell.'

'I didn't know that; and I am afraid that only a severe illness would have justified my coming!'

'Yes . . . yes. And I almost wish you had not come! It is a little too soon—that's all I mean. Still, let us make the best of it. You haven't heard about the school, I suppose?'

'No—what about it?'

'Only that I am going away from here to another place. The managers and I don't agree, and we are going to part—that's all.'

Sue did not for a moment, either now or later, suspect what troubles had resulted to him from letting her go; it never once seemed to cross her mind, and she had received no news whatever from Shaston. They talked on slight and ephemeral subjects, and when his tea was brought up he told the amazed little servant that a cup was to be set for Sue. That young person was much more interested in their history than they supposed, and as she descended the stairs she lifted her eyes and hands in grotesque amazement. While they sipped Sue went to the window and thoughtfully said, 'It is such a beautiful sunset, Richard.'

'They are mostly beautiful from here, owing to the rays crossing the mist of the Vale. But I lose them all, as they don't shine into this gloomy corner where I lie.'

'Wouldn't you like to see this particular one? It is like heaven opened.'

'Ah yes! But I can't.'

'I'll help you to.'

'No—the bedstead can't be shifted.'

'But see how I mean.'

She went to where a swing-glass stood, and taking it in her hands carried it to a spot by the window where it could catch the sunshine, moving the glass till the beams were reflected into Phillotson's face.

'There—you can see the great red sun now!' she said. 'And I am sure it will cheer you—I do so hope it will!' She spoke with a child-like, repentant kindness, as if she could not do too much for him.

Phillotson smiled sadly. 'You are an odd creature!' he murmured as the sun glowed in his eyes. 'The idea of your coming to see me after what has passed!'

'Don't let us go back upon that!' she said quickly. 'I have to catch the omnibus for the train, as Jude doesn't know I have come; he was out when I started; so I must return home almost directly. Richard, I am so very glad you are better. You don't hate me, do you? You have been such a kind friend to me!'

'I am glad to know you think so,' said Phillotson huskily. 'No. I don't hate you!'

It grew dusk quickly in the gloomy room during their intermittent chat, and when candles were brought and it was time to leave she put her hand in his—or rather allowed it to flit through his; for she was significantly light in touch. She had nearly closed the door when he said, 'Sue!' He had noticed that in turning away from him, tears were on her face and a quiver in her lip.

It was bad policy to recall her—he knew it while he pursued it. But he could not help it. She came back.

'Sue,' he murmured, 'do you wish to make it up, and stay? I'll forgive you and condone everything!'

'O you can't, you can't!' she said hastily. 'You can't condone it now!'

'*He* is your husband now, in effect, you mean, of course?'

'You may assume it. He is obtaining a divorce from his wife Arabella.'

'His wife! It is altogether news to me that he has a wife.'

'It was a bad marriage.'

'Like yours.'

'Like mine. He is not doing it so much on his own account as on hers. She wrote and told him it would be a kindness to her, since then she could marry and live respectably. And Jude has agreed.'

'A wife. . . . A kindness to her. Ah, yes; a kindness to her to release her altogether. . . . But *I* don't like the sound of it. *I* can forgive, Sue.'

'No, no! You can't have me back now I have been so wicked—as to do what I have done!'

There had arisen in Sue's face that incipient fright which showed itself whenever he changed from friend to husband, and which made her adopt any line of defence against marital feeling in him. 'I *must* go now. I'll come again—may I?'

'I don't ask you to go, even now. I ask you to stay.'

'I thank you, Richard; but I must. As you are not so ill as I thought, I *cannot* stay!'

'She's his—his from lips to heel!' said Phillotson; but so faintly that in closing the door she did not hear it. The dread of a reactionary change in the schoolmaster's sentiments coupled, perhaps, with a faint shamefacedness at letting even him know what a slipshod lack of thoroughness, from a man's point of view, characterized her transferred allegiance, prevented her telling him of her, thus far, incomplete relations with Jude; and Phillotson lay writhing like a man in hell as he pictured the prettily dressed, maddening compound of sympathy and averseness who bore his name, returning impatiently to the home of her lover.

Gillingham was so interested in Phillotson's affairs, and so seriously concerned about him, that he walked up the hillside to Shaston two or three times a week, although, there and back, it was a journey of nine miles, which had to be performed between tea and supper, after a hard day's work in school. When he called on the next occasion after Sue's visit his friend was downstairs, and Gillingham noticed that his restless mood had been supplanted by a more fixed and composed one.

'She's been here since you called last,' said Phillotson.

'Not Mrs Phillotson?'

'Yes.'

'Ah! You have made it up?'

'No. . . . She just came, patted my pillow with her little white hand, played the thoughtful nurse for half-an-hour, and went away.'

'Well—I'm hanged! A little hussy!'

'What do you say?'

'O—nothing!'

'What do you mean?'

'I mean, what a tantalizing, capricious little woman! If she were not your wife—'

'She is not; she's another man's except in name and law. And I have been thinking—it was suggested to me by a conversation I had with her—that, in kindness to her, I ought to dissolve the legal tie altogether; which, singularly enough, I think I can do, now she has been back, and refused my request to stay after I said I had forgiven her. I believe that fact would afford me opportunity of doing it, though I did not see it at the moment. What's the use of keeping her chained on to me if she doesn't belong to me? I know—I feel absolutely certain—that she would welcome my taking such a step as the greatest charity to her. For though as a fellow-creature she sympathizes with, and pities me, and even weeps for me, as a husband she cannot endure me—she loathes me—there's no use in mincing words—she loathes me, and my only manly, and dignified, and merciful course is to complete what I have begun. . . . And for worldly reasons, too, it will be better for her to be independent. I have hopelessly ruined my prospects because of my decision as to what was best for us, though she does not know it; I see only dire poverty ahead from my feet to the grave; for I can be accepted as teacher no more. I shall probably have enough to do to make both ends meet during the remainder of my life, now my occupation's gone; and I shall be better able to bear it alone. I may as well tell you that what has suggested my letting her go is some news she brought me—the news that Fawley is doing the same.'

'O—he had a spouse, too? A queer couple, these lovers!'

'Well—I don't want your opinion on that. What I was going to say is that my liberating her can do her no possible harm, and will open up a chance of happiness for her which she has never dreamt of hitherto. For then they'll be able to marry, as they ought to have done at first.'

Gillingham did not hurry to reply. 'I may disagree with your motive,' he said gently, for he respected views he could not share. 'But I think you are right in your determination—if you can carry it out. I doubt, however, if you can.'

PART FIFTH

AT ALDBRICKHAM AND ELSEWHERE

'Thy aerial part, and all the fiery parts which are mingled in thee, though by nature they have an upward tendency, still in obedience to the disposition of the universe they are overpowered here in the compound mass the body.'

—M. Antoninus (Long)

I

How Gillingham's doubts were disposed of will most quickly appear by passing over the series of dreary months and incidents that followed the events of the last chapter, and coming on to a Sunday in the February of the year following.

Sue and Jude were living in Aldbrickham, in precisely the same relations that they had established between themselves when she left Shaston to join him the year before. The proceedings in the Law-Courts had reached their consciousness but as a distant sound, and an occasional missive which they hardly understood.

They had met, as usual, to breakfast together in the little house with Jude's name on it, that he had taken at fifteen pounds a year, with three-pounds-ten extra for rates and taxes, and furnished with his aunt's ancient and lumbering goods, which had cost him about their full value to bring all the way from Marygreen. Sue kept house, and managed everything.

As he entered the room this morning Sue held up a letter she had just received.

'Well; and what is this about?' he said after kissing her.

'That the decree *nisi* in the case of Phillotson *versus* Phillotson and Fawley, pronounced six months ago, has just been made absolute.'

'Ah,' said Jude, as he sat down.

The same concluding incident in Jude's suit against Arabella had occurred about a month or two earlier. Both cases had been too insignificant to be reported in the papers, further than by name in a long list of other undefended cases.

'Now then, Sue, at any rate, you can do what you like!' He looked at his sweetheart curiously.

'Are we—you and I—just as free now as if we had never married at all?'

'Just as free—except, I believe, that a clergyman may object personally to re-marry you, and hand the job on to somebody else.'

'But I wonder—do you think it is really so with us? I know it is generally. But I have an uncomfortable feeling that my freedom has been obtained under false pretences!'

'How?'

'Well—if the truth about us had been known, the decree wouldn't have been pronounced. It is only, is it, because we have made no defence and have led them into a false supposition? Therefore is my freedom lawful, however proper it may be?'

'Well—why did you let it be under false pretences? You have only yourself to blame,' he said mischievously.

'Jude—don't! You ought not to be so touchy about that still. You must take me as I am.'

'Very well, darling: so I will. Perhaps you were right. As to your question, we were not obliged to prove anything. That was their business. Anyhow we are living together.'

'Yes. Though not in their sense.'

'One thing is certain, that however the decree may be brought about, a marriage is dissolved when it is dissolved. There is this advantage in being poor obscure people like us—that these things are done for us in a rough and ready fashion. It was the same with me and Arabella. I was afraid her criminal second marriage would have been discovered, and she punished; but nobody took any interest in her—nobody inquired, nobody suspected it. If we'd been patented nobilities we should have had infinite trouble, and days and weeks would have been spent in investigations.'

By degrees Sue acquired her lover's cheerfulness at the sense of freedom, and proposed that they should take a walk in the fields, even if they had to put up with a cold dinner on account of it. Jude agreed, and Sue went upstairs and prepared to start, putting on a joyful coloured gown in observance of her liberty; seeing which Jude put on a lighter tie.

'Now we'll strut arm in arm,' he said, 'like any other engaged couple. We've a legal right to.'

They rambled out of the town, and along a path over the low-lying lands that bordered it, though these were frosty now, and the extensive seed-fields were bare of colour and produce. The pair, however, were so absorbed in their own situation that their surroundings were little in their consciousness.

'Well, my dearest, the result of all this is that we can marry after a decent interval.'

'Yes; I suppose we can,' said Sue, without enthusiasm.

'And aren't we going to?'

'I don't like to say no, dear Jude; but I feel just the same about it now as I have done all along. I have just the same dread lest an iron contract should extinguish your tenderness for me, and mine for you, as it did between our unfortunate parents.'

'Still, what can we do? I do love you, as you know, Sue.'

'I know it abundantly. But I think I would much rather go on living always as lovers, as we are living now, and only meeting by day. It is so much sweeter—for the woman at least, and when she is sure of the man. And henceforward we needn't be so particular as we have been about appearances.'

'Our experiences of matrimony with others have not been encouraging, I own,' said he with some gloom; 'either owing to our own dissatisfied, unpractical natures, or by our misfortune. But we two—'

'Should be two dissatisfied ones linked together, which would be twice as bad as before. . . . I think I should begin to be afraid of you, Jude, the moment you had contracted to cherish me under a Government stamp, and I was licensed to be loved on the premises by you—Ugh, how horrible and sordid! Although, as you are, free, I trust you more than any other man in the world.'

'No, no—don't say I should change!' he expostulated; yet there was misgiving in his own voice also.

'Apart from ourselves, and our unhappy peculiarities, it is foreign to a man's nature to go on loving a person when he is told that he must and shall be that person's lover. There would be a much likelier chance of his doing it if he were told not to love. If the marriage ceremony consisted in an oath and signed contract between the parties to cease loving from that day forward, in consideration of personal possession being given, and to avoid each other's society as much as possible in public, there would be more loving couples than there are now. Fancy the secret meetings between the perjuring husband and wife, the denials of having seen each other, the clambering in at the bedroom windows, and the hiding in closets! There'd be little cooling then.'

'Yes; but admitting this, or something like it, to be true, you are not the only one in the world to see it, dear little Sue. People go on marrying because they can't resist natural forces, although many of them may know perfectly well that they are possibly buying a month's pleasure with a life's discomfort. No doubt my father and mother, and your father and mother, saw it, if they at all resembled us in habits of observation. But then they went and married just the same, because they had ordinary passions. But you, Sue, are such a phantasmal, bodiless creature, one who—if you'll allow me to say it—has so little animal passion in you, that you can act upon reason in the matter, when we poor unfortunate wretches of grosser substance can't.'

'Well,' she sighed, 'you've owned that it would probably end in misery for us. And I am not so exceptional a woman as you think. Fewer women like marriage than you suppose, only they enter into it for the dignity it is assumed to confer, and the social advantages it gains them sometimes—a dignity and an advantage that I am quite willing to do without.'

Jude fell back upon his old complaint—that, intimate as they were, he had never once had from her an honest candid declaration that she loved or could love him. 'I really fear sometimes that you cannot,' he said, with a dubiousness approaching anger. 'And you are so reticent. I know that women are taught by other women that they must never admit the full truth to a man. But the highest form of affection is based on full sincerity on both sides. Not being men, these women don't know that in looking back on those he has had tender relations with, a man's heart returns closest to her who was the soul of truth in her conduct. The better class of man, even if caught by airy affectations of dodging and parrying, is not retained by them. A Nemesis attends the woman who plays the game of elusiveness too often, in the utter contempt for her that, sooner or later, her old admirers feel; under which they allow her to go unlamented to her grave.'

Sue, who was regarding the distance, had acquired a guilty look; and she suddenly replied in a tragic voice: 'I don't think I like you to-day as well as I did, Jude!'

'Don't you? Why?'

'O, well—you are not nice—too sermony. Though I suppose I am so bad and worthless that I deserve the utmost rigour of lecturing!'

'No, you are not bad. You are a dear. But as slippery as an eel when I want to get a confession from you.'

'O yes I am bad, and obstinate, and all sorts! It is no use your pretending I am not! People who are good don't want scolding as I do. . . . But now that I have nobody but you, and nobody to defend me, it is *very* hard that I mustn't have my own way in deciding how I'll live with you, and whether I'll be married or no!'

'Sue, my own comrade and sweetheart, I don't want to force you either to marry or to do the other thing—of course I don't! It is too wicked of you to be so pettish! Now we won't say any more about it, and go on just the same as we have done; and during the rest of our walk we'll talk of the meadows only, and the floods, and the prospect of the farmers this coming year.'

After this the subject of marriage was not mentioned by them for several days, though living as they were with only a landing between them it was constantly in their minds. Sue was assisting Jude very materially now: he had latterly occupied himself on his own account in working and lettering headstones, which he kept in a little yard at the back of his little house, where in the intervals of domestic duties she marked out the letters full size for him, and blacked them in after he had cut them. It was a lower class of handicraft than were his former performances as a cathedral mason, and his only patrons were the poor people who lived in his own neighbourhood, and knew what a cheap man this 'Jude Fawley: Monumental Mason' (as he called himself on his front door) was to employ for the simplest memorials they required for their dead. But he seemed more independent than before, and it was the only arrangement under which Sue, who particularly wished to be no burden on him, could render any assistance.

II

It was an evening at the end of the month, and Jude had just returned home from hearing a lecture on ancient history in the public hall not far off. When he entered Sue, who had been keeping indoors during his absence, laid out supper for him. Contrary to custom she did not speak. Jude had taken up some illustrated paper, which he perused till, raising his eyes, he saw her face was troubled.

'Are you depressed, Sue?' he said.

She paused a moment. 'I have a message for you,' she answered.

'Somebody has called?'

'Yes. A woman.' Sue's voice quavered as she spoke, and she suddenly sat down from her preparations, laid her hands in her lap, and looked into the fire. 'I don't know whether I did right or not!' she continued. 'I said you were not at home, and when she said she would wait, I said I thought you might not be able to see her.'

'Why did you say that, dear? I suppose she wanted a headstone. Was she in mourning?'

'No. She wasn't in mourning, and she didn't want a headstone; and I thought you couldn't see her.' Sue looked critically and imploringly at him.

'But who was she? Didn't she say?'

'No. She wouldn't give her name. But I know who she was—I think I do! It was Arabella!'

'Heaven save us! What should Arabella come for? What made you think it was she?'

'O, I can hardly tell. But I know it was! I feel perfectly certain it was—by the light in her eyes as she looked at me. She was a fleshy, coarse woman.'

'Well—I should not have called Arabella coarse exactly, except in speech, though she may be getting so by this time under the duties of the public-house. She was rather handsome when I knew her.'

'Handsome! But yes!—so she is!'

'I think I heard a quiver in your little mouth. Well, waiving that, as she is nothing to me, and virtuously married to another man, why should she come troubling us?'

'Are you sure she's married? Have you definite news of it?'

'No, not definite news. But that was why she asked me to release her. She and the man both wanted to lead a proper life, as I understood.'

'O Jude—it was, it *was* Arabella!' cried Sue, covering her eyes with her hand. 'And I am so miserable! It seems such an ill-omen, whatever she may have come for. You could not possibly see her, could you?'

'I don't really think I could. It would be so very painful to talk to her now—for her as much as for me. However, she's gone. Did she say she would come again?'

'No. But she went away very reluctantly.'

Sue, whom the least thing upset, could not eat any supper, and when Jude had finished his he prepared to go to bed. He had no sooner raked out the fire, fastened the doors, and got to the top of the stairs than there came a knock. Sue instantly emerged from her room, which she had but just entered.

'There she is again!' Sue whispered in appalled accents.

'How do you know?'

'She knocked like that last time.'

They listened, and the knocking came again. No servant was kept in the house, and if the summons were to be responded to one of them would have to do it in person. 'I'll open a window,' said Jude. 'Whoever it is cannot be expected to be let in at this time.'

He accordingly went into his bedroom and lifted the sash. The lonely street of early retiring work-people was empty from end to end save of one figure—that of a woman walking up and down by the lamp a few yards off.

'Who's there?' he asked.

'Is that Mr Fawley?' came up from the woman, in a voice which was unmistakably Arabella's.

Jude replied that it was.

'Is it she?' asked Sue from the door, with lips apart.

'Yes, dear,' said Jude. 'What do you want, Arabella?' he inquired.

'I beg your pardon, Jude, for disturbing you,' said Arabella humbly. 'But I called earlier—I wanted particularly to see you to-night, if I could. I am in trouble and have nobody to help me!'

'In trouble, are you?'

'Yes.'

There was a silence. An inconvenient sympathy seemed to be rising in Jude's breast at the appeal. 'But aren't you married?' he said.

Arabella hesitated. 'No, Jude, I am not,' she returned. 'He wouldn't, after all. And I am in great difficulty. I hope to get another situation as barmaid soon. But it takes time, and I really am in great distress, because of a sudden responsibility that's been sprung upon me from Australia; or I wouldn't trouble you—believe me I wouldn't. I want to tell you about it.'

Sue remained at gaze, in painful tension, hearing every word, but speaking none.

'You are not really in want of money, Arabella?' he asked in a distinctly softened tone.

'I have enough to pay for the night's lodgings I have obtained, but barely enough to take me back again.'

'Where are you living?'

'In London still.' She was about to give the address, but she said, 'I am afraid somebody may hear, so I don't like to call out particulars of myself so loud. If you could come down and walk a little way with me towards the Prince Inn, where I am staying to-night, I would explain all. You may as well, for old time's sake!'

'Poor thing!—I must do her the kindness of hearing what's the matter, I suppose,' said Jude in much perplexity. 'As she's going back to-morrow it can't make much difference.'

'But you can go and see her to-morrow Jude! Don't go now, Jude!' came in plaintive accents from the doorway. 'O, it is only to entrap you, I know it is, as she did before! Don't, don't go, dear!

She is such a low-passioned woman—I can see it in her shape, and hear it in her voice!'

'But I shall go,' said Jude. 'Don't attempt to detain me, Sue. God knows I love her little enough now, but I don't want to be cruel to her.' He turned to the stairs.

'But she's not your wife!' cried Sue distractedly. 'And I—'

'And you are not either, dear, yet,' said Jude.

'O, but are you going to her? Don't! Stay at home! Please, please stay at home, Jude, and not go to her, now she's not your wife any more than I!'

'Well, she is, rather more than you, come to that,' he said, taking his hat determinedly. 'I've wanted you to be, and I've waited with the patience of Job, and I don't see that I've got anything by my self-denial. I shall certainly give her something, and hear what it is she is so anxious to tell me; no man could do less!'

There was that in his manner which she knew it would be futile to oppose. She said no more, but, turning to her room as meekly as a martyr, heard him go downstairs, unbolt the door and close it behind him. With a woman's disregard to her dignity when in the presence of nobody but herself, she also trotted down, sobbing articulately as she went. She listened. She knew exactly how far it was to the inn that Arabella had named as her lodging. It would occupy about seven minutes to get there at an ordinary walking pace; seven to come back again. If he did not return in fourteen minutes he would have lingered. She looked at the clock. It was twenty-five minutes to eleven. He *might* enter the inn with Arabella, as they would reach it before closing time; she might get him to drink with her; and Heaven only knew what disasters would befall him then.

In a still suspense she waited on. It seemed as if the whole time had nearly elapsed when the door was opened again, and Jude appeared.

Sue gave a little ecstatic cry. 'O, I knew I could trust you!—how good you are!'—she began.

'I can't find her anywhere in this street, and I went out in my slippers only. She has walked on, thinking I've been so hard-hearted as to refuse her requests entirely, poor woman. I've come back for my boots as it is beginning to rain.'

'O, but why should you take such trouble for a woman who has served you so badly!' said Sue in a jealous burst of disappointment.

'But, Sue, she's a woman, and I once cared for her; and one can't be a brute in such circumstances.'

'She isn't your wife any longer!' exclaimed Sue, passionately excited. 'You *mustn't* go out to find her! It isn't right! You *can't* join her, now she's a stranger to you. How can you forget such a thing, my dear, dear one!'

'She seems much the same as ever—an erring, careless, unreflecting fellow-creature,' he said, continuing to pull on his boots. 'What those legal fellows have been playing at in London makes no difference in my real relations to her. If she was my wife while she was away in Australia with another husband she's my wife now.'

'But she wasn't! That's just what I hold! There's the absurdity!—Well—you'll come straight back, after a few minutes, won't you, dear? She is too low, too coarse for you to talk to long, Jude, and was always!'

'Perhaps I am too coarse too, worse luck! I have the germs of every human infirmity in me, I verily believe—that was why I saw it was so preposterous of me to think of being a curate. I have cured myself of drunkenness I think; but I never know in what new form a suppressed vice will break out in me! I do love you, Sue, though I have danced attendance on you so long for such poor returns! All that's best and noblest in me loves you, and your freedom from everything that's gross has elevated me, and enabled me to do what I should never have dreamt myself capable of, or any man, a year or two ago. It is all very well to preach about self-control, and the wickedness of coercing a woman. But I should just like a few virtuous people who have condemned me in the past, about Arabella and other things, to have been in my tantalizing position with you through these late weeks!—they'd believe, I think, that I have exercised some little restraint in always giving in to your wishes—living here in one house, and not a soul between us.'

'Yes, you have been good to me, Jude; I know you have, my dear protector.'

'Well—Arabella has appealed to me for help. I must go out and speak to her, Sue, at least!'

'I can't say any more!—O, if you must, you must!' she said, bursting out into sobs that seemed to tear her heart. 'I have nobody but you, Jude, and you are deserting me! I didn't know you were like this—I can't bear it, I can't! If she were yours it would be different!'

'Or if you were.'

'Very well then—if I must I must. Since you will have it so, I agree! I will be. Only I didn't mean to! And I didn't want to marry again, either! . . . But, yes—I agree, I agree! I do love you. I ought to have known that you would conquer in the long run, living like this!'

She ran across and flung her arms round his neck. 'I am not a cold-natured, sexless creature, am I, for keeping you at such a distance? I am sure you don't think so! Wait and see! I do belong to you, don't I? I give in!'

'And I'll arrange for our marriage to-morrow, or as soon as ever you wish.'

'Yes, Jude.'

'Then I'll let her go,' said he, embracing Sue softly. 'I do feel that it would be unfair to you to see her, and perhaps unfair to her. She is not like you, my darling, and never was: it is only bare justice to say that. Don't cry any more. There; and there; and there!' He kissed her on one side, and on the other, and in the middle, and rebolted the front door.

The next morning it was wet.

'Now, dear,' said Jude gaily at breakfast; 'as this is Saturday I mean to call about the banns at once, so as to get the first publishing done to-morrow, or we shall lose a week. Banns will do? We shall save a pound or two.'

Sue absently agreed to banns. But her mind for the moment was running on something else. A glow had passed away from her, and depression sat upon her features.

'I feel I was wickedly selfish last night!' she murmured. 'It was sheer unkindness in me—or worse—to treat Arabella as I did. I didn't care about her being in trouble, and what she wished to tell you! Perhaps it was really something she was justified in telling you. That's some more of my madness, I suppose! Love has its own dark morality when rivalry enters in—at least, mine has, if other people's hasn't. . . . I wonder how she got on? I hope she reached the inn all right, poor woman.'

'O yes: she got on all right,' said Jude placidly.

'I hope she wasn't shut out, and that she hadn't to walk the streets in the rain. Do you mind my putting on my waterproof and going to see if she got in? I've been thinking of her all the morning.'

'Well—is it necessary? You haven't the least idea how Arabella is able to shift for herself. Still, darling, if you want to go and inquire you can.'

There was no limit to the strange and unnecessary penances which Sue would meekly undertake when in a contrite mood; and this going to see all sorts of extraordinary persons whose relation to her was precisely of a kind that would have made other people shun them, was her instinct ever, so that the request did not surprise him.

'And when you come back,' he added, 'I'll be ready to go about the banns. You'll come with me?'

Sue agreed, and went off under cloak and umbrella, letting Jude kiss her freely, and returning his kisses in a way she had never done before. Times had decidedly changed. 'The little bird is caught at last!' she said, a sadness showing in her smile.

'No—only nested,' he assured her.

She walked along the muddy street till she reached the public-house mentioned by Arabella, which was not so very far off. She was informed that Arabella had not yet left, and in doubt how to announce herself so that her predecessor in Jude's affections would recognize her, she sent up word that a friend from Spring Street had called, naming the place of Jude's residence. She was asked to step upstairs, and on being shown into a room found that it was Arabella's bedroom, and that the latter had not yet risen. She halted on the turn of her toe till Arabella cried from the bed, 'Come in and shut the door,' which Sue accordingly did.

Arabella lay facing the window, and did not at once turn her head: and Sue was wicked enough, despite her penitence, to wish for a moment that Jude could behold her forerunner now, with the daylight full upon her. She may have seemed handsome enough in profile under the lamps, but a frowsiness was apparent this morning; and the sight of her own fresh charms in the looking-glass made Sue's manner bright, till she reflected what a meanly sexual emotion this was in her, and hated herself for it.

'I've just looked in to see if you got back comfortably last night, that's all,' she said gently. 'I was afraid afterwards that you might have met with any mishap?'

'O—how stupid this is! I thought my visitor was—your friend—your husband—Mrs Fawley, as I suppose you call yourself?' said Arabella, flinging her head back upon the pillows with a disappointed toss, and ceasing to retain the dimple she had just taken the trouble to produce.

'Indeed I don't,' said Sue.

'Oh, I thought you might have, even if he's not really yours. Decency is decency, any hour of the twenty-four.'

'I don't know what you mean,' said Sue stiffly. 'He is mine, if you come to that!'

'He wasn't yesterday.'

Sue coloured roseate, and said 'How do you know?'

'From your manner when you talked to me at the door. Well, my dear, you've been quick about it, and I expect my visit last night helped it on—ha-ha! But I don't want to get him away from you.'

Sue looked out at the rain, and at the dirty toilet-cover, and at the detached tail of Arabella's hair hanging on the looking-glass, just as it had done in Jude's time; and wished she had not come. In the pause there was a knock at the door, and the chambermaid brought in a telegram for 'Mrs Cartlett'.

Arabella opened it as she lay, and her ruffled look disappeared.

'I am much obliged to you for your anxiety about me,' she said blandly when the maid had gone; 'but it is not necessary you should feel it. My man finds he can't do without me after all, and agrees to stand by the promise to marry again over here that he has made me all along. See here! This is in answer to one from me.' She held out the telegram for Sue to read, but Sue did not take it. 'He asks me to come back. His little corner public in Lambeth would go to pieces without me, he says. But he isn't going to knock me about when he has had a drop, any more after we are spliced by English law than before! . . . As for you, I should coax Jude to take me before the parson straight off, and have done with it, if I were in your place. I say it as a friend, my dear.'

'He's waiting to, any day,' returned Sue, with frigid pride.

'Then let him, in Heaven's name. Life with a man is more business-like after it, and money matters work better. And then, you see, if you have rows, and he turns you out of doors, you can get the law to protect you, which you can't otherwise, unless he half runs you through with a knife, or cracks your noddle with a poker. And if he bolts away from you—I say it friendly, as woman to woman, for there's never any knowing what a man med do—you'll have the sticks o' furniture, and won't be looked upon as a thief. I shall marry my man over again, now he's willing, as there was a little flaw in the first ceremony. In my telegram last night which this is an answer to, I told him I had almost made it up with Jude; and that frightened him, I expect! Perhaps I should quite have done it if it hadn't been for you,' she said laughing; 'and then how different our histories might have been from to-day! Never such a tender fool as Jude is if a woman seems in trouble, and coaxes him a bit! Just as he used to be about birds and things. However, as it happens, it is just as well as if I had made it up, and I forgive you. And, as I say, I'd advise you to get the business legally done as soon as possible. You'll find it an awful bother later on if you don't.'

'I have told you he is asking me to marry him—to make our natural marriage a legal one,' said Sue, with yet more dignity. 'It was quite by my wish that he didn't the moment I was free.'

'Ah yes—you are a oneyer too, like myself,' said Arabella, eyeing her visitor with humorous criticism. 'Bolted from your first, didn't you, like me?'

'Good morning!—I must go,' said Sue hastily.

'And I, too, must up and off!' replied the other, springing out of bed so suddenly that the soft parts of her person shook. Sue jumped aside in trepidation. 'Lord, I am only a woman—not a six-foot sojer! . . . Just a moment, dear,' she continued, putting her hand on Sue's arm. 'I really did want to consult Jude on a little matter of business, as I told him. I came about that more than anything else. Would he run up to speak to me at the station as I am going? You think not. Well, I'll write to him about it. I didn't want to write, but never mind—I will.'

III

When Sue reached home Jude was awaiting her at the door to take the initial step towards their marriage. She clasped his arm, and they went along silently together, as true comrades ofttimes do. He saw that she was preoccupied, and forbore to question her.

'O Jude—I've been talking to her,' she said at last. 'I wish I hadn't! And yet it is best to be reminded of things.'

'I hope she was civil.'

'Yes. I—I can't help liking her—just a little bit! She's not an ungenerous nature; and I am so glad her difficulties have all suddenly ended.' She explained how Arabella had been summoned back, and would be enabled to retrieve her position. 'I was referring to our old question. What Arabella has been saying to me has made me feel more than ever how hopelessly vulgar an institution legal marriage is—a sort of trap to catch a man—I can't bear to think of it. I wish I hadn't promised to let you put up the banns this morning!'

'O, don't mind me. Any time will do for me. I thought you might like to get it over quickly, now.'

'Indeed, I don't feel any more anxious now than I did before. Perhaps with any other man I might be a little anxious; but among the very few virtues possessed by your family and mine, dear, I think I may set staunchness. So I am not a bit frightened about losing you, now I really am yours and you really are mine. In fact, I am easier in my mind than I was, for my conscience is clear about Richard, who now has a right to his freedom. I felt we were deceiving him before.'

'Sue, you seem when you are like this to be one of the women of some grand old civilization, whom I used to read about in my bygone, wasted, classical days, rather than a denizen of mere Christian country. I almost expect you to say at these times that you have just been talking to some friend whom you met in the Via Sacra, about the latest news of Octavia or Livia; or have been listening to Aspasia's eloquence, or have been watching Praxiteles chiselling away at his latest Venus, while Phryne made complaint that she was tired of posing.'

They had now reached the house of the parish-clerk. Sue stood back, while her lover went up to the door. His hand was raised to knock when she said: 'Jude!'

He looked round.

'Wait a minute, would you mind?'

He came back to her.

'Just let us think,' she said timidly. 'I had such a horrid dream one night . . . And Arabella—'

'What did Arabella say to you?' he asked.

'O, she said that when people were tied up you could get the law of a man better if he beat you—and how when couples quarrelled. . . . Jude, do you think that when you *must* have me with you by law, we shall be so happy as we are now? The men and women of our families are very generous when everything depends upon their good-will, but they always kick against compulsion. Don't you dread the attitude that insensibly arises out of legal obligation? Don't you think it is destructive to a passion whose essence is its gratuitousness?'

'Upon my word, love, you are beginning to frighten me, too, with all this foreboding! Well, let's go back and think it over.'

Her face brightened. 'Yes—so we will!' said she. And they turned from the clerk's door, Sue taking his arm and murmuring as they walked on homeward:

> 'Can you keep the bee from ranging,
> Or the ring-dove's neck from changing?
> No! Nor fetter'd love . . .'

They thought it over, or postponed thinking. Certainly they postponed action, and seemed to live on in a dreamy paradise. At the end of a fortnight or three weeks matters remained unadvanced, and no banns were announced to the ears of any Aldbrickham congregation.

Whilst they were postponing and postponing thus a letter and a newspaper arrived before breakfast one morning from Arabella. Seeing the handwriting Jude went up to Sue's room and told her, and as soon as she was dressed she hastened down. Sue opened the newspaper; Jude the letter. After glancing at the paper she held across the first page to him with her finger on a paragraph; but he was so absorbed in his letter that he did not turn awhile.

'Look!' she said.

He looked and read. The paper was one that circulated in South London only, and the marked advertisement was simply the announcement of a marriage at St John's Church, Waterloo Road, under the names, 'Cartlett—Donn'; the united pair being Arabella and the innkeeper.

'Well, it is satisfactory,' said Sue complacently. 'Though, after this, it seems rather low to do likewise, and I am glad— However, she is provided for now in a way, I suppose, whatever her faults, poor thing. It is nicer that we are able to think that, than to be uneasy about her. I ought, too, to write to Richard and ask him how he is getting on, perhaps?'

But Jude's attention was still absorbed. Having merely glanced at the announcement he said in a disturbed voice: 'Listen to this letter. What shall I say or do?

The Three Horns, Lambeth

Dear Jude (I won't be so distant as to call you Mr Fawley),—I send to-day a newspaper, from which useful document you will learn that I was married over again to Cartlett last Tuesday. So that business is settled right and tight at last. But what I write about more particular is that private affair I wanted to speak to you on when I came down to Aldbrickham. I couldn't very well tell it to your lady friend, and should much have liked to let you know it by word of mouth, as I could have explained better than by letter. The fact is, Jude, that, though I have never informed you before, there was a boy born of our marriage, eight months after I left you, when I was at Sydney, living with my father and mother. All that is easily provable. As I had separated from you before I thought such a thing was going to happen, and I was over there, and our quarrel had been sharp, I did not think it convenient to write about the birth. I was then looking out for a good situation, so my parents took the child, and he has been with them ever since. That was why I did not mention it when I met you in Christminster, nor at the law proceedings. He is now of an intelligent age, of course, and my mother and father have lately written to say that, as they have rather a hard struggle over there, and I am settled comfortably here, they don't see why they should be encumbered with the child any longer, his parents being alive. I would have him with me here in a moment, but he is not old enough to be of any use in the bar, nor will be for years and years, and naturally Cartlett might think him in the way. They have, however, packed him off to me in charge of some friends who happened to be coming home, and I must ask you to take him when he arrives, for I don't know what to do with him. He is lawfully yours, that I solemnly swear. If anybody says he isn't, call them brimstone liars, for my sake. Whatever I may have done before or afterwards, I was honest to you from the time we were married till I went away, and I remain, yours, &c.,

Arabella Cartlett

Sue's look was one of dismay. 'What will you do, dear?' she asked faintly.

Jude did not reply, and Sue watched him anxiously, with heavy breaths.

'It hits me hard!' said he in an under-voice. 'It *may* be true! I can't make it out. Certainly, if his birth was exactly when she says, he's mine. I cannot think why she didn't tell me when I met her at Christminster, and came on here that evening with her! . . . Ah—I do remember now that she said something about having a thing on her mind that she would like me to know, if ever we lived together again.'

'The poor child seems to be wanted by nobody!' Sue replied, and her eyes filled.

Jude had by this time come to himself. 'What a view of life he must have, mine or not mine!' he said. 'I must say that, if I were better off, I should not stop for a moment to think whose he might be. I would take him and bring him up. The beggarly question of parentage—what is it, after all? What does it matter, when you come to think of it, whether a child is yours by blood or not? All the little ones of our time are collectively the children of us adults of the time, and entitled to our general care. That excessive regard of parents for their own children, and their dislike of other people's, is, like class-feeling, patriotism, save-your-own-soul-ism, and other virtues, a mean exclusiveness at bottom.'

Sue jumped up and kissed Jude with passionate devotion. 'Yes—so it is, dearest! And we'll have him here! And if he isn't yours it makes it all the better. I do hope he isn't—though perhaps I ought not to feel quite that! If he isn't, I should like so much for us to have him as an adopted child!'

'Well, you must assume about him what is most pleasing to you, my curious little comrade!' he said. 'I feel that, anyhow, I don't like to leave the unfortunate little fellow to neglect. Just think of his life in a Lambeth pothouse, and all its evil influences, with a parent who doesn't want him, and has, indeed, hardly seen him, and a stepfather who doesn't know him. "Let the day perish wherein I was born, and the night in which it was said, There is a man child conceived!" That's what the boy—*my* boy, perhaps, will find himself saying before long!'

'O no!'

'As I was the petitioner, I am really entitled to his custody, I suppose.'

'Whether or no, we must have him. I see that. I'll do the best I can to be a mother to him, and we can afford to keep him somehow. I'll work harder. I wonder when he'll arrive?'

'In the course of a few weeks, I suppose.'

'I wish—When shall we have courage to marry, Jude?'

'Whenever you have it, I think I shall. It remains with you entirely, dear. Only say the word, and it's done.'

'Before the boy comes?'

'Certainly.'

'It would make a more natural home for him, perhaps,' she murmured.

Jude thereupon wrote in purely formal terms to request that the boy should be sent on to them as soon as he arrived, making no remark whatever on the surprising nature of Arabella's information, nor vouchsafing a single word of opinion on the boy's paternity, nor on whether, had he known all this, his conduct towards her would have been quite the same.

In the down train that was timed to reach Aldbrickham station about ten o'clock the next evening, a small, pale child's face could be seen in the gloom of a third-class carriage. He had large, frightened eyes, and wore a white woollen cravat, over which a key was suspended round his neck by a piece of common string: the key attracting attention by its occasional shine in the lamplight. In the band of his hat his half-ticket was stuck. His eyes remained mostly fixed on the back of the seat opposite, and never turned to the window even when a station was reached and called. On the other seats were two or three passengers, one of them a working woman who held a basket on her lap, in which was a tabby kitten. The woman opened the cover now and then, whereupon the kitten would put out its head, and indulge in playful antics. At these the fellow-passengers laughed, except the solitary boy bearing the key and ticket, who, regarding the kitten with his saucer eyes, seemed mutely to say: 'All laughing comes from misapprehension. Rightly looked at there is no laughable thing under the sun.'

Occasionally at a stoppage the guard would look into the compartment and say to the boy, 'All right, my man. Your box is safe in the van.' The boy would say, 'Yes,' without animation, would try to smile, and fail.

He was Age masquerading as Juvenility, and doing it so badly that his real self showed through crevices. A ground swell from ancient years of night seemed now and then to lift the child in this his morning-life, when his face took a back view over some great Atlantic of Time, and appeared not to care about what it saw.

When the other travellers closed their eyes, which they did one by one—even the kitten curling itself up in the basket, weary of its too circumscribed play—the boy remained just as before. He then seemed to be doubly awake, like an enslaved and dwarfed Divinity, sitting passive and regarding his companions as if he saw their whole rounded lives rather than their immediate figures.

This was Arabella's boy. With her usual carelessness she had postponed writing to Jude about him till the eve of his landing, when she could absolutely postpone no longer, though she had known for weeks of his approaching arrival, and had, as she truly said, visited Aldbrickham mainly to reveal the boy's existence and his near home-coming to Jude. This very day on which she received her former husband's answer at some time in the afternoon, the child reached the London Docks, and the family in whose charge he had come, having put him into a cab for Lambeth, and directed the cabman to his mother's house, bade him good-bye, and went their way.

On his arrival at the Three Horns, Arabella had looked him over with an expression that was as good as saying, 'You are very much what I expected you to be,' had given him a good meal, a little money, and, late as it was getting, despatched him to Jude by the next train, wishing her husband Cartlett, who was out, not to see him.

The train reached Aldbrickham, and the boy was deposited on the lonely platform beside his box. The collector took his ticket and, with a meditative sense of the unfitness of things, asked him where he was going by himself at that time of night.

'Going to Spring Street,' said the little one impassively.

'Why, that's a long way from here; a'most out in the country; and the folks will have gone to bed.'

'I've got to go there.'

'You must have a fly for your box.'

'No. I must walk.'

'O well: you'd better leave your box here and send for it. There's a 'bus goes half-way, but you'll have to walk the rest.'

'I am not afraid.'

'Why didn't your friends come to meet 'ee?'

'I suppose they didn't know I was coming.'

'Who is your friends?'

'Mother didn't wish me to say.'

'All I can do, then, is to take charge of this. Now walk as fast as you can.'

Saying nothing further the boy came out into the street, looking round to see that nobody followed or observed him. When he had walked some little distance he asked for the street of his destination. He was told to go straight on quite into the outskirts of the place.

The child fell into a steady mechanical creep which had in it an impersonal quality—the movement of the wave, or of the breeze, or of the cloud. He followed his directions literally, without an inquiring gaze at anything. It could have been seen that the boy's ideas of life were different from those of the local boys. Children begin with detail, and learn up to the general; they begin with the contiguous, and gradually comprehend the universal. The boy seemed to have begun with the generals of life, and never to have concerned himself with the particulars. To him the houses, the willows, the obscure fields beyond, were apparently regarded not as brick residences, pollards, meadows; but as human dwellings in the abstract, vegetation, and the wide dark world.

He found the way to the little lane, and knocked at the door of Jude's house. Jude had just retired to bed, and Sue was about to enter her chamber adjoining when she heard the knock and came down.

'Is this where father lives?' asked the child.

'Who?'

'Mr Fawley, that's his name.'

Sue ran up to Jude's room and told him, and he hurried down as soon as he could, though to her impatience he seemed long.

'What—is it he—so soon?' she asked as Jude came.

She scrutinized the child's features, and suddenly went away into the little sitting-room adjoining. Jude lifted the boy to a level with himself, keenly regarded him with gloomy tenderness, and telling him he would have been met if they had known of his coming so soon, set him provisionally in a chair whilst he went to look for Sue, whose super-sensitiveness was disturbed, as he knew. He found her in the dark, bending over an arm-chair. He enclosed her with his arm, and putting his face by hers, whispered, 'What's the matter?'

'What Arabella says is true—true! I see you in him!'

'Well: that's one thing in my life as it should be, at any rate.'

'But the other half of him is—*she*! And that's what I can't bear! But I ought to—I'll try to get used to it; yes, I ought!'

'Jealous little Sue! I withdraw all remarks about your sexlessness. Never mind! Time may right things. . . . And Sue, darling; I have an idea! We'll educate and train him with a view to the University. What I couldn't accomplish in my own person perhaps I can carry out through him? They are making it easier for poor students now, you know.'

'O you dreamer!' said she, and holding his hand returned to the child with him. The boy looked at her as she had looked at him. 'Is it you who's my *real* mother at last?' he inquired.

'Why? Do I look like your father's wife?'

'Well, yes; 'cept he seems fond of you, and you of him. Can I call you mother?'

Then a yearning came over the child and he began to cry. Sue thereupon could not refrain from instantly doing likewise, being a harp which the least wind of emotion from another's heart could make to vibrate as readily as a radical stir in her own.

'You may call me mother, if you wish to, my poor dear!' she said, bending her cheek against his to hide her tears.

'What's this round your neck?' asked Jude with affected calmness.

'The key of my box that's at the station.'

They bustled about and got him some supper, and made him up a temporary bed, where he soon fell asleep. Both went and looked at him as he lay.

'He called you mother two or three times before he dropped off,' murmured Jude. 'Wasn't it odd that he should have wanted to!'

'Well—it was significant,' said Sue. 'There's more for us to think about in that one little hungry heart than in all the stars of the sky. . . . I suppose, dear, we *must* pluck up courage, and get that ceremony over? It is no use struggling against the current, and I feel myself getting intertwined with my kind. O Jude, you'll love me dearly, won't you, afterwards! I do want to be kind to this child, and to be a mother to him; and our adding the legal form to our marriage might make it easier for me.'

IV

Their next and second attempt thereat was more deliberately made, though it was begun on the morning following the singular child's arrival at their home.

Him they found to be in the habit of sitting silent, his quaint and weird face set, and his eyes resting on things they did not see in the substantial world.

'His face is like the tragic mask of Melpomene,' said Sue. 'What is your name, dear? Did you tell us?'

'Little Father Time is what they always called me. It is a nick-name; because I look so aged, they say.'

'And you talk so, too,' said Sue tenderly. 'It is strange, Jude, that these preternaturally old boys almost always come from new countries. But what were you christened?'

'I never was.'

'Why was that?'

'Because, if I died in damnation, 'twould save the expense of a Christian funeral.'

'O—your name is not Jude, then?' said his father with some disappointment.

The boy shook his head. 'Never heerd on it.'

'Of course not,' said Sue quickly; 'since she was hating you all the time!'

'We'll have him christened,' said Jude; and privately to Sue: 'The day we are married.' Yet the advent of the child disturbed him.

Their position lent them shyness, and having an impression that a marriage at a Superintendent Registrar's office was more private than an ecclesiastical one, they decided to avoid a church this time. Both Sue and Jude together went to the office of the district to give notice: they had become such companions that they could hardly do anything of importance except in each other's company.

Jude Fawley signed the form of notice, Sue looking over his shoulder and watching his hand as it traced the words. As she read the four-square undertaking, never before seen by her, into which her own and Jude's names were inserted, and by which that very volatile essence, their love for each other, was supposed to be made permanent, her face seemed to grow painfully apprehensive. 'Names and Surnames of the Parties'—(they were to be parties now, not lovers, she thought). 'Condition'—(a horrid idea)—'Rank or Occupation'—'Age'—'Dwelling at'—'Length of Residence'—'Church or Building in which the Marriage is to be solemnized'—'District and County in which the Parties respectively dwell.'

'It spoils the sentiment, doesn't it!' she said on their way home. 'It seems making a more sordid business of it even than signing the contract in a vestry. There is a little poetry in a church. But we'll try to get through with it, dearest, now.'

'We will. "For what man is he that hath betrothed a wife and hath not taken her? Let him go and return unto his house, lest he die in the battle, and another man take her." So said the Jewish law-giver.'

'How you know the Scriptures, Jude! You really ought to have been a parson. I can only quote profane writers!'

During the interval before the issuing of the certificate Sue, in her housekeeping errands, sometimes walked past the office, and furtively glancing in saw affixed to the wall the notice of the purposed clinch to their union. She could not bear its aspect. Coming after her previous experience of matrimony, all the romance of their attachment seemed to be starved away by placing her present case in the same category. She was usually leading little Father Time by the hand, and fancied that people thought him hers, and regarded the intended ceremony as the patching up of an old error.

Meanwhile Jude decided to link his present with his past in some slight degree by inviting to the wedding the only person remaining on earth who was associated with his early life at Marygreen—the aged widow Mrs Edlin, who had been his great-aunt's friend and nurse in her last illness. He hardly expected that she would come; but she did, bringing singular presents, in the form of apples, jam, brass snuffers, an ancient pewter dish, a warming-pan, and an enormous bag of goose feathers towards a bed. She was allotted the spare room in Jude's house, whither she retired early, and where they could hear her through the ceiling below, honestly saying the Lord's Prayer in a loud voice, as the Rubric directed.

As, however, she could not sleep, and discovered that Sue and Jude were still sitting up—it being in fact only ten o'clock—she dressed herself again, and came down; and they all sat by the fire till a late hour—Father Time included; though, as he never spoke, they were hardly conscious of him.

'Well, I ain't set against marrying as your great-aunt was,' said the widow. 'And I hope 'twill be a jocund wedding for ye in all respects this time. Nobody can hope it more, knowing what I do of your families, which is more, I suppose, than anybody else now living. For they have been unlucky that way, God knows.'

Sue breathed uneasily.

'They was always good-hearted people, too—wouldn't kill a fly if they knowed it,' continued the wedding guest. 'But things happened to thwart 'em, and if everything wasn't vitty they were upset. No doubt that's how he that the tale is told of came to do what 'a did—if he *were* one of your family.'

'What was that?' said Jude.

'Well—that tale, ye know; he that was gibbeted just on the brow of the hill by the Brown House—not far from the milestone between Marygreen and Alfredston, where the other road branches off. But Lord, 'twas in my grandfather's time; and it needn't have been one of your folk at all.'

'I know where the gibbet is said to have stood, very well,' murmured Jude. 'But I never heard of this. What—did this man—my ancestor and Sue's—kill his wife?'

''Twer not that exactly. She ran away from him, with their child, to her friends; and while she was there the child died. He wanted the body, to bury it where his people lay, but she wouldn't give it up. Her husband then came in the night with a cart, and broke into the house to steal the coffin away; but he was catched, and being obstinate, wouldn't tell what he broke in for. They brought it in burglary, and that's why he was hanged and gibbeted on Brown

House Hill. His wife went mad after he was dead. But it medn' be true that he belonged to ye more than to me.'

A small slow voice rose from the shade of the fireside, as if out of the earth: 'If I was you, mother, I wouldn't marry father!' It came from little Time, and they started, for they had forgotten him.

'O, it is only a tale,' said Sue cheeringly.

After this exhilarating tradition from the widow on the eve of the solemnization they rose, and, wishing their guest good-night, retired.

The next morning Sue, whose nervousness intensified with the hours, took Jude privately into the sitting-room before starting. 'Jude, I want you to kiss me, as a lover, incorporeally,' she said, tremulously nestling up to him, with damp lashes. 'It won't be ever like this any more, will it! I wish we hadn't begun the business. But I suppose we must go on. How horrid that story was last night! It spoilt my thoughts of to-day. It makes me feel as if a tragic doom overhung our family, as it did the house of Atreus.'

'Or the house of Jeroboam,' said the quondam theologian.

'Yes. And it seems awful temerity in us two to go marrying! I m going to vow to you in the same words I vowed in to my other husband, and you to me in the same as you used to your other wife; regardless of the deterrent lesson we were taught by those experiments!'

'If you are uneasy I am made unhappy,' said he. 'I had hoped you would feel quite joyful. But if you don't, you don't. It is no use pretending. It is a dismal business to you, and that makes it so to me!'

'It is unpleasantly like that other morning—that's all,' she murmured. 'Let us go on now.'

They started arm in arm for the office aforesaid, no witness accompanying them except for the Widow Edlin. The day was chilly and dull, and a clammy fog blew through the town from 'Royal-tower'd Thame'. On the steps of the office there were the muddy footmarks of people who had entered, and in the entry were damp umbrellas. Within the office several persons were gathered, and our couple perceived that a marriage between a soldier and a young woman was just in progress. Sue, Jude, and the widow stood in the background while this was going on, Sue reading the notices of marriage on the wall. The room was a dreary place to two of their temperament, though to its usual frequenters it doubtless seemed ordinary enough. Law-books in musty calf covered one wall, and elsewhere were Post-Office Directories, and other books of reference. Papers in packets tied with red tape were pigeon-holed around, and some iron safes filled a recess; while the bare wood floor was, like the doorstep, stained by previous visitors.

The soldier was sullen and reluctant: the bride sad and timid; she was soon, obviously, to become a mother, and she had a black eye. Their little business was soon done, and the twain and their friends straggled out, one of the witnesses saying casually to Jude and Sue in passing, as if he had known them before: 'See the couple just come in? Ha, ha! That fellow is just out of gaol this morning. She met him at the gaol gates, and brought him straight here. She's paying for everything.'

Sue turned her head and saw an ill-favoured man, closely cropped, with a broad-faced, pock-marked woman on his arm, ruddy with liquor and the satisfaction of being on the brink of a gratified desire. They jocosely saluted the outgoing couple, and went forward in front of Jude and Sue, whose diffidence was increasing. The latter drew back and turned to her lover, her mouth shaping itself like that of a child about to give way to grief:

'Jude—I don't like it here! I wish we hadn't come! The place gives me the horrors: it seems so unnatural as the climax of our love! I wish it had been at church, if it had to be at all. It is not so vulgar there!'

'Dear little girl,' said Jude. 'How troubled and pale you look!'

'It must be performed here now, I suppose?'

'No—perhaps not necessarily.'

He spoke to the clerk, and came back. 'No—we need not marry here or anywhere, unless we like, even now,' he said. 'We can be married in a church, if not with the same certificate with another he'll give us, I think. Anyhow, let us go out till you are calmer, dear, and I too, and talk it over.'

They went out stealthily and guiltily, as if they had committed a misdemeanour, closing the door without noise, and telling the widow, who had remained in the entry, to go home and await them; that they would call in any casual passers as witnesses, if necessary. When in the street they turned into an unfrequented side alley, where they walked up and down as they had done long ago in the Market-house at Melchester.

'Now, darling, what shall we do? We are making a mess of it, it strikes me. Still, *anything* that pleases you will please me.'

'But Jude, dearest, I am worrying you! You wanted it to be there, didn't you?'

'Well, to tell the truth, when I got inside I felt as if I didn't care much about it. The place depressed me almost as much as it did you—it was ugly. And then I thought of what you had said this morning as to whether we ought.'

They walked on vaguely, till she paused, and her little voice began anew: 'It seems so weak, too, to vacillate like this! And yet how much better than to act rashly a second time. . . . How terrible that scene was to me! The expression in that flabby woman's face, leading her on to give herself to that gaol-bird, not for a few hours, as she would, but for a lifetime, as she must. And the other poor soul—to escape a nominal shame which was owing to the weakness of her character, degrading herself to the real shame of bondage to a tyrant who scorned her—a man whom to avoid for ever was her only chance of salvation. . . . This is our parish church, isn't it? This is where it would have to be, if we did it in the usual way? A service or something seems to be going on.'

Jude went up and looked in at the door. 'Why—it is a wedding here too,' he said. 'Everybody seems to be on our tack to-day.'

Sue said she supposed it was because Lent was just over, when there was always a crowd of marriages. 'Let us listen,' she said, 'and find how it feels to us when performed in a church.'

They stepped in, and entered a back seat, and watched the proceedings at the altar. The contracting couple appeared to belong to the well-to-do middle class, and the wedding altogether was of ordinary prettiness and interest. They could see the flowers tremble in the bride's hand, even at that distance, and could hear her mechanical murmur of words whose meaning her brain seemed to gather not at all under the pressure of her self-consciousness. Sue and Jude listened, and deservedly saw themselves in time past going through the same form of self-committal.

'It is not the same to her, poor thing, as it would be to me doing it over again with my present knowledge,' Sue whispered. 'You see, they are fresh to it, and take the proceedings as a matter of course. But having been awakened to its solemnity as we have, or at least as I have, by experience, and to my own too squeamish feelings perhaps sometimes, it really does seem immoral in me to go and undertake the same thing again with open eyes. Coming in here and seeing this has frightened me from a church wedding as much as the other did from a registry one. . . . We are a weak, tremulous pair, Jude, and what others may feel confident in I feel doubts of—my being proof against the sordid conditions of a business contract again!'

Then they tried to laugh, and went on debating in whispers the object-lesson before them. And Jude said he also thought they were both too thin-skinned—that they ought never to have been born—much less have come together for the most preposterous of all joint-adventures for *them*—matrimony.

His betrothed shuddered; and asked him earnestly if he indeed felt that they ought not to go in cold blood and sign that life-undertaking again? 'It is awful if you think we have found ourselves not strong enough for it, and knowing this, are proposing to perjure ourselves,' she said.

'I fancy I do think it—since you ask me,' said Jude. 'Remember I'll do it if you wish, own darling.' While she hesitated he went on to confess that, though he thought they ought to be able to do it, he felt checked by the dread of incompetency just as she did—from their peculiarities, perhaps, because they were unlike other people. 'We are horribly sensitive; that's really what's the matter with us, Sue!' he declared.

'I fancy more are like us than we think!'

'Well, I don't know. The intention of the contract is good, and right for many, no doubt; but in our case it may defeat its own ends because we are the queer sort of people we are—folk in whom domestic ties of a forced kind snuff out cordiality and spontaneousness.'

Sue still held that there was not much queer or exceptional in them: that all were so. 'Everybody is getting to feel as we do. We are a little beforehand, that's all. In fifty, a hundred, years the descendants of these two will act and feel worse than we. They will see weltering humanity still more vividly than we do now, as

Shapes like our own selves hideously multiplied,

and will be afraid to reproduce them.'

'What a terrible line of poetry! . . . though I have felt it myself about my fellow-creatures, at morbid times.'

Thus they murmured on, till Sue said more brightly:

'Well—the general question is not our business, and why should we plague ourselves about it? However different our reasons are we come to the same conclusion; that for us particular two, an irrevocable oath is risky. Then, Jude, let us go home without killing our dream! Yes? How good you are, my friend: you give way to all my whims!'

'They accord very much with my own.'

He gave her a little kiss behind a pillar while the attention of everybody present was taken up in observing the bridal procession entering the vestry; and then they came outside the building. By the door they waited till two or three carriages, which had gone away for a while, returned, and the new husband and wife came into the open daylight. Sue sighed.

'The flowers in the bride's hand are sadly like the garland which decked the heifers of sacrifice in old times!'

'Still, Sue, it is no worse for the woman than for the man. That's what some women fail to see, and instead of protesting against the conditions they protest against the man, the other victim; just as a woman in a crowd will abuse the man who crushes against her, when he is only the helpless transmitter of the pressure put upon him.'

'Yes—some are like that, instead of uniting with the man against the common enemy, coercion.' The bride and the bridegroom had by this time driven off, and the two moved away with the rest of the idlers. 'No—don't let's do it,' she continued. 'At least just now.'

They reached home, and passing the window arm in arm saw the widow looking out at them. 'Well,' cried their guest when they entered, 'I said to myself when I zeed ye coming so loving up to the door, "They made up their minds at last, then!" '

They briefly hinted that they had not.

'What—and ha'n't ye really done it? Chok' it all, that I should have lived to see a good old saying like "marry in haste and repent at leisure" spoiled like this by you two! 'Tis time I got back again to Marygreen—sakes if tidden—if this is what the new notions be leading us to! Nobody thought o' being afeard o' matrimony in my time, nor of much else but a cannon-ball or empty cupboard! Why when I and my poor man were married we thought no more o't than of a game o' dibs!'

'Don't tell the child when he comes in,' whispered Sue nervously. 'He'll think it has all gone on right, and it will be better that he should not be surprised and puzzled. Of course it is only put off for reconsideration. If we are happy as we are, what does it matter to anybody?'

V

THE purpose of a chronicler of moods and deeds does not require him to express his personal views upon the grave controversy above given. That the twain were happy—between their times of sadness—was indubitable. And when the unexpected apparition of Jude's child in the house had shown itself to be no such disturbing event as it had looked, but one that brought into their lives a new and tender interest of an ennobling and unselfish kind, it rather helped than injured their happiness.

To be sure, with such pleasing anxious beings as they were, the boy's coming also brought with it much thought for the future, particularly as he seemed at present to be singularly deficient in all the usual hopes of childhood. But the pair tried to dismiss, for a while at least, a too strenuously forward view.

There is in Upper Wessex an old town of nine or ten thousand souls; the town may be called Stoke-Barehills. It stands with its gaunt, unattractive, ancient church, and its new red brick suburb, amid the open, chalk-soiled cornlands, near the middle of an imaginary triangle which has for its three corners the towns of Aldbrickham and Wintoncester, and the important military station of Quartershot. The great western highway from London passes through it, near a point where the road branches into two, merely to unite again some twenty miles further westward. Out of this bifurcation and reunion there used to arise among wheeled travellers, before railway days, endless questions of choice between the respective ways. But the question is now as dead as the scot-and-lot freeholder, the road waggoner, and the mail coachman who disputed it; and probably not a single inhabitant of Stoke-Barehills is now even aware that the two roads which part in his town ever meet again; for nobody now drives up and down the great western highway daily.

The most familiar object in Stoke-Barehills nowadays is its cemetery, standing among some picturesque mediaeval ruins beside the railway; the modern chapels, modern tombs, and modern shrubs, having a look of intrusiveness amid the crumbling and ivy-covered decay of the ancient walls.

On a certain day, however, in the particular year which has now been reached by this narrative—the month being early June—the features of the town excite little interest, though many visitors arrive by the trains; some down trains, in especial, nearly emptying themselves here. It is the week of the Great Wessex Agricultural Show, whose vast encampment spreads over the open outskirts of the town like the tents of an investing army. Rows of marquees, huts, booths, pavilions, arcades, porticoes—every kind of structure short of a permanent one—cover the green field for the space of a square half-mile, and the crowds of arrivals walk through the town in a mass, and make straight for the exhibition ground. The way thereto is lined with shows, stalls, and hawkers on foot, who make a market-place of the whole roadway to the show proper, and lead some of the improvident to lighten their pockets appreciably before they reach the gates of the exhibition they came expressly to see.

It is the popular day, the shilling day, and of the fast arriving excursion trains two from different directions enter the two contiguous railway-stations at almost the same minute. One, like several which have preceded it, comes from London: the other by a cross-line from Aldbrickham; and from the London train alights a couple; a short, rather bloated man, with a globular stomach and small legs, resembling a top on two pegs, accompanied by a woman of rather fine figure and rather red face, dressed in black material, and covered with beads from bonnet to skirt, that made her glisten as if clad in chain-mail.

They cast their eyes around. The man was about to hire a fly as some others had done, when the woman said, 'Don't be in such a hurry, Cartlett. It isn't so very far to the show-yard. Let us walk down the street into the place. Perhaps I can pick up a cheap bit of furniture or odd china. It is years since I was here—never since I lived as a girl at Aldbrickham, and used to come across for a trip sometimes with my young man.'

'You can't carry home furniture by excursion train,' said, in a thick voice, her husband, the landlord of The Three Horns, Lambeth; for they had both come down from the tavern in that 'excellent, densely populated, gin-drinking neighbourhood', which they had occupied ever since the advertisement in those words had attracted them thither. The configuration of the landlord showed that he, too, like his customers, was becoming affected by the liquors he retailed.

'Then I'll get it sent, if I see any worth having,' said his wife.

They sauntered on, but had barely entered the town when her attention was attracted by a young couple leading a child, who had come out from the second platform, into which the train from Aldbrickham had steamed. They were walking just in front of the innkeepers.

'Sakes alive!' said Arabella.

'What's that?' said Cartlett.

'Who do you think that couple is? Don't you recognize the man?'

'No.'

'Not from the photos I have showed you?'

'Is it Fawley?'

'Yes—of course.'

'Oh, well. I suppose he was inclined for a little sight-seeing like the rest of us.' Cartlett's interest in Jude, whatever it might have been when Arabella was new to him, had plainly flagged since her charms and her idiosyncrasies, her super-numerary hair-coils, and her optional dimples, were becoming as a tale that is told.

Arabella so regulated her pace and her husband's as to keep just in the rear of the other three, which it was easy to do without notice in such a stream of pedestrians. Her answers to Cartlett's remarks were vague and slight, for the group in front interested her more than all the rest of the spectacle.

'They are rather fond of one another and of their child, seemingly,' continued the publican.

'*Their* child! 'Tisn't their child,' said Arabella with a curious, sudden covetousness. 'They haven't been married long enough for it to be theirs!'

But although the smouldering maternal instinct was strong enough in her to lead her to quash her husband's conjecture, she was not disposed on second thoughts to be more candid than necessary. Mr Cartlett had no other idea than that his wife's child by her first husband was with his grandparents at the Antipodes.

'O I suppose not. She looks quite a girl.'

'They are only lovers, or lately married, and have the child in charge, as anybody can see.'

All continued to move ahead. The unwitting Sue and Jude, the couple in question, had determined to make this Agricultural Exhibition within twenty miles of their own town the occasion of a day's excursion which should combine exercise and amusement with instruction, at small expense. Not regardful of themselves alone, they had taken care to bring Father Time, to try every means of making him kindle and laugh like other boys, though he was to some extent a hindrance to the delightful unreserved intercourse in their pilgrimages which they so much enjoyed. But they soon ceased to consider him an observer, and went along with that tender attention to each other which the shyest can scarcely disguise, and which these, among entire strangers as they imagined, took less trouble to disguise than they might have done at home. Sue, in her new summer clothes, flexible and light as a bird, her little thumb stuck up by the stem of her white cotton sunshade, went along as if she hardly touched the ground, and as if a moderately strong puff of wind would float her over the hedge into the next field. Jude, in his light grey holiday-suit, was really proud of her companionship, not more for her external attractiveness than for her sympathetic words and ways. That complete mutual understanding, in which every glance and movement was as effectual as speech for conveying intelligence between them, made them almost the two parts of a single whole.

The pair with their charge passed through the turnstiles, Arabella and her husband not far behind them. When inside the enclosure the publican's wife could see that the two ahead began to take trouble with the youngster, pointing out and explaining the many objects of interest, alive and dead; and a passing sadness would touch their faces at every failure to disturb his indifference.

'How she sticks to him!' said Arabella. 'O no—I fancy they are not married, or they wouldn't be so much to one another as that.... I wonder!'

'But I thought you said he did marry her?'

'I heard he was going to—that's all, going to make another attempt, after putting it off once or twice.... As far as they themselves are concerned they are the only two in the show. I should be ashamed of making myself so silly if I were he!'

'I don't see as how there's anything remarkable in their behaviour. I should never have noticed their being in love, if you hadn't said so.'

'You never see anything,' she rejoined. Nevertheless Cartlett's view of the lovers' or married pair's conduct was undoubtedly that of the general crowd, whose attention seemed to be in no way attracted by what Arabella's sharpened vision discerned.

'He's charmed by her as if she were some fairy!' continued Arabella. 'See how he looks round at her, and lets his eyes rest on her. I am inclined to think that she don't care for him quite so much as he does for her. She's not a particular warm-hearted creature to my thinking, though she cares for him pretty middling much—as much as she's able to; and he could make her heart ache a bit if he liked to try—which he's too simple to do. There—now they are going across to the cart-horse sheds. Come along.'

'I don't want to see the cart-horses. It is no business of ours to follow these two. If we have come to see the show let us see it in our own way, as they do in theirs.'

'Well—suppose we agree to meet somewhere in an hour's time—say at that refreshment tent over there, and go about independent? Then you can look at what you choose to, and so can I.'

Cartlett was not loth to agree to this, and they parted—he proceeding to the shed where malting processes were being exhibited, and Arabella in the direction taken by Jude and Sue. Before, however, she had regained their wake a laughing face met her own, and she was confronted by Anny, the friend of her girlhood.

Anny had burst out in hearty laughter at the mere fact of the chance recounter. 'I am still living down there,' she said, as soon as she was composed. 'I am soon going to be married, but my intended couldn't come up here to-day. But there's lots of us come by excursion, though I've lost the rest of 'em for the present.'

'Have you met Jude and his young woman, or wife, or whatever she is? I saw 'em by now.'

'No. Not a glimpse of un for years!'

'Well, they are close by here somewhere. Yes—there they are—by that grey horse!'

'O, that's his present young woman—wife did you say? Has he married again?'

'I don't know.'

'She's pretty, isn't she!'

'Yes—nothing to complain of; or jump at. Not much to depend on, though; a slim, fidgety little thing like that.'

'He's a nice-looking chap, too! You ought to ha' stuck to un, Arabella.'

'I don't know but I ought,' murmured she.

Anny laughed. 'That's you, Arabella! Always wanting another man than your own.'

'Well, and what woman don't I should like to know? As for that body with him—she don't know what love is—at least what I call love! I can see in her face she don't.'

'And perhaps, Abby dear, you don't know what she calls love.'

'I'm sure I don't wish to! . . . Ah—they are making for the Art Department. I should like to see some pictures myself. Suppose we go that way?—Why, if all Wessex isn't here, I verily believe! There's Dr Vilbert. Haven't seen him for years, and he's not looking a day older than when I used to know him. How do you do, Physician? I was just saying that you don't look a day older than when you knew me as a girl.'

'Simply the result of taking my own pills regular, ma'am. Only two and threepence a box—warranted efficacious by the Government stamp. Now let me advise you to purchase the same immunity from the ravages of Time by following my example? Only two-and-three.'

The physician had produced a box from his waistcoat pocket, and Arabella was induced to make the purchase.

'At the same time,' continued he, when the pills were paid for, 'you have the advantage of me, Mrs—Surely not Mrs Fawley, once Miss Donn, of the vicinity of Marygreen?'

'Yes. But Mrs Cartlett now.'

'Ah—you lost him, then? Promising young fellow! A pupil of mine, you know. I taught him the dead languages. And believe me, he soon knew nearly as much as I.'

'I lost him; but not as you think,' said Arabella drily. 'The lawyers untied us. There he is, look, alive and lusty; along with that young woman, entering the Art exhibition.'

'Ah—dear me! Fond of her, apparently.'

'They *say* they are cousins.'

'Cousinship is a great convenience to their feelings, I should say?'

'Yes. So her husband thought, no doubt, when he divorced her. . . . Shall we look at the pictures too?'

The trio followed across the green and entered. Jude and Sue, with the child, unaware of the interest they were exciting, had gone up to a model at one end of the building, which they regarded with considerable attention for a long while before they went on. Arabella and her friends came to it in due course, and the inscription it bore was: 'Model of Cardinal College, Christminster; by J. Fawley and S. F. M. Bridehead'.

'Admiring their own work,' said Arabella. 'How like Jude—always thinking of Colleges and Christminster, instead of attending to his business!'

They glanced cursorily at the pictures, and proceeded to the band-stand. When they had stood a little while listening to the music of the military performers, Jude, Sue, and the child came up on the other side. Arabella did not care if they should recognize her; but they were too deeply absorbed in their own lives, as translated into emotion by the military band, to perceive her under her beaded veil. She walked round the outside of the listening throng, passing behind the lovers, whose movements had an unexpected fascination for her to-day. Scrutinizing them narrowly from the rear she noticed that Jude's hand sought Sue's as they stood, the two standing close together so as to conceal, as they supposed, this tacit expression of their mutual responsiveness.

'Silly fools—like two children!' Arabella whispered to herself morosely, as she rejoined her companions, with whom she preserved a preoccupied silence.

Anny meanwhile had jokingly remarked to Vilbert on Arabella's hankering interest in her first husband.

'Now,' said the physician to Arabella, apart; 'do you want anything such as this, Mrs Cartlett? It is not compounded out of my regular pharmacopoeia, but I am sometimes asked for such a thing.' He produced a small phial of clear liquid. 'A love-philtre, such as was used by the Ancients with great effect. I found it out by study of their writings, and have never known it to fail.'

'What is it made of?' asked Arabella curiously.

'Well—a distillation of the juices of doves' hearts—otherwise pigeons'—is one of the ingredients. It took nearly a hundred hearts to produce that small bottle full.'

'How do you get pigeons enough?'

'To tell a secret, I get a piece of rock-salt, of which pigeons are inordinately fond, and place it in a dovecote on my roof. In a few hours the birds come to it from all points of the compass—east, west, north, and south—and thus I secure as many as I require. You use the liquid by contriving that the desired man shall take about ten drops of it in his drink. But remember, all this is told you because I gather from your questions that you mean to be a purchaser. You must keep faith with me?'

'Very well—I don't mind a bottle—to give some friend or other to try it on her young man.' She produced five shillings, the price asked, and slipped the phial in her capacious bosom. Saying presently that she was due at an appointment with her husband she sauntered away towards the refreshment bar, Jude, his companion, and the child having gone on to the horticultural tent, where Arabella caught a glimpse of them standing before a group of roses in bloom.

She waited a few minutes observing them, and then proceeded to join her spouse with no very amiable sentiments. She found him seated on a stool by the bar, talking to one of the gaily dressed maids who had served him with spirits.

'I should think you had enough of this business at home!' Arabella remarked gloomily. 'Surely you didn't come fifty miles from your own bar to stick in another? Come, take me round the show, as other men do their wives! Dammy, one would think you were a young bachelor, with nobody to look after but yourself!'

'But we agreed to meet here; and what could I do but wait?'

'Well, now we have met, come along,' she returned, ready to quarrel with the sun for shining on her. And they left the tent together, this pot-bellied man and florid woman, in the antipathetic, recriminatory mood of the average husband and wife of Christendom.

In the meantime the more exceptional couple and the boy still lingered in the pavilion of flowers—an enchanted palace to their appreciative taste—Sue's usually pale cheeks reflecting the pink of the tinted roses at which she gazed; for the gay sights, the air, the music, and the excitement of a day's outing with Jude, had quickened her blood and made her eyes sparkle with vivacity. She adored roses, and what Arabella had witnessed was Sue detaining Jude almost against his will while she learnt the names of this variety and that, and put her face within an inch of their blooms to smell them.

'I should like to push my face quite into them—the dears!' she had said. 'But I suppose it is against the rules to touch them—isn't it, Jude?'

'Yes, you baby,' said he: and then playfully gave her a little push, so that her nose went among the petals.

'The policeman will be down on us, and I shall say it was my husband's fault!'

Then she looked up at him, and smiled in a way that told so much to Arabella.

'Happy?' he murmured.

She nodded.

'Why? Because you have come to the great Wessex Agricultural Show—or because *we* have come?'

'You are always trying to make me confess all sorts of absurdities. Because I am improving my mind, of course, by seeing all these steam-ploughs, and threshing-machines, and chaff-cutters, and cows, and pigs, and sheep.'

Jude was quite content with a baffle from his ever evasive companion. But when he had forgotten that he had put the question, and because he no longer wished for an answer, she went on: 'I feel that we have returned to Greek joyousness, and have blinded ourselves to sickness and sorrow, and have forgotten what twenty-five centuries have taught the race since their time, as one of your Christminster luminaries says. . . . There is one immediate shadow, however—only one.' And she looked at the aged child, whom, though they had taken him to everything likely to attract a young intelligence, they had utterly failed to interest.

He knew what they were saying and thinking. 'I am very, very sorry, father and mother,' he said. 'But please don't mind!—I can't help it. I should like the flowers very much, if I didn't keep on thinking they'd be all withered in a few days!'

VI

The unnoticed lives that the pair had hitherto led began, from the day of the suspended wedding onwards, to be observed and discussed by other persons than Arabella. The society of Spring Street and the neighbourhood generally did not understand, and probably could not have been made to understand, Sue and Jude's private minds, emotions, positions, and fears. The curious facts of a child coming to them unexpectedly, who called Jude father, and Sue mother, and a hitch in a marriage ceremony intended for quietness to be performed at a registrar's office, together with rumours of the undefended cases in the law-courts, bore only one translation to plain minds.

Little Time—for though he was formally turned into 'Jude', the apt nickname stuck to him—would come home from school in the evening, and repeat inquiries and remarks that had been made to him by the other boys; and cause Sue, and Jude when he heard them, a great deal of pain and sadness.

The result was that shortly after the attempt at the registrar's the pair went off—to London it was believed—for several days, hiring somebody to look to the boy. When they came back they let it be understood indirectly, and with total indifference and weariness of mien, that they were legally married at last. Sue, who had previously been called Mrs Bridehead, now openly adopted the name of Mrs Fawley. Her dull, cowed, and listless manner for days seemed to substantiate all this.

But the mistake (as it was called) of their going away so secretly to do the business, kept up much of the mystery of their lives; and they found that they made not such advances with their neighbours as they had expected to do thereby. A living mystery was not much less interesting than a dead scandal.

The baker's lad and the grocer's boy, who at first had used to lift their hats gallantly to Sue when they came to execute their errands, in these days no longer took the trouble to render her that homage, and the neighbouring artizans' wives looked straight along the pavement when they encountered her.

Nobody molested them, it is true; but an oppressive atmosphere began to encircle their souls, particularly after their excursion to the Show, as if that visit had brought some evil influence to bear on them. And their temperaments were precisely of a kind to suffer from this atmosphere, and to be indisposed to lighten it by vigorous and open statements. Their apparent attempt at reparation had come too late to be effective.

The headstone and epitaph orders fell off: and two or three months later, when autumn came, Jude perceived that he would have to return to journey-work again, a course all the more unfortunate just now, in that he had not as yet cleared off the debt he had unavoidably incurred in the payment of the law-costs of the previous year.

One evening he sat down to share the common meal with Sue and the child as usual. 'I am thinking,' he said to her, 'that I'll hold on here no longer. The life suits us, certainly; but if we could get away to a place where we are unknown, we should be lighter hearted, and have a better chance. And so I am afraid we must break it up here, however awkward for you, poor dear!'

Sue was always much affected at a picture of herself as an object of pity, and she saddened.

'Well—I am not sorry,' said she presently. 'I am much depressed by the way they look at me here. And you have been keeping on this house and furniture entirely for me and the boy! You don't want it yourself, and the expense is unnecessary. But whatever we do, wherever we go, you won't take him away from me, Jude dear? I could not let him go now! The cloud upon his young mind makes him so pathetic to me; I do hope to lift it some day! And he loves me so. You won't take him away from me?'

'Certainly I won't, dear little girl! We'll get nice lodgings, wherever we go. I shall be moving about probably—getting a job here and a job there.'

'I shall do something too, of course, till—till—Well, now I can't be useful in the lettering it behoves me to turn my hand to something else.'

'Don't hurry about getting employment,' he said regretfully. 'I don't want you to do that. I wish you wouldn't, Sue. The boy and yourself are enough for you to attend to.'

There was a knock at the door, and Jude answered it. Sue could hear the conversation:

'Is Mr Fawley at home? . . . Biles and Willis the building contractors sent me to know if you'll undertake the relettering of the Ten Commandments in a little church they've been restoring lately in the country near here.'

Jude reflected, and said he could undertake it.

'It is not a very artistic job,' continued the messenger. 'The clergyman is a very old-fashioned chap, and he has refused to let anything more be done to the church than cleaning and repairing.'

'Excellent old man!' said Sue to herself, who was sentimentally opposed to the horrors of over-restoration.

'The Ten Commandments are fixed to the east end,' the messenger went on, 'and they want doing up with the rest of the wall there, since he won't have them carted off as old materials belonging to the contractor, in the usual way of the trade.'

A bargain as to terms was struck, and Jude came indoors. 'There, you see,' he said cheerfully. 'One more job yet, at any rate, and you can help in it—at least you can try. We shall have all the church to ourselves, as the rest of the work is finished.'

Next day Jude went out to the church, which was only two miles off. He found that what the contractor's clerk had said was true. The tables of the Jewish law towered sternly over the utensils of Christian grace, as the chief ornament of the chancel end, in the fine dry style of the last century. And as their framework was constructed of ornamental plaster they could not be taken down for repair. A portion, crumbled by damp, required renewal; and when this had been done, and the whole cleansed, he began to renew the lettering. On the second morning Sue came to see what assistance she could render, and also because they liked to be together.

The silence and emptiness of the building gave her confidence, and, standing on a safe low platform erected by Jude, which she was nevertheless timid at mounting, she began painting in the letters of the first Table while he set about mending a portion of the second. She was quite pleased at her powers; she had acquired them in the days she painted illumined texts for the church-fitting shop at Christminster. Nobody seemed likely to disturb them; and the pleasant twitter of birds, and rustle of October leafage, came in through an open window, and mingled with their talk.

They were not, however, to be left thus snug and peaceful for long. About half-past twelve there came footsteps on the gravel without. The old vicar and his churchwarden entered, and, coming up to see what was being done, seemed surprised to discover that a young woman was assisting. They passed on into an aisle, at which time the door again opened, and another figure entered—a small one, that of little Time, who was crying. Sue had told him where he might find her between schoolhours, if he wished. She came down from her perch, and said, 'What's the matter, my dear?'

'I couldn't stay to eat my dinner in school, because they said—' He described how some boys had taunted him about his nominal mother, and Sue, grieved, expressed her indignation to Jude aloft. The child went into the churchyard, and Sue returned to her work. Meanwhile the door had opened again, and there shuffled in with a business-like air the white-aproned woman who cleaned the church. Sue recognized her as one who had friends in Spring Street, whom she visited. The church-cleaner looked at Sue, gaped, and lifted her hands; she had evidently recognized Jude's companion as the latter had recognized her. Next came two ladies, and after talking to the charwoman they also moved forward, and as Sue stood reaching upward, watched her hand tracing the letters, and critically regarded her person in relief against the white wall, till she grew so nervous that she trembled visibly.

They went back to where the others were standing, talking in undertones: and one said—Sue could not hear which—'She's his wife, I suppose?'

'Some say Yes: some say No,' was the reply from the charwoman.

'Not? Then she ought to be, or somebody's—that's very clear!'

'They've only been married a very few weeks, whether or no.'

'A strange pair to be painting the Two Tables! I wonder Biles and Willis could think of such a thing as hiring those!'

The churchwarden supposed that Biles and Willis knew of nothing wrong, and then the other, who had been talking to the old woman, explained what she meant by calling them strange people.

The probable drift of the subdued conversation which followed was made plain by the churchwarden breaking into an anecdote, in a voice that everybody in the church could hear, though obviously suggested by the present situation:

'Well, now, it is a curious thing, but my grandfather told me a strange tale of a most immoral case that happened at the painting of the Commandments in a church out by Gaymead—which is quite within a walk of this one. In them days Commandments were mostly done in gilt letters on a black ground, and that's how they were out where I say, before the owld church was rebuilded. It must have been somewhere about a hundred years ago that them Commandments wanted doing up, just as ours do here, and they had to get men from Aldbrickham to do 'em. Now they wished to get the job finished by a particular Sunday, so the men had to work late Saturday night, against their will, for over-time was not paid then as 'tis now. There was no true religion in the country at that date, neither among pa'sons, clerks, nor people, and to keep the men up to their work the vicar had to let 'em have plenty of drink during the afternoon. As the evening drawed on they sent for some more themselves; rum, by all account. It got later and later, and they got more and more fuddled, till at last they went a putting their rum-bottle and rummers upon the Communion table, and drawed up a trestle or two, and sate round comfortable, and poured out again right hearty bumpers. No sooner had they tossed off their glasses than, so the story goes, they fell down senseless, one and all. How long they bode so they didn't know, but when they came to themselves there was a terrible thunderstorm a-raging, and they seemed to see in the gloom a dark figure with very thin legs and a curious voot, a-standing on the ladder, and finishing their work. When it got daylight they could see that the work was really finished, and couldn't at all mind finishing it themselves. They went home, and the next thing they heard was that a great scandal had been caused in the church that Sunday morning, for when the people came and service began, all saw that the Ten Commandments wez painted with the "Nots" left out. Decent people wouldn't attend service there for a long time, and the Bishop had to be sent for to re-consecrate the church. That's the tradition as I used to hear it as a child. You must take it for what it is wo'th, but this case to-day has reminded me o't, as I say.'

The visitors gave one more glance, as if to see whether Jude and Sue had left the Nots out likewise, and then severally left the church, even the old woman at last. Sue and Jude, who had not stopped working, sent back the child to school, and remained without speaking; till, looking at her narrowly, he found she had been crying silently.

'Never mind, comrade!' he said. 'I know what it is!'

'I can't *bear* that they, and everybody, should think people wicked because they may have chosen to live their own way! It is really these opinions that make the best intentioned people reckless, and actually become immoral!'

'Never be cast down! It was only a funny story.'

'Ah, but we suggested it! I am afraid I have done you mischief, Jude, instead of helping you by coming!'

To have suggested such a story was certainly not very exhilarating, in a serious view of their position. However, in a few minutes Sue seemed to see that their position this morning had a ludicrous side, and wiping her eyes she laughed.

'It is droll, after all,' she said, 'that we two, of all people, with our queer history, should happen to be here painting the Ten Commandments! You a reprobate, and I—in my condition. . . . O dear!' . . . And with her hand over her eyes she laughed again silently and intermittently, till she was quite weak.

'That's better,' said Jude gaily. 'Now we are right again, aren't we, little girl!'

'O but it is serious, all the same!' she sighed as she took up the brush and righted herself. 'But do you see they don't think we are married? They *won't* believe it! It is extraordinary!'

'I don't care whether they think so or not,' said Jude. 'I shan't take any more trouble to make them.'

They sat down to lunch—which they had brought with them not to hinder time—and having eaten it were about to set to work anew when a man entered the church and Jude recognized in him the contractor Willis. He beckoned to Jude, and spoke to him apart.

'Here—I've just had a complaint about this,' he said, with rather breathless awkwardness. 'I don't wish to go into the matter—as of course I didn't know what was going on—but I am afraid I must ask you and her to leave off, and let somebody else finish this! It is best, to avoid all unpleasantness. I'll pay you for the week, all the same.'

Jude was too independent to make any fuss; and the contractor paid him, and left. Jude picked up his tools, and Sue cleansed her brush. Then their eyes met.

'How could we be so simple as to suppose we might do this!' said she, dropping to her tragic note. 'Of course we ought not—I ought not—to have come!'

'I had no idea that anybody was going to intrude into such a lonely place and see us!' Jude returned. 'Well, it can't be helped, dear; and of course I wouldn't wish to injure Willis's trade-connection by staying.' They sat down passively for a few minutes, proceeded out of the church, and overtaking the boy pursued their thoughtful way to Aldbrickham.

Fawley had still a pretty zeal in the cause of education, and, as was natural with his experiences, he was active in furthering 'equality of opportunity' by any humble means open to him. He had joined an Artizans' Mutual Improvement Society established in the town about the time of his arrival there; its members being young men of all creeds and denominations, including Churchmen, Congregationalists, Baptists, Unitarians, Positivists, and others—Agnostics had scarcely been heard of at this time—their one common wish to enlarge their minds forming a sufficiently close bond of union. The subscription was small, and the room homely; and Jude's activity, uncustomary acquirements, and above all, singular intuition on what to read and how to set about it—begotten of his years of struggle against malignant stars—had led to his being placed on the committee.

A few evenings after his dismissal from the church repairs, and before he had obtained any more work to do, he went to attend a meeting of the aforesaid committee. It was late when he arrived: all the others had come, and as he entered they looked dubiously at him, and hardly uttered a word of greeting. He guessed that something bearing on himself had been either discussed or mooted. Some ordinary business was transacted, and it was disclosed that the number of subscriptions had shown a sudden falling off for that quarter. One member—a really well-meaning and upright man—began speaking in enigmas about certain possible causes: that it behoved them to look well into their constitution; for if the committee were not respected, and had not at least, in their differences, a common standard of *conduct*, they would bring the institution to the ground. Nothing further was said in Jude's presence, but he knew what this meant; and turning to the table wrote a note resigning his office there and then.

Thus the supersensitive couple were more and more impelled to go away. And then bills were sent in, and the question arose, what could Jude do with his great-aunt's heavy old furniture, if he left the town to travel he knew not whither? This, and the necessity of ready money, compelled him to decide on an auction, much as he would have preferred to keep the venerable goods.

The day of the sale came on; and Sue for the last time cooked her own, the child's, and Jude's breakfast in the little house he had furnished. It chanced to be a wet day; moreover Sue was unwell, and not wishing to desert her poor Jude in such gloomy circumstances, for he was compelled to stay awhile, she acted on the suggestion of the auctioneer's man, and ensconced herself in an upper room, which could be emptied of its effects, and so kept closed to the bidders. Here Jude discovered her; and with the child, and their few trunks, baskets, and bundles, and two chairs and a table that were not in the sale, the two sat in meditative talk.

Footsteps began stamping up and down the bare stairs, the comers inspecting the goods, some of which were of so quaint and ancient a make as to acquire an adventitious value as art. Their door was tried once or twice, and to guard themselves against intrusion Jude wrote 'Private' on a scrap of paper, and stuck in upon the panel.

They soon found that, instead of the furniture, their own personal histories and past conduct began to be discussed to an unexpected and intolerable extent by the intending bidders. It was not till now that they really discovered what a fools' paradise of supposed unrecognition they had been living in of late. Sue silently took her companion's hand, and with eyes on each other they heard these passing remarks—the quaint and mysterious personality of Father Time being a subject which formed a large ingredient in the hints and innuendoes. At length the auction began in the room below, whence they could hear each familiar article knocked down, the highly prized ones cheaply, the unconsidered at an unexpected price.

'People don't understand us,' he sighed heavily. 'I am glad we have decided to go.'

'The question is, where to?'

'It ought to be to London. There one can live as one chooses.'

'No—not London, dear! I know it well. We should be unhappy there.'

'Why?'

'Can't you think?'

'Because Arabella is there?'

'That's the chief reason.'

'But in the country I shall always be uneasy lest there should be some more of our late experience. And I don't care to lessen it by explaining, for one thing, all about the boy's history. To cut him off from his past I have determined to keep silence. I am sickened of ecclesiastical work now; and I shouldn't like to accept it, if offered me!'

'You ought to have learnt Classic. Gothic is barbaric art, after all. Pugin was wrong, and Wren was right. Remember the interior of Christminster Cathedral—almost the first place in which we looked in each other's faces. Under the picturesqueness of those Norman details one can see the grotesque childishness of uncouth people trying to imitate the vanished Roman forms, remembered by dim tradition only.'

'Yes—you have half converted me to that view by what you have said before. But one can work, and despise what one does. I must do something, if not church-gothic.'

'I wish we could both follow an occupation in which personal circumstances don't count,' she said, smiling up wistfully. 'I am as disqualified for teaching as you are for ecclesiastical art. You must fall back upon railway stations, bridges, theatres, music-halls, hotels—everything that has no connection with conduct.'

'I am not skilled in those. . . . I ought to take to breadbaking. I grew up in the baking business with aunt, you know. But even a baker must be conventional, to get customers.'

'Unless he keeps a cake and gingerbread stall at markets and fairs, where people are gloriously indifferent to everything except the quality of the goods.'

Their thoughts were diverted by the voice of the auctioneer:

'Now this antique oak settle—a unique example of old English furniture, worthy the attention of all collectors!'

'That was my great-grandfather's,' said Jude. 'I wish we could have kept the poor old thing!'

One by one the articles went, and the afternoon passed away. Jude and the other two were getting tired and hungry, but after the conversation they had heard they were shy of going out while the purchasers were in their line of retreat. However, the later lots drew on, and it became necessary to emerge into the rain soon, to take on Sue's things to their temporary lodging.

'Now the next lot: two pairs of pigeons, all alive and plump—a nice pie for somebody for next Sunday's dinner!'

The impending sale of these birds had been the most trying suspense of the whole afternoon. They were Sue's pets, and when it was found that they could not possibly be kept, more sadness was caused than by parting from all the furniture. Sue tried to think away her tears as she heard the trifling sum that her dears were deemed to be worth advanced by small stages to the price at which they were finally knocked down. The purchaser was a neighbouring poulterer, and they were unquestionably doomed to die before the next market day.

Noting her dissembled distress Jude kissed her, and said it was time to go and see if the lodgings were ready. He would go on with the boy, and fetch her soon.

When she was left alone she waited patiently, but Jude did not come back. At last she started, the coast being clear, and on passing the poulterer's shop, not far off, she saw her pigeons in a hamper by the door. An emotion at sight of them, assisted by the growing dusk of evening, caused her to act on impulse, and first looking around her quickly, she pulled out the peg which fastened down the cover, and went on. The cover was lifted within, and the pigeons flew away with a clatter that brought the chagrined poulterer cursing and swearing to the door.

Sue reached the lodging trembling, and found Jude and the boy making it comfortable for her. 'Do the buyers pay before they bring away the things?' she asked breathlessly.

'Yes, I think. Why?'

'Because, then, I've done such a wicked thing!' And she explained, in bitter contrition.

'I shall have to pay the poulterer for them, if he doesn't catch them,' said Jude. 'But never mind. Don't fret about it, dear.'

'It was so foolish of me! O why should Nature's law be mutual butchery!'

'Is it so, mother?' asked the boy intently.

'Yes!' said Sue vehemently.

'Well, they must take their chance, now, poor things,' said Jude. 'As soon as the sale-account is wound up, and our bills paid, we go.'

'Where do we go to?' asked Time, in suspense.

'We must sail under sealed orders, that nobody may trace us. . . . We mustn't go to Alfredston, or to Melchester, or to Shaston, or to Christminster. Apart from those we may go anywhere.'

'Why mustn't we go there, father?'

'Because of a cloud that has gathered over us; though "we have wronged no man, corrupted no man, defrauded no man"! Though perhaps we have "done that which was right in our own eyes".'

VII

From that week Jude Fawley and Sue walked no more in the town of Aldbrickham.

Whither they had gone nobody knew, chiefly because nobody cared to know. Any one sufficiently curious to trace the steps of such an obscure pair might have discovered without great trouble that they had taken advantage of his adaptive craftsmanship to enter on a shifting, almost nomadic, life, which was not without its pleasantness for a time.

Wherever Jude heard of freestone work to be done, thither he went, choosing by preference places remote from his old haunts and Sue's. He laboured at a job, long or briefly, till it was finished; and then moved on.

Two whole years and a half passed thus. Sometimes he might have been found shaping the mullions of a country mansion, sometimes setting the parapet of a town-hall, sometimes ashlaring an hotel at Sandbourne, sometimes a museum at Casterbridge, sometimes as far down as Exonbury, sometimes at Stoke-Barehills. Later still he was at Kennetbridge, a thriving town not more than a dozen miles south of Marygreen, this being his nearest approach to the village where he was known; for he had a sensitive dread of being questioned as to his life and fortunes by those who had been acquainted with him during his ardent young manhood of study and promise, and his brief and unhappy married life at that time.

At some of these places he would be detained for months, at others only a few weeks. His curious and sudden antipathy to ecclesiastical work, both episcopal and nonconformist, which had risen in him when suffering under a smarting sense of misconception, remained with him in cold blood, less from any fear of renewed censure than from an ultra-conscientiousness which would not allow him to seek a living out of those who would disapprove of his ways; also, too, from a sense of inconsistency between his former dogmas and his present practice, hardly a shred of the beliefs with which he had first gone up to Christminster now remaining with him. He was mentally approaching the position which Sue had occupied when he first met her.

On a Saturday evening in May, nearly three years after Arabella's recognition of Sue and himself at the Agricultural Show, some of those who there encountered each other met again.

It was the spring fair at Kennetbridge, and, though this ancient trade-meeting had much dwindled from its dimensions of former times, the long straight street of the borough presented a lively scene about midday. At this hour a light trap, among other vehicles, was driven into the town by the north road, and up to the door of a temperance inn. There alighted two women, one the driver, an ordinary country person, the other a finely built figure in the deep mourning of a widow. Her sombre suit, of pronounced cut, caused her to appear a little out of place in the medley and bustle of a provincial fair.

'I will just find out where it is, Anny,' said the widow-lady to her companion, when the horse and cart had been taken by a man who came forward: 'and then I'll come back, and meet you here; and we'll go in and have something to eat and drink. I begin to feel quite a sinking.'

'With all my heart,' said the other. 'Though I would sooner have put up at the Chequers or The Jack. You can't get much at these temperance houses.'

'Now, don't you give way to gluttonous desires, my child,' said the woman in weeds reprovingly. 'This is the proper place. Very well: we'll meet in half-an-hour, unless you come with me to find out where the site of the new chapel is?'

'I don't care to. You can tell me.'

The companions then went their several ways, the one in crape walking firmly along with a mien of disconnection from her miscellaneous surroundings. Making inquiries she came to a hoarding, within which were excavations denoting the foundations of a building; and on the boards without one or two large posters announcing that the foundation-stone of the chapel about to be erected would be laid that afternoon at three o'clock by a London preacher of great popularity among his body.

Having ascertained thus much the immensely weeded widow retraced her steps, and gave herself leisure to observe the movements of the fair. By and by her attention was arrested by a little stall of cakes and gingerbreads, standing between the more pretentious erections of trestles and canvas. It was covered with an immaculate cloth, and tended by a young woman apparently unused to the business, she being accompanied by a boy with an octogenarian face, who assisted her.

'Upon my—senses!' murmured the widow to herself. 'His wife Sue—if she is so!' She drew nearer to the stall. 'How do you do, Mrs Fawley?' she said blandly.

Sue changed colour and recognized Arabella through the crape veil.

'How are you, Mrs Cartlett?' she said stiffly. And then perceiving Arabella's garb her voice grew sympathetic in spite of herself. 'What?—you have lost—'

'My poor husband. Yes. He died suddenly, six weeks ago, leaving me none too well off, though he was a kind husband to me. But whatever profit there is in public-house keeping goes to them that brew the liquors, and not to them that retail 'em. . . . And you, my little old man! You don't know me, I expect?'

'Yes, I do. You be the woman I thought wer my mother for a bit, till I found you wasn't,' replied Father Time, who had learned to use the Wessex tongue quite naturally by now.

'All right. Never mind. I am a friend.'

'Juey,' said Sue suddenly, 'go down to the station platform with this tray—there's another train coming in, I think.'

When he was gone Arabella continued: 'He'll never be a beauty, will he, poor chap! Does he know I am his mother really?'

'No. He thinks there is some mystery about his parentage—that's all. Jude is going to tell him when he is a little older.'

'But how do you come to be doing this? I am surprised.'

'It is only a temporary occupation—a fancy of ours while we are in a difficulty.'

'Then you are living with him still?'

'Yes.'

'Married?'

'Of course.'

'Any children?'

'Two.'

'And another coming soon, I see.'

Sue writhed under the hard and direct questioning, and her tender little mouth began to quiver.

'Lord—I mean goodness gracious—what is there to cry about? Some folks would be proud enough!'

'It is not that I am ashamed—not as you think! But it seems such a terribly tragic thing to bring beings into the world—so presumptuous—that I question my right to do it sometimes!'

'Take it easy, my dear. . . . But you don't tell me why you do such a thing as this? Jude used to be a proud sort of chap—above any business almost, leave alone keeping a standing.'

'Perhaps my husband has altered a little since then. I am sure he is not proud now!' And Sue's lips quivered again. 'I am doing this because he caught a chill early in the year while putting up some stone-work of a music-hall, at Quartershot, which he had to do in the rain, the work having to be executed by a fixed day. He is better than he was; but it has been a long, weary time! We had an old widow friend with us to help us through it; but she's leaving soon.'

'Well, I am respectable too, thank God, and of a serious way of thinking since my loss. Why did you choose to sell gingerbreads?'

'That's a pure accident. He was brought up to the baking business, and it occurred to him to try his hand at these, which he can make without coming out of doors. We call them Christminster cakes. They are a great success.'

'I never saw any like 'em. Why, they are windows and towers, and pinnacles! And upon my word they are very nice.' She had helped herself, and was unceremoniously munching one of the cakes.

'Yes. They are reminiscences of the Christminster Colleges. Traceried windows, and cloisters, you see. It was a whim of his to do them in pastry.'

'Still harping on Christminster—even in his cakes!' laughed Arabella. 'Just like Jude. A ruling passion. What a queer fellow he is, and always will be!'

Sue sighed, and she looked her distress at hearing him criticized.

'Don't you think he is? Come now; you do, though you are so fond of him!'

'Of course Christminster is a sort of fixed vision with him, which I suppose he'll never be cured of believing in. He still thinks it a great centre of high and fearless thought, instead of what it is, a nest of commonplace schoolmasters whose characteristic is timid obsequiousness to tradition.'

Arabella was quizzing Sue with more regard of how she was speaking than of what she was saying. 'How odd to hear a woman selling cakes talk like that!' she said. 'Why don't you go back to school-keeping?'

Sue shook her head. 'They won't have me.'

'Because of the divorce, I suppose?'

'That and other things. And there is no reason to wish it. We gave up all ambition, and were never so happy in our lives till his illness came.'

'Where are you living?'

'I don't care to say.'

'Here in Kennetbridge?'

Sue's manner showed Arabella that her random guess was right.

'Here comes the boy back again,' continued Arabella. 'My boy and Jude's!'

Sue's eyes darted a spark. 'You needn't throw that in my face!' she cried.

'Very well—though I half feel as if I should like to have him with me! . . . But Lord, I don't want to take him from 'ee—ever I should sin to speak so profane—though I should think you must have enough of your own! He's in very good hands, that I know; and I am not the woman to find fault with what the Lord has ordained. I've reached a more resigned frame of mind.'

'Indeed! I wish I had been able to do so.'

'You should try,' replied the widow, from the serene heights of a soul conscious not only of spiritual but of social superiority. 'I make no boast of my awakening, but I'm not what I was. After

Cartlett's death I was passing the chapel in the street next ours, and went into it for shelter from a shower of rain. I felt a need of some sort of support under my loss, and, as 'twas righter than gin, I took to going there regular, and found it a great comfort. But I've left London now, you know, and at present I am living at Alfredston, with my friend Anny, to be near my own old country. I'm not come here to the fair to-day. There's to be the foundation-stone of a new chapel laid this afternoon by a popular London preacher, and I drove over with Anny. Now I must go back to meet her.'

Then Arabella wished Sue good-bye, and went on.

VIII

In the afternoon Sue and the other people bustling about Kennetbridge fair could hear singing inside the placarded hoarding further down the street. Those who peeped through the opening saw a crowd of persons in broadcloth, with hymn-books in their hands, standing round the excavations for the new chapel-walls. Arabella Cartlett and her weeds stood among them. She had a clear, powerful voice, which could be distinctly heard with the rest, rising and falling to the tune, her inflated bosom being also seen doing likewise.

It was two hours later on the same day that Anny and Mrs Cartlett, having had tea at the Temperance hotel, started on their return journey across the high and open country which stretches between Kennetbridge and Alfredston. Arabella was in a thoughtful mood; but her thoughts were not of the new chapel, as Anny at first surmised.

'No—it is something else,' at last said Arabella sullenly. 'I came here to-day never thinking of anybody but poor Cartlett, or of anything but spreading the Gospel by means of this new tabernacle they've begun this afternoon. But something has happened to turn my mind another way quite. Anny, I've heard of un again, and I've seen *her*!'

'Who?'

'I've heard of Jude, and I've seen his wife. And ever since, do what I will, and though I sung the hymns wi' all my strength, I have not been able to help thinking about 'n; which I've no right to do as a chapel member.'

'Can't ye fix your mind upon what was said by the London preacher to-day, and try to get rid of your wandering fancies that way?'

'I do. But my wicked heart will ramble off in spite of myself!'

'Well—I know what it is to have a wanton mind o' my own, too! If you on'y knew what I do dream sometimes o' nights quite against my wishes, you'd say I had my struggles!' (Anny, too, had grown rather serious of late, her lover having jilted her.)

'What shall I do about it?' urged Arabella morbidly.

'You could take a lock of your late-lost husband's hair, and have it made into a mourning brooch, and look at it every hour of the day.'

'I haven't a morsel!—and if I had 'twould be no good. . . . After all that's said about the comforts of this religion, I wish I had Jude back again!'

'You must fight valiant against the feeling, since he's another's. And I've heard that another good thing for it, when it afflicts volupshious widows, is to go to your husband's grave in the dusk of evening, and stand a long while a-bowed down.'

'Pooh! I know as well as you what I should do; only I don't do it!'

They drove in silence along the straight road till they were within the horizon of Marygreen, which lay not far to the left of their route. They came to the junction of the highway and the cross-lane leading to that village, whose church-tower could be seen athwart the hollow. When they got yet further on, and were passing the lonely house in which Arabella and Jude had lived during the first months of their marriage, and where the pig-killing had taken place, she could control herself no longer.

'He's more mine than hers!' she burst out. 'What right has she to him, I should like to know! I'd take him from her if I could!'

'Fie, Abby! And your husband only six weeks gone! Pray against it!'

'Be damned if I do! Feelings are feelings! I won't be a creeping hypocrite any longer—so there!'

Arabella had hastily drawn from her pocket a bundle of tracts which she had brought with her to distribute at the fair, and of which she had given away several. As she spoke she flung the whole remainder of the packet into the hedge. 'I've tried that sort o' physic and have failed wi' it. I must be as I was born!'

'Hush! You be excited, dear! Now you come along home quiet,

and have a cup of tea, and don't let us talk about un no more. We won't come out this road again, as it leads to where he is, because it inflames 'ee so. You'll be all right again soon.'

Arabella did calm herself down by degrees; and they crossed the Ridge-way. When they began to descend the long, straight hill, they saw plodding along in front of them an elderly man of spare stature and thoughtful gait. In his hand he carried a basket; and there was a touch of slovenliness in his attire, together with that indefinable something in his whole appearance which suggested one who was his own housekeeper, purveyor, confidant, and friend, through possessing nobody else at all in the world to act in those capacities for him. The remainder of the journey was down-hill, and guessing him to be going to Alfredston they offered him a lift, which he accepted.

Arabella looked at him, and looked again, till at length she spoke. 'If I don't mistake I am talking to Mr Phillotson?'

The wayfarer faced round and regarded her in turn. 'Yes; my name is Phillotson,' he said. 'But I don't recognize you, ma'am.'

'I remember you well enough when you used to be schoolmaster out at Marygreen, and I one of your scholars. I used to walk up there from Cresscombe every day, because we had only a mistress down at our place, and you taught better. But you wouldn't remember me as I should you?—Arabella Donn.'

He shook his head. 'No,' he said politely, 'I don't recall the name. And I should hardly recognize in your present portly self the slim school child no doubt you were then.'

'Well, I always had plenty of flesh on my bones. However, I am staying down here with some friends at present. You know, I suppose, who I married?'

'No.'

'Jude Fawley—also a scholar of yours—at least a night scholar—for some little time I think? And known to you afterwards, if I am not mistaken.'

'Dear me, dear me,' said Phillotson, starting out of his stiffness. '*You* Fawley's wife? To be sure—he had a wife! And he—I understood—'

'Divorced her—as you did yours—perhaps for better reasons.'

'Indeed?'

'Well—he med have been right in doing it—right for both; for I soon married again, and all went pretty straight till my husband died lately. But you—you were decidedly wrong!'

'No,' said Phillotson, with sudden testiness. 'I would rather not talk of this, but—I am convinced I did only what was right, and just, and moral. I have suffered for my act and opinions, but I hold to them; though her loss was a loss to me in more ways than one!'

'You lost your school and good income through her, did you not?'

'I don't care to talk of it. I have recently come back here—to Marygreen, I mean.'

'You are keeping the school there again, just as formerly?'

The pressure of a sadness that would out unsealed him. 'I am there,' he replied. 'Just as formerly, no. Merely on sufferance. It was a last resource—a small thing to return to after my move upwards, and my long indulged hopes—a returning to zero, with all its humiliations. But it is a refuge. I like the seclusion of the place, and the vicar having known me before my so-called eccentric conduct towards my wife had ruined my reputation as a schoolmaster, he accepted my services when all other schools were closed against me. However, although I take fifty pounds a year here after taking above two hundred elsewhere, I prefer it to running the risk of having my old domestic experiences raked up against me, as I should do if I tried to make a move.'

'Right you are. A contented mind is a continual feast. She has done no better.'

'She is not doing well, you mean?'

'I met her by accident at Kennetbridge this very day, and she is anything but thriving. Her husband is ill, and she anxious. You made a fool of a mistake about her, I tell 'ee again, and the harm you did yourself by dirting your own nest serves you right, excusing the liberty.'

'How?'

'She was innocent.'

'But nonsense! They did not even defend the case!'

'That was because they didn't care to. She was quite innocent of what obtained you your freedom, at the time you obtained it. I saw her just afterwards, and proved it to myself completely by talking to her.'

Phillotson grasped the edge of the spring-cart, and appeared to be much stressed and worried by the information. 'Still—she wanted to go,' he said.

'Yes. But you shouldn't have let her. That's the only way with these fanciful women that chaw high—innocent or guilty. She'd have come round in time. We all do! Custom does it! it's all the same in the end! However, I think she's fond of her man still—whatever he med be of her. You were too quick about her. *I* shouldn't have let her go! I should have kept her chained on—her spirit for kicking would have been broke soon enough! There's nothing like bondage and a stone-deaf taskmaster for taming us women. Besides, you've got the laws on your side. Moses knew. Don't you call to mind what he says?'

'Not for the moment, ma'am, I regret to say.'

'Call yourself a schoolmaster! I used to think o't when they read it in church, and I was carrying on a bit. "Then shall the man be guiltless; but the woman shall bear her iniquity." Damn rough on us women; but we must grin and put up wi' it!—Haw haw!—Well; she's got her deserts now.'

'Yes,' said Phillotson, with biting sadness. 'Cruelty is the law pervading all nature and society; and we can't get out of it if we would!'

'Well—don't you forget to try it next time, old man.'

'I cannot answer you, madam. I have never known much of womankind.'

They had now reached the low levels bordering Alfredston, and passing through the outskirts approached a mill, to which Phillotson said his errand led him; whereupon they drew up, and he alighted, bidding them good-night in a preoccupied mood.

In the meantime Sue, though remarkably successful in her cake-selling experiment at Kennetbridge fair, had lost the temporary brightness which had begun to sit upon her sadness on account of that success. When all her 'Christminster' cakes had been disposed of she took upon her arm the empty basket, and the cloth which had covered the standing she had hired, and giving the other things to the boy left the street with him. They followed a lane to a distance of half a mile, till they met an old woman carrying a child in short clothes, and leading a toddler in the other hand.

Sue kissed the children, and said, 'How is he now?'

'Still better!' returned Mrs Edlin cheerfully. 'Before you are upstairs again your husband will be well enough—don't 'ee trouble.'

They turned, and came to some old, dun-tiled cottages with gardens and fruit-trees. Into one of these they entered by lifting the latch without knocking, and were at once in the general living-room. Here they greeted Jude, who was sitting in an armchair, the increased delicacy of his normally delicate features, and the childishly expectant look in his eyes, being alone sufficient to show that he had been passing through a severe illness.

'What—you have sold them all?' he said, a gleam of interest lighting up his face.

'Yes. Arcades, gables, east windows and all.' She told him the pecuniary results, and then hesitated. At last, when they were left alone, she informed him of the unexpected meeting with Arabella, and the latter's widowhood.

Jude was discomposed. 'What—is she living here?' he said.

'No; at Alfredston,' said Sue.

Jude's countenance remained clouded. 'I thought I had better tell you?' she continued, kissing him anxiously.

'Yes. . . . Dear me! Arabella not in the depths of London, but down here! It is only a little over a dozen miles across the country to Alfredston. What is she doing there?'

She told him all she knew. 'She has taken to chapel-going,' Sue added; 'and talks accordingly.'

'Well,' said Jude, 'perhaps it is for the best that we have almost decided to move on. I feel much better to-day, and shall be well enough to leave in a week or two. Then Mrs Edlin can go home again—dear faithful old soul—the only friend we have in the world!'

'Where do you think to go to?' Sue asked, a troublousness in her tones.

Then Jude confessed what was in his mind. He said it would

surprise her, perhaps, after his having resolutely avoided all the old places for so long. But one thing and another had made him think a great deal of Christminster lately, and, if she didn't mind, he would like to go back there. Why should they care if they were known? It was over-sensitive of them to mind so much. They could go on selling cakes there, if he couldn't work. He had no sense of shame at mere poverty; and perhaps he would be as strong as ever soon, and able to set up stone-cutting for himself there.

'Why should you care so much for Christminster?' she said pensively. 'Christminster cares nothing for you, poor dear!'

'Well, I do, and I can't help it. I love the place—although I know how it hates all men like me—the so-called Self-taught,—how it scorns our laboured acquisitions, when it should be the first to respect them; how it sneers at our false quantities and mispronunciations, when it should say, I see you want help, my poor friend! . . . Nevertheless, it is the centre of the universe to me, because of my early dream: and nothing can alter it. Perhaps it will soon wake up, and be generous. I pray so! . . . I should like to go back to live there—perhaps to die there! In two or three weeks I might, I think. It will then be June, and I should like to be there by a particular day.'

His hope that he was recovering proved so far well grounded that in three weeks they had arrived in the city of many memories; were actually treading its pavements, receiving the reflection of the sunshine from its wasting walls.

PART SIXTH

AT CHRISTMINSTER AGAIN

. . . And she humbled her body greatly, and all the places of her joy she filled with her torn hair.'

—ESTHER (*Apoc.*)

'There are two who decline, a woman and I,
And enjoy our death in the darkness here.'

—R. BROWNING

I

On their arrival the station was lively with straw-hatted young men, welcoming young girls who bore a remarkable family likeness to their welcomers, and who were dressed up in the brightest and lightest of raiment.

'The place seems gay,' said Sue. 'Why—it is Remembrance Day!—Jude—how sly of you—you come to-day on purpose!'

'Yes,' said Jude quietly, as he took charge of the small child, and told Arabella's boy to keep close to them, Sue attending to their own eldest. 'I thought we might as well come to-day as on any other.'

'But I am afraid it will depress you!' she said, looking anxiously at him up and down.

'O, I mustn't let it interfere with our business; and we have a good deal to do before we shall be settled here. The first thing is lodgings.'

Having left their luggage and his tools at the station they proceeded on foot up the familiar street, the holiday people all drifting in the same direction. Reaching the Fourways they were about to turn off to where accommodation was likely to be found when, looking at the clock and the hurrying crowd, Jude said: 'Let us go and see the procession, and never mind the lodgings just now? We can get them afterwards.'

'Oughtn't we to get a house over our heads first?' she asked.

But his soul seemed full of the anniversary, and together they went down Chief Street, their smallest child in Jude's arms, Sue leading her little girl, and Arabella's boy walking thoughtfully and silently beside them. Crowds of pretty sisters in airy costumes, and meekly ignorant parents who had known no College in their youth, were under convoy in the same direction by brothers and sons bearing the opinion written large on them, that no properly qualified human beings had lived on earth till they came to grace it here and now.

'My failure is reflected on me by every one of those young fellows,' said Jude. 'A lesson on presumption is awaiting me to-day!—Humiliation Day for me! . . . If you, my dear darling, hadn't come to my rescue, I should have gone to the dogs with despair!'

She saw him from his face that he was getting into one of his tempestuous, self-harrowing moods. 'It would have been better if we had gone at once about our own affairs, dear,' she answered. 'I am sure this sight will awaken old sorrows in you, and do no good!'

'Well—we are near; we will see it now,' said he.

They turned in on the left by the church with the Italian porch, whose helical columns were heavily draped with creepers, and pursued the lane till there arose on Jude's sight the circular theatre with that well-known lantern above it, which stood in his mind as the sad symbol of his abandoned hopes; for it was from that outlook that he had finally surveyed the City of Colleges on the afternoon of his great meditation, which convinced him at last of the futility of his attempt to be a son of the University.

To-day, in the open space stretching between this building and the nearest college, stood a crowd of expectant people. A passage was kept clear through their midst by two barriers of timber, extending from the door of the college to the door of the large building between it and the theatre.'

'Here is the place—they are just going to pass!' cried Jude in sudden excitement. And pushing his way to the front he took up a position close to the barrier, still hugging the youngest child in his arms, while Sue and the others kept immediately behind him. The crowd filled in at their back, and fell to talking, joking, and laughing as carriage after carriage drew up at the lower door of the college, and solemn stately figures in blood-red robes began to alight. The sky had grown overcast and livid, and thunder rumbled now and then.

Father Time shuddered. 'It do seem like Judgment Day!' he whispered.

'They are only learned Doctors,' said Sue.

While they waited big drops of rain fell on their heads and shoulders, and the delay grew tedious. Sue again wished not to stay.

'They won't be long now,' said Jude, without turning his head.

But the procession did not come forth, and somebody in the crowd, to pass the time, looked at the façade of the nearest college, and said he wondered what was meant by the Latin inscription in its midst. Jude, who stood near the inquirer, explained it, and finding that the people all round him were listening with interest, went on to describe the carving of the frieze (which he had studied years before), and to criticize some details of masonry in other college fronts about the city.

The idle crowd, including the two policemen at the doors, stared like the Lycaonians at Paul, for Jude was apt to get too enthusiastic over any subject in hand, and they seemed to wonder how the stranger should know more about the buildings of their town than they themselves did; till one of them said: 'Why, I know that man; he used to work here years ago—Jude Fawley, that's his name! Don't you mind he used to be nicknamed Tutor of St Slums, d'ye mind?—because he aimed at that line o'business? He's married, I suppose, then, and that's his child he's carrying. Taylor would know him, as he knows everybody.'

The speaker was a man named Jack Stagg, with whom Jude had formerly worked in repairing the college masonries; Tinker Taylor was seen to be standing near. Having his attention called the latter cried across the barriers to Jude: 'You've honoured us by coming back again, my friend!'

Jude nodded.

'An' you don't seem to have done any great things for yourself by going away?'

Jude assented to this also.

'Except found more mouths to fill!' This came in a new voice, and Jude recognized its owner to be Uncle Joe, another mason whom he had known.

Jude replied good-humouredly that he could not dispute it; and from remark to remark something like a general conversation arose between him and the crowd of idlers, during which Tinker Taylor asked Jude if he remembered the Apostles' Creed in Latin still, and the night of the challenge in the public-house.

'But Fortune didn't lie that way?' threw in Joe. 'Yer powers wasn't enough to carry 'ee through?'

'Don't answer them any more!' entreated Sue.

'I don't think I like Christminster!' murmured little Time mournfully, as he stood submerged and invisible in the crowd.

But finding himself the centre of curiosity, quizzing, and comment, Jude was not inclined to shrink from open declarations of what he had no great reason to be ashamed of; and in a little while was stimulated to say in a loud voice to the listening throng generally:

'It is a difficult question, my friends, for any young man—that question I had to grapple with, and which thousands are weighing at the present moment in these uprising times—whether to follow uncritically the track he finds himself in, without considering his aptness for it, or to consider what his aptness or bent may be, and re-shape his course accordingly. I tried to do the latter, and I failed. But I don't admit that my failure proved my view to be a wrong one, or that my success would have made it a right one; though that's how we appraise such attempts nowadays—I mean, not by their essential soundness, but by their accidental outcomes. If I had ended by becoming like one of these gentlemen in red and black that we saw dropping in here by now, everybody would have said: "See how wise that young man was, to follow the bent of his nature!" But having ended no better than I began they say: "See what a fool that fellow was in following a freak of his fancy!"

'However it was my poverty and not my will that consented to be beaten. It takes two or three generations to do what I tried to do in one; and my impulses—affections—vices perhaps they should be called—were too strong not to hamper a man without advantages; who should be as cold-blooded as a fish and as selfish as a pig to have a really good chance of being one of his country's worthies. You may ridicule me—I am quite willing that you should—I am a fit subject, no doubt. But I think if you knew what I have gone through these last few years you would rather pity me. And if they knew'—he nodded towards the college at which the Dons were severally arriving—'it is just possible they would do the same.'

'He do look ill and worn-out, it is true!' said a woman.

Sue's face grew more emotional; but though she stood close to Jude she was screened.

'I may do some good before I am dead—be a sort of success as a frightful example of what not to do; and so illustrate a moral story,' continued Jude, beginning to grow bitter, though he had opened serenely enough. 'I was, perhaps, after all, a paltry victim to the spirit of mental and social restlessness, that makes so many unhappy in these days!'

'Don't tell them that!' whispered Sue with tears, at perceiving Jude's state of mind. 'You weren't that. You struggled nobly to acquire knowledge, and only the meanest souls in the world would blame you!'

Jude shifted the child into a more easy position on his arm, and concluded: 'And what I appear, a sick and poor man, is not the worst of me. I am in a chaos of principles—groping in the dark—acting by instinct and not after example. Eight or nine years ago when I came here first, I had a neat stock of fixed opinions, but they dropped away one by one; and the further I get the less sure I am. I doubt if I have anything more for my present rule of life than following inclinations which do me and nobody else any harm, and actually give pleasure to those I love best. There, gentlemen, since you wanted to know how I was getting on, I have told you. Much good may it do you! I cannot explain further here. I perceive there is something wrong somewhere in our social formulas: what it is can only be discovered by men or women with greater insight than mine,—if, indeed, they ever discover it—at least in our time. "For who knoweth what is good for man in this life?—and who can tell a man what shall be after him under the sun?" '

'Hear, hear,' said the populace.

'Well preached!' said Tinker Taylor. And privately to his neighbours: 'Why, one of them jobbing pa'sons swarming about here, that takes the services when our head Reverends want a holiday, wouldn't ha' discoursed such doctrine for less than a guinea down? Hey? I'll take my oath not one o' 'em would! And then he must have had it wrote down for 'n. And this only a working man!'

As a sort of objective commentary on Jude's remarks there drove up at this moment with a belated Doctor, robed and panting, a cab whose horse failed to stop at the exact point required for setting down the hirer, who jumped out and entered the door. The driver, alighting, began to kick the animal in the belly.

'If that can be done,' said Jude, 'at college gates in the most religious and educational city in the world, what shall we say as to how far we've got?'

'Order!' said one of the policemen, who had been engaged with a comrade in opening the large doors opposite the college. 'Keep yer tongue quiet, my man, while the procession passes.' The rain came on more heavily, and all who had umbrellas opened them. Jude was not one of these, and Sue only possessed a small one, half sunshade. She had grown pale, though Jude did not notice it then.

'Let us go on, dear,' she whispered, endeavouring to shelter him. 'We haven't any lodgings yet, remember, and all our things are at the station; and you are by no means well yet. I am afraid this wet will hurt you!'

'They are coming now. Just a moment, and I'll go!' said he.

A peal of six bells struck out, human faces began to crowd the windows around, and the procession of Heads of Houses and new Doctors emerged, their red and black gowned forms passing across the field of Jude's vision like inaccessible planets across an object glass.

As they went their names were called by knowing informants; and when they reached the old round theatre of Wren a cheer rose high.

'Let's go that way!' cried Jude, and though it now rained steadily he seemed not to know it, and took them round to the Theatre. Here they stood upon the straw that was laid to drown the discordant noise of wheels, where the quaint and frost-eaten stone busts encircling the building looked with pallid grimness on the proceedings, and in particular at the bedraggled Jude, Sue, and their children, as at ludicrous persons who had no business there.

'I wish I could get in!' he said to her fervidly. 'Listen—I may catch a few words of the Latin speech by staying here; the windows are open.'

However, beyond the peals of the organ, and the shouts and hurrahs between each piece of oratory, Jude's standing in the wet did not bring much Latin to his intelligence more than, and now and then, a sonorous word in *um* or *ibus*.

'Well—I'm an outsider to the end of my days!' he sighed after a while. 'Now I'll go, my patient Sue. How good of you to wait in the rain all this time—to gratify my infatuation! I'll never care any more about the infernal cursed place, upon my soul I won't! But what made you tremble so when we were at the barrier? And how pale you are, Sue!'

'I saw Richard amongst the people on the other side.'

'Ah—did you!'

'He is evidently come up to Jerusalem to see the festival like the rest of us: and on that account is probably living not so very far away. He had the same hankering for the University that you had, in a milder form. I don't think he saw me, though he must have heard you speaking to the crowd. But he seemed not to notice.'

'Well—suppose he did. Your mind is free from worries about him now, my Sue?'

'Yes, I suppose so. But I am weak. Although I know it is all right with our plans, I felt a curious dread of him; an awe, or terror, of conventions I don't believe in. It comes over me at times like a sort of creeping paralysis, and makes me so sad!'

'You are getting tired, Sue. O—I forgot, darling! Yes, we'll go on at once.'

They started in quest of the lodging, and at last found something that seemed to promise well, in Mildew Lane—a spot which to Jude was irresistible—though to Sue it was not so fascinating—a narrow lane close to the back of a college, but having no communication with it. The little houses were darkened to gloom by the high collegiate buildings, within which life was so far removed from that of the people in the lane as if it had been on opposite sides of the globe; yet only a thickness of wall divided them. Two or three of the houses had notices of rooms to let, and the newcomers knocked at the door of one, which a woman opened.

'Ah—listen!' said Jude suddenly, instead of addressing her.

'What?'

'Why the bells—what church can that be? The tones are familiar.'

Another peal of bells had begun to sound out at some distance off.

'I don't know!' said the landlady tartly. 'Did you knock to ask that?'

'No; for lodgings,' said Jude, coming to himself.

The householder scrutinized Sue's figure a moment. 'We haven't any to let,' said she, shutting the door.

Jude looked discomfited, and the boy distressed. 'Now, Jude,' said Sue, 'let me try. You don't know the way.'

They found a second place hard by; but here the occupier, observing not only Sue, but the boy and the small children, said civilly, 'I am sorry to say we don't let where there are children;' and also closed the door.

The small child squared its mouth and cried silently, with an instinct that trouble loomed. The boy sighed. 'I don't like Christminster!' he said. 'Are the great old houses goals?'

'No; colleges,' said Jude; 'which perhaps you'll study in some day.'

'I'd rather not!' the boy rejoined.

'Now we'll try again,' said Sue. 'I'll pull my cloak more round me. . . . Leaving Kennetbridge for this place is like coming from Caiaphas to Pilate! . . . How do I look now, dear?'

'Nobody would notice it now,' said Jude.

There was one other house, and they tried a third time. The woman here was more amiable; but she had little room to spare, and could only agree to take in Sue and the children if her husband could go elsewhere. This arrangement they perforce adopted, in the stress from delaying their search till so late. They came to terms with her, though her price was rather high for their pockets. But they could not afford to be critical till Jude had time to a get a more permanent abode; and in this house Sue took possession of a back room on the second floor with an inner closet-room for the children. Jude stayed and had a cup of tea; and was pleased to find that the window commanded the back of another of the colleges. Kissing all four he went to get a few necessaries and look for lodgings for himself.

When he was gone the landlady came up to talk a little with Sue, and gather something of the circumstances of the family she had taken in. Sue had not the art of prevarication, and, after admitting several facts as to their late difficulties and wanderings, she was startled by the landlady saying suddenly:

'Are you really a married woman?'

Sue hesitated; and then impulsively told the woman that her husband and herself had each been unhappy in their first marriages, after which, terrified at the thought of a second irrevocable union, and lest the conditions of the contract should kill their love, yet wishing to be together, they had literally not found the courage to repeat it, though they had attempted it two or three times. Therefore, though in her own sense of the words she was a married woman, in the landlady's sense she was not.

The housewife looked embarrassed, and went downstairs. Sue sat by the window in a reverie, watching the rain. Her quiet was broken by the noise of some one entering the house, and then the voices of a man and woman in conversation in the passage below. The landlady's husband had arrived, and she was explaining to him the incoming of the lodgers during his absence.

His voice rose in sudden anger. 'Now who wants such a woman here? and perhaps a confinement! . . . Besides, didn't I say I wouldn't have children? The hall and stairs fresh painted, to be kicked about by them! You must have known all was not straight with 'em—coming like that. Taking in a family when I said a single man.'

The wife expostulated, but, as it seemed, the husband insisted on his point; for presently a tap came to Sue's door, and the woman appeared.

'I am sorry to tell you, ma'am,' she said, 'that I can't let you have the room for the week after all. My husband objects; and therefore I must ask you to go. I don't mind your staying over to-night, as it is getting late in the afternoon; but I shall be glad if you can leave early in the morning.'

Though she knew that she was entitled to the lodging for a

week, Sue did not wish to create a disturbance between the wife and husband, and she said she would leave as requested. When the landlady had gone Sue looked out of the window again. Finding that the rain had ceased she proposed to the boy that, after putting the little ones to bed, they should go out and search about for another place, and bespeak it for the morrow, so as not to be so hard driven then as they had been that day.

Therefore, instead of unpacking her boxes, which had just been sent on from the station by Jude, they sallied out into the damp though not unpleasant streets, Sue resolving not to disturb her husband with the news of her notice to quit while he was perhaps worried in obtaining a lodging for himself. In the company of the boy she wandered into this street and into that; but though she tried a dozen different houses she fared far worse alone than she had fared in Jude's company, and could get nobody to promise her a room for the following day. Every householder looked askance at such a woman and child inquiring for accommodation in the gloom.

'I ought not to be born, ought I?' said the boy with misgiving.

Thoroughly tired at last Sue returned to the place where she was not welcome, but where at least she had temporary shelter. In her absence Jude had left his address; but knowing how weak he still was she adhered to her determination not to disturb him till the next day.

II

Sue sat looking at the bare floor of the room, the house being little more than an old intramural cottage, and then she regarded the scene outside the uncurtained window. At some distance opposite, the outer walls of Sarcophagus College—silent, black and windowless—threw their four centuries of gloom, bigotry, and decay into the little room she occupied, shutting out the moonlight by night and the sun by day. The outlines of Rubric College also were discernible beyond the other, and the tower of a third further off still. She thought of the strange operation of a simple-minded man's ruling passion, that it should have led Jude, who loved her and the children so tenderly, to place them here in this depressing purlieu, because he was still haunted by this dream. Even now he did not distinctly hear the freezing negative that those scholared walls had echoed to his desire.

The failure to find another lodging, and the lack of room in this house for his father, had made a deep impression on the boy;—a brooding undemonstrative horror seemed to have seized him. The silence was broken by his saying: 'Mother, *what* shall we do to-morrow!'

'I don't know!' said Sue despondently. 'I am afraid this will trouble your father.'

'I wish father was quite well, and there had been room for him! Then it wouldn't matter so much! Poor father!'

'It wouldn't!'

'Can I do anything?'

'No! All is trouble, adversity and suffering!'

'Father went away to give us children room, didn't he?'

'Partly.'

'It would be better to be out o' the world than in it, wouldn't it?'

'It would almost, dear.'

''Tis because of us children, too, isn't it, that you can't get a good lodging?'

'Well—people do object to children sometimes.'

'Then if children make so much trouble, why do people have 'em?'

'O—because it is a law of nature.'

'But we don't ask to be born?'

'No indeed.'

'And what makes it worse with me is that you are not my real mother, and you needn't have had me unless you liked. I oughtn't to have come to 'ee—that's the real truth! I troubled 'em in Australia, and I trouble folk here. I wish I hadn't been born!'

'You couldn't help it, my dear.'

'I think that whenever children be born that are not wanted they should be killed directly, before their souls come to 'em, and not allowed to grow big and walk about!'

Sue did not reply. She was doubtfully pondering how to treat this too reflective child.

She at last concluded that, so far as circumstances permitted, she would be honest and candid with one who entered into her difficulties like an aged friend.

'There is going to be another in our family soon,' she hesitatingly remarked.

'How?'

'There is going to be another baby.'

'What!' The boy jumped up wildly. 'O God, mother, you've never a-sent for another; and such trouble with what you've got!'

'Yes, I have, I am sorry to say!' murmured Sue, her eyes glistening with suspended tears.

The boy burst out weeping. 'O you don't care, you don't care!' he cried in bitter reproach. 'How *ever* could you, mother, be so wicked and cruel as this, when you needn't have done it till we was better off, and father well!—To bring us all into *more* trouble! No room for us, and father a-forced to go away, and we turned out to-morrow; and yet you be going to have another of us soon! . . .'Tis done o' purpose!—'tis—'tis!' He walked up and down sobbing.

'Y-you must forgive me, little Jude!' she pleaded, her bosom heaving now as much as the boy's. 'I can't explain—I will when you are older. It does seem—as if I had done it on purpose, now we are in these difficulties! I can't explain, dear! But it—is not quite on purpose—I can't help it!'

'Yes it is—it must be! For nobody would interfere with us, like that, unless you agreed! I won't forgive you, ever, ever! I'll never believe you care for me, or father, or any of us any more!'

He got up, and went away into the closet adjoining her room, in which a bed had been spread on the floor. There she heard him say: 'If we children was gone there'd be no trouble at all!'

'Don't think that, dear,' she cried, rather peremptorily. 'But go to sleep!'

The following morning she awoke at a little past six, and decided to get up and run across before breakfast to the inn which Jude had informed her to be his quarters, to tell him what had happened before he went out. She arose softly, to avoid disturbing the children, who, as she knew, must be fatigued by their exertions of yesterday.

She found Jude at breakfast in the obscure tavern he had chosen as a counterpoise to the expense of her lodging: and she explained to him her homelessness. He had been so anxious about her all night, he said. Somehow, now it was morning, the request to leave the lodgings did not seem such a depressing incident as it had seemed the night before, nor did even her failure to find another place affect her so deeply as at first. Jude agreed with her that it would not be worth while to insist upon her right to stay a week, but to take immediate steps for removal.

'You must all come to this inn for a day or two,' he said. 'It is a rough place, and it will not be so nice for the children, but we shall have more time to look round. There are plenty of lodgings in the suburbs—in my old quarter of Beersheba. Have breakfast with me now you are here, my bird. You are sure you are well? There will be plenty of time to get back and prepare the children's meal before they wake. In fact, I'll go with you.'

She joined Jude in a hasty meal, and in a quarter of an hour they started together, resolving to clear out from Sue's too respectable lodging immediately. On reaching the place and going upstairs she found that all was quiet in the children's room, and called to the landlady in timorous tones to please bring up the tea-kettle and something for their breakfast. This was perfunctorily done, and producing a couple of eggs which she had brought with her she put them into the boiling kettle, and summoned Jude to watch them for the youngsters, while she went to call them, it being now about half-past eight o'clock.

Jude stood bending over the kettle, with his watch in his hand, timing the eggs, so that his back was turned to the little inner chamber where the children lay. A shriek from Sue suddenly caused him to start round. He saw that the door of the room, or rather closet—which had seemed to go heavily upon its hinges as she pushed it back—was open, and that Sue had sunk to the floor just within it. Hastening forward to pick her up he turned his eyes to the little bed spread on the boards; no children were there. He looked in bewilderment round the room. At the back of the door were fixed two hooks for hanging garments, and from these the forms of the two youngest children were suspended, by a piece of box-cord round each of their necks, while from a nail a few yards off the body of little Jude was hanging in a similar manner. An overturned chair was near the elder boy, and his glazed eyes were slanted into the room; but those of the girl and the baby were closed.

Half paralyzed by the strange and consummate horror of the scene he let Sue lie, cut the cords with his pocket-knife and threw the three children on the bed; but the feel of their bodies in the momentary handling seemed to say that they were dead. He caught up Sue, who was in fainting fits, and put her on the bed in the other room, after which he breathlessly summoned the landlady and ran out for a doctor.

When he got back Sue had come to herself, and the two helpless women, bending over the children in wild efforts to restore them, and the triplet of little corpses, formed a sight which overthrew his self-command. The nearest surgeon came in, but, as Jude had inferred, his presence was superfluous. The children were past saving, for though their bodies were still barely cold it was conjectured that they had been hanging more than an hour. The probability held by the parents later on, when they were able to reason on the case, was that the elder boy, on waking, looked into the outer room for Sue, and, finding her absent, was thrown into a fit of aggravated despondency that the events and information of the evening before had induced in his morbid temperament. Moreover a piece of paper was found upon the floor, on which was written, in the boy's hand, with the bit of lead pencil that he carried:

Done because we are too menny.

At sight of this Sue's nerves utterly gave way, an awful conviction that her discourse with the boy had been the main cause of the tragedy, throwing her into a convulsive agony which knew no abatement. They carried her away against her wish to a room on the lower floor: and there she lay, her slight figure shaken with her gasps, and her eyes staring at the ceiling, the woman of the house vainly trying to soothe her.

They could hear from this chamber the people moving about above, and she implored to be allowed to go back, and was only kept from doing so by the assurance that, if there were any hope, her presence might do harm, and the reminder that it was necessary to take care of herself lest she should endanger a coming life. Her inquiries were incessant, and at last Jude came down and told her there was no hope. As soon as she could speak she informed him what she had said to the boy, and how she thought herself the cause of this.

'No,' said Jude. 'It was in his nature to do it. The doctor says there are such boys springing up amongst us—boys of a sort unknown in the last generation—the outcome of new views of life. They seem to see all its terrors before they are old enough to have staying power to resist them. He says it is the beginning of the coming universal wish not to live. He's an advanced man, the doctor: but he can give no consolation to—'

Jude had kept back his own grief on account of her; but he now broke down; and this stimulated Sue to efforts of sympathy which in some degree distracted her from her poignant self-reproach. When everybody was gone, she was allowed to see the children.

The boy's face expressed the whole tale of their situation. On that little shape had converged all the inauspiciousness and shadow which had darkened the first union of Jude, and all the accidents, mistakes, fears, errors of the last. He was their nodal point, their focus, their expression in a single term. For the rashness of those parents he had groaned, for their ill-assortment he had quaked, and for the misfortunes of these he had died.

When the house was silent, and they could do nothing but await the coroner's inquest, a subdued, large, low voice spread into the air of the room from behind the heavy walls at the back.

'What is it?' said Sue, her spasmodic breathing suspended.

'The organ of the College chapel. The organist practising I suppose. It's the anthem for the seventy-third Psalm; "Truly God is loving unto Israel".'

She sobbed again. 'O, O my babies! They had done no harm! Why should they have been taken away, and not I!'

There was another stillness—broken at last by two persons in conversation somewhere without.

'They are talking about us, no doubt!' moaned Sue. ' "We are made a spectacle unto the world, and to angels, and to men!" '

Jude listened—'No—they are not talking of us,' he said. 'They are two clergymen of different views, arguing about the eastward position. Good God—the eastward position, and all creation groaning!'

Then another silence, till she was seized with another uncontrollable fit of grief. 'There is something external to us which says, "You shan't!" First it said, "You shan't learn!" Then it said, "You shan't labour!" Now it says, "You shan't love!" '

He tried to soothe her by saying, 'That's bitter of you, darling.'

'But it's true!'

Thus they waited, and she went back again to her room. The baby's frock, shoes, and socks, which had been lying on a chair at the time of his death, she would not now have removed, though Jude would fain have got them out of her sight. But whenever he touched them she implored him to let them lie, and burst out almost savagely at the woman of the house when she also attempted to put them away.

Jude dreaded her dull apathetic silences almost more than her paroxysms. 'Why don't you speak to me, Jude?' she cried out, after one of these. 'Don't turn away from me! I can't *bear* the loneliness of being out of your looks!'

'There, dear; here I am,' he said, putting his face close to hers.

'Yes. . . . O my comrade, our perfect union—our two-in-oneness—is now stained with blood!'

'Shadowed by death—that's all.'

'Ah; but it was I who incited him really, though I didn't know I was doing it! I talked to the child as one should only talk to people of mature age. I said the world was against us, that it was better to be out of life than in it at this price; and he took it literally. And I told him I was going to have another child. It upset him. O how bitterly he upbraided me!'

'Why did you do it, Sue?'

'I can't tell. It was that I wanted to be truthful. I couldn't bear deceiving him as to the facts of life. And yet I wasn't truthful, for with a false delicacy I told him too obscurely.—Why was I half wiser than my fellow-women? and not entirely wiser! Why didn't I tell him pleasant untruths, instead of half realities? It was my want of self-control, so that I could neither conceal things nor reveal them!'

'Your plan might have been a good one for the majority of cases; only in our peculiar case it chanced to work badly perhaps. He must have known sooner or later.'

'And I was just making my baby darling a new frock; and now I shall never see him in it, and never talk to him any more! . . . My eyes are so swollen that I can scarcely see; and yet little more than a year ago I called myself happy! We went about loving each other too much—indulging ourselves to utter selfishness with each other! We said—do you remember?—that we would make a virtue of joy. I said it was Nature's intention, Nature's law and *raison d'être* that we should be joyful in what instincts she afforded us—instincts which civilization had taken upon itself to thwart. What dreadful things I said! And now Fate has given us this stab in the back for being such fools as to take Nature at her word!'

She sank into a quiet contemplation, till she said, 'It is best, perhaps, that they should be gone.—Yes—I see it is! Better that they should be plucked fresh than stay to wither away miserably!'

'Yes,' replied Jude. 'Some say that the elders should rejoice when their children die in infancy.'

'But they don't know! ... O my babies, my babies, could you be alive now! You may say the boy wished to be out of life, or he wouldn't have done it. It was not unreasonable for him to die; it was part of his incurably sad nature, poor little fellow! But then the others—my *own* children and yours!'

Again Sue looked at the hanging little frock, and at the socks and shoes; and her figure quivered like a string. 'I am a pitiable creature,' she said, 'good neither for earth nor heaven any more! I am driven out of my mind by things! What ought to be done?' She stared at Jude, and tightly held his hand.

'Nothing can be done,' he replied. 'Things are as they are, and will be brought to their destined issue.'

She paused. 'Yes! Who said that?' she asked heavily.

'It comes in the chorus of the *Agamemnon*. It has been in my mind constantly since this happened.'

'My poor Jude—how you've missed everything!—you more than I, for I did get you! To think you should know that by your unassisted reading, and yet be in poverty and despair!'

After such momentary diversions her grief would return in a wave.

The jury duly came and viewed the bodies, the inquest was held; and next arrived the melancholy morning of the funeral. Accounts in the newspapers had brought to the spot curious idlers, who stood apparently counting the window-panes and the stones of the walls. Doubt of the real relations of the couple added zest to their curiosity. Sue had declared that she would follow the two little ones to the grave, but at the last moment she gave way, and the coffins were quietly carried out of the house while she was lying down. Jude got into the vehicle, and it drove away, much to the relief of the landlord, who now had only Sue and her luggage remaining on his hands, which he hoped to be also clear of later on in the day, and so to have freed his house from the exasperating notoriety it had acquired during the week through his wife's unlucky admission of these strangers. In the afternoon he privately consulted with the owner of the house, and they agreed that if any objection to it arose from the tragedy which had occurred there they would try to get its number changed.

When Jude had seen the two little boxes—one containing little Jude, and the other the two smallest—deposited in the earth he hastened back to Sue, who was still in her room, and he therefore did not disturb her just then. Feeling anxious, however, he went again about four o'clock. The woman thought she was still lying down, but returned to him to say that she was not in her bedroom after all. Her hat and jacket, too, were missing: she had gone out. Jude hurried off to the public-house where he was sleeping. She had not been there. Then bethinking himself of possibilities he went along the road to the cemetery, which he entered, and crossed to where the interments had recently taken place. The idlers who had followed to the spot by reason of the tragedy were all gone now. A man with a shovel in his hands was attempting to earth in the common grave of the three children, but his arm was held back by an expostulating woman who stood in the half-filled hole. It was Sue, whose coloured clothing, which she had never thought of changing for the mourning he had bought, suggested to the eye a deeper grief than the conventional garb of bereavement could express.

'He's filling them in, and he shan't till I've seen my little ones again!' she cried wildly when she saw Jude. 'I want to see them once more. O Jude—please Jude—I want to see them! I didn't know you would let them be taken away while I was asleep! You said perhaps I should see them once more before they were screwed down; and then you didn't, but took them away! O Jude, you are cruel to me too!'

'She's been wanting me to dig out the grave again, and let her get to the coffins,' said the man with the spade. 'She ought to be took home, by the look o' her. She is hardly responsible, poor thing, seemingly. Can't dig 'em up again now, ma'am. Do ye go home with your husband, and take it quiet, and thank God that there'll be another soon to swage yer grief.'

But Sue kept asking piteously: 'Can't I see them once more—

just once! Can't I? Only just one little minute, Jude? It would not take long! And I should be so glad, Jude! I will be so good, and not disobey you ever any more, Jude, if you will let me? I would go home quietly afterwards, and not want to see them any more! Can't I? Why can't I?'

Thus she went on. Jude was thrown into such acute sorrow that he almost felt he would try to get the man to accede. But it could do no good, and might make her still worse; and he saw that it was imperative to get her home at once. So he coaxed her, and whispered tenderly, and put his arm round her to support her; till she helplessly gave in, and was induced to leave the cemetery.

He wished to obtain a fly to take her back in, but economy being so imperative she deprecated his doing so, and they walked along slowly, Jude in black crape, she in brown and red clothing. They were to have gone to a new lodging that afternoon, but Jude saw that it was not practicable, and in course of time they entered the now hated house. Sue was at once got to bed, and the doctor sent for.

Jude waited all the evening downstairs. At a very late hour the intelligence was brought to him that a child had been prematurely born, and that it, like the others, was a corpse.

III

Sue was convalescent, though she had hoped for death, and Jude had again obtained work at his old trade. They were in other lodgings now, in the direction of Beersheba, and not far from the Church of Ceremonies—Saint Silas.

They would sit silent, more bodeful of the direct antagonism of things than of their insensate and stolid obstructiveness. Vague and quaint imaginings had haunted Sue in the days when her intellect scintillated like a star, that the world resembled a stanza or melody composed in a dream; it was wonderfully excellent to the half-aroused intelligence, but hopelessly absurd at the full waking; that the First Cause worked automatically like a somnambulist, and not reflectively like a sage; that at the framing of the terrestrial conditions there seemed never to have been contemplated such a development of emotional perceptiveness among the creatures subject to those conditions as that reached by thinking and educated humanity. But affliction makes opposing forces loom anthropomorphous; and those ideas were now exchanged for a sense of Jude and herself fleeing from a persecutor.

'We must conform!' she said mournfully. 'All the ancient wrath of the Power above us has been vented upon us, His poor creatures, and we must submit. There is no choice. We must. It is no use fighting against God!'

'It is only against man and senseless circumstance,' said Jude.

'True!' she murmured. 'What have I been thinking of! I am getting as superstitious as a savage! . . . But whoever or whatever our foe may be, I am cowed into submission. I have no more fighting strength left; no more enterprize. I am beaten, beaten! . . . "We are made a spectacle unto the world, and to angels, and to men!" I am always saying that now.'

'I feel the same!'

'What shall we do? You are in work now; but remember, it may only be because our history and relations are not absolutely known. . . . Possibly, if they knew our marriage had not been formalized they would turn you out of your job as they did at Aldbrickham!'

'I hardly know. Perhaps they would hardly do that. However, I think that we ought to make it legal now—as soon as you are able to go out.'

'You think we ought?'

'Certainly.'

And Jude fell into thought. 'I have seemed to myself lately,' he said, 'to belong to that vast band of men shunned by the virtuous—the men called seducers. It amazes me when I think of it! I have not been conscious of it, or of any wrong-doing towards you, whom I love more than myself. Yet I *am* one of those men! I wonder if any other of them are the same purblind, simple creatures as I? . . . Yes, Sue—that's what I am. I seduced you. . . . You were a distinct type—a refined creature, intended by Nature to be left intact. But I couldn't leave you alone!'

'No, no, Jude!' she said quickly. 'Don't reproach yourself with being what you are not. If anybody is to blame it is I.'

'I supported you in your resolve to leave Phillotson; and without me perhaps you wouldn't have urged him to let you go.'

'I should have, just the same. As to ourselves, the fact of our not having entered into a legal contract is the saving feature in our union. We have thereby avoided insulting, as it were, the solemnity of our first marriages.'

'Solemnity?' Jude looked at her with some surprise, and grew conscious that she was not the Sue of their earlier time.

'Yes,' she said, with a little quiver in her words, 'I have had dreadful fears, a dreadful sense of my own insolence of action. I have thought—that I am still his wife!'

'Whose?'

'Richard's.'

'Good God, dearest!—why?'

'O I can't explain! Only the thought comes to me.'

'It is your weakness—a sick fancy, without reason or meaning! Don't let it trouble you.'

Sue sighed uneasily.

As a set-off against such discussions as these there had come an improvement in their pecuniary position, which earlier in their experience would have made them cheerful. Jude had quite unexpectedly found good employment at his old trade almost directly he arrived, the summer weather suiting his fragile constitution; and outwardly his days went on with that monotonous uniformity which is in itself so grateful after vicissitude. People seemed to have forgotten that he had ever shown any awkward aberrancies: and he daily mounted to the parapets and copings of colleges he could never enter, and renewed the crumbling freestones of mullioned windows he would never look from, as if he had known no wish to do otherwise.

There was this change in him; that he did not often go to any service at the churches now. One thing troubled him more than any other; that Sue and himself had mentally travelled in opposite directions since the tragedy: events which had enlarged his own views of life, laws, customs, and dogmas, had not operated in the same manner on Sue's. She was no longer the same as in the independent days, when her intellect played like lambent lightning over conventions and formalities which he at that time respected, though he did not now.

On a particular Sunday evening he came in rather late. She was not at home, but she soon returned, when he found her silent and meditative.

'What are you thinking of, little woman?' he asked curiously.

'O I can't tell clearly! I have thought that we have been selfish, careless, even impious, in our courses, you and I. Our life has been a vain attempt at self-delight. But self-abnegation is the higher road. We should mortify the flesh—the terrible flesh—the curse of Adam!'

'Sue!' he murmured. 'What has come over you?'

'We ought to be continually sacrificing ourselves on the altar of duty! But I have always striven to do what has pleased me. I well deserved the scourging I have got! I wish something would take the evil right out of me, and all my monstrous errors, and all my sinful ways!'

'Sue—my own too suffering dear!—there's no evil woman in you. Your natural instincts are perfectly healthy; not quite so impassioned, perhaps, as I could wish; but good, and dear, and pure. And as I have often said, you are absolutely the most ethereal, least sensual woman I ever knew to exist without inhuman sexlessness. Why do you talk in such a changed way? We have not been selfish, except when no one could profit by our being otherwise. You used to say that human nature was noble and long-suffering, not vile and corrupt, and at last I thought you spoke truly. And now you seem to take such a much lower view!'

'I want a humble heart; and a chastened mind; and I have never had them yet!'

'You have been fearless, both as a thinker and as a feeler, and you deserved more admiration than I gave. I was too full of narrow dogmas at that time to see it.'

'Don't say that, Jude! I wish my every fearless word and thought could be rooted out of my history. Self-renunciation—that's everything! I cannot humiliate myself too much. I should like to prick myself all over with pins and bleed out the badness that's in me!'

'Hush!' he said, pressing her little face against his breast as if she were an infant. 'It is bereavement that has brought you to this! Such remorse is not for you, my sensitive plant, but for the wicked ones of the earth—who never feel it!'

'I ought not to stay like this,' she murmured, when she had remained in the position a long while.

'Why not?'

'It is indulgence.'

'Still on the same track! But is there anything better on earth than that we should love one another?'

'Yes. It depends on the sort of love; and yours—ours—is the wrong.'

'I won't have it, Sue! Come, when do you wish our marriage to be signed in a vestry?'

She paused, and looked up uneasily. 'Never,' she whispered.

Not knowing the whole of her meaning he took the objection serenely, and said nothing. Several minutes elapsed, and he thought she had fallen asleep; but he spoke softly, and found that she was wide awake all the time. She sat upright and sighed.

'There is a strange, indescribable perfume or atmosphere about you to-night, Sue,' he said. 'I mean not only mentally, but about your clothes, also. A sort of vegetable scent, which I seem to know, yet cannot remember.'

'It is incense.'

'Incense?'

'I have been to the service at St Silas', and I was in the fumes of it.'

'Oh—St Silas.'

'Yes. I go there sometimes.'

'Indeed. You go there!'

'You see, Jude, it is lonely here in the week-day mornings, when you are at work, and I think and think of—of my—' She stopped till she could control the lumpiness of her throat. 'And I have taken to go in there, as it is so near.'

'O well—of course, I say nothing against it. Only it is odd, for you. They little think what sort of chiel is amang them!'

'What do you mean, Jude?'

'Well—a sceptic, to be plain.'

'How can you pain me so, dear Jude, in my trouble! Yet I know you didn't mean it. But you ought not to say that.'

'I won't. But I am much surprised!'

'Well—I want to tell you something else, Jude. You won't be angry, will you? I have thought of it a good deal since my babies died. I don't think I ought to be your wife—or as your wife—any longer.'

'What? . . . But you *are*!'

'From your point of view; but—'

'Of course we were afraid of the ceremony, and a good many others would have been in our places, with such strong reasons for fears. But experience has proved how we misjudged ourselves, and overrated our infirmities; and if you are beginning to respect rites and ceremonies, as you seem to be, I wonder you don't say it shall be carried out instantly? You certainly *are* my wife, Sue, in all but law. What do you mean by what you said?'

'I don't think I am!'

'Not? But suppose we *had* gone through the ceremony? Would you feel that you were then?'

'No. I should not feel even then that I was. I should feel worse than I do now.'

'Why so—in the name of all that's perverse, my dear?'

'Because I am Richard's.'

'Ah—you hinted that absurd fancy to me before!'

'It was only an impression with me then; I feel more and more convinced as time goes on that—I belong to him, or to nobody.'

'My good heavens—how we are changing places!'

'Yes. Perhaps so.'

Some few days later, in the dusk of the summer evening, they were sitting in the same small room downstairs, when a knock came to the front door of the carpenter's house where they were lodging, and in a few moments there was a tap at the door of their room. Before they could open it the comer did so, and a woman's form appeared.

'Is Mr Fawley here?'

Jude and Sue started as he mechanically replied in the affirmative, for the voice was Arabella's.

He formally requested her to come in, and she sat down in the window bench, where they could distinctly see her outline against the light; but no characteristic that enabled them to estimate her general aspect and air. Yet something seemed to denote that she was not quite so comfortably circumstanced, nor so bouncingly attired, as she had been during Cartlett's lifetime.

The three attempted an awkward conversation about the tragedy, of which Jude had felt it to be his duty to inform her immediately, though she had never replied to his letter.

'I have just come from the cemetery,' she said. 'I inquired and found the child's grave. I couldn't come to the funeral—thank you for inviting me all the same. I read all about it in the papers, and I felt I wasn't wanted. . . . No—I couldn't come to the funeral,' repeated Arabella, who, seeming utterly unable to reach the ideal of a catastrophic manner, fumbled with iterations. 'But I am glad I found the grave. As 'tis your trade, Jude, you'll be able to put up a handsome stone to 'em.'

'I shall put up a headstone,' said Jude drearily.

'He was my child, and naturally I feel for him.'

'I hope so. We all did.'

'The others that weren't mine I didn't feel so much for, as was natural.'

'Of course.'

A sigh came from the dark corner where Sue sat.

'I had often wished I had mine with me,' continued Mrs Cartlett. 'Perhaps 'twouldn't have happened then! But of course I didn't wish to take him away from your wife.'

'I am not his wife,' came from Sue.

The unexpectedness of her words struck Jude silent.

'O I beg your pardon, I'm sure,' said Arabella. 'I thought you were!'

Jude had known from the quality of Sue's tone that her new and transcendental views lurked in her words; but all except their obvious meaning was, naturally, missed by Arabella. The latter, after evincing that she was struck by Sue's avowal, recovered herself, and went on to talk with placid bluntness about 'her' boy, for whom, though in his lifetime she had shown no care at all, she now exhibited a ceremonial mournfulness that was apparently sustaining to the conscience. She alluded to the past, and in making some remark appealed again to Sue. There was no answer: Sue had invisibly left the room.

'She said she was not your wife?' resumed Arabella in another voice. 'Why should she do that?'

'I cannot inform you,' said Jude shortly.

'She is, isn't she? She once told me so.'

'I don't criticize what she says.'

'Ah—I see! Well, my time is up. I am staying here to-night, and thought I could do no less than call, after our mutual affliction. I am sleeping at the place where I used to be barmaid, and to-morrow I go back to Alfredston. Father is come home again, and I am living with him.'

'He has returned from Australia?' said Jude with languid curiosity.

'Yes. Couldn't get on there. Had a rough time of it. Mother died of dys——what do you call it—in the hot weather, and father and two of the young ones have just got back. He has got a cottage near the old place, and for the present I am keeping house for him.'

Jude's former wife had maintained a stereotyped manner of strict good breeding even now that Sue was gone, and limited her stay to a number of minutes that should accord with the highest respectability. When she had departed Jude, much relieved, went to the stairs and called Sue—feeling anxious as to what had become of her.

There was no answer, and the carpenter who kept the lodgings said that she had not come in. Jude was puzzled, and became quite alarmed at her absence, for the hour was growing late. The carpenter called his wife, who conjectured that Sue might have gone to St Silas' church, as she often went there.

'Surely not at this time o' night?' said Jude. 'It is shut.'

'She knows somebody who keeps the key, and she has it whenever she wants it.'

'How long has she been going on with this?'

'Oh, some few weeks, I think.'

Jude went vaguely in the direction of the church, which he had never once approached since he lived out that way years before, when his young opinions were more mystical than they were now. The spot was deserted, but the door was certainly unfastened; he lifted the latch without noise, and pushing to the door behind him, stood absolutely still inside. The prevalent silence seemed to contain a faint sound, explicable as a breathing, or a sobbing, which came from the other end of the building. The floor-cloth deadened his footsteps as he moved in that direction through the obscurity, which was broken only by the faintest reflected night-light from without.

High overhead, above the chancel steps, Jude could discern a huge, solidly constructed Latin cross—as large, probably, as the original it was designed to commemorate. It seemed to be suspended in the air by invisible wires; it was set with large jewels, which faintly glimmered in some weak ray caught from outside, as the cross swayed to and fro in a silent and scarcely perceptible motion. Underneath, upon the floor, lay what appeared to be a heap of black clothes, and from this was repeated the sobbing that he had heard before. It was his Sue's form, prostrate on the paving.

'Sue!' he whispered.

Something white disclosed itself; she had turned up her face.

'What—do you want with me here, Jude?' she said almost sharply. 'You shouldn't come! I wanted to be alone! Why did you intrude here?'

'How can you ask!' he retorted in quick reproach, for his full heart was wounded to its centre at this attitude of hers towards him. 'Why do I come? Who has a right to come, I should like to know, if I have not! I, who love you better than my own self—better—O far better—than you have loved me! What made you leave me to come here alone?'

'Don't criticize me, Jude—I can't bear it!—I have often told you so. You must take me as I am. I am a wretch—broken by my distractions! I couldn't *bear* it when Arabella came—I felt so utterly miserable I had to come away. She seems to be your wife still, and Richard to be my husband!'

'But they are nothing to us!'

'Yes, dear friend, they are. I see marriage differently now. My babies have been taken from me to show me this! Arabella's child killing mine was a judgment—the right slaying the wrong. What, *what* shall I do! I am such a vile creature—too worthless to mix with ordinary human beings!'

'This is terrible!' said Jude, verging on tears. 'It is monstrous and unnatural for you to be so remorseful when you have done no wrong!'

'Ah—you don't know my badness!'

He returned vehemently: 'I do! Every atom and dreg of it! You make me hate Christianity, or mysticism, or Sacerdotalism, or whatever it may be called, if it's that which has caused this deterioration in you. That a woman-poet, a woman-seer, a woman whose soul shone like a diamond—whom all the wise of the world would have been proud of, if they could have known you—should degrade herself like this! I am glad I had nothing to do with Divinity—damn glad—if it's going to ruin you in this way!'

'You are angry, Jude, and unkind to me, and don't see how things are.'

'Then come along home with me, dearest, and perhaps I shall. I am over-burdened—and you, too, are unhinged just now.' He put his arm round her and lifted her; but though she came, she preferred to walk without his support.

'I don't dislike you, Jude,' she said in a sweet and imploring voice. 'I love you as much as ever! Only—I ought not to love you—any more. O I must not any more!'

'I can't own it.'

'But I have made up my mind that I am not your wife! I belong to him—I sacramentally joined myself to him for life. Nothing can alter it!'

'But surely we are man and wife, if ever two people were in this world? Nature's own marriage it is, unquestionably!'

'But not Heaven's. Another was made for me there, and ratified eternally in the church at Melchester.'

'Sue, Sue—affliction has brought you to this unreasonable state! After converting me to your views on so many things, to find you suddenly turn to the right-about like this—for no reason whatever, confounding all you have formerly said through sentiment merely! You root out of me what little affection and reverence I had left in me for the Church as an old acquaintance. . . . What I can't understand in you is your extraordinary blindness now to your old logic. Is it peculiar to you, or is it common to woman? Is a woman a thinking unit at all, or a fraction always wanting its integer? How you argued that marriage was only a clumsy contract—which it is—how you showed all the objections to it—all the absurdities! If two and two made four when we were happy together, surely they make four now? I can't understand it, I repeat!'

'Ah, dear Jude; that's because you are a totally deaf man observing people listening to music. You say "What are they regarding? Nothing is there." But something is.'

'That is a hard saying from you; and not a true parallel! You threw off old husks of prejudices, and taught me to do it; and now you go back upon yourself. I confess I am utterly stultified in my estimate of you.'

'Dear friend, my only friend, don't be hard with me! I can't help being as I am, I am convinced I am right—that I see the light at last. But O, how to profit by it!'

They walked along a few more steps till they were outside the building, and she had returned the key. 'Can this be the girl,' said Jude when she came back, feeling a slight renewal of elasticity now that he was in the open street; 'can this be the girl who brought the Pagan deities into this most Christian city?—who mimicked Miss Fontover when she crushed them with her heel?—quoted Gibbon, and Shelley, and Mill? Where are dear Apollo, and dear Venus now!'

'O don't, don't be so cruel to me, Jude, and I so unhappy!' she sobbed. 'I can't bear it! I was in error—I cannot reason with you. I was wrong—proud in my own conceit! Arabella's coming was the finish. Don't satirize me: it cuts like a knife!'

He flung his arms round her and kissed her passionately there in the silent street, before she could hinder him. They went on till they came to a little coffee-house. 'Jude,' she said with suppressed tears, 'would you mind getting a lodging here?'

'I will—if, if you really wish? But do you? Let me go to our door and understand you.'

He went and conducted her in. She said she wanted no supper, and went in the dark upstairs and struck a light. Turning she found that Jude had followed her, and was standing at the chamber door. She went to him, put her hand in his, and said 'Good-night.'

'But Sue! Don't we live here?'

'You said you would do as I wished!'

'Yes. Very well! . . . Perhaps it was wrong of me to argue distastefully as I have done! Perhaps as we couldn't conscientiously marry at first in the old-fashioned way, we ought to have parted. Perhaps the world is not illuminated enough for such experiments as ours! Who were we, to think we could act as pioneers!'

'I am so glad you see that much, at any rate. I never deliberately meant to do as I did. I slipped into my false position through jealousy and agitation!'

'But surely through love—you loved me?'

'Yes. But I wanted to let it stop there, and go on always as mere lovers; until—'

'But people in love couldn't live for ever like that!'

'Women could: men can't, because they—won't. An average woman is in this superior to an average man—that she never instigates, only responds. We ought to have lived in mental communion, and no more.'

'I was the unhappy cause of the change, as I have said before! . . . Well, as you will! . . . But human nature can't help being itself.'

'O yes—that's just what it has to learn—self-mastery.'

'I repeat—if either were to blame it was not you but I.'

'No—it was I. Your wickedness was only the natural man's desire to possess the woman. Mine was not the reciprocal wish till envy stimulated me to oust Arabella. I had thought I ought in charity to let you approach me—that it was damnably selfish to torture you as I did my other friend. But I shouldn't have given way if you hadn't broke me down by making me fear you would go back to her. . . . But don't let us say any more about it! Jude, will you leave me to myself now?'

'Yes. . . . But Sue—my wife, as you are!' he burst out; 'my old reproach to you was, after all, a true one. You have never loved me as I love you—never—never! Yours is not a passionate heart—your heart does not burn in a flame! You are, upon the whole, a sort of fay, or sprite—not a woman!'

'At first I did not love you, Jude; that I own. When I first knew you I merely wanted you to love me. I did not exactly flirt with you; but that inborn craving which undermines some women's morals almost more than unbridled passion—the craving to attract and captivate, regardless of the injury it may do the man—was in me; and when I found I had caught you, I was frightened. And then—I don't know how it was—I couldn't bear to let you go—possibly to Arabella again—and so I got to love you, Jude. But you see, however fondly it ended, it began in the selfish and cruel wish to make your heart ache for me without letting mine ache for you.'

'And now you add to your cruelty by leaving me!'

'Ah—yes! The further I flounder, the more harm I do!'

'O Sue!' said he with a sudden sense of his own danger. 'Do not do an immoral thing for moral reasons! You have been my social salvation. Stay with me for humanity's sake! You know what a weak fellow I am. My two Arch Enemies you know—my weakness for womankind and my impulse to strong liquor. Don't abandon me to them, Sue, to save your own soul only! They have been kept entirely at a distance since you became my guardian-angel! Since I have had you I have been able to go into any temptations of the sort, without risk. Isn't my safety worth a little sacrifice of dogmatic principle? I am in terror lest, if you leave me, it will be with me another case of the pig that was washed turning back to his wallowing in the mire!'

Sue burst out weeping. 'O but you must not. Jude! You won't! I'll pray for you night and day!'

'Well—never mind; don't grieve,' said Jude generously. 'I did suffer, God knows, about you at that time; and now I suffer again. But perhaps not so much as you. The woman mostly gets the worst of it in the long run!'

'She does.'

'Unless she is absolutely worthless and contemptible. And this one is not that, anyhow!'

Sue drew a nervous breath or two. 'She is—I fear! . . . Now Jude—good-night,—please!'

'I mustn't stay?—Not just once more? As it has been so many times—O Sue, my wife, why not!'

'No—no—not wife! . . . I am in your hands, Jude—don't tempt me back now I have advanced so far!'

'Very well. I do your bidding. I owe that to you, darling, in penance for how I over-ruled it at the first time. My God, how selfish I was! Perhaps—perhaps I spoilt one of the highest and purest loves that ever existed between man and woman! . . . Then let the veil of our temple be rent in two from this hour!'

He went to the bed, removed one of the pair of pillows thereon, and flung it to the floor.

Sue looked at him, and bending over the bed-rail wept silently. 'You don't see that it is a matter of conscience with me, and not of dislike to you!' she brokenly murmured. 'Dislike to you! But I can't say any more—it breaks my heart—it will be undoing all I have begun! Jude—good-night!'

'Good-night,' he said, and turned to go.

'O but you shall kiss me!' said she, starting up. 'I can't—bear—!'

He clasped her, and kissed her weeping face as he had scarcely ever done before, and they remained in silence till she said, 'Good-bye, good-bye!' And then gently pressing him away she got free, trying to mitigate the sadness by saying: 'We'll be dear friends just the same, Jude, won't we? And we'll see each other sometimes—Yes!—and forget all this, and try to be as we were long ago?'

Jude did not permit himself to speak, but turned and descended the stairs.

IV

The man whom Sue, in her mental volte-face, was now regarding as her inseparable husband, lived still at Marygreen.

On the day before the tragedy of the children, Phillotson had seen both her and Jude as they stood in the rain at Christminster watching the procession to the Theatre. But he had said nothing of it at the moment to his companion Gillingham, who, being an old friend, was staying with him at the village aforesaid, and had, indeed, suggested the day's trip to Christminster.

'What are you thinking of?' said Gillingham, as they went home. 'The University degree you never obtained?'

'No, no,' said Phillotson gruffly. 'Of somebody I saw to-day.' In a moment he added, 'Susanna.'

'I saw her, too.'

'You said nothing.'

'I didn't wish to draw your attention to her. But, as you did see her, you should have said: "How d'ye do, my dear-that-was?" '

'Ah, well. I might have. But what do you think of this: I have good reason for supposing that she was innocent when I divorced her—that I was all wrong. Yes, indeed! Awkward, isn't it?'

'She has taken care to set you right since, anyhow, apparently.'

'H'm. That's a cheap sneer. I ought to have waited, unquestionably.'

At the end of the week, when Gillingham had gone back to his school near Shaston, Phillotson, as was his custom, went to Alfredston market; ruminating again on Arabella's intelligence as he walked down the long hill which he had known before Jude knew it, though his history had not beaten so intensely upon its incline. Arrived in the town he bought his usual weekly local paper; and when he had sat down in an inn to refresh himself for the five miles' walk back, he pulled the paper from his pocket and read awhile. The account of the 'Strange suicide of a stone-mason's children' met his eye.

Unimpassioned as he was, it impressed him painfully, and puzzled him not a little, for he could not understand the age of the elder child being what it was stated to be. However, there was no doubt that the newspaper report was in some way true.

'Their cup of sorrow is now full!' he said: and thought and thought of Sue, and what she had gained by leaving him.

Arabella having made her home at Alfredston, and the schoolmaster coming to market there every Saturday, it was not wonderful that in a few weeks they met again—the precise time being just after her return from Christminster, where she had stayed much longer than she had at first intended, keeping an interested eye on Jude, though Jude had seen no more of her. Phillotson was on his way homeward when he encountered Arabella, and she was approaching the town.

'You like walking out this way, Mrs Cartlett?' he said.

'I've just begun to again,' she replied. 'It is where I lived as maid and wife, and all the past things of my life that are interesting to my feelings are mixed up with this road. And they have been stirred up in me too, lately; for I've been visiting at Christminster. Yes; I've seen Jude.'

'Ah! How do they bear their terrible affliction?'

'In a ve-ry strange way—ve-ry strange! She don't live with him any longer. I only heard of it as a certainty just before I left; though I had thought things were drifting that way from their manner when I called on them.'

'Not live with her husband? Why, I should have thought 'twould have united them more.'

'He's not her husband, after all. She has never really married him although they have passed as man and wife so long. And now, instead of this sad event making 'em hurry up, and get the thing done legally, she's took in a queer religious way, just as I was in my affliction at losing Cartlett, only hers is of a more 'sterical sort than mine. And she says, so I was told, that she's your wife in the eye of Heaven and the Church—yours only; and can't be anybody else's by an act of man.'

'Ah—indeed? . . . Separated, have they!'

'You see, the eldest boy was mine—'

'O—yours!'

'Yes, poor little fellow—born in lawful wedlock, thank God. And perhaps she feels, over and above other things, that I ought to have been in her place. I can't say. However, as for me, I am soon off from here. I've got father to look after now, and we can't live in such a humdrum place as this. I hope soon to be in a bar again at Christminster, or some other big town.'

They parted. When Phillotson had ascended the hill a few steps he stopped, hastened back, and called her.

'What is, or was, their address?'

Arabella gave it.

'Thank you. Good afternoon.'

Arabella smiled grimly as she resumed her way, and practised dimple-making all along the road from where the pollard willows begin to the old almshouses in the first street of the town.

Meanwhile Phillotson ascended to Marygreen, and for the first time during a lengthened period he lived with a forward eye. On crossing under the large trees of the green to the humble school-house to which he had been reduced he stood a moment, and pictured Sue coming out of the door to meet him. No man had ever suffered more inconvenience from his own charity, Christian or heathen, than Phillotson had done in letting Sue go. He had been knocked about from pillar to post at the hands of the virtuous almost beyond endurance; he had been nearly starved, and was now dependent entirely upon the very small stipend from the school of this village (where the parson had got ill-spoken of for befriending him). He had often thought of Arabella's remarks that he should have been more severe with Sue, that her recalcitrant spirit would soon have been broken. Yet such was his obstinance and illogical disregard of opinion, and of the principles in which he had been trained, that his convictions on the rightness of his course with his wife had not been disturbed.

Principles which could be subverted by feeling in one direction were liable to the same catastrophe in another. The instincts which had allowed him to give Sue her liberty now enabled him to regard her as none the worse for her life with Jude. He wished for her still, in his curious way, if he did not love her, and, apart from policy, soon felt that he would be gratified to have her again as his, always provided that she came willingly.

But artifice was necessary, he had found, for stemming the cold and inhumane blast of the world's contempt. And here were the materials ready made. By getting Sue back and remarrying her on the respectable plea of having entertained erroneous views of her, and gained his divorce wrongfully, he might acquire some comfort, resume his old courses, perhaps return to the Shaston school, if not even to the Church as a licentiate.

He thought he would write to Gillingham to inquire his views, and what he thought of his, Phillotson's, sending a letter to her. Gillingham replied, naturally, that now she was gone it were best to let her be; and considered that if she were anybody's wife she was the wife of the man to whom she had borne three children and owed such tragical adventures. Probably, as his attachment to her seemed unusually strong, the singular pair would make their union legal in course of time, and all would be well, and decent, and in order.

'But they won't—Sue won't!' exclaimed Phillotson to himself. 'Gillingham is so matter-of-fact. She's affected by Christminster sentiment and teaching. I can see her views on the indissolubility of marriage well enough, and I know where she got them. They are not mine; but I shall make use of them to further mine.'

He wrote a brief reply to Gillingham. 'I know I am entirely wrong, but I don't agree with you. As to her having lived and had three children by him, my feeling is (though I can advance no logical or moral defence of it, on the old lines) that it has done little more than finish her education. I shall write to her, and learn whether what that woman said is true or no.'

As he had made up his mind to do this before he had written to his friend, there had not been much reason for writing to the latter at all. However, it was Phillotson's way to act thus.

He accordingly addressed a carefully considered epistle to Sue, and, knowing her emotional temperament, threw a Rhadamanthine strictness into the lines here and there, carefully hiding his heterodox feelings, not to frighten her. He stated that, it having come to his knowledge that her views had considerably changed, he felt compelled to say that his own, too, were largely modified by events subsequent to their parting. He would not conceal from her that passionate love had little to do with his communication. It arose from a wish to make their lives, if not a success, at least no such disastrous failure as they threatened to become, through his acting on what he had considered at the time a principle of justice, charity, and reason.

To indulge one's instinctive and uncontrolled sense of justice and right, was not, he had found, permitted with impunity in an old civilization like ours. It was necessary to act under an acquired and cultivated sense of the same, if you wished to enjoy an average share of comfort and honour; and to let crude loving-kindness take care of itself.

He suggested that she should come to him there at Marygreen.

On second thoughts he took out the last paragraph but one; and having re-written the letter he despatched it immediately, and in some excitement awaited the issue.

A few days after a figure moved through the white fog which enveloped the Beersheba suburb of Christminster, towards the quarter in which Jude Fawley had taken up his lodging since his division from Sue. A timid knock sounded upon the door of his abode.

It was evening—so he was at home; and by a species of divination he jumped up and rushed to the door himself.

'Will you come out with me? I would rather not come in. I want to—to talk with you—and to go with you to the cemetery.'

It had been in the trembling accents of Sue that those words came. Jude put on his hat. 'It is dreary for you to be out,' he said. 'But if you prefer not to come in, I don't mind.'

'Yes—I do. I shall not keep you long.'

Jude was too much affected to go on talking at first; she, too, was now such a mere cluster of nerves that all initiatory power seemed to have left her, and they proceeded through the fog like Acherontic shades for a long while, without sound or gesture.

'I want to tell you,' she presently said, her voice now quick, now slow, 'so that you may not hear of it by chance. I am going back to Richard. He has—so magnanimously—agreed to forgive all.'

'Going back? How can you go—'

'He is going to marry me again. That is for form's sake, and to satisfy the world, which does not see things as they are. But of course I *am* his wife already. Nothing has changed that.'

He turned upon her with an anguish that was well-nigh fierce.

'But you are *my* wife! Yes, you are. You know it. I have always regretted that feint of ours in going away and pretending to come back legally married, to save appearances. I loved you, and you loved me; and we closed with each other; and that made the marriage. We still love—you as well as I—I *know* it, Sue! Therefore our marriage is not cancelled.'

'Yes; I know how you see it,' she answered with despairing self-suppression. 'But I am going to marry him again, as it would be called by you. Strictly speaking you, too,—don't mind my saying it, Jude!—you should take back—Arabella.'

'I should? Good God—what next! But how if you and I had married legally, as we were on the point of doing?'

'I should have felt just the same—that ours was not a marriage. And I would go back to Richard without repeating the sacrament, if he asked me. But "the world and its ways have a certain worth" (I suppose): therefore I concede a repetition of the ceremony. . . . Don't crush all the life out of me by satire and argument, I implore you! I was strongest once, I know, and perhaps I treated you cruelly. But Jude, return good for evil! I am the weaker now. Don't retaliate upon me, but be kind. O be kind to me—a poor wicked woman who is trying to mend!'

He shook his head hopelessly, his eyes wet. The blow of her bereavement seemed to have destroyed her reasoning faculty. The once keen vision was dimmed. 'All wrong, all wrong!' he said huskily. 'Error—perversity! It drives me out of my senses. Do you care for him? Do you love him? You know you don't! It will be a fanatic prostitution—God forgive me, yes—that's what it will be!'

'I don't love him—I must, must, own it, in deepest remorse! But I shall try to learn to love him by obeying him.'

Jude argued, urged, implored; but her conviction was proof against all. It seemed to be the one thing on earth on which she was firm, and that her firmness in this had left her tottering in every other impulse and wish she possessed.

'I have been considerate enough to let you know the whole truth, and to tell it you myself,' she said in cut tones; 'that you might not consider yourself slighted by hearing of it at second-hand. I have even owned the extreme fact that I do not love him. I did not think you would be so rough with me for doing so! I was going to ask you . . .'

'To give you away.'

'No. To send—my boxes to me—if you would. But I suppose you won't.'

'Why, of course I will. What—isn't he coming to fetch you—to marry you from here? He won't condescend to do that?'

'No—I won't let him. I go to him voluntarily, just as I went away from him. We are to be married at this little church at Marygreen.'

She was so sadly sweet in what he called her wrongheadedness that Jude could not help being moved to tears more than once for pity of her. 'I never knew such a woman for doing impulsive penances as you, Sue! No sooner does one expect you to go straight on, as the one rational proceeding, than you double round the corner!'

'Ah, well; let that go! . . . Jude, I must say good-bye! But I wanted you to go to the cemetery with me. Let our farewell be there—beside the graves of those who died to bring home to me the error of my views.'

They turned in the direction of the place, and the gate was opened to them on application. Sue had been there often, and she knew the way to the spot in the dark. They reached it, and stood still.

'It is here—I should like to part,' said she.

'So be it!'

'Don't think me hard because I have acted on conviction. Your generous devotion to me is unparalleled, Jude! Your worldly failure, if you have failed, is to your credit rather than to your blame. Remember that the best and greatest among mankind are those who do themselves no worldly good. Every successful man is more or less a selfish man. The devoted fail. . . . "Charity seeketh not her own." '

'In that chapter we are at one, ever-beloved darling, and on it we'll part friends. Its verses will stand fast when all the rest that you call religion has passed away!'

'Well—don't discuss it. Good-bye, Jude; my fellow-sinner, and kindest friend!'

'Good-bye, my mistaken wife. Good-bye!'

V

The next afternoon the familiar Christminster fog still hung over all things. Sue's slim shape was only just discernible going towards the station.

Jude had no heart to go to his work that day. Neither could he go anywhere in the direction by which she would be likely to pass. He went in an opposite one, to a dreary, strange, flat scene, where boughs dripped, and coughs and consumption lurked, and where he had never been before.

'Sue's gone from me—gone!' he murmured miserably.

She in the meantime had left by the train, and reached Alfredston Road, where she entered the steam-tram and was conveyed into the town. It had been her request to Phillotson that he should not meet her. She wished, she said, to come to him voluntarily, to his very house and hearthstone.

It was Friday evening, which had been chosen because the schoolmaster was disengaged at four o'clock that day till the Monday morning following. The little car she hired at The Bear to drive her to Marygreen set her down at the end of the lane, half-a-mile from the village, by her desire, and preceded her to the schoolhouse with such portion of her luggage as she had brought. On its return she encountered it, and asked the driver if he had found the master's house open. The man informed her that he had, and that her things had been taken in by the schoolmaster himself.

She could now enter Marygreen without exciting much observation. She crossed by the well and under the trees to the pretty new school on the other side, and lifted the latch of the dwelling without knocking. Phillotson stood in the middle of the room, awaiting her, as requested.

'I've come, Richard,' said she, looking pale and shaken, and sinking into a chair. 'I cannot believe—you forgive your—wife!'

'Everything, darling Susanna,' said Phillotson.

She started at the endearment, though it had been spoken advisedly without fervour. Then she nerved herself again.

'My children—are dead—and it is right that they should be! I am glad—almost. They were sin-begotten. They were sacrificed to teach me how to live!—their death was the first stage of my purification. That's why they have not died in vain! . . . You will take me back?'

He was so stirred by her pitiful words and tone that he did more than he had meant to do. He bent and kissed her cheek.

Sue imperceptibly shrank away, her flesh quivering under the touch of his lips.

Phillotson's heart sank, for desire was renascent in him. 'You still have an aversion to me!'

'O no, dear—I—have been driving through the damp, and I was chilly!' she said, with a hurried smile of apprehension. 'When are we going to have the marriage? Soon?'

'To-morrow morning, early, I thought—if you really wish. I am sending round to the vicar to let him know you are come. I have told him all, and he highly approves—he says it will bring our lives to a triumphant and satisfactory issue. But—are you sure of yourself? It is not too late to refuse now if—you think you can't bring yourself to it, you know?'

'Yes, yes, I can! I want it done quick. Tell him, tell him at once! My strength is tried by the undertaking—I can't wait long!'

'Have something to eat and drink then, and go over to your room at Mrs Edlin's. I'll tell the vicar half-past eight to-morrow, before anybody is about—if that's not too soon for you? My friend Gillingham is here to help us in the ceremony. He's been good enough to come all the way from Shaston at great inconvenience to himself.'

Unlike a woman in ordinary, whose eye is so keen for material things, Sue seemed to see nothing of the room they were in, or any detail of her environment. But on moving across the parlour to put down her muff she uttered a little 'O!' and grew paler than before. Her look was that of the condemned criminal who catches sight of his coffin.

'What?' said Phillotson.

The flap of the bureau chanced to be open, and in placing her muff upon it her eye had caught a document which lay there. 'O—only a—funny surprise!' she said, trying to laugh away her cry as she came back to the table.

'Ah! yes,' said Phillotson. 'The license. . . . It has just come.'

Gillingham now joined them from his room above, and Sue nervously made herself agreeable to him by talking on whatever she thought likely to interest him, except herself, though that interested him most of all. She obediently ate some supper, and prepared to leave for her lodging hard by. Phillotson crossed the green with her, bidding her good-night at Mrs Edlin's door.

The old woman accompanied Sue to her temporary quarters, and helped her to unpack. Among other things she laid out a nightgown tastefully embroidered.

'O—I didn't know *that* was put in!' said Sue quickly. 'I didn't mean it to be. Here is a different one.' She handed a new and absolutely plain garment, of coarse and unbleached calico.

'But this is the prettiest,' said Mrs Edlin. 'That one is no better than very sackcloth o' Scripture!'

'Yes—I meant it to be. Give me the other.'

She took it, and began rending it with all her might, the tears resounding through the house like a screech-owl.

'But my dear, dear!—whatever . . .'

'It is adulterous! It signifies what I don't feel—I bought it long ago—to please Jude. It must be destroyed!'

Mrs Edlin lifted her hands, and Sue excitedly continued to tear the linen into strips, laying the pieces in the fire.

'You med ha' give it to me!' said the widow. 'It do make my heart ache to see such pretty open-work as that a-burned by the flames—not that ornamental night-rails can be much use to a' ould 'ooman like I. My days for such be all past and gone!'

'It is an accursed thing—it reminds me of what I want to forget!' Sue repeated. 'It is only fit for the fire.'

'Lord, you be too strict! What do ye use such words for, and condemn to hell your dear little innocent children that's lost to 'ee! Upon my life I don't call that religion!'

Sue flung her face upon the bed, sobbing. 'O, don't, don't! That kills me!' She remained shaken with her grief, and slipped down upon her knees.

'I'll tell 'ee what—you ought not to marry this man again!' said Mrs Edlin indignantly. 'You are in love wi' t' other still!'

'Yes I must—I am his already!'

'Pshoo! You must be t' other man's. If you didn't like to commit yourselves to the binding vow again, just at first, 'twas all the more credit to your consciences, considering your reasons, and you med ha' lived on, and made it all right at last. After all, it concerned nobody but your own two selves.'

'Richard says he'll have me back, and I'm bound to go! If he had refused, it might not have been so much my duty to—give up Jude. But—' She remained with her face in the bedclothes, and Mrs Edlin left the room.

Phillotson in the interval had gone back to his friend Gillingham, who still sat over the supper-table. They soon rose, and walked out on the green to smoke awhile. A light was burning in Sue's room, a shadow moving now and then across the blind.

Gillingham had evidently been impressed with the indefinable charm of Sue, and after a silence he said, 'Well: you've all but got her again at last. She can't very well go a second time. The pear has dropped into your hand.'

'Yes! . . . I suppose I am right in taking her at her word. I confess there seems a touch of selfishness in it. Apart from her being what she is, of course, a luxury for a fogey like me, it will set me right in the eyes of the clergy and orthodox laity, who have never forgiven me for letting her go. So I may get back in some degree into my old track.'

'Well—if you've got any sound reason for marrying her again, do it now in God's name! I was always against your opening the cage-door and letting the bird go in such an obviously suicidal way. You might have been a school inspector by this time, or a reverend, if you hadn't been so weak about her.'

'I did myself irreparable damage—I know it.'

'Once you've got her housed again, stick to her.'

Phillotson was more evasive to-night. He did not care to admit clearly that his taking Sue to him again had at bottom nothing to do with repentance of letting her go, but was, primarily, a human instinct flying in the face of custom and profession. He said, 'Yes—I shall do that. I know woman better now. Whatever justice there was in releasing her, there was little logic, for one holding my views on other subjects.'

Gillingham looked at him, and wondered whether it would ever happen that the reactionary spirit induced by the world's sneers and his own physical wishes would make Phillotson more orthodoxly cruel to her than he had erstwhile been informally and perversely kind.

'I perceive it won't do to give way to impulse,' Phillotson resumed, feeling more and more every minute the necessity of acting up to his position. 'I flew in the face of the Church's teaching; but I did it without malice prepense. Women are so strange in their influence, that they tempt you to misplaced kindness. However, I know myself better now. A little judicious severity, perhaps. . . .'

'Yes; but you must tighten the reins by degrees only. Don't be too strenuous at first. She'll come to any terms in time.'

The caution was unnecessary, though Phillotson did not say so. 'I remember what my vicar at Shaston said, when I left after the row that was made about my agreeing to her elopement. "The only thing you can do to retrieve your position and hers is to admit your error in not restraining her with a wise and strong hand, and to get her back again if she'll come, and be firm in the future." But I was so headstrong at that time that I paid no heed. And that after the divorce she should have thought of doing so I did not dream.'

The gate of Mrs Edlin's cottage clicked, and somebody began crossing in the direction of the school. Phillotson said 'Good-night.'

'O, is that Mr Phillotson,' said Mrs Edlin. 'I was going over to see 'ee. I've been upstairs with her, helping her to unpack her things; and upon my word, sir, I don't think this ought to be!'

'What—the wedding?'

'Yes. She's forcing herself to it, poor dear little thing; and you've no notion what she's suffering. I was never much for religion nor against it, but it can't be right to let her do this, and you ought to persuade her out of it. Of course everybody will say it was very good and forgiving of 'ee to take her to 'ee again. But for my part I don't.'

'It's her wish, and I am willing,' said Phillotson with grave reserve, opposition making him illogically tenacious now. 'A great piece of laxity will be rectified.'

'I don't believe it. She's his wife if anybody's. She's had three children by him, and he loves her dearly; and it's a wicked shame to egg her on to this, poor little quivering thing! She's got nobody on her side. The one man who'd be her friend the obstinate creature won't allow to come near her. What first put her into this mood o' mind, I wonder!'

'I can't tell. Not I certainly. It is all voluntary on her part. Now that's all I have to say.' Phillotson spoke stiffly. 'You've turned round, Mrs Edlin. It is unseemly of you!'

'Well. I knowed you'd be affronted at what I had to say; but I don't mind that. The truth's the truth.'

'I'm not affronted, Mrs Edlin. You've been too kind a neighbour for that. But I must be allowed to know what's best for myself and Susanna. I suppose you won't go to church with us, then?'

'No. Be hanged if I can. . . . I don't know what the times be coming to! Matrimony have growed to be that serious in these days that one really do feel afeared to move in at all. In my time we took it more careless; and I don't know that we was any the worse for it! When I and my poor man were jined in it we kept up the junketing all the week, and drunk the parish dry, and had to borrow half-a-crown to begin housekeeping!'

When Mrs Edlin had gone back to her cottage Phillotson spoke moodily. 'I don't know whether I ought to do it—at any rate quite so rapidly.'

'Why?'

'If she is really compelling herself to this against her instincts—merely from this new sense of duty or religion—I ought perhaps to let her wait a bit.'

'Now you've got so far you ought not to back out of it. That's my opinion.'

'I can't very well put it off now; that's true. But I had a qualm when she gave that little cry at sight of the license.'

'Now, never you have qualms, old boy. I mean to give her away to-morrow morning, and you mean to take her. It has always been on my conscience that I didn't urge more objections to your letting her go, and now we've got to this stage I shan't be content if I don't help you to set the matter right.'

Phillotson nodded, and seeing how staunch his friend was, became more frank. 'No doubt when it gets known what I've done I shall be thought a soft fool by many. But they don't know Sue as I do. Though so elusive, hers is such an honest nature at bottom that I don't think she has ever done anything against her conscience. The fact of her having lived with Fawley goes for nothing. At the time she left me for him she thought she was quite within her right. Now she thinks otherwise.'

The next morning came, and the self-sacrifice of the woman on the altar of what she was pleased to call her principles was acquiesced in by these two friends, each from his own point of view. Phillotson went across to the Widow Edlin's to fetch Sue a few minutes after eight o'clock. The fog of the previous day or two on the lowlands had travelled up here by now, and the trees on the green caught armfuls, and turned them into showers of big drops. The bride was waiting, ready; bonnet and all on. She had never in her life looked so much like the lily her name connoted as she did in that pallid morning light. Chastened, world-weary, remorseful, the strain on her nerves had preyed upon her flesh and bones, and she appeared smaller in outline than she had formerly done, though Sue had not been a large woman in her days of rudest health.

'Prompt,' said the schoolmaster, magnanimously taking her hand. But he checked his impulse to kiss her, remembering her start of yesterday, which unpleasantly lingered in his mind.

Gillingham joined them, and they left the house, Widow Edlin continuing steadfast in her refusal to assist in the ceremony.

'Where is the church?' said Sue. She had not lived there for any length of time since the old church was pulled down, and in her preoccupation forgot the new one.

'Up here,' said Phillotson; and presently the tower loomed large and solemn in the fog. The vicar had already crossed to the building, and when they entered he said pleasantly: 'We almost want candles.'

'You do—wish me to be yours, Richard?' gasped Sue in a whisper.

'Certainly, dear: above all things in the world.'

Sue said no more; and for the second or third time she felt he was not quite following out the humane instinct which had induced him to let her go.

There they stood, five altogether: the parson, the clerk, the couple and Gillingham; and the holy ordinance was re-solemnized forthwith. In the nave of the edifice were two or three villagers, and when the clergyman came to the words, 'What God hath joined,' a woman's voice from among these was heard to utter audibly:

'God hath jined indeed!'

It was like a re-enactment by the ghosts of their former selves of the similar scene which had taken place at Melchester years before. When the books were signed the vicar congratulated the husband and wife on having performed a noble, and righteous, and mutually forgiving act. 'All's well that ends well,' he said smiling. 'May you long be happy together, after thus having been "saved as by fire".'

They came down the nearly empty building, and crossed to the schoolhouse. Gillingham wanted to get home that night, and left early. He, too, congratulated the couple. 'Now,' he said in parting from Phillotson, who walked out a little way, 'I shall be able to tell the people in your native place a good round tale; and they'll all say "Well done," depend on it.'

When the schoolmaster got back Sue was making a pretence of doing some housewifery as if she lived there. But she seemed timid at his approach, and compunction wrought on him at sight of it.

'Of course, my dear, I shan't expect to intrude upon your personal privacy any more than I did before,' he said gravely. 'It is for our good socially to do this, and that's its justification, if it was not my reason.'

Sue brightened a little.

VI

The place was the door of Jude's lodging in the outskirts of Christminster—far from the precincts of St Silas' where he had formerly lived, which saddened him to sickness. The rain was coming down. A woman in shabby black stood on the doorstep talking to Jude, who held the door in his hand.

'I am lonely, destitute, and houseless—that's what I am! Father has turned me out of doors after borrowing every penny I'd got, to put it into his business, and then accusing me of laziness when I was only waiting for a situation. I am at the mercy of the world! If you can't take me and help me, Jude, I must go to the workhouse, or to something worse. Only just now two undergraduates winked at me as I came along. 'Tis hard for a woman to keep virtuous where there's so many young men!'

The woman in the rain who spoke thus was Arabella, the evening being that of the day after Sue's re-marriage with Phillotson.

'I am sorry for you, but I am only in lodgings,' said Jude coldly.

'Then you turn me away?'

'I'll give you enough to get food and lodging for a few days.'

'O, but can't you have the kindness to take me in? I cannot endure going to a public-house to lodge; and I am so lonely. Please, Jude, for old times' sake!'

'No, no,' said Jude hastily. 'I don't want to be reminded of those things; and if you talk about them I shall not help you.'

'Then I suppose I must go!' said Arabella. She bent her head against the doorpost and began sobbing.

'The house is full,' said Jude. 'And I have only a little extra room to my own—not much more than a closet—where I keep my tools, and templates, and the few books I have left!'

'That would be a palace for me!'

'There is no bedstead in it.'

'A bit of a bed could be made on the floor. It would be good enough for me.'

Unable to be harsh with her, and not knowing what to do, Jude called the man who let the lodgings, and said this was an acquaintance of his in great distress for want of temporary shelter.

'You may remember me as barmaid at the Lamb and Flag formerly?' spoke up Arabella. 'My father has insulted me this afternoon, and I've left him, though without a penny!'

The housekeeper said he could not recall her features. 'But still, if you are a friend of Mr Fawley's we'll do what we can for a day or two—if he'll make himself answerable?'

'Yes, yes,' said Jude. 'She has really taken me quite unawares; but I should wish to help her out of her difficulty.' And an arrangement was ultimately come to under which a bed was to be thrown down in Jude's lumber-room, to make it comfortable for Arabella till she could get out of the strait she was in—not by her own fault, as she declared—and return to her father's again.

While they were waiting for this to be done Arabella said: 'You know the news, I suppose?'

'I guess what you mean; but I know nothing.'

'I had a letter from Anny at Alfredston to-day. She had just heard that the wedding was to be yesterday: but she didn't know if it had come off.'

'I don't wish to talk of it.'

'No, no: of course you don't. Only it shows what kind of woman—'

'Don't speak of her I say! She's a fool!—And she's an angel, too, poor dear!'

'If it's done, he'll have a chance of getting back to his old position, by everybody's account, so Anny says. All his well-wishers will be pleased, including the bishop himself.'

'Do spare me, Arabella.'

Arabella was duly installed in the little attic, and at first she did not come near Jude at all. She went to and fro about her own business, which, when they met for a moment on the stairs or in the passage, she informed him was that of obtaining another place in the occupation she understood best. When Jude suggested

London as affording the most likely opening in the liquor trade, she shook her head. 'No—the temptations are too many,' she said. 'Any humble tavern in the country before that for me.'

On the Sunday morning following, when he breakfasted later than on other days, she meekly asked him if she might come in to breakfast with him, as she had broken her teapot, and could not replace it immediately, the shops being shut.

'Yes, if you like,' he said indifferently.

While they sat without speaking she suddenly observed: 'You seem all in a brood, old man. I'm sorry for you.'

'I am all in a brood.'

'It is about her, I know. It's no business of mine, but I could find out all about the wedding—if it really did take place—if you wanted to know.'

'How could you?'

'I wanted to go to Alfredston to get a few things I left there. And I could see Anny, who'll be sure to have heard all about it, as she had friends at Marygreen.'

Jude could not bear to acquiesce in this proposal; but his suspense pitted itself against his discretion, and won in the struggle. 'You can ask about it if you like,' he said. 'I've not heard a sound from there. It must have been very private, if—they have married.'

'I am afraid I haven't enough cash to take me there and back, or I should have gone before. I must wait till I have earned some.'

'O—I can pay the journey for you,' he said impatiently. And thus his suspense as to Sue's welfare, and the possible marriage, moved him to despatch for intelligence the last emissary he would have thought of choosing deliberately.

Arabella went, Jude requesting her to be home not later than by the seven o'clock train. When she had gone he said: 'Why should I have charged her to be back by a particular time! She's nothing to me:—nor the other neither!'

But having finished work he could not help going to the station to meet Arabella, dragged thither by feverish haste to get the news she might bring, and know the worst. Arabella had made dimples most successfully all the way home, and when she stepped out of the railway carriage she smiled. He merely said 'Well?' with the very reverse of a smile.

'They are married.'

'Yes—of course they are!' he returned. She observed, however, the hard strain upon his lip as he spoke.

'Anny says she has heard from Belinda, her relation out at Marygreen, that it was very sad, and curious!'

'How do you mean sad? She wanted to marry him again, didn't she?—and he her!'

'Yes—that was it. She wanted to in one sense, but not in the other. Mrs Edlin was much upset by it all, and spoke out her mind at Phillotson. But Sue was that excited about it that she burnt her best embroidery that she'd worn with you, to blot you out entirely. Well—if a woman feels like it, she ought to do it. I commend her for it, though others don't.' Arabella sighed. 'She felt he was her only husband, and that she belonged to nobody else in the sight of God A'mighty while he lived. Perhaps another woman feels the same about herself, too!' Arabella sighed again.

'I don't want any cant!' exclaimed Jude.

'It isn't cant,' said Arabella. 'I feel exactly the same as she!'

He closed that issue by remarking abruptly: 'Well—now I know all I wanted to know. Many thanks for your information. I am not going back to my lodgings just yet.' And he left her straightaway.

In his misery and depression Jude walked to well-nigh every spot in the city that he had visited with Sue; thence he did not know whither, and then thought of going home to his usual evening meal. But having all the vices of his virtues, and some to spare, he turned into a public-house, for the first time during many months. Among the possible consequences of her marriage Sue had not dwelt on this.

Arabella, meanwhile, had gone back. The evening passed, and Jude did not return. At half-past nine Arabella herself went out, first proceeding to an outlying district near the river where her father lived, and had opened a small and precarious pork-shop lately.

'Well,' she said to him, 'for all your rowing me that night, I've called in, for I have something to tell you. I think I shall get married and settled again. Only you must help me: and you can do no less, after what I've stood 'ee.'

'I'll do anything to get thee off my hands!'

'Very well. I am now going to look for my young man. He's on the loose I'm afraid, and I must get him home. All I want you to do to-night is not to fasten the door, in case I should want to sleep here, and should be late.'

'I thought you'd soon get tired of giving yourself airs and keeping away!'

'Well—don't do the door. That's all I say.'

She then sallied out again, and first hastening back to Jude's to make sure that he had not returned, began her search for him. A shrewd guess as to his probable course took her straight to the tavern which Jude had formerly frequented, and where she had been barmaid for a brief term. She had no sooner opened the door of the 'Private Bar' than her eyes fell upon him—sitting in the shade at the back of the compartment, with his eyes fixed on the floor in a blank stare. He was drinking nothing stronger than ale just then. He did not observe her, and she entered and sat beside him.

Jude looked up, and said without surprise: 'You've come to have something, Arabella? . . . I'm trying to forget her: that's all! But I can't; and I am going home.' She saw that he was a little way on in liquor, but only a little as yet.

'I've come entirely to look for you, dear boy. You are not well. Now you must have something better than that.' Arabella held up her finger to the barmaid. 'You shall have a liqueur—that's better fit for a man of education than beer. You shall have maraschino, or curaçoa dry or sweet, or cherry brandy. I'll treat you, poor chap!'

'I don't care which! Say cherry brandy. . . . Sue has served me badly, very badly. I didn't expect it of Sue! I stuck to her, and she ought to have stuck to me. I'd have sold my soul for her sake, but she wouldn't risk hers a jot for me. To save her own soul she lets mine go damn! . . . But it isn't her fault, poor little girl—I am sure it isn't!'

How Arabella had obtained money did not appear, but she

ordered a liqueur each, and paid for them. When they had drunk these Arabella suggested another; and Jude had the pleasure of being, as it were, personally conducted through the varieties of spirituous delectation by one who knew the landmarks well. Arabella kept very considerably in the rear of Jude; but though she only sipped where he drank, she took as much as she could safely take without losing her head—which was not a little, as the crimson upon her countenance showed.

Her tone towards him to-night was uniformly soothing and cajoling; and whenever he said 'I don't care what happens to me,' a thing he did continually, she replied, 'But I do very much!' The closing hour came, and they were compelled to turn out; whereupon Arabella put her arm round his waist, and guided his unsteady footsteps.

When they were in the streets she said: 'I don't know what our landlord will say to my bringing you home in this state. I expect we are fastened out, so that he'll have to come down and let us in.'

'I don't know—I don't know.'

'That's the worst of not having a home of your own. I tell you, Jude, what we had best do. Come round to my father's—I made it up with him a bit to-day. I can let you in, and nobody will see you at all; and by to-morrow morning you'll be all right.'

'Anything—anywhere,' replied Jude. 'What the devil does it matter to me?'

They went along together, like any other fuddling couple, her arm still round his waist, and his, at last, round hers; though with no amatory intent; but merely because he was weary, unstable, and in need of support.

'This—is th' Martyrs'—burning-place,' he stammered as they dragged across a broad street. I remember—in old Fuller's *Holy State*—and I am reminded of it—by our passing by here—old Fuller in his *Holy State* says, that at the burning of Ridley, Doctor Smith—preached sermon, and took as his text "*Though I give my body to be burned, and have not charity, it profiteth me nothing.*"—Often think of it as I pass here. Ridley was a—'

'Yes. Exactly. Very thoughtful of you, deary, even though it hasn't much to do with our present business.'

'Why, yes it has! I'm giving *my* body to be burned! But—ah—you don't understand!—it wants Sue to understand such things! And I was her seducer—poor little girl! And she's gone—and I don't care about myself! Do what you like with me! . . . And yet she did it for conscience' sake, poor little Sue!'

'Hang her!—I mean, I think she was right,' hiccupped Arabella. 'I've my feelings too, like her; and I feel I belong to you in Heaven's eye, and to nobody else, till death us do part! It is—hic—never too late—hic—to mend!'

They had reached her father's house, and she softly unfastened the door, groping about for a light within.

The circumstances were not altogether unlike those of their entry into the cottage at Cresscombe, such a long time before. Nor were perhaps Arabella's motives. But Jude did not think of that, though she did.

'I can't find the matches, dear,' she said when she had fastened up the door. 'But never mind—this way. As quiet as you can, please.'

'It is as dark as pitch,' said Jude.

'Give me your hand, and I'll lead you. That's it. Just sit down here, and I'll pull off your boots. I don't want to wake him.'

'Who?'

'Father. He'd make a row, perhaps.'

She pulled off his boots. 'Now,' she whispered, 'take hold of me—never mind your weight. Now—first stair, second stair—'

'But,—are we out in our old house by Marygreen?' asked the stupefied Jude. 'I haven't been inside it for years till now! Hey? And where are my books? That's what I want to know?'

'We are at my house, dear, where there's nobody to spy out how ill you are. Now—third stair, fourth stair—that's it. Now we shall get on.'

VII

Arabella was preparing breakfast in the downstairs back room of this small, recently hired tenement of her father's. She put her head into the little pork-shop in front, and told Mr Donn it was ready. Donn, endeavouring to look like a master pork-butcher, in a greasy blue blouse, and with a strap round his waist from which a steel dangled, came in promptly.

'You must mind the shop this morning,' he said casually. 'I've to go and get some inwards and half a pig from Lumsdon, and to call elsewhere. If you live here you must put your shoulder to the wheel, at least till I get the business started!'

'Well, for to-day I can't say.' She looked deedily into his face. 'I've got a prize upstairs.'

'Oh?—What's that?'

'A husband—almost.'

'No!'

'Yes. It's Jude. He's come back to me.'

'Your old original one? Well, I'm damned!'

'Well, I always did like him, that I will say.'

'But how does he come to be up there?' said Donn, humour-struck, and nodding to the ceiling.

'Don't ask inconvenient questions, father. What we've to do is to keep him here till he and I are—as we were.'

'How was that?'

'Married.'

'Ah. . . . Well it is the rummest thing I ever heard of—marrying an old husband again, and so much new blood in the world! He's no catch, to my thinking. I'd have had a new one while I was about it.'

'It isn't rum for a woman to want her old husband back for respectability, though for a man to want his old wife back—well, perhaps it is funny, rather!' And Arabella was suddenly seized with a fit of loud laughter, in which her father joined more moderately.

'Be civil to him, and I'll do the rest,' she said when she had recovered seriousness. 'He told me this morning that his head ached fit to burst, and he hardly seemed to know where he was. And no wonder, considering how he mixed his drink last night. We must keep him jolly and cheerful here for a day or two, and not let him go back to his lodging. Whatever you advanced I'll pay back to you again. But I must go up and see how he is now, poor deary.'

Arabella ascended the stairs, softly opened the door of the first bedroom, and peeped in. Finding that her shorn Samson was asleep she entered to the bedside and stood regarding him. The fevered flush on his face from the debauch of the previous evening lessened the fragility of his ordinary appearance, and his long lashes, dark brows, and curly black hair and beard against the white pillow, completed the physiognomy of one whom Arabella, as a woman of rank passions, still felt it worth while to recapture, highly important to recapture as a woman straitened both in means and in reputation. Her ardent gaze seemed to affect him; his quick breathing became suspended, and he opened his eyes.

'How are you now, dear?' said she. 'It is I—Arabella.'

'Ah!—where—O yes, I remember! You gave me shelter. . . . I am stranded—ill—demoralized—damn bad! That's what I am!'

'Then do stay there. There's nobody in the house but father and me, and you can rest till you are thoroughly well. I'll tell them at the stone-works that you are knocked up.'

'I wonder what they are thinking at the lodgings!'

'I'll go round and explain. Perhaps you had better let me pay up, or they'll think we've run away?'

'Yes. You'll find enough money in my pocket there.'

Quite indifferent, and shutting his eyes because he could not bear the daylight in his throbbing eyeballs, Jude seemed to doze again. Arabella took his purse, softly left the room, and putting on her outdoor things went off to the lodgings she and he had quitted the evening before.

Scarcely half-an-hour had elapsed ere she reappeared round the corner, walking beside a lad wheeling a truck on which were piled all Jude's household possessions, and also a few of Arabella's things which she had taken to the lodging for her short sojurn there. Jude was in such physical pain from his unfortunate breakdown of the previous night, and in such mental pain from the loss of Sue and from having yielded in his half-somnolent state to Arabella, that when he saw his few chattels unpacked and standing before his eyes in this strange bedroom, intermixed with woman's apparel, he scarcely considered how they had come there, or what their coming signalized.

'Now,' said Arabella to her father downstairs, 'we must keep plenty of good liquor going in the house these next few days. I know his nature, and if he once gets into that fearfully low state that he does get into sometimes, he'll never do the honourable thing by me in this world, and I shall be left in the lurch. He must be kept cheerful. He had a little money in the savings-bank, and he has given me his purse to pay for anything necessary. Well, that will be the license; for I must have that ready at hand, to catch him the moment he's in the humour. You must pay for the liquor. A few friends, and a quiet convivial party would be the thing, if we could get it up. It would advertise the shop, and help me too.'

'That can be got up easy enough by anybody who'll afford victuals and drink.... Well yes—it would advertise the shop—that's true.'

Three days later, when Jude had recovered somewhat from the fearful throbbing of his eyes and brain, but was still considerably confused in his mind by what had been supplied to him by Arabella during the interval—to keep him jolly, as she expressed it—the quiet convivial gathering suggested by her, to wind Jude up to the striking point, took place.

Donn had only just opened his miserable little pork and sausage shop, which had as yet scarce any customers; nevertheless that party advertised it well, and the Donns acquired a real notoriety among a certain class in Christminster who knew not the colleges, nor their works, nor their ways. Jude was asked if he could suggest any guest in addition to those named by Arabella and her father, and in a saturnine humour of perfect recklessness mentioned Uncle Joe, and Stagg, and the decayed auctioneer, and others whom he remembered as having been frequenters of the well-known tavern during his bout therein years before. He also suggested Freckles and Bower o' Bliss. Arabella took him at his word so far as the men, but drew the line at the ladies.

Another man they knew, Tinker Taylor, though he lived in the same street, was not invited; but as he went homeward from a late job on the evening of the party, he had occasion to call at the shop for trotters. There were none in, but he was promised some the next morning. While making his inquiry Taylor glanced into the back room, and saw the guests sitting round, card-playing, and drinking, and otherwise enjoying themselves at Donn's expense. He went home to bed, and on his way out next morning wondered how the party went off. He thought it hardly worth while to call at the shop for his provisions at that hour, Donn and his daughter being probably not up, if they caroused late the night before. However, he found in passing that the door was open, and he could hear voices within, though the shutters of the meat-stall were not down. He went and tapped at the sitting-room door, and opened it.

'Well—to be sure!' he said, astonished.

Hosts and guests were sitting card-playing, smoking, and talking, precisely as he had left them eleven hours earlier; the gas was burning and the curtains drawn, though it had been broad daylight for two hours out of doors.

'Yes!' cried Arabella, laughing. 'Here we are, just the same. We ought to be ashamed of ourselves, oughtn't we! But it is a sort of housewarming, you see; and our friends are in no hurry. Come in, Mr Taylor, and sit down.'

The tinker, or rather reduced ironmonger, was nothing loth, and entered and took a seat. 'I shall lose a quarter, but never mind,' he said. 'Well, really, I could hardly believe my eyes when I looked in! It seemed as if I was flung back again into last night, all of a sudden.'

'So you are. Pour out for Mr Taylor.'

He now perceived that she was sitting beside Jude, her arm being round his waist. Jude, like the rest of the company, bore on his face the signs of how deeply he had been indulging.

'Well, we've been waiting for certain legal hours to arrive, to tell the truth,' she continued bashfully, and making her spirituous crimson look as much like a maiden blush as possible. 'Jude and I have decided to make up matters between us by tying the knot again, as we find we can't do without one another after all. So, as a bright notion, we agreed to sit on till late enough, and go and do it off-hand.'

Jude seemed to pay no great heed to what she was announcing, or indeed to anything whatever. The entrance of Taylor infused fresh spirit into the company, and they remained sitting, till Arabella whispered to her father: 'Now we may as well go.'

'But the parson don't know?'

'Yes, I told him last night that we might come between eight and nine, as there were reasons of decency for doing it as early and quiet as possible; on account of it being our second marriage, which might make people curious to look on if they knew. He highly approved.'

'O very well: I'm ready,' said her father, getting up and shaking himself.

'Now, old darling,' she said to Jude. 'Come along, as you promised.'

'When did I promise anything?' asked he, whom she had made so tipsy by her special knowledge of that line of business as almost to have made him sober again—or to seem so to those who did not know him.

'Why!' said Arabella, affecting dismay. 'You've promised to marry me several times as we've sat here to-night. These gentlemen have heard you.'

'I don't remember it,' said Jude doggedly. 'There's only one woman—but I won't mention her in this Capharnaum!'

Arabella looked towards her father. 'Now, Mr Fawley, be honourable,' said Donn. 'You and my daughter have been living here together these three or four days, quite on the understanding that you were going to marry her. Of course I shouldn't have had such goings on in my house if I hadn't understood that. As a point of honour you must do it now.'

'Don't say anything against my honour!' enjoined Jude hotly, standing up. 'I'd marry the W—— of Babylon rather than do anything dishonourable! No reflection on you, my dear. It is a mere rhetorical figure—what they call in the books, hyperbole.'

'Keep your figures for your debts to friends who shelter you,' said Donn.

'If I am bound in honour to marry her—as I suppose I am—though how I came to be here with her I know no more than a dead man—marry her I will, so help me God! I have never behaved dishonourably to a woman or to any living thing. I am not a man who wants to save himself at the expense of the weaker among us!'

'There—never mind him, deary,' said she, putting her cheek against Jude's. 'Come up and wash your face, and just put yourself tidy, and off we'll go. Make it up with father.'

They shook hands. Jude went upstairs with her, and soon came down looking tidy and calm. Arabella, too, had hastily arranged herself, and accompanied by Donn away they went.

'Don't go,' she said to the guests at parting. 'I've told the little maid to get the breakfast while we are gone; and when we come back we'll all have some. A good strong cup of tea will set everybody right for going home.'

When Arabella, Jude and Donn had disappeared on their matrimonial errand the assembled guests yawned themselves wider awake, and discussed the situation with great interest. Tinker Taylor, being the most sober, reasoned the most lucidly.

'I don't wish to speak against friends,' he said. 'But it do seem a rare curiosity for a couple to marry over again! If they couldn't get on the first time when their minds were limp, they won't the second, by my reckoning.'

'Do you think he'll do it?'

'He's been put upon his honour by the woman, so he med.'

'He'd hardly do it straight off like this. He's got no license nor anything.'

'She's got that, bless you. Didn't you hear her say so to her father?'

'Well,' said Tinker Taylor, re-lighting his pipe at the gas-jet. 'Take her all together, limb by limb, she's not such a bad-looking piece—particular by candlelight. To be sure, half-pence that have been in circulation can't be expected to look like new ones from the Mint. But for a woman that's been knocking about the four hemispheres for some time, she's passable enough. A little bit thick in the flitch perhaps; but I like a woman that a puff o' wind won't blow down.'

Their eyes followed the movements of the little girl as she spread the breakfast-cloth on the table they had been using, without wiping up the slops of the liquor. The curtains were undrawn, and the expression of the house made to look like morning. Some of the guests, however, fell asleep in the chairs. One or two went to the door, and gazed along the street more than once. Tinker Taylor was the chief of these, and after a time he came in with a leer on his face.

'By Gad, they are coming! I think the deed's done!'

'No,' said Uncle Joe, following him in. 'Take my word, he turned rusty at the last minute. They are walking in a very onusual way; and that's the meaning of it!'

They waited in silence till the wedding party could be heard entering the house. First into the room came Arabella boisterously; and her face was enough to show that her strategy had succeeded.

'Mrs Fawley, I presume?' said Tinker Taylor with mock courtesy.

'Certainly. Mrs Fawley again,' replied Arabella blandly, pulling off her glove and holding out her left hand. 'There's the padlock, see.... Well, he was a very nice, gentlemanly man indeed. I mean the clergyman. He said to me as gentle as a babe when all was done: "Mrs Fawley, I congratulate you heartily," he says. "For having heard your history, and that of your husband, I think you have both done the right and proper thing. And for your past errors as a wife, and his as a husband, I think you ought now to be forgiven by the world, as you have forgiven each other," says he. Yes: he was a very nice, gentlemanly man. "The Church don't recognize divorce in her dogma, strictly speaking," he says: "and bear in mind the words of the Service in your goings out and your comings in: What God hath joined together let no man put asunder." Yes: he was a very nice, gentlemanly man.... But, Jude, my dear, you were enough to make a cat laugh! You walked that straight, and held yourself that steady that one would have thought you were going 'prentice to a judge; though I knew you were seeing double all the time, from the way you fumbled with my finger.'

'I said I'd do anything to—save a woman's honour,' muttered Jude. 'And I've done it!'

'Well now, old deary, come along and have some breakfast.'

'I want—some—more whisky,' said Jude stolidly.

'Nonsense, dear. Not now! There's no more left. The tea will take the muddle out of our heads, and we shall be as fresh as larks.'

'All right. I've—married you. She said I ought to marry you again, and I have straightaway. It is true religion! Ha—ha—ha!'

VIII

Michaelmas came and passed, and Jude and his wife, who had lived but a short time in her father's house after their re-marriage, were in lodgings on the top floor of a dwelling nearer to the centre of the city.

He had done a few days' work during the two or three months since the event, but his health had been indifferent, and it was now precarious. He was sitting in an arm-chair before the fire, and coughed a good deal.

'I've got a bargain for my trouble in marrying thee over again!' Arabella was saying to him. 'I shall have to keep 'ee entirely,—that's what 'twill come to! I shall have to make black-pot and sausages, and hawk 'em about the street, all to support an invalid husband I'd no business to be saddled with at all. Why didn't you keep your health, deceiving one like this? You were well enough when the wedding was!'

'Ah, yes!' said he, laughing acridly. 'I have been thinking of my foolish feeling about the pig you and I killed during our first marriage. I feel now that the greatest mercy that could be vouchsafed to me would be that something should serve me as I served that animal.'

This was the sort of discourse that went on between them every day now. The landlord of the lodging, who had heard that they were a queer couple, had doubted if they were married at all, especially as he had seen Arabella kiss Jude one evening when she had taken a little cordial; and he was about to give them notice to quit, till by chance overhearing her one night haranguing Jude in rattling terms, and ultimately flinging a shoe at his head, he recognized the note of genuine wedlock; and concluding that they must be respectable, said no more.

Jude did not get any better, and one day he requested Arabella, with considerable hesitation, to execute a commission for him. She asked him indifferently what it was.

'To write to Sue.'

'What in the name—do you want me to write to her for?'

'To ask her how she is, and if she'll come to see me, because I'm ill, and should like to see her—once again.'

'It is like you to insult a lawful wife by asking such a thing!'

'It is just in order not to insult you that I ask you to do it. You know I love Sue. I don't wish to mince the matter—there stands the fact: I love her. I could find a dozen ways of sending a letter to her without your knowledge. But I wish to be quite above-board with you, and with her husband. A message through you asking her to come is at least free from any odour of intrigue. If she retains any of her old nature at all, she'll come.'

'You've no respect for marriage whatever, or its rights and duties!'

'What *does* it matter what my opinions are—a wretch like me! Can it matter to anybody in the world who comes to see me for half-an-hour—here with one foot in the grave! . . . Come, please write, Arabella!' he pleaded. 'Repay my candour by a little generosity!'

'I should think *not*!'

'Not just once?—O do!' He felt that his physical weakness had taken away all his dignity.

'What do you want *her* to know how you are for? She don't want to see 'ee. She's the rat that forsook the sinking ship!'

'Don't, don't!'

'And I stuck to un—the more fool I! Have that strumpet in the house indeed!'

Almost as soon as the words were spoken Jude sprang from the chair, and before Arabella knew where she was he had her on her back upon a little couch which stood there, he kneeling above her.

'Say another word of that sort,' he whispered, 'and I'll kill you—here and now! I've everything to gain by it—my own death not being the least part. So don't think there's no meaning in what I say!'

'What do you want me to do?' gasped Arabella.

'Promise never to speak of her.'

'Very well. I do.'

'I take your word,' he said scornfully as he loosened her. 'But what it is worth I can't say.'

'You couldn't kill the pig, but you could kill me!'

'Ah—there you have me! No—I couldn't kill you—even in a passion. Taunt away!'

He then began coughing very much, and she estimated his life with an appraiser's eye as he sank back ghastly pale. 'I'll send for her,' Arabella murmured, 'if you'll agree to my being in the room with you all the time she's here.'

The softer side of his nature, the desire to see Sue, made him unable to resist the offer even now, provoked as he had been; and he replied breathlessly: 'Yes, I agree. Only send for her!'

In the evening he inquired if she had written.

'Yes,' she said; 'I wrote a note telling her you were ill, and asking her to come to-morrow or the day after. I haven't posted it yet.'

The next day Jude wondered if she really did post it, but would not ask her; and foolish Hope, that lives on a drop and a crumb, made him restless with expectation. He knew the times of the possible trains, and listened on each occasion for sounds of her.

She did not come; but Jude would not address Arabella again thereon. He hoped and expected all the next day; but no Sue appeared; neither was there any note of reply. Then Jude decided in the privacy of his mind that Arabella had never posted hers, although she had written it. There was something in her manner which told it. His physical weakness was such that he shed tears at the disappointment when she was not there to see. His suspicions were, in fact, well founded. Arabella, like some other nurses, thought that your duty towards your invalid was to pacify him by any means short of really acting upon his fancies.

He never said another word to her about her wish or his conjecture. A silent, undiscerned resolve grew up in him, which gave him, if not strength, stability and calm. One mid-day when, after an absence of two hours, she came into the room, she beheld the chair empty.

Down she flopped on the bed, and sitting, meditated. 'Now where the devil is my man gone to!' she said.

A driving rain from the north-east had been falling with more or less intermission all the morning, and looking from the window at the dripping spouts it seemed impossible to believe that any sick man would have ventured out to almost certain death. Yet a conviction possessed Arabella that he had gone out, and it became a certainty when she had searched the house. 'If he's such a fool, let him be!' she said. 'I can do no more.'

Jude was at that moment in a railway train that was drawing near to Alfredston, oddly swathed, pale as a monumental figure in alabaster, and much stared at by other passengers. An hour later this thin form, in the long great-coat and blanket he had come with, but without an umbrella, could have been seen walking along the five-mile road to Marygreen. On his face showed the determined purpose that alone sustained him, but to which his weakness afforded a sorry foundation. By the uphill walk he was quite blown, but he pressed on; and at half-past three o'clock stood by the familiar well at Marygreen. The rain was keeping everybody indoors; Jude crossed the green to the church without observation, and found the building open. Here he stood, looking forth at the school, whence he could hear the usual sing-song tones of the little voices that had not learnt Creation's groan.

He waited till a small boy came from the school—one evidently allowed out before hours for some reason or other. Jude held up his hand, and the child came.

'Please call at the schoolhouse and ask Mrs Phillotson if she will be kind enough to come to the church for a few minutes.'

The child departed, and Jude heard him knock at the door of the dwelling. He himself went further into the church. Everything was new, except a few pieces of carving preserved from the wrecked old fabric, now fixed against the new walls. He stood by these: they seemed akin to the perished people of that place who were his ancestors and Sue's.

A light footstep, which might have been accounted no more than an added drip to the rainfall, sounded in the porch, and he looked round.

'O—I didn't think it was you! I didn't—O Jude!' A hysterical catch in her breath ended in a succession of them. He advanced, but she quickly recovered and went back.

'Don't go—don't go!' he implored. 'This is my last time! I thought it would be less intrusive than to enter your house. And I shall never come again. Don't then be unmerciful. Sue, Sue! we are acting by the letter; and "the letter killeth"!'

'I'll stay—I won't be unkind!' she said, her mouth quivering and her tears flowing as she allowed him to come closer. 'But why did you come, and do this wrong thing, after doing such a right thing as you have done?'

'What right thing?'

'Marrying Arabella again. It was in the Alfredston paper. She has never been other than yours, Jude—in a proper sense. And therefore you did so well—O so well!—in recognizing it—and taking her to you again.'

'God above—and is that all I've come to hear? If there is anything more degrading, immoral, unnatural, than another in my life, it is this meretricious contract with Arabella which has been called doing the right thing! And you too—you call yourself Phillotson's wife! *His* wife! You are mine.'

'Don't make me rush away from you—I can't bear much! But on this point I am decided.'

'I cannot understand how you did it—how you think it—I cannot!'

'Never mind that. He is a kind husband to me—And I—I've wrestled and struggled, and fasted, and prayed. I have nearly brought my body into complete subjection. And you mustn't—will you—wake—'

'O you darling little fool; where is your reason? You seem to have suffered the loss of your faculties! I would argue with you if I didn't know that a woman in your state of feeling is quite beyond all appeals to her brains. Or is it that you are humbugging yourself, as so many women do about these things; and don't actually believe what you pretend to, and only are indulging in the luxury of the emotion raised by an affected belief?'

'Luxury! How can you be so cruel!'

'You dear, sad, soft, most melancholy wreck of a promising human intellect that it has ever been my lot to behold! Where is your scorn of convention gone? I *would* have died game!'

'You crush, almost insult me, Jude! Go away from me!' She turned off quickly.

'I will. I would never come to see you again, even if I had the strength to come, which I shall not have any more. Sue, Sue, you are not worth a man's love!'

Her bosom began to go up and down. 'I can't endure you to say that!' she burst out, and her eye resting on him a moment, she turned back impulsively. 'Don't, don't scorn me! Kiss me, O kiss me lots of times, and say I am not a coward and a contemptible humbug—I can't bear it!' She rushed up to him and, with her mouth on his, continued: 'I must tell you—O I must—my darling Love! It has been—only a church marriage—an apparent marriage I mean! He suggested it at the very first!'

'How?'

'I mean it is a nominal marriage only. It hasn't been more than that at all since I came back to him!'

'Sue!' he said. Pressing her to him in his arms he bruised her lips with kisses: 'If misery can know happiness, I have a moment's happiness now! Now, in the name of all you hold holy, tell me the truth, and no lie. You do love me still?'

'I do! You know it too well! . . . But I *mustn't* do this!—I mustn't kiss you back as I would!'

'But do!'

'And yet you are so dear!—and you look so ill—'

'And so do you! There's one more, in memory of our dead little children—yours and mine!'

The words struck her like a blow, and she bent her head. 'I *mustn't*—I *can't* go on with this!' she gasped presently. 'But there, there, darling; I give you back your kisses; I do, I do! . . . And now I'll *hate* myself for ever for my sin!'

'No—let me make my last appeal. Listen to this! We've both remarried out of our senses. I was made drunk to do it. You were the same. I was gin-drunk; you were creed-drunk. Either form of intoxication takes away the nobler vision. . . . Let us then shake off our mistakes, and run away together!'

'No; again no! . . . Why do you tempt me so far, Jude! It is too merciless! . . . But I've got over myself now. Don't follow me—don't look at me. Leave me, for pity's sake!'

She ran up the church to the east end, and Jude did as she requested. He did not turn his head, but took up his blanket, which she had not seen, and went straight out. As he passed the end of the church she heard his coughs mingling with the rain on the windows, and in a last instinct of human affection, even now unsubdued by her fetters, she sprang up as if to go and succour him. But she knelt down again, and stopped her ears with her hands till all possible sound of him had passed away.

He was by this time at the corner of the garden, from which the path ran across the fields in which he had scared rooks as a boy. He turned and looked back, once, at the building which still contained Sue; and then went on, knowing that his eyes would light on that scene no more.

There are cold spots up and down Wessex in autumn and winter weather; but the coldest of all when a north or east wind is blowing is the crest of the down by the Brown House, where the road to Alfredston crosses the old Ridgeway. Here the first winter sleets and snows fall and lie, and here the spring frost lingers last unthawed. Here in the teeth of the north-east wind and rain Jude now pursued his way, wet through, the necessary slowness of his walk from lack of his former strength being insufficient to maintain his heat. He came to the milestone, and, raining as it was, spread his blanket and lay down there to rest. Before moving on he went and felt at the back of the stone for his own carving. It was still there; but nearly obliterated by moss. He passed the spot where the gibbet of his ancestors and Sue's had stood, and descended the hill.

It was dark when he reached Alfredston, where he had a cup of tea, the deadly chill that began to creep into his bones being too much for him to endure fasting. To get home he had to travel by a steam tramcar, and two branches of railway, with much waiting at a junction. He did not reach Christminster till ten o'clock.

IX

On the platform stood Arabella. She looked him up and down.

'You've been to see her?' she asked.

'I have,' said Jude, literally tottering with cold and lassitude.

'Well, now you'd best march along home.'

The water ran out of him as he went, and he was compelled to lean against the wall to support himself while coughing.

'You've done for yourself by this, young man,' said she. 'I don't know whether you know it.'

'Of course I do. I meant to do for myself.'

'What—to commit suicide?'

'Certainly.'

'Well, I'm blest! Kill yourself for a woman.'

'Listen to me, Arabella. You think you are the stronger; and so you are, in a physical sense, now. You could push me over like a ninepin. You did not send that letter the other day, and I could not resent your conduct. But I am not so weak in another way as you think. I made up my mind that a man confined to his room by inflammation of the lungs, a fellow who had only two wishes left in the world, to see a particular woman, and then to die, could neatly accomplish those two wishes at one stroke by taking this journey in the rain. That I've done. I have seen her for the last time, and I've finished myself—put an end to a feverish life which ought never to have been begun!'

'Lord—you do talk lofty! Won't you have something warm to drink?'

'No thank you. Let's get home.'

They went along by the silent colleges, and Jude kept stopping.

'What are you looking at?'

'Stupid fancies. I see, in a way, those spirits of the dead again, on this my last walk, that I saw when I first walked here!'

'What a curious chap you are!'

'I seem to see them, and almost hear them rustling. But I don't revere all of them as I did then. I don't believe in half of them. The theologians, the apologists, and their kin the metaphysicians, the high-handed statesmen, and others, no longer interest me. All that has been spoilt for me by the grind of stern reality!'

The expression of Jude's corpse-like face in the watery lamplight was indeed as if he saw people where there was nobody. At moments he stood still by an archway, like one watching a figure walk out; then he would look at a window like one discerning a familiar face behind it. He seemed to hear voices, whose words he repeated as if to gather their meaning.

'They seem laughing at me!'

'Who?'

'O—I was talking to myself! The phantoms all about here, in the college archways, and windows. They used to look friendly in the old days, particularly Addison, and Gibbon, and Johnson, and Dr Browne, and Bishop Ken—'

'Come along do! Phantoms! There's neither living nor dead hereabouts except a damn policeman! I never saw the streets emptier.'

'Fancy! The Poet of Liberty used to walk here, and the great Dissector of Melancholy there!'

'I don't want to hear about 'em! They bore me.'

'Walter Raleigh is beckoning to me from that lane—Wycliffe—Harvey—Hooker—Arnold—and a whole crowd of Tractarian Shades—'

'I *don't want* to know their names, I tell you! What do I care about folk dead and gone? Upon my soul you are more sober when you've been drinking than when you have not!'

'I must rest a moment,' he said; and as he paused, holding to the railings, he measured with his eye the height of a college front. 'This is old Rubric. And that Sarcophagus; and up that lane Crozier and Tudor; and all down there is Cardinal with its long front, and its windows with lifted eyebrows, representing the polite surprise of the University at the efforts of such as I.'

'Come along, and I'll treat you!'

'Very well. It will help me home, for I feel the chilly fog from the meadows of Cardinal as if death-claws were grabbing me through and through. As Antigone said, 'I am neither a dweller among men nor ghosts. But, Arabella, when I am dead, you'll see my spirit flitting up and down here among these!'

'Pooh! You mayn't die after all. You are tough enough yet, old man.'

It was night at Marygreen, and the rain of the afternoon showed no sign of abatement. About the time at which Jude and Arabella were walking the streets of Christminster homeward, the Widow Edlin crossed the green, and opened the back door of the schoolmaster's dwelling, which she often did now before bedtime, to assist Sue in putting things away.

Sue was muddling helplessly in the kitchen, for she was not a good housewife, though she tried to be, and grew impatient of domestic details.

'Lord love 'ee, what do ye do that yourself for, when I've come o' purpose! You knew I should come.'

'O—I don't know—I forgot! No, I didn't forget. I did it to discipline myself. I have scrubbed the stairs since eight o'clock. I *must* practice myself in my household duties. I've shamefully neglected them!'

'Why should ye? He'll get a better school, perhaps be a parson, in time, and you'll keep two servants. 'Tis a pity to spoil them pretty hands.'

'Don't talk of my pretty hands, Mrs Edlin. This pretty body of mine has been the ruin of me already!'

'Pshoo—you've got no body to speak of! You put me more in mind of a sperrit. But there seems something wrong to-night, my dear. Husband cross?'

'No. He never is. He's gone to bed early.'

'Then what is it?'

'I cannot tell you. I have done wrong to-day. And I want to eradicate it. . . . Well—I will tell you this—Jude had been here this afternoon, and I find I still love him—O, grossly! I cannot tell you more.'

'Ah!' said the widow. 'I told 'ee how 'twould be!'

'But it shan't be! I have not told my husband of his visit; it is not necessary to trouble him about it, as I never mean to see Jude any more. But I am going to make my conscience right on my duty to Richard—by doing a penance—the ultimate thing. I must!'

'I wouldn't—since he agrees to it being otherwise, and it has gone on three months very well as it is.'

'Yes—he agrees to my living as I choose; but I feel it is an indulgence I ought not to exact from him. It ought not to have been accepted by me. To reverse it will be terrible—but I must be more just to him. O why was I so unheroic!'

'What is it you don't like in him?' asked Mrs Edlin curiously.

'I cannot tell you. It is something . . . I cannot say. The mournful thing is, that nobody would admit it as a reason for feeling as I do; so that no excuse is left me.'

'Did you ever tell Jude what it was?'

'Never.'

'I've heard strange tales o' husbands in my time,' observed the widow in a lowered voice. 'They say that when the saints were upon the earth devils used to take husbands' forms o' nights, and get poor women into all sorts of trouble. But I don't know why that should come into my head, for it is only a tale. . . . What a wind and rain it is to-night! Well—don't be in a hurry to alter things, my dear. Think it over.'

'No, no! I've screwed my weak soul up to treating him more courteously—and it must be now—at once—before I break down!'

'I don't think you ought to force your nature. No woman ought to be expected to.'

'It is my duty. I will drink my cup to the dregs!'

Half-an-hour later when Mrs Edlin put on her bonnet and shawl to leave, Sue seemed to be seized with vague terror.

'No, no—don't go, Mrs Edlin,' she implored, her eyes enlarged, and with a quick nervous look over her shoulder.

'But it is bed-time, child.'

'Yes, but—there's the little spare room—my room that was. It is quite ready. Please stay, Mrs Edlin!—I shall want you in the morning.'

'O well—I don't mind, if you wish. Nothing will happen to my four old walls, whether I be there or no.'

She then fastened up the doors, and they ascended the stairs together.

'Wait here, Mrs Edlin,' said Sue. 'I'll go into my old room a moment by myself.'

Leaving the widow on the landing Sue turned to the chamber which had been hers exclusively since her arrival at Marygreen, and pushing to the door knelt down by the bed for a minute or two. She then arose, and taking her nightgown from the pillow undressed and came out to Mrs Edlin. A man could be heard snoring in the room opposite. She wished Mrs Edlin good-night, and the widow entered the room that Sue had just vacated.

Sue unlatched the other chamber door, and, as if seized with faintness, sank down outside it. Getting up again she half opened the door, and said 'Richard.' As the word came out of her mouth she visibly shuddered.

The snoring had quite ceased for some time, but he did not reply. Sue seemed relieved, and hurried back to Mrs Edlin's chamber. 'Are you in bed, Mrs Edlin?' she asked.

'No, dear,' said the widow, opening the door. 'I be old and slow, and it takes me a long while to un-ray. I han't unlaced my jumps yet.'

'I—don't hear him! And perhaps—perhaps—'

'What, child?'

'Perhaps he's dead!' she gasped. 'And then—I should be *free*, and I could go to Jude! . . . Ah—no—I forgot *her*—and God!'

'Let's go and hearken. No—he's snoring again. But the rain and the wind is so loud that you can hardly hear anything but between whiles.'

Sue had dragged herself back. 'Mrs Edlin, good night again! I am sorry I called you out.' The widow retreated a second time.

The strained, resigned look returned to Sue's face when she was alone. 'I must do it—I must! I must drink to the dregs!' she whispered. 'Richard!' she said again.

'Hey—what? Is that you, Susanna?'

'Yes.'

'What do you want? Anything the matter? Wait a moment.' He pulled on some articles of clothing, and came to the door. 'Yes?'

'When we were at Shaston I jumped out of the window rather than that you should come near me. I have never reversed that treatment till now—when I have come to beg your pardon for it, and ask you to let me in.'

'Perhaps you only think you ought to do this? I don't wish you to come against your impulses, as I have said.'

'But I beg to be admitted.' She waited a moment, and repeated, 'I beg to be admitted! I have been in error—even to-day. I have exceeded my rights. I did not mean to tell you, but perhaps I ought. I sinned against you this afternoon.'

'How?'

'I met Jude! I didn't know he was coming. And—'

'Well?'

'I kissed him, and let him kiss me.'

'O—the old story!'

'Richard, I didn't know we were going to kiss each other till we did!'

'How many times?'

'A good many. I don't know. I am horrified to look back on it, and the least I can do after it is to come to you like this.'

'Come—this is pretty bad, after what I've done! Anything else to confess?'

'No.' She had been intending to say: 'I called him my darling Love.' But, as a contrite woman always keeps back a little, that portion of the scene remained untold. She went on: 'I am never going to see him any more. He spoke of some things of the past: and it overcame me. He spoke of—the children.—But, as I have said, I am glad—almost glad I mean—that they are dead, Richard. It blots out all that life of mine!'

'Well—about not seeing him again any more. Come—you really mean this?' There was something in Phillotson's tone now which seemed to show that his three months of remarriage with Sue had somehow not been so satisfactory as his magnanimity or amative patience had anticipated.

'Yes, yes!'

'Perhaps you'll swear it on the New Testament?'

'I will.'

He went back to the room and brought out a little brown Testament. 'Now then: So help you God!'

She swore.

'Very good!'

'Now I supplicate you, Richard, to whom I belong, and whom I wish to honour and obey, as I vowed, to let me in.'

'Think it over well. You know what it means. Having you back in the house was one thing—this another. So think again.'

'I have thought—I wish this!'

'That's a complaisant spirit—and perhaps you are right. With a lover hanging about, a half-marriage should be completed. But I repeat my reminder this third and last time.'

'It is my wish! . . . O God!'

'What did you say O God for?'

'I don't know!'

'Yes you do! But . . .' He gloomily considered her thin and fragile form a moment longer as she crouched before him in her night-clothes. 'Well, I thought it might end like this,' he said presently. 'I owe you nothing, after these signs; but I'll take you in at your word, and forgive you.'

He put his arm round her to lift her up. Sue started back.

'What's the matter?' he asked, speaking for the first time sternly. 'You shrink from me again?—just as formerly!'

'No, Richard—I—I—was not thinking—'

'You wish to come in here?'

'Yes.'

'You still bear in mind what it means?'

'Yes. It is my duty!'

Placing the candlestick on the chest of drawers he led her through the doorway, and lifting her bodily, kissed her. A quick look of aversion passed over her face, but clenching her teeth she uttered no cry.

Mrs Edlin had by this time undressed, and was about to get into bed when she said to herself: 'Ah—perhaps I'd better go and see if the little thing is all right. How it do blow and rain!'

The widow went out on the landing, and saw that Sue had disappeared. 'Ah! Poor soul! Weddings be funerals 'a b'lieve nowadays. Fifty-five years ago, come Fall, since my man and I married! Times have changed since then!'

X

Despite himself Jude recovered somewhat, and worked at his trade for several weeks. After Christmas, however, he broke down again.

With the money he had earned he shifted his lodgings to a yet more central part of the town. But Arabella saw that he was not likely to do much work for a long while, and was cross enough at the turn affairs had taken since her re-marriage to him. 'I'm hanged if you haven't been clever in this last stroke!' she would say, 'to get a nurse for nothing by marrying me!'

Jude was absolutely indifferent to what she said, and, indeed, often regarded her abuse in a humorous light. Sometimes his mood was more earnest, and as he lay he often rambled on upon the defeat of his early aims.

'Every man has some little power in some one direction,' he would say. 'I was never really stout enough for the stone trade, particularly the fixing. Moving the blocks away used to strain me, and standing the trying draughts in buildings before the windows are in, always gave me colds, and I think that began the mischief inside. But I felt I could do one thing if I had the opportunity. I could accumulate ideas, and impart them to others. I wonder if the Founders had such as I in their minds—a fellow good for nothing else but for that particular thing? . . . I hear that soon there is going to be a better chance for such helpless students as I was. There are schemes afoot for making the University less exclusive, and extending its influence. I don't know much about it. And it is too late, too late for me! Ah—and for how many worthier ones before me!'

'How you keep a-mumbling!' said Arabella. 'I should have thought you'd have got over all that craze about books by this time. And so you would, if you'd had any sense to begin with. You are as bad now as when we were first married.'

On one occasion while soliloquizing thus he called her 'Sue' unconsciously.

'I wish you'd mind who you are talking to!' said Arabella indignantly. 'Calling a respectable married woman by the name of that—' She remembered herself and he did not catch the word.

But in the course of time, when she saw how things were going, and how very little she had to fear from Sue's rivalry, she had a fit of generosity. 'I suppose you want to see your—Sue?' she said. 'Well, I don't mind her coming. You can have her here if you like.'

'I don't wish to see her again.'

'O—that's a change!'

'And don't tell her anything about me—that I'm ill, or anything. She has chosen her course. Let her go!'

One day he received a surprise. Mrs Edlin came to see him, quite on her own account. Jude's wife, whose feelings as to where his affections were centred had reached absolute indifference by this time, went out, leaving the old woman alone with Jude. He impulsively asked how Sue was, and then said bluntly, remembering what Sue had told him: 'I suppose they are still only husband and wife in name?'

Mrs Edlin hesitated. 'Well, no—it's different now. She's begun it quite lately—all of her own free will.'

'When did she begin?' he asked quickly.

'The night after you came. But as a punishment to her poor self. He didn't wish it, but she insisted.'

'Sue, my Sue—you darling fool—this is almost more than I can endure! . . . Mrs Edlin—don't be frightened at my rambling—I've got to talk to myself lying here so many hours alone—she was once a woman whose intellect was to mine like a star to a benzoline lamp: who saw all *my* superstitions as cobwebs that she could brush away with a word. Then bitter affliction came to us, and her intellect broke, and she veered round to darkness. Strange difference of sex, that time and circumstance, which enlarge the views of most men, narrow the views of women almost invariably. And now the ultimate horror has come—her giving herself like this to what she loathes, in her enslavement to forms!—she, so sensitive, so shrinking, that the very wind seemed to blow on her with a touch of deference. . . . As for Sue and me when we were at our own best, long ago—when our minds were clear, and our love of truth fearless—the time was not ripe for us! Our ideas were fifty years too soon to be any good to us. And so the resistance they met with brought reaction in her, and recklessness and ruin on me! . . . There—this, Mrs Edlin, is how I go on to myself continually, as I lie here. I must be boring you awfully.'

'Not at all, my dear boy. I could hearken to 'ee all day.'

As Jude reflected more and more on her news, and grew more restless, he began in his mental agony to use terribly profane language about social conventions, which started a fit of coughing. Presently there came a knock at the door downstairs. As nobody answered it Mrs Edlin herself went down.

The visitor said blandly: 'The doctor.' The lanky form was that of Physician Vilbert, who had been called in by Arabella.

'How is my patient at present?' asked the physician.

'O bad—very bad! Poor chap, he got excited, and do blaspeam terribly, since I let out some gossip by accident—the more to my blame. But there—you must excuse a man in suffering for what he says, and I hope God will forgive him.'

'Ah. I'll go up and see him. Mrs Fawley at home?'

'She's not in at present, but she'll be here soon.'

Vilbert went; but though Jude had hitherto taken the medicines of that skilful practitioner with the greatest indifference whenever poured down his throat by Arabella, he was now so brought to bay by events that he vented his opinion of Vilbert to the physician's face, and so forcibly, and with such striking epithets, that Vilbert soon scurried downstairs again. At the door he met Arabella, Mrs Edlin having left. Arabella inquired how he thought her husband was now, and seeing that the doctor looked ruffled, asked him to take something. He assented.

'I'll bring it to you here in the passage,' she said. 'There's nobody but me about the house to-day.'

She brought him a bottle and a glass, and he drank. Arabella began shaking with suppressed laughter. 'What is this, my dear?' he asked, smacking his lips.

'O—a drop of wine—and something in it.' Laughing again she said: 'I poured your own love-philter into it, that you sold me at the Agricultural Show, don't you remember?'

'I do, I do! Clever woman! But you must be prepared for the consequences.' Putting his arm round her shoulders he kissed her there and then.

'Don't, don't,' she whispered, laughing good-humouredly. 'My man will hear.'

She let him out of the house, and as she went back she said to herself: 'Well! Weak women must provide for a rainy day. And if my poor fellow upstairs do go off—as I suppose he will soon—it's well to keep chances open. And I can't pick and choose now as I could when I was younger. And one must take the old if one can't get the young.'

XI

THE last pages to which the chronicler of these lives would ask the reader's attention are concerned with the scene in and out of Jude's bedroom when leafy summer came round again.

His face was now so thin that his old friends would hardly have known him. It was afternoon, and Arabella was at the looking-glass curling her hair, which operation she performed by heating an umbrella-stay in the flame of a candle she had lighted, and using it upon the flowing lock. When she had finished this, practised a dimple, and put on her things, she cast her eyes round upon Jude. He seemed to be sleeping, though his position was an elevated one, his malady preventing him lying down.

Arabella, hatted, gloved, and ready, sat down and waited, as if expecting some one to come and take her place as nurse.

Certain sounds from without revealed that the town was in festivity, though little of the festival, whatever it might have been, could be seen here. Bells began to ring, and the notes came into the room through the open window, and travelled round Jude's head in a hum. They made her restless, and at last she said to herself: 'Why ever doesn't father come!'

She looked again at Jude, critically gauged his ebbing life, as she had done so many times during the late months, and glancing at his watch, which was hung up by way of timepiece, rose impatiently. Still he slept, and coming to a resolution she slipped from the room, closed the door noiselessly, and descended the stairs. The house was empty. The attraction which moved Arabella to go abroad had evidently drawn away the other inmates long before.

It was a warm, cloudless, enticing day. She shut the front door, and hastened round into Chief Street, and when near the Theatre could hear the notes of the organ, a rehearsal for a coming concert being in progress. She entered under the archway of Oldgate College, where men were putting up awnings round the quadrangle for a ball in the Hall that evening. People who had come up from the country for the day were picnicking on the grass, and Arabella walked along the gravel paths and under the aged limes. But finding this place rather dull she returned to the streets, and watched the carriages drawing up for the concert, numerous Dons and their wives, and under-graduates with gay female companions, crowding up likewise. When the doors were closed, and the concert began, she moved on.

The powerful notes of that concert rolled forth through the swinging yellow blinds of the open windows, over the housetops, and into the still air of the lanes. They reached so far as to the room in which Jude lay; and it was about this time that his cough began again and awakened him.

As soon as he could speak he murmured, his eyes still closed: 'A little water, please.'

Nothing but the deserted room perceived his appeal, and he coughed to exhaustion again—saying still more feebly: 'Water—some water—Sue—Arabella!'

The room remained still as before. Presently he gasped again: 'Throat—water—Sue—darling—drop of water—please—O please!'

No water came, and the organ notes, faint as a bee's hum, rolled in as before.

While he remained, his face changing, shouts and hurrahs came from somewhere in the direction of the river.

'Ah—yes! The Remembrance games,' he murmured. 'And I here. And Sue defiled!'

The hurrahs were repeated, drowning the faint organ notes. Jude's face changed more: he whispered slowly, his parched lips scarcely moving:

'*Let the day perish wherein I was born, and the night in which it was said, There is a man child conceived.*'

('Hurrah!')

'*Let that day be darkness; let not God regard it from above, neither let the light shine upon it. Lo, let that night be solitary, let no joyful voice come therein.*'

('Hurrah!')

'Why died I not from the womb? Why did I not give up the ghost when I came out of the belly? . . . For now should I have lain still and been quiet. I should have slept: then had I been at rest!'

('Hurrah!')

'There the prisoners rest together; they hear not the voice of the oppressor. . . . The small and the great are there; and the servant is free from his master. Wherefore is light given to him that is in misery, and life unto the bitter in soul?'

Meanwhile Arabella, in her journey to discover what was going on, took a short cut down a narrow street and through an obscure nook into the quad of Cardinal. It was full of bustle, and brilliant in the sunlight with flowers and other preparations for a ball here also. A carpenter nodded to her, one who had formerly been a fellow-workman of Jude's. A corridor was in course of erection from the entrance to the Hall staircase, of gay red and buff bunting. Waggon-loads of boxes containing bright plants in full bloom were being placed about, and the great staircase was covered with red cloth. She nodded to one workman and another, and ascended to the Hall on the strength of their acquaintance, where they were putting down a new floor and decorating for the dance. The cathedral bell close at hand was sounding for five o'clock service.

'I should not mind having a spin there with a fellow's arm round my waist,' she said to one of the men. 'But Lord, I must be getting home again—there's a lot to do. No dancing for me!'

When she reached home she was met at the door by Stagg, and one or two other of Jude's fellow stone-workers. 'We are just going down to the river,' said the former, 'to see the boat-bumping. But we've called round on our way to ask how your husband is.'

'He's sleeping nicely, thank you,' said Arabella.

'That's right. Well now, can't you give yourself half-an-hour's relaxation, Mrs Fawley, and come along with us? 'Twould do you good.'

'I should like to go,' said she. 'I've never seen the boat-racing, and I hear it is good fun.'

'Come along!'

'How I *wish* I could!' She looked longingly down the street.

'Wait a minute, then. I'll just run up and see how he is now. Father is with him, I believe; so I can most likely come.'

They waited, and she entered. Downstairs the inmates were absent as before, having, in fact, gone in a body to the river where the procession of boats was to pass. When she reached the bedroom she found that her father had not even now come.

'Why couldn't he have been here!' she said impatiently. 'He wants to see the boats himself—that's what it is!'

However, on looking round to the bed she brightened, for she saw that Jude was apparently sleeping, though he was not in the usual half-elevated posture necessitated by his cough. He had slipped down, and lay flat. A second glance caused her to start, and she went to the bed. His face was quite white, and gradually becoming rigid. She touched his fingers; they were cold, though his body was still warm. She listened at his chest. All was still within. The bumping of near thirty years had ceased.

After her first appalled sense of what had happened the faint notes of a military or other brass band from the river reached her ears; and in a provoked tone she exclaimed, 'To think he should die just now! Why did he die just now!' Then meditating another moment or two she went to the door, softly closed it as before, and again descended the stairs.

'Here she is!' said one of the workmen. 'We wondered if you were coming after all. Come along; we must be quick to get a good place. . . . Well, how is he? Sleeping well still? Of course, we don't want to drag 'ee away if—'

'O yes—sleeping quite sound. He won't wake yet,' she said hurriedly.

They went with the crowd down Cardinal Street, where they presently reached the bridge, and the gay barges burst upon their view. Thence they passed by a narrow slit down to the riverside path—now dusty, hot, and thronged. Almost as soon as they had arrived the grand procession of boats began; the oars smacking with a loud kiss on the face of the stream, as they were lowered from the perpendicular.

'O, I say—how jolly! I'm glad I've come,' said Arabella. 'And—it can't hurt my husband—my being away.'

On the opposite side of the river, on the crowded barges, were gorgeous nosegays of feminine beauty, fashionably arrayed in green, pink, blue, and white. The blue flag of the Boat Club denoted the centre of interest, beneath which a band in red uniform gave out the notes she had already heard in the death-chamber. Collegians of all sorts, in canoes with ladies, watching keenly for 'our' boat, darted up and down. While she regarded the lively scene somebody touched Arabella in the ribs, and looking round she saw Vilbert.

'That philter is operating, you know!' he said with a leer. 'Shame on 'ee to wreck a heart so!'

'I shan't talk of love to-day.'

'Why not? It is a general holiday.'

She did not reply. Vilbert's arm stole round her waist, which act could be performed unobserved in the crowd. An arch expression overspread Arabella's face at the feel of the arm, but she kept her eyes on the river as if she did not know of the embrace.

The crowd surged, pushing Arabella and her friends sometimes nearly into the river, and she would have laughed heartily at the horse-play that succeeded, if the imprint on her mind's eye of a pale, statuesque countenance she had lately gazed upon had not sobered her a little.

The fun on the water reached the acme of excitement; there were immersions, there were shouts; the race was lost and won, the pink and blue and yellow ladies retired from the barges, and the people who had watched began to move.

'Well—it's been awfully good,' cried Arabella. 'But I think I must get back to my poor man. Father is there, so far as I know; but I had better get back.'

'What's your hurry?'

'Well, I must go. . . . Dear, dear, this is awkward!'

At the narrow gangway where the people ascended from the riverside path to the bridge the crowd was literally jammed into one hot mass—Arabella and Vilbert with the rest; and here they remained motionless, Arabella exclaiming, 'Dear, dear!' more and more impatiently; for it had just occurred to her mind that if Jude were discovered to have died alone an inquest might be deemed necessary.

'What a fidget you are, my love,' said the physician, who, being pressed close against her by the throng, had no need of personal effort for contact. 'Just as well have patience: there's no getting away yet!'

It was nearly ten minutes before the wedged multitude moved sufficiently to let them pass through. As soon as she got up into the street Arabella hastened on, forbidding the physician to accompany her further that day. She did not go straight to her house; but to the abode of a woman who performed the last necessary offices for the poorer dead; where she knocked.

'My husband has just gone, poor soul,' she said. 'Can you come and lay him out?'

Arabella waited a few minutes; and the two women went along, elbowing their way through the stream of fashionable people pouring out of Cardinal meadow, and being nearly knocked down by the carriages.

'I must call at the sexton's about the bell, too,' said Arabella. 'It is just round here, isn't it? I'll meet you at my door.'

By ten o'clock that night Jude was lying on the bedstead at his lodging covered with a sheet, and straight as an arrow. Through the partly opened window the joyous throb of a waltz entered from the ball-room at Cardinal.

Two days later, when the sky was equally cloudless, and the air equally still, two persons stood beside Jude's open coffin in the same little bedroom. On one side was Arabella, on the other the Widow Edlin. They were both looking at Jude's face, the worn old eyelids of Mrs Edlin being red.

'How beautiful he is!' said she.

'Yes. He's a handsome corpse,' said Arabella.

The window was still open to ventilate the room, and it being about noontide the clear air was motionless and quiet without. From a distance came voices; and an apparent noise of persons stamping.

'What's that?' murmured the old woman.

'Oh, that's the doctors of the Theatre, conferring Honorary degrees on the Duke of Hamptonshire and a lot more illustrious gents of that sort. It's Remembrance Week, you know. The cheers come from the young men.'

'Ay; young and strong-lunged! Not like our poor boy here.'

An occasional word, as from some one making a speech, floated from the open windows of the Theatre across to this quiet corner, at which there seemed to be a smile of some sort upon the marble features of Jude; while the old, superseded, Delphin editions of Virgil and Horace, and the dog-eared Greek Testament on the neighbouring shelf, and the few other volumes of the sort that he had not parted with, roughened with stone-dust where he had been in the habit of catching them up for a few minutes between his labours, seemed to pale to a sickly cast at the sounds. The bells struck out joyously; and their reverberations travelled round the bedroom.

Arabella's eyes removed from Jude to Mrs Edlin. 'D'ye think she will come?' she asked.

'I could not say. She swore not to see him again.'

'How is she looking?'

'Tired and miserable, poor heart. Years and years older than when you saw her last. Quite a staid, worn woman now. 'Tis the man;—she can't stomach un, even now!'

'If Jude had been alive to see her, he would hardly have cared for her any more, perhaps.'

'That's what we don't know. . . . Didn't he ever ask you to send for her, since he came to see her in that strange way?'

'No. Quite the contrary. I offered to send, and he said I was not to let her know how ill he was.'

'Did he forgive her?'

'Not as I know.'

'Well—poor little thing, 'tis to be believed she's found forgiveness somewhere! She said she had found peace!'

'She may swear that on her knees to the holy cross upon her necklace till she's hoarse, but it won't be true!' said Arabella. 'She's never found peace since she left his arms, and never will again till she's as he is now!'

A Note on the Type

The principal text of this Modern Library edition was set in a digitized version of Janson, a typeface that dates from about 1690 and was cut by Nicholas Kis, a Hungarian working in Amsterdam. The original matrices have survived and are held by the Stempel foundry in Germany. Hermann Zapf redesigned some of the weights and sizes for Stempel, basing his revisions on the original design.